Praise for

THE LIES OF LOCKE LAMORA

#1 Reader's Choice for Best Novel of 2006 on SFSite.com
Nominated for the Compton Crook Award for Best First
Novel, 2006

"Fafhrd and the Grey Mouser would have felt right at
home with the Gentleman Bastards.... This is a fresh, original, and engrossing tale by a bright new voice in the fantasy genre. Locke Lamora makes for an engaging rogue,
and Camorr a fascinating and gorgeously realized setting, a
city to rival Lankhmar, Amber, and Viriconium. I look forward to returning there for many more visits."

—George R. R. Martin

"Tough, funny, and inventive. You *will* be entertained."

—Kate Elliott

"A quirky, high-octane fantasy caper... Here there are titled nobles, elaborate schemes, multiple disguises and horrible fates enough for any piece of Shakespeare, but all laid
out in a finely imagined otherworld and told at the narra-
tive pace and pitch of *Pirates of the Caribbean*. A great,
swashbuckling yarn of a novel." —Richard Morgan

"Scott Lynch's first novel, *The Lies of Locke Lamora*, exports
the suspense and wit of a cleverly constructed crime caper
into an exotic realm of fantasy, and the result is engagingly
entertaining.... It is a remarkably stylish debut, and it comes
as no surprise that Hollywood has snapped up the rights."

—*Times* (London)

"Big summer-release books aren't all bulky, bad or bathetic; some summer stuff's several strata slier, standouts from the usual suspects. Scott Lynch's first novel is one of those standouts.... The dialogue is cleverly and articulately picturesque, colorful and profane."
—*San Diego Union-Tribune*

"Even on the 'high concept' level, Lynch distinguishes himself.... *The Lies of Locke Lamora* is a 'fantasy' *Ocean's 11*.... And Lynch delivers an appallingly enjoyable shtick that is itself witty enough to make you believe his characters' wit as well.... Damn entertaining." —*Agony Column*

"With a world so vividly realized that it's positively tactile, and characters so richly drawn that they threaten to walk right off the page... With this debut novel, Lynch immediately establishes himself as a gifted and fearless storyteller, unafraid of comparisons to Silverberg and Jordan, not to mention David Liss and even Dickens.... This is a true genre bender, at home on almost any kind of fiction shelf. Expect it to be among the year's most impressive debuts."
—*Booklist* (starred review)

"A picaresque fantasy...reminiscent of new weirdists Steven Erikson and China Miéville...Locke's resilience and wit give the book the tragicomic air of a traditional picaresque, rubbery ethics and all." —*Publishers Weekly*

"This impossible-to-put-down tale is a first novel, and I hope others are working their way out of this very fertile brain." —*Philadelphia Weekly Press*

Praise for
RED SEAS UNDER RED SKIES

"Charming, unpredictable and fast on its feet."
—*Publishers Weekly*

"Genuine 'seat of your pants' adventure, true and breathless thrill-seeking fiction that digs deep into our sense of wonder and rewards with every turn of the page. At the risk of overdosing on superlatives and clichés, *Red Seas Under Red Skies* resoundingly proves that Scott Lynch is no flash-in-the-pan, one-hit wonder—instead, he is very much the real deal. Very highly recommended." —SFRevu.com

"Grand, grandiose, grandiloquent, filled with swordplay and wordplay, swindles, confidence tricks, bluff and double bluff, contests of wit and rodomontade, sea battles, land battles, battles with foes and former friends, intrigues, gambits, tavern brawls, amorous idylls, poisonings...No critic is likely to fault Lynch on his overflowing qualities of inventiveness, audacious draftsmanship, and sympathetic characterization." —*Locus*

"The kind of witty romp that reminds you exactly how much fun heroic fantasy is supposed to be. Packed to the brim with memorable set-pieces...plenty of rip-roaring entertainment and the rambunctious friendship between Locke and Jean is fast turning into one of the most engaging pairings in epic fantasy." —SFX.com

"Fast-paced, colorful, funny, with a fiendishly intricate plot containing plenty of right-angle turns...Lynch hasn't merely imagined a far-off world, he's created it, put it all down on paper—the smells, the sounds, the people, the feel of the place. The novel is a virtuoso performance, and sf/fantasy fans will gobble it up, though they'll have to fight with caper novel aficionados for every crumb."

—*Booklist* (starred review)

"*Red Seas Under Red Skies* is not only a worthy sophomore effort, it is with little doubt the superior book. Too infrequent is our chance to read great pirate stories...and Lynch supplies an addition to that list."

—FantasyBookSpot.com

"*Red Seas Under Red Skies* firmly proves that Scott Lynch isn't a one-hit wonder, and if the author is able to maintain this level of competence in resulting volumes, while also continuing to up his game, then it'll only be a matter of time before Scott Lynch is mentioned in the same breath as George R. R. Martin and Steven Erikson."

—FantasyBookCritic.com

"Fast-paced...For fans of *Robin Hood; Ocean's Eleven; Pirates of the Caribbean.*"—*Entertainment Weekly*

Also by Scott Lynch

THE LIES OF LOCKE LAMORA

RED SEAS UNDER RED SKIES

SCOTT LYNCH

BANTAM BOOKS

RED SEAS UNDER RED SKIES
A Bantam Spectra Book

PUBLISHING HISTORY
Originally published in Great Britain in 2007 by
The Orion Publishing Group, Ltd.
Bantam Spectra hardcover edition published August 2007
Bantam Spectra mass market edition / August 2008

Published by Bantam Dell
A Division of Random House, Inc.
New York, New York

This is a work of fiction. Names, characters, places, and incidents
either are the product of the author's imagination or are used fictitiously.
Any resemblance to actual persons, living or dead,
events, or locales is entirely coincidental.

Library of Congress Catalog Card Number: 2007018597

Bantam Books and the rooster colophon are registered trademarks
and Spectra and the portrayal of a boxed "s" are trademarks of
Random House, Inc.

ISBN: 978-0-553-58895-8

Printed in the United States of America

www.bantamdell.com

OPM 10 9 8 7 6 5

For Matthew Woodring Stover,
a friendly sail on the horizon.
Non destiti, nunquam desistam.

Karthain

Lashain

Salon Corbeau

Vel Najara Isles

Vel Virazzo

Tal Verrar

Tamalek

Talisham

Pearls of Iono

Issara

Nicora

Ghostwind Isles

Port Prodigal

Okanti Nera

Unknown Ghostwinds

The
Sea
of
Brass

Landside

The Midden Deep

Blackhands Crescent

The Savrola   The Midden

The Portable Quarter   Istrian Crescent

Alchemists'   Mara
Crescent   Verraria

Great Gallery

The Mon Magisteria

The Golden Steps   Merchants   Castellana
Crescent

The Sinspire   Emerald
Galleries

Main   Artificers'
Anchorage   Crescent

Windward
Rock   Sword Marina   Galezzo

Glass Reefs

Arsenale   Windward
Crescent

Silver Marina

The Sea
of
Brass

Tal Verrar

RED SEAS
UNDER
RED SKIES

PROLOGUE

A Strained Conversation

1

Locke Lamora stood on the pier in Tal Verrar with the hot wind of a burning ship at his back and the cold bite of a loaded crossbow's bolt at his neck.

He grinned and concentrated on holding his own crossbow level with the left eye of his opponent; they were close enough that they would catch most of each other's blood, should they both twitch their fingers at the same time.

"Be reasonable," said the man facing him. Beads of sweat left visible trails as they slid down his grime-covered cheeks and forehead. "Consider the disadvantages of your situation."

Locke snorted. "Unless your eyeballs are made of iron, the disadvantage is mutual. Wouldn't you say so, Jean?"

They were standing two-by-two on the pier, Locke beside Jean, their assailants beside one another. Jean and his foe were toe-to-toe with their crossbows similarly poised; four cold metal bolts were cranked and ready scant inches away from the heads of four understandably nervous men. Not one of them could miss at this range, not if all the gods above or below the heavens willed it otherwise.

"All four of us would seem to be up to our balls in quicksand," said Jean.

On the water behind them, the old galleon groaned and creaked as the roaring flames consumed it from the inside out. Night was made day for hundreds of yards around; the hull was crisscrossed with the white-orange lines of seams coming apart. Smoke boiled out of those hellish cracks in little black eruptions, the last shuddering breaths of a vast wooden beast dying in agony. The four men stood at the very end of their pier, strangely alone in the midst of light and noise that was drawing the attention of the entire city.

"Lower your piece, for the love of the gods," said Locke's opponent. "We've been instructed not to kill you, if we don't have to."

"And I'm sure you'd be honest if it were otherwise, of course," said Locke. His smile grew. "I make it a point never to trust men with weapons at my windpipe. Sorry."

"Your hand will start to shake long before mine does."

"I'll rest the tip of my quarrel against your nose when I get tired. Who sent you after us? What are they paying you? We're not without funds; a happy arrangement could be reached."

"Actually," said Jean, "I know who sent them."

"Really?" Locke flicked a glance at Jean before locking eyes with his adversary once again.

"And an arrangement has been reached, but I wouldn't call it happy."

"Ah . . . Jean, I'm afraid you've lost me."

"No." Jean raised one hand, palm out, to the man opposite him. He then slowly, carefully shifted his aim to his left—until his crossbow was pointing at Locke's head. The man he'd previously been threatening blinked in surprise. "You've lost me, Locke."

"Jean," said Locke, the grin vanishing from his face, "this isn't funny."

"I agree. Hand your piece over to me."

"Jean—"

"Hand it over now. Smartly. You there, are you some kind of moron? Get that thing out of my face and point it at him."

Jean's former opponent licked his lips nervously, but didn't move. Jean ground his teeth together. "Look, you sponge-witted dock ape, I'm doing your job for you. Point your crossbow at my gods-damned partner so we can get off this pier!"

"Jean, I would describe this turn of events as less than helpful," said Locke, and he would have said more, except that Jean's opponent chose that moment to take Jean's advice.

It seemed to Locke that sweat was now veritably cascading down his face, as though his own treacherous moisture were abandoning the premises before anything worse happened.

"There. Three on one." Jean spat on the pier and waved toward the two assailants with his free hand. "You gave me no choice but to cut a deal with the employer of these gentlemen before we set out—gods damn it, you forced me. I'm sorry. I thought they'd make contact before they drew down on us. Now give your weapon over."

"Jean, what the hell do you think you're—"

"Don't. Don't say another fucking thing. Don't try to finesse me; I know you too well to let you have your say. Silence, Locke. Finger off the trigger and hand it over."

Locke stared at the steel-tipped point of Jean's quarrel, his mouth open in disbelief. The world around him seemed to fade to that tiny, gleaming point, alive with the orange reflection of the inferno blazing in the anchorage behind him. Jean would have given him a hand signal if he were lying. . . . Where the hell was the hand signal?

"I don't believe this," he whispered. "This is impossible."

"This is the last time I'm going to say this, Locke." Jean ground his teeth together and held his aim steady, directly between Locke's eyes. "Take your finger off the trigger and hand over your gods-damned weapon. Right now."

I

CARDS IN THE HAND

"If you must play, decide upon three things at the start:
the rules of the game, the stakes, and the quitting time."

Chinese Proverb

CHAPTER ONE

LITTLE GAMES

1

THE GAME WAS CAROUSEL HAZARD, the stakes were roughly half of all the wealth they commanded in the entire world, and the plain truth was that Locke Lamora and Jean Tannen were getting beaten like a pair of dusty carpets.

"Last offering for the fifth hand," said the velvet-coated attendant from his podium on the other side of the circular table. "Do the gentlemen choose to receive new cards?"

"No, no—the gentlemen choose to confer," said Locke, leaning to his left to place his mouth close to Jean's ear. He lowered his voice to a whisper. "What's your hand look like?"

"A parched desert," Jean murmured, casually moving his right hand up to cover his mouth. "How's yours?"

"A wasteland of bitter frustration."

"Shit."

"Have we been neglecting our prayers this week? Did one of us fart in a temple or something?"

"I thought the expectation of losing was all part of the plan."

"It is. I just expected we'd be able to put up a better fight than *this*."

The attendant coughed demurely into his left hand, the card-table equivalent of slapping Locke and Jean across the backs of their heads. Locke leaned away from Jean, tapped his cards lightly against the lacquered surface of the table, and grinned the best knew-what-he-was-doing sort of grin he could conjure from his facial arsenal. He sighed inwardly, glancing at the sizable pile of wooden markers that was about to make the short journey from the center of the table to his opponents' stacks.

"We are of course prepared," he said, "to meet our fate with heroic stoicism, worthy of mention by historians and poets."

The dealer nodded. "Ladies and gentlemen both decline last offering. House calls for final hands."

There was a flurry of shuffling and discarding as the four players formed their final hands and set them, face-down, on the table before them.

"Very well," said the attendant. "Turn and reveal."

The sixty or seventy of Tal Verrar's wealthiest idlers who had crowded the room behind them to watch every turn of Locke and Jean's unfolding humiliation now leaned forward as one, eager to see how embarrassed they would be this time.

2

TAL VERRAR, the Rose of the Gods, at the westernmost edge of what the Therin people call the civilized world.

If you could stand in thin air a thousand yards above Tal Verrar's tallest towers, or float in lazy circles there like the nations of gulls that infest the city's crevices and rooftops, you could see how its vast dark islands have given this place its ancient nickname. They seem to whirl outward from the city's heart, a series of crescents steadily increasing in size, like the stylized petals of a rose in an artist's mosaic.

They are not natural, in the sense that the mainland looming a few miles to the northeast is natural. The mainland cracks before wind and weather, showing its age. The islands of Tal Verrar are unweathered, possibly unweatherable—they are the black glass of the Eldren, unimaginable quantities of it, endlessly tiered and shot through with passages, glazed with layers of stone and dirt from which a city of men and women springs.

This Rose of the Gods is surrounded by an artificial reef, a broken circle three miles in diameter, shadows under shadowed waves. Against this hidden wall the restless Sea of Brass is gentled for the passage of vessels flying the banners of a hundred kingdoms and dominions. Their masts and yards rise in a forest, white with furled sails, far beneath your feet.

If you could turn your eye to the city's western island, you would see that its interior surfaces are sheer black walls, plunging hundreds of feet to the softly lapping harbor waves, where a network of wooden docks clings to the base of the cliffs. The seaward side of the island, however, is tiered along its entire length. Six wide, flat ledges sit one atop the other with smooth fifty-foot escarpments backing all but the highest.

The southernmost district of this island is called the Golden Steps—its six levels are thick with alehouses, dicing dens, private clubs, brothels, and fighting pits. The Golden Steps are heralded as the gambling capital of the Therin city-states, a place where men and women may lose money on anything from the mildest vices to the wickedest felonies. The authorities of Tal Verrar, in a magnanimous gesture of hospitality, have decreed that no foreigner upon the Golden Steps may be impressed into slavery. As a result, there are few places west of Camorr where it is safer for strangers to drink their brains out and fall asleep in the gutters and gardens.

There is rigid stratification on the Golden Steps; with each successively higher tier, the quality of the establishments rises, as do the size, number, and vehemence of the guards at the doors. Crowning the Golden Steps are a dozen baroque mansions of old stone and witchwood, embedded in the wet green luxury of manicured gardens and miniature forests.

These are the "chance houses of quality"—exclusive clubs where men and women of funds may gamble in the style to which their letters of credit entitle them. These houses have been informal centers of power for centuries, where nobles, bureaucrats, merchants, ships' captains, legates, and spies gather to wager fortunes, both personal and political.

Every possible amenity is contained within these houses. Notable visitors board carriage-boxes at exclusive docks at the base of the inner harbor cliffs, and are hauled up by gleaming brass water engines, thereby avoiding the narrow, twisting, crowd-choked ramps leading up the five lower Steps on their seaward face. There is even a public dueling green—a broad expanse of well-kept grass lying dead-center on the top tier, so that cooler heads need not be given any chance to prevail when someone has their blood up.

The houses of quality are sacrosanct. Custom older and firmer than law forbids soldiers or constables to set foot within them, save for response to the most heinous crimes. They are the envy of a continent: no foreign club, however luxurious or exclusive, can quite recapture the particular atmosphere of a genuine Verrari chance house. And they are, one and all, put to shame by the Sinspire.

Nearly one hundred and fifty feet tall, the Sinspire juts skyward at the southern end of the topmost tier of the Steps, which is itself more than two hundred and fifty feet above the harbor. The Sinspire is an Elderglass tower, glimmering with a pearly black sheen. A wide balcony decked with alchemical lanterns circles each of its nine levels. At night, the Sinspire is a constellation of lights in scarlet and twilight-sky blue, the heraldic colors of Tal Verrar.

The Sinspire is the most exclusive, most notorious, and most heavily guarded chance house in the world, open from sunset to sunrise for those powerful, wealthy, or beautiful enough to make it past the whims of the doorkeepers. Each ascending floor outdoes the one beneath it for luxury, exclusivity, and the risk ceiling of the games allowed. Access to each higher floor must be earned with good credit, amusing behavior, and impeccable play. Some aspirants spend years of their lives and thousands of solari trying to catch the attention of the Sinspire's master, whose ruthless hold on his unique position has made him the most powerful arbiter of social favor in the city's history.

The code of conduct at the Sinspire is unwritten, but as rigid as that of a religious cult. Most simply, most incontrovertibly, it is death to be caught cheating here. Were the archon of Tal Verrar himself to be detected with a card up his sleeve, he would find no appeal this side of the gods themselves from the consequences. Every few months, the tower's attendants discover some would-be exception to the rule, and yet another person dies quietly of an alchemical overdose in their carriage, or tragically "slips" from the balcony nine stories above the hard, flat stones of the Sinspire's courtyard.

It has taken Locke Lamora and Jean Tannen two years and a completely new set of false identities to carefully cheat their way up to the fifth floor.

They are, in fact, cheating at this very moment, trying hard to keep up with opponents who have no need to do likewise.

3

"LADIES SHOW a run of Spires and a run of Sabers, crowned with the Sigil of the Sun," said the attendant. "Gentlemen show a run of Chalices and a mixed hand, crowned with the five of Chalices. Fifth hand is to the ladies."

Locke bit the inside of his cheek as a wave of applause rippled through the warm air of the room. The ladies had taken four of the five hands so far, and the crowd had barely deigned to notice Locke and Jean's sole victory.

"Well, damn," said Jean, in credible mock surprise.

Locke turned to the opponent on his right. Maracosa Durenna was a slender, dark-complexioned woman in her late thirties, with thick hair the color of oil smoke and several visible scars on her neck and forearms. In her right hand she held a thin black cigar wrapped with gold thread, and on her face she wore a tight smile of detached contentment. The game was clearly not demanding her utmost exertion.

The attendant flicked Locke and Jean's little pile of lost wooden counters toward the ladies' side of the table with a long-handled crop. He then used the same crop to sweep all the cards back into his hands; it was strictly forbidden for players to touch the cards after the attendant had called for the reveal.

"Well, Madam Durenna," said Locke, "my congratulations on the increasingly robust state of your finances. Your purse would seem to be the only thing growing faster than my impending hangover." Locke knuckle-walked one of his markers over the fingers of his right hand. The little wooden disk was worth five solari, roughly eight months' pay for a common laborer.

"My condolences on a particularly unfortunate run of cards, Master Kosta." Madam Durenna took a long drag from her cigar, then slowly exhaled a stream of smoke so that it hung in the air between Locke and Jean, just far enough away to avoid direct insult. Locke had come to recognize that she used the cigar smoke as her *strat péti*, her "little game"—an ostensibly civilized mannerism actually cultivated to distract or annoy opponents at a gaming table, and goad them into mistakes. Jean had planned to use his own cigars for the same purpose, but Durenna's aim was better.

"No run of cards could be considered truly unfortunate in the presence of such a lovely pair of opponents," said Locke.

"I could almost admire a man who can stay so charmingly dishonest while being bled of all his silver," said Durenna's partner, who was seated on Durenna's right, between her and the dealer.

Izmila Corvaleur was nearly of a size with Jean, wide and florid, prodigiously rounded in every place a woman *could* be round. She was undeniably attractive, but the intelligence that shone out of her eyes was sharp and contemptuous. In her Locke recognized a contained pugnacity akin to that of a street brawler—a honed appetite for hard contests. Corvaleur nibbled constantly from a silver-gilded box of cherries coated in powdered chocolate, sucking her fingers loudly after each one. Her own *strat péti*, of course.

She was purpose-built for Carousel Hazard, thought Locke. A mind for the cards and a frame capable of withstanding the game's unique punishment for losing a hand.

"Default," said the attendant. Within his podium, he tripped the mechanism that set the carousel spinning. This device, in the center of the table, was a set of circular brass frames that held row upon row of tiny glass vials, each one capped in silver. It whirled under the soft lantern light of the gaming parlor, until it became continuous streaks of silver within brass, and then—a clinking sound of mechanisms beneath the table, the rattle of many tiny vessels of thick glass colliding with one another, and the carousel spat out two of its vials. They rolled toward Locke and Jean and clattered against the slightly upraised outer rim of the table.

Carousel Hazard was a game for two teams of two; an *expensive* game, for the clockwork carousel mechanism came very dear. At the end of each hand, the losing team was randomly dispensed two vials from the carousel's great store of little bottles; these held liquor, mixed with sweet oils and fruit juice to disguise the potency of any given drink. The cards were only one aspect of the game. Players also had to maintain concentration under the increasing effects of the devilish little vials. The only way a game could end was for a player to become too drunk to keep playing.

Theoretically, the game could not be cheated. The Sinspire maintained the mechanism and prepared the vials; the little silver caps were fastened tight over wax seals. Players were not permitted to touch the carousel, or another player's vials, on pain of immediate default. Even the chocolates and cigars being consumed by the players had to be provided by the house. Locke and Jean could even have refused to allow Madam Corvaleur the luxury of her sweets, but that would have been a bad idea for several reasons.

"Well," said Jean as he cracked the seal on his tiny libation, "here's to charming losers, I suppose."

"If only we knew where to find some," said Locke, and in unison they tossed back their drinks. Locke's left a warm, plum-flavored trail down his throat—it was one of the potent ones. He sighed and set the empty vial down before him. Four vials to one, and the way his concentration seemed to be unraveling at the edges meant that he was beginning to feel it.

As the attendant sorted and shuffled the cards for the next hand, Madam Durenna took another long, satisfied draw on her cigar and flicked the ashes into a solid-gold pot set on a pedestal behind her right hand. She exhaled two lazy streams of smoke through her nose and stared at the carousel from behind a gray veil. Durenna was a natural ambush predator, Locke thought, always most comfortable behind some camouflage. His information said that she was only recently arrived in the life of a city-bound merchant speculator. Her previous profession had been the command of bounty-privateers, hunting and sinking the slaver ships of Jerem on the high seas. She hadn't acquired those scars drinking tea in anyone's parlor.

It would be very, very unfortunate if a woman like her were to realize that Locke and Jean were counting on what Locke liked to call "discreetly unorthodox methods" to win the game—hell, it would be preferable to simply lose the old-fashioned way, or to be caught cheating by the Sinspire attendants. They, at least, would probably be quick and efficient executioners. They had a very busy establishment to run.

"Hold the cards," said Madam Corvaleur to the attendant, interrupting Locke's musings. "Mara, the gentlemen have indeed had several hands of unfortunate luck. Might we not allow them a recess?"

Locke concealed his instant excitement; the pair of Carousel Hazard partners that held the lead could offer their opponents a short break from the game, but the courtesy was rarely extended, for the obvious reason that it allowed the losers precious time to shake the effects of their liquor. Was Corvaleur trying to cover for some distress of her own?

"The gentlemen *have* seen a great deal of strenuous effort on our behalf, counting all those markers and pushing them over to us again and again." Durenna drew smoke, expelled it. "You would honor us, gentlemen, if you would consent to a short pause to refresh and recover yourselves."

Ah. Locke smiled and folded his hands on the table before him. So that was the game—play to the crowd and show off how little regard the ladies truly had for their opponents, how inevitable they considered their own victory. This was etiquette fencing, and Durenna had performed the equivalent of a lunge for the throat. Outright refusal would be terrible form; Locke and Jean's parry would have to be delicate.

"How could anything be more refreshing," said Jean, "than to continue our game against such an excellent partnership?"

"You're too kind, Master de Ferra," said Madam Durenna. "But would you have it said that we were heartless? You've refused us neither of our comforts." She used her cigar to gesture at Madam Corvaleur's sweets. "Would you refuse us our desire to give a comfort in exchange?"

"We would refuse you nothing, madam, and yet we would beg leave to answer your *greater* desire, for which you've troubled yourselves to come here tonight—the desire to play."

"There are many hands yet before us," added Locke, "and it would wound Jerome and myself to inconvenience the ladies in any way." He made eye contact with the dealer as he spoke.

"You have thus far presented no inconvenience," said Madam Corvaleur sweetly.

Locke was uncomfortably aware that the attention of the crowd was indeed hanging on this exchange. He and Jean had challenged the two women widely regarded as the best Carousel Hazard players in Tal Verrar, and a substantial audience had packed all the other tables on the fifth floor of the Sinspire. Those tables should have been hosting games of their own, but by some unspoken understanding between the house and its patrons, other action in the parlor had ceased for the duration of the slaughter.

"Very well," said Durenna. "We've no objection to continuing, for our sakes. Perhaps your luck may even turn."

Locke's relief that she had abandoned her conversational ploy was faint; she did, after all, have every expectation of continuing to thrash money out of him and Jean, like a cook might beat weevils from a bag of flour.

"Sixth hand," said the attendant. "Initial wager will be ten solari." As each player pushed forward two wooden coins, the attendant tossed three cards down in front of them.

Madam Corvaleur finished another chocolate-dusted cherry and sucked the sweet residue from her fingers. Before touching his cards, Jean slid the fingers of his left hand briefly under the lapel of his coat and moved them, as though scratching an itch. After a few seconds, Locke did the same. Locke caught Madam Durenna watching them, and saw her roll her eyes. Signals between players were perfectly acceptable, but a bit more subtlety was preferred.

Durenna, Locke, and Jean peeked at their cards almost simultaneously; Corvaleur was a moment behind them, with her fingers still wet. She laughed quietly. Genuine good fortune or *strat péti*? Durenna looked eminently satisfied, but Locke had no doubt she maintained that precise expression even in her sleep. Jean's face revealed nothing, and Locke for his part tried on a thin smirk, although his three opening cards were pure trash.

Across the room, a curving set of brass-railed stairs, with a large attendant guarding their foot, led up toward the sixth floor, briefly expanding into a sort of gallery on the way. A flicker of movement from this gallery caught Locke's attention; half concealed in shadow was a slight, well-dressed figure. The warm golden light of the room's lanterns was reflected in a pair of optics, and Locke felt a shivery thrill of excitement along his spine.

Could it be? Locke tried to keep one eye on the shadowy figure while pretending to fixate on his cards. The glare on those optics didn't waver or shift—the man was staring at their table, all right.

At last, he and Jean had attracted (or stumbled into, and by the gods they'd take that bit of luck) the attention of the man who kept his offices on the ninth floor—master of the Sinspire, clandestine ruler of all Tal Verrar's thieves, a man with an iron grip on the worlds of larceny and luxury both. In Camorr they would have called him *capa*, but here he affected no title save his own name.

Requin.

Locke cleared his throat, turned his eyes back to the table, and prepared to lose another hand with grace. Out on the dark water, the soft echo of ships' bells could be heard, ringing the tenth hour of the evening.

4

"EIGHTEENTH HAND," said the dealer. "Initial wager will be ten solari." Locke had to push aside the eleven little vials before him, with a visibly shaking hand, to slide his buy-in forward. Madam Durenna, steady as a dry-docked ship, was working on her fourth cigar of the night. Madam Corvaleur seemed to be wavering in her seat; was she perhaps more red-cheeked than usual? Locke tried not to stare too intently as she placed her initial wager; perhaps the waver came solely from his own impending inebriation. It was nearing midnight, and the smoke-laced air of the stuffy room scratched at Locke's eyes and throat like wool.

The dealer, emotionless and alert as ever—he seemed to have more clockwork in him than the carousel did—flicked three cards to the tabletop before Locke. Locke ran his fingers under his coat lapel, then peeked at his cards and said "Ahhhh-ha," with a tone of interested pleasure. They were an astonishing constellation of crap; his worst hand yet. Locke blinked and squinted, wondering if the alcohol was somehow masking a set of decent cards, but alas—when he concentrated again, they were still worthless.

The ladies had been forced to drink last, but unless Jean concealed a major miracle on the tabletop to Locke's left, it was a good bet that another little vial would soon be rolling merrily across the table toward Locke's wobbling hand.

Eighteen hands, thought Locke, to lose nine hundred and eighty solari thus far. His mind, well wet by the Sinspire's liquor, wandered off on its own calculations. A year of fine new clothes for a man of high station. A small ship. A very large house. The complete lifetime earnings of an honest artisan, like a stonemason. Had he ever pretended to be a stonemason?

"First options," said the dealer, snapping him back to the game.

"Card," said Jean. The attendant slid one to him; Jean peeked at it, nodded, and slid another wooden chit toward the center of the table. "Bid up."

"Hold fast," said Madam Durenna. She moved two wooden chits forward from her substantial pile. "Partner reveal." She showed two cards from her hand to Madam Corvaleur, who was unable to contain a smile.

"Card," said Locke. The attendant passed him one, and he turned up an edge just far enough to see what it was. The two of Chalices, worth precisely one wet shit from a sick dog in this situation. He forced himself to smile. "Bid up," he said, sliding two markers forward. "I'm feeling blessed."

All eyes turned expectantly to Madam Corvaleur, who plucked a chocolate-dusted cherry from her dwindling supply, popped it into her mouth, and then rapidly sucked her fingers clean. "Oh-ho," she said, staring down at her cards and drumming one set of sticky fingers gently on the table. "Oh...ho...oh...Mara, this is...the oddest..."

And then she slumped forward, settling her head onto her large pile of wooden markers on the tabletop. Her cards fluttered down, faceup, and she slapped at them, without coordination, trying to cover them up.

"Izmila," said Madam Durenna, a note of urgency in her voice. "Izmila!" She reached over and shook her partner by her heavy shoulders.

"'Zmila," Madam Corvaleur agreed in a sleepy, blubbering voice. Her mouth lolled open and she drooled remnants of chocolate and cherry onto her five-solari chits. "Mmmmmmillllaaaaaaaaaa. Verrry...odd...oddest..."

"Play sits with Madam Corvaleur." The dealer couldn't keep his surprise out of his voice. "Madam Corvaleur must state a preference."

"Izmila! Concentrate!" Madam Durenna spoke in an urgent whisper.

"There are...cards...," mumbled Corvaleur. "Look out, Mara.... Soooo...many...cards. On table."

She followed that up with, "Blemble...na...fla...gah." And then she was out cold.

"Final default," said the dealer after a few seconds. With his crop, he swept all of Madam Durenna's markers away from her, counting rapidly. Locke and Jean would take everything on the table. The looming threat of a thousand-solari loss had just become a gain of equal magnitude, and Locke sighed with relief.

The dealer considered the spectacle of Madam Corvaleur using her wooden markers as a pillow, and he coughed into his hand.

"Gentlemen," he said, "the house will, ah, provide new chits of the appropriate value in place of...those still in use."

"Of course," said Jean, gently patting the little mountain

of Durenna's markers suddenly piled up before him. In the crowd behind them, Locke could hear noises of bewilderment, consternation, and surprise. A light ripple of applause was eventually coaxed into existence by some of the more generous observers, but it died quickly. They were faintly embarrassed, rather than exhilarated, to see a notable like Madam Corvaleur inebriated by a mere six drinks.

"Hmmmph," said Madam Durenna, stubbing out her cigar in the gold pot and rising to her feet. She made a show of straightening her jacket—black brocaded velvet decorated with platinum buttons and cloth-of-silver, worth a good fraction of everything she'd bet that night. "Master Kosta, Master de Ferra... it appears we must admit to being outmatched."

"But certainly not outplayed," said Locke, summoning up a snake-charming smile along with the pulverized remnants of his wits. "You very nearly had us... um, sewn up."

"And the whole world is wobbling around me," said Jean, whose hands were as steady as a jeweler's, and had been throughout the entire game.

"Gentlemen, I have appreciated your stimulating company," said Madam Durenna in a tone of voice that indicated she hadn't. "Another game later this week, perhaps? Surely you must allow us a chance at revenge, for honor's sake."

"Nothing would please us more," said Jean, to which Locke nodded enthusiastically, making the contents of his skull ache. At that, Madam Durenna coldly held out her hand and consented for the two of them to kiss the air above it. When they had done so, as though making obeisance to a particularly irritable snake, four of Requin's attendants appeared to help move the snoring Madam Corvaleur somewhere more decorous.

"Gods, it must be tedious, watching us try to drink one

another under the table night after night," said Jean. He flipped the dealer a five-solari chit; it was customary to leave a small gratuity for the attendant.

"I don't believe so, sir. How would you like your change?"

"What change?" Jean smiled. "Keep the whole thing."

The attendant betrayed human emotions for the second time that night; relatively well-off as he was, one little wooden chit was half his annual salary. He stifled a gasp when Locke threw him another dozen.

"Fortune is a lady who likes to be passed around," said Locke. "Buy a house, maybe. I'm having a little trouble counting at the moment."

"Sweet gods—*many* thanks, gentlemen!" The attendant took a quick glance around, and then spoke under his breath. "Those two ladies don't lose very often, you know. In fact, this is the first time I can remember."

"Victory has its price," said Locke. "I suspect my head will be paying it when I wake up tomorrow."

Madam Corvaleur was hauled carefully down the stairs, with Madam Durenna following to keep a close eye on the men carrying her card partner. The crowd dispersed; those observers who remained at their tables called for attendants, food, new decks of cards for games of their own.

Locke and Jean gathered their markers (fresh ones, sans slobber, were swiftly provided by the attendants to replace Madam Corvaleur's) in the customary velvet-lined wooden boxes and made their way to the stairs.

"Congratulations, gentlemen," said the attendant guarding the way up to the sixth floor. The tinkle of glass on glass and the murmur of conversation could be heard filtering down from above.

"Thank you," said Locke. "I'm afraid that something in Madam Corvaleur gave way just a hand or two before I might have done the same."

He and Jean slowly made their way down the stairs that curved all the way around the inside of the Sinspire's exterior wall. They were dressed as men of credit and consequence in the current height of Verrari summer fashion. Locke (whose hair had been alchemically shifted to a sunny shade of blond) wore a caramel-brown coat with a cinched waist and flaring knee-length tails; his huge triple-layered cuffs were paneled in orange and black and decorated with gold buttons. He wore no waistcoat; just a sweat-soaked tunic of the finest silk, under a loose black neck-cloth. Jean was dressed similarly, though his coat was the grayish blue of a sea under clouds, and his belly was cinched up with a wide black sash, the same color as the short, curly hairs of his beard.

Down past floors of notables they went . . . past queens of Verrari commerce with their decorative young companions of both sexes on their arms like pets. Past men and women with purchased Lashani titles, staring across cards and wine decanters at lesser dons and doñas from Camorr; past Vadran shipmasters in tight black coats, with sea tans like masks over their sharp, pale features. Locke recognized at least two members of the Priori, the merchant council that theoretically ruled Tal Verrar. Deep pockets seemed to be the primary qualification for membership.

Dice fell and glasses clinked; celebrants laughed and coughed and cursed and sighed. Currents of smoke moved languidly in the warm air, carrying scents of perfume and wine, sweat and roast meats, and here and there the resiny hint of alchemical drugs.

Locke had seen genuine palaces and mansions before; the Sinspire, opulent as it was, was not so very much more handsome than the homes many of these people would be returning to when they finally ran out of night to play in. The real magic of the Sinspire was woven from its capricious exclusivity; deny something to enough people and sooner or later it will grow a mystique as thick as fog.

Nearly hidden at the rear of the first floor was a heavy wooden booth manned by several unusually large attendants. Luckily, there was no line. Locke set his box down on the countertop beneath the booth's only window, a bit too forcefully.

"All to my account."

"My pleasure, Master Kosta," said the chief attendant as he took the box. Leocanto Kosta, merchant speculator of Talisham, was well known in this kingdom of wine fumes and wagers. The attendant swiftly changed Locke's pile of wooden chits into a few marks on a ledger. In beating Durenna and Corvaleur, even minus his tip to the dealer, Locke's cut of the winnings came to nearly five hundred solari.

"I understand that congratulations are in order to the both of you, Master de Ferra," said the attendant as Locke stepped back to let Jean approach the counter with his own box. Jerome de Ferra, also of Talisham, was Leocanto's boon companion. They were a pair of fictional peas in a pod.

Suddenly, Locke felt a hand fall onto his left shoulder. He turned warily and found himself facing a woman with curly dark hair, richly dressed in the same colors as the Sinspire attendants. One side of her face was sublimely beautiful—the other side was a leathery brown half-mask, wrinkled, as though it had been badly burned. When she smiled, the damaged side of her lips failed to move. It seemed to Locke as though a living woman was somehow struggling to emerge from within a rough clay sculpture.

Selendri, Requin's majordomo.

The hand that she had placed on his shoulder (her left, on the burned side) wasn't real. It was a solid brass simulacrum, and it gleamed dully in the lantern light as she withdrew it.

"The house congratulates you," she said in her eerie, lisping voice, "for good manners as well as considerable fortitude, and wishes you and Master de Ferra to know that you would both be welcome on the sixth floor, should you choose to exercise the privilege."

Locke's smile was quite genuine. "Many thanks, on behalf of myself and my partner," he said with tipsy glibness. "The kind regard of the house is, of course, extremely flattering."

She nodded noncommittally, then slipped away into the crowd as quickly as she'd come. Eyebrows went up appreciatively here and there—few of Requin's guests, to Locke's knowledge, were apprised of their increasing social status by Selendri herself.

"We're a commodity in demand, my dear Jerome," he said as they made their way through the crowd toward the front doors.

"For the time being," said Jean.

"Master de Ferra," beamed the head doorman as they approached, "and Master Kosta. May I call for a carriage?"

"No need, thanks," said Locke. "I'll fall over sideways if I don't flush my head with some night air. We'll walk."

"Very good then, sir."

With military precision, four attendants held the doors open for Locke and Jean to pass. The two thieves stepped carefully down a wide set of stone steps covered with a red velvet carpet. That carpet was thrown out and replaced each night. As a result, in Tal Verrar alone could one find armies of beggars routinely sleeping on piles of red velvet scraps.

The view was breathtaking; to their right, the whole crescent sweep of the island was visible beyond the silhouettes of other chance houses. There was relative darkness in the north, in contrast to the auralike glow of the Golden Steps. Beyond the city—to the south, west, and north—the Sea of Brass gleamed phosphorescent silver, lit by three moons in a cloudless sky. Here and there the sails of distant ships reached up from the quicksilver tableau, ghostly pale.

Locke could gaze downward to his left and see across the staggered rooftops of the island's five lower tiers, a vertigo-inducing view despite the solidity of the stones beneath his feet. All around him was the murmur of human pleasure and the clatter of horse-drawn carriages on cobbles; there were at least a dozen moving or waiting along the straight avenue atop the sixth tier. Above, the Sinspire reared up into the opalescent darkness with its alchemical lanterns bright, like a candle meant to draw the attentions of the gods.

"And now, my dear professional pessimist," said Locke as they stepped away from the Sinspire and acquired relative privacy, "my worry-merchant, my tireless font of doubt and derision . . . what do you have to say to *that*?"

"Oh, very little, to be sure, Master Kosta. It's so hard to think, overawed as I am with the sublime genius of your plan."

"That bears some vague resemblance to sarcasm."

"Gods forfend," said Jean. "You wound me! Your inexpressible criminal virtues have triumphed again, as inevitably as the tides come and go. I cast myself at your feet and beg for absolution. Yours is the genius that nourishes the heart of the world."

"And now you're—"

"If only there was a leper handy," interrupted Jean, "so you could lay your hands on and magically heal him."

"Oh, you're just farting out your mouth because you're jealous."

"It's possible," said Jean. "Actually, we are substantially enriched, not caught, not dead, more famous, and welcome on the next floor up. I must admit that I was wrong to call it a silly scheme."

"Really? Huh." Locke reached under his coat lapels as he spoke. "Because I have to admit, it *was* a silly scheme. Damned irresponsible. One drink more and I would have been finished. I'm actually pretty bloody surprised we pulled it off."

He fumbled beneath his coat for a second or two, then pulled out a little pad of wool about as wide and long as his thumb. A puff of dust was shaken from the wool when Locke slipped it into one of his outer pockets, and he wiped his hands vigorously on his sleeves as they walked along.

"Nearly lost is just another way to say finally won," said Jean.

"Nonetheless, the liquor almost did me in. Next time I'm that optimistic about my own capacity, correct me with a hatchet to the skull."

"I'll be glad to correct you with *two*."

It was Madam Izmila Corvaleur who'd made the scheme possible. Madam Corvaleur, who'd first crossed paths with "Leocanto Kosta" at a gaming table a few weeks earlier, who had the reliable habit of eating with her fingers to annoy her opponents while she played cards.

Carousel Hazard really *couldn't* be cheated by any traditional means. None of Requin's attendants would stack a deck, not once in a hundred years, not even in exchange for a dukedom. Nor could any player alter the carousel, select one vial in favor of another, or serve a vial to anyone else. With all the usual means of introducing a foreign substance to another player guarded against, the only remaining possibility was for a player to do herself in by slowly, willingly taking in something subtle and unorthodox. Something delivered by a means beyond the ken of even a healthy paranoia.

Like a narcotic powder, dusted on the playing cards in

minute quantities by Locke and Jean, then gradually passed around the table to a woman continually licking her fingers as she played.

Bela paranella was a colorless, tasteless alchemical powder also known as "the night friend." It was popular with rich people of a nervous disposition, who took it to ease themselves into deep, restful slumber. When mixed with alcohol, *bela paranella* was rapidly effective in tiny quantities; the two substances were as complementary as fire and dry parchment. It would have been widely used for criminal purposes, if not for the fact that it sold for twenty times its own weight in white iron.

"Gods, that woman had the constitution of a war galley," said Locke. "She must have started getting some of the powder by the third or fourth hand...probably could've killed a pair of wild boars in heat with less."

"At least we got what we wanted," said Jean, removing his own powder reservoir from his coat. He considered it for a moment, shrugged, and slipped it in a pocket.

"We did indeed...and I saw him!" said Locke. "Requin. He was on the stairs, watching us for most of the hands in the middle game. We *must* have excited a personal interest." The exciting ramifications of this helped clear some of the haze from Locke's thoughts. "Why else send Selendri herself to pat our backs?"

"Well, assume you're correct. So what now? Do you want to push on with it, like you mentioned, or do you want to take it slow? Maybe gamble around on the fifth and sixth floors for a few more weeks?"

"A few more weeks? To hell with that. We've been kicking around this gods-damned city for two years now; if we've finally cracked Requin's shell, I say we bloody well go for it."

"You're going to suggest tomorrow night, aren't you?"

"His curiosity's piqued. Let's strike while the blade is fresh from the forge."

"I suspect that drink has made you impulsive."

"Drink makes me see funny; the gods made me impulsive."

"You there," came a voice from the street in front of them. "Hold it!"

Locke tensed. "I beg your pardon?"

A young, harried-looking Verrari man with long black hair was holding his hands out, palms facing toward Locke and Jean. A small, well-dressed crowd seemed to have gathered beside him, at the edge of a trim lawn that Locke recognized as the dueling green.

"Hold it, sirs, I beg of you," said the young man. "I'm afraid it's an affair, and there may be a bolt flying past. Might I beg of you to wait but a moment?"

"Oh. *Oh.*" Locke and Jean relaxed simultaneously. If someone was dueling with crossbows, it was common courtesy as well as good sense to wait beside the dueling ground until the shots were taken. That way, neither participant would be distracted by movement in the background, or accidentally bury a bolt in a passerby.

The dueling green was about forty yards long and half as wide, lit at each of its four corners by a soft white lantern hanging in a black iron frame. Two duelists stood in the center of the green with their seconds, each man casting four pale gray shadows in a crisscross pattern. Locke had little personal inclination to watch, but he reminded himself that he was supposed to be Leocanto Kosta, a man of worldly indifference to strangers punching holes in one another. He and Jean squeezed into the crowd of spectators as unobtrusively as possible; a similar crowd had formed on the other side of the green.

One of the duelists was a very young man, dressed in fine loose gentleman's clothing of a fashionable cut; he wore optics, and his hair hung to his shoulders in well-tended ringlets.

His red-jacketed opponent was a great deal older, a bit hunched over and weathered. He looked active and determined enough to pose a threat, however. Each man held a lightweight crossbow—what Camorri thieves would call an alley-piece.

"Gentlemen," said the younger duelist's second. "Please. Can there be no accommodation?"

"If the Lashani gentleman will withdraw his imprecation," added the younger duelist. His voice was high and nervous. "I would be eminently satisfied, with the merest recognition—"

"No, there *cannot*," said the man standing beside the older duelist. "His Lordship is not in the habit of tendering apologies for mere statements of obvious fact."

"...with the *merest recognition*," continued the young duelist, desperately, "that the incident was an unfortunate misunderstanding, and that it need not—"

"Were he to condescend to speak to you again," said the older duelist's second, "his Lordship would no doubt also note that you wail like a *bitch*, and would inquire as to whether you're equally capable of biting like one."

The younger duelist stood speechless for a few seconds, then gestured rudely toward the older men with his free hand.

"I am forced," said his second, "I am, ah, forced... to allow that there may be no accommodation. Let the gentlemen stand... back-to-back."

The two opponents walked toward each other—the older man marched with vigor while the younger still stepped hesitantly—and turned their backs to each other.

"You shall have ten paces," said the younger man's second, with bitter resignation. "Wait then, and on my signal, you may turn and loose."

Slowly he counted out the steps; slowly the two opponents walked away from each other. The younger man was shaking very badly indeed. Locke felt a ball of unaccustomed tension growing in his own stomach. Since when had he become such a damned softhearted fellow? Just because he preferred not to watch didn't mean he should be afraid to do so...yet the feeling in his stomach paid no heed to the thoughts in his head.

"...nine...ten. Stand fast," said the young duelist's second. "Stand fast.... *Turn and loose!*"

The younger man whirled first, his face a mask of terror; he threw out his right hand and let fly. A sharp twang sounded across the green. His opponent didn't even jerk back as the bolt hissed through the air beside his head, missing by at least the width of a hand.

The red-jacketed old man completed his own turn more slowly, his eyes bright and his mouth set into a scowl. His younger opponent stared at him for several seconds, as though trying to will his bolt to come flying back like a trained bird. He shuddered, lowered his crossbow, and then threw it down to the grass. With his hands on his hips, he stood waiting, breathing in deep and noisy gulps.

His opponent regarded him briefly, then snorted. "Be fucked," he said, and he raised his crossbow in both hands. His shot was perfect; there was a wet crack and the younger duelist toppled with a feathered bolt dead in the center of his chest. He fell onto his back, clawing at his coat and tunic, spitting up dark blood. Half a dozen spectators rushed toward him, while one young woman in a silver evening gown fell to her knees and screamed.

"We'll get back just in time for dinner," said the older duelist to nobody in particular. He tossed his own crossbow carelessly to the ground behind him and stomped off toward one of the nearby chance houses, with his second at his side.

"Sweet fucking Perelandro," said Locke, forgetting Leocanto Kosta for a moment and thinking out loud. "What a way to manage things."

"You don't approve, sir?" A lovely young woman in a black silk dress regarded Locke with disconcertingly penetrating eyes. She couldn't have been more than eighteen or nineteen. "I understand that some differences of opinion need to be settled with steel," said Jean, butting in, appearing to recognize that Locke was still a bit too tipsy for his own good. "But standing before a crossbow bolt seems foolish. Blades strike me as a more honest test of skill."

"Rapiers are tedious; all that back and forth, and rarely a killing strike right away," said the young woman. "Bolts are fast, clean, and merciful. You can hack at someone all night with a rapier and fail to kill them."

"I am quite compelled to agree with you," muttered Locke.

The woman raised an eyebrow but said nothing; a moment later she was gone, vanishing into the dispersing crowd.

The contented murmur of the night—the laughter and chatter of the small clusters of men and women making time beneath the stars—had died briefly while the duel took place, but now it rose up once again. The woman in the silver dress beat her fists against the grass, sobbing, while the crowd around the fallen duelist seemed to sag in unison. The bolt's work was clearly done.

"Fast, clean, and merciful," said Locke softly. "Idiots."

Jean sighed. "Neither of us has any right to offer that sort of observation, since 'gods-damned idiots' is likely to be inscribed on our grave-markers."

"I've had reasons for doing what I've done, and so did you."

"I'm sure those duelists felt the same way."

"Let's get the hell out of here," said Locke. "Let's walk off the fumes in my head and get back to the inn. Gods, I feel old and sour. I see things like this and I wonder if I was that bloody stupid when I was that boy's age."

"You were worse," said Jean. "Until quite recently. Probably still are."

5

LOCKE'S MELANCHOLY slowly evaporated, along with more of his alcoholic haze, as they made their way down and across the Golden Steps, north by northeast to the Great Gallery. The Eldren craftsmen (Crafts-women? Crafts-*things*?) responsible for Tal Verrar had covered the entire district with an open-sided Elderglass roof that sloped downward from its peak atop the sixth tier and plunged into the sea at the western island's base, leaving at least thirty feet of space beneath it at all points in between. Strange twisted glass columns rose up at irregular intervals, looking like leafless climbing vines carved from ice. The glass ceiling of the Gallery was easily a thousand yards from end to end the long way.

Beyond the Great Gallery, on the lower layers of the island, was the Portable Quarter—open-faced tiers on which the miserably destitute were allowed to set up squatters' huts and whatever shelters they could construct from castoff materials. The trouble was that any forceful wind from the north, especially in the rainy winter, would completely rearrange the place.

Perversely, the district above and immediately southeast of the Portable Quarter, the Savrola, was a pricey expatriate's enclave, full of foreigners with money to waste. All the best inns were there, including the one Locke and Jean were currently using for their well-heeled alternate identities. The Savrola was sealed off from the Portable Quarter by high stone walls, and heavily patrolled by Verrari constables and private mercenaries.

By day, the Great Gallery was the marketplace of Tal Verrar. A thousand merchants set up their stalls beneath it every morning, and there was room for five thousand more, should the city ever grow so vast. Visitors rooming in the Savrola who didn't travel by boat were forced, by cunning coincidence, to walk across the full breadth of the market to travel to or from the Golden Steps.

An east wind was up, blowing out from the mainland, across the glass islands and into the Gallery. Locke and Jean's footsteps echoed in the darkness of the vast hollow space; soft lamps on some of the glass pillars made irregular islands of light. Scraps of trash blew past their feet, and wisps of wood smoke from unseen fires. Some merchants kept family members sleeping in particularly desirable stall locations all night...and of course there were always vagrants from the Portable Quarter, seeking privacy in the shadows of the empty Gallery. Patrols stomped through the Gallery tiers several times each night, but there were none in sight at the moment.

"What a strange wasteland this place becomes after dark," said Jean. "I can't decide if I mislike it or if it enchants me."

"You'd probably be less inclined to enchantment if you didn't have a pair of hatchets stuffed up the back of your coat."

"Mmm."

They walked on for another few minutes. Locke rubbed his stomach and muttered to himself.

"Jean—are you hungry, by chance?"

"I usually am. Need some more ballast for that liquor?"

"I think it might be a good idea. Damn that carousel. Another losing hand and I might have proposed marriage to that gods-damned smoking dragoness. Or just fallen out of my chair."

"Well, let's raid the Night Market."

On the topmost tier of the Great Gallery, toward the northeastern end of the covered district, Locke could see the flickering light of barrel fires and lanterns, and the shadowy shapes of several people. Commerce never truly ground to a halt in Tal Verrar; with thousands of people coming and going from the Golden Steps, there was enough coin floating around for a few dozen nocturnal stall-keepers to stake out a spot just after sunset every evening. The Night Market could be a great convenience, and it was invariably more eccentric than its daytime counterpart.

As Locke and Jean strolled toward the bazaar with the night breeze blowing against them, they had a fine view of the inner harbor with its dark forest of ships' masts. Beyond that, the rest of the city's islands lay sensibly sleeping, dotted here and there with specks of light rather than the profligate glow of the Golden Steps. At the heart of the city, the three crescent islands of the Great Guilds (Alchemists, Artificers, and Merchants) curled around the base of the high, rocky Castellana like slumbering beasts. And atop the Castellana, like a looming stone hill planted in a field of mansions, was the dim outline of the Mon Magisteria, the fortress of the archon.

Tal Verrar was supposedly ruled by the Priori, but in reality a significant degree of power rested in the man who resided in that palace, the city's master of arms. The office of the archon had been created following Tal Verrar's early disgraces in the Thousand-Day War against Camorr, to take command of the army and navy out of the hands of the bickering merchant councils. But the trouble with creating military dictators, Locke reflected, was getting rid of them after the immediate crisis was past. The first archon had "declined" retirement, and his successor was, if any-thing, even more interested in interfering with civic affairs. Outside guarded bastions of frivolity like the Golden Steps and expatriate havens like the Savrola, the disagreements between archon and Priori kept the city on edge.

"Gentlemen!" came a voice from their left, breaking into Locke's chain of thought. "Honored sirs. A walk across the Great Gallery cannot possibly be complete without re-freshment." Locke and Jean had reached the fringes of the Night Market; there were no other customers in sight, and the faces of at least a dozen merchants stared keenly out at them from within their little circles of fire or lamplight.

The first Verrari to throw his pitch against the gates of their good judgment was a one-armed man getting on in years, with long white hair braided down to his waist. He waved a wooden ladle at them, indicating four small casks set atop a portable counter not unlike a flat-topped wheel-barrow.

"What's your fare?"

"Delicacies from the table of Iono himself, the sweetest taste the sea has to offer. Sharks' eyes in brine; all fresh plucked. Crisp the shells, soft the humors, sweet the juices."

"Sharks' eyes? Gods, no." Locke grimaced. "Have you more common flesh? Liver? Gills? A gill pie would be wel-come."

"Gills? Sir, gills have none of the virtues of the eyes; it is the eyes that tone the muscles, prevent cholera, and firm up a man's mechanisms for certain, ah, marital duties."

"I have no need of any mechanism-firming in that re-spect," said Locke. "And I'm afraid my stomach is too un-settled for the splendor of sharks' eyes at just the moment."

"A pity, sir. For your sake, I wish I had some bit of gill to offer you, but it's the eyes that I get, and little else. Yet I do have several types—scythe sharks, wolf sharks, blue wid-ower...."

"We must pass, friend," said Jean as he and Locke walked on.

"Fruit, worthy masters?" The next merchant along was a slender young woman comfortably ensconced in a cream-colored frock coat several sizes too large for her; she also wore a four-cornered hat with a small alchemical globe dangling on a chain, hanging down just above her left shoulder. She stood watch over a number of woven baskets. "Alchemical fruit, fresh hybrids. Have you ever seen the Sofia Orange of Camorr? It makes its own liquor, very sweet and powerful."

"We are . . . acquainted," said Locke. "And more liquor is not what I had in mind. Anything to recommend for an unsettled stomach?"

"Pears, sir. The world would have no unsettled stomachs if only we were all wise enough to eat several every day."

She took up one basket, about half-full, and held it up before him. Locke sifted through the pears, which seemed firm and fresh enough, and drew out three. "Five centira," said the fruit seller.

"A full volani?" Locke feigned outrage. "Not if the archon's favorite whore held them between her legs and wiggled for me. One centira is too much for the lot."

"One centira wouldn't buy you the stems. At least I won't lose money for four."

"It would be an act of supreme pity," said Locke, "for me to give you two. Fortunately for you I'm brimming with largesse; the bounty is yours."

"Two would be an insult to the men and women who grew those, in the hot glass gardens of the Blackhands Crescent. But surely we can meet at three?"

"Three," said Locke with a smile. "I have never been robbed in Tal Verrar before, but I'm just hungry enough to allow you the honor." He passed two of the pears to Jean without looking while fumbling in one of his coat pockets for copper. When he tossed three coins to the fruit seller, she nodded.

"A good evening to you, Master Lamora."

Locke froze and fixed his eyes on her. "I beg your pardon?"

"A good evening to you, is all I said, worthy master."

"You didn't..."

"Didn't what?"

"Ah, nothing." Locke sighed nervously. "I had a bit much to drink, is all. A fair evening to you, as well."

He and Jean strolled away, and Locke took a tentative bite of his pear. It was in a fine state, neither too firm and dry nor too ripe and sticky. "Jean," he said between bites, "did you hear what she said to me, just now?"

"I'm afraid I heard nothing but the death cry of this unfortunate pear. Listen closely: 'Noooo, don't eat me, please, nooo....'" Jean had already reduced his first pear to its core; as Locke watched, he popped this into his mouth, crunched it loudly, and swallowed it all but for the stem, which he flicked away.

"Thirteen gods," said Locke, "*must* you do that?"

"I like the cores," said Jean sulkily. "All the little crunchy bits."

"*Goats* eat the gods-damned crunchy bits."

"You're not my mother."

"Well, true. Your mother would be ugly. Oh, don't give me that look. Go on, eat your other core; it's got a nice juicy pear wrapped around it."

"What did the woman say?"

"She said...oh, gods, she said nothing. I'm tipsy, is all."

"Alchemical lanterns, sirs?" A bearded man held his arm out toward them; at least half a dozen little lanterns in ornamental gilt frames hung from it. "A pair of well-dressed gentlemen should not be without light; only scrubs scuttle about in darkness with no way to see! You'll find no better lanterns in all the Gallery, not by night or day."

Jean waved the man off while he and Locke finished their pears. Locke carelessly tossed his core over his shoulder, while Jean popped his into his mouth, taking pains to ensure that Locke was watching when he did.

"Mmmmmm," he muttered with a half-full mouth, "ambrosial. But you'll never know, you and all your fellow culinary cowards."

"Gentlemen. Scorpions?"

That brought Locke and Jean up short. The speaker was a cloaked, bald-headed man with the coffee-colored skin of an Okanti islander; the man was several thousand miles from home. His well-kept white teeth stood out as he smiled and bowed slightly over his wares. He stood over a dozen small wooden cages; dark shapes could be seen moving about in several of them.

"Scorpions? Real scorpions? Live ones?" Locke bent down to get a better look at the cages, but kept his distance. "What on earth for?"

"Why, you must be fresh visitors here." The man's Therin had a slight accent. "Many on the Sea of Brass are only too familiar with the gray rock scorpion. Can you be Karthani? Camorri?"

"Talishani," said Jean. "These are gray rock scorpions, from here?"

"From the mainland," said the merchant. "And their use is primarily, ahh, recreational."

"Recreational? Are they pets?"

"Oh no, not really. The sting, you see—the sting of the gray rock scorpion is a complex thing. First there is pain, sharp and hot, as you might expect. But after a few minutes, there is a pleasant numbness, a dreamy sort of fever. It is not unlike some of the powders smoked by Jeremites.

After a few stings, a body grows more used to it. The pain lessens and the dreams deepen."

"Astonishing!"

"Commonplace," said the merchant. "Quite a few men and women in Tal Verrar keep one close at hand, even if they don't speak of it in public. The effect is as pleasing as liquor, yet ultimately far less costly."

"Hmmm." Locke scratched his chin. "Never had to stab myself with a bottle of wine, though. And this isn't just some ruse, some amusement for visitors who wouldn't know any better?"

The merchant's smile broadened. He extended his right arm and pulled back the sleeve of his cloak; the dark skin of his slender forearm was dotted with little circular scars. "I would never offer a product for which I was not prepared to vouch myself."

"Admirable," said Locke. "And fascinating, but . . . perhaps there are some customs of Tal Verrar best left unexplored."

"To your own tastes be true." Still smiling, the man pulled his cloak sleeve back up and folded his hands before him. "After all, a scorpion *hawk* was never to your liking, Master Lamora."

Locke felt a sudden cold pressure in his chest. He flicked a glance at Jean, and found the larger man instantly tense as well. Struggling to maintain his outward calm, Locke cleared his throat. "I beg your pardon?"

"I'm sorry." The merchant blinked at him guilelessly. "I merely wished you a pleasant night, gentlemen."

"Right." Locke eyed him for a moment or two longer, then stepped back, turned on his heel, and began to walk across the Night Market once more. Jean was at his side immediately.

"You heard that," whispered Locke.

"Very clearly," said Jean. "I wonder who our friendly scorpion merchant works for?"

"It's not just him," muttered Locke. "The fruit seller called me 'Lamora' as well. You didn't hear that one, but I damn well did."

"Shit. Want to double back and grab one of them?"

"Going somewhere, Master Lamora?"

Locke almost whirled on the middle-aged female merchant who stepped toward them from their right; he managed to keep the six-inch stiletto concealed up his coat sleeve from flying reflexively into his hand. Jean put one arm beneath the back of his coat.

"You seem to be mistaken, madam," said Locke. "My name is Leocanto Kosta."

The woman made no further move toward them; she merely smiled and chuckled. "Lamora... Locke Lamora."

"Jean Tannen," said the scorpion merchant, who had stepped out from behind his little cage-covered table. Other merchants were moving slowly behind them, staring fixedly at Locke and Jean.

"There seems to be a, ah, *misunderstanding* afoot," said Jean. He slid his right hand back out from under his coat; Locke knew from long experience that the head of one of his hatchets would be cupped in his palm, with the handle concealed up his sleeve.

"No misunderstanding," said the scorpion merchant.

"Thorn of Camorr...," said a little girl who stepped out to block their progress toward the Savrola side of the Great Gallery.

"Thorn of Camorr...," said the middle-aged woman.

"Gentlemen Bastards," said the scorpion merchant. "Far from home."

Locke glanced around, his heart hammering in his chest. Deciding that the time for discretion was past, he let his stiletto fall into his itching fingers. All the merchants in the Night Market seemed to have taken an interest in them; they were surrounded, and the merchants were slowly tightening the circle. They cast long dark shadows upon the stones at Locke and Jean's feet. Was Locke imagining things, or were some of the lights dimming? Already the Night Gallery seemed darker—damn, some of the lanterns were indeed going out right before his eyes.

"That is *far enough*." Jean let his hatchet fall visibly into his right hand; he and Locke pressed their backs against one another.

"No closer," shouted Locke. "Cut the weird shit, or there's going to be blood!"

"There has already been blood . . . ," said the little girl.

"Locke Lamora . . . ," muttered a soft chorus of the people surrounding them.

"There has already been blood, Locke Lamora," said the middle-aged woman.

The last alchemical lanterns within the periphery of the Night Market dimmed; the last few fires banked down, and now Locke and Jean faced the circle of merchants solely by the wan light coming from the inner harbor, and from the eerie flicker of distant lamps beneath the vast, deserted Gallery, much too far away for comfort.

The little girl took one last step toward them, her eyes gray and unblinking.

"Master Lamora, Master Tannen," she said in her clear, soft voice, "the Falconer of Karthain sends his regards."

6

LOCKE STARED at the little girl, jaw half-open. She glided forward like an apparition, until just two paces separated them. Locke felt a pang of foolishness at holding a stiletto on a girl not yet three feet high, but then she smiled coldly in the near darkness, and the malice behind that smile steadied his hand on the hilt of the blade. The little girl reached up to touch her chin.

"Though he cannot speak," she said.

"Though he cannot speak for himself . . . ," chorused the circle of merchants, now motionless in the darkness.

"Though he is mad," said the girl, slowly spreading her hands toward Locke and Jean, palms out.

"Mad beyond measure . . . ," whispered the circle.

"His friends remain," said the girl. "His friends remember."

Jean moved beside Locke, and then both of his hatchets were out, blackened steel heads naked to the night. "These people are puppets. There are Bondsmagi somewhere around us," he hissed.

"Show yourselves, you fucking cowards!" said Locke, speaking to the girl.

"We show our power," she replied.

"What more do you need?" whispered the chorus in their ragged circle, their eyes empty as reflecting pools.

"What more do you need to see, Master Lamora?" The little girl gave a sinister parody of a curtsy.

"Whatever you want," said Locke, "leave these people out of it. Just fucking talk to us. We don't want to hurt these people."

"Of *course*, Master Lamora. . . ."

"Of course . . . ," whispered the circle.

"Of course, that's the *point*," said the girl. "So you must hear what we have to say."

"State your gods-damned business, then."

"You must answer," said the girl.

"Answer for the Falconer," said the chorus.

"You must answer. Both of you."

"Of all the . . . *fuck you*!" said Locke, his voice rising to a shout. "We *did* answer for the Falconer. Our answer was ten lost fingers and a lost tongue, for three dead friends. You got him back alive and it was more than he deserved!"

"Not for you to judge," hissed the girl.

"...judge the Magi of Karthain...," whispered the circle.

"Not for you to judge, nor for you to presume a grasp of our laws," said the girl.

"All the world knows it's death to slay a Bondsmage," said Jean. "That, and little else. We let him live and took pains to return him to you. Our business is ended. If you wanted a more complicated treatment than that, you should have sent a fucking letter."

"This is not business," said the girl.

"But personal," said the circle.

"*Personal,*" repeated the girl. "A brother has been blooded; we cannot let this stand unanswered."

"You sons of bitches," said Locke. "You really think you're fucking gods, don't you? I didn't mug the Falconer in an alley and take his purse. *He helped murder my friends!* I'm not sorry he's mad and I'm *not* sorry for the rest of you! Kill us and get on with your business, or piss off and let these people go free."

"No," said the scorpion merchant. A whispered chorus of "no" came from around the circle.

"Cowards. Pissants!" Jean pointed one of his hatchets at the little girl as he spoke. "You can't scare us with this penny-theater bullshit!"

"If you force us to," said Locke, "we'll fight you with the weapons in our hands, all the way to Karthain. You bleed like the rest of us. Seems to me all you *can* do is kill us."

"No," said the girl, giggling.

"We can do worse," said the fruit seller.

"We can let you live," said the scorpion merchant.

"Live, uncertain," said the girl.

"Uncertain...," said the chorus of merchants as they began to step backward, widening their circle.

"Watched," said the girl.

"Followed," said the circle.

"Now wait," said the girl. "Run your little games, and chase your little fortunes...."

"And wait," whispered the chorus. "Wait for our answer."

"Wait for our time."

"You are always in our reach," said the little girl, "and you are always in our sight."

"Always," whispered the circle, slowly dispersing back to their stalls, back to the positions they'd held just a few minutes earlier.

"You will meet misfortune," said the little girl as she slipped away. "For the Falconer of Karthain."

Locke and Jean said nothing as the merchants around them resumed their places in the Night Market, as the lanterns and barrel fires gradually rose once more to flush the area with warm light. Then the affair was ended; the merchants resumed their former attitudes of keen interest or watchful boredom, and the babble of conversation rose up around them again. Locke and Jean slipped their weapons out of sight before anyone seemed to notice them.

"Gods," said Jean, shuddering visibly.

"I suddenly feel," Locke said quietly, "that I didn't drink nearly enough from that bloody carousel." There was mist at the edges of his vision; he put a hand to his cheeks and was surprised to find himself crying. "Bastards," he muttered. "Infants. Wretched cowardly show-offs."

"Yes," said Jean.

Locke and Jean began to walk forward once again, glancing warily around. The little girl who had done most of the speaking for the Bondsmagi was now sitting beside an elderly man, sorting through little baskets of dried figs under his supervision. She smiled shyly as they passed.

"I hate them," whispered Locke. "I hate *this*. Do you think they've really got something planned for us, or was that just a put-on?"

"I suppose it works either way," said Jean with a sigh. "Gods. *Strat péti*. Do we flinch, or do we keep betting? Worst case, we've got a few thousand solari on record at the 'Spire. We could cash out, take a ship, be gone before noon tomorrow."

"Where to?"

"Anywhere else."

"There's no running from these assholes, not if they're serious."

"Yes, but—"

"Fuck Karthain." Locke clenched his fists. "You know, I think I understand. I think I understand how the Gray King could feel the way he did. I've never even been there, but if I could *smash* Karthain, burn the fucking place, make the sea swallow it . . . I'd do it. Gods help me, I'd do it."

Jean suddenly came to a complete stop.

"There's . . . another problem, Locke. Gods forgive me."

"What?"

"Even if you stay . . . I shouldn't. I'm the one who should be gone, as far from you as possible."

"What the *fuck* nonsense is this?"

"They know my name!" Jean grabbed Locke by his shoulders, and Locke winced; that stone-hard grip didn't agree with the old wound beneath his left clavicle. Jean immediately realized his mistake and loosened his fingers, but his voice remained urgent. "My real name, and they can use it. They can make me a puppet, like these poor people. I'm a threat to you every moment I'm around you."

"I don't bloody well care that they know your name! Are you mad?"

"No, but you're still drunk, and you're not thinking straight."

"I certainly am! Do you *want* to leave?"

"No! Gods, no, of course not! But I'm—"

"Shutting up right this second if you know what's good for you."

"You need to understand that you're in danger!"

"Of course I'm in danger. I'm *mortal*. Jean, gods love you, I will *not* fucking send you away, and I will not let you send yourself away! We lost Calo, Galdo, and Bug. If I send you away, I lose the last friend I have in the world. Who wins then, Jean? Who's protected *then*?"

Jean's shoulders slumped, and Locke suddenly felt the beginning of the transition from fading inebriation to pounding headache. He groaned.

"Jean, I will never stop feeling awful for what I put you through in Vel Virazzo. And I will never forget how long you stayed with me when you should have tied weights around my ankles and thrown me in the bay. Gods help me, I will *never* be better off without you. I don't care how many Bondsmagi know your damned name."

"I wish I could be sure you knew best about this."

"This is our life," said Locke. "This is our game, that we've put *two years* into. That's our fortune, waiting for us to steal it at the Sinspire. That's all our hopes for the future. So fuck Karthain. They want to kill us, we can't stop them. So what else can we do? I won't jump at shadows on account of those bastards. *On with it!* Both of us together."

Most of the Night Market merchants had taken note of the intensity of Locke and Jean's private conversation, and had avoided making further pitches. But one of the last merchants on the northern fringe of the Night Market was either less sensitive or more desperate for a sale, and called out to them.

"Carved amusements, gentlemen? Something for a

woman or a child in your lives? Something artful from the City of Artifice?" The man had dozens of exotic little toys on an upturned crate. His long, ragged brown coat was lined on the inside with quilted patches in a multitude of garish colors—orange, purple, cloth-of-silver, mustard yellow. He dangled the painted wood figure of a spear-carrying soldier by four cords from his left hand, and with little gestures of his fingers he made the figure thrust at an imaginary enemy. "A marionette? A little puppet, for memory of Tal Verrar?"

Jean stared at him for a few seconds before responding. "For memory of Tal Verrar," he said quietly, "I would want anything, beg pardon, before I would want a puppet."

Locke and Jean said nothing else to each other. With an ache around his heart to match the one growing in his head, Locke followed the bigger man out of the Great Gallery and into the Savrola, eager to be back behind high walls and locked doors, for what little it might prove to be worth.

REMINISCENCE

The Capa of Vel Virazzo

1

Locke Lamora had arrived in Vel Virazzo nearly two years earlier, wanting to die, and Jean Tannen had been inclined to let him have his wish.

Vel Virazzo is a deepwater port about a hundred miles southeast of Tal Verrar, carved out of the high rocky cliffs that dominate the mainland coast on the Sea of Brass. A city of eight or nine thousand souls, it has long been a sullen tributary of the Verrari, ruled by a governor appointed directly by the archon.

A line of narrow Elderglass spires rises two hundred feet out of the water just offshore, one more Eldren artifact of inscrutable function on a coast thick with abandoned wonders. The glass pylons have fifteen-foot platforms atop them and are now used as lighthouses, manned by petty convicts. Boats will leave them to climb up the knotted rope ladders that hang down the pylons. That accomplished, they winch up their provisions and settle in for a few weeks of exile, tending red alchemical lamps the size of small huts. Not all of them come back down right in the head, or live to come back down at all.

Two years before that fateful game of Carousel Hazard,

a heavy galleon swept in toward Vel Virazzo under the red glow of those offshore lights. The hands atop the galleon's yardarms waved, half in pity and half in jest, at the lonely figures atop the pylons. The sun had been swallowed by thick clouds on the western horizon, and a soft, dying light rippled across the water beneath the first stars of evening.

A warm wet breeze was blowing from shore to sea, and little threads of mist seemed to be leaking out of the gray rocks to either side of the old port town. The galleon's yellowed canvas topsails were close-reefed as she prepared to lay to about half a mile offshore. A little harbormaster's skiff scudded out to meet the galleon, green and white lanterns bobbing in its bow to the rhythm of the eight heaving oarsmen.

"What vessel?" The harbormaster stood up beside her bow lanterns and shouted through a speaking trumpet from thirty yards away.

"*Golden Gain;* Tal Verrar," came the return shout from the galleon's waist.

"Do you wish to put in?"

"No! Passengers only, coming off by boat."

The lower stern cabin of the *Golden Gain* smelled strongly of sweat and illness. Jean Tannen was newly returned from the upper deck, and had lost some of his tolerance for the odor, which lent further edge to his bad mood. He flung a patched blue tunic at Locke and folded his arms.

"For fuck's sake," he said, "we're here. We're getting off this bloody ship and back onto good solid stone. Put the bloody tunic on; they're lowering a boat."

Locke shook the tunic out with his right hand and frowned. He was sitting on the edge of a bunk, dressed only in his breeches, and was thinner and dirtier than Jean had ever seen him. His ribs stood out beneath his pale skin like the hull timbers of an unfinished ship. His hair was dark with grease, long and unkempt on every side, and a fine thistle of beard fringed his face.

His upper left arm was crisscrossed with the glistening red lines of barely sealed wounds; there was a scabbed puncture on his left forearm, and beneath that a dirty cloth brace was wound around his wrist. His left hand was a mess of fading bruises. A discolored bandage partially covered an ugly-looking injury on his left shoulder, a scant few inches above his heart. Their three weeks at sea had done much to reduce the swelling of Locke's cheeks, lips, and broken nose, but he still looked as though he'd tried to kiss a kicking mule. Repeatedly.

"Can I get a hand, then?"

"No, you can do it for yourself. You should've been exercising this past week, getting ready. I can't always be here to hover about like your fairy fucking nursemaid."

"Well, let me shove a gods-damn rapier through your shoulder and wiggle it for you, and then let's see how keen you are to exercise."

"I *took* my cuts, you sobbing piss-wallow, and I did exercise 'em." Jean lifted his own tunic; above the substantially reduced curve of his once-prodigious belly was the fresh, livid scar of a long slash across his ribs. "I don't care how much it hurts; you have to move around, or they heal tight like a caulk-seal and then you're really in the shit."

"So you keep telling me." Locke threw the shirt down on the deck beside his bare feet. "But unless that tunic animates itself, or you do the honors, it seems I go to the boat like this."

"Sun's going down. Summer or not, it's going to be cool out there. But if you want to be an idiot, I guess you do go like that."

"You're a son of a bitch, Jean."

"If you were healthy, I'd rebreak your nose for that, you self-pitying little—"

"Gentlemen?" A crew-woman's muffled voice came

through the door, followed by a loud knock. "Captain's compliments, and the boat is ready."

"Thank you," yelled Jean. He ran a hand through his hair and sighed. "Why did I bother saving your life, again? I could've brought the Gray King's corpse. Would've been better fucking company."

"Please," said Locke forcefully, gesturing with his good arm. "We can meet in the middle. I'll pull with my good arm and you handle the bad side. Get me off this ship and I'll get to exercising."

"Can't come soon enough," said Jean, and after another moment's hesitation he bent down for the tunic.

2

JEAN'S TOLERANCE rose for a few days with their release from the wet, smelly, heaving world of the galleon; even for paying customers, long-distance sea transit still had more in common with a prison sentence than a vacation.

With their handful of silver volani (converted from Camorri solons at an extortionate rate by the first mate of the *Golden Gain,* who'd argued that it was still preferable to the numismatic mugging they'd get from the town's moneychangers), he and Locke secured a third-floor room at the Silver Lantern, a sagging old inn on the waterfront.

Jean immediately set about securing a source of income. If Camorr's underworld had been a deep lake, Vel Virazzo's was a stagnant pond. He had little trouble sussing out the major dockside gangs and the relationships between them. There was little organization in Vel Virazzo, and no boss-of-bosses to screw things up. A few nights of drinking in all the right dives, and he knew exactly who to approach.

They called themselves the Brass Coves, and they

skulked about in an abandoned tannery down on the city's eastern docks, where the sea lapped against the pilings of rotting piers that had seen no legitimate use in twenty years. By night, they were an active crew of sneak-thieves, muggers, and coat-charmers. By day, they slept, diced, and drank away most of their profits. Jean kicked in their door (though it hung loosely in its frame, and wasn't locked) at the second hour of the afternoon on a bright, sunny day.

There were an even dozen of them in the old tannery, young men between the ages of fifteen and twenty-odd. Standard membership for a local-trouble sort of gang. Those who weren't awake were slapped back to consciousness by their associates as Jean strolled into the center of the tannery floor.

"Good afternoon!" He gave a slight bow, from the neck, then spread his arms wide. "Who's the biggest, meanest motherfucker here? Who's the best bruiser in the Brass Coves?"

After a few seconds of silence and surprised stares, a relatively stocky young man with a crooked nose and a shaved head leapt down onto the dusty floor from an open staircase. The boy walked up to Jean and smirked.

"You're lookin' at him."

Jean nodded, smiled, then whipped both of his arms around so that his cupped hands cracked against both of the boy's ears. He staggered, and Jean took a firm hold of his head, lacing his fingers tightly behind the rear arch of his skull. He pulled the tough's head sharply downward and fed him a knee—once, twice, three times. As the boy's face met Jean's kneecap for the last time, Jean let go, and the tough sprawled backward on the tannery floor, senseless as a side of cold, salted meat.

"Wrong," said Jean, not even breathing heavily. "*I'm* the meanest motherfucker here. *I'm* the biggest bruiser in the Brass Coves."

"You ain't in the Brass Coves, asshole," shouted another boy, who nonetheless had a look of awed disquiet on his face.

"Let's kill this piece of shit!"

A third boy, wearing a tattered four-cornered cap and a set of handmade necklaces threaded with small bones, darted toward Jean with a stiletto drawn back in his right hand. When the thrust came, Jean stepped back, caught the boy by the wrist, and yanked him forward into a backfist from his other hand. While the boy spat blood and tried to blink tears of pain from his eyes, Jean kicked him in the groin, then swept his legs out from under him. The boy's stiletto appeared in Jean's left hand as if by magic, and he twirled it slowly.

"Surely you boys can do simple sums," he said. "One plus one equals *don't fuck with me*."

The boy who'd charged at him with the knife sobbed, then threw up.

"Let's talk taxes." Jean walked around the periphery of the tannery floor, kicking over a few empty wine bottles; there were dozens of them scattered around. "Looks like you boys pull in enough coin to eat and drink; that's good. I'll have forty percent of it; cold metal. I don't want goods. You'll pay your taxes every other day, starting today. Cough up your purses and turn out your pockets."

"Fuck that!"

Jean stalked toward the boy who'd spoken; the youth was standing against the far wall of the tannery with his arms crossed. "Don't like it? Hit me, then."

"Uh…"

"You don't think that's fair? You mug people for a living, right? Make a fist, son."

"Uh…"

Jean grabbed him, spun him around, took hold of him by his neck and by the top of his breeches, and rammed him headfirst into the thick wood of the tannery's outer wall several times. The boy hit the ground with a thud when Jean let go; he was unable to fight back when Jean patted down his tunic and came up with a small leather purse.

"Added penalty," said Jean, "for damaging the wall of my tannery with your head." He emptied the purse into his own, then tossed it back down beside the boy. "Now, all of you get down here and line up. Line up! Four-tenths isn't much. Be honest; you can guess what I'll do if I find out that you're not."

"Who the hell *are* you?"

The first boy to approach Jean with coins in his hand offered up the question along with the money.

"You can call me—"

As Jean began to speak, the boy conjured a dagger in his other hand, dropped the coins, and lunged. The bigger man shoved the boy's extended arm to the outside, bent nearly in half, and slammed his right shoulder into the boy's stomach. He then lifted the boy effortlessly on his shoulder and dropped him over his back, so that the boy struck the floor of the tannery nearly facefirst. He ended up writhing in pain beside the last Cove who'd pulled a blade on Jean.

"... Callas. Tavrin Callas, actually." Jean smiled. "That was a good thought, coming at me while I was talking. That at least I can respect." Jean shuffled backward several paces to block the door. "But it seems to me that the subtle philosophical concept I'm attempting to descant upon may be going over your heads. Do I really have to kick all your asses before you take the hint?"

There was a chorus of mutterings and a healthy number of boys shaking their heads, however reluctantly.

"Good." The extortion went smoothly after that; Jean wound up with a satisfying collection of coins, surely enough to keep him and Locke ensconced at their inn for another week. "I'm off, then. Rest easy and work well tonight. I'll be back tomorrow, at the second hour of the afternoon. We can start talking about how things are going to be now that I'm the new boss of the Brass Coves."

3

NATURALLY, THEY all armed themselves, and at the second hour of the afternoon the next day they were waiting in ambush for Jean.

To their surprise, he strolled into the old tannery with a Vel Virazzo constable at his side. The woman was tall and muscular, dressed in a plum-purple coat reinforced with a lining of fine iron chain; she had brass epaulettes on her shoulders, and long brown hair pulled back in a tight swordswoman's tail with brass rings. Four more constables took up a position just outside the door; they wore similar coats, but also carried long lacquered sticks and heavy wooden shields slung over their backs.

"Hello, lads," said Jean. All around the room, daggers, stilettos, broken bottles, and sticks were disappearing from sight. "I'm sure some of you recognize Prefect Levasto and her men."

"Boys," said the prefect offhandedly, hooking her thumbs into her leather sword-belt. Alone of all the constables, she carried a cutlass in a plain black sheath.

"Prefect Levasto," said Jean, "is a wise woman, and she leads wise men. They happen to enjoy money, which I am now providing as a consideration for the hardship and tedium of their duties. If anything should chance to happen to me, why, they would lose a new source of the very thing they enjoy."

"It would be heartbreaking," said the prefect.

"And it would have consequences," said Jean.

The prefect set one of her boots on an empty wine bottle and applied steady pressure until it shattered beneath her heel. "Heartbreaking," she repeated with a sigh.

"I'm sure you're all bright lads," said Jean. "I'm sure you've all enjoyed the prefect's visit."

"Shouldn't like to have to repeat it," said Levasto with a grin. She turned slowly and ambled back out the door. The sound of her squad marching away soon receded into the distance.

The Brass Coves looked down at Jean glumly. The four boys closest to the door, with their hands behind their backs, were the ones wearing livid black and green bruises from before.

"Why the fuck are you doing this to us?" grumbled one of them.

"I'm not your enemy, boys. Believe it or not, I think you'll really come to appreciate what I can do for you. Now shut up and listen.

"First," said Jean, raising his voice so everyone could hear, "I'd like to say that it's rather sad, how long you've been around without getting the city watch on the take. They were so *eager* for it when I made the offer. Like sad, neglected little puppies."

Jean was wearing a long black vest over a stained white tunic. He reached up beneath his back, under the vest, with his right hand.

"But," he continued, "at least the fact that your first thought was to kill me shows some spirit. Let's see those toys again. Come on, show 'em off."

Sheepishly, the boys drew out their weapons once again, and Jean inspected them with a sweep of his head. "Mmmm. Gimp steel, broken bottles, little sticks, a hammer...Boys, the trouble with this setup is that you think those are threats. They're not. They're insults."

He started moving while the last few words were still coming out of his mouth; his left hand slid up beneath his vest beside his right. Both of his arms came out and up in a blur, and then he grunted as he let fly with both of his hatchets, overhand.

There was a pair of half-full wineskins hanging on pegs on the far wall; each one exploded in a gout of cheap Verrari red that spattered several boys nearby. Jean's hatchets had impaled the wineskins dead center, and stuck in the wood behind them without quivering.

"That was a threat," he said, cracking his knuckles. "And that's why *you* now work for *me*. Anyone else really want to dispute that at this point?"

The boys standing closest to the wineskins edged backward as Jean stepped over and wrenched his hatchets out of the wall. "Didn't think so. But don't take it amiss," Jean continued. "It works in your favor, too. A boss needs to protect what's his if he's going to stay the boss. If anyone other than *me* tries to shove you around, let me know. I'll pay them a visit. That's my job."

The next day, the Brass Coves grudgingly lined up to pay their taxes. The last boy in line, as he dropped his copper coins into Jean's hands, muttered, "You said you'd help if someone else gave us the business. Some of the Coves got kicked around this morning by the Black Sleeves, from over on the north side."

Jean nodded sagely and slipped his takings into his coat pocket.

The next night, after making inquiries, he sauntered into a north-side dive called the Sign of the Brimming Cup. The only thing the tavern was brimming with was thugs, a good seven or eight of them, all with dirty black cloths tied around the arms of their jackets and tunics. They were the only customers, and they looked up with suspicion as he closed the door behind him and carefully slid home the wooden bolt.

"Good evening!" He smiled and cracked his knuckles.

"I'm curious. Who's the biggest, meanest motherfucker in the Black Sleeves?"

The day after that, he collected his taxes from the Brass Coves with the bruised knuckles of his right hand wrapped in a poultice. For the first time, most of the boys paid enthusiastically. A few even started to call him "Tav."

4

BUT LOCKE did not exercise his wounds, as he'd promised.

Locke's thin supply of coins was parceled out for wine; his poison of choice was a particularly cheap local slop. More purple than red, with a bouquet like turpentine, its scent soon saturated the room he shared with Jean at the Silver Lantern. Locke took it constantly "for the pain"; Jean remarked one evening that his pain must be increasing as the days went on, for the empty skins and bottles were multiplying proportionally. They quarreled—or more accurately rekindled their ongoing quarrel—and Jean stomped off into the night, for neither the first nor the last time.

Those first few days in Vel Virazzo, Locke would totter down the steps to the common room some nights, where he would play a few desultory hands of cards with some of the locals. He conned them mirthlessly with whatever fast-fingers tricks he could manage with just one good hand. Soon enough they began to shun his games and his bad attitude, and he retreated back to the third floor, to drink alone in silence. Food and cleanliness remained afterthoughts. Jean tried to get a dog-leech in to examine Locke's wounds, but Locke drove the man out with a string of invective that made Jean (whose speech could be colorful enough to strike fire from damp tinder) blush.

"Of your friend, I can find no trace," said the man. "He seems to have been eaten by one of the thin hairless apes from the Okanti isles; all it does is screech at me. What became of the last leech to take a look at him?"

"We left him in Talisham," said Jean. "I'm afraid my friend's attitude moved him to bring an early end to his own sea voyage."

"Well, I might have done the same. I waive my fee, in profound sympathy. Keep your silver—you shall need it for wine. Or poison."

More and more, Jean found himself spending time with the Brass Coves for no better reason than to avoid Locke. A week passed, then another. "Tavrin Callas" was becoming a known and solidly respected figure in Vel Virazzo's crooked fraternity. Jean's arguments with Locke became more circular, more frustrating, more pointless. Jean instinctively recognized the downward arc of terminal self-pity, but had never dreamed that he'd have to drag Locke, of all people, out of it. He avoided the problem by training the Coves.

At first, he passed on just a few hints—how to use simple hand signals around strangers, how to set distractions before picking pockets, how to tell real gems from paste and avoid stealing the latter. Inevitably, he began to receive respectful entreaties to "show them a thing or two" of the tricks he'd used to pound four Coves into the ground. First in line with these requests were the four who'd been pounded.

A week after that, the alchemy was fully under way. Half a dozen boys were rolling around in the dust of the tannery floor while Jean coached them on all the essentials—leverage, initiative, situational awareness. He began to demonstrate the tricks, both merciful and cruel, that had kept him alive over half a lifetime spent making his points with his fists and hatchets.

Under Jean's influence, the boys began to take more of an interest in the state of their old tannery. He explicitly encouraged them to start viewing it as a headquarters, which demanded certain comforts. Alchemical lanterns appeared hanging from the rafters. Fresh oilpaper was nailed up over the broken windows, and new planks and straw were raised up to the roof to plug holes. The boys stole cushions, cheap tapestries, and portable shelves.

"Find me a hearthstone," said Jean. "Steal me a big one, and I'll teach you poor little bastards how to cook, too. You can't beat Camorr for chefs; even the thieves are chefs back there. I had years of training."

He stared around at the increasingly well-maintained tannery, at the increasingly eager band of young thieves living in it, and he spoke wistfully to himself. "We all did."

He'd tried to interest Locke in the project of the Brass Coves, but had been rebuffed. That night he tried again, explaining about their ever-increasing nightly take, their headquarters, the tips and training he was giving them. Locke stared at him for a long time, sitting on the bed with a chipped glass half-full of purple wine in his hands.

"Well," he said at last. "Well, I can see you've found your replacements, haven't you?"

Jean was too startled to say anything. Locke drained his glass and continued, his voice flat and humorless.

"That was certainly quick. Quicker than I expected. A new gang, a new burrow. Not a glass one, but you can probably fix that if you look around long enough. So here you are, playing Father Chains, lighting a fire under that kettle of happy horse-shit all over again."

Jean exploded across the room and slapped the empty glass out of Locke's hand; it shattered against the wall and showered half the room with glittering fragments, but Locke didn't even blink. Instead, he leaned back against his sweat-stained pillows and sighed.

"Got any twins yet? How about a new Sabetha? A new *me*?"

"To *hell* with you!" Jean clenched his fists until he could feel the warm, slick blood seeping out beneath his nails. "To hell with you, Locke! I didn't save your gods-damned life so you could sulk in this gods-damned hovel and pretend you're the man who invented grief. You're not that gods-damned special!"

"Why *did* you save me then, Saint Jean?"

"Of all the stupid fucking questions—"

"Why?" Locke heaved himself up off the bed and shook his fists at Jean; the effect would have been comical, but all the murder in the world was in his eyes. "I told you to *leave* me! Am I supposed to be grateful for this? This bloody room?"

"I didn't make this room your whole world, Locke. You did."

"*This* is what I was rescued for? Three weeks sick at sea, and now Vel Virazzo, asshole of Tal Verrar? It's the joke of the gods, and I'm the punchline. Dying with the Gray King was better. I told you to fucking leave me there!

"And I miss them," he said, his voice nearly a whisper. "Gods, I miss them. It's my fault they're dead. I can't . . . I can't stand it. . . ."

"Don't you dare," growled Jean.

He shoved Locke in the chest, forcefully. Locke fell backward across his bed and hit the wall of the room hard enough to rattle the window shutters.

"Don't you dare use them as an excuse for what you're doing to yourself! Don't you fucking *dare*."

Without another word, Jean spun on his heels, walked out the door, and slammed it behind him.

5

LOCKE SANK down against the bed, put his face in his hands, and listened to the creak of Jean's footsteps recede from the hall outside.

To his surprise, that creak returned a few minutes later, growing steadily louder. Jean threw the door open, face grim, and marched directly over to Locke with a tall wooden bucket of water in his hands. Without warning, he threw this all over Locke, who gasped in surprise and fell backward against the wall again. He shook his head like a dog and pushed his sopping hair out of his eyes.

"Jean, are you out of your fucking—"

"You needed a bath," Jean interrupted. "You were covered in self-pity."

He threw the bucket down and moved around the room, plucking up any bottle or wineskin that still contained liquid. He was finished before Locke realized what he was doing; he then swiped Locke's coin purse from the room's little table and tossed a thin leather package down in its place.

"Hey, Jean, Jean, you can't—that's mine!"

"Used to be 'ours,'" said Jean coldly. "I liked that better."

When Locke tried to jump up from the bed again, Jean pushed him back down effortlessly. He then stormed out once more, and pulled the door shut behind him. There was a curious clicking noise, and then nothing—not even a creak on the floorboards. Jean was waiting right outside the door.

Snarling, Locke moved across the room and tried to pull the door open, but it held fast in its frame. He frowned in puzzlement and rattled it a few more times. The bolt was on this side, and it wasn't shot.

"It's a curious fact," Jean said through the door, "that the rooms of the Silver Lantern can be locked from the outside with a special key only the innkeeper has. In case he wants to keep an unruly guest at bay while he calls for the watch, you see."

"Jean, open this fucking door!"

"No. You open it."

"I can't! You told me yourself you've got the special key!"

"The Locke Lamora I used to know would *spit* on you," said Jean. "Priest of the Crooked Warden. *Garrista* of the Gentlemen Bastards. Student of Father Chains. Brother to Calo, Galdo, and Bug! Tell me, what would *Sabetha* think of you?"

"You . . . you bastard! Open this door!"

"Look at yourself, Locke. You're a fucking disgrace. Open it yourself."

"You. Have. The. Godsdamnedmotherfuckingkey."

"You know how to charm a lock, right? I left you some picks on the table. You want your wine back, you work the bloody door yourself."

"You son of a *bitch*!"

"My mother was a saint," said Jean. "The sweetest jewel Camorr ever produced. The city didn't deserve her. I can wait out here all night, you know. It'll be easy. I've got all your wine and all *your* money."

"Gaaaaaaaaaaah!"

Locke snatched the little leather wallet off the table; he wiggled the fingers of his good right hand and regarded his left hand more dubiously; the broken wrist was mending, but it ached constantly.

He bent over the lock mechanism by the door, scowled, and went to work. He was surprised at how quickly the muscles of his back began to protest his uncomfortable posture. He stopped long enough to pull the room's chair over so he could sit on it while he worked.

As his picks rattled around inside the lock and he bit his tongue in concentration, he heard the heavy creak of movement outside the door and a series of loud thumps.

"Jean?"

"Still here, Locke," came Jean's voice, now cheerful.

"Gods, you're taking your sweet time. Oh, I'm sorry—have you even started yet?"

"When I get this door open, you're dead, Jean!"

"When you get that door open? I look forward to many long years of life, then."

Locke redoubled his concentration, falling back into the rhythm he'd learned over so many painstaking hours as a boy—moving the picks slightly, feeling for sensations. That damn creaking and thumping had started up on the other side of the door again! What was Jean playing at now? Locke closed his eyes and tried to block the sound out of his mind...tried to let his world narrow down to the message of the picks against his fingers.

The mechanism clicked open. Locke stumbled up from his chair, jubilant and furious, and yanked the door open.

Jean had vanished, and the narrow corridor outside the room was packed wall to wall with wooden crates and barrels—an impassable barrier about three feet from Locke's face.

"Jean, what the *hell* is this?"

"I'm sorry, Locke." Jean was obviously standing directly behind his makeshift wall. "I borrowed a few things from the keeper's larder, and got a few of the boys you cheated at cards last week to help me carry it all up here."

Locke gave the wall a good shove, but it didn't budge; Jean was probably putting his full weight against it. There was a faint chorus of laughter from somewhere on the other side, probably down in the common room. Locke ground his teeth together and beat the flat of his good hand against a barrel.

"What the hell's the matter with you, Jean? You're making a gods-damned scene!"

"Not really. Last week I told the keeper you were a Camorri don traveling incognito, trying to recover from a bout of madness. Just now I set an awful lot of silver on his bar. You do remember silver, don't you? How we used to steal it from people, back when you were pleasant company?"

"This has ceased to amuse me, Jean! Give me back my gods-damned wine!"

"Gods-damned, it is. And I'm afraid that if you want it, you're going to have to climb out your window."

Locke took a step back and stared at the makeshift wall, dumbfounded.

"Jean, you can't be serious."

"I've never been more serious."

"Go to hell. Go to hell! I can't climb out a bloody window. My wrist—"

"You fought the Gray King with one arm nearly cut off. You climbed out a window five hundred feet up in Raven's Reach. And here you are, three stories off the ground, helpless as a kitten in a grease barrel. Crybaby. Pissant."

"You are deliberately trying to provoke me!"

"No shit," said Jean. "Sharp as a cudgel, you are."

Locke stomped back into the room, fuming. He stared at the shuttered window, bit his tongue, and stormed back to Jean's wall.

"Please let me out," he said, as evenly as he could manage. "Your point is driven home."

"I'd drive it home with a blackened steel pike if I had one," said Jean. "Why are you talking to me when you should be climbing out the window?"

"Gods *damn* you!"

Back to the room; Locke paced furiously. He swung his arms about tentatively; the cuts on his left arm ached, and the deep wound on his shoulder still twinged cruelly. His battered left wrist felt as though it *might* almost serve. Pain or no pain...he curled his left-hand fingers into a fist, stared down at them, and then looked up at the window with narrowed eyes.

"Fuck it," he said. "I'll show you a thing or three, you son of a bloody silk merchant."

Locke tore his bedding apart, knotting sheet-ends to blankets, inviting twinges from his injuries. The pain only seemed to drive him on faster. He tightened his last knot, threw open the shutters, and tossed his makeshift rope out the window. He tied the end in his hands to his bed frame. It wasn't a terribly sturdy piece of furniture, but then, he didn't weigh all that much.

Out the window he went.

Vel Virazzo was an old, low city; Locke's impressions as he swung there, three stories above the faintly misted street, came in flashes. Flat-topped, sagging buildings of stone and plaster...reefed sails on black masts in the harbor...white moonlight gleaming on dark water...red lights burning atop glass pylons, in a line receding out toward the horizon. Locke shut his eyes, clung to his sheets, and bit his tongue to avoid throwing up.

It seemed easiest to simply let himself slide downward; he did so in fits and starts, letting his palms grow warm against the sheets and blankets before stopping. Down ten feet...twenty...he balanced precariously on the top sill of the inn's common-room window and gasped in a few deep breaths before continuing. Warm as the night was, he was getting chilly from the soaking he'd received.

The last end of the last sheet ended about six feet off the ground; Locke slid down as far as he could, then let himself drop. His heels slapped against the cobblestones, and he found that Jean Tannen was already waiting for him, with a cheap gray cloak in his hands. Before Locke could move, Jean flung the cloak around his shoulders.

"You son of a bitch," cried Locke, pulling the cloak around himself with both hands. "You snake-souled, dirty-minded *son of a bitch*! I hope a shark tries to suck your cock!"

"Why, Master Lamora, look at you," said Jean. "Charming a lock, climbing out a window. Almost as though you used to be a thief."

"I was pulling off hanging offenses when you were still teeth-on-tits in your mother's arms!"

"And I've been pulling off hanging offenses while you've been sulking in your room, drinking away your skills."

"I'm the best thief in Vel Virazzo," growled Locke, "drunk or sober, awake or asleep, and you damn well know it."

"I might have believed that once," said Jean. "But that was a man I knew in Camorr, and he hasn't been with me for some time."

"Gods *damn* your ugly face," yelled Locke as he stepped up to Jean and punched him in the stomach. More surprised than hurt, Jean gave him a solid shove. Locke flew backward, cloak whirling as he tried to keep his balance—until he collided with a man who'd been coming down the street.

"Mind your fucking step!" The stranger, a middle-aged man in a long orange coat and the prim clothes of a clerk or a lawscribe, wrestled for a few seconds with Locke, who clutched at him for support.

"A thousand pardons," said Locke, "A thousand pardons, sir. My friend and I were merely having a discussion; the fault is all mine."

"I daresay it is," said the stranger, at last succeeding in prying Locke from his coat lapels and thrusting him away. "You have breath like a wine cask! Bloody Camorri."

Locke watched until the man was a good twenty or thirty yards down the street, then whirled back toward Jean, dangling a little black leather purse in the air before him. It jingled with a healthy supply of heavy coins.

"Ha! What do you say to that, hmmm?"

"I say it was bloody child's play. Doesn't mean a gods-damned thing."

"Child's play? Die screaming, Jean, that was—"

"You're mangy," said Jean. "You're dirtier than a Shades' Hill orphan. You've lost weight, though where from is a great mystery. You haven't been exercising your wounds or letting anyone tend to them for you. You've been hiding in a room, letting your condition slip away, and you've been drunk for two straight weeks. You're not what you were, and it's your own damn fault."

"So." Locke scowled at Jean, slipped the purse into a tunic pocket, and straightened the cloak on his shoulders. "You require a demonstration. Fine. Get back inside and take down your silly wall, and wait for me in the room. I'll be back in a few hours."

"I—"

But Locke had already thrown up the hood of his cloak, turned, and begun to stride down the street, into the warm Vel Virazzo night.

6

JEAN CLEARED the barrier from the third-floor hall-way, left a few more coins (from Locke's purse) with the bemused innkeeper, and bustled about the room, allowing some of the smell of drunken enclosure to evaporate out the open window. Upon reflection, he went down to the bar and came back with a glass decanter of water.

Jean was pacing, worriedly, when Locke burst back in about four hours later, just past the third hour of the morning. He set a huge wicker basket down on the table, threw off his cloak, grabbed the bucket Jean had used to douse him, and noisily threw up in it.

"My apologies," he muttered when he finished. He was flushed and breathing heavily, as wet as he'd been when he'd left, but now with warm sweat. "The wine has not entirely left my head . . . and my wind has all but deserted me."

Jean passed him the decanter, and Locke slurped from it as shamelessly as a horse at a trough. Jean helped him into the chair. Locke said nothing for a few seconds, then suddenly seemed to notice Jean's hand on his shoulder, and he recoiled. "Here we are, then," he gasped. "See what happens when you provoke me? I think we're going to have to flee the city."

"What the—what have you done?"

Locke tore the lid from his basket; it was the sort commonly used by merchants to haul small loads of goods to and from a street market. A prodigious assortment of odds and ends lay inside, and Locke began to list them off as he pulled them out and showed them to Jean.

"What's this? Why, it's a pile of purses . . . one-two-three-*four* of them, all plucked from sober gentlemen in open streets. Here's a knife, two bottles of wine, a pewter ale mug—dented a bit, but still good metal. A brooch, three gold pins, two earrings—*earrings,* Master Tannen, plucked from *ears,* and I'd like to see you try that. Here's a little bolt of nice silk, a box of sweetmeats, two loaves of bread—the crusty kind with all the spices baked in that you like so much. And now, specially for the edification of a certain pessimistic, peace-breaking son of a bitch who shall remain nameless . . ."

Locke held up a glittering necklace, a braided band of gold and silver supporting a heavy gold pendant, studded with sapphires in the stylized pattern of a floral blossom. The little phalanx of stones flashed like blue fire even by the light of the room's single soft lantern.

"That's a sweet piece," said Jean, briefly forgetting to be aggravated. "You didn't snatch that off a street."

"No," said Locke, before taking another deep draught of

the warm water in the decanter. "I got it from the neck of the governor's mistress."

"You can't be serious."

"In the governor's manor."

"Of all the—"

"In the governor's bed."

"Damned lunatic!"

"With the governor sleeping next to her."

The night quiet was broken by the high, distant trill of a whistle, the traditional swarming noise of city watches everywhere. Several other whistles joined in a few moments later.

"It is possible," said Locke with a sheepish grin, "that I have been slightly too bold."

Jean sat down on the bed and ran both of his hands through his hair. "Locke, I've spent the past few weeks making a name for Tavrin Callas as the biggest, brightest thing to come along in this city's sad little pack of Right People for ages! When the watch starts asking questions, someone's going to point me out...and someone's going to mention all the time I spend here, and the time I spend with you...and if we try to fence a piece of metal like that in a place this small..."

"As I said, I think we're going to have to flee the city."

"Flee the city?" Jean jumped up and pointed an accusatory finger at Locke. "You've screwed up weeks of work! I've been training the Coves—signals, tricks, teasing, fighting, the whole bit! I was going to...I was going to start teaching them how to cook!"

"Oooh, this is serious. I take it the marriage proposal wasn't far behind?"

"Dammit, this *is* serious! I've been *building* something! I've been out working while you've been sobbing and sulking and pissing your time away in here."

"You're the one who lit a fire under me because he

wanted to see me dance. Now I've danced, and I believe I've made my point. Will you be apologizing?"

"Apologizing? You're the one who's been an insufferable little shit! Letting you live is apology enough! All my work..."

"Capa of Vel Virazzo? Is that how you saw yourself, Jean? Another Barsavi?"

"Another *anything*," said Jean. "There's worse things to be—Capa Lamora, for example, Lord of One Smelly Room. I won't be a bloody knockabout, Locke. I am an honest working thief and I'll do what I have to, to keep a roof over our heads!"

"So let's go somewhere and get back to something really lucrative," said Locke. "You want honest crooked work? Fine. Let's go hook a big fish just like we used to in Camorr. You wanted to see me steal, let's go out and *steal*!"

"But Tavrin Callas..."

"Has died before," said Locke. "Seeker into Aza Guilla's mysteries, right? Let him seek again."

"Dammit." Jean stepped over to the window and took a peek out; there was still whistling coming from several directions. "It might take a few days to arrange a berth on a ship, and we won't get out by land with what you've stolen—they'll be checking everyone at the gates, probably for a week or two to come."

"Jean," said Locke, "now you're disappointing *me*. Gates? Ships? Please. This is *us* we're talking about. We could smuggle a live cow past every constable in this city, at high noon. Without clothes."

"Locke? Locke *Lamora*?" Jean rubbed his eyes with exaggerated motions. "Why, where have you been all these weeks? Here I thought I'd been rooming with a miserable self-absorbed asshole who—"

"Right," said Locke. "Fine. Ha. Yeah, maybe I deserved that kick in the face. But I'm serious, getting us out is as easy as a bit of cooking. Get down to the innkeeper. Wake him up and throw some more silver at him—there's plenty in those purses. I'm a mad Camorri don, right? Tell him I've got a mad whim. Get me some more dirty cloth, some apples, a hearthstone, and a black iron pot full of water."

"Apples?" Jean scratched his beard. "Apples? You mean . . . the apple mash trick?"

"Just so," said Locke. "Get me that stuff, and I'll get boiling, and we can be out of here by dawn."

"Huh." Jean opened the door, slipped out into the hall, and turned once before leaving for good. "I take some of it back," he said. "You might still be a lying, cheating, lowdown, greedy, grasping, conniving, pocket-picking son of a bitch."

"Thanks," said Locke.

7

A DRIZZLE was pattering softly around them as they walked out through Vel Virazzo's north gate a few hours later. Sunrise was a watery line of yellow on the eastern horizon, under scudding charcoal clouds. Purple-jacketed soldiers stared down in revulsion from atop the city's fifteen-foot wall; the heavy wooden door of the small sallyport slammed shut behind them as though it too was glad to be quit of them.

Locke and Jean were both dressed in tattered cloaks, and wrapped in bandagelike fragments from a dozen torn-up sheets and pieces of clothing. A thin coating of boiled apple mash, still warm, soaked through some of the "bandages" on their arms and chests, and was plastered liberally over their faces. Sloshing around wearing a layer of the stuff under cloth was disgusting, but there was no better disguise to be had in all the world.

Slipskin was a painful, incurable disease, and those

afflicted with it were even less tolerated than lepers. Had Locke and Jean approached from outside Vel Virazzo's walls, they never would have been let in. As it was, the guards had no interest in how they'd entered the city in the first place; they'd nearly stumbled over themselves in their haste to see them gone.

The outer city was an unhappy-looking place: a few blocks of crumbling one- and two-story buildings, decorated here and there with the makeshift windmill towers favored in these parts for driving bellows over forges and ovens. Smoke sketched a few curling gray lines in the wet air overhead, and thunder rumbled in the distance. Beyond the city, where the cobbles of the old Therin Throne road became a wet dirt track, Locke could see scrubland, interrupted here and there by rocky clefts and piles of debris.

Their coins—and all of their other small goods worth transporting—were tucked into a little bag tied under Jean's clothes, where no guardsman would dare search, not even if a superior stood behind him with a drawn sword and ordered it on pain of death.

"Gods," Locke muttered as they trudged along beside the road, "I'm getting too tired to think straight. I really have let myself slouch out of condition."

"Well," said Jean, "you're going to get some exercise these next few days, whether you like it or not. How're the wounds?"

"They itch," said Locke. "This damn mush does them little good, I suspect. Still, it's not as bad as it was. A few hours of motion seems to have had some benefit."

"Wise in the ways of all such things is Jean Tannen," said Jean. "Wiser by far than most; especially most named Lamora."

"Shut your fat, ugly, inarguably wiser face," said Locke. "Mmmm. Look at those idiots scamper away from us."

"Would you do otherwise, if you saw a pair of real slip-skinners by the side of the road?"

"Eh. I suppose not. Damn these aching feet, too."

"Let's get a mile or two outside town, then find a place to rest. Once we've put some leagues under our heels, we can ditch this mush and pose as respectable travelers again. Any idea where you want to strike out for?"

"I should've thought it was obvious," said Locke. "These little towns are for pikers. We're after gold and white iron, not clipped coppers. Let's make for Tal Verrar. Something's bound to present itself there."

"Mmm. Tal Verrar. Well, it is close."

"Camorri have a long and glorious history of kicking the piss out of our poor Verrari cousins, so I say, on to Tal Verrar," said Locke. "And glory." They walked on a ways under the tickling mist of the morning drizzle. "And baths."

CHAPTER TWO

REQUIN

1

THOUGH LOCKE SAW that Jean remained as unsettled by their experience in the Night Market as he was, they spoke no further of the matter. There was a job to be done, and they were up at the crack of dusk the next day.

The close of the working day for honest men and women in Tal Verrar was just the beginning of theirs. It had been strange at first, getting used to the rhythm of a city where the sun simply fell beneath the horizon like a quiescent murder victim each night, without the glow of Falselight to mark its passing. But Tal Verrar had been built to different tastes or needs than Camorr, and its Elderglass simply mirrored the sky, raising no light of its own.

Their suite at the Villa Candessa was high-ceilinged and opulent; at five silver volani a night nothing less was to be expected. Their fourth-floor window overlooked a cobbled courtyard in which carriages, studded with lanterns and outriding mercenary guards, came and went with echoing clatters.

"Bondsmagi," muttered Jean as he tied on his neckcloths before a looking glass. "I'll never hire one of the bastards to do so much as heat my tea, not if I live to be richer than the duke of Camorr."

"Now there's a thought," said Locke, who was already dressed and sipping coffee. A full day of sleep had done wonders for his head. "If we were richer than the duke of Camorr, we could hire a whole pack of them and give them instructions to go lose themselves on a desolate fucking island somewhere."

"Mmm. I don't think the gods made any islands desolate enough for my tastes."

Jean finished his neck-cloths with one hand and reached for his breakfast with the other. One of the odder services the Villa Candessa provided for its long-term guests was its "likeness cakes"—little frosted simulacra fashioned after the guests by the inn's Camorr-trained pastry sculptor. On a silver tray beside the looking glass, a little sweetbread Locke (with raisin eyes and almond-butter blond hair) sat beside a rounder Jean with dark chocolate hair and beard. The baked Jean's legs were already missing.

A few moments later, Jean was brushing the last buttery crumbs from the front of his coat. "Alas, poor Locke and Jean."

"They died of consumption," said Locke.

"I do wish I could be there to see it when you talk to Requin and Selendri, you know."

"Hmmm. Can I trust you to still be in Tal Verrar by the time I get finished?" He tried to leaven the question with a smile, only partially succeeding.

"You know I won't go anywhere," said Jean. "I'm still not sure it's wise. But you know I won't."

"I do. I'm sorry." He finished his coffee and set the cup down. "And my chat with Requin isn't going to be that terribly interesting."

"Nonsense. I heard a smirk in your voice. Other people

smirk when their work is finished; you grin like an idiot just before yours really begins."

"Smirking? I'm as slack-cheeked as a corpse. I'm just looking forward to being done with it. Tedious business. I anticipate a dull meeting."

"Dull meeting, my ass. Not after you walk straight up to the lady with the brass bloody hand and say, 'Excuse me, madam, but...'"

2

"I HAVE been cheating," said Locke. "Steadily. At every single game I've played since my partner and I first came to the Sinspire, two years ago."

Receiving a piercing stare from Selendri was a curious thing; her left eye was nothing but a dark hollow, half-covered with a translucent awning that had once been a lid. Her single good eye did the work of two, and damned if it wasn't unnerving.

"Are you deaf, madam? Every single one. Cheating. All the way up and down this precious Sinspire, cheating floor after floor, taking your other guests for a very merry ride."

"I wonder," she said in her slow, witchy whisper, "if you truly understand what it means to say that to me, Master Kosta. Are you drunk?"

"I'm as sober as a suckling infant."

"Is this something you've been put up to?"

"I am completely serious," said Locke. "And it's your master I would speak to about my motivations. Privately."

The sixth floor of the Sinspire was quiet. Locke and Selendri were alone, with four of Requin's uniformed attendants waiting about twenty feet away. It was still too early in the evening for this level's rarefied crowd to have finished their slow, carousing migration up through the livelier levels.

At the heart of the sixth floor was a tall sculpture within a cylinder of transparent Elderglass. Though the glass could not be worked by human arts, there were literally millions of cast-off fragments and shaped pieces scattered around the world, some of which could be conveniently fitted to human use. There were Elderglass scavenging guilds in several cities, capable of filling special needs in exchange for exorbitant fees.

Within the cylinder was something Locke could only describe as a *copperfall*—it was a sculpture of a rocky waterfall, taller than a man, in which the rocks were shaped entirely from silver volani coins, and the "water" was a constant heavy stream of copper centira, thousands upon thousands of them. The clatter within the soundproof glass enclosure must have been tremendous, but for those on the outside the show proceeded in absolute silence. Some mechanism in the floor was catching the stream of coins and recirculating it up the back of the silver "rocks." It was eccentric and hypnotic.... Locke had never before known anyone to decorate a room with a literal pile of money.

"Master? You presume that I have one."

"You know I mean Requin."

"He would be the first to correct your presumption. Violently."

"A private audience would give us a chance to clear up several misunderstandings, then."

"Oh, Requin will certainly speak to you—*very* privately." Selendri snapped the fingers of her right hand twice and the four attendants converged on Locke. Selendri pointed up; two of them took firm hold of his arms, and together they began to lead him up the stairs. Selendri followed a few steps behind.

The seventh floor was dominated by another sculpture within an even wider Elderglass enclosure. This one seemed to be a circle of volcanic islands, again built from silver volani, floating in a sea of solid-gold solari. Each of the silver peaks had a stream of gold coins bubbling from its top, to fall back down into the churning, gleaming "ocean." Requin's guards maintained a pace too vigorous for Locke to catch many more details of the sculpture or the room; they passed another pair of uniformed attendants beside the stairwell and continued up.

At the heart of the eighth floor was a third spectacle within glass, the largest yet. Locke blinked several times and suppressed an appreciative chuckle.

It was a stylized sculpture of Tal Verrar, silver islands nestled in a sea of gold coins. Standing over the model city, bestriding it like a god, was a life-sized marble sculpture of a man Locke recognized immediately. The statue, like the man, had prominent curving cheekbones that lent the narrow face a sense of mirth—plus a round protruding chin, wide eyes, and large ears that seemed to have been jammed into the head at right angles. Requin, whose features bore a fair resemblance to a marionette put together in haste by a somewhat irate puppeteer.

The statue's hands were held outward at the waist, spread forward, and from the flaring stone cuffs around them two solid streams of gold coins were continually gushing onto the city below.

Locke, staring, only avoided tripping over his own feet because the attendants holding him chose that moment to tighten their grip. Atop the eighth-floor stairs was a pair of lacquered wooden doors. Selendri strode past Locke and the attendants. To the left of the door was a small silver panel in the wall; Selendri slid her brass hand into it, let it settle into some sort of mechanism, and then gave it a half-turn to the left. There was a clatter of clockwork devices within the wall, and the doors cracked open.

"Search him," she said as she vanished through the doors without turning around.

Locke was rapidly stripped of his coat; he was then poked, prodded, sifted, and patted down more thoroughly than he'd been during his last visit to a brothel. His sleeve-stiletto (a perfectly ordinary thing for a man of consequence to carry) was confiscated, his purse was shaken out, his shoes were slipped off, and one attendant even ran his hands through Locke's hair. When this process was finished, Locke (shoeless, coatless, and somewhat disheveled) was given a less-than-gentle shove toward the doors Selendri had vanished through.

Past them was a dark space not much larger than a wardrobe closet. A winding black iron staircase, wide enough for one person, rose up from the floor toward a square of soft yellow light. Locke padded up the stairs and emerged into Requin's office.

This place took up the whole of the ninth floor of the Sinspire; an area against the far wall, curtained off with silk drapes, probably served as a bedroom. There was a balcony door on the right-hand wall, covered by a sliding mesh screen. Locke could see a wide, darkened sweep of Tal Verrar through it, so he presumed it looked east.

Every other wall of the office, as he'd heard, was liberally decorated with oil paintings—nearly twenty of them around the visible periphery of the room, in elaborate frames of gilded wood—masterworks of the late Therin Throne years, when nearly every noble at the emperor's court had kept a painter or sculptor on the leash of patronage, showing them off like pets. Locke hadn't the training to tell one from another by sight, but rumor had it that there were two Morestras and a Ventathis on Requin's walls. Those two artists—along with all their sketches, books of theory, and apprentices—had died centuries before, in the firestorm that had consumed the imperial city of Therim Pel.

Selendri stood beside a wide wooden desk the color of a fine coffee, cluttered with books and papers and miniature clockwork devices. A chair was pushed out behind it, and Locke could see the remnants of a dinner—some sort of fish on a white iron plate, paired with a half-empty bottle of pale golden wine.

Selendri touched her flesh hand to her brass simulacrum, and there was a clicking noise. The hand folded apart like the petals of a gleaming flower. The fingers locked into place along the wrist and revealed a pair of blackened-steel blades, six inches long, previously concealed at the heart of the hand. Selendri waved these like a claw and gestured for Locke to stand before the desk, facing it.

"Master Kosta." The voice came from somewhere behind him, within the silk-curtained enclosure. "What a pleasure! Selendri tells me you've expressed an interest in getting *killed*."

"Hardly, sir. All I told your assistant was that I had been cheating steadily, along with my partner, at the games we've been playing in your Sinspire. For nearly the last two years."

"Every game," said Selendri. "You said every single game."

"Ah, well," said Locke with a shrug, "it just sounded more dramatic that way. It was more like *nearly* every game."

"This man is a clown," whispered Selendri.

"Oh, no," said Locke. "Well, maybe occasionally. But not now."

Locke heard footsteps moving toward his back across the room's hardwood floor. "You're here on a bet," said Requin, much closer.

"Not in the way that you mean, no."

Requin stepped around Locke and stood before him, hands behind his back, peering at Locke very intently. The man was a virtual twin of his statue on the floor below; perhaps a few pounds heavier, with the bristling curls of steel-gray hair atop his head receding more sharply. His narrow frock coat was crushed black velvet, and his hands were covered with brown leather gloves. He wore optics, and Locke was surprised to see that the glimmer he had taken for reflected light the night before was actually imbued within the glass. They glowed a translucent orange, giving a demonic cast to the wide eyes behind them. Some fresh, expensive alchemy Locke had never heard of, no doubt.

"Did you drink anything unusual tonight, Master Kosta? An unfamiliar wine, perhaps?"

"Unless the water of Tal Verrar itself intoxicates, I'm as dry as baked sand."

Requin moved behind his desk, picked up a small silver fork, speared a white morsel of fish, and pointed at Locke with it.

"So, if I'm to believe you, you've been successfully cheating here for two years, and aside from the sheer impossibility of that claim, now you just want to give yourself up to me. Case of conscience?"

"Not even remotely."

"An earnest wish for an elaborate suicide?"

"I aim to leave this office alive."

"Oh, you wouldn't necessarily be dead until you hit the cobblestones nine stories below."

"Perhaps I can convince you I'm worth more to you intact."

Requin chewed his fish before speaking again.

"Just how have you been cheating, Master Kosta?"

"Fast-fingers work, mostly."

"Really? I can tell a cardsharp's fingers at a glance. Let's see that right hand of yours." Requin held out his gloved left hand, and Locke hesitantly put his own forward, as though they might shake.

Requin snatched Locke's right hand above the wrist and slammed it down atop his desk—but rather than the sharp rap Locke expected, his hand tipped aside some sort of disguised panel and slid into an aperture just beneath the surface of the desk. There was a loud *clack* of clockwork, and a cold pressure pinched his wrist. Locke jerked back, but the desk had swallowed his hand like the unyielding maw of a beast. Selendri's twin steel claws turned casually toward him, and he froze.

"There now. Hands, hands, hands. They get their owners into such trouble, Master Kosta. Selendri and I are two who would know." Requin turned to the wall behind his desk and slid back a lacquered wood panel, revealing a long, shallow shelf set into the wall.

Within were dozens of sealed glass jars, each holding something dark and withered. Dead spiders? No, Locke corrected himself—human hands. Severed, dried, and stored as trophies, with rings still gleaming on many of their curled and desiccated fingers.

"Before we proceed to the inevitable, that's what we usually do," Requin said in a lightly conversational tone. "Right hand, ta-ta. I've got it down to a pretty process. Used to have carpets in here, but the damn blood made for *such* a mess."

"Very prudent of you." Locke felt a single bead of sweat start its slow slide down his forehead. "I am as awed and chastised as you no doubt hoped. Might I have my hand back?"

"In its original condition? I doubt it. But answer some questions, and we'll see. Now, fast-fingers work, you say.

But forgive me—my attendants are extremely adept at spotting cardsharps."

"I'm sure your attendants mean well." Locke knelt down before the desk, the most comfortable position possible, and smiled. "But I can finger-dance a live cat into a standard deck of fifty-six, and slip it back out at leisure. Other players might complain about the noise, but they'd never spot the source."

"Set a live cat on my desk, then."

"It was, ah, a colorful figure of speech. Live cats, unfortunately, aren't in fashion as evening accessories for gentlemen of Tal Verrar this season."

"Pity. But hardly a surprise. I've had quite a few dead men kneeling where you are now, offering colorful figures of speech and little else."

Locke sighed. "Your boys removed my coat and my shoes, and if they'd patted me down any more thoroughly they would have been fingering my liver. But what's this?"

He shook out his left sleeve, and held up his left hand to show that a deck of cards had somehow fallen into it.

Selendri shoved her blades toward Locke's throat, but Requin waved her back with a smile on his face. "He can hardly kill me with a pack of cards, darling. Not bad, Master Kosta."

"Now," said Locke, "let's see." He held his arm straight out to the side, with the deck held firmly upright between his thumb and all four fingers. A twist of the wrist, a flick of his thumb, and the deck was cut. He began to flex and splay his fingers, steadily increasing his tempo until they moved like a spider taking fencing lessons. Cut and shuffle, cut and shuffle—he sliced the deck apart and slid it back together no fewer than a dozen times. Then, with one smooth flourish, he slapped it down on the desk and spread it in a long arc, displacing several of Requin's knick-knacks.

"Pick one," said Locke. "Any one you like. Look at it, but don't show it to me."

Requin did as instructed. While he peeked at the card he'd drawn, Locke gathered the rest of the deck with a reverse slide across Requin's desktop; he shuffled and cut once more, then split the deck and left half on top of the desk. "Go ahead and place your chosen card atop that half of the deck. Remember it, now."

When Requin returned the card, Locke slapped the other half of the deck down on top of it. Taking the full deck in his left hand, he did his one-handed cut-and-shuffle another five times. Then, he slid the top card from the deck—the four of Chalices—onto Requin's desk and smiled. "This, master of the Sinspire, is your card."

"No," said Requin with a smirk.

"Shit." Locke flicked out the next card from the top, the Sigil of the Sun. "Aha—I knew it was around there, somewhere."

"No," said Requin.

"Damn me," said Locke, and he rapidly went through the next half dozen from the top of the deck. "Eight of Spires? Three of Spires? Three of Chalices? Sigil of the Twelve Gods? Five of Sabers? Shit. Mistress of Flowers?" Requin shook his head for each one.

"Huh. Excuse me." Locke set the deck of cards down on Requin's desk, then fumbled at the clasp of his right sleeve with his left hand. After a few seconds, he slid the sleeve back above his elbow and reset the clasp. Suddenly, there was another deck of cards in his left hand.

"Let's see. . . . Seven of Sabers? Three of Spires? No, we already did that one. . . . Two of Chalices? Six of Chalices? Master of Sabers? Three of Flowers? Damn, damn. That deck wasn't so good after all."

Locke set the second deck down beside the first on Requin's desk, appeared to scratch an itch near the slender black sash above his breeches, and then held up a third deck of cards. He grinned at Requin and raised his eyebrows.

"This trick might work even better if I could have the use of my right hand."

"Why, when you seem to be doing so well without it?"

Locke sighed and flicked the top card from the new deck onto the growing pile atop the desk. "Nine of Chalices! Look familiar?"

Requin laughed and shook his head. Locke set the third deck down beside the ones already on Requin's desk, stood up, and conjured another from somewhere in the vicinity of his breeches.

"But your attendants would of course know," said Locke, "if I were loaded down with four concealed decks of cards, they being so *adept* at spotting something like that on a man with no jacket or shoes . . . wait, four? I may have miscounted. . . ."

He produced a fifth deck from somewhere within his silk tunic, which joined the little tower of cards perched ever more precariously on the edge of the desk.

"Surely I couldn't have hidden *five* decks of cards from your guards, Master Requin. Five would be quite ridiculous. Yet there they are—though I'm afraid that's as good as it gets. To conjure more, I would have to begin producing them from somewhere disagreeable.

"And, I'm sorry to say, I don't seem to have the card you took. But wait. . . . I do know where it might be found. . . ."

He reached across Requin's desk, nudged the wine bottle at its base, and seemed to pluck a facedown card from underneath it.

"Your card," he said, twirling it in the fingers of his left hand. "Ten of Sabers."

"Well," laughed Requin, showing a wide arc of yellowing teeth below the fire-orange circles of his optics. "Very fine, very fine. And one-handed, too. But even if I grant that you could perform such tricks, continuously, in front of my attendants and my other guests...you and Master de Ferra have spent a great deal of time at games that are more rigorously controlled than the open card tables."

"I can tell you how we beat those, too. Simply free me."

"Why relinquish a clear advantage?"

"Then trade it to gain another. Free my right hand," said Locke, mustering every last bit of passionate sincerity he could pour into his words, "and I shall tell you *exactly* why you must never again trust the security of your Sinspire as it stands."

Requin stared down at him, laced his gloved fingers together, and finally nodded to Selendri. She withdrew her blades—though she kept them pointed at Locke—and pressed a switch behind the desk. Locke was suddenly free to stumble back to his feet, rubbing his right wrist.

"Most kind," said Locke with a breeziness that was pure conjuring. "Now, yes, we have played at quite a bit more than the open tables. But which games have we scrupulously avoided? Reds-and-Blacks. Count to Twenty. Fair Maiden's Wish. All the games in which a guest plays against the Sinspire, rather than against another guest. Games mathematically contrived to give the house a substantial edge."

"Hard to make a profit otherwise, Master Kosta."

"Yes. And useless for the purposes of a cheat like myself; I need flesh and blood to fool. I don't care how much clockwork and how many attendants you throw in. In a game between guests, larceny *always* finds a way, sure as water pushes through a ship's seams."

"More bold speech," said Requin. "I admire glibness in the doomed, Master Kosta. But you and I both know that there is no way to cheat at, say, Carousel Hazard, barring four-way complicity between the participants, which would render the game absolutely pointless."

"True. There is no way to cheat the carousel or the cards, at least not here in your spire. But when one cannot cheat the game, one must cheat the players. Do you know what *bela paranella* is?"

"A soporific. Expensive alchemy."

"Yes. Colorless, tasteless, and doubly effective when taken with liquor. Jerome and I were dusting our fingers with it before we handled our cards during each hand last night. Madam Corvaleur has a well-known habit of eating and licking her fingers while playing. Sooner or later, she was bound to take in enough of the drug to pass out."

"Well!" Requin looked genuinely taken aback. "Selendri, do you know anything about this?"

"I can vouch for Corvaleur's habits, at least," she whispered. "It seemed to be her preferred method of irritating her opponents."

"That it did," said Locke. "It was quite a pleasure to see her do herself in."

"I'll grant your story is remotely plausible," said Requin. "I had been . . . curious about Izmila's strange incapacity."

"Indeed. The woman's built like an Elderglass boathouse. Jerome and I had more empty vials than her side did; what she'd had wouldn't have gotten her eyelashes alone drunk, if not for the powder."

"Perhaps. But let's discuss other games. What of Blind Alliances?"

A game of Blind Alliances was played at a circular table with tall, specially designed barriers before each player's hands so that everyone but the person directly across from them (their partner) could see at least some of their cards. Each silent participant set his or her right foot atop the left foot of the person on their right, all around the table, so no player could tap signals to a partner below the table.

Partners therefore had to play by instinct and desperate inference, cut off from each other's sight, voice, and touch.

"A child's stratagem. Jerome and I had special boots constructed, with iron-shod toes beneath the leather. We could slide our feet carefully out the backs of them, and the iron would continue to provide the sensation of a full boot to the person beside us. We could tap entire books to one another with the code we've got. Have you ever known anyone to dominate that game as thoroughly as we did?"

"You can't be serious."

"I can show you the boots."

"Well. You did seem to have an extraordinary run of luck.... But what about billiards? You scored a rather famous victory against Lord Landreval. How could you have finessed that? My house provides all the balls, the sticks, and the handling."

"Yes, so naturally those three things couldn't be fiddled. I paid Lord Landreval's consulting physiker ten solari for insight into his medical complaints. Turns out he's allergic to lemons. Jerome and I rubbed our necks, cheeks, and hands with sliced lemons each night before we played him, and used other oils to mostly cover up the scent. Half an hour in our presence and he'd be so puffed up he could barely see. I'm not sure he ever realized what the problem was."

"You say you won a thousand solari with a few slices of *lemon*? Nonsense."

"Of course you're right. I asked politely if he'd lend me a thousand solari, and he offered to let us publicly humiliate him at his favorite game out of the kindness of his heart."

"Hmmmph."

"How often did Landreval lose before he met Jerome and myself? Once in fifty games?"

"Lemons. I'll be damned."

"Yes. When you can't cheat the game, you'd best find a means to cheat the player. Given information and preparation, there's not a player in your spire Jerome and I can't dance along like a finger-puppet. Hell, someone with my talents who knew enough about me could probably string me right along, too."

"It's a good story, Master Kosta." Requin reached across his desk and took a sip of his wine. "I suppose I can charitably believe at least some of what you claim. I suspected that you and your friend were no more merchant speculators than I am, but at my tower you may claim to be a duke or a three-headed dragon provided you have solid credit. You certainly did before you stepped into my office this evening. Which brings us only to the most important question of all—why the hell are you telling me this?"

"I needed your attention."

"You already had it."

"I needed more than that. I needed you to understand my skills and my inclinations."

"And now you have that as well, inasmuch as I accept your story. What *exactly* do you think that gets you?"

"A chance that what I'm going to say next will actually sink in."

"Oh?"

"I'm not really here to take your guests for a few thousand solari here and a few thousand solari there, Requin. It's been fun, but it's secondary to my actual goal."

Locke spread his hands and smiled apologetically.

"I've been hired to break into your vault, just as soon as I find a way to haul everything in it from right out under your nose."

3

REQUIN BLINKED.

"Impossible!"

"Inevitable."

"This isn't legerdemain or lemons we're talking about now, Master Kosta. Explain yourself."

"My feet are beginning to hurt," said Locke. "And my throat is somewhat dry."

Requin stared at him, then shrugged. "Selendri. A chair for Master Kosta. And a glass."

Frowning, Selendri turned and took a finely wrought dark wood chair with a thin leather cushion from its place on the wall. She placed it behind Locke, and he settled into it with a smile on his face. She then bustled about behind him for a few moments, and returned with a crystal goblet, which she passed to Requin. He picked up the wine bottle and poured a generous stream of red liquid into the goblet. *Red* liquid? Locke blinked—and then relaxed. Kameleona, the shifting wine, of course. One of the hundreds of Tal Verrar's famous alchemical vintages. Requin passed him the goblet, then sat down atop his desk with his arms folded.

"To your health," said Requin. "It needs all the assistance it can get."

Locke took a long sip of the warm wine and allowed himself a few seconds of contemplation. He marveled at the way the taste of apricots transmuted to the sharper flavor of slightly tart apple in midswallow. That sip had been worth twenty volani, if his knowledge of the liquor market was still accurate. He gave a genuinely appreciative nod to Requin, who waved a hand nonchalantly.

"It cannot have escaped your attention, Master Kosta, that my vault is the most secure in Tal Verrar—the single most redundantly protected space in the entire city, in fact, not excepting the private chambers of the archon himself." Requin tugged at the skintight leather of his right glove with the fingers of his left hand. "Or that it is encased within a structure of pristine Elderglass, and accessible only through several layers of metallurgical and clockwork artifice that are, if I may be permitted to stroke my own breechclout, peerless. Or that half the Priori council regards it so highly that they entrust much of their personal fortunes to it."

"Of course," said Locke. "I congratulate you on a very flattering clientele. But your vault doors are guarded by gears, and gears are shaped by men. What one man locks another will sooner or later unlock."

"I say again, impossible."

"And I correct you again. *Difficult.* 'Difficult' and 'impossible' are cousins often mistaken for one another, with very little in common."

"You have more chance of giving birth to a live hippopotamus," said Requin, "than the best thief alive has of making it past the cordon drawn around my vault. But this is silly—we could sit here all night contrasting cocklengths. I say mine is five feet long, you say yours is six, and shoots fire upon command. Let's hurry back to significant conversation. You admit that cheating the mechanisms of my games is out of the question. My vault is the most secure of all mechanisms; am *I* therefore the flesh and blood you were presuming to fool?"

"It's possible this conversation represents me giving up that hope."

"What does cheating my guests have to do with plotting entry into my vault?"

"Originally," said Locke, "we gamed merely to blend in and cover our observance of your operations. Time passed and we made no progress. The cheating was a lark to make the games more interesting."

"My house bores you?"

"Jerome and I are thieves. We've been sharping cards and lifting goods east and west, here to Camorr and back again, for years. Spinning carousels with the well-heeled is only amusing for so long, and we weren't getting far with our job, so we had to stay amused somehow."

"Job. Yes, you said you were hired to come here. Elaborate."

"My partner and I were sent here as the point men of something very elaborate. *Someone* out there wants your vault emptied. Not merely penetrated, but pillaged. Plucked and left behind like an empty honeycomb."

"Someone?"

"Someone. I haven't the faintest notion who; Jerome and I are dealt with through fronts. All of our efforts to penetrate them have been in vain. Our employer is as anonymous to us now as he was two years ago."

"Do you frequently work for anonymous employers, Master Kosta?"

"Only the ones that pay me large piles of good, cold metal. And I can assure you—this one has been paying us very well."

Requin sat down behind his desk, removed his optics, and rubbed his eyes with his gloved hands. "What's this new game, Master Kosta? Why favor me with all of this?"

"I tire of our employer. I tire of Jerome's company. I find Tal Verrar much to my taste, and I wish to arrange a new situation for myself."

"You wish to turn your coat?"

"If you must put it that way, yes."

"What do you suggest I have to gain from this?"

"First, a means to work against my current employer. Jerome and I aren't the only agents set against you. Our job is the vault, and nothing else. All the information we gather on your operations is being passed to someone else. They're waiting for us to come up with a means to crack your money-box, and then they've got further plans for you."

"Go on."

"The other benefit would be mutual. I want a job. I'm tired of running from city to city chasing after work. I want to settle in Tal Verrar, find a home, maybe a woman. After I help you deal with my current employer, I want to work for you, here."

"As an entertainer, perhaps?"

"You need a floor boss, Requin. Tell me truly, are you as complacent about your security as you were before I came up your stairs? I know how to cheat every single game that *can* be cheated here, and if I weren't sharper than your attendants I'd already be dead. Who better to keep your guests playing fairly?"

"Your request is . . . logical. Your willingness to shrug off your employer isn't. Don't you fear their retribution?"

"Not if I can help you put us both beyond it. Identification is the problem. Once identified, any man or woman in the world can be dealt with. You have every gang in Tal Verrar under your thumb, and you have the ear of the Priori. Surely you could make the arrangements if we could come up with names."

"And your partner, Master de Ferra?"

"We've worked well together," said Locke. "But we quarreled, not long ago, over an intensely personal matter. He believes his insult is forgiven; I assure you it is anything but. I want to be quits with him when our current employer is dealt with. I want him to know before he dies that I've had the best of him. If possible, I'd like to kill him myself. That and the job are my only requests."

"Mmm. What do you think of all this, Selendri?"

"Some mysteries are better off with their throats slit," she whispered.

"You might fear that I'm trying to displace you," said Locke. "I assure you, when I said floor boss I meant floor boss. I don't want your job."

"And you could never *have* it, Master Kosta, even if you

did want it." Requin ran his fingers down Selendri's right forearm and squeezed her undamaged hand. "I admire your boldness only to a point."

"Forgive me, both of you. I had no intention of presuming too much. Selendri, for what it's worth, I agree with you. In your position, getting rid of me might seem like wisdom. Mysteries *are* dangerous to people in our profession. I am no longer pleased with the mystery of my employment. I want a more predictable life. What I ask and what I offer are straightforward."

"And in return," said Requin, "I receive possible insight into an alleged threat against a vault I have enhanced by my own design to be impenetrable."

"A few minutes ago, you expressed the same confidence concerning your attendants and their ability to spot cardsharps."

"Have you penetrated my vault security as thoroughly as you say you've danced around my attendants, Master Kosta? Have you penetrated it at all?"

"All I need is time," said Locke. "Give it to me and a way will make itself plain, sooner or later. I'm not giving up because it's too hard; I'm giving up because it pleases me. But don't just take my word on my sincerity; look into the activities of Jerome and myself. Make inquiries about everything we've been doing in your city for the past two years. We have made some progress that might open your eyes."

"I shall," said Requin. "And in the meantime, what am I to do with you?"

"Nothing extraordinary," said Locke. "Make your inquiries. Keep your eyes on Jerome and myself. Continue to let us play at your spire—I promise to play more fairly, at least for the coming few days. Allow me to think on my plans and gather whatever information I can about my anonymous employer."

"Let you walk out of here, unscathed? Why not hold you

somewhere secure, while I exercise my curiosity about your background?"

"If you take me seriously enough to consider any part of my offer," said Locke, "then you must take the possible threat of my employer seriously as well. Any tip-off to them that I've been compromised, and Jerome and I might be cast loose. So much for your opportunity."

"So much for your usefulness, you mean. I am to take a great deal on faith, from a man offering to betray and kill his business partner."

"You hold my purse, as surely as your desk held my hand. All the coin I have in Tal Verrar, I keep here with your Sinspire. You may look for my name at any countinghouse in the city, and you will not find it. I give you that leverage over me, willingly."

"A man with a grudge, a genuine grudge, might piss on all the white iron in the world for one chance at his real target, Master Kosta. I have been that target too many times to forget this."

"I am *not* crass," said Locke, taking back one of his decks of cards from Requin's desktop. He shuffled it a few times without looking at it. "Jerome insulted me without good cause. Pay me well and treat me well, and I will never give you any reason for displeasure."

Locke whisked the top card off his desk, flipped it, and set it down faceup beside the remnants of Requin's dinner. It was the Master of Spires.

"I deliberately choose to throw in with you, if you'll have me. Place a bet, Master Requin. The odds are favorable."

Requin pulled his optics out of his coat pocket and slipped them back on. He seemed to brood over the card; nothing was said by anyone for some time. Locke sipped quietly from his glass of wine, which had turned pale blue and now tasted of juniper.

"Why," said Requin at last, "all other considerations aside, should I allow you to violate the cardinal rule of my spire on your own initiative and suffer nothing in exchange?"

"Only because I imagine that cheaters are ordinarily discovered by your attendants while other guests are watching," said Locke, attempting to sound as sincere and contrite as possible. "Nobody knows about my confession, outside this office. Selendri didn't even tell your attendants why they were hauling me up here."

Requin sighed, then drew a gold solari from within his scarlet coat and set it down atop Locke's Master of Spires.

"I shall hold fast with a small wager for now," said Requin. "Do anything unusual or alarming, and you will not survive long enough to reconsider. At the slightest hint that anything you've told me has been a lie, I will have molten glass poured down your throat."

"Uh . . . that seems fair."

"How much money do you currently have on the ledger here?"

"Just over three thousand solari."

"Two thousand of that is no longer yours. It will remain on the ledger so Master de Ferra doesn't get suspicious, but I'm going to issue instructions that it is not to be released to you. Consider it a reminder that my rules are not to be broken on anyone's recognition but my own."

"Ouch. I suppose I should be grateful. I mean, I am. Thank you."

"You walk on eggshells with me, Master Kosta. Step delicately."

"Then I may go? And I may think of myself as in your service?"

"You may go. And you may consider yourself on my *sufferance*. We will speak again when I know more about your recent past. Selendri will accompany you back down to the first floor. Get out of my sight."

With an air of faint disappointment, Selendri folded the brass fingers of her artificial hand up, until it was whole once again and the blades were hidden. She gestured toward the stairs with that hand, and with the look in her good eye she told him precisely how much patience she had to spare for him if Requin's should start to wane.

4

JEAN TANNEN sat reading in a private booth at the Gilded Cloister, a club on the second tier of the Savrola, just a few blocks down from the Villa Candessa. The Cloister was a labyrinth of dark wood enclosures, well padded with leather and quilting, for the benefit of diners wishing an unusual degree of solitude. The waitstaff, in their leather aprons and drooping red caps, were forbidden to speak, answering all customer requests with either a nod or a shake of the head.

Jean's dinner, smoked rock eel in caramel brandy sauce, lay chopped into fragments and scattered like debris from a battle. He was making his way slowly through dessert, a cluster of marzipan dragonflies with crystallized sugar wings that glimmered by the steady glow of the booth's candles. He was absorbed in a leather-bound copy of Lucarno's *Tragedy of the Ten Honest Turncoats,* and he didn't notice Locke until the smaller man was already seated across from him in the booth.

"Leocanto! You gave me a start."

"Jerome." They both spoke in a near whisper. "You really were nervous, weren't you? Nose buried in a book to keep you from going mad. Some things never change."

"I wasn't nervous. I was merely reasonably concerned."

"You needn't have been."

"Is it done, then? Am I successfully betrayed?"

"Quite betrayed. Absolutely sold out. A dead man walking."

"Wonderful! And his attitude?"

"Guarded. Ideal, I'd say. Had he been too enthusiastic, I would be worried. And had he not been enthusiastic at all, well..." Locke mimicked shoving a knife into his chest and wiggling it several times. "Is this smoked eel?"

"Help yourself. It's stuffed with apricots and soft yellow onions. Not entirely to my taste."

Locke took up Jean's fork and helped himself to a few bites of the eel; he was more partial to the stuffing than Jean had been. "We're going to lose two-thirds of my account, it seems," he said after making some progress on the dish. "A tax on cheating to remind me not to presume too much on Requin's patience."

"Well, it's not as though we expected to get out of the city with the money in those accounts. Might've been nice to have it for a few more weeks, at least."

"True. But I think the alternative would have been desktop surgery, whether I needed a hand amputated or not. What're you reading?"

Jean showed him the title and Locke feigned choking. "Lucarno? Why is it always Lucarno? You drag him everywhere we go, his damn romances. Your brains will go soft with that mush. You'll end up more fit for tending flower gardens than for running confidence games."

"Well," said Jean, "I shall be sure to criticize your reading habits, Master Kosta, should I ever see you develop any."

"I've read quite a bit!"

"History and biography, mostly what Chains prescribed for you."

"What could possibly be wrong with those subjects?"

"As for history, we are living in its ruins. And as for biographies, we are living with the consequences of all the decisions ever made in them. I tend not to read them for pleasure. It's not unlike carefully scrutinizing the map when one has already reached the destination."

"But romances aren't real, and surely never were. Doesn't that take away some of the savor?"

"What an interesting choice of words. 'Not real, and never were.' Could there be any more appropriate literature for men of our profession? Why are you always so averse to fiction, when we've made it our meal ticket?"

"I live in the real world," said Locke, "and my methods are of the real world. They are, just as you say, a profession. A practicality, not some romantic whim."

Jean set the book down before him and tapped its cover. "This is where we're headed, *Thorn*—or at least you are. Look for us in history books and you'll find us in the margins. Look for us in legends, and you might just find us celebrated."

"Exaggerated, you mean. Lied about. Trumped up, or stamped down. The truth of anything we do will die with us and nobody else will ever have a bloody clue."

"Better that than obscurity! I recall you once had quite a taste for drama. For plays, if nothing else."

"Yes." Locke folded his hands on the table and lowered his voice even further. "And you know what happened to it."

"Forgive me," said Jean with a sigh. "I should have known better than to bring up that particular redheaded subject once again."

A waiter appeared at the entrance to the little booth, looking attentively at Locke.

"Oh, no," said Locke, and set Jean's fork back on the eel plate. "Nothing for me, I'm afraid. I'm just here waiting for my friend to finish his little candy wasps."

"Dragonflies." Jean popped the last one into his mouth,

swallowed it nearly whole, and tucked his book away within his coat. "Give over the bill, and I'll settle up with you."

The waiter nodded, cleared away the used dishes, and left a scrap of paper pinned to a small wooden tablet.

"Well," said Locke as Jean counted copper coins from his purse, "We've no responsibilities for the rest of the evening. Requin is no doubt setting eyes on us as we speak. I think a night or two of light relaxation would be in order, to avoid upsetting him."

"Great," said Jean. "Why don't we wander around a bit, and maybe catch a boat over to the Emerald Galleries? They've got coffeehouses there, and music. Would it be in character for Leo and Jerome to get a bit tipsy and chase tavern dancers?"

"Jerome can murder as much ale as he likes, and bother tavern dancers until the sun chases us home to bed. Leo will sit and watch the festivities."

"Maybe play spot-the-shadow with Requin's people?"

"Maybe. Damn, I wish we had Bug to lurk on a few rooftops for us. We could use a pair of top-eyes; there's not a trustworthy one in this damn city."

"I wish we still had Bug, period," said Jean with a sigh.

They made their way to the foyer of the club, chatting quietly of imaginary business between Masters Kosta and de Ferra, batting little improvisations back and forth for the sake of any prying ears. It was just after midnight when they stepped out into the familiar quiet order and high walls of the Savrola. The place was artificially clean—no knackers here, no blood in the alleys, no piss in the gutters. The gray brick streets were well lit by silvery lanterns in swaying iron frames; the whole district seemed framed in bright moonlight, though the sky tonight was occluded by a high ceiling of dark clouds.

The woman was waiting for them in the shadows on Locke's left.

She matched pace with him as he and Jean moved down the street. One of Locke's sleeve-stilettos fell into the palm of his hand before he could control the reflex, but she stayed a full yard away, with her hands folded behind her back. She was youngish, short and slender with dark hair pulled back into a long tail. She wore a vaguely fashionable dark coat and a four-cornered hat with a long gray silk scarf that trailed behind her like a ship's pennant as she walked.

"Leocanto Kosta," she said in a pleasant, even voice. "I know you and your friend are armed. Let's not be difficult."

"I beg your pardon, madam?"

"Move that blade in your hand, and it's a shaft through the neck for you. Tell your friend to keep his hatchets under his coat. Let's just keep walking."

Jean began to move his left hand beneath his coat; Locke caught him with his right hand and swiftly shook his head. They were not alone on the street; people hurried here and there on business or pleasure, but some of them were staring at him and Jean. Some of them were standing in alleys and shadows, wearing unseasonably heavy cloaks, unmoving.

"Shit," Jean muttered. "Rooftops."

Locke glanced up briefly. Across the street, atop the three- and four-story stone buildings, he could see the silhouettes of at least two men moving slowly along with them, carrying thin, curved objects in their hands. Longbows.

"You appear to have us at a disadvantage, madam," said Locke, slipping his stiletto into a coat pocket and showing her his empty hand. "To what do we owe the pleasure of your attention?"

"Someone wants to have a conversation with you."

"Clearly they knew where to find us. Why not simply join us for dinner?"

"Conversation should be private, don't you think?"

"Did a man in a rather tall tower send you?"

She smiled but said nothing. A moment later, she gestured ahead of them. "At the next corner, take a left. You'll see an open door, first building on your right. Go there. Follow directions."

Sure enough, the promised open door was waiting just past the next crossroads, a rectangle of yellow light casting a pale twin across the ground. The woman went in first. Locke, conscious of the presence of at least four or five nearby lurkers in addition to the rooftop archers, sighed and passed Jean a quick hand signal—*easy, easy*.

The place looked like a shop, disused but otherwise in good repair. There were six more people inside the room, men and women in silver-banded leather doublets with their backs up against the walls. Four of them held loaded crossbows, which neatly quashed any thoughts of resistance Locke might have been teasing around inside his head. Even Jean couldn't balance those odds.

One of the crossbowmen quietly closed the door, and the woman who'd led Locke and Jean in turned. The front of her coat fell open and Locke could see that she, too, was wearing reinforced leather armor. She held out her hands.

"Weapons," she said, politely but firmly. "Smartly, now."

When Locke and Jean glanced at each other, she laughed.

"Don't be dense, gentlemen. If we wanted you dead you'd already be pinned to the wall. I'll take good care of your property for you."

Slowly, resignedly, Locke shook his two stilettos out of his coat, and Jean followed suit with his matched pair of hatchets and no fewer than three daggers of his own.

"I do like men who travel prepared," said the woman.

She passed their weapons to one of the men behind her and drew two lightweight cloth hoods out of her coat. She tossed one to Locke and one to Jean.

"On over your heads, please. Then we can get on with our business."

"Why?" Jean sniffed at his hood suspiciously, and Locke followed suit. The cloth seemed to be clean.

"For your own protection. Do you really want your faces out in the open if we drag you through the streets under guard?"

"I suppose not," said Locke. Frowning, he slipped the hood on and found that it put him in total darkness.

There was a sound of footsteps and the swirl of moving coats. Strong hands seized Locke's arms and forced them together behind his back. A moment later, he felt something being woven tightly around his wrists. There was a louder tumult and a number of irritated grunts from beside him; presumably they had ganged up on Jean in heavy numbers.

"There," came the voice of the woman, now behind Locke. "Now, step lively. Don't worry about falling over—you'll be assisted."

By "assisted" she clearly meant that they'd be seized and carried along by the arms. Locke felt hands close around his biceps, and he cleared his throat.

"Where are we going?"

"For a boat ride, Master Kosta," said the woman. "Don't ask any more questions, because I won't answer them. Let's be on our way."

There was a creak as the door was thrown open once again, and a brief whirling sensation as he was pushed around and reoriented by the people holding him. Then they were moving back out into the muggy Verrari night, and Locke could feel heavy beads of sweat begin to slide their ticklish paths down his forehead.

REMINISCENCE

Best-Laid Plans

1

"Shit," said Locke as the deck of cards exploded outward from his sore left hand. Jean flinched back from the blizzard of paper that fluttered around the compartment of the carriage.

"Try again," said Jean. "Perhaps the eighteenth time's the charm."

"I used to be so damned good at this one-handed shuffle." Locke began plucking up cards and reorganizing them into a neat pile. "I bet I could do it better than Calo and Galdo, even. Damn, my hand aches."

"Well, I know I pushed you to exercise," said Jean, "but you were a little out of practice even before you got hurt. Give it time."

A hard rain was falling around the jouncing black luxury carriage as it threaded its way along the old Therin Throne road through the foothills just east of the Tal Verrar coast. A hunched middle-aged woman worked the reins of the six-horse team from her open box atop the cabin, with the cowl of her oilcloak pulled forward to protect the smoldering bowl of her pipe. Two outrider guards huddled in misery on the rear footboard, secured by wide leather straps around their waists.

Jean was peering over a sheaf of notes, flipping parchment pages back and forth, muttering to himself. The rain was beating hard against the right side of the closed cabin, but they were able to keep the left-hand window open, with its mesh screens and leather shutters drawn back to admit muggy air that smelled of manured fields and salt marshes. A little yellow alchemical globe on the padded seat beside Jean provided reading light.

They were two weeks out from Vel Virazzo, a good hundred miles to the northwest, and well past the need to paint themselves up with apple mash to move freely.

"Here's what all my sources say," said Jean when Locke had finished recovering all of his cards. "Requin's somewhere in his forties. Native Verrari, but he speaks a bit of Vadran and supposedly he's a genius at Throne Therin. He's an art collector, mad about the painters and sculptors from the very last years of the empire. Nobody knows what he did prior to twenty years ago. Apparently he won the Sinspire on a bet and threw the previous owner out a window."

"And he's tight with the Priori?"

"Most of them, it seems."

"Any idea how much he keeps in his vaults?"

"Conservative estimate," said Jean, "at least enough to pay out any debts the house might incur. He could never allow himself to be embarrassed in that respect—so let's say fifty thousand solari, at least. Plus his personal fortune, plus the combined goods and fortunes of a great many people. He doesn't pay interest like the best counting-houses, but he doesn't keep transaction ledgers for the taxmen, either. Supposedly he has one book, hidden gods know where, amended only by his own hand. This is mostly hearsay, of course."

"That fifty thousand doesn't cover anything but the house's operating funds, right? So how much do you presume the *total* contents of his vault would be worth?"

"It's pure entrail-reading, without the entrails, even, but . . . three hundred thousand? Three hundred fifty?"

"Seems reasonable."

"Yes, well, the details on the vault itself are much more solid. Apparently, Requin doesn't mind letting some of the facts get out. Thinks it dissuades thieves."

"They always do, don't they?"

"In this case, they may be onto something. Listen. The Sinspire is nearly sixty yards high, one thick Elderglass cylinder. You know about those; you tried to jump off one about two months ago. Goes down another hundred feet or so into a glass hill. It's got one door at street level, and exactly one door into the vault beneath the tower. One. No secrets, no side entrances. The ground is pristine Elderglass; no tunneling through it, not in a thousand years."

"Mmmm-hmmm."

"Requin's got at least four attendants on each floor at any given time, plus dozens of table minders, card dealers, and waiters. There's a lounge on the third floor where he keeps more out of sight. So figure, at a minimum, fifty or sixty loyal workers on duty with another twenty to thirty he can call out. Lots of nasty brutes, too. He likes to recruit from ex-soldiers, mercenaries, city thieves, and such. He gives cushy positions to his Right People for jobs well done, and he pays them like he was their doting mother. Plus, there are stories of dealers getting a year's wages in tips from lucky blue bloods in just a night or two. Bribery won't be likely to work on anyone."

"Mmmm-hmmm."

"He's got three layers of vault doors, all of them iron-shod witchwood, three or four inches thick. Last set of doors is supposedly backed with blackened steel, so even if you had a week to chop through the other two, you'd never get past the third. All of them have clockwork mechanisms, the best and most expensive Verrari stuff, private designs from masters of the Artificers' Guild. The standing orders are, not one set of doors opens unless he's there himself to see it; he watches every deposit and every withdrawal. Opens the doors a couple times per day at most. Behind the first set of doors are four to eight guards, in rooms with cots, food, and water. They can hold out there for a week, under siege."

"Mmmm-hmmm."

"The inner sets of doors don't open except for a key he keeps around his neck. The outer doors won't open except for a key he always gives to his majordomo. So you'd need them both to get anywhere."

"Mmmm-hmmm."

"And the traps...they're demented, or at least the rumors are. Pressure plates, counterweights, crossbows in the walls and ceilings. Contact poisons, sprays of acid, chambers full of venomous serpents or spiders...One fellow even said that there's a chamber before the last door that fills up with a cloud of powdered strangler's orchid petals, and while you're choking to death on that, a bit of twist-match falls out and lights the whole mess on fire, so then you burn to a crisp. Insult to injury."

"Mmmm-hmmm."

"Worst of all, the inner vault is guarded by a live dragon, attended by fifty naked women armed with poisoned spears, each of them sworn to die in Requin's service. All redheads."

"You're just making that up, Jean."

"I wanted to see if you were listening. But what I'm saying is, I don't care if he's got a million solari in there, packed in bags for easy hauling. I'm inclined to the idea that this vault might not be breakable, not unless you've got three hundred soldiers, six or seven wagons, and a team of master clockwork artificers you're not telling me about."

"Right."

"*Do* you have three hundred soldiers, six or seven wagons, and a team of master clockwork artificers you're not telling me about?"

"No, I've got you, me, the contents of our coin purses, this carriage, and a deck of cards." He attempted a complicated manipulation of the cards, and they erupted out of his hand yet again, scattering against the opposite seat. "Fuck me with a poleax!"

"Then if I might persist, Lord of Legerdemain, perhaps there's some other target in Tal Verrar we might consider—"

"I'm not sure that'd be wise. Tal Verrar's got no twit-riddled aristocracy for us to fool around with. The archon's a military tyrant on a long leash—he can bend the laws as he sees fit, so I'd rather not yank his breechclout. The Priori council is all merchants from common stock, and they'll be damned hard to cheat. There's plenty of likely subjects for small-time games, but if we want a big game, Requin's the best one to hit. He's got what we want, right there for the taking."

"Yet his vault..."

"Let me tell you," said Locke, "exactly what we're going to do about his vault."

Locke spoke for a few minutes while he put his deck of cards together, outlining the barest details of his scheme. Jean's eyebrows strained upward, attempting to take to the air above his head.

"...so that's that. Now what do you say, Jean?"

"I'll be damned. That might just work. If..."

"If?"

"Are you sure you remember how to work a climbing harness? I'm a bit rusty myself."

"We'll have quite a while to practice, won't we?"

"Hopefully. Hmmm. And we'll need a carpenter. One outside Tal Verrar itself, obviously."

"We can go looking into that as well, once we've got a bit of coin back in our pockets."

Jean sighed, and all the banter went out of him like wine from a punctured skin. "I suppose...that just leaves...damn."

"What?"

"I, ah...well, hell. Are you going to break down on me again? Are you going to stay reliable?"

"Stay *reliable*? Jean, you can...Damn it, look for yourself! What have I been doing? Exercising, planning—and apologizing all the damn time! I'm sorry, Jean, I really am. Vel Virazzo was a bad time. I miss Calo, Galdo, and Bug."

"As do I, but..."

"I know. I let my sorrow get the best of me. It was damned selfish, and I *know* you must ache like I do. I said some stupid things. But I thought I'd been forgiven.... Did I misunderstand?" Locke's voice hardened. "Shall I now understand that forgiveness is something prone to going in and out like the tide?"

"Now that's hardly fair. Just—"

"Just what? Am I special, Jean? Am I our only liability? When have I ever doubted your skills? When have I ever treated you like a child? You're not my fucking mother, and you're certainly not Chains. We can't work as partners if you're going to sit in judgment of me like this."

The two of them stared at each other, each trying to muster an attitude of cold indignation, and each failing. The mood within the little cabin turned morose, and Jean turned to stare sullenly out the window for a few moments while Locke dejectedly shuffled his cards. He attempted another one-handed cut, and neither he nor Jean seemed surprised when a little blizzard of paper chits settled into the seat beside Jean.

"I'm sorry," Locke said as his cards fluttered down. "That was another shitty thing to say. Gods, when did we discover how easy it is to be cruel to one another?"

"You're right," Jean said softly. "I'm not Chains and I'm certainly not your mother. I shouldn't push you."

"No, you should. You pushed me off that galleon and you pushed me out of Vel Virazzo. *You* were right. I behaved terribly, and I can understand if you're still...nervous about me. I was so wrapped up in what I'd lost, I forgot what I still had. I'm glad you still worry enough about me to kick my ass when I need it."

"I, ah, look—I apologize as well. I just—"

"Damn it, don't interrupt me when I'm feeling virtuously self-critical. I'm ashamed of how I behaved in Vel Virazzo. It was a slight to everything we've been through together. I promise to do better. Does that put you at ease?"

"Yes. Yes, it does." Jean began to pick up the scattered cards, and the ghost of a smile reappeared on his face. Locke settled back in his seat and rubbed his eyes.

"Gods. We need a target, Jean. We need a *game*. We need someone to go to work on, as a team. Don't you see? It's not just about what we can charm out of Requin. I want it to be us against the world, lively and dangerous, just like it used to be. Where there's no room for this sort of second-guessing, you know?"

"Because we're constantly inches from a horrible bloody death, you mean."

"Right. The good times."

"This plan might take a year," said Jean, slowly. "Maybe two."

"For a game this interesting, I'm *willing* to spend a year or two. You have any other pressing engagements?"

Jean shook his head, passed the collected cards back to

Locke, and went back to his sheaf of notes, a deeply thoughtful expression on his face. Locke slowly traced the outline of the deck of cards with the fingers of his left hand, which felt slightly less useful than a crab claw. He could feel the still-fresh scars itching beneath his cotton tunic—scars so extensive it looked as though most of his left side had been sewn together from rag parts. Gods *damn* it, he was ready to be healed *now*. He was ready to have his old careless agility back. He imagined that he felt like a man of twice his years.

He tried another one-handed shuffle, and the deck fell apart in his hands. At least it hadn't shot apart in all directions. Was that improvement?

He and Jean were silent for several minutes.

Eventually, the carriage rattled around a final small hill and suddenly Locke was looking across a green checkerboard land, sloping downward to sea-cliffs perhaps five or six miles distant. Specks of gray and white and black dotted the landscape, thickening toward the horizon, where the landside of Tal Verrar crowded against the cliff edges. The coastal section of the city seemed pressed down beneath the rain; great silvery curtains were sweeping past behind it, blotting out the islands of Tal Verrar proper. Lightning crackled blue and white in the distance, and soft peals of thunder rolled toward them across the fields.

"We're here," said Locke.

"Landside," said Jean without looking up. "Might as well find an inn when we get there; we'll be hard pressed to find a boat to the islands in weather like this."

"Who shall we be, when we get there?"

Jean looked up and chewed his lip before taking the bait of their old game. "Let's be something other than Camorri for a while. Camorr's brought us nothing good of late."

"Talishani?"

"Seems good to me." Jean adjusted his voice slightly,

adopting the faint but characteristic accent of the city of Talisham. "Anonymous Unknown of Talisham, and his associate Unknown Anonymous, also of Talisham."

"What names did we leave on the books at Meraggio's?"

"Well, Lukas Fehrwight and Evante Eccari are right out. Even if those accounts haven't been confiscated by the state, they'll be watched. You trust the Spider not to get a burr up her ass if she finds out we're active in Tal Verrar?"

"No," said Locke. "I seem to recall... Jerome de Ferra, Leocanto Kosta, and Milo Voralin."

"I opened the Milo Voralin account myself. He's supposed to be Vadran. I think we might leave him in reserve."

"And that's what we have left? Three useful accounts?"

"Sadly, yes. But it's more than most thieves get. I'll be Jerome."

"I suppose I'll be Leocanto, then. What are we doing in Tal Verrar, Jerome?"

"We're... hired men for a Lashani countess. She's thinking of buying a summer home in Tal Verrar and we're there to hunt one down for her."

"Hmmm. That might be good for a few months, but after we've looked at all the available properties, then what? And there's lots of actual work involved, if we don't want everyone to know right away that we're lying through our teeth. What if we call ourselves... merchant speculators?"

"Merchant speculators. That's good. It doesn't have to mean a damn thing."

"Exactly. If we spend all our time lounging around the chance houses cutting cards, well, we're just passing time waiting for market conditions to ripen."

"Or we're so good at our jobs we hardly need to work at all."

"Our lines write themselves. How did we meet, and how long have we been together?"

"We met five years ago." Jean scratched his beard. "On a

sea voyage. We became business partners out of sheer boredom. Since then we've been inseparable."

"Except that my plan calls for me to be plotting your death."

"Yes, but I don't know that, do I? Boon companion! I suspect nothing."

"Chump! I can hardly wait to see you get yours."

"And the loot? Assuming we do manage to work our way into Requin's confidence, and we do manage to call the dance properly, and we do manage to get out of his city with everything intact...we haven't really talked about what comes after that."

"We'll be old thieves, Jean." Locke squinted and tried to pick out details of the rain-swept landscape as the carriage made its final turn down the long, straight road into Tal Verrar. "Old thieves of seven-and-twenty, or perhaps eight-and-twenty, when we finish this. I don't know. How would you feel about becoming a viscount?"

"Lashain," Jean mused. "Buy a pair of titles, you mean? Settle there for good?"

"Not sure if I'd go that far. But last I heard, poor titles were running about ten thousand solari, and better ones fifteen to twenty. It'd give us a home and some clout. We could do whatever we wanted from there. Plot more games. Grow old in comfort."

"Retirement?"

"We can't run around false-facing forever, Jean. I think we both realize that. Sooner or later we'll need to favor another style of crime. Let's tease a nice big score out of this place and then sink it into something *useful*. Build something again. Whatever comes after...well, we can charm that lock when we come to it."

"Viscount Anonymous Unknown of Lashain—and his neighbor, Viscount Unknown Anonymous. There are worse fates, I suppose."

"There certainly are—Jerome. So are you with me?"

"Of course, Leocanto. You know that. Maybe another two years of honest thieving will leave me *ready* to retire. I could get back into silks and shipping, like mother and father—perhaps look up some of their old contacts, if I can remember them right."

"I think Tal Verrar will be good for us," said Locke. "It's a pristine city. We've never worked out of it and it's never seen our like. Nobody knows us; nobody expects us. We'll have total freedom of movement."

The carriage clattered along under the rain, jostling against patches where the weathered stones of the Therin Throne road had been washed clean of their protective layers of dirt. Lightning lit the sky in the distance, but the gray veil swirled thick between land and sea, and the great mass of Tal Verrar was hidden from their eyes as they rode down into it for the first time.

"You're almost certainly right, Locke. I think we *do* need a game." Jean set his notes on his lap and cracked his knuckles. "Gods, but it'll be good to be out and around. It'll be good to be the predators again."

CHAPTER THREE

WARM HOSPITALITY

1

THE CHAMBER WAS a rough brick cube about eight feet on a side. It was completely dark, and an arid sauna heat was radiating from the walls, which were too hot to touch for more than a few seconds. Locke and Jean had been sweltering inside it for only the gods knew how long—probably hours.

"Agh." Locke's voice was cracked. He and Jean were seated back to back in the blackness, leaning against each other for support, with their folded coats beneath them. Locke beat his heels against the stones of the floor, not for the first time.

"Gods damn it!" Locke yelled. "Let us out. You've made your point!"

"What point," rasped Jean, "could that possibly be?"

"I don't know." Locke coughed. "I don't care. Whatever it is, they've damn well made it, don't you think?"

2

THE REMOVAL of their hoods had been a relief, for about two heartbeats.

First had come an interminable interval spent stumbling around in stifling darkness, pulled and prodded along by captors who seemed to be in some haste. Next, there was indeed a boat ride; Locke could smell the warm salt mists rising off the city's harbor, while the deck swayed gently beneath him and oars creaked rhythmically in their locks.

Eventually, that too came to an end; the boat rocked as someone rose and moved about. The oars were drawn in and an unfamiliar voice called for poles. A few moments later, the boat bumped against something, and strong hands again hoisted Locke to his feet. When he'd been helped from the boat to a firm stone surface, the hood was suddenly whisked off his head. He looked around, blinked at the sudden light, and said, "Oh, shit."

At the heart of Tal Verrar, between the three crescent islands of the Great Guilds, lay the Castellana, fortified estate of the dukes of Tal Verrar centuries earlier. Now that the city had dispensed with titled nobility, the mansion-covered Castellana was home to a new breed of well-heeled gentry—the Priori councilors, the independently rich, and those guildmasters whose social positions required the most ostentatious displays of spending power.

At the very heart of the Castellana, guarded by a moat of empty air like a circular Elderglass canyon, was the Mon Magisteria, the palace of the archon—a towering human achievement springing upward from alien grandeur. An elegant stone weed growing in a glass garden.

Locke and Jean had been brought to a point directly beneath it. Locke guessed that they stood within the hollow space that separated the Mon Magisteria from the surrounding island; a million-faceted cavern of darkened Elderglass soared upward around them, and the open air of the upper island lay fifty or sixty feet above their heads. The channel that the boat had traveled through wound away to his left, and the sound of the lapping water was drowned out by a distant rumbling noise with no visible cause.

There was a wide stone landing at the base of the Mon Magisteria's private island, with several boats tied up alongside it, including an enclosed ceremonial barge with silk awnings and gilded woodwork. Soft blue alchemical lamps in iron posts filled the space with light, and behind those posts a dozen soldiers stood at attention. Even if a quick glance upward hadn't told Locke the identity of their captor, those soldiers would have revealed everything.

They wore dark blue doublets and breeches, with black leather bracers, vests, and boots all chased with raised designs in gleaming brass. Blue hoods were drawn up around the backs of their heads, and their faces were covered with featureless oval masks of polished bronze. Grids of tiny pinholes permitted them to see and breathe, but from a distance every impression of humanity was erased—the soldiers were faceless sculptures brought to life.

The Eyes of the Archon.

"Here you are then, Master Kosta, Master de Ferra." The woman who'd waylaid Locke and Jean stepped up onto the landing between them and took them by the elbows, smiling as though they were out for a night on the town. "Is this not a more private place for a conversation?"

"What," said Jean, "have we done to warrant our transport here?"

"I'm the wrong person to ask," said the woman as she pushed them gently forward. "My job is to retrieve, and deliver."

She released Locke and Jean just before the front rank of the archon's soldiers. Their own disquieted expressions were reflected back at them in a dozen gleaming bronze masks.

"And sometimes," said the woman as she returned to the boat, "when guests don't come back out again, my job is to forget that I ever saw them at all."

The Eyes of the Archon moved without apparent signal; Locke and Jean were enveloped and secured by several soldiers apiece. One of them spoke—another woman, her voice echoing ominously. "We will go up. You must not struggle and you must not speak."

"Or what?" said Locke.

The Eye who'd spoken stepped over to Jean without hesitation and punched him in the stomach. The big man exhaled in surprise and grimaced while the female Eye turned back to Locke. "If either of you causes any trouble, I'm instructed to punish the *other* one. Do I make myself clear?"

Locke ground his teeth together and nodded.

A wide set of switchback stairs led upward from the landing; the glass underfoot was rough as brick. Flight by flight the archon's soldiers led Locke and Jean up past gleaming walls, until the moist night breeze of the city was on their faces once again.

They emerged within the perimeter defined by the glass chasm. A guardhouse stood just this side of the thirty-foot gap, beside a drawbridge currently hauled straight up into the air and set inside a heavy wood frame. Locke presumed that was the usual means of entrance to the archon's domain.

The Mon Magisteria was a ducal fortress in the true Therin Throne style, easily fifteen stories high at its peak and three or four times as wide. Layer after layer of crenellated battlements rose up, formed from flat black stones that seemed to absorb the fountains of light thrown up by dozens of lanterns burning on the castle's grounds.

Columned aqueducts circled the walls and towers at every level, and decorative streams of water cascaded down from sculptures of dragons and sea monsters set at the fortress' corners.

The Eyes of the Archon led Locke and Jean toward the front of the palace, down a wide path dusted with white gravel. There were lush green lawns on either side of the path, set behind decorative stone borders that made the lawns seem like islands. More blue-robed and black-armored guards in bronze masks stood unmoving along the path, holding up blackened-steel halberds with alchemical lights built into their wooden shafts.

Where most castles would have a front gate the Mon Magisteria had a rushing waterfall wider than the path on which they stood; this was the source of the noise Locke had heard echoing at the boat landing below. Multiple torrents of water crashed out of huge, dark apertures set in a line running straight up the castle wall. These joined and fell into a churning moat at the very base of the structure, a moat even wider than the glass-sided canyon that cut the castle grounds off from the rest of the Castellana.

A bridge, slightly arched, vanished into the pounding white waterfall about halfway over the moat. Warm mist wafted up around them as their party approached the edge of this bridge, which Locke could now see had some sort of niche cut into it, running right down its center for its full visible length. Beside the bridge was an iron pull-chain hanging from the top of a narrow stone pillar. The Eye officer reached up for this and gave it three swift tugs.

A moment later there came a metallic rattling noise from the direction of the bridge. A dark shape loomed within the waterfall, grew, and then burst out toward them with mist and water exploding off its roof. It was a giant box of iron-ribbed wood, fifteen feet high and as wide as the bridge. Rumbling, it slid along the track carved into the bridge until it halted with a squeal of metal on metal just before them. Doors popped open toward them, pushed from the inside by two attendants in dark blue coats with silver-braid trim.

Locke and Jean were ushered into the roomy conveyance, which had windows set into the end facing the castle. Through them, Locke could see nothing but rushing water. The waterfall pounded off the roof; the noise was like being in a carriage during a heavy storm.

When Locke and Jean and all the Eyes had stepped into the box, the attendants drew the doors closed. One of them pulled a chain set into the right-hand wall, and with a lurching rumble the box was drawn back to where it had come from. As they passed through it, Locke guessed that the waterfall was fifteen to twenty feet long. An unprotected man would never be able to pass it without being knocked into the moat, which he supposed was precisely the point.

That, and it was a hell of a way to show off.

They soon pushed through the other side of the falls. Locke could see that they were being drawn into a huge hemispherical hall, with a curved far wall and a ceiling about thirty feet high. Alchemical chandeliers shed light on the hall, silver and white and gold, so that the place gleamed like a treasure vault through the distortion of the water-covered windows. When the conveyor box ground to a halt, the attendants manipulated unseen latches to crack open the forward windows like a pair of giant doors.

Locke and Jean were prodded out of the box, but more gently than before. The stones at their feet were slick with water, and they followed the example of the guards in treading carefully. The waterfall roared at their back for a moment longer, and then two huge doors slammed together behind the conveyor box, and the deafening noise became a dull echo.

Some sort of water engine could be seen in a wall niche to Locke's left. Several men and women stood before gleaming cylinders of brass, working levers attached to mechanical contrivances whose functions were well beyond Locke's capability to guess. Heavy iron chains disappeared into dark holes in the floor, just beside the track the huge wooden box rode in. Jean, too, cocked his head for a closer look at this curiosity, but once past the danger of the slick stones, the soldiers' brief spate of tolerance passed and they shoved the two thieves along at a good clip once again.

Through the entrance hall, wide and grand enough to host several balls at once, they passed at speed. The hall had no windows open to the outside, but rather, artificial panoramas of stained glass, lit from behind. Each window seemed to be a stylized view of what *would* be seen through a real hole cut in the stone—white buildings and mansions, dark skies, the tiers of islands across the harbor, dozens of sails in the main anchorage.

Locke and Jean were escorted down a side hall, up a flight of steps, and down another hall, past blue-coated guards standing stiffly at attention. Was it Locke's imagination, or did something more than ordinary respect creep into their faces when the bronze masks of the Eyes swept past them? There was no more time to ponder, for they were suddenly halted before their evident destination. In a corridor full of wooden doorways, they stood before one made of metal.

An Eye stepped forward, unlocked the door, and pushed it open. The room beyond was small and dark. Soldiers rapidly undid the bonds on Locke and Jean's hands, and then the two of them were shoved forward into the little room.

"Hey, wait just a damn—," said Locke, but the door slammed shut behind them and the sudden blackness was absolute.

"Perelandro," said Jean. He and Locke spent a few seconds stumbling into each other before they managed to regain some balance and dignity. "How on earth did we attract the attention of *these* bloody assholes?"

"I don't know, Jerome." Locke emphasized the pseudonym very slightly. "But maybe the walls have ears. Hey! Bloody assholes! No need to be coy! We're perfectly well behaved when civilly incarcerated."

Locke stumbled toward the remembered location of the nearest wall to pound his fists against it. He discovered for the first time that it was rough brick. "Damnation," he muttered, and sucked at a scraped knuckle.

"Odd," said Jean.

"What?"

"I can't be sure."

"What?"

"Is it just me, or does it seem to be getting warmer in here?"

3

TIME WENT by with all the speed of a sleepless night.

Locke was seeing colors flashing and wobbling in the darkness, and while part of him knew they weren't real, that part of him was getting less and less assertive with every passing minute. The heat was like a weight pressing in on every inch of his skin. His tunic was wide open, and he'd slipped his neck-cloths off so he could wrap them around his hands to steady himself as he leaned back against Jean.

When the door clicked open, it took him a few seconds to realize that he wasn't imagining things. The crack of white light grew into a square, and he flinched back with his hands over his eyes. The air from the corridor fell across him like a cool autumn breeze.

"Gentlemen," said a voice from beyond the square of light, "there has been a terrible misunderstanding."

"Ungh gah ah," was all the response Locke could muster as he tried to remember just how his knees worked. His mouth felt dryer than if it had been packed with cornmeal.

Strong, cool hands reached out to help him to his feet; the room swam around him as he and Jean were helped back out into the bliss of the corridor. They were surrounded once again by blue doublets and bronze masks, but Locke squinted against the light and felt more ashamed than afraid. He *knew* he was confused, almost as though he were drunk, and he was powerless to do anything more than grasp at the vague realization. He was carried along corridors and up stairs (Stairs! Gods! How many sets could there be in one bloody palace?), with his legs only sometimes bearing their fair share of his weight. He felt like a puppet in a cruel comedy with an unusually large stage set.

"Water," he managed to gasp out.

"Soon," said one of the soldiers carrying him. "Very soon."

At last he and Jean were ushered through tall black doors into a softly lit office that seemed to have walls made up of thousands upon thousands of tiny glass cells filled with little flickering shadows. Locke blinked and cursed his condition; he'd heard sailors talk of "dry drunk"—the stupidity, weakness, and irritability that seized a man in great want of water—but he'd never imagined he'd experience it firsthand. It was making everything very strange indeed; no doubt it was embellishing the details of a perfectly ordinary room.

The office held a small table and three plain wooden chairs. Locke steered himself toward one of them gratefully, but was firmly restrained and held upright by the soldiers at his arms.

"You must wait," said one of them.

Though not for long; a scant few heartbeats later, another door opened into the office. A man in long fur-trimmed robes of deepwater blue strode in, clearly agitated.

"Gods defend the archon of Tal Verrar," said the four soldiers in unison.

Maxilan Stragos, came Locke's dazed realization, the gods-damned supreme warlord of Tal Verrar.

"For pity's sake, let these men have their chairs," said the archon. "We have already done them a grievous wrong, Sword Prefect. We shall now extend them every possible courtesy. After all . . . we are not Camorri."

"Of course, Archon."

Locke and Jean were quickly helped into their seats. When the soldiers were reasonably certain that they wouldn't topple over immediately, they stepped back and stood at attention behind them. The archon waved his hand irritably.

"Dismissed, Sword Prefect."

"But . . . Your Honor . . ."

"Out of my sight. You have already conjured a serious embarrassment from my very clear instructions for these men. As a result, they are in no shape to be any threat to me."

"But . . . yes, Archon."

The sword prefect gave a stiff bow, which the other three soldiers repeated. The four of them hurriedly left the office, closing the door behind them with the elaborate click-clack of a clockwork mechanism.

"Gentlemen," said the archon, "you must accept my deepest apologies. My instructions were misconstrued. You were to be given every courtesy. Instead, you were shown to the sweltering chamber, which is reserved for criminals of the lowest sort. I would trust my Eyes to be the equal of ten times their number in any fight, yet in this simple matter they have dishonored me. I must take responsibility. You must forgive this misunderstanding, and allow me the honor of showing you a better sort of hospitality."

Locke mustered his will to attempt a suitable response, and whispered a silent prayer of thanks to the Crooked Warden when Jean spoke first.

"The honor is ours, Protector." His voice was hoarse, but his wits seemed to be returning faster than Locke's. "The chamber was a small price to pay for the pleasure of such an, an unexpected audience. There is nothing to forgive."

"You are an uncommonly gracious man," said Stragos. "Please, dispense with the superfluities. It will do to call me 'Archon.' "

There was a soft knock at the door through which the archon had entered the office.

"Come," he said, and in bustled a short, bald man in elaborate blue-and-silver livery. He carried a silver tray on which there were three crystal goblets and a large bottle of some pale amber liquid. Locke and Jean fixed their gazes on this bottle with the intensity of hunters about to fling their last javelins at some charging beast.

When the servant set the tray down and reached for the bottle, the archon gestured for him to withdraw and took up the bottle himself.

"Go," he said, "I am perfectly capable of serving these poor gentlemen myself."

The attendant bowed and vanished back through the door. Stragos withdrew the already loosened cork from the bottle and filled two goblets to their brims with its contents. That wet gurgle and splash brought an expectant ache to the insides of Locke's cheeks.

"It is customary," said Stragos, "for the host to drink first when serving in this city . . . to establish a basis for trust in what he happens to be serving." He dashed two fingers of liquid into the third goblet, lifted it to his lips, and swallowed it at a gulp.

"Ahh," he said as he passed the full goblets over to Locke and Jean without further hesitation. "There now. Drink up. No need to be delicate. I'm an old campaigner."

Locke and Jean were anything but delicate; they gulped down the offered drinks with grateful abandon. Locke wouldn't have cared if the offering had been squeezed earthworm juice, but it was in fact some sort of pear cider, with just the slightest bite. A child's liquor, barely capable of intoxicating a sparrow, and an astute choice, given their condition. The tart, cold cider coated the inside of Locke's tortured throat, and he shuddered with pleasure.

He and Jean thrust out their empty goblets without thinking, but Stragos was already waiting with the bottle in hand. He refilled their cups, smiling benevolently. Locke inhaled half of his new goblet, then forced himself to make the second half last. Already a new strength seemed to be radiating outward from his stomach, and he sighed with relief.

"Many thanks, Archon," he said. "May I, ah, presume to ask how Jerome and I have offended you?"

"Offended me? Not at all." Stragos, still smiling, set down the bottle and seated himself behind the little table. He reached toward the wall and pulled a silk cord; a shaft of pale amber light fell from the ceiling, illuminating the center of the table. "What you've done, young fellows, is catch my interest."

Stragos sat framed by the shaft of light, and Locke studied him for the first time. A man of very late middle years, surely nearing sixty if not already past it. A strangely precise man, with squared-off features. His skin was pink and weathered, his hair a flat gray roof. In Locke's experience, most powerful men were either ascetics or gluttons; Stragos seemed neither—a man of balance. And his eyes were shrewd, shrewd as a usurer with a client in need. Locke sipped at his pear cider and prayed for wit.

The golden light was caught and reflected by the glass cells that walled the room, and when Locke let his eyes wander for a moment he was startled to see their contents moving. The little fluttering shadows were butterflies, moths, beetles—hundreds of them, perhaps thousands. Each one in its own little glass prison.... The archon's study was walled in with the largest insect collection Locke had ever heard of, let alone seen with his own eyes. Beside him, Jean gasped, evidently having noticed the same thing. The archon chuckled indulgently.

"My collection. Is it not striking?"

He reached toward the wall again and pulled another silken cord; soft white light grew behind the glass walls, until the full details of each specimen became plainly visible. There were butterflies with scarlet wings, blue wings, green wings...some with multicolored patterns more intricate than tattoos. There were gray, black, and gold moths, with curled antennae. There were beetles with burnished carapaces that gleamed like precious metals, and wasps with translucent wings flickering above their sinister tapered bodies.

"It's incredible," said Locke. "How can it be possible?"

"Oh, it isn't. They're all artificial, the best artistry and artisanry can provide. A clockwork mechanism several floors below works a set of bellows, sending gusts of air up shafts behind the walls of this office. Each cell has a tiny aperture at the rear. The fluttering of the wings seems quite random and realistic.... In semidarkness, one might never realize the truth."

"It's no less incredible," said Jean.

"Well, this is the City of Artifice," said the archon. "Living creatures can require such tedious care. You might think of my Mon Magisteria as a repository of artificial things. Here, drink up, and let me pour you the last of the bottle."

Locke and Jean obliged, and Stragos was able to give them each a few fingers more before the bottle was drained. He settled himself back down behind his table and pulled something off the silver tray—a slim file of some sort, wrapped in a brown cover with broken wax seals on three sides.

"Artificial things. Just as you are artificial things, Master Kosta and Master de Ferra. Or should I say, Master Lamora and Master Tannen?"

If Locke had possessed the strength to crush heavy Verrari crystal with his bare hands, the archon would have lost a goblet.

"I beg your pardon," said Locke, adopting a helpful, slightly confused smile, "but I don't know anyone by those names. Jerome?"

"There must be some mistake," said Jean, picking up Locke's exact tone of polite bewilderment.

"No mistake, gentlemen," said the archon. He slipped the file open and briefly examined the contents, about a dozen pages of parchment covered in neat black script. "I received a very curious letter several days ago, through secure channels within my intelligence apparatus. A letter rich with the most singular collection of stories. From a personal acquaintance—a source within the hierarchy of the Bondsmagi of Karthain."

Not even Jean's hands could squeeze a Verrari crystal goblet to fragments, Locke thought, or that moment might have seen the archon's office decorated with an exploding cloud of shards and blood.

Locke gamely raised an eyebrow, refusing to give in just yet. "The Bondsmagi? Gods, that sounds ominous.

But, ah, what would Bondsmagi have to do with Jerome and myself?"

Stragos stroked his chin while he skimmed the documents in the file. "Apparently, you're both thieves from some sort of secret enclave formerly operating out of the House of Perelandro in Camorr's Temple District—cheeky, that. You operated without the permission of Capa Vencarlo Barsavi, no longer among the breathing. You stole tens of thousands of crowns from several dons of Camorr. You are jointly responsible for the death of one Luciano Anatolius, a buccaneer captain who hired a Bondsmage to aid his plans. Perhaps most importantly, you foiled those plans and crippled that Bondsmage. Overcame him, at close quarters. Extraordinary. You shipped him back to Karthain half-dead and quite mad. No fingers, no tongue."

"Actually, Leocanto and I are from Talisham, and we're—"

"You're both from Camorr. Jean Estevan Tannen, which is your real name, and Locke Lamora—which *isn't* yours. That's emphasized for some reason. You're in my city as part of a scheme against that scrub Requin—supposedly, you've been making preparations to break into his vault. *Best* of luck there. Need we continue with your charade? I have many more details. It seems that the Bondsmagi have it in for you."

"Those assholes," muttered Locke.

"I see you *are* personally acquainted with them," said Stragos. "I've hired a few of them in the past. They're a touchy bunch. So you'll admit to the truth of this report? Come, Requin is no friend of mine. He's in with the Priori; might as well be on their damn councils."

Locke and Jean looked at each other, and Jean shrugged. "Very well," said Locke. "You seem to have us at quite a disadvantage, Archon."

"To be precise, I have you at three. I have this report

extensively documenting your activities. I have you here at the center of all my power. And now, for the sake of my own comfort, I have you on a leash."

"Meaning what?" said Locke.

"Perhaps my Eyes did *not* embarrass me, gentlemen. Perhaps you two were *intended* to spend a few hours in the sweltering chamber, to help you work up a thirst that needed quenching." He gestured at Locke and Jean's goblets, which now held only dregs.

"You put something else in the cider," said Jean.

"Of course," said Stragos. "An excellent little poison."

4

FOR A moment, the room was utterly silent, save for the soft fluttering of artificial insect wings. Then Locke and Jean stumbled up from their chairs in unison, but Stragos didn't so much as twitch. "Sit down. Unless you'd prefer *not* to hear exactly what's going on."

"You drank from the same bottle," said Locke, still standing.

"Of course I did. It wasn't actually in the cider. It was in your goblets, painted into the bottoms. Colorless and tasteless. A proprietary alchemical substance, quite expensive. You should be flattered. I've increased your net personal worth, heh."

"I know a thing or two about poisons. What is it?"

"What would be the sense in telling you anything more? You might attempt to have someone assemble an antidote. As it stands, your only possible source for your antidote is me." He smiled, every pretense of contrite gentility shed from his features like a molted insect's husk. A very different Stragos was with them now, and there was a lash in his voice. "Sit down. You're at my disposal now, obviously. You're not what I might have wanted, by the gods, but perhaps just what I can best put to use."

Locke and Jean settled back into their chairs uneasily. Locke threw his goblet down onto the carpet, where it bounced and rolled to a halt beside Stragos' table.

"You might as well know," said Locke, "that I've been poisoned for coercive purposes before."

"Have you? How convenient. Then surely you'll agree it's better than being poisoned for murderous ones."

"What would you have us do?"

"Something useful," said Stragos. "Something grand. According to this report, you're the Thorn of Camorr. My agents brought me stories of you...the most ridiculous rumors, which now turn out to have been true. I thought you were a myth."

"The Thorn of Camorr *is* a myth," said Locke. "And it was never just me. We've always worked as a group, as a team."

"Of course. No need to stress Master Tannen's importance to me. It's all here, in this file. I shall keep you both alive while I prepare for the task I have in mind for you. I'm not ready to discuss it yet, so let us say that I'm keeping you on retainer in the meantime. Go about your business. When I call, you will come."

"Will we?" spat Locke.

"Oh, it's well within your power to leave the city—and if you do, you will both die rather slow and miserable deaths before another season passes. And that would disappoint us all."

"You could be bluffing," said Jean.

"Yes, yes, but if you're rational men, a bluff would hold you as surely as a real poison, would it not? But come now, Tannen. I have the resources *not* to bluff."

"And what's to keep us from running after we've received the antidote?"

"The poison is latent, Lamora. It slumbers within the body for many, many months, if not years. I will dole out your antidote at intervals so long as you please me."

"And what guarantee do we have that you'll continue to give us the antidote once we've done whatever task you'd set us to?"

"You have none."

"And no better alternatives."

"Of course not."

Locke closed his eyes and gently massaged them with the knuckles of his index fingers. "Your alleged poison. Will it interfere with our daily lives in any way? Will it complicate matters of judgment, agility, or health?"

"Not at all," said Stragos. "You won't notice a thing until the time for the antidote is well past, and then you'll notice a great deal all at once. Until then, your affairs will be unimpeded."

"But you have *already* impeded our affairs," said Jean. "We're at a very delicate point in our dealings with Requin."

"He gave us strict orders," said Locke, "to do nothing suspicious while he sniffs around our recent activities. Disappearing from the streets in the care of the archon's people would *probably* qualify as suspicious."

"Already taken into consideration," said the archon. "Most of the people who pulled you two off the street are in one of Requin's gangs. He just doesn't know they work for me. They'll report seeing you out and about, even if others do not."

"Are you confident that Requin is blind to their true loyalty?"

"Gods bless your amusing insolence, Lamora, but I'm not going to justify my every order to you. You'll accept them like my other soldiers, and if you must trust, trust in the judgment that has kept me seated as archon for fifteen years."

"It's our lives under Requin's thumb if you're wrong, Stragos."

"It's your lives under *my* thumb, regardless."

"Requin is no fool!"

"Then why are you attempting to steal from him?"

"We flatter ourselves," said Jean, "that we're—"

"I'll tell you why," Stragos interrupted. He closed his file and folded his hands atop it. "You're not just greedy. You two have an unhealthy lust for excitement. The contemplation of long odds must positively get you drunk. Or else why choose the life you have, when you could have obviously succeeded as thieves of a more mundane stripe, within the limits allowed by that Barsavi?"

"If you think that little pile of papers gives you enough knowledge to presume so much—"

"You two are risk-takers. Exceptional, professional risk-takers. I have just the risk for you to take. You might even enjoy it."

"That might have been true," said Locke, "before you told us about the cider."

"Obviously I know that what I've done will give you cause to bear me malice. Appreciate my position. I've done this to you because I respect your abilities. I *can't* afford to have you in my service without controls. You're a lever and a fulcrum, you two, looking for a city to turn upside down."

"Why the hell couldn't you just hire us?"

"How would money be sufficient leverage for two men who can conjure it as easily as you?"

"So the fact that you're screwing us like a Jeremite cot doxy is really a very sweet compliment?" said Jean. "You fucking—"

"Calm down, Tannen," said Stragos.

"Why should he?" Locke straightened his sweat-rumpled

tunic and began tying his wrinkled neck-cloths back on in an agitated huff. "You poison us, lay a mysterious task at our feet, and offer no pay. You complicate our lives as Kosta and de Ferra, and you expect to summon us at your leisure when you condescend to reveal this chore. Gods. What about expenses, should we incur them?"

"You shall have any funds and material you require to operate in my service. And before you get excited, remember that you'll account for every last centira properly."

"Oh, splendid. And what other perquisites does this job of yours entail? Complimentary luncheon at the barracks of your Eyes? Convalescent beds when Requin cuts our balls off and has them sewn into our eye sockets?"

"I am not accustomed to being spoken to in this—"

"*Get* accustomed to it," snapped Locke, rising out of his chair and beginning to dust off his coat. "I have a counterproposal, one I urge you to entertain quite seriously."

"Oh?"

"Forget about this, Stragos." Locke drew on his coat, shook his shoulders to settle it properly, and gripped it by the lapels. "Forget about this whole ridiculous scheme. Give us enough antidote, if there is one, to settle us for the time being. Or let us know what it is and we'll have our own alchemist see to it, with our own funds. Send us back to Requin, for whom you profess no love, and let us get on with robbing him. Bother us no further, and we'll return the favor."

"What could that possibly gain me?"

"My point is more that it would allow you to keep everything you have now."

"My dear Lamora," laughed Stragos with a soft, dry sound like an echo inside a coffin, "your bluster may be sufficient to convince some sponge-spined Camorri mongrel don to hand over his coin purse. It might even be enough to see you through the task I have in mind. But you're mine now, and the Bondsmagi were rather clear on how you might be humbled."

"Oh? How's that, then?"

"Threaten me one more time and I shall have Jean returned to the sweltering room for the rest of the night. You may wait, chained outside in perfect comfort, imagining what it must be like for him. And the reverse, Jean, should *you* decide to wax rebellious."

Locke clenched his jaw and looked down at his feet. Jean sighed, reached over, and patted him on the arm. Locke nodded very slightly.

"Good." Stragos smiled without warmth. "Just as I respect your abilities, I respect your loyalty to one another. I respect it enough to use it, for good and for ill. So you *will* want to come at my summons, and accept the task I have for you. . . . It's when I *refuse* to see you that you will begin to have cause for concern."

"So be it," said Locke. "But I want you to remember."

"Remember what?"

"That I offered to let this go," said Locke. "That I offered to simply walk away."

"Gods, but you *do* think highly of yourself, don't you, Master Lamora?"

"Just highly enough. No higher than the Bondsmagi, I'd say."

"Are you suggesting that Karthain fears you, Master Lamora? Please. If that were so, they would have killed you already. No. They don't fear you—they want to see you *punished*. Giving you over to me to suit my own purposes seems to accomplish that in their eyes. I daresay you've good reason to bear them malice."

"Indeed," said Locke.

"Consider for a moment," said Stragos, "the possibility that I might not like them any more than you do. And that while I might use them, out of necessity, and freely accept windfalls they send in my direction...your service on my behalf might actually come to work against them. Doesn't that intrigue you?"

"Nothing you say can be taken in good faith." Locke glowered.

"Ahhh. That's where you're wrong, Lamora. With the benefit of time, you'll see how little need I have to lie about anything. Now, this audience is over. Reflect on your situation, and don't do anything rash. You may remove yourselves from the Mon Magisteria and return when summoned."

"Wait," said Locke. "Just—"

The archon rose, tucked the file under his arm, turned, and left the room through the same door he'd used to enter. It swung shut immediately behind him with the clatter of steel mechanisms.

"Hell," said Jean.

"I'm sorry," muttered Locke. "I was *so* keen to come to Tal fucking Verrar."

"It's not your fault. We were both eager to hop in bed with the wench; it's just shit luck she turned out to have the clap."

The main doors to the office creaked open, revealing a dozen Eyes waiting in the hall beyond.

Locke stared at the Eyes for several seconds, then grinned and cleared his throat. "Oh, good. Your master has left strict instructions placing you at our disposal. We're to have a boat, eight rowers, a hot meal, five hundred solari, six women who know how to give a proper massage, and—"

One thing Locke would say for the Eyes was that when they seized him and Jean to "escort" them from the Mon Magisteria, they were firm without being needlessly cruel. Their clubs remained at their belts, and there were a minimal number of body blows to soften the resolve of their prisoners. All in all, a very efficient bunch to be manhandled by.

5

THEY WERE rowed back to the lower docks of the Savrola in a long gig with a covered gallery. It was nearly dawn, and a watery orange light was coming up over the landside of Tal Verrar, peeking over the islands and making their seaward faces seem darker by contrast. Surrounded by the archon's oarsmen and watched by four Eyes with crossbows, Locke and Jean said nothing.

Their exit was quick; the boat simply drew up to the edge of one deserted quay and Locke and Jean hopped out. One of the archon's soldiers threw a leather sack out onto the stones at their feet, and then the gig was backing away, and the whole damnable episode was over. Locke felt a strange daze and he rubbed his eyes, which felt dry within their sockets.

"Gods," said Jean. "We must look as though we've been mugged."

"We have been." Locke reached down, picked up the sack, and examined its contents—Jean's two hatchets and their assortment of daggers. He grunted. "Magi. Gods-damned *Bondsmagi*!"

"This must be what they had in mind."

"I hope it's *all* they have in mind."

"They're not all-knowing, Locke. They must have weaknesses."

"Must they really? And do you know what they are? Might one of them be allergic to exotic foods, or suffer poor relations with his mother? Some good that does us, when they're well beyond dagger reach! Crooked Warden, why don't dog's assholes like Stragos ever want to simply hire us for money? I'd be *happy* to work for fair pay."

"No, you wouldn't."

"Feh."

"Quit scowling and think for a moment. You heard Stragos' report. The Bondsmagi knew about the preparations we've made for going after Requin's vault, but they didn't know the *whole* story. The important part."

"Right . . . but what need would there be for them to tell Stragos everything?"

"None, of course, but also . . . they knew where we were operating from in Camorr, but he didn't mention our history. Stragos spoke of Barsavi, but not Chains. Perhaps because Chains died before the Falconer ever came to Camorr and started observing us? I don't think the Bondsmagi can read our thoughts, Locke. I think they're magnificent spies, but they're not infallible. We still have some secrets."

"Hmmm. Forgive me if I find that a cold comfort, Jean. You know who waxes philosophical about the tiniest weaknesses of enemies? The *powerless.*"

"You seem resigned to that without much of a—"

"I'm not resigned, Jean. I'm angry. We need to cease being powerless as soon as possible."

"Right. So where do we start?"

"Well, I'm going to go back to the inn. I'm going to pour a gallon of cold water down my throat. I'm going to get into bed, put a pillow over my head, and stay there until sunset."

"I approve."

"Good. Then we'll both be well rested when it comes time to get up and find a black alchemist. I want a second opinion on latent poisons. I want to know everything there is to know about the subject, and whether there are any antidotes we can start trying."

"Agreed."

"After that, we can add one more small item to our agenda for this Tal Verrar holiday of ours."

"Kick the archon in the teeth?"

"Gods yes," said Locke, smacking a fist into an open palm. "Whether or not we finish the Requin job first. Whether or not there really is a poison! I'm going to take his whole bloody palace and shove it so far up his ass he'll have stone towers for tonsils!"

"Any plans to that effect?"

"No idea. I've no idea whatsoever. I'll *reflect* on it, that's for damn sure. But as for not being rash, well, no promises."

Jean grunted. The two of them turned and began to plod along the quay, toward the stone steps that would lead laboriously to the island's upper tier. Locke rubbed his stomach and felt his skin crawling . . . felt *violated* somehow, knowing that something lethal might be slipping unfelt into the darkest crevices of his own body, waiting to do mischief.

On their right the sun was a burning bronze medallion coming up over the city's horizon, perched there like one of the archon's faceless soldiers, gazing steadily down upon them.

REMINISCENCE

The Lady of the Glass Pylon

1

Azura Gallardine was not an easy woman to speak to. To be sure, hers was a well-known title (second mistress of the Great Guild of Artificers, Reckoners, and Minutiary Artisans), and her address was common knowledge (the intersection of Glassbender Street and the Avenue of the Cog-Scrapers, West Cantezzo, Fourth Tier, Artificers' Crescent), but anyone approaching that home had to walk forty feet off the main pedestrian thoroughfare.

Those forty feet were one *hell* of a thing to contemplate.

Six months had passed since Locke and Jean had come to Tal Verrar; the personalities of Leocanto Kosta and Jerome de Ferra had evolved from bare sketches to comfortable second skins. Summer had been dying when they'd clattered down the road toward the city for the first time, but now the hard, dry winds of winter had given way to the turbulent breezes of early spring. It was the month of Saris, in the seventy-eighth year of Nara, the Plaguebringer, Mistress of Ubiquitous Maladies.

Jean rode in a padded chair at the stern of a hired luxury scull, a low, sleek craft crewed by six rowers. It sliced across the choppy waters of Tal Verrar's main anchorage like an insect in haste, ducking and weaving between larger vessels in accordance with the shouted directions of a teenage girl perched in its bow.

It was a windy day, with the milky light of the sun pouring down without warmth from behind high veils of clouds. Tal Verrar's anchorage was crowded with cargo lighters, barges, small boats, and the great ships of a dozen nations. A squadron of galleons from Emberlain and Parlay rode low in the water with the aquamarine-and-gold banners of the Kingdom of the Seven Marrows fluttering at their sterns. A few hundred yards away, Jean could see a brig flying the white flag of Lashain, and beyond that a galley with the banner of the Marrows over the smaller pennant of the Canton of Balinel, which was just a few hundred miles north up the coast from Tal Verrar.

Jean's scull was rounding the southern tip of the Merchants' Crescent, one of three sickle-shaped islands that surrounded the Castellana at the city's center like the encompassing petals of a flower. His destination was the Artificers' Crescent, home of the men and women who had raised the art of clockwork mechanics from an eccentric hobby to a vibrant industry. Verrari clockwork was more delicate, more subtle, more durable—more *anything*, as required—than that fashioned by all but a handful of masters anywhere else in the known world.

Strangely, the more familiar Jean grew with Tal Verrar, the odder the place seemed to him. Every city built on Eldren ruins acquired its own unique character, in many cases shaped directly by the nature of those ruins. Camorri lived on islands separated by nothing more than canals, or at most the Angevine River, and their existence was shoulder-to-shoulder compared to the great wealth of space Tal Verrar had to offer. The hundred-odd thousand souls on Tal Verrar's seaward islands made full use of that space, dividing themselves into tribes with unusual precision.

In the west, the poor clung to spots in the Portable Quarter, where those willing to tolerate constant re-arrangement of all their belongings by hard sea-weather could at least live free of rent. In the east, they crowded the Istrian District and provided labor for the tiered gardens of the Blackhands Crescent. There they grew luxury crops they could not afford, on plots of alchemically enriched soil they could never own.

Tal Verrar had only one graveyard, the ancient Midden of Souls, which took up most of the city's eastern island, opposite the Blackhands Crescent. The Midden had six tiers, studded with memorial stones, sculptures, and mausoleums like miniature mansions. The dead were as strictly sifted in death as they'd been in life, with each successive tier claiming a better class of corpse. It was a morbid mirror of the Golden Steps across the bay.

The Midden itself was almost as large as the entire city of Vel Virazzo, and it sported its own strange society—priests and priestesses of Aza Guilla, gangs of mourners-for-hire (all of whom would loudly proclaim their ceremonial specialties or particular theatrical flourishes to anyone within shouting distance), mausoleum sculptors, and the oddest of all, the Midden Vigilants. The Vigilants were criminals convicted of grave robbery. In place of execution, they were locked into steel masks and clanking scale armor and forced to patrol the Midden of Souls as part of a sullen constabulary. Each would be freed only when another grave robber was captured to take his or her place. Some would have to wait years.

Tal Verrar had no hangings, no beheadings, and none of the fights between convicted criminals and wild animals that were popular virtually everywhere else. In Tal Verrar those convicted of capital crimes simply vanished, along with most of the city's garbage, into the Midden Deep. This was an open square pit, forty feet on a side, located to the north of the Midden of Souls. Its Elderglass walls plunged into absolute darkness, giving no hint as to how far down they truly went. Popular lore held that it was bottomless, and criminals prodded off the execution planks usually went screaming and pleading. The worst rumor about the place, of course, was that those thrown down into the Deep did *not* die...but somehow continued falling. Forever.

"Hard larboard!" cried the girl at the bow of the scull. The rowers on Jean's left yanked their oars out of the water and the ones on the right pulled hard, sliding the craft just out of the way of a cargo galley crammed with fairly alarmed cattle. A man at the side rail of the galley shook his fist down at the scull as it passed, perhaps ten feet beneath the level of his boots.

"Get the shit out of your eyes, you undergrown cunt!"

"Go back to pleasuring your cattle, you soft-dicked cur!"

"You bitch! You cheeky bitch! Heave-to and I'll show you who's soft-dicked! Begging your pardon, gracious sir."

Seated in his thronelike chair, dressed in a velvet frock coat with enough gold fripperies to sparkle even in the weak light of an overcast day, Jean looked very much a man of consequence. It was important for the man on the galley to ensure that his verbal salvoes were accurately received; while they were an accepted part of life on the harbor in Tal Verrar, the moneyed class were always treated as though they were somehow levitating above the water, entirely independent of the vessels and laborers carrying them. Jean waved nonchalantly.

"I don't need to get any closer to know it's soft, lard-cock!" The girl made a rude gesture with both hands. "I can see how disappointed your fucking cows are from here!"

With that, the scull was out of range of any audible

reply; the galley fell away to the stern, and the southwestern edge of the Artificers' Crescent grew before them.

"For that," said Jean, "an extra silver volani for everyone here."

As the increasingly cheerful girl and her enthusiastic team pulled him steadily toward the docks of the Artificers' Crescent, Jean's eyes were drawn by a tumult on the water a few hundred yards to his left. A cargo lighter flagged with some sort of Verrari guild banner Jean didn't recognize was surrounded by at least a dozen smaller craft. Men and women from the boats were trying to clamber aboard the cargo lighter while the outnumbered crew of the larger vessel attempted to fend them off with oars and a water pump. A boat full of constables seemed to be approaching, but was still several minutes off.

"Now, what the hell's that?" Jean yelled to the girl.

"What? Where? Oh, that. That's the Quill Pen Rebellion, up to business as usual."

"Quill Pen Rebellion?"

"The Guild of Scribes. That cargo boat's flying a Guild of Letter-Pressers' flag. It must be carrying a printing press from the Artificers' Crescent. You ever seen a press?"

"Heard of them. For the first time just a few months ago, in fact."

"The scribes don't like 'em. Think they'll put their trade out of business. So they've been running ambushes when the Letter-Pressers try to get one across the bay. There must be six or seven of those new presses on the bottom of the water by now. Plus a few bodies. It's a big fat weeping mess, you ask me."

"I'm inclined to agree."

"Well, hopefully they won't come up with anything that can replace a good team of honest rowers. Here's your dock, sir, quite a bit ahead of schedule if I'm correct. You want us to wait around?"

"By all means," said Jean. "Amusing help is so hard to find. I expect I won't be but an hour."

"At your service, then, Master de Ferra."

2

THE CRESCENT was not exclusive to the Great Guild of Artificers, though it was where the majority of them chose to settle, and where their private halls and clubs loomed on virtually every street corner, and where they were most tolerated in their habit of leaving incomprehensible and occasionally hazardous devices out in plain sight.

Jean made his way up the steep steps of the Avenue of the Brass Cockatrice, past candle merchants and blade sharpeners and veniparsifers (mystics who claimed to be able to read the full sweep of someone's destiny from the pattern of blood vessels visible on their hands and forearms). At the top of the avenue he dodged away from a slim young woman in a four-cornered hat and sun veil walking a *valcona* on a reinforced leather leash. *Valcona* were flightless attack birds, larger than hunting hounds. With their vestigial wings folded back along their stout bodies, they hopped about on claws that could tear out fist-sized chunks of human flesh. They bonded like affectionate babies to one person and were perfectly happy to kill anyone else in the entire world, at any time.

"Good killer bird," muttered Jean. "Pretty threat to life and limb. What a lovely little girl or boy or thing you are."

The creature chirruped a little warning at him and scampered after its mistress.

Huffing and sweating, Jean made his way up another set of switchback stairs and made an irritated mental note that a few hours of training would do his spreading gut some good. Jerome de Ferra was a man who viewed exercise solely as a means of getting from bed to the gambling tables and back again. Forty feet, sixty feet, eighty feet... up from the waterfront, up the second and third tiers of the island, up to the fourth and topmost, where the eccentric influence of the Artificers was at its strongest.

The shops and houses on the fourth tier of the Crescent were provided with water by an extremely elaborate network of aqueducts. Some of them were the stones and pillars of the Therin Throne era, while some were merely leather chutes supported by wooden struts. Waterwheels, windmills, gears, counterweights, and pendulums swung everywhere Jean looked. Rearranging the water supply was a game the Artificers played amongst themselves; the only rule was that nobody's supply was to be cut off at the point of final delivery. Every few days, a new offshoot of some duct or a new pumping apparatus would appear, stealing water from an older duct or pumping apparatus. A few days later another artificer would divert water through another new channel and the battle would continue. Tropical storms would invariably litter the streets of the Crescent with cogs and mechanisms and ductwork, and the artificers would invariably rebuild their water channels twice as strangely as before.

Glassbender Street ran the full length of the topmost tier. Jean turned to his left and hurried along the cobbles. The strange smells of glassmaking wafted out at him from shop fronts; through open doors he could see artisans spinning glowing orange shapes at the ends of long poles. A small crowd of alchemists' assistants brushed past him, hogging the street. They wore the trademark red skullcaps of their profession and displayed the chemical burns along their hands and faces that were their badges of pride.

He passed the Avenue of the Cog-Scrapers, where a small crowd of laborers were seated before their shops, cleaning and polishing pieces of metal. Some were under the direct scrutiny of impatient artificers, who grumbled unhelpful directions and stamped their feet nervously. This intersection was the southwestern end of the fourth tier; there was nowhere else to go except down—or out along the forty-foot walk to the home of Azura Gallardine.

At the cul-de-sac end to Glassbender Street was an arc of shop fronts with one gap like a tooth knocked out of a smile. Jutting beyond this gap was an Elderglass pylon, anchored to the stone of the fourth tier for some unfathomable Eldren reason. The pylon was about a foot and a half wide, flat-topped, and forty feet long. It speared out into the empty air, fifteen yards above the rooftops of a winding street down on the third tier.

The house of Azura Gallardine was perched at the far end of that pylon like a three-story bird's nest on the tip of a branch. The second mistress of the Great Guild of Artificers had discovered an ideal means of assuring her privacy—only those with very serious business, or very sincere need of her skills, would be mad enough to scamper out along the pylon that led to her front door.

Jean swallowed, rubbed his hands together, and said a brief prayer to the Crooked Warden before stepping out onto the Elderglass. "It can't be that hard," he muttered. "I've been through worse. It's just a short little walk. No need to look down. I'm as steady as a laden galleon."

With his hands held out at his sides for balance, he began to make his way carefully across the pylon. It was curious, how the breeze seemed to pick up as he crossed, and how the sky seemed suddenly wider above him. . . . He fixed his eyes firmly on the door before him, and (unbeknownst to himself) ceased to breathe until his hands were planted firmly on that door. He gasped in a deep breath and wiped his brow, which had sprung an embarrassing quantity of sweat.

Azura Gallardine's house was solidly crafted from white

stone blocks. It had a high peaked roof crowned with a squeaking windmill and a large leather rain-collection bladder in a wooden frame. The door was decorated with relief carvings of gears and other clockwork mechanisms, and beside it a brass plate was set into the stone. Jean pressed the plate, and heard a gong echoing within the house. Smoke from cookfires below curled up past him while he stood there waiting for some response.

He was about to press the plate again when the door creaked open. A short, scowling woman appeared in the gap between the door and its frame, staring up at him. She had to be on the downside of sixty, Jean thought—her reddish skin was lined like the joints of an aged leather garment. She was heavyset, with a vaguely froglike bulge of flesh at her throat and jowly features drooping like sculptor's putty from her high cheekbones. Her white hair was tightly braided with alternating rings of brass and black iron, and most of the visible flesh on her hands, forearms, and neck was covered in elaborate, slightly faded tattoos.

Jean set his right foot before his left and bowed at a forty-five-degree angle, with his left hand flung out and his right tucked beneath his stomach. He was about to start conjuring verbal flowers when Guildmistress Gallardine seized him by his collar and dragged him into her house.

"Ow! Madam, please! Allow me to introduce myself!"

"You're too fat and well dressed to be an apprentice after patronage," she replied, "so you must be here to beg a favor, and when your kind says hello, it tends to take a while. No, shut up."

Her house smelled like oil, sweat, stone dust, and heated metal. The interior was one tall hollow, the strangest cluttered conglomeration Jean had ever seen. There were man-sized arched windows on the right-hand and left-hand walls, but every other inch of wall space was taken up with a sort of scaffolding that supported a hundred wooden shelves crammed with tools, materials, and junk. At the top of the scaffolding, set atop a makeshift floor of planks, Jean could see a sleeping pallet and a desk beneath a pair of hanging alchemical lamps. Ladders and leather cords hung down in several places; books and scrolls and half-empty corked bottles covered most of the floor.

"If I've come at a bad time..."

"It's usually a bad time, Young Master Interloper. A client with an interesting request is about the only thing that ever changes that. So what's it to be?"

"Guildmistress Gallardine, everyone I've asked has sworn that the most subtle, most accomplished, most imitated artificer in all of Tal Verrar is none other than y—"

"Quit bathing me with your flattery, boy," said the old woman, waving her hands. "Look around you. Gears and levers, weights and chains. You don't need to lick them with pretty words to make them work—nor me."

"As you wish," said Jean, straightening up and reaching within his coat. "I couldn't live with myself if I didn't extend one small courtesy, however."

From within his coat he brought forth a small package wrapped in cloth-of-silver. The neat corners of the wrapping were drawn together beneath a red wax seal, stamped into a curled disc of shaved gold.

Jean's informants had all mentioned Gallardine's single human failing: a taste for presents as strong as her distaste for flattery and interruptions. She knitted her eyebrows, but did manage a ghost of an anticipatory smile as she took the package in her tattooed hands.

"Well," she said, "well, we must all certainly be able to live with ourselves...."

She popped the disc seal and pried the cloth of silver apart with the eagerness of a little girl. The package contained a brass-stoppered rectangular bottle filled with milky white liquid. She sucked in her breath when she read the label.

"White Plum Austershalin," she whispered. "Twelve gods. Who *have* you been speaking to?"

Brandy mixes were a Tal Verrar peculiarity; fine brandies from elsewhere (in this case, the peerless Austershalin of Emberlain) were mixed with local liquor from rare alchemical fruits (and there were none rarer than the heavenly white plum), then bottled and aged to produce cordials that could blast the tongue into numbness with the richness of their flavor. The bottle held perhaps two glasses of White Plum Austershalin, and it was worth forty-five solari.

"A few knowledgeable souls," said Jean, "who said you might appreciate a modest draught."

"This is hardly modest, Master..."

"De Ferra. Jerome de Ferra, at your service."

"Quite the opposite, Master de Ferra. What did you want me to do for you?"

"Well—if you'd really prefer to get to the nub of the matter, I don't have a specific need just yet. What I have are...questions."

"About what?"

"Vaults."

Guildmistress Gallardine cradled her brandy mix like a new baby and said, "Vaults, Master de Ferra? Simple storage vaults, with mechanical conveniences, or *secure* vaults, with mechanical defenses?"

"My taste, madam, runs more toward the latter."

"What is it you wish to guard?"

"Nothing," said Jean. "It is more a matter of something I wish to *un*guard."

"Are you locked out of a vault? Needing someone to loosen it up a bit for you?"

"Yes, madam. It's just..."

"Just what?"

Jean licked his lips again and smiled. "I had heard, well, credible rumors that you might be amenable to the sort of work I might suggest."

She fixed him with a knowing stare. "Are you implying that you don't necessarily *own* the vault that you're locked out of?"

"Heh. Not necessarily, no."

She paced around the floor of her house, stepping over books and bottles and mechanical devices.

"The law of the Great Guild," she said at last, "forbids any one of us from directly interfering with the work of another, save by invitation, or at the need of the state." There was another pause. "However . . . it's not unknown for advice to be given, schematics to be examined . . . in the interest of advancing the craft, you understand. It's a form of testing to destruction. It's how we critique one another, as it were."

"Advice would be all that I ask," said Jean. "I don't even need a locksmith; I just need information to *arm* a locksmith."

"There are few who could better arm such a one than myself. Before we discuss the matter of compensation, tell me—do you know the designer of the vault you've got your eyes on?"

"I do."

"And it is?"

"Azura Gallardine."

The guildmistress took a step away from him, as though a forked tongue had suddenly flicked out between his lips.

"Help you circumvent my own work? Are you mad?"

"I had hoped," said Jean, "that the identity of the vault owner might be one that wouldn't raise any particular pangs of sympathy."

"Who and where?"

"Requin. The Sinspire."

"Twelve gods, you *are* mad!" Gallardine glanced around as though checking the room for spies before she continued. "That certainly *does* raise pangs of sympathy! Sympathy for myself!"

"My pockets are deep, Guildmistress. Surely there must be a sum which would alleviate your qualms?"

"There is no sum in this world," said the old woman, "large enough to convince me to give you what you ask for. Your accent, Master de Ferra . . . I believe I place it. You're from Talisham, are you not?"

"Yes."

"And Requin—you've studied him, have you?"

"Thoroughly, of course."

"Nonsense. If you'd studied him thoroughly, you wouldn't be here. Let me tell you a little something about Requin, you poor rich Talishani simpleton. Do you know that woman of his, Selendri? The one with the brass hand?"

"I've heard that he keeps no other close to him."

"And that's all you know?"

"Ah, more or less."

"Until several years ago," said Gallardine, "it was Requin's custom to host a grand masque at the Sinspire each Day of Changes. A mad revel, in thousand-solari costumes, of which his were always the grandest. Well, one year he and that beautiful young woman of his decided to switch costumes and masks. On a whim.

"An assassin," she continued, "had dusted the inside of Requin's costume with something devilish. The blackest sort of alchemy, a kind of *aqua regia* for human flesh. It was just a powder . . . it needed sweat and warmth to bring it to life. And so that woman wore it for nearly half an hour, until she'd just begun to sweat and enjoy herself. And that's when she started to *scream*.

"I wasn't there. But there were artificers of my acquaintance in the crowd, and they say she screamed and screamed until her voice broke. Until there was nothing coming from her throat but a hiss, and still she kept trying to scream. Only one side of the costume was doused with the stuff...a perverse gesture. Her skin bubbled and ran like hot tar. Her flesh *steamed*, Master de Ferra. No one had the courage to touch her, except Requin. He cut her costume off, demanded water, worked over her feverishly. He wiped her burning skin clean with his jacket, with scraps of cloth, with his bare hands. He was so badly burned himself that he wears gloves to this day, to hide his own scars."

"Astonishing," said Jean.

"He saved her life," said Gallardine, "what was left of it to save. Surely you've seen her face. One eye evaporated, like a grape in a bonfire. Her toes required amputation. Her fingers were burnt twigs, her hand a blistered waste. It had to go as well. They had to cut off a *breast*, Master de Ferra. I assure you, you can have no conception of quite what that means—it would mean much to me now, and it has been many long years since I was last thought comely.

"When she was abed, Requin passed the word to all of his gangs, all of his thieves, all of his contacts, all of his friends among the rich and the powerful. He offered a thousand solari, no questions asked, for anyone who could give him the identity of the would-be poisoner. But there was quite a bit of fear concerning this particular assassin, and Requin was not nearly as respected then as he is now. He received no answer. The next night, he offered five thousand solari, no questions asked, and still received no answer. The third night, he repeated his offer, for ten thousand solari, fruitlessly. On the fourth night, he offered twenty thousand...and not one person came forward.

"And so the murders started the very next night. At random. Among the thieves, among the alchemists, among the servants of the Priori. Anyone who might have access to useful information. One a night, silent work, absolutely professional. Each victim had his or her skin peeled off with a knife, on their left side. As a reminder.

"And so his gangs, and his gamblers, and his associates begged him to stop. 'Find me an assassin,' he told them, 'and I will.' And they pleaded, and they made their inquiries, and came back with nothing. So he began to kill two people per night. He began to kill wives, husbands, children, friends. One of his gangs rebelled, and they were found dead the next morning. All of them. He tightened his grip on his gangs and purged them of the weakhearted. He killed and killed and killed, until the entire city was in a frenzy to turn over every rock, to kick in every door for him. Until nothing could be worse than to keep disappointing him. At last, a man was brought before him who satisfied his questions.

"Requin," said Gallardine with a long dry sigh, "set that man inside a wooden frame, chained there, on his left side. The frame was filled with alchemical cement, which was allowed to harden. The frame was tipped up—so you see, the man was half sealed into a stone wall, all along his left side, from his feet to the top of his head. He was tipped up and left standing in Requin's vault to die. Requin would go in himself and force water down the man's throat each day. His trapped limbs rotted, festered, made him sick. He died slowly, starving and gangrenous, sealed into the most perfectly hideous physical torture I have ever heard of in all my long years.

"So you will forgive me," she said, taking Jean gently by the arm and leading him toward the left-hand window, "if Requin is one client with whom I intend to maintain absolute faith until the Lady Most Kind sweeps my soul out of this old sack of bones."

"But surely, there's no need for him to know?"

"And just as surely, Master de Ferra, there is the fact that I would never chance it. Never."

"But surely, a small consideration——"

"Have you heard," interrupted Gallardine, "of what happens to those caught cheating at his tower, Master de Ferra? He collects their hands, and then he drops them onto a stone courtyard and bills their families or business partners to have the bodies cleaned up. And what about the last man who started a fight inside the Sinspire, and drew blood? Requin had him tied to a table. His kneecaps were cut out by a dog-leech, and red ants were poured into the wounds. The kneecaps were lashed back down with twine. That man *begged* to have his throat slit. His request was not granted.

"Requin is a power unto himself. The archon can't touch him for fear of aggravating the Priori, and the Priori find him far too useful to turn on him. Since Selendri nearly died, he's become an artist of cruelty the likes of which this city has never seen. There is *no mortal reward* that I would consider worth provoking that man."

"I take all that very seriously, madam. So can we not carefully minimize your involvement? Settle for a basic schematic of the vault mechanisms, the most general overview? The sort of thing that could never be specifically tied to you?"

"You haven't really been listening." She shook her head and gestured toward the left-hand window of her house. "Let me ask you something else, Master de Ferra. Can you see the view of Tal Verrar out this window?"

Jean stepped forward to gaze out through the pane of glass. The view was southward, over the western tip of the Artificers' Crescent, across the anchorage and the glimmering silver-white water to the Sword Marina. There the archon's navy rode at anchor, protected by high walls and catapults.

"It's a . . . very lovely view," he said.

"Isn't it? Now, you must consider this my final statement on the matter. Do you know anything of counterweights?"

"I can't say that I—"

At that moment, the guildmistress yanked on one of the leather cords that hung down from her ceiling.

The first notion Jean had that the floor had opened up beneath his feet was when the view of Tal Verrar suddenly seemed to move up toward the ceiling; his senses conferred hastily on just what this meant, and were stumped for a split second until his stomach weighed in with nauseous confirmation that the *view* wasn't doing the moving.

He plunged through the floor and struck a hard square platform suspended just beneath Gallardine's house by iron chains at the corners. His first thought was that it must be some sort of lift—and then it began to plummet toward the street forty-odd feet below.

The chains rattled and the sudden breeze washed over him; he fell prone and clung to the platform with white-knuckled alarm. Roofs and carts and cobblestones rushed up toward him and he braced himself for the sharp pain of impact—but it didn't come. The platform was slowing down with impossible smoothness: sure death slowed to possible injury and then to mere embarrassment. The descent ended a bare few feet above the street, when the chains on Jean's left stayed taut while the others went slack. The platform tilted with a lurch and dumped him in a heap on the cobbles.

He sat up and sucked in a grateful breath; the street was spinning slightly around him. He looked up and saw that the chain platform was rapidly ascending back to its former position. A split second before it drew home into the underside of Gallardine's floor, something small and shiny tumbled out of the trap door above it. Jean managed to flinch away and cover his face just before glass shards and liquor from the exploding bottle of brandy mix sprayed over him.

He wiped a good few solari worth of White Plum Austershalin out of his hair as he stumbled to his feet, wide-eyed and cursing.

"A fine afternoon to you, sir. But wait, don't tell me. Let me guess. Proposal not accepted by the guildmistress?"

Jean, befuddled, found a smiling beer seller not five feet to his right, leaning against the wall of a closed and un-marked two-story building. The man was a tanned scare-crow with a broad-brimmed leather hat that drooped with age until it nearly touched his bony shoulders. He drummed the fingers of one hand on a large wheeled cask, to which several wooden mugs were attached by long chains.

"Um, something like that," said Jean. A hatchet slipped out of his coat and clattered against the cobblestones. Red-faced, he bent, retrieved it, and made it vanish again.

"You might call this self-serving, and I'd certainly be the first to agree with you, sir. But you look to me like a man in need of a drink. A drink that won't bust open against the cobbles and damn near break your skull, that is."

"Do I? What have you got?"

"Burgle, sir. Presuming you've heard of it, it's a Verrari specialty, and if you've had it in Talisham you haven't had it at all. Nothing at all against Talishani, of course. Why, I've got family in Talisham, you know."

Burgle was a thick dark beer usually flavored with a few drops of almond oil. It had a kick comparable to many wines. Jean nodded. "A full mug, if you please."

The beer seller opened the tap on his cask and filled one of the chained mugs with liquid that looked almost black. He passed this to Jean with one hand and tipped his cap with the other.

"She does it a few times a week, you know."

Jean quaffed the warm beer and let the yeasty, nutty flavor flow down the back of his throat. "A few times a week?"

"She's a mite impatient with some of her visitors. Doesn't wait to terminate conversation with all the usual niceties. But then you knew that already."

"Mmm-hmmm. This is pretty tolerable stuff."

"Thank you kindly, sir. One centira the full mug... thank you, thank you kindly. I do a brisk business with folks falling out of Madam Gallardine's floor. I usually try to stake this spot out just in case it rains a customer or two. I'm very sorry you didn't find satisfaction in your meeting with her."

"Satisfaction? Well, she might have gotten rid of me before I expected, but I think I did what I set out to do." Jean poured the last of the beer down his throat, wiped his mouth on his sleeve, and passed the mug back. "I'm really just planting a seed for the future, is all."

CHAPTER FOUR

BLIND ALLIANCES

1

"MASTER KOSTA, please be reasonable. Why would I be holding anything back from you? If I had a treatment to suggest, it would mean a fair bit more gold in my pocket, now wouldn't it?"

Pale Therese, the consulting poisoner, kept a rather comfortable parlor in which to discuss confidential business with her clients. Locke and Jean were seated cross-legged on soft, wide cushions, holding (but not sipping from) little porcelain cups of thick Jereshti coffee. Pale Therese—a serious, ice-eyed Vadran of about thirty—had hair the color of new sail canvas that bobbed against the collar of her black velvet coat as she paced the room across from her guests. Her bodyguard, a well-dressed Verrari woman with a basket-hilted rapier and a lacquered wooden club hanging from her belt, lounged against the wall beside the room's single locked door, silent and watchful.

"Of course," said Locke. "I beg your pardon, madam, if I'm a bit out of sorts. I hope you can appreciate *our* situation... *possibly* poisoned, with no means to tell in the first place, let alone begin securing an antidote."

"Yes, Master Kosta. It's certainly an anxious position you're in."

"This is the second time I've been poisoned for coercive purposes. I was lucky enough to escape the first."

"Pity it's such an effective means of keeping someone on a chain, isn't it?"

"You needn't sound so satisfied, madam."

"Oh, come now, Master Kosta. You mustn't think me unsympathetic." Pale Therese held up her left hand, showing off a collection of rings and alchemical scars, and Locke was surprised to see that the fourth finger of that hand was missing. "A careless accident, when I was an apprentice, working with something unforgiving. I had ten heartbeats to choose—my finger or my life. Fortunately there was a heavy knife very close at hand. I know what it means to taste the fruits of my art, gentlemen. I know what it is to feel sickly and anxious and desperate, waiting to see what happens next."

"Of course," said Jean. "Forgive my partner. It's just... well, the artistry of our apparent poisoning surely left us hoping for some equally miraculous solution."

"As a rule of thumb, it's always easier to poison than it is to cure." Therese idly rubbed the stump of her missing finger, a gesture that looked like an old familiar tic. "Antidotes are delicate things; in many cases, they're poisons in their own right. There is no panacea, no cure-all, no cleansing that can blunt every venom known to my trade. And since the substance you describe does indeed seem to be proprietary, I'd sooner just cut your throats than attempt random antidote treatments. They could prolong your misery, or even enhance the effect of the substance already within you."

Jean cupped his chin in one hand and gazed around the parlor. Therese had decorated one wall with a shrine to fat, sly Gandolo, Lord of Coin and Commerce, heavenly father of business transactions. On the opposite wall was a shrine to veiled Aza Guilla, Lady of the Long Silence, Goddess of Death. "But you said there are known substances that linger on like the one we're supposed to be afflicted with. Might they not narrow the field of worthwhile treatments?"

"There are such substances, yes. Twilight rose essence sleeps in the body for several months and deadens the nerves if the subject doesn't take a regular antidote. Witherwhite steals the nourishment from all food and drink; the victims can gorge themselves all they like and still waste away to nothing. *Anuella* dust makes the victim bleed out through their skin weeks after they breathe it. . . . But don't you see the problem? Three lingering poisons, three very different means of causing harm. An antidote for, say, a poison of the blood might well kill you if your poison works by some other means."

"Damn," said Locke. "All right, then. I feel silly bringing this up, but Jerome, you said there was one more possibility. . . ."

"Bezoars," said Jean. "I read a great deal about them as a child."

"Bezoars are, sadly, a myth." Therese folded her hands in front of her and sighed. "Just a fairy story, like the Ten Honest Turncoats, the Heart-Eating Sword, the Clarion Horn of Therim Pel, and all that wonderful nonsense. I'm sure I read the same books, Master de Ferra. I'm sorry. In order to extract magic stones from the stomachs of dragons, we'd have to have living dragons somewhere, wouldn't we?"

"They do seem to be in short supply."

"If it's miraculous and expensive you're looking for," said Therese, "there is one more course of action I could suggest."

"Anything . . . ," said Locke.

"The Bondsmagi of Karthain. I have credible reports

that they *do* have means to halt poisonings that we alchemists cannot. For those who can afford their fees, of course."

"... except that," muttered Locke.

"Well," said Therese with a certain resigned finality. "Though it aids neither my pocketbook nor my conscience to set you back on the street without a solution, I fear I can do little else, given how thin our information is. You are absolutely confident the poisoning happened but recently?"

"Last night, madam, was the very first opportunity our ... tormentor ever had."

"Then take what little comfort I can give. Stay useful to this individual and you probably have weeks or months of safety ahead. In that time, some lucky stroke may bring you more information on the substance in question. Watch and listen keenly for whatever clues you may. Return with more solid information for me, and I will instruct my people to take you in at any hour, night or day, to see what I might do."

"That's quite gracious of you, madam," said Locke.

"Poor gentlemen! I offer you my best prayers for good fortune. I know you shall live for some time with a weight on your shoulders ... and should you eventually find no solution forthcoming, I can always offer you my *other* services. Turnabout, as they say, is fair play."

"You're our kind of businesswoman," said Jean, rising to his feet. He set down his little cup of coffee, and beside it placed a gold solari coin. "We appreciate your time and hospitality."

"No trouble, Master de Ferra. Are you ready to go out, then?"

Locke stood up and adjusted his long coat. He and Jean nodded in unison.

"Very well, then. Valista will see you back out the way

you came. Apologies once again for the blindfolds, but...
some precautions are for your benefit as well as mine."

The actual location of Pale Therese's parlor was a secret,
tucked away somewhere amongst the hundreds of respectable businesses, coffeehouses, taverns, and homes in
the wooden warrens of the Emerald Galleries, where sunlight and moonlight alike filtered down a soothing sea
green through the mushrooming, intersecting Elderglass
domes that roofed the district. Therese's guards led
prospective clients to her, blindfolded, along a lengthy series of passageways. The armed young woman stood away
from the door, a pair of blindfolds in hand.

"We understand completely," said Locke. "And never
fear. We're becoming quite accustomed to being led around
by our noses in the dark."

2

LOCKE AND Jean skulked about the Savrola for two
nights after that, keeping their eyes on every rooftop and
every alley, but neither Bondsmagi nor agents of the archon came forward and conveniently announced themselves. They *were* being followed and observed by several
teams of men and women; that much was clear. Locke's
guess was that these were Requin's people, given instructions to let just enough of their activities slip to keep him
and Jean on their toes.

On the third night, they decided they might as well return to the Sinspire and put on their brave faces. Decked
out in several hundred solari worth of finery apiece, they
walked up the red velvet carpet and placed silver volani in
the hands of the door-guards while a sizable crowd of well-
dressed nobodies stood nearby hoping for a glimmer of social mercy.

Locke's practiced eye picked out the ringers among

them; men and women with worse teeth, leaner faces, and warier eyes than the rest of the crowd, dressed in evening clothes that didn't look precisely tailored, or wearing the wrong accessories, or the wrong colors. Requin's Right People, out for a night at his Sinspire as a reward for some job well done. They'd be let in in good time, but not allowed past the second floor. Their presence was just one more component of the tower's mystique; a chance for the great and good to mingle with the dirty and dangerous.

"Masters Kosta and de Ferra," said one of the doormen, "welcome back."

When the wide doors swung open toward Locke and Jean, a wave of noise and heat and smells washed out over them into the night—the familiar exhalation of decadence.

The first floor was merely crowded, but the second floor was a wall-to-wall sea of flesh and fine clothes. The crowd began on the stairs, and Locke and Jean had to use elbows and threats to make their way up into the mess.

"What in Perelandro's name is going on?" Locke asked of a man pressed against him. The man turned, grinning excitedly.

"It's a cage spectacle!"

In the center of the second floor was a brass cage that could be lowered from the ceiling, locking into apertures in the floor to create a sturdy cube about twenty feet on a side. Tonight the cage was also covered with a very fine mesh—no, Locke corrected himself, two layers of mesh, one inside the cage and one outside. A lucky minority of the Sinspire patrons in the room were watching from elevated tables along the outer walls; it was standing-room only for at least a hundred others.

Locke and Jean made their way through the crowd counterclockwise, attempting to get close enough to see what the spectacle was. The excited murmur of conversation surrounded them, more frantic than Locke had ever heard it within these walls. But as he and Jean approached the cage, he suddenly realized that not all of the noise was coming from the crowd.

Something the size of a sparrow beat its wings against the mesh and buzzed angrily, a low thrumming sound that sent a shiver of pure animal dread up Locke's spine. "That's a fucking stiletto wasp," he whispered to Jean, who nodded vigorously in agreement.

Locke had never been unfortunate enough to encounter one of the insects personally. They were the bane of several large tropical islands a few thousand miles to the east, far past Jerem and Jeresh and the lands detailed on most Therin maps. Years before, Jean had found a gruesome account of the creatures in one of his natural philosophy books and read it aloud to the other Gentlemen Bastards, ruining their sleep for several nights.

They were called stiletto wasps on account of descriptions the rare survivors gave of being stung by them. They were as heavy as songbirds, bright red in color, and their stinging abdomens were longer than a grown man's middle finger. Possession of a stiletto wasp queen in any Therin city-state was punishable by death, lest the things should ever gain a foothold on Therin soil. Their hives were said to be the size of houses.

A young man ducked and wove inside the cage, dressed in nothing more protective than a silk tunic, cotton breeches, and short boots. Thick leather gauntlets were his weapons as well as his only armor; they were wedded to bracers buckled around his forearms, and he kept his hands up before his face like a boxer. With gloves like that a man could certainly contemplate swatting or crushing a stiletto wasp—but he would have to be very quick and very sure of himself.

On a table at the opposite side of the cage sat a heavy wooden cabinet fronted with dozens of mesh-covered cells, a few of which were already open. The rest, judging by the noise, were crammed full of highly agitated stiletto wasps just waiting to be released.

"Master Kosta! Master de Ferra!"

The shout carried across the noisy crowd but even so was hard to pinpoint. Locke had to look around several times before he could spot the source—Maracosa Durenna, waving to him and Jean from her place at one of the tables against a far wall.

Her black hair was pulled back into a sort of fantail around a gleaming silver ornament, and she was smoking from a curved silver pipe almost as long as her arm. Bands of white iron and jade slid against one another on her left wrist as she beckoned Locke and Jean across the room. They raised eyebrows at each other but pushed their way through the crowd toward her, and were soon standing beside her table.

"Where have you been these past few nights? Izmila has been indisposed, but I've been cruising the waters with other games in mind."

"Our apologies, Madam Durenna," said Jean. "Matters of business have kept us elsewhere. We occasionally consult on a freelance basis for very . . . demanding clients."

"There was a brief trip over water," added Locke.

"Negotiations concerning futures in pear cider," said Jean.

"We came highly recommended by former associates," said Locke.

"Pear cider futures? What a romantic and dangerous sort of trade you two must ply. And are you as accomplished at stake-placing in futures as you are at Carousel Hazard?"

"It stands to reason," said Jean, "or else we wouldn't have the funds to play Carousel Hazard."

"Well then, how about a demonstration? The cage duel.

Which participant do you believe to have a happier prospect for the future?"

In the cage, the free stiletto wasp darted toward the young man, who swatted it out of the air and crushed it beneath one of his boots with an audible juicy crack. Most of the crowd cheered.

"Apparently, it's too late for our opinion to matter one way or the other," said Locke. "Or is there more to the show?"

"The show's only just started, Master Kosta. That hive has one hundred and twenty cells. There's a clockwork device opening the doors, mostly at random. He might get one at a time; he might get six. Eye-catching, isn't it? He can't leave the cage until he's got one hundred and twenty wasps dead at his feet, or ..."

She punctuated the sentence with a deep intake of smoke from her pipe and a raising of both her eyebrows.

"I believe he's killed eight so far," she finished.

"Ah," said Locke. "Well ... if I had to choose, I'd be inclined to favor the boy. Call me an optimist."

"I do." She let two long streams of smoke fall out of her nose like faint gray waterfalls, and she smiled. "I would take the wasps. Shall we call it a wager? Two hundred solari from me, one hundred apiece from each of you?"

"I'm as fond of a small wager as the next man, but let's ask the next man—Jerome?"

"If it's your pleasure, madam, our coin purses are yours to command."

"What a font of gracious untruths you two are." She beckoned one of Requin's attendants, and the three of them pledged their credit with the house for markers. They received four short wooden sticks engraved with ten rings apiece. The attendant recorded their names on a tablet and moved on; the tempo of the betting around the room was still rising.

In the cage, two more murderously annoyed insects wriggled out of their enclosures and took wing toward the young man.

"Did I mention," said Durenna as she set her pair of markers down atop her little table, "that the death of nearby wasps seems to excite the others to a higher state of frenzy? That boy's opponents will get angrier and angrier as the fight goes on."

The pair currently free in the enclosure seemed angry enough; the boy was dancing a lively jig to keep them away from his back and flanks. "Fascinating," said Jean, working a series of specific hand gestures into his mannerisms as he craned his neck to watch the duel. There were a few creative uses of fairly limited signals in Jean's message, but Locke eventually sorted the gist of it out:

Do we really have to stay to watch this with her?

He was about to answer when a familiar hard weight fell on his left shoulder.

"Master Kosta," said Selendri before Locke had even finished turning. "One of the Priori wishes to speak to you on the sixth floor. A small matter. Something concerning... card tricks. He said you'd understand."

"Madam," said Locke, "I, ah, would be only too happy to attend. Can you let him know that I'll be with him shortly?"

"Better," she said with a half-smile that didn't move the devastated side of her face at all. "I can escort you myself, to greatly speed your passage."

Locke smiled as though that were exactly what he would have wished, and he turned back to Madam Durenna with his hands spread out before him.

"You *do* move in interesting circles, Master Kosta. Best hurry; Jerome can tend your wager, and share a drink with me."

"A most unlooked-for pleasure," said Jean, already beckoning an attendant to order that drink.

Selendri didn't waste another moment; she turned and stepped into the crowd, setting course for the stairs on the far side of the circular room. She moved quickly, with her brass hand cradled in her flesh hand before her like an offering, and the throng parted almost miraculously. Locke hurried along in her wake, keeping just ahead of the crowd as it closed up again behind him like some colony of scuttling creatures briefly disturbed in its chores. Glasses clinked, ragged layers of smoke twirled in the air, and wasps buzzed.

Up the stairs to the third floor; again the well-dressed masses melted away before Requin's majordomo. On the south side of the third floor was a service area filled with attendants bustling about shelves of liquor bottles. At the rear of the service room was a narrow wooden door with a brass wall-plate beside it. Selendri slid her artificial hand into this plate, and the door cracked open on a dark space barely larger than a coffin. She stepped in first, put her back against the wall of the enclosure, and beckoned him in.

"The climbing closet," she said. "Much easier than the stairs and the crowds."

It was a tight fit; Jean would have been unable to share the compartment with her. Locke was crammed in against her left side, and he could feel the heavy weight of her brass hand against his upper back. She reached past him with her other hand and drew the compartment closed. They were locked in warm darkness, and Locke became intensely aware of their smells—his fresh sweat and her feminine musk, and something in her hair, like the smoke from a burning pine log. Woodsy, tingly, not at all unpleasant.

"Well," he said softly, "this is where I'd have an accident, right? If I had an accident coming?"

"It wouldn't be an accident, Master Kosta." She spoke

softly as well, as though it was some rule of the enclosure. "But no, you're not to have it on the way up."

She moved, and he heard the clicking of some mechanism from the wall on her right. A moment later, the walls of the compartment shuddered, and a faint creaking noise grew above them.

"You dislike me," Locke said on a whim. There was a brief silence.

"I've known many traitors," she said at last, "but perhaps none so glib."

"Only those who initiate treachery are traitors," said Locke, injecting a hurt tone into his voice. "What I desire is redress for a grievance."

"You would have your rationalizations," she whispered.

"I've offended you somehow."

"Call it whatever you like."

Locke concentrated furiously on the tone of his next few words. In darkness, facing away from her, his voice would be detached from all the cues of his face and his mannerisms. It would never have a more effective theater of use. Like an alchemist, he mingled long-practiced deceptions into the desired emotional compound—regret, abashedness, longing.

"If I have offended you, madam—I would unsay what I said, or undo what I did." The briefest hesitation, just the thing for conveying sincerity. The trustiest tool in his verbal kit. "I would do it the moment you told me how, if you only gave me the chance."

She shuffled ever so slightly against him; the brass hand pressed harder for a heartbeat. Locke closed his eyes and willed his ears, his skin, and his pure animal instincts to pluck whatever slightest clue they could out of the darkness. Would she scorn pity, or did she crave it? He could feel the shuddering beat of his own heart, hear the faint pulse in his own temples.

"There is nothing to unsay or undo," she replied, faintly.

"I almost wish that there were. So that I could put you at ease."

"You cannot." She sighed. "You could not."

"And you won't even let me try?"

"You talk the way you perform card tricks, Master Kosta. Far too smoothly. I fear you may be even better at hiding things with words than you are with your hands. If you must know, it's your possible usefulness against your employer—and that alone—that preserves my consent for letting you live."

"I don't want to be your enemy, Selendri. I don't even want to be trouble."

"Words are cheap. Cheap and meaningless."

"I can't..." Judicious pause again. Locke was as careful as a master sculptor placing crow's-feet around the edges of a stone statue's eye. "Look, maybe I am glib. I can't speak otherwise, Selendri." Repeated use of her proper name, a compulsion, almost a spell. More intimate and effective than titles. "I am who I am."

"And you wonder that I distrust you for it?"

"I wonder more if there's anything that you *don't* distrust."

"Distrust everyone," she said, "and you can never be betrayed. Opposed, but never betrayed."

"Hmmm." Locke bit his tongue and thought rapidly. "But you don't distrust *him,* do you, Selendri?"

"That's no gods-damned business of yours, Master Kosta."

There was a loud rattle from the ceiling of the climbing closet. The room gave a last heavy shudder, and then fell still.

"Forgive me, again," said Locke. "Not the sixth floor, of course. The ninth?"

"The ninth."

In a second she would push past him and open the door. They had one last moment alone in the intimate darkness. He weighed his options, hefted his last conversational dart. Something risky, but potentially disquieting.

"I used to think much less of him, you know. Before I found out that he was wise enough to really love you." Another pause, and he lowered his voice to the barest edge of audibility. "I think you must be the bravest woman I've ever met."

He counted his own heartbeats in the darkness until she responded.

"What a pretty presumption," she whispered, and there was acid beneath her words. There was a click, and a line of yellow light split the blackness, stinging his eyes. She gave him a firm push with her artificial hand, against the door that opened out into the lamplit heart of Requin's office.

Well, let her roll his words over in her thoughts for a while. Let her give him the signals that would tell him how to proceed. He had no specific goal in mind; it would be enough to keep her uncertain, simply less inclined to stick a knife in his back. And if some small part of him felt sour at twisting her emotions (gods damn it, that part of him had rarely spoken up before!), well—he reminded himself that he could do as he pleased and feel as he pleased while he was Leocanto Kosta. Leocanto Kosta wasn't real.

He stepped out of the climbing closet, unsure if he was any more convinced by himself than Selendri was.

3

"MASTER KOSTA! My mysterious new associate. What a busy man you've been."

Requin's office was as cluttered as it had been on Locke's last visit. Locke was gratified to see his decks of cards stacked haphazardly at various points on and near Requin's desk. The climbing closet opened out of a wall niche between two paintings, a niche Locke certainly hadn't noticed on his previous visit.

Requin was standing gazing out through the mesh screen that covered the door to his balcony, wearing a heavy maroon frock coat with black lapels. He scratched at his chin with one gloved hand and glanced sideways at Locke.

"Actually," said Locke, "Jerome and I have had a quiet few days. As I believe I promised you."

"I don't mean just these past few days. I've been making those inquiries into your past two years in Tal Verrar."

"As I'd hoped. Enlightening?"

"Most educational. Let's be direct. Your associate tried to shake down Azura Gallardine for information concerning my vault. Something more than a year ago. You know who she is?"

Selendri was pacing the room to Locke's left, slowly, watching him over her right shoulder.

"Of course. One of the high muck-a-shits of the Artificers' Guild. I told Jerome where to find her."

"And how did you know that she'd had a hand in the design of my vault?"

"It's amazing, how much you can learn by buying drinks in artificer bars and pretending that every story you hear is incredibly fascinating."

"I see."

"The old bitch didn't tell him anything, though."

"She wouldn't have. And she would have been content at that; she didn't even tell me about the inquiry he'd made. But I put out the question a few nights ago, and it turns out that a beer-seller on my list of reliable eyes once saw someone answering your associate's description fall out of the sky."

"Yes. Jerome said the guildmistress had a unique method of interrupting conversations."

"Well, Selendri had an uninterrupted conversation with her yesterday evening. She was enticed to remember everything she could about Jerome's visit."

"Enticed?"

"Financially, Master Kosta."

"Ah."

"I have also come to understand that you made inquiries with some of my gangs over in the Silver Marina. Starting around the time Jerome visited Guildmistress Gallardine."

"Yes. I spoke to an older fellow named Drava, and a woman named . . . what was it . . ."

"Armania Cantazzi."

"Yes, that was her. Thank you. Gorgeous woman; I tried to get past business and get a bit friendlier with her, but she didn't seem to appreciate my charms."

"Armania wouldn't have; she prefers the company of other women."

"Now there's a relief. I thought I was losing my touch."

"You were curious about shipping, the sort customs officials never get to hear about. You discussed a few terms with my people and never followed up. Why?"

"Jerome and I agreed, upon reflection, that securing shipping from outside Tal Verrar would be wisest. We could then simply hire a few small barges to move whatever we stole from you, and avoid the more complicated dealings involved in getting a lighter."

"If I were planning to rob myself, I suppose I would agree. Now, the matter of alchemists. I have reliable information placing you at several over the past year. Reputable and otherwise."

"Of course. I conducted a few experiments with fire oils and acids, on secondhand clockwork mechanisms. I thought it might save some tedious lock-picking."

"Did these experiments bear fruit?"

"I'd share that information with an employer," said Locke, grinning.

"Mmmm. Leave that for now. But it does indeed appear that you've been up to something. So many disparate activities that do add up to support your story. There's just one thing more."

"Which is?"

"I'm curious. How *was* old Maxilan doing when you saw him three nights ago?"

Locke was suddenly aware that Selendri was no longer pacing. She had placed herself just a few steps directly behind him, unmoving. Crooked Warden, give me a golden line of bullshit and the wisdom to know when to stop spinning it, he thought.

"Uh, well, he's a prick."

"That's no secret. Any child on the street could tell me that. But you admit you were at the Mon Magisteria?"

"I was. I had a private audience with Stragos. Incidentally, he's under the impression that his agents among your gangs are undetected."

"As per my intentions. But you do get around, Leocanto. Just what *would* the archon of Tal Verrar want with you and Jerome? In the middle of the night, no less? On the very night we had such an *interesting* conversation ourselves?"

Locke sighed to buy himself a few seconds to think. "I can tell you," he said when he'd hesitated as long as was prudent, "but I doubt you're going to like it."

"Of course I won't like it. Let's have it anyway."

Locke sighed. Headfirst into a lie, or headfirst out the window.

"Stragos is the one who's been paying Jerome and myself. The fronts we've been dealing with are his agents. *He's* the man who's so keen to see your vault looking like a larder after a banquet. He thought it was time to crack the whip on us."

Faint lines appeared on Requin's face as he ground his teeth together, and he put his hands behind his back. "You heard that from his own mouth?"

"Yes."

"What an astonishing regard he must feel for you, to give you a personal briefing on his affairs. And your proof?"

"Well, you know, I did ask for a signed affidavit concerning his intentions to rake you over the coals, and he was happy to provide me with one, but clumsy me . . . I lost it on my way over here tonight!" Locke turned to his left and scowled. He could see that Selendri was watching him keenly, with her flesh hand resting on something under her jacket. "For fuck's sake, if you don't believe me I can jump out the window right now and save us all a great deal of time."

"No . . . no need to paint the cobblestones with your brains just yet." Requin held up one hand. "It is, however, unusual for someone in Stragos' position to deal directly with agents that must be, ah, somewhat lowly placed within his hierarchy, and in his regard. No offense."

"None taken. If I might hazard a guess, I think Stragos is impatient for some reason. I suspect he wants faster results. And . . . I'm fairly sure that Jerome and myself are no longer intended to outlive any success we achieve on his behalf. It's the only reasonable presumption."

"And it would save him a fair bit of money, I'd guess. Stragos' sort are ever more parsimonious with gold than they are with lives." Requin cracked his knuckles beneath his thin leather gloves. "The damnable thing is, this all makes a great deal of sense. I have a rule of thumb—if you have a puzzle and the answers are elegant and simple, it means someone is trying to fuck you over."

"My only remaining question," said Selendri, "is why

Stragos would deal with you *personally*, knowing full well you could now implicate him if put to ... persuasion."

"There is one thing I hadn't thought to mention," said Locke, looking abashed. "It is ... a matter of great embarrassment to Jerome and myself. Stragos gave us cider to drink during our audience. Not daring to be inhospitable, we drank quite a bit of it. He claims to have laced it with a poison, something subtle and latent. Something that will require Jerome and I to take an antidote from his hand at regular intervals, or else die unpleasantly. So now he has us by the hip, and if we want the antidote, we must be his good little creatures."

"An old trick," said Requin. "Old and reliable."

"I said we were duly embarrassed. And so you see," said Locke, "he already has a means to dispose of us when we've served his purpose. I'm sure he feels very confident of our loyalty for the time being."

"And yet you still wish to turn against him?"

"Be honest, Requin. If you were Stragos, would you give us the antidote and send us on our merry way? We're already dead to him. So now I have the burden of two revenges to carry out before I die. Even if I do succumb to Stragos' damn cider, I want my last moment with Jerome. And I want the archon to suffer. *You* are still the best means I have to either end."

"A reasonable presumption," purred Requin, growing slightly warmer in his manner.

"I'm glad you think so, because apparently I know less about the politics of this city than I thought I did. What the hell is going on, Requin?"

"The archon and the Priori are gnashing their teeth at one another again. Now, half the Priori store large portions of their personal fortunes in my vault, making it impossible for the archon's spies to know the true extent of their resources. Emptying my vault would not only strip them of funds, but put me in their bad graces. Right now, Stragos could *never* put me out of business without major provocation, for fear of initiating a civil war. But sponsoring an apparent third party to hit my vault... oh yes, that'd do the trick nicely. I'd be busy hunting you and Jerome, the Priori would be busy trying to have me drawn and quartered, and *then* Stragos could simply..."

Requin illustrated what the archon could do by placing a balled fist inside an open palm and squeezing hard.

"I was under the impression," said Locke, "that the archon was subordinate to the Priori council."

"Technically, he is. The Priori have a lovely piece of parchment that says so. Stragos has an army and a navy that afford him a dissenting opinion."

"Great. So now what do we do?"

"Good question. No more suggestions from you, no more schemes, no more card tricks, Master Kosta?"

Locke decided it was a good time to make Leocanto Kosta a bit more human. "Look," he said. "When my employer was just an anonymous someone who sent a bag of coins every month, I knew exactly what I was doing. But now something else is happening, knives are coming out, and you can see all the angles that I don't. So tell me what to do and I'll do it."

"Hmmmm. Stragos. Did he ask about the conversation you and I had?"

"He didn't even mention it. I don't think he knew about it. I think Jerome and I were scheduled to get picked up and brought in that night regardless."

"You're sure?"

"I'm as sure as I can be."

"Tell me something, Leocanto. If Stragos had revealed himself to you before you'd had a chance to perform your card tricks for me... if you'd known it was him you were betraying, would you still have done it?"

"Well..." Locke pretended to think. "I can't say what I might think if I actually liked him, or trusted him. Maybe I'd just give Jerome a knife in the back and work for him if I did. But...we're rats to Stragos, aren't we? We're fucking insects. Stragos is one presumptuous son of a bitch. He thinks he knows Jerome and me. I just...don't like him, not a bit, even without the poison to consider."

"He must have spoken to you at length, to inspire such distaste," said Requin with a smile. "So be it. If you want to buy your way into my organization, there will be a price. That price is Stragos."

"Oh, gods. What the hell does *that* mean?"

"When Stragos is either verifiably dead or in my custody, you may have what you ask. A place at the Sinspire assisting with my games. A salary. All the assistance I can offer you with his poison. And Jerome de Ferra crying under your knife. Is that agreeable?"

"How am I supposed to do that?"

"I don't want you to do it all yourself. But Maxilan has clearly ruled long enough. Assist me in enabling his retirement by any means you can, or any means I order. Then I suppose I'll have a new floor boss."

"Best thing I've heard in a long while. And the, ah, money in my account, locked away by your command?"

"Will remain locked away, lost by your own actions. I am not a man of charity, Leocanto. Remember that, if you would serve me."

"Of course. Of course. But now indulge me, please, in a question of my own. Why aren't you worried that I might be double-timing you for Stragos? That I might run back and tell him all this?"

"Why do you presume that *I'm* not playing *you* falsely on that very presumption?" Requin smiled, broadly, in genuine amusement.

"All these possibilities make my head hurt," said Locke.

"I prefer cardsharping to intrigue. If you're not on the up-and-up, logically, I might as well go home and hang myself tonight."

"Yes. But I'll give you a better answer. What could you possibly tell Stragos? That I dislike him, bank for his enemies, and wish him dead? So he'd have confirmation of my hostility? No point. He *knows* I'm hostile. He knows the underworld of Tal Verrar is an impediment to him if he wants to assert his power. My *felantozzi* prefer the rule of the guilds to the possibility of rule by uniforms and spears; there's less money in dictatorship by arms."

Felantozzi was a Throne Therin term for foot soldiers; Locke had heard it used to refer to criminals a few times before, but he'd never heard them using it among themselves.

"All that remains," said Requin, "is for your other judge to concur that you are still a risk worth taking."

"Other judge?"

Requin gestured toward Selendri. "You've heard everything, my dear. Do we put Leocanto out the window, or do we send him back down to where you fetched him from?"

Locke met her gaze, folded his arms, and smiled in what he hoped was his most agreeable harmless-puppy fashion. She scowled inscrutably for a few moments, then sighed.

"There's so much to distrust here. But if there's a chance to place a turncoat relatively close to the archon . . . I suppose it costs us little enough. We may as well take it."

"There, Master Kosta." Requin stepped over and placed a hand on Locke's shoulder. "How's that for a ringing endorsement of your character?"

"I'll take what I can get." Locke tried not to let too much of his genuine relief show.

"Then for the time being, your task will be to keep the archon happy. And, presumably, feeding you your antidote."

"I shall, gods willing." Locke scratched his chin thoughtfully. "I'll have to let him know that we've made our personal acquaintance; he must have other eyes in your spire who'll figure it out sooner or later. Best have it explained sooner."

"Of course. Is he likely to bring you back to the Mon Magisteria soon?"

"I don't know how soon, but yes. Very much more than likely."

"Good. That means he might blather on about his plans again. Now, let's get you back down to Master de Ferra and your evening's business. Cheating anyone tonight?"

"We'd only just arrived. We were taking in the cage spectacle."

"Oh, the wasps. Quite a windfall, those monsters."

"Dangerous property."

"Yes, a Jeremite captain had a seed hive and a queen he was trying to sell. My people tipped off customs, had him executed, burnt the queen, and the rest vanished into my keeping after they were impounded. I knew I'd find some sort of use for them."

"And the young man facing them?"

"Some eighth son of a titled nobody with sand for brains and debts to the 'Spire. He said he'd cover his markers or die trying, and I took him at his word."

"Well. I've got a hundred solari on him, so I hope he lives to cover those markers." He turned back toward Selendri. "The climbing closet again?"

"Only to the sixth floor. You can walk back down from there." She smirked slightly. "By yourself."

4

WHEN LOCKE managed to elbow his way back down to the second floor at last, the young man in the cage was limping, bleeding, and wobbling on his feet. Half a dozen stiletto wasps were free in the enclosure, hovering and darting around him. Locke sighed as he pushed through the crowd.

"Master Kosta! Returned to us just in time for the issue to be settled, I believe."

Madam Durenna smiled over the top of her drink, some milky orange liquor in a slender glass vessel nearly a foot high. Jean was sipping from a smaller tumbler of something pale brown, and he passed an identical glass to Locke, who took it up with a grateful nod. Honeyed rum—hard enough to avoid Durenna's scorn, but not quite powerful enough to start beating anyone's better judgment down for the evening.

"Is it about that time? My apologies for my absence. Silly little business."

"Silly? With one of the Priori involved?"

"I made the mistake of showing him a card trick last week," said Locke. "Now he's making arrangements for me to perform the same trick for, ah, a friend of his."

"It must be an impressive trick, then. More impressive than what you usually do at a card table?"

"I doubt it, madam." Locke took a long sip from his drink. "For one thing, I don't have to worry about such excellent opposition when I'm performing a card trick."

"Has anyone ever tried to cut out that disgustingly silver tongue of yours, Master Kosta?"

"It's become a traditional pastime in several cities I could mention."

In the cage, the mad buzzing of the wasps grew louder as more of them exploded from their cells: two, three, four.... Locke shuddered and watched helplessly as the blurry dark shapes hurtled around the meshed cage. The young man tried to stand his ground, then panicked and began to flail wildly. One wasp met his glove and was slapped to the floor, but another alighted on his lower back and drove its body down. The boy howled, slapped at it, and arched his back. The crowd grew deadly silent in mingled horror and anticipation.

It was fast, but Locke would never have called it merciful. The wasps swarmed the young man, darting and stinging, digging their clawed legs into his blood-soaked shirt. One on his chest, one on his arm, its abdomen pulsing madly up and down...one fluttered about his hair, and another drove its sting home into the nape of his neck. The boy's wild screams became wet choking noises. Foam trickled from his mouth, blood ran in rivulets down his face and chest, and at last he fell over, twitching wildly. The wasps buzzed and stalked atop his body, looking horribly like blood-colored ants as they went about their business, still stinging and biting.

Locke's stomach revolted against the small breakfast he'd eaten at the Villa Candessa, and he bit down hard on one of his curled fingers, using the pain to assert some self-control. When he turned back to Madam Durenna, his face was once again placid.

"Well," she said, waving the four wooden sticks at him and Jean, "this is a tolerable salve for the wounds I still bear from our last meeting. But when shall we have the pleasure of full redress?"

"It can't possibly come soon enough," said Locke. "But if you'll excuse us for the evening, we've got some...political difficulties to discuss. And before we leave I'm going to dispose of my drink on the body of the man who's cost us two hundred solari."

Madam Durenna waved airily, and was reloading her silver pipe from a leather pouch before Locke and Jean had taken two steps.

Locke's queasiness rose again as he approached the cage. The crowd was breaking up around him, trading marker sticks and enthusiastic babble. The last few paces around the cage, though, were already clear. The noise and movement in the room around them was keeping the wasps agitated. As Locke approached the cage, a pair leapt back into the air and hovered menacingly, beating loudly against the inner layer of mesh and following him along. Their black eyes seemed to stare right into his. He cringed despite himself.

He knelt as close to the young man's body as he could get, and in seconds half the free wasps in the enclosure were buzzing and batting against the mesh just a foot or two from his face. Locke threw the remaining half of his rum on the wasp-covered corpse. Behind him, there was an eruption of laughter.

"That's the spirit, friend," came a slurred voice. "Clumsy son of a bitch cost me five hundred solari. Take a piss on him while you're down there!"

"Crooked Warden," Locke muttered under his breath, speaking quickly. "A glass poured on the ground for a stranger without friends. Lord of gallants and fools, ease this man's passage to the Lady of the Long Silence. This was a hell of a way to die. Do this for me and I'll try not to ask for anything for a while. I really do mean that this time."

Locke kissed the back of his left hand and stood up. With the blessing said, suddenly it seemed that he couldn't be far enough away from the cage.

"Where now?" asked Jean quietly.

"The hell away from these gods-damned bugs."

5

THE SKY was clear over the sea and roofed in by clouds to the east; a high pearlescent ceiling hung there like frozen smoke beneath the moons. A hard breeze was blowing past them as they trudged across the docks that fringed the inner side of the Great Gallery, whipping discarded papers and other bits of junk about their feet. A ship's bell echoed across the lapping silver water.

On their left, a dark Elderglass wall rose story after story like a looming cliff, crossed here and there by rickety stairs with faint lanterns to guide the way of those stumbling up and down them. At the top of those heights was the Night Market, and the edge of the vast roof that covered the tiers of the island down to the waves on its other side.

"Oh, fantastic," said Jean when Locke had finished his recounting of what had transpired in Requin's office. "So now we've got Requin thinking that Stragos is out to get him. I've never helped precipitate a civil war before. This should be fun."

"I didn't have much choice," said Locke. "Can you think of any other convincing reasons for Stragos to take a personal interest in us? Without a good explanation, I was going out that window, that much was clear."

"If only you'd landed on your head, you'd have nothing to fear but the bill for damaged cobblestones. Do you think Stragos needs to know that Requin's not as blind to his agents as he thought?"

"Oh, fuck the son of a bitch."

"Didn't think so."

"Besides, for all we know Stragos really is out to get Requin. They're certainly not friends, and trouble's brewing all over this damn city. On the assets side of the ledger," said Locke, "I think Selendri can be sweet-talked, at least a little bit. And it seems that Requin really thinks of me as *his.*"

"Well, good on that. Do you think it's time to give him the chairs?"

"Yeah, the chairs...the chairs. Yes. Let's do it, before Stragos decides to push us around some more."

"I'll have them taken out of storage and brought round in a cart, whenever you like."

"Good. I'll deliver them later this week, then. You mind avoiding the Sinspire for a night or two?"

"Of course not. Any particular reason?"

"I just want to disappoint Durenna and Corvaleur for a bit. Until we're a little more secure with our situation, I'd really prefer not to waste another night losing money and getting drunk. The *bela paranella* trick might rouse suspicion if we pull it again."

"If you put it that way, I can't say no. How about if I poke around in a few other places, and see if I can catch any whispers about the archon and the Priori? I think we might arm ourselves with a little more of this city's history."

"Lovely. What the hell's this?"

They were not alone on the dockside; in addition to occasional strangers hurrying here and there on business, there were boatmen sleeping under cloaks beside their tied-up craft, and a fair number of drunks and derelicts curled up beneath any shelter they could claim. A pile of crates lay just a few paces to their left, and in its shadow sat a thin figure covered in layers of torn rags, near a tiny alchemical globe that shone a pale red. The figure clutched a small burlap sack and beckoned to them with one pale hand.

"Sirs, sirs!" The loud, croaking voice seemed to be a woman's. "For pity's sake, you fine gentlemen. For pity's sake, for Perelandro's sake. A coin, any coin, thin copper would do. Have pity, for Perelandro's sake."

Locke's hand went to his purse, just inside his frock coat. Jean had taken his coat off and now carried it folded over his right arm; he seemed content to let Locke see to the evening's act of charity.

"For Perelandro's sake, madam, you may have more than just a centira."

Temporarily distracted by the warm glow of his own affected gallantry, Locke was holding out three silver volani before the first little warning managed to register. The beggar would be happy to have one thin copper, and had a loud voice . . . why hadn't they heard her speaking to any of the strangers who'd passed by just ahead of them?

And why was she reaching out with the burlap sack rather than an open hand?

Jean was faster than he was, and with no more elegant way to get Locke to safety, he raised his left arm and gave Locke a hard shove. A crossbow bolt punched a neat dark hole in the burlap sack and hissed through the air between them; Locke felt it tug at his coattails as he fell sideways. He toppled over a smaller crate and landed clumsily on his back.

He sat up just in time to see Jean kick the beggar in the face. The woman's head snapped back, but she planted her hands on the ground and scissored her legs, sweeping Jean off his feet. As Jean hit the ground and tossed his folded coat away, the beggar drew her legs straight up, kicked them down, and seemed to fling herself forward in an arc. She was on her feet in a second, casting off her rags.

Ah, shit. She's a foot-boxer—a bloody *chassoneur*, Locke thought, stumbling to his feet. Jean hates that. Locke twitched his coat-sleeves, and a stiletto fell into each hand. Moving warily, he skipped across the stones toward Jean's attacker, who was kicking Jean in the ribs as the big man attempted to roll away. Locke was within three paces of the *chassoneur* when the slap of boot-leather against the ground warned of a presence close behind him. He raised the stiletto in his right hand as though to strike Jean's assailant, then ducked and whirled, lunging blindly to his rear with the left-hand blade.

Locke was instantly glad he'd ducked; something whirled past his head close enough to tear painfully at his hair. His new attacker was another "beggar," a man close to his own stature, and he'd just missed a swing with a long iron chain that would have opened Locke's skull like an egg. The force of the man's attack helped carry him onto the point of Locke's stiletto, which plunged in up to the hilt just beneath the man's right armpit. The man gasped, and Locke pressed his advantage ruthlessly, bringing his other blade down overhand and burying it in the man's left clavicle.

Locke wrenched both of his blades as savagely as he could, and the man moaned. The chain slipped from his fingers and hit the stones with a clatter; a second later Locke worked his blades out of the man's body as though he were pulling skewers from meat and let the poor fellow slump to the ground. He raised his bloody stilettos, turned, and with a sudden burst of ill-advised self-confidence, charged Jean's assailant.

She kicked out from the hip, barely sparing him a glance. Her foot struck his sternum; it felt like walking into a brick wall. He stumbled back, and she took the opportunity to step away from Jean (who looked to have been rather pummeled) and advance on Locke.

Her rags were discarded. Locke saw that she was a young woman, probably younger than he was, wearing loose dark clothing and a thin, well-fashioned ribbed leather vest. She was Therin, relatively dark-skinned, with tightly braided black hair that circled her head like a crown. She had a poise that said she'd killed before.

No problem, thought Locke as he moved backward. So have I. That's when he tripped over the body of the man he'd just stabbed.

She took instant advantage of his misstep. Just as he regained his balance, she snapped out in an arc with her right leg. Her foot landed like a hammer against Locke's left forearm, and he swore as his stiletto flew from suddenly nerveless fingers. Incensed, he lunged with his right-hand blade.

Moving as deftly as Jean ever had, she grabbed his right wrist with her left hand, pulled him irresistibly forward, and slammed the heel of her right hand into his chin. His remaining stiletto whirled into the darkness like a man diving from a tall building, and suddenly the dark sky above him was replaced with looming gray stones. He made their acquaintance hard enough to rattle his teeth like dice in a cup.

She kicked him once to roll him over onto his back, then planted a foot on his chest to pin him down. She'd caught one of his blades, and he watched in a daze as she bent forward to put it to use. His hands were numb, traitorously slow, and he felt an unbearable itching sensation on his unprotected neck as his own stiletto dipped toward it.

Locke didn't hear Jean's hatchet sink into her back, but he saw its effect and guessed the cause. The woman jerked upright, arched backward, and let the stiletto slip. It clattered against the ground just beside Locke's face, and he flinched. His assailant sank down to her knees just beside him, breathing in swift shallow gasps, and then twisted away. He could see one of Jean's Wicked Sisters buried in a spreading dark stain on her lower back, just to the right of her spine.

Jean stepped over Locke, reached down, and yanked the hatchet from the woman's back. She gasped, fell forward, and was viciously yanked back upright by Jean, who stood behind her and placed the blade of his hatchet against her throat.

"Lo . . . Leo! Leocanto. Are you all right?"

"With this much pain," Locke gasped, "I know I can't be dead."

"Good enough." Jean applied more force to the hatchet, which he was holding just behind its head, like a barber wielding a beard-scraper. "Start talking. I can help you die without further pain, or I can even help you live. You're no simple bandit. Who put you here?"

"My back," sobbed the woman, her voice trembling and utterly without threat. "Please, please, it hurts."

"It's supposed to. Who put you here? Who hired you?"

"Gold," said Locke, coughing. "White iron. We can pay you. Double. Just give us a name."

"Oh, gods, it hurts..."

Jean seized her by the hair with his free hand and pulled; she cried out and straightened up. Locke blinked as he saw what appeared to be a dark feathered shape burst out of her chest; the wet thud of the crossbow quarrel's impact didn't register until a split second later. Jean leapt back, dumbfounded, and dropped the woman to the ground. A moment later, he looked past Locke and gestured threateningly with his hatchet.

"You!"

"At your service, Master de Ferra."

Locke craned his head back far enough to catch an upside-down glimpse of the woman who'd stolen them off the street and delivered them to the archon a few nights before. Her dark hair fluttered freely behind her in the breeze. She wore a tight black jacket over a gray waistcoat and a gray skirt, and held a discharged crossbow in her left hand. She was walking toward them at a leisurely pace, from the direction they'd come. Locke groaned and rolled over until she was right side up.

Beside him, the beggar-*chassoneur* gave one last wet cough and died.

"Gods *damn* it," cried Jean, "I was about to get some answers from her!"

"No, you weren't," said the archon's agent. "Take a look at her right hand."

Locke, climbing shakily to his feet, and Jean both did so; a slender knife with a curved blade glistened there by the faint light of the moons and the few dockside lamps.

"I was assigned to watch over you two," the woman said as she stepped up beside Locke, beaming contentedly.

"Fine fucking job," said Jean, rubbing his ribs with his left hand.

"You seemed to be doing well enough until the end." She looked down at the little knife and nodded. "Look, this knife has an extra groove right alongside the cutting edge. That usually means something nasty on the blade. She was buying time to slip it out and stick you with it."

"I know what a groove along the blade means," mumbled Jean petulantly. "Do you know who the hell these two work for?"

"I have some theories, yes."

"And would you mind sharing them?" asked Locke.

"If I were given orders to that effect," she said sweetly.

"Gods damn all Verrari, and give them more sores on their privates than hairs on their heads," muttered Locke.

"I was born in Vel Virazzo," said the woman.

"Do you have a name?" asked Jean.

"Lots. All of them lovely and none of them true," she replied. "You two can call me Merrain."

"Merrain. Ow." Locke winced and massaged his left forearm with his right hand. Jean set a hand on his shoulder.

"Anything broken, Leo?

"Not much. Perhaps my dignity and my previous presumptions of divine benevolence." Locke sighed. "We've seen people following us for the past few nights, Merrain. I suppose we must have seen you."

"I doubt it. You gentlemen should collect your things and start walking. Same direction you were moving before. There'll be constables here soon enough, and the constables don't take orders from my employer."

Locke retrieved his wet stilettos and wiped them on the trousers of the man he'd killed before returning them to his sleeves. Now that the anger of the fight had run cold, Locke felt his gorge rising at the sight of the corpse, and he scuttled away as fast as he could.

Jean gathered up his coat and slipped his hatchet into it. Soon enough the three of them were walking along, Merrain in the middle with her elbows linked in theirs.

"My employer," she said after a few moments, "wished me to watch over you tonight, and when convenient show you down to a boat."

"Wonderful," said Locke. "Another private conversation."

"I can't say. But if I were to conjecture, I'd guess that he's found a job for the pair of you."

Jean spared a quick glance for the two bodies lying in the darkness far behind them, and he coughed into his clenched fist. "Splendid," he growled. "This place has been so dull and uncomplicated so far."

REMINISCENCE

The Amusement War

1

Six days north up the coast road from Tal Verrar, the demi-city of Salon Corbeau lies within an unusually verdant cleft in the black seaside rocks. More than a private estate, not quite a functional village, the demi-city clings to its peculiar life in the smoldering shadow of Mount Azar.

In the time of the Therin Throne Azar exploded to life, burying three living villages and ten thousand souls in a matter of minutes. These days it seems content merely to rumble and brood, sending twisting charcoal plumes out to sea, and flights of ravens wheel without concern beneath the tired old volcano's smoke. Here begin the hot, dusty plains called the Adra Morcala, inhabited by few and loved by none. They roll like a cracked dry sea all the way to the southern boundaries of Balinel, most westerly and desolate canton of the Kingdom of the Seven Marrows.

Locke Lamora rode into Salon Corbeau on the ninth day of Aurim, in the Seventy-eighth Year of Nara. A mild westerly winter. A fruitful year (and more) had passed since he and Jean had first set foot in Tal Verrar, and in the armored strongbox at the rear of Locke's rented carriage rattled a thousand gold solari, stolen at billiards from a certain Lord Landreval of Espara who was unusually sensitive to lemons.

The little harbor that served the demi-city was thick with small craft—yachts and pleasure-barges and coasting galleys with square silk sails. Farther out, upon the open sea a galleon and a sloop rode at anchor, each flying the pennant of Lashain under family crests and colors Locke didn't recognize. The breeze was slight and the sun was pale, more silver than gold behind the hazy exhalations of the mountain.

"Welcome to Salon Corbeau," said a footman in livery of black and olive green, with a tall hat of pressed black felt. "How are you styled, and how must you be announced?"

A liveried woman placed a wooden block beneath the open door to Locke's carriage and he stepped out, bracing his hands in the small of his back and stretching with relief before hopping to the ground. He wore a drooping black moustache beneath black-rimmed optics and slick black hair; his heavy black coat was tight in the chest and shoulders but flared out from waist to knees, fluttering behind him like a cape. He had eschewed the more refined hose and shoes for gray pantaloons tucked into knee-high field boots, dull black beneath a faint layer of road dust.

"I am Mordavi Fehrwright, a merchant of Emberlain," he said. "I doubt that I shall require announcement, as I have no title of any consequence."

"Very good, Master Fehrwright," said the footman smoothly. "The Lady Saljesca appreciates your visit to Salon Corbeau and earnestly wishes you good fortune in your affairs."

Appreciates your visit, noted Locke, rather than *would be most pleased to receive your audience.* Countess Vira Saljesca of Lashain was the absolute ruler of Salon Corbeau; the demi-city was built on one of her estates.

Equally distant from Balinel, Tal Verrar, and Lashain, just out of convenient rulership by any of them, Salon Corbeau was more or less an autonomous resort state for the wealthy of the Brass Coast.

In addition to the constant arrival of carriages along the coast roads and pleasure-vessels from the sea, Salon Corbeau attracted one other noteworthy form of traffic, which Locke had meditated on in a melancholy fashion during his journey.

Ragged groups of peasants, urban poor and rural wretches alike, trudged wearily along the dusty roads to Lady Saljesca's domain. They came in intermittent but ceaseless streams, flowing to the strange private city beneath the dark heights of the mountain.

Locke imagined that he already knew exactly what they were coming for, but his next few days in Salon Corbeau would prove that understanding to be woefully incomplete.

2

LOCKE HAD originally expected that a sea voyage to Lashain or even Issara might be necessary to secure the final pieces of his Sinspire scheme, but conversation with several wealthier Verrari had convinced him that Salon Corbeau might have exactly what he needed.

Picture a seaside valley carved from night-dark stone, perhaps three hundred yards in length and a hundred wide. Its little harbor lies on its western side, with a crescent beach of fine black sand. At its eastern end, an underground stream pours out of a fissure in the rocks, rushing down a stepped arrangement of stones. The headlands above this stream are commanded by Countess Saljesca's residence, a stone manor house above two layers of crenellated walls—a minor fortress.

The valley walls of Salon Corbeau are perhaps twenty yards in height, and for nearly their full length they are terraced with gardens. Thick ferns, twisting vines, blossoming orchids, and fruit and olive trees flourish there, a healthy curtain of brown and green in vivid relief against the black, with little water ducts meandering throughout to keep Saljesca's artificial paradise from growing thirsty.

In the very center of the valley is a circular stadium, and the gardens on both sides of this stone structure share the walls with several dozen sturdy buildings of polished stone and lacquered wood. A miniature city rests on stilts and platforms and terraces, charmingly enclosed by walkways and stairs at every level.

Locke strolled these walkways on the afternoon of his arrival, looking for his ultimate goal with a stately lack of haste—he expected to be here for many days, perhaps even weeks. Salon Corbeau, like the chance houses of Tal Verrar, drew the idle rich in large numbers. Locke walked among Verrari merchants and Lashani nobles, among scions of the western Marrows, past Nesse ladies-in-waiting (or perhaps more accurately, ladies-weighted-down, in more cloth-of-gold than Locke would have previously thought possible) and the landed families they served. Here and there he was sure he even spotted Camorri, olive-skinned and haughty, though thankfully none were important enough for him to recognize.

So many bodyguards, and so many bodies to guard! Rich bodies and faces; people who could afford proper alchemy and physik for their ailments. No weeping sores or sagging facial tumors, no crooked teeth lolling out of bleeding gums, no faces pinched by emaciation. The Sinspire crowd might be more exclusive, but these folk were even more refined, even more pampered. Hired musicians followed some of them, so that even little journeys of thirty or forty yards need not threaten a second of boredom. Rich men and women were hemorrhaging money all around Locke, to the strains of music. Even a man like Mordavi Fehrwight might spend less to eat for a month than some of them would throw away just to be noticed at breakfast each day.

He'd come to Salon Corbeau because of these folk; not to rob them, for once, but to make use of their privileged existence. Where the rich nested like bright-feathered birds, the providers of the luxuries and services they relied upon followed. Salon Corbeau had a permanent community of tailors, clothiers, instrument makers, glassbenders, alchemists, caterers, entertainers, and carpenters. A small community, to be sure, but one of the highest reputation, fit for aristocratic patronage and priced accordingly.

Almost in the middle of Salon Corbeau's south gallery, Locke found the shop he had come all this way to visit—a rather long, two-story stone building without windows along its walkway face. The wooden sign above the single door said:

M. BAUMONDAIN AND DAUGHTERS
HOUSEHOLD DEVICES AND FINE FURNITURE
BY APPOINTMENT

On the door of the Baumondain shop was a scrollwork decoration, the crest of the Saljesca family (as Locke had glimpsed on banners fluttering here and there, and on the cross-belts of Salon Corbeau's guards), implying Lady Vira's personal approval of the work that went on there. Meaningless to Locke, since he knew too little of Saljesca's taste to judge it . . . but the Baumondain reputation stretched all the way to Tal Verrar.

He would send a messenger first thing in the morning, as was appropriate, and request an appointment to discuss the matter of some peculiar chairs he needed built.

3

AT THE second hour of the next afternoon a warm soft rain was falling; a weak and wispy thing that hung in the air more like damp gauze than falling water. Vague columns of mist swirled among the plants and atop the valley, and the walkways were for once clear of most of their well-heeled traffic. Gray clouds necklaced the tall black mountain to the northwest. Locke stood outside the door to the Baumondain shop with water dripping down the back of his neck and rapped sharply three times.

The door swung inward immediately; a wiry man of about fifty peered out at Locke through round optics. He wore a simple cotton tunic cinched up above his elbows, revealing guild tattoos in faded green and black on his lean forearms, and a long leather apron with at least six visible pockets on the front. Most of them held tools; one held a gray kitten, with only its little head visible.

"Master Fehrwright? Mordavi Fehrwright?"

"So pleased you could make the time for me," began Locke. He spoke with a faint Vadran accent, just enough to suggest an origin in the far north. He'd decided to be lazy, and let this Fehrwright be as fluent in Therin as possible. Locke stretched out his right hand to shake. In his left he carried a black leather satchel with an iron lock upon its flap. "Master Baumondain, I presume?"

"None other. Come in directly, sir, out of the rain. Will you take coffee? Allow me to trade you a cup for your coat."

"With pleasure." The foyer of the Baumondain shop was a high, cozily paneled room lit with little golden lanterns in wall sconces. A counter with one swinging door ran across the rear of the room, and behind it Locke could see shelves piled high with samples of wood, cloth, wax, and oils in glass jars. The placed smelled of sanded wood, a sharp and pleasant tang. There was a little sitting area before the counter, where two superbly wrought chairs with black velvet cushions stood upon a floor tapestry.

Locke set his satchel at his feet, turned to allow Baumondain to help him shrug out of his damp black coat, picked up his satchel once again, and settled himself in the chair nearest to the door. The carpenter hung Locke's coat on a brass hook on the wall. "Just a moment, if you please," he said, and went behind the counter. From his new vantage point, Locke could see that a canvas-covered door led from behind the counter to what he presumed must be the workshop. Baumondain pushed the canvas flap aside and yelled, "Lauris! The coffee!"

Some muffled reply that he evidently found satisfactory came back to him from the workshop, and he hurried around the counter to take his place in the chair across from Locke, crinkling his seamy face into a welcoming smile. A few moments later, the canvas flew aside once again and out from the workshop came a freckled girl of fifteen or sixteen years, chestnut-haired, slim in the manner of her father but more firmly muscled about the arms and shoulders. She carried a wooden tray before her set with cups and silver pots, and when she stepped through the door in the counter Locke saw the tray had legs like a very short table.

She placed the coffee service between Locke and her father, just to the side, and gave Locke a respectful nod.

"My oldest daughter, Lauris," said Master Baumondain. "Lauris, this is Master Fehrwight, of the House of bel Sarethon, from Emberlain."

"Charmed," said Locke. Lauris was close enough for him to see that her hair was full of curly little wood shavings.

"Your servant, Master Fehrwight." Lauris nodded again, prepared to withdraw, and then caught sight of the gray kitten sticking out of her father's apron pocket. "Father, you've forgotten Lively. Surely you didn't mean to have him sit in on the coffee?"

"Have I? Oh, dear, I see that I have." Baumondain reached down and eased the kitten out of his apron. Locke was astonished to see how limply it hung in his hands, with its legs and tail drooping and its little head lolling; what self-respecting cat would sleep while plucked up and carried through the air? Then Locke saw the answer, as Lauris took Lively in her own hands and turned to go. The kitten's little eyes were wide open, and stark white.

"That creature was Gentled," said Locke in a low voice when Lauris had returned to the workshop.

"I'm afraid so," said the carpenter.

"I've never seen such a thing. What purpose does it serve, in a cat?"

"None, Master Fehrwight, none." Baumondain's smile was gone, replaced by a wary and uncomfortable expression. "And it certainly wasn't my doing. My youngest daughter, Parnella, found him abandoned behind the Villa Verdante." Baumondain referred to the huge luxury inn where the intermediate class of Salon Corbeau's visitors stayed, the wealthy who were not private guests of the Lady Saljesca. Locke himself was rooming there.

"Damned strange."

"We call him Lively, as a sort of jest, though he does little. He must be coaxed to eat, and prodded to . . . to excrete, you see. Parnella thought it would be kinder to smash his skull, but Lauris would not hear of it and so I could not refuse. You must think me weak and doting."

"Not at all," said Locke, shaking his head. "The world is cruel enough without our compounding it; I approve. I meant that it was damned strange that anyone should do such a thing at all."

"Master Fehrwight." The carpenter licked his lips nervously. "You seem a humane man, and you must understand... our position here brings us a steady and lucrative business. My daughters will have quite an inheritance, when I turn this shop over to them. There are... there are things about Salon Corbeau, things that go on, that we artisans... do not pry into. *Must* not. If you take my meaning."

"I do," said Locke, eager to keep the man in a good humor. However, he made a mental note to perhaps poke around in pursuit of whatever was disturbing the carpenter. "I do indeed. So let us speak no more of the matter, and instead look to business."

"Most kind," said Baumondain, with obvious relief. "How do you take your coffee? I have honey and cream."

"Honey, please."

Baumondain poured steaming coffee from the silver pot into a thick glass cup, and spooned in honey until Locke nodded. Locke sipped at his cup while Baumondain bombarded his own with enough cream to turn it leather brown. It was quality brew, rich and very hot.

"My compliments," Locke mumbled over a slightly scalded tongue.

"It's from Issara. Lady Saljesca's household has an endless thirst for the stuff," said the carpenter. "The rest of us buy pecks and pinches from her sellers when they come around. Now, your messenger said that you wished to discuss a commission that was, in her words, very *particular*."

"Yes, indeed," said Locke. "Particular, to a design and an end that may strike you as eccentric. I assure you I am in grave earnest."

Locke set down his coffee and lifted his satchel into his lap, then pulled a small key from his waistcoat pocket to open the lock. He reached inside and drew out a few pieces of folded parchment.

"You must be familiar," Locke continued, "with the style of the last few years of the Therin Throne? The very last few, just before Talathri died in battle against the Bondsmagi?"

He passed over one of his sheets of parchment, which Baumondain removed his optics to examine.

"Oh, yes," the carpenter said slowly. "The Talathri Baroque, also called the Last Flowering. Yes, I've done pieces in this fashion before.... Lauris has as well. You have an interest in this style?"

"I require a suite of chairs," said Locke. "Four of them, leather-backed, lacquered shear-crescent with real gold insets."

"Shear-crescent is a somewhat delicate wood, fit only for occasional use. For more regular sitting I'm sure you'd want witchwood."

"My master," said Locke, "has very exact tastes, however peculiar. He insisted upon shear-crescent, several times, to ensure that his wishes were clear."

"Well, if you wished them carved from marzipan, I suppose I should have to do it... with the clear understanding, of course, that I did warn you against hard use."

"Naturally. I assure you, Master Baumondain, you won't be held liable for anything that happens to these chairs after they leave your workshop."

"Oh, I would never do less than vouch for our work, but I cannot make a soft wood hard, Master Fehrwright. Well, then, I do have some books with excellent illustrations of this style. Your artist has done well to start with, but I'd like to give you more variety to choose from...."

"By all means," said Locke, and he sipped his coffee contentedly as the carpenter rose and returned to the workshop door. "Lauris," Baumondain cried, "my three volumes of Velonetta.... Yes, those."

He returned a moment later cradling three heavy, leather-bound tomes that smelled of age and some spicy alchemical preservative. "Velonetta," he said as he settled the books on his lap. "You are familiar with her? No? She was the foremost scholar of the Last Flowering. There are only six sets of her work in all the world, as far as I know. Most of these pages are on sculpture, painting, music, alchemy...but there are fine passages on furniture, gems worth mining. If you please..."

They spent half an hour poring over the sketches Locke had provided and the pages Baumondain wished to show him. Together, they hammered out an agreeable compromise on the design of the chairs that "Master Fehrwight" would receive. Baumondain fetched a stylus of his own and scrawled notes in an illegible chicken scratch. Locke had never before considered how many details might go into something as straightforward as a chair; by the time they had finished their discussion of legs, bracings, cushion filling, leathers, scrollwork, and joinery, Locke's brain was in full revolt.

"Excellent, Master Baumondain, excellent," is nonetheless what he said. "The very thing, in shear-crescent, lacquered black, with gold leaf to gild the incised decorations and the rivets. They must look as though they had been plucked from Emperor Talathri's court just yesterday, new and unburnt."

"Ah," said the carpenter, "a delicate subject arises, then. Without meaning to give the slightest offense, I must make it clear that these will never pass for originals. They will be exact reconstructions of the style, perfect facsimiles, of a quality to match *any* furnishings in the world—but an expert could tell. They are few, and far between, but such a one would never confuse a brilliant reconstruction for even a modest original. They have had centuries to weather; these will be plainly new."

"I take your meaning, Master Baumondain. Never fear; I am ordering these for eccentric purposes, not for deceptive ones. These chairs will never be alleged to be originals, on my word. And the man who will receive them *is* such an expert, in fact."

"Very good, then, very good. Is there anything else?"

"Yes," said Locke, who had withheld two sketch-covered sheets of parchment and passed them over. "Now that we've settled on a design for the suite of chairs, this—or something very much like it, subject to your more expert adjustments—*must* be included in the plans."

As Baumondain absorbed the implications of the sketches, his eyebrows rose steadily, until it seemed that they were being drawn up to the fullest possible extent of his forehead's suppleness, and must be flung back down to the floor like crossbow bolts when they reached their zenith.

"This is a prodigious curiosity," he said at last. "A very strange thing to incorporate. . . . I'm not at all sure—"

"It is essential," said Locke. "That, or something very much like it, within the bounds of your own discretion. It is absolutely necessary. My master simply will not place an order for the chairs unless these features are built into them. Cost is no object."

"It's possible," said the carpenter after a few seconds of further contemplation. "Possible, with some adjustments to these designs. I believe I see your intention, but I can improve upon this scheme . . . must, if the chairs are to function as chairs. May I ask why this is necessary?"

"My master is a dear old fellow, but as you must have gathered, quite eccentric, and morbidly afraid of fire. He fears to be trapped in his study or his library tower by flames. Surely you can see how these mechanisms might help set his mind at ease?"

"I suppose I can," muttered Baumondain, his puzzled reluctance turning to interest in a professional challenge as he spoke.

After that, it was merely a matter of haggling, however politely, over finer and finer details, until Locke was finally able to coax a suggested price out of Baumondain.

"What coin would you wish to settle in, Master Fehrwight?"

"I presumed solari would be convenient."

"Shall we say...six solari per chair?" Baumondain spoke with feigned nonchalance; that was a cheeky initial offer, even for luxury craftsmanship. Locke would be expected to haggle it down. Instead, he smiled and nodded.

"If six per chair is what you require, then six you will have."

"Oh," said Baumondain, almost too surprised to be pleased. "Oh. Well then! I should be only too happy to accept your note."

"While that would be fine in ordinary circumstances, let's do something more convenient for both of us." Locke reached inside the satchel and drew out a coin purse, from which he counted twenty-four gold solari onto the little coffee table while Baumondain watched with growing excitement. "There you are, in advance. I prefer to carry hard coinage when I come to Salon Corbeau. This little city needs a moneylender."

"Well, thank you, Master Fehrwight, thank you! I didn't expect...well, let me get a work order and some papers for you to take with you, and we'll be set."

"Now, let me ask—do you have all the materials you need for my master's order?"

"Oh yes! I know that off the top of my head."

"Warehoused here, at your shop?"

"Yes indeed, Master Fehrwight."

"About how long might I expect the construction to take?"

"Hmmm...given my other duties, and your requirements...six weeks, possibly seven. Will you be returning for them yourself, or will we need to arrange shipping?"

"In that, too, I was hoping for something a little more convenient."

"Ah, well...you having been so very civil, I'm sure I could shift my schedule. Five weeks, perhaps?"

"Master Baumondain, if you and your daughters were to work on my master's order more or less exclusively, starting this afternoon, at your best possible speed...how long then would you say it might take?"

"Oh, Master Fehrwight, Master Fehrwight, you must understand, I have other orders pending, for clients of some standing. *Significant* people, if you take my meaning."

Locke set four more gold coins atop the coffee table.

"Master Fehrwight, be reasonable! These are just chairs! I will bend every effort to finishing your order as fast as possible, but I cannot simply displace my existing clients or their pieces—"

Locke set four more coins down, next to the previous pile.

"Master Fehrwight, please, we would give you our exclusive efforts for far less, if *only* we didn't already have clients to satisfy! How could I possibly explain this to them?"

Locke set six more coins directly in the middle of the two stacks of four, building a little tower. "What is that now, Baumondain? Forty solari, when you were so pleased to get just twenty-four?"

"Sir, please, my sole consideration is that clients who placed their orders before your master's must, in all courtesy, have precedence."

Locke sighed, and dumped ten more solari onto the coffee table, upsetting his little tower and emptying the purse. "You can have a shortage of materials. Some essential wood or oil or leather. You need to send away for it; six days to Tal Verrar and six days back. Surely it's happened before. Surely you can explain."

"Oh, but the aggravation; they'll be so annoyed...."

Locke drew a second coin purse from his satchel and held it poised like a dagger in the air before him. "Refund some of their money. Here, have more of mine." He shook out even more coins, haphazardly. The *clink-clink-clink* of metal falling upon metal echoed in the foyer.

"Master Fehrwight," said the carpenter, "who *are* you?"

"A man who's dead serious about chairs." Locke dropped the half-full purse atop the pile of gold next to the coffeepot. "One hundred solari, even. Put off your other appointments, set aside your other jobs, make your excuses and your refunds. How long would it take?"

"Perhaps a week," said Baumondain, in a defeated whisper.

"Then you agree? Until my four chairs are finished, this is the Fehrwight Furniture Shop? I have more gold in the Villa Verdante's strongbox. You will have to kill me to stop forcing it upon you if you say no. So do we have a deal?"

"Gods help us both, yes!"

"Then shake on it. You get carving, and I'll start wasting time back at my inn. Send messengers if you need me to inspect anything. I'll stay until you're finished."

4

"AS YOU can see, my hands are empty, and it is unthinkable that anything should be concealed within the sleeves of such a finely tailored tunic."

Locke stood before the full-length mirror in his suite at the Villa Verdante, wearing nothing but his breeches and a light tunic of fine silk. The cuffs of the tunic were drawn away from his wrists, and he stared intently at his own reflection.

"It would, of course, be impossible for me to produce a deck of cards from thin air ... but what's this?"

He moved his right hand toward the mirror, with a flourish, and a deck of cards slipped clumsily out of it, coming apart in a fluttering mess as it fell to the floor.

"Oh, fucking hell," Locke muttered.

He had a week of empty time on his hands, and his legerdemain was improving with torturous slowness. Locke soon turned his attention to the curious institution at the heart of Salon Corbeau, the reason so many idle rich made pilgrimage to the place, and the reason so many desperate and downtrodden ate their carriage dust as they trudged to the same destination.

They called it the Amusement War.

Lady Saljesca's stadium was a miniature of the legendary *stadia ultra* of Therim Pel, complete with twelve marble idols of the gods gracing the exterior in high stone niches. Ravens perched on their divine heads and shoulders, cawing halfheartedly down at the bustling crowd around the gates. As he made his way through the tumult Locke noted every species of attendant known to man. There were physikers clucking over the elderly, litter bearers hauling the infirm (or the unabashedly lazy), musicians and jugglers, guards, translators, and dozens of men and women waving fans or hoisting wide silk parasols, looking like nothing so much as fragile human-sized mushrooms as they chased their patrons under the growing morning sun.

While it was said that the floor of the Imperial Arena had been too wide for even the strongest archer to send an arrow across, the floor of Saljesca's recreation was just fifty yards in diameter. There were no common seats; the smooth stone walls rose twenty feet above the smooth stone floor, and were topped with luxury galleries whose cloth sunscreens flapped gently in the breeze.

Three times per day, Lady Saljesca's liveried guards would open the public gates to the better class of Salon Corbeau's visitors. There was a single standing gallery (which even had a decent view) to which admission was free, but the vast majority of spectators at the stadium would take nothing less than the luxury seats and boxes, which needed to be reserved at some considerable expense. Unfashionable as it was, Locke elected to stand for his first visit to the Amusement War. A relative nonentity like Mordavi Fehrwright had no reputation to protect.

On the floor of the arena was a gleaming grid of black and white marble squares, each one yard on a side. The squares were set twenty by twenty, like a gigantic Catch-the-Duke board. Where little carved pieces of wood or ivory were used in that game, Saljesca's playing field featured living pieces. The poor and destitute would man that field, forty to a side, wearing white or black tabards to distinguish themselves. This strange employment was the reason they risked the long, hard trudge to Salon Corbeau.

Locke had already discovered that there were two large barracks behind Lady Saljesca's stadium, heavily guarded, where the poor were taken upon arrival in Salon Corbeau. There they were made to clean themselves up, and were given two simple meals a day for the duration of their stay, which could be indefinite. Each "aspirant," as they were known, was assigned a number. Three times per day, random drawings were held to select two teams of forty for the coming Amusement War. The only rule of the war was that the living pieces had to be able to stand, move, and obey orders; children of eight or nine were about the youngest taken. Those who refused to participate when their number was drawn, even once, were thrown out of Saljesca's demi-city immediately and barred from returning. Without supplies and preparation, being cast out onto the roads in this dry land could be a death sentence.

The aspirants were marched into the arena by two dozen of Saljesca's guards, who were armed with curved shields and lacquered wooden sticks. They were robust men and women who moved with the easy assurance of hard experience; even a general uprising of the aspirants would stand no chance against them. The guards lined the aspirants up in their starting positions on the board, forty white "pieces" and forty black "pieces," with sixteen squares separating each double-ranked army.

At opposite ends of the stadium were two special gallery boxes, one draped in black silk curtains and the other in white. These boxes were reserved far in advance by a waiting list, much as patrons of a chance house would lay claim to billiards tables or private rooms at certain hours. Whoever reserved a box gained the right to absolute command of that color for the duration of a war.

That morning's White warmistress was a young Lashani viscountess whose retinue looked as nervous with the affair as she was enthusiastic; they appeared to be scribbling notes and consulting charts. The Black warmaster was a middle-aged Iridani with the well-fed, calculating look of a prosperous merchant. He had a young son and daughter with him in his gallery.

Although the living pieces could be hung (by the agreement of both players) with special tabards that gave them unusual privileges or movement allowances, the rules of this particular Amusement War seemed to be plain Catch-the-Duke with no variations. The controllers began calling orders and the game slowly developed, with white and black pieces trudging nervously toward one another, very gradually closing the distance between the opposing forces. Locke found himself puzzled by the reaction of the stadium crowd.

There were easily sixty or seventy spectators in the boxes, with twice as many servants, bodyguards, assistants, and messengers on hand, not to mention caterers in Saljesca's livery hurrying to and fro to serve their wants. Their buzz of eager anticipation seemed totally incongruous given the plodding nature of the contest shaping up on the squares.

"What," Locke muttered to himself in Vadran, "is so damn fascinating?"

Then the first piece was taken, and the Demons came out to the arena floor.

The White warmistress deliberately placed one of her "pieces," a middle-aged man, in harm's way. More of her army lurked behind him in an obvious trap, but the Black warmaster apparently decided it was a worthwhile exchange. Under the shouted orders of the Black adjutant, a teenaged girl in black stepped from a diagonal square and touched the middle-aged man on the shoulder. He hung his head, and the appreciative clapping of the crowd was drowned out a moment later by a wild shrieking that arose from the far left side of Locke's view of the stadium.

Six men ran onto the arena floor from a side portal, dressed in elaborate leather costumes with black-and-orange fluting; their faces were covered with grotesque flame-orange masks trailing wild manes of black hair. They threw their arms in the air, screaming and hollering meaninglessly, and the crowd cheered back as they ran across the arena toward the cringing man in white. The Demons seized him by the arms and by the hair; he was thrust, sobbing, to the side of the game board and exhibited to the crowd like a sacrificial animal. One of the Demons, a man with a booming voice, pointed to the Black warmaster and shouted, "Cry the default!"

"I want to cry it," said the little boy in the merchant's gallery.

"We agreed that your sister would go first. Theodora, name the default." The little girl peered down to the arena floor in concentration, then whispered up to her father. He cleared his throat and shouted, "She wants the guards to beat him with their clubs. On his legs!"

And so it was; the Demons held the writhing, screaming man with his limbs spread while two guards obligingly laid into him. The fall of their sticks echoed across the arena; they thoroughly bruised his thighs, shins, and calves until the chief Demon waved his hands to clear them off. The audience applauded politely (though not with particular enthusiasm, noted Locke), and the Demons hauled the quivering, bleeding man off the stadium floor.

They came back soon enough; one of the Whites removed a Black on the next move. "Cry the default!" echoed once again across the arena.

"I'll sell the right for five solari," shouted the Lashani viscountess. "First taker."

"I'll pay it," cried an old man in the stands, dressed in layers of velvet and cloth-of-gold. The chief Demon pointed up at him, and he beckoned to a frock-coated attendant standing just behind him. The attendant threw a purse down to one of Saljesca's guards, who carried it over to the White warmistress' side of the field and threw it into her gallery. The Demons then hauled the young woman in black over for the old man's examination. After a moment of exaggerated contemplation, he shouted, "Get rid of her dress!"

The young woman's black tabard and dirty cotton dress were ripped apart by the grasping hands of the Demons; in seconds, she was naked. She seemed determined to give less of a demonstration than the man who'd gone before; she glared stonily up at the old man, be he minor lord or merchant prince, and said nothing.

"Is that all?" cried the chief Demon.

"Oh no," said the old man. "Get rid of her hair, too!"

The crowd burst into applause and cheers at that, and the woman betrayed real fear for the first time. She had a thick mane of glossy black hair down to the small of her back, something to be proud of even among the penniless—perhaps all she had to be proud of in the world. The chief Demon played to the crowd, hoisting a gleaming, crooked dagger over his head and howling with glee. The woman attempted to struggle against the five pairs of arms that held her, to no avail. Swiftly, painfully, the chief Demon slashed at her long black locks—they fluttered down until the ground was thick with them and the woman's scalp was covered with nothing but a chopped, irregular stubble. Trickles of blood ran down her face and neck as she was dragged, too numb for further struggle, out of the arena.

So it went, as Locke watched in growing unease, as the pitiless sun crept across the sky and the shadows shortened. The living pieces moved on the gleaming-hot squares, without water and without relief, until they were taken from the board and subjected to a default of the opposing warmaster's choosing. It soon became apparent to Locke that the default could be virtually anything, short of death. The Demons would follow orders with frenzied enthusiasm, playing up each new injury or humiliation for the appreciative crowd.

Gods, Locke realized, barely any of them are here for the game at all. They've only come to see the defaults.

The rows of armored guards would dissuade all possibility of refusal or rebellion. Those "pieces" who refused to hurry along to their appointed places, or dared to step off their squares without instructions, were simply beaten until they obeyed. Obey they did, and the cruelty of the defaults did not wane as the game went on.

"Rotten fruit," the little boy in the Black warmaster's box yelled, and so it was; an elderly woman with a white tabard was thrown against the stadium wall and pelted with apples, pears, and tomatoes by four of the Demons. They knocked her off her feet and continued the barrage until the woman was a shuddering heap, curled up beneath her frail arms for protection, and great spatters of sour pulp and juice were dripping from the wall behind her.

The white player's retaliation was swift. She took a stocky young man in black colors and for once reserved the choice of default to herself. "We must keep our hostess' stadium clean. Take him to the wall with the fruit stains," she shouted, "and let him clean it with his tongue!"

The crowd broke into wild applause at that; the man on the arena floor was pushed up to the wall by the chief Demon. "Start licking, scum!"

His first efforts were halfhearted. Another Demon produced a whip that ended in seven knotted cords and lashed the man across the shoulders, knocking him into the wall hard enough to bloody his nose. "Earn your fucking pay, worm," screamed the Demon, whipping him once again. "Haven't you ever had a lady tell you to get down and use your tongue before?"

The man ran his tongue desperately up and down the wall, gagging every few seconds, which would bring another crack of the Demon's whip. The man was a bleeding, retching nervous wreck by the time he was finally hauled from the arena floor.

So it went, all morning long.

"Gods, why do they bear it? Why do they take this?" Locke stood in the free gallery, alone, staring out at the wealthy and powerful, at their guards and servants, and at the thinning ranks of the living pieces in the game beneath them. He brooded, sweating in his heavy black garments.

Here were the richest and freest people in the Therin world, those with positions and money but no political duties to constrict them, gathered together to do what law and custom forbade beyond Saljesca's private fiefdom—to humiliate and brutalize their lessers however they saw fit, for their own gleeful amusement. The arena and the

Amusement War itself were obviously just frames. Means to an end.

There was no order to it, no justice. Gladiators and prisoners fighting before a crowd were there for a reason, risking their lives for glory or paying the price for having been caught. Men and women hung from a gibbets because the Crooked Warden had only so much help to give to the foolish, the slow, and the unlucky. But this was wanton.

Locke felt his anger growing like a chancre in his guts.

They had no idea who he was or what he was really capable of. No idea what the *Thorn of Camorr* could do to them, unleashed on Salon Corbeau, with Jean to aid him! Given months to plan and observe, the Gentlemen Bastards could take the place *apart,* find ways to cheat the Amusement War, surely—rob the participants, rob the Lady Saljesca, embarrass and humiliate the bastards, blacken the demi-city's reputation so thoroughly that nobody would ever want to visit again.

But...

"Crooked Warden," Locke whispered, "why now? Why show me this *now*?"

Jean was waiting for him back in Tal Verrar, and they were already neck-deep in a game that had taken a year to put together. Jean didn't know anything about what really went on at Salon Corbeau. He would be expecting Locke to return in short order with a set of chairs, so the two of them could carry on with the plan they'd agreed to, a plan that was already desperately delicate.

"Gods damn it," said Locke. "Gods damn it all to hell."

5

CAMORR, YEARS before. The wet, seeping mists enclosed Locke and Father Chains in curtains of midnight gray as the old man led the boy back home from his first meeting with Capa Vencarlo Barsavi. Locke, drunk and sweat-soaked, clung to the back of his Gentled goat for dear life.

"...you don't belong to Barsavi," Chains said. "He's good enough for what he is, a good ally to have on your side, and a man that you must appear to obey at all times. But he certainly doesn't own you. In the end, neither do I."

"So I don't have to—"

"Obey the Secret Peace? Be a good little *pezon*? Only for pretend, Locke. Only to keep the wolves from the door. Unless your eyes and ears have been stitched shut with rawhide these past two days, by now you must have realized that I intend you and Calo and Galdo and Sabetha to be nothing less," Chains confided through a feral grin, "than a fucking ballista bolt right through the heart of Vencarlo's precious Secret Peace."

"Uh..." Locke collected his thoughts for several moments. "Why?"

"Heh. It's...complicated. It has to do with what I am, and what I hope you'll someday be. A priest in the sworn service of the Crooked Warden."

"Is the Capa doing something wrong?"

"Well," said Chains, "well, lad, now there's a question. Is he doing right by the Right People? Gods, yes—the Secret Peace tames the city watch, calms everyone down, gets less of us hung.

"Still, every priesthood has what we call mandates: laws handed down by the gods themselves to those who serve them. In most temples, these are complex, messy, annoying things. In the priesthood of the Benefactor, things are easy. We only have two. The first one is *thieves prosper*. Simple as that. We're ordered to aid one another, hide one another, make peace whenever possible, and see to it that our kind flourishes, by hook or by crook. Barsavi's got that mandate covered, never doubt that.

"But the second mandate," said Chains, lowering his voice and glancing around into the fog to make doubly sure that they were not overheard, "is this—*the rich remember*."

"Remember what?"

"That they're not invincible. That locks can be picked and treasures can be stolen. Nara, Mistress of Ubiquitous Maladies, may Her hand be stayed, sends disease among men so that men will never forget that they are not gods. We're sort of like that, for the rich and powerful. We're the stone in their shoe, the thorn in their side, a little bit of reciprocity this side of divine judgment. That's our second mandate, and it's as important as the first."

"And . . . the Secret Peace protects the nobles, and so you don't like it?"

"It's not that I don't like it." Chains mulled his next few words over before he let them out. "Barsavi's not a priest of the Thirteenth. He's not sworn to the mandates like I am; he's got to be practical. And while I can accept that, I can't just let it go. It's my divine duty to see that the blue bloods with their pretty titles get a little bit of what life hands the rest of us as a matter of routine—a nice, sharp jab in the ass every now and again."

"And, Barsavi . . . doesn't need to know about this?"

"Bleeding shits, no. As I see it, if Barsavi takes care of *thieves prosper* and I look after *the rich remember,* this'll be one holy, holy city in the eyes of the Crooked Warden."

6

"WHY DO they bear it? I know they get paid, but the defaults! Gods . . . er, Holy Marrows, why do they come here and put up with it? Humiliated, beaten, stoned, befouled . . . to what end?"

Locke paced agitatedly around the Baumondain

family's workshop, clenching and unclenching his fists. It was the afternoon of his fourth day in Salon Corbeau.

"As you said, they get paid, Master Fehrwight." Lauris Baumondain rested one hand gently on the back of the half-finished chair Locke had come in to see. With the other she stroked poor motionless Lively, tucked away inside a pocket of her apron. "If you're selected for a game, you get a copper centira. If you're given a default, you get a silver volani. There's also a random drawing; one person per war, one in eighty, gets a gold solari."

"They must be desperate," said Locke.

"Farms fail. Businesses fail. Tenant lands get repossessed. Plagues knock all the money and health out of cities. When they've got nowhere else to come, they come here. There's a roof to sleep under, meals, hope of gold or silver. All you have to do is go out there often enough and...amuse them."

"It's perverse. It's infamous."

"You have a soft heart, for what you're spending on just four chairs, Master Fehrwight." Lauris looked down and wrung her hands together. "Forgive me. I spoke well out of turn."

"Speak as you will. I'm not a rich man, Lauris. I'm just my master's servant. But even he...We're frugal people, damn it. Frugal and fair. We might be eccentric, but we're not cruel."

"I've seen nobles from the Marrows at the Amusement War many times, Master Fehrwight."

"*We're* not nobles. We're merchants...merchants of Emberlain. I can't speak for our nobles, and often don't want to. Look, I've seen many cities. I know how people live. I've seen gladiatorial fights, executions, misery and poverty and desperation. But I've never seen *anything* like that—the faces of those spectators. The way they watched and cheered. Like jackals, like crows, like something... something so very *wrong*."

"There are no laws here but Lady Saljesca's laws," said Lauris. "Here they can behave however they choose. At the Amusement War they can do *exactly* what they want to do to the poor folk and the simple folk. Things forbidden elsewhere. All you're seeing is what they look like when they stop pretending they give a damn about anything. Where do you think Lively came from? I saw a noblewoman having kittens Gentled so her sons could torture them with knives. Because they were *bored at tea.* So welcome to Salon Corbeau, Master Fehrwright. I'm sorry it's not the paradise it looks like from a distance. Does our work on the chairs meet with your approval?"

"Yes," said Locke slowly. "Yes, I suppose it does."

"If I were to presume to give you advice," said Lauris, "I'd suggest that you stay away from the Amusement War for the rest of your stay. Do what the rest of us here do. Ignore it. Paint a great cloud of fog over it in your mind's eye and pretend that it's not there."

"As you say, Madam Baumondain." Locke sighed. "I might just do so."

7

BUT LOCKE could not stay away. Morning, afternoon, and evening, he found himself in the public gallery, standing alone, eating and drinking nothing. He saw crowd after crowd, war after war, humiliation after humiliation. The Demons made gruesome mistakes on several occasions; beatings and stranglings got out of control. Those aspirants who were accidentally roughed up beyond hope of recovery had their skulls crushed on the spot, to the polite applause of the crowd. It would not do to be unmerciful.

"Crooked Warden," Locke muttered to himself the first

time it happened. "They don't even have a priest...not a single one...."

He realized, dimly, what he was doing to himself. He felt the stirring within, as though his conscience were a deep, still lake with a beast struggling to rise to its surface. Each brutal humiliation, each painful default excitedly decreed by some spoiled noble child while their parents laughed in appreciation, gave strength to that beast as it beat itself against his better judgment, his cold calculation, his willingness to *stick to the plan.*

He was trying to make himself angry enough to give in.

The Thorn of Camorr had been a mask he'd halfheartedly worn as a game. Now it was almost a separate entity, a hungry thing, an increasingly insistent ghost prying at his resolve to stand up for the mandate of his faith.

Let me out, it whispered. Let me out. The rich must remember. By the gods, I can make damn sure they never forget.

"I hope you'll pardon my intrusion if I observe that you don't seem to be enjoying yourself!"

Locke was snapped out of his brooding by the appearance of another man in the free gallery. The stranger was tanned and fit-looking, perhaps five or six years older than Locke, with brown curls down to his collar and a precisely trimmed goatee. His long velvet coat was lined with cloth-of-silver, and he held a gold-topped cane behind his back with both hands.

"But forgive me. Fernand Genrusa, peer of the Third, of Lashain."

Peer of the third order—a baron—a purchased Lashani patent of nobility, just as Locke and Jean had toyed with possibly acquiring. Locke bent slightly at the waist and inclined his head. "Mordavi Fehrwright, m'lord. Of Emberlain."

"A merchant, then? You must be doing well for yourself, Master Fehrwright, to take your leisure here. So what's behind your long face?"

"What makes you think I'm displeased?"

"You stand here alone, taking no refreshment, and you watch each new war with such an expression on your face...as though someone were slipping hot coals into your breechclout. I've seen you several times from my own gallery. Are you losing money? I might be able to share some insights I've cultivated on how to best place wagers at the Amusement War."

"I have no wagers outstanding, m'lord. I am merely... unable to stop watching."

"Curious. Yet it does not please you."

"No." Locke turned slightly toward Baron Genrusa and swallowed nervously. Etiquette demanded that a lowborn like Mordavi Fehrwright, and a Vadran at that, should defer even to a banknote baron like Genrusa and offer no unpleasant conversation, but Genrusa seemed to be inviting explanation. Locke wondered how much he might get away with. "Have you ever seen a carriage accident, m'lord, or a man run over by a team of horses? Seen the blood and wreckage and been completely unable to take your eyes off the spectacle?"

"I can't say that I have."

"There I would beg to differ. You have a private gallery to see it three times a day if you wish. M'lord."

"Ahhhh. So you find the Amusement War, what, undecorous?"

"Cruel, m'lord Genrusa. Most uncommonly cruel."

"Cruel? Compared to what? War? Times of plague? Have you ever seen Camorr, by chance? Now there's a basis for comparison that might have you thinking more soundly, Master Fehrwright."

"Even in Camorr," said Locke, "I don't believe anyone is allowed to beat old women in broad daylight on a whim.

Or tear their clothes off, stone them, rape them, slash their hair off, splash them with alchemical caustics.... It's like ... like children tearing off an insect's wings. So they might watch and laugh."

"Who forced them to come here, Fehrwight? Who put a sword to their backs and made them march all the way to Salon Corbeau along those hot, empty roads? That pilgrimage takes days from anywhere worthy of note."

"What choice do they have, m'lord? They're only here because they're desperate. Because they could not sustain themselves where they were. Farms fail, businesses fail ... it's desperation, is all. They cannot simply decide not to eat."

"Farms fail, businesses fail, ships sink, empires fall." Genrusa brought his cane out from behind his back and punctuated his statements by gesturing at Locke with the gold head. "That's life, under the gods, by the will of the gods. Perhaps if they'd prayed harder, or saved more, or been less thoughtless with what they had, they wouldn't need to come crawling here for Saljesca's charity. Seems only fair that she should require most of them to earn it."

"Charity?"

"They have a roof over their heads, food to eat, and the chance of money. Those that earn the gold prizes seem to have no trouble taking their coin and leaving."

"One in eighty wins a solari, m'lord. No doubt more money than they've ever seen at once in their lives. And for the other seventy-nine that gold is just a promise, holding them here day after day, week after week, default after default. And those that die because the Demons get out of hand? What good is gold or the promise of gold to them? Anywhere else, it would be plain murder."

"It's Aza Guilla that takes them from the arena floor, not you or I or anyone mortal, Fehrwight." Genrusa's brows were furrowed and his cheeks were reddening.

"And yes, anywhere else, it might be plain murder. But this is Salon Corbeau, and they're here of their own free will. As are you and I. They could simply choose not to come—"

"And starve and die elsewhere."

"Please. I have seen the world, Master Fehrwight. I might recommend it to you for perspective. Certainly, some of them must be down on their luck. But I wager you'd find that most of them are just hungry for gold, hoping for an easy break. Look out at those on the arena floor now . . . quite a few young and healthy ones, aren't there?"

"Who else might be expected to make the journey here on foot without extraordinary luck, m'lord Genrusa?"

"I can see there's no talking sense to sentiment, Master Fehrwight. I'd thought you coin-kissers from Emberlain were a harder lot than this."

"Hard perhaps, but not vulgar."

"Now mind yourself, Master Fehrwight. I wanted a word because I was genuinely curious about your disposition; I think I can see now what it stems from. A bit of advice: Salon Corbeau might not be the healthiest place to harbor your sort of resentment."

"My business here will be . . . shortly concluded."

"All for the better, then. But perhaps your business at the Amusement War might be curtailed even sooner. I'm not the only one who's taken an interest in you. Lady Saljesca's guards are . . . sensitive about discontent. *Above* the arena floor as well as on it."

I could leave you penniless and sobbing, whispered the voice in Locke's head. *I could have you pawning your piss-buckets to keep your creditors from slitting your throat.*

"Forgive me, my lord. I will take what you say most seriously," muttered Locke. "I doubt . . . that I shall trouble anyone here again."

8

ON THE morning of Locke's ninth day in Salon Corbeau, the Baumondains were finished with his chairs.

"They look magnificent," said Locke, running his fingers lightly over the lacquered wood and padded leather. "Very fine, as fine as I had reason to hope. And the . . . additional features?"

"Built to your specifications, Master Fehrwight. *Exactly* to your specifications." Lauris stood beside her father in the Baumondain workshop while ten-year-old Parnella was struggling to brew tea over an alchemical hearthstone, at a corner table covered in unidentifiable tools and half-empty jars of woodworking oils. Locke made a mental note to smell any tea offered to him very carefully before drinking.

"You have outdone yourselves, all of you."

"We were, ah, financially inspired, Master Fehrwight," said the elder Baumondain.

"I like building weird things," Parnella added from the corner.

"Heh. Yes, I suppose these would qualify." Locke stared at his suite of four matching chairs and sighed in mingled relief and aggravation. "Well, then. If you'd be so kind as to ready them for transport, I shall hire two carriages and take my leave this afternoon."

"In that much of a hurry to leave?"

"I hope you'll forgive me if I say that every unnecessary moment I spend in this place weighs on me. Salon Corbeau and I do not agree." Locke removed a leather purse from his coat pocket and tossed it to Master Baumondain. "An additional twenty solari. For your silence, and for these chairs to never have existed. Is this clear?"

"I . . . well, I'm sure we can accommodate your request. . . . I must say, your generosity is—"

"A subject that needs no further discussion. Humor me, now. I'll be gone soon enough."

So that's all, said the voice in Locke's head. Stick to the plan. Leave this all behind, and do nothing, and return to Tal Verrar with my tail between my legs.

While he and Jean enriched themselves at Requin's expense and cheated their way up the luxurious floors of the Sinspire, on the stone floor of Lady Saljesca's arena the defaults would go on, and the faces of the spectators would be the same, day after day. Children tearing the wings from insects to laugh at how they flailed and bled . . . and stepping on one every now and again.

"Thieves prosper," muttered Locke under his breath. He tightened his neck-cloths and prepared to go summon his carriages, feeling sick to his stomach.

CHAPTER FIVE

ON A CLOCKWORK RIVER

1

THE GLASS-FRONTED transport box erupted out of the Mon Magisteria's waterfall once again and slid home with a lurch just inside the palace. Water hissed through iron pipes, the high gates behind the box slammed shut, and the attendants pushed the front doors open for Locke, Jean, and Merrain.

A dozen Eyes of the Archon were waiting for them in the entrance hall. They fell in wordlessly on either side of Locke and Jean as Merrain led them forward.

Though not to the same office as before, it seemed. Locke glanced around from time to time as they passed through dimly lit halls and up twisting staircases. The Mon Magisteria was truly more fortress than palace; the walls outside the grand hall were devoid of decoration, and the air smelled mainly of humidity, sweat, leather, and weapon oils. Water rumbled through unseen channels behind the walls. Occasionally they would troop past servants, who would stand with their backs to the wall and their heads bowed toward their feet until the Eyes were past.

Merrain led them to an iron-reinforced door in a nondescript corridor several floors up from the entrance. Faint silver moonlight could be seen rippling through an arched window at the far end of the hall. . . . Locke squinted and realized that a stream of water from the palace's circling aqueducts was falling down the glass.

Merrain pounded on the door three times. When it opened with a click, allowing a crack of soft yellow light into the hall, she dismissed the Eyes with a wave of her hand. As they marched away down the corridor, she pushed the door open slightly and pointed toward it with her other hand.

"At last. I might have hoped to see you sooner. You must have been away from your usual haunts when Merrain found you." Stragos looked up from where he sat, on one of only two chairs in the small, bare room, and shuffled the papers he'd been examining. His bald attendant sat on the other with several files in hand, saying nothing.

"They were having a bit of trouble on the inner docks of the Great Gallery," said Merrain as she closed the door behind Locke and Jean. "A pair of fairly motivated assassins."

"Really?" Stragos seemed genuinely annoyed. "What business might that be in relation to?"

"I only wish we knew," said Locke. "Our chance for an interrogation took a crossbow bolt in the chest when Merrain showed up."

"The woman was about to stick one of these two with a poisoned knife, Protector. I thought you'd prefer to have them both intact for the time being."

"Hmmm. A pair of assassins. Were you at the Sinspire tonight?"

"Yes," said Jean.

"Well, it wouldn't be Requin, then. He'd simply have taken you while you were there. So it's some other business. Something you should have told me about before, Kosta?"

"Oh, begging your pardon, Archon. I thought that

between your little friends the Bondsmagi and all the spies you must have slinking about at our backsides, you'd know more than you do."

"This is serious, Kosta. I aim to make use of you; it doesn't suit my needs to have someone else's vendetta on my hands. You don't know who might have sent them?"

"Truthfully, we have no bloody clue."

"You left the bodies of these assassins on the docks?"

"The constables have them by now, surely," said Merrain.

"They'll throw the bodies in the Midden Deep, but first they'll inter them at the death-house for a day or two," said Stragos. "I want someone down there to have a look at them. Note their descriptions, plus any tattoos or other markings that might be meaningful."

"Of course," said Merrain.

"Tell the officer of the watch to see to that now. You'll know where to find me when you're finished."

"Your will...Archon." Merrain looked as though she might say something else, then turned, opened the door, and hurried out.

"You called me Kosta," said Locke when the door had slammed closed once again. "She doesn't know our real names, does she? Curious. Don't you trust your people, Stragos? Seems like it'd be easy enough to get your hooks into them the same way you got them into us."

"I'll wager," said Jean, "that you never take up your master's offer of a friendly drink when you're off duty, eh, baldy?" Stragos' attendant scowled but still said nothing.

"By all means," said Stragos lightly, "taunt my personal alchemist, the very man responsible for me 'getting my hooks into you,' not to mention the preparation of your antidotes."

The bald man smiled thinly. Locke and Jean cleared

their throats and shuffled their feet in unison, a habit they'd synchronized as boys.

"You seem a reasonable fellow," said Locke. "And I for one have always found a hairless brow to be a noble thing, sensible in every climate...."

"Shut up, Lamora. Do we have the people we need, then?" Stragos passed his papers over to his attendant.

"Yes, Archon. Forty-four of them, all told. I'll see that they're moved by tomorrow evening."

"Good. Leave us the vials and you may go."

The man nodded and gathered his papers. He handed two small glass vials over to the archon, then left without another word, sliding the door respectfully closed behind him.

"Well, you two." Stragos sighed. "You seem to attract attention, don't you? You're certain you've *no* idea who else might be trying to kill you? Some old score to settle from Camorr?"

"There are so *many* old scores to settle," said Locke.

"There would be, wouldn't there? Well, my people will continue to protect you as best they can. You two, however, will have to be more...circumspect."

"That sentiment is not exactly unprecedented," said Locke.

"Confine your movements to the Golden Steps and the Savrola until further notice. I'll have extra people placed on the inner docks; use those when you must travel."

"Gods damn it, we can*not* operate like that! For a few days, perhaps, but not for the rest of our stay in Tal Verrar, however long it might be."

"In that, you're more right than you know, Locke. But if someone else is after you, I can't let it interfere with my needs. Curtail your movements or I'll have them curtailed for you."

"You said there'd be no further complication of our game with Requin!"

"No, I said that the *poison* wouldn't further complicate your game with Requin."

"You seem pretty confident of our good behavior for a man who's all alone with us in a little stone room," said Jean, taking a step forward. "Your alchemist's not coming back, is he? Nor Merrain?"

"Should I be worried? You've absolutely nothing to gain by harming me."

"Except immense personal satisfaction," said Locke. "You *presume* that we're in our right minds. You *presume* that we give a shit about your precious poison, and that we wouldn't tear you limb from limb on general principle and take the consequences afterward."

"Must we do this?" Stragos remained seated, one leg crossed over the other, a mildly bored expression on his face. "It occurred to me that the two of you might be stubborn enough to nurse a bit of mutiny in your hearts. So listen carefully—if you leave this room without me, the Eyes in the hall outside will kill you on sight. And if you otherwise harm me in any way, I repeat my earlier promise. I'll revisit the same harm on one of you, tenfold, while the other is forced to watch."

"You," said Locke, "are a goat-faced wad of slipskinner's shit."

"Anything's possible," said Stragos. "But if you're thoroughly in my power, pray tell me, what does that make *you*?"

"Downright embarrassed," muttered Locke.

"Very likely. Can you, both of you, set aside this childish need to avenge your self-regard and accept the mission I have for you? Will you hear the plan and keep civil tongues?"

"Yes." Locke closed his eyes and sighed. "I suppose we truly have no choice. Jean?"

"I wish I didn't have to agree."

"Just so long as you do." Stragos stood up, opened the door to the corridor, and beckoned for Locke and Jean to follow. "My Eyes will see you along to my gardens. I have something I want to show the two of you . . . while we speak more privately about your mission."

"What exactly do you intend to do with us?" asked Jean.

"Simply put, I have a navy riding at anchor in the Sword Marina, accomplishing little. Inasmuch as I still depend on the Priori to help pay and provision it, I can't send it out in force without a proper excuse." Stragos smiled. "So I'm going to send *you two* out onto the sea to find that excuse for me."

"Out to *sea*?" said Locke. "Are you out of your fu—"

"Take them to my garden," said Stragos, spinning on his heel.

2

IT WAS less a garden than a forest, stretching for what must have been hundreds of yards on the northern side of the Mon Magisteria. Hedges entwined with softly glowing Silver Creeper vines marked the paths between the swaying blackness of the trees; by some natural alchemy the vines shed enough artificial moonlight for the two thieves and their guards to step easily along the gravel paths. The moons themselves were out, but had now fallen behind the looming fifteen-story darkness of the palace itself and could not be seen from Locke and Jean's position.

The perfumed air was humid and heavy; there was rain lurking in the creeping arc of clouds enclosing the eastern sky. There was a buzzing flutter of unseen wings from the darkness of the trees, and here and there pale gold and scarlet lights seemed to drift around the trunks like some fairy mischief.

"Lantern beetles," said Jean, mesmerized despite himself.

"Think on how much dirt they must have had to haul up here, to cover the Elderglass deeply enough to let these trees grow...," whispered Locke.

"It's good to be a duke," said Jean. "Or an archon."

At the center of the garden was a low structure like a boathouse, lit by hanging alchemical lanterns in the heraldic blue of Tal Verrar. Locke heard the faint lapping of water against stone, and soon enough saw that there was a dark channel perhaps twenty feet wide cut into the ground just beyond the little structure. It meandered into the darkness of the forest-garden like a miniature river. In fact, Locke realized, the lantern-lit structure *was* a boathouse.

More guards appeared out of the darkness, a team of four being half led and half dragged by two massive black dogs in armored harnesses. These creatures, waist-high at the shoulders and nearly as broad, bared their fangs and sniffed disdainfully at the two thieves, then snorted and pulled their handlers along into the archon's garden.

"Very good," said Stragos, appearing out of the darkness a few strides behind the dog team. "Everything's prepared. You two, come with me. Sword-prefect, you and yours are dismissed."

The Eyes turned as one and marched off toward the palace, their boots crunching faintly on the gravel underfoot. Stragos beckoned to Locke and Jean, then led them down to the water's edge. There, a boat floated on the still water, lashed to a little post behind the boathouse. The craft seemed to be built for four, with a leather-padded bench up front and another at the stern. Stragos gestured again, for Locke and Jean to climb down into the forward bench.

Locke had to admit it was pleasant enough, settling against the cushions and resting his arm against the gunwale of the sturdy little craft. Stragos rocked the boat slightly as he stepped down behind them, untied the lashing, and settled on his own bench. He took up an oar and dipped it over the left gunwale. "Tannen," he said, "be so kind as to light our bow lantern."

Jean glanced over his shoulder and spotted a fist-sized alchemical lantern in a faceted glass hanging off his side of the boat. He fiddled with a brass dial atop the lantern until the vapors inside mingled and sputtered to life, like a sky-blue diamond casting ghosts of the lantern's facets on the water below.

"This was here when the dukes of the Therin Throne built their palace," said Stragos. "A channel cut down into the glass, eight yards deep, like a private river. These gardens were built around it. We archons inherited this place along with the Mon Magisteria. While my predecessor was content with still waters, I have made modifications."

As he spoke, the sound of the water lapping against the sides of the channel became louder and more irregular. Locke realized that the rushing, gurgling noise slowly rising around them was the sound of a current flowing through the river. The bow lantern's reflected light bobbed and shifted as the water beneath it undulated like dark silk.

"Sorcery?" asked Locke.

"Artifice, Lamora." The boat began to slide gently away from the side of the channel, and Stragos used the oar to align them in the center of the miniature river. "There's a strong breeze blowing from the east tonight, and windmills at the far side of my garden. They can be used to drive waterwheels beneath the surface of the channel. In still air, forty or fifty men can crank the mechanisms by hand. I can call the current up as I see fit."

"Any man can fart in a closed room and say that he

commands the wind," said Locke. "Though I will admit, this whole garden is...more elegant than I would have given you credit for."

"How pleasant, to have your good opinion of my aesthetic sense." Stragos steered them in silence for a few minutes after that, around a wide turn, past hanging banks of silver creeper and the rustle of leaves on low-hanging branches. The smell of the artificial river rose up around them as the current strengthened—not unpleasant, but more stale and less *green,* somehow, than the scent of natural ponds and rivers Locke recalled.

"I presume this river is a closed circuit," said Jean.

"A meandering one, but yes."

"Then, ah...forgive me, but where exactly are you taking us?"

"All in good time," said Stragos.

"Speaking of where you're taking us," said Locke, "would you care to return to our earlier subject? One of your guards must have struck me on the head; I thought I heard you say that you wanted us to go to sea."

"So I do. And so you shall."

"To what *possible* end?"

"Are you familiar," said Stragos, "with the story of the Free Armada of the Ghostwind Isles?"

"Vaguely," said Locke."

"The pirate uprising on the Sea of Brass," mused Jean. "Six or seven years ago. It was put down."

"*I* put it down," said the archon. "Seven years ago, those damn fools down in the Ghostwinds got it into their heads to make a bid for power. Claimed to have the right to levy taxes on shipping on the Sea of Brass, if by taxes you mean boarding and plundering anything with a hull. They had a dozen fit vessels, and a dozen more-or-less fit crews."

"Bonaire," said Jean. "That was the captain they all followed, wasn't it? Laurella Bonaire?"

"It was," said Stragos. "Bonaire and her *Basilisk;* she was one of my officers, and that was one of my ships, before she turned her coat."

"And you such a pleasant, unassuming fellow to work for," said Locke.

"That squadron of brigands hit Nicora and Vel Virazzo and just about every little village on the nearby coast; they took ships in sight of this palace and hauled sail for the horizon when my galleys went out to meet them. It was the greatest aggravation this city had faced since the war against Camorr, in my predecessor's time."

"I don't recall it lasting long," said Jean.

"Half a year, perhaps. That declaration was their downfall; freebooters can run and skulk well enough, but when you make declarations you usually end up in battle to uphold them. Pirates are no match for real naval men and women when it's line against line on the open sea. We hammered them just off Nicora, sank half their fleet, and sent the rest pissing their breeches all the way back to the Ghostwinds. Bonaire wound up in a crow's cage dangling over the Midden Deep. After she watched all of her crew go in, I cut the rope that held her up myself."

Locke and Jean said nothing. There was a faint watery creak as Stragos adjusted the course of their boat. Another bend in the artificial river was looming ahead.

"Now, that little demonstration," the archon continued, "made piracy a fairly unpopular trade on the Sea of Brass. It's been a good time for honest merchants since then; of course there are still pirates in the Ghostwinds, but they don't come within three hundred miles of Tal Verrar, nor anywhere near Nicora or the coast. My navy hasn't had anything more serious than customs incidents and plague ships to deal with for nigh on three or four years. A quiet time ... a prosperous time."

"Isn't it your job to provide just that?" said Jean.

"You seem a well-read man, Tannen. Surely, your readings must have taught you that when men and women of arms have bled to secure a time of peace, the very people who most benefit from that peace are also the most likely to forget the bleeding."

"The Priori," said Locke. "That victory made them nervous, didn't it? People like victories. That's what makes generals popular... and dictators."

"Astute, Lamora. Just as it was in the interests of the merchant councils to send me out to deliver them from piracy," said Stragos, "it was in their interest to wring my navy dry soon afterward. Dividends of peace... they paid off half the ships, put them up in ordinary, loosed a few hundred trained sailors from the muster rolls, and let the merchants snap them up. The taxes of Tal Verrar paid to train them, and the Priori and their partners were happy to steal them. So it was, and so it is, with the Sea of Brass at peace, the Marrows squabbling, Lashain without a navy and Karthain far beyond the need to even consider one. This corner of the world is calm."

"If you and the Priori are so very unhappy with one another, why don't they just run you out of funds completely?" Locke settled back against his corner of the boat and let his left hand hang far over the gunwale, trailing in the warm water.

"I'm sure they would if they could," said Stragos. "But the charter of the city guarantees me a certain minimal budget, from general revenues. Though every finnicker and comptroller in the city is one of *theirs*, and they contrive some damned elaborate lies to trim even that. My own ledger-folk have their hands full chasing after them. But it's discretionary funds they won't cut loose. In a time of need they could swell my forces with gold and supplies at a moment's notice. In a time of peace, they begrudge me every last centira. They have forgotten why the archonate was instituted in the first place."

"It does occur to me," said Locke, "that your predecessor was supposed to sort of . . . *dissolve* the office when Camorr agreed to stop kicking your ass."

"A standing force is the only professional force, Lamora. There must be a continuity of experience and training in the ranks; a worthwhile army or navy cannot simply be conjured out of nothing. Tal Verrar might not have the luxury of three or four years to build a defense when the next crisis comes along. And the Priori, the ones who prattle the loudest about 'opposing dictatorship' and 'civic guarantees,' would be the first to slip away like rats, loaded down with their fortunes, to take ship for whatever corner of the world would give them refuge. They would never stand or die with the city. And so the enmity between us is more than personal, for my part."

"While I've known too many grand merchants to dispute your general idea of their character," said Locke, "I've had a sudden sharp realization about where this conversation has been going."

"As have I," said Jean, clearing his throat. "Seems to me that with your power on the wane, this would be a terribly *convenient* time for new trouble to surface somewhere out on the Sea of Brass, wouldn't it?"

"Very good," said Stragos. "Seven years ago, the pirates of the Ghostwinds rose up and gave the people of Tal Verrar reason to be glad of the navy I command. It *would* be convenient if they might be convinced to trouble us once again . . . and be crushed once again."

"Send us out to sea to find an excuse for you, that's what you said," said Locke. "Send *us* out to *sea*. Has your brain swelled against the inside of your skull? How the screaming fucking hell do you expect the two of us to raise a bloody pirate armada in a place we've never been and convince it to come merrily *die* at the hands of the navy that bent it over the table and fucked it in the ass last time?"

"You convinced the nobles of Camorr to throw away a fortune on your schemes," said Stragos without a hint of anger. "They love their money. Yet you shook it out of them like ripe fruit from a tree. You outwitted a Bondsmage. You outwitted Capa Barsavi to his very face. You evaded the trap that caught your Capa Barsavi and his entire court."

"Only some of us," whispered Locke. "Only some of us got away, asshole."

"I need more than agents. I need *provocateurs*. You two fell into my hands at an ideal time. Your task, your mission, will be to raise hell on the Sea of Brass. I want ships sacked from here to Nicora. I want the Priori pounding on my door, pleading with me to take more gold, more ships, more responsibility. I want commerce south of Tal Verrar to set full sail and run for port. I want underwriters soiling their breeches. I know I might not get all that, but by the gods, I'll take whatever you can give me. Raise me a pirate scare the likes of which we haven't had in years."

"You are *cracked*," said Jean.

"We can rob nobles. We can do second-story work. We can slide down chimneys and slip locks and rob coaches and break vaults and do a fine spread of card tricks," said Locke. "I could cut your balls off, if you had any, and replace them with marbles, and you wouldn't notice for a week. But I hate to tell you that the one class of criminal we really haven't associated with, *ever,* is fucking pirates!"

"We're at a bit of a loss when it comes to the particulars of making their acquaintance," added Jean.

"In this, as in so much, I'm well ahead of you," said Stragos. "You should have no trouble making the acquaintance of the Ghostwind pirates, because you yourselves will *become* perfectly respectable pirates. Captain and first mate of a pirate sloop, as a matter of fact."

3

"YOU ARE beyond mad," said Locke after several moments of silent, furious thought. "Full-on barking madness is a state of rational bliss to which you may not aspire. Men living in gutters and drinking their own piss would shun your company. *You* are a prancing lunatic."

"That's not the sort of thing I'd expect to hear from a man who genuinely wants his antidote."

"Well, what a magnificent choice you've given us— death by slow poison or death by insane misadventure!"

"Come now," said Stragos. "That's also not the sort of thing I'd expect to hear from a man with your proven ability for slipping out of extremely complicated situations."

"I'm getting a bit annoyed," said Locke, "with those who praise our previous escapades as an excuse for forcing us into even riskier ones. Look, if you want us to run a job, give us one within our field of experience. Isn't it broad enough for you? All we're saying is that we don't know the first bloody thing about wind, weather, ships, pirates, the Sea of Brass, the Ghostwind Isles, sails, ropes, er... weather, ships..."

"Our sole experience with ships," said Jean, "consists of getting on, getting seasick, and getting off."

"I'd thought of that," said Stragos. "The captain of a criminal crew must have, above all other things, charisma. Leadership. A sense of decision. Rogues must be ruled. I believe you can do that, Lamora... by faking it, if necessary. That makes you the best possible choice in some respects. You can *fake* confidence when a sincere man might be inclined to panic. And your friend Jean can enforce your leadership; a good infighter is someone to be respected on a ship."

"Sure, great," said Locke. "I'm charming; Jean's tough. That just leaves all the other things I named—"

"As for the nautical arts, I will provide you with an experienced sailing master. A man who can train you in the essentials and make the proper decisions for you once you're at sea, all the while pretending the orders come from you. Don't you see? All I'm doing is asking you to play a role; he'll provide the knowledge to make that role convincing."

"Sweet Venaportha," said Locke. "You *really* intend for us to go out there, and you *genuinely* wish us to succeed?"

"Absolutely," said Stragos.

"And the poison," said Jean, "you'll just put enough antidote in our hands to allow us to roam the Sea of Brass, as we will?"

"Hardly. You'll need to call at Tal Verrar once every two months. My alchemist tells me that sixty-two to sixty-five days is really as far as you should push it."

"Now, wait just a damn minute," said Locke. "It's not enough that we'll be clueless sailors masquerading as hardened pirates, trusting another man to make us look competent. Or that we're going to be out risking gods know what at sea, with our plans for Requin postponed. Now you expect us to be tied to Mother's apron strings every two months?"

"It's two or three weeks to the Ghostwinds, and the same time back. You'll have ample time to do your business each trip, for however many months it takes. How closely you wish to shave your schedule is, of course, your own concern. Surely you see that it has to be this way."

"No," Locke laughed, "frankly, I don't!"

"I'll want progress reports. I may have new orders and information for you. You may have new requests or suggestions. It makes a great deal of sense to stay in regular contact."

"And what if we chance across one of those patches

of...damn, Jean, what are they called? No wind whatsoever?"

"Doldrums," said Jean.

"Exactly," said Locke. "Even *we* know that you can't presume a constant speed with wind and sails; you get what the gods send you. We could be stuck on a flat ocean fifty miles from Tal Verrar, on day sixty-three, dying for no reason at all."

"Remotely possible, but unlikely. I'm well aware that there's a great element of risk in the task I'm handing you; the possibility of a vast return compels me to play the odds. Now...speak no more of this for the time being. Here's what I've brought you out to see."

There was a golden ripple on the black water ahead, and faint golden lines that seemed to sway in the air above it. As they drew closer, Locke saw that a wide, dark shape covered the artificial river completely, from one bank to the other. A building of some sort...and the golden lines appeared to be cracks in curtains that hung down to the water. The boat reached this barrier and pushed through with little trouble; Locke shoved heavy damp canvas away from his face, and as it fell aside the boat burst into broad daylight.

They were inside a walled and roofed garden, at least forty feet high, filled with willow, witchwood, olive, citrus, and amberthorn trees. Black, brown, and gray trunks stood in ranks beside one another, their vine-tangled branches reaching up in vast constellations of bright leaves that entwined above the river like a roof beneath the roof.

As for the roof itself, it was scintillant, sky blue and bright as noon, with wisps of white clouds drifting past half-visible between the branches. The sun burned painfully bright on Locke's right as he turned around to stare straight ahead, and it sent rays of golden light down through the silhouetted leaves...though surely it was still the middle of the night outside.

"This is alchemy, or sorcery, or both," said Jean.

"Some alchemy," said Stragos in a soft, enthusiastic voice. "The ceiling is glass, the clouds are smoke, the sun is a burning vessel of alchemical oils and mirrors."

"Bright enough to keep this forest alive under a roof? Damn," said Locke.

"It may indeed be bright enough, Lamora," said the archon, "but if you'll look closely, you'll see that nothing under this roof besides ourselves is *alive*."

As Locke and Jean glanced around in disbelief, Stragos steered the boat up against one of the garden's riverbanks. The waterway narrowed here to a mere ten feet, to allow room for the trees and vines and bushes on either side. Stragos reached out to grasp a trunk and halt the boat, and he pointed into the air as he spoke.

"A clockwork garden for my clockwork river. There's not a real plant in here. It's wood and clay and wire and silk; paint and dye and alchemy. All of it engineered to my design; it took the artificers and their assistants six years to construct it all. My little glen of mechanisms."

Incredulously, Locke realized that the archon was telling the truth. Other than the movement of white smoke clouds far overhead, the place was unnaturally still, almost eerie. And the air in the enclosed garden was inert, smelling of stale water and canvas. It should have been bursting with forest scents, with the rich odors of dirt and flowering and decay.

"Do I still strike you as a man farting in an enclosed room, Lamora? In here, I *do* command the wind...."

Stragos raised his right arm high above his head, and a rustling noise filled the artificial garden. A current of air plucked at Locke's scalp, and steadily rose until there was a firm breeze against his face. The leaves and branches around them swayed gently.

"And the rain," cried Stragos. His voice echoed off the

water and was lost in the depths of the suddenly lively forest. A moment later a faint warm mist began to descend, a ticklish haze of water that swirled in ghostly curves throughout the imaginary greenery and enveloped their boat. Then drops began to fall with a soft pitter-patter, rippling the surface of the clockwork river. Locke and Jean huddled beneath their coats as Stragos laughed.

"I can do more," said Stragos. "Perhaps I can even call up a storm!" A stronger breath of air began to beat the rain and mist against them; the little river churned as a countercurrent surged from somewhere ahead of them. Little whitecaps burst beneath the boat as though the water were boiling; Stragos clung to his chosen tree trunk with both hands as the boat rocked nauseatingly. The raindrops grew heavier and harder; Locke had to shield his eyes to see. Clouds of thick dark mist boiled overhead, dimming the artificial sun. The forest had come to life, flailing at the misty air with branches and leaves as though the faux greenery was at war with unseen ghosts.

"But only after a fashion," said Stragos, and without any apparent further signals from him the rain faded away. Gradually, the flailing of the forest died down to a soft rustling, and then to stillness; the surging currents of the river beneath them subsided, and in minutes the mechanical garden was restored to relative peace. Fingers of fading mist swirled around the trees, the sun peeked out from behind the thinning "clouds," and the enclosure echoed with the not-unpleasant sound of water dripping from a thousand branches and fronds and trunks.

Locke shook himself and pushed his wet hair back out of his eyes. "It's . . . it's gods-damned singular, Archon. I'll give it that. I've never even imagined anything like this."

"A bottled garden with bottled weather," mused Jean.

"Why?" Locke asked the question for both of them.

"As a reminder." Stragos released his hold on the tree

trunk and let the boat drift gently into the middle of the stream once again. "Of what the hands and minds of human beings can achieve. Of what *this* city, alone in all the world, is capable of producing. I told you my Mon Magisteria was a repository of artificial things. Think of them as the fruits of order... order I must secure and safeguard."

"How the hell does interfering with Tal Verrar's ocean commerce secure and safeguard order?"

"Short-term sacrifice for long-term gain. There is something latent in this city that will flower, Lamora. Something that will *bloom*. Can you imagine the wonders the Therin Throne might have produced, given centuries of peace, had it not been shattered into all our warring, scrabbling city-states? Something is preparing to emerge out of all our misfortune at last, and it will be *here*. The alchemists and artificers of Tal Verrar are peerless, and the scholars of the Therin Collegium are just a few days away.... It *must* be here!"

"Maxilan, darling." Locke raised one eyebrow and smiled. "I knew you were driven, but I had no idea you could *smolder*. Come, take me now! Jean won't mind; he'll avert his eyes like a gentleman."

"Mock me as you will, Lamora, but hear the words I speak. *Comprehend,* damn you. What you just witnessed," said Stragos, "required sixty men and women to achieve. Spotters watching for my signals. Alchemists to tend the smoke-pots, and hidden crews to work the bellows and fans that produce the wind. There were several dozen merely pulling strings, as it were; the branches of my artificial trees are threaded with metal wire, like puppets, so that they may shake more convincingly. A small army of trained workers, straining to produce a five-minute spectacle for three men in a boat. And even that was not possible with the art and artifice of previous centuries.

"What more might we achieve, given time? What if thirty people could produce the same result? Or ten? Or one? What if better devices could give stronger winds, more driving rain, a harder current? What if our mechanisms of control grew so subtle and so powerful that they ceased to be a spectacle at all? What if we could harness them to change anything, control anything, even ourselves? Our bodies? Our *souls*? We cower in the ruins of the Eldren world, and cower in the shadow of the Magi of Karthain. But common men and women could equal their power. Given centuries, given the good grace of the gods, common men and women could *eclipse* their power."

"And all of these grandiose notions," said Jean, "somehow require the two of us to go out and pretend to be pirates on your behalf?"

"Tal Verrar will never be strong so long as its fate is vouchsafed by those who would squeeze gold from it like milk from a cow, then flee for the horizons at the first sign of danger. I *need* more power, and to speak plainly, I must seize or trick it out of my enemies, with the will of the people behind me. Your mission, if successful, would turn a key in the lock of a door that bars the way to greater things." Stragos chuckled and spread his hands. "You are thieves. I am offering you a chance to help steal history itself."

"Which is of little comfort," said Locke, "compared to money in a countinghouse and a roof over one's head."

"You hate the magi of Karthain," said Stragos flatly.

"I suppose I do," said Locke.

"The last emperor of the Therin Throne tried to fight them with magic; sorcery against sorcery. He died for his failure. Karthain can never be conquered by the arts it commands; they have ensured that no power in our world will ever have sorcerers numerous or powerful enough to match them. They must be fought with this." He set down his oar and spread his hands. "Machines. Artifice. Alchemy and engineering—the fruits of the mind."

"All of this," said Locke, "this whole ridiculous scheme ... a more powerful Tal Verrar, conquering this corner of the world ... all to hurt Karthain? I can't say I find the idea unpleasant, but why? What did they do to you, to make you imagine this?"

"Do either of you know," said Stragos, "of the ancient art of illusionism? Have you ever read about it in books of history?"

"A little," said Locke. "Not very much."

"Once upon a time the performance of illusions—imaginary magic, not real sorcery at all, just clever tricks—was widespread, popular, and lucrative. Commoners paid to see it on street corners; nobles of the Therin Throne paid to see it in their courts. But that culture is dead. The art no longer exists, except as trifles for cardsharps. The Bondsmagi haunt our city-states like wolves, ready to crush the slightest hint of competition. No sensible person would ever stand up in public and declare themselves to be capable of magic. Fear killed the entire tradition, hundreds of years ago.

"The Bondsmagi distort our world with their very presence. They rule us in many ways that have nothing to do with politics; the fact that we can hire them to do our bidding is immaterial. That little guild *looms* over everything we plan, everything we dream. Fear of the magi poisons our people to the very marrow of their ambitions. It prevents them from imagining a larger destiny ... from the hope of reforging the empire we once had. I know that you consider what I've done to you unforgivable. But believe it or not, I admire you for standing up to the Bondsmagi. They turned you over to me as a means of punishment. Instead, I ask you to help me strike at them."

"Grand abstracts," said Jean. "You make it sound like

this is some sort of incredible privilege for us, being pressed into service without our consent."

"I don't need an excuse to hate the Bondsmagi," said Locke. "Not to hate them, nor to fight them. I've taunted them to their faces, more or less. Jean and I both. But you have to be some kind of madman, to think they'll ever let you build anything openly powerful enough to knock them down."

"I don't expect to live to see it," said Stragos. "I only expect to plant the seed. Look at the world around you, Lamora. Examine the clues they've given us. Alchemy is revered in every corner of our world, is it not? It lights our rooms, salves our injuries, preserves our food...enhances our cider." He favored Locke and Jean with a self-satisfied smile. "Alchemy is a low-grade form of magic, but the Bondsmagi have never once tried to curtail or control it."

"Because they just don't give a damn," said Locke.

"Wrong," said Stragos. "Because it's so necessary to so many things. It would be like trying to deny us the right to water, or fire. It would push us *too far*. No matter the cost, no matter the carnage, it would force us to fight back against them for the sake of our very existence. And they know it. Their power has limits. Someday, we'll surpass those limits, if we're only given a chance."

"That's a fine bedtime story," said Locke. "If you wrote a book on that subject, I'd pay for ten copies to be scribed. But here and now, you're interfering with our lives. You're tearing us away from something we've worked long and hard to achieve."

"I am prepared to expand on my earlier terms," said Stragos, "and offer a financial reward for the successful completion of your task."

"How much?" said Locke and Jean simultaneously.

"No promises," said Stragos. "Your reward will be

proportional to your achievement. I shall make you as happy as you make me. Is that understood?"

Locke stared at Stragos for several seconds, scratching his neck. Stragos was using a confidence trick—an appeal to high ideals, followed by an appeal to greed. And this was a *classic* fuck-the-agent situation; Stragos had no compulsion whatsoever to follow through on his promise, and nothing to lose by making it, and no reason at all to let him and Jean live once their task was finished. He made eye contact with Jean and stroked his chin several times, a simple hand signal:

Lying. Jean sighed, and tapped his fingers a few times against the gunwale on his side of the boat. He seemed to share Locke's thought that elaborate signals would best be avoided with Stragos just a few feet away. His answer was equally simple:

Agreed.

"That's good news," said Locke, conjuring a note of guarded optimism in his voice. The knowledge that he and Jean were of one mind always gave him renewed energy for false-facing. "A pile of solari when this is all over would go a long way toward mitigating our distaste for the circumstances of our employment."

"Good. My sole concern is that the mission may benefit from more enthusiasm on your part."

"This mission, to be frank, is going to need all the help it can get."

"Don't dwell on the matter, Lamora. And look out behind—we're coming to the far side of my little glen."

The boat was sliding toward another curtain-barrier of hanging canvas; by Locke's casual estimate, the entire artificial garden enclosure must have been about eighty yards long.

"Say farewell to the sun," said the archon, and then they were slipping through the canvas, back out into the muggy black-and-silver night, with its flitting lantern-flies and genuine forest perfume. A guard dog barked nearby, growled, and went silent in response to a hushed command. Locke rubbed his eyes as they slowly adjusted once again to the darkness.

"You'll begin training this week," said Stragos.

"What do you mean, training? There's a pile of questions you haven't answered," said Locke. "Where's our ship? Where's our crew? How do we make ourselves known as pirates? There's a thousand damn details to go over. . . ."

"All in good time," said Stragos. His voice had an air of unmistakable satisfaction now that Locke was speaking constructively of carrying out his plan. "I'm told you two frequently take meals at the Gilded Cloister. Spend a few days returning to a schedule of rising with the sun. On Throne's Day, have breakfast at the Cloister. Wait for Merrain to find you. She'll see you to your destination with her usual discretion, and you'll begin your lessons. They'll take up most of your days, so don't make any plans."

"Damn it," said Jean, "why not let us finish our affair with Requin? It won't take more than a few weeks. Then we can do whatever you like, without distraction."

"I've thought about it," said Stragos, "but no. Postpone it. I want you to have something to look forward to after you complete my mission. And I don't have a few weeks to wait. I need you at sea in a month. Six weeks at the very latest."

"A *month* to go from gratefully ignorant landlubbers to fucking professional pirates?" said Jean. "Gods."

"It will be a busy month," said Stragos.

Locke groaned.

"Are you up for the task? Or shall I simply deny you your antidote and give you a prison cell from which to observe the results?"

"Just see to it that that fucking antidote is ready and

waiting each time we come back," said Locke. "And give a serious *ponder* to just how much money would best send us away happy when this affair is concluded. I'm guessing that you're likely to be the underestimating type in that regard, so I'd think *big*."

"Rewards proportional to results, Lamora. That and your lives. When the red flag is seen again in my city's waters, and the Priori are begging me to save them, you may turn your thoughts to the matter of reward. Then and no sooner. Understood?"

Lying, Locke signaled to Jean, sure it was unnecessary but equally sure Jean would appreciate a bit of cheek. "Your will then, I suppose. If the gods are kind we'll poke a stick into whatever hornets' nest is left to be stirred up down in the Ghostwinds. After all, we have no choice, do we?"

"As it should be," said Stragos.

"You know, Locke," said Jean in a lightly conversational tone of voice, "I like to imagine that there are thieves out there who only ever get caught up in perfectly ordinary, uncomplicated escapades. We should consider finding some and asking them what their secret is, one of these days."

"It's probably as simple as staying the hell away from assholes like this," said Locke, gesturing at the archon.

4

A SQUAD of Eyes was waiting beside the boathouse when the little craft completed its circuit of the artificial river.

"Here," said Stragos after one of his soldiers took the oar from him. He removed two glass vials from his pockets and held one out to each Camorri thief. "Your first stay of execution. The poison's had time to work its way into you. I don't want to have to worry about you for the next few weeks."

Locke and Jean complied, each gagging as they drank. "Tastes like chalk," said Locke, wiping his mouth.

"If only it were that inexpensive," said the archon. "Now give the vials back. Caps, too."

Locke sighed. "I suppose it was too much to hope you'd forget that part."

The two thieves were being hauled back toward the Mon Magisteria as Stragos lashed the boat to the piling once again.

Stragos stood up, stretched, and felt the old familiar creaks, the twinges in his hips and knees and wrists. Damn rheumatism... by rights he was still outrunning his age, still ahead of most men nearing threescore years, but he knew deep in his heart that there would never be any way of running fast enough. Sooner or later, the Lady of the Long Silence would call a dance for Maxilan Stragos, whether or not his work here was done.

Merrain was waiting in the shadows of the unlit side of the boathouse, still and quiet as a hunting spider until she stepped out beside him. Long practice enabled him to avoid flinching.

"My thanks for saving those two, Merrain. You've been very useful to me, these past few weeks."

"Just as I was instructed to be," she said. "But are you sure they really suit the needs of this plan of yours?"

"They're at every disadvantage in this city, my dear." Stragos squinted at the blurry forms of Locke, Jean, and their escorts as they disappeared into the garden. "The Bondsmagi sewed them up for us, and we have them second-guessing their every step. I don't believe those two are used to being controlled. Out on their own, I know they'll perform as required."

"Your reports give you that much confidence?"

"Not merely my reports," said Stragos. "Requin certainly hasn't killed them yet, has he?"

"I suppose not."

"They'll serve," said Stragos. "I know their hearts. As the days go by, the resentment will fade and the novelty will gain on them. They'll be enjoying themselves soon enough. And when they start to enjoy themselves . . . I honestly think they can do it. If they live. It's for damn sure I've no other agents suitable to the task."

"Then I may report to my masters that the plan is under way?"

"Yes, I suppose this commits us. You may do just that." Stragos eyed the shadowed shape of the slender woman beside him and sighed. "Let them know that everything begins in a month or so. I hope for their sake they're ready for the consequences."

"*Nobody's* ready for the consequences," said Merrain. "It's going to mean more blood than anyone's seen in two hundred years. All we can do is hope that by setting things off we can ensure that *others* reap most of the trouble. By your leave, Archon, I'd like to go compose my messages to them now."

"Of course," said Stragos. "Send my regards along with your report, and my prayers that we might continue to prosper . . . together."

LAST REMINISCENCE

By Their Own Rope

1

"Oh, this is a *wonderful* spot to fling ourselves to our deaths from," said Locke.

Six months had passed since his return from Salon Corbeau; the suite of four exquisitely crafted chairs was safely locked away in a private storage room at the Villa Candessa. Tal Verrar's version of late winter held the region in the grip of temperatures so brisk that folk had to engage in actual labor to break a sweat.

About an hour's hard ride north of Tal Verrar, just past the village of Vo Sarmara and its surrounding fields, a scrubby forest of gnarled witchwood and amberthorn trees rose beside a wide, rocky vale. The walls of this vale were the grayish color of corpse-flesh, giving the place the look of a giant wound in the earth. The thin olive-colored grass abandoned the struggle for life about ten feet from the edge of the cliffs above this vale, where Locke and Jean stood contemplating the sheer hundred-foot drop to the gravel floor far below.

"I suppose we should've kept more in practice with this," said Jean, starting to shrug his way out of the half dozen coils of rope draped from his right shoulder to his left hip. "But then, I don't recall many opportunities to put it to use in the past few years."

"Most places in Camorr, we could just hand-over-hand it, up and down," said Locke. "I don't think you were even with us that night we used ropes, to get up Lady de Marre's tower at that horrible old estate of hers. . . . Calo and Galdo and I nearly got pecked to bloody shreds by pigeons working that one. Must've been five, six years ago."

"Oh, I was with you, remember? On the ground, keeping watch. I saw the bit with the pigeons. Hard to play sentry when you're pissing yourself laughing."

"Wasn't funny at all from up top. Beaky little bastards were vicious!"

"The Death of a Thousand Pecks," said Jean. "You would have been legends, dying so gruesomely. I'd have written a book on the man-eating pigeons of Camorr and joined the Therin Collegium. Gone respectable. Bug and I would've built a memorial statue to the Sanzas, with a nice plaque."

"What about me?"

"Footnote on the plaque. Space permitting."

"Hand over some rope or I'll show you the edge of the cliff, *space permitting.*"

Jean tossed a coil to Locke, who plucked it out of the air and walked back toward the edge of the forest, about thirty feet from the cliff. The rope was tightly woven demi-silk, much lighter than hemp and *much* more expensive. At the rim of the forest, Locke selected a tall old witchwood, about as broad around as Jean's shoulders. He pulled a goodly length of his line free, passed it around the tree trunk, and stared at the slightly frayed end for a few seconds, trying to rekindle his memories of knot-tying.

As his fingers slipped into hesitant motion, he took a quick glance around at the melancholy state of the world. A stiff wind was blowing from the northwest, and the sky was one vast cataract of wet-looking haze. Their hired carriage was parked at the far end of the woods, perhaps three hundred yards away. He and Jean had set the driver up with a clay jug of beer and a splendid basket lunch from the Villa Candessa, promising to be gone for a few hours at most.

"Jean," muttered Locke as the bigger man stepped up beside him, "this is a proper anchor-noose, right?"

"Certainly looks like it." Jean hefted the elaborate knot that secured the rope in a bight around the tree and nodded. He took the working end of the rope and added an additional half-hitch for safety. "There. Just right."

He and Locke worked together for a few minutes, repeating the anchor-noose knot with three further lengths of rope, until the old witchwood tree seemed thoroughly decorated with taut demi-silk. Their spare coils of rope were set aside. The two men then slipped out of their long frock coats and their vests, revealing heavy leather belts studded with iron rings at their waists.

The belts weren't quite like the custom climbing harnesses treasured by the more responsible burglars of Camorr; these were actually nautical in origin, used by those happy sailors whose ship owners cared enough to spend a bit of money to preserve their health. The belts had been available on the cheap, and had spared Locke and Jean the need to suss out a contact in Tal Verrar's underworld who could make a pair to order...but remember the transaction. There were a few things Requin would be better off not knowing until the chance came to finally spring the game on him.

"Right, then. Here's your descender." Jean passed Locke a fairly heavy bit of iron, a figure eight with one side larger than the other, with a thick bar right down the middle. He also kept one for himself; he'd had them knocked up by a blacksmith in Tal Verrar's Istrian Crescent a few weeks earlier. "Let's get you rigged up first. Main line, then belay."

Locke clipped his descender into one of his harness rings and threaded it through with one of the demi-silk lines leading back to the tree. The other end of this line was left free and tossed toward the cliff. A second line was lashed tight to a harness ring above Locke's opposite hip. Many Camorri thieves on working jobs "danced naked," without the added safety of a belay line in case their primary rope broke, but for today's practice session Locke and Jean were in firm agreement that they were going to play it safe and boring.

It took a few minutes to rig Jean up in a similar fashion; soon enough they were each attached to the tree by two lines, like a pair of human puppets. The two thieves wore little save their tunics, breeches, field boots, and leather gloves, though Jean did pause to slip his reading optics on.

"Now then," he said. "Seems a fine day for abseiling. Care to do the honors before we kiss solid earth farewell?"

"Crooked Warden," said Locke, "men are stupid. Protect us from ourselves. If you can't, let it be quick and painless."

"Well said." Jean took a deep breath. "Crazy part on three?"

"On three."

Each of them took up their coiled main line and tossed the free end over the cliff; the two ropes went over and uncoiled with a soft hiss.

"One," said Locke.

"Two," said Jean.

"Three," they said together. Then they ran for the cliff and threw themselves off, whooping as they went.

For one brief moment Locke's stomach and the misty gray sky seemed to be turning a somersault in unison. Then his line was taut and the cliff face was rushing toward him just a little too eagerly for his taste. Like a human pendulum, he swung in, raised his legs, and hit the rock wall about eight feet beneath the rim, keeping his knees bent to absorb the shock of impact. That much, at least, he remembered very well. Jean hit with a heavier *whoomp* about two feet below him.

"Heh," said Locke, his heartbeat pounding in his ears, loud enough to match the whisper of the wind. "There's got to be an easier way to test whether or not we have an honest rope-weaver, Jean."

"Whew!" Jean shifted his feet slightly, keeping a hold on his line with both hands. The use of the descenders made it easy for them to apply enough friction to the rope to slow or stop at will. The little devices were a marked improvement on what they'd been taught as boys. While they could still no doubt slide down a rope using their own bodies for friction, as they once had, it was easy to abrade a certain protruding portion of the male anatomy with that approach if one was careless or unlucky.

For a few moments they simply hung there, feet against the cliffside, enjoying their new vantage point as the vaporous clouds rolled by overhead. The ropes waving in the air beneath them only hung down about half the distance to the ground, but they didn't intend to get there today anyway. There would be plenty of time to work up to longer drops, in future practice sessions.

"You know," said Locke, "this is the only part of the plan, I must admit, that I wasn't terribly sure of. It's so much easier to contemplate abseiling from a height like this than it is to actually run off a cliff with just two lengths of rope between you and Aza Guilla."

"Ropes and cliffs are no problem," said Jean. "What we need to watch out for up here are your carnivorous pigeons."

"Oh, bend over and bite your own ass."

"I'm serious. I'm terrified. I'll keep a sharp lookout, lest the last thing we feel in this life should be that *terrible swift pecking—*"

"Jean, your belay line must be weighing you down. Here, let me cut it for you...."

They kicked and shoved good-naturedly against one another for a few minutes, Locke scrambling around and trying to use his agility to balance out Jean's far greater strength and mass. Strength and mass seemed to be winning the day, however, so in a fit of self-preservation he suggested they actually practice descending.

"Sure," said Jean, "let's go down five or six feet, nice and smooth, and stop on my mark, shall we?"

Each of them gripped his taut main line and released a bit of tension on his descender. Slowly, smoothly, they slipped down a good two yards, and Jean cried, "Hold!"

"Not bad," said Locke. "The knack seems to come back quick, doesn't it?"

"I suppose. I was never really keen on this after I got back from my little holiday at Revelation House. This was more your thing, and the Sanzas', than mine. And, ah, Sabetha's, of course."

"Yeah," said Locke, wistfully. "Yeah, she was so mad... so mad and so lovely. I used to love watching her climb. She didn't like ropes. She'd... take her boots off, and let her hair out, and wouldn't even wear gloves, sometimes. Just her breeches and her blouse... and I would just..."

"Sit there hypnotized," said Jean. "Struck dumb. Hey, my eyes worked back then too, Locke."

"Heh. I suppose it must have been obvious. Gods." Locke stared at Jean and laughed nervously. "Gods, I'm actually bringing her up myself. I don't believe it." His expression turned shrewd. "Are we all right with each other, Jean? Back to being comfortable, I mean?"

"Hell, we're hanging together eighty feet above a messy death, aren't we? I don't do that with people I don't like."

"That's good to hear."

"And yeah, I'd say we're—"

"Gentlemen! Hello down there!"

The voice was Verrari, with a rough rustic edge. Locke and Jean glanced up in surprise and saw a man standing at the edge of the cliff, arms akimbo, silhouetted against the churning sky. He wore a threadbare cloak with the hood thrown up.

"Er, hello up there," said Locke.

"Fine day for a bit of sport, ain't it?"

"That's exactly what we thought," cried Jean.

"A fine day indeed, beggin' your pardons, sirs. And a fine set o' coats and vests you've gone and left up here. I like them very much, exceptin' that there ain't no purses in the pockets."

"Of course not, we're not stu— Hey, come on now. Kindly don't mess with our things," said Jean. As if by some unspoken signal, he and Locke reached out to brace themselves against the cliff, finding hand- and footholds as quickly as they could.

"Why not? They're such fine things, sirs, I just can't help but feel sort of drawn to them, like."

"If you'll just wait right there," said Locke, preparing to begin climbing, "one of us should be up in a few minutes, and I'm sure we can discuss this civilly."

"I'm also sort of drawn to the idea of keepin' you two down there, if it's all the same to you, gents." The man moved slightly, and a hatchet appeared in his right hand. "It's a mighty fine pair of choppers you've left up here with your coats, too. Damned fine. Ain't never seen the like."

"That's very polite of you to say," yelled Locke.

"Oh, sweet jumping fuck," muttered Jean.

"I might point out, however," continued Locke, "that our man at the carriage is due to check on us soon, and he'll have his crossbow with him."

"Oh, you mean the unconscious fellow I like jacked over

the head with a rock, sir? Sorry to report that he was drunk."

"I don't believe you. We didn't give him that much beer!"

"Beggin' pardon, but he weren't all that much *man*, gents. Skinny fellow, if you savvy. As it is, he's sleepin' now. And he didn't have no crossbow anyway. I checked."

"Well, I hope you don't blame us for trying," said Locke.

"I don't, not one little bit. Good try. Very creditable, like. But I'm sort of interested, if you don't mind, in the wheresabouts of your purses."

"Safely down here with us," said Locke. "We might be convinced to surrender them, but you'll have to help haul us up if you want them."

"Now on that subject," said the stranger, "you an' I have a sort of difference in outlook, like. Since I know you've got 'em, now, I think it's easier to just chop you down and collect 'em at my ease."

"Unless you're a much better rock climber than you look," said Jean, "it's one hell of a climb down and back for the sake of our little purses!"

"And they are little," said Locke. "Our rock-climbing purses. Specially made not to weigh us down. Hardly hold anything!"

"I think we probably got different ideas of what *anythin'* is. And I wouldn't have to climb," said the stranger. "There's easier ways down to that valley floor, if you know where to go."

"Ah, don't be foolish," said Jean. "These ropes are demisilk. It'll take you some time to cut through them. Longer than it will take for us to climb back up, surely."

"Probably," said the man in the cloak. "But I'm still up here if you do, ain't I? I can just crack you over the edge and make your skulls into soup bowls, like. See if I don't!"

"But if we stay down here, we'll die anyway, so we might as well come up and die fighting," said Locke.

"Well, have it your way, sir. Whole conversation's gettin' sort of circular, if you don't mind me sayin', so I'm just gonna start cuttin' rope now. Me, I'd stay put and go quiet, was I you."

"Yeah, well, you're a miserable cur," shouted Locke. "Any child of three could murder helpless men hanging over a cliff. Time was when a bandit would have the balls to fight us face-to-face and earn his pay!"

"What do I rightly look like, sir, an honest tradesman? Guild tats on my arms?" He knelt down and began to chop at something, steadily, with Jean's hatchet. "Splattin' you against those rocks below seems a fine way of earnin' my pay. Even finer, if you're gonna speak so unkind."

"You're a wretch," cried Locke. "A cringing dog, a scrub, damned not just for avarice but for cowardice! The gods spit on those without honor, you know! It'll be a cold hell, and a dark one, for you!"

"I'm chock-full of honor, sir. Got lots of it. Keep it right here between my empty stomach and my puckered white ass, which you may kiss, by the way."

"Fine, fine," said Locke. "I merely wanted to see if you could be goaded to misjudgment. I applaud your restraint! But surely, there's more profit to be had in hoisting us up and holding us for ransom!"

"We're important people," said Jean.

"With rich, important friends. Why not just hold us prisoner and send a letter with a ransom demand?"

"Well," said the man, "for one thing, I can't read nor write."

"We'd be happy to write the demand for you!"

"Can't rightly see how that'd work. You could just write anythin' you like, couldn't you? Ask for constables and soldiers instead of gold, if you take my meanin'. I said I can't read, not that I got worm piss for brains."

"Whoa! Hold it! Stop cutting!" Jean heaved himself up another foot and braced his rope within the descender to hold him. "Stop cutting! I have a serious question!"

"What's that, then?"

"Where the hell did you come from?"

"Roundabouts, here and there, by way of my mother's womb, original like," said the man, who continued chopping.

"No, I mean, do you always watch these cliffs for climbers? Seems bloody unlikely they'd be common enough to skulk in ambush for."

"Oh, they isn't, sir. Ain't never seen any, before you two. Was so curious I just had to come down and take a peek, and ain't I glad I did." *Chop, chop, chop.* "No, mostly I hide in the woods, sometimes the hills. Watch the roads."

"All by yourself?"

"I'd be cuttin' you down faster if I wasn't by myself, wouldn't I?"

"So you watch the roads. Looking to rob what, carriages?"

"Mostly."

"You have a bow or a crossbow?"

"Sadly, no. Think maybe I might buy a piece if I can get enough for your things."

"You hide in the woods, all by yourself, and try to ambush carriages without a real weapon?"

"Well," said the man a bit hesitantly, "has been a while since I got one. But today's my lucky day, ain't it?"

"I should say so. Crooked Warden, you must be the worst highwayman under the sun."

"What did you say?"

"He said," said Locke, "that in his highly educated opinion you're the—"

"No, the other part."

"He mentioned the Crooked Warden," said Locke. "Does that mean something to you? We're members of the same fraternity, friend! The Benefactor, the Thiefwatcher, the Nameless Thirteenth, patron of you and I and all who take the twisty path through life. We're actually conse-crated servants of the Crooked Warden! There's no need for animosity, and no need for you to cut us down!"

"Oh yes there is," said the man vehemently, "now I'm *definitely* cuttin' you down."

"What? Why?"

"Bloody fuckin' heretics, you are! There ain't no Thirteenth! Ain't naught but the Twelve, that's truth! Yeah, I been to Verrar a couple times, met up with lads and lasses from the cuttin' crews what tried to tell me 'bout this Thirteenth. I don't hold with it. Ain't right like I was raised. So down you go, boys!" The man began hacking at the demi-silk ropes with a vengeance.

"Shit. Want to try and snag him in the belay lines?" Jean swung over beside Locke and spoke with soft urgency. Locke nodded. The two thieves took hold of their ends of their belay lines, stared upward, and at Jean's whispered signal, yanked them downward.

It was hardly an efficient trap; the lines were slack, and coiled up above the cliffs. Their tormentor looked down at his feet, hopped up, and stepped away as seven or eight feet of each belay line slipped over the cliff's edge.

"Ha! You'll have to get up earlier than that, gents, if you don't mind my sayin' so!" Whistling tunelessly, he vanished out of sight and continued chopping. A moment later he gave a cry of triumph, and Locke's coiled belay line flew over the edge of the cliff. Locke averted his face as the rope fell just past him; it was soon dangling in thin air from his waistbelt, its frayed far end still too many feet above the ground for safety.

"Shit," said Locke. "Right, Jean. Here's what we do. He should cut my main line next. Let's hook arms. I'll slide down your main line, knot what's left of mine to the bottom, and that should probably get us within twenty feet or so of the ground. If I haul up my belay line and knot that on the end of the other two, we can make it all the way down."

"Depends on how quickly that asshole cuts. You think you can tie knots fast enough?"

"I think I've got no choice. My hands feel up to the task, at least. Even if I just get one line lashed, twenty feet's a happier fall than eighty."

At that moment, there was a faint rumble of thunder overhead. Locke and Jean looked up at just the right moment to feel the first few drops of rain on their faces.

"It's possible," said Locke, "that this would be really fucking amusing right now, were it anyone but us down on these ropes."

"At the moment, I think I'd take my chances with your pigeons if I could," said Jean. "Damn, I'm sorry for leaving the Wicked Sisters up there, Locke."

"Why in Venaportha's name would you have brought them down? There's nothing to apologize for."

"Although," said Jean, "maybe there is one other thing I could try. You carrying sleeve steel?"

"Yeah, but it's in my boot." The rain was beating down fairly hard now, soaking through their tunics and wetting their lines. Their light dress and the stiff breeze made it seem colder than it really was. "Yourself?"

"Got mine right here." Locke saw a flash of bright metal in Jean's right hand. "Yours balanced for throwing, Locke?"

"Shit, no. Sorry."

"No worries. Hold it in reserve, then. And give us a good silent prayer." Jean paused to pluck off his optics and tuck them into his tunic collar, then raised his voice. "Hey! Sheep-lover! A word if you please!"

"I sort of thought we was done talkin'," came the man's voice from above the cliff's edge.

"No doubt! I'll wager using so many words in so short a time makes your brain feel like a squeezed lemon, doesn't it? You wouldn't have the wit to find the fucking ground if I threw you out of a bloody window! Are you listening? You'd have to take your shoes and breeches off to count to twenty-one! You'd have to look up to see the underside of cockroach shit!"

"Does it help, yellin' at me like that? Seems like you should be prayin' to your useless Thirteenth or somethin', but what would I know? I ain't one of you big-time Verrari *felantozzers* or whatever, am I?"

"You want to know why you shouldn't kill us? You want to know why you shouldn't let us hit that valley floor?" Jean hollered at the top of his lungs while bracing his feet more firmly against the cliffside and pulling back his right arm. Thunder echoed overhead. "See this, you idiot? See what I've got in my hands? Something you'll see only once in a lifetime! Something you'll never forget!"

A few seconds later, the man's head and torso appeared over the edge of the cliff. Jean let out a cry as he flung his knife with all of his strength. The cry became triumphant as he saw the blurred shape of his weapon strike home in their tormentor's face . . . and changed yet again to a frustrated groan as he saw the knife bounce back and fall away into thin air. It had struck hilt-first.

"Fucking rain!" yelled Jean.

The bandit was in serious pain, at least. He moaned and clutched his face, teetering forward. A nice hard smack in the eye? Jean fervently hoped so—perhaps he still had a few seconds to try again.

"Locke, your knife, quickly!"

Locke was reaching into his right boot when the man thrust his arms out for balance, lost it, and toppled screaming over the edge of the cliff. He got one hand around Locke's main line a second later and fell directly into the crook of Locke's waist and rope, where they met at the iron descender on his belt. The shock knocked Locke's legs away from the cliff as it knocked the breath from his lungs, and for a second he and the bandit were in free fall, flailing and screaming in a tangle of arms and legs, with no proper pressure on the line in the descender.

Straining himself to the utmost, Locke curled his left hand around the free side of the line and tugged hard, putting enough strain on the rope to snap them to a halt. They swung into the cliff face together, the bandit taking the brunt of the impact, and dangled there in a struggling mess of limbs while Locke fought to breathe and make sense of the world. The bandit kicked and screamed.

"*Stop that,* you fucking moron!" They seemed to have fallen about fifteen feet; Jean slipped rapidly down beside them, alighted on the cliff, and reached out with one hand to grab the bandit by the hair. With the hood thrown back, Locke could see that the fellow was grizzled like an underfed hound, perhaps forty, with long greasy hair and a gray beard as scrubby as the grass on the cliff's edge. His left eye was swelling shut. "Stop kicking, you idiot! Hold still!"

"Oh, gods, please don't drop me! Please don't kill me, sir!"

"Why the *fuck* not?" Locke groaned, dug his heels into the cliff, and managed to reach the edge of his right boot with his right hand. A moment later he had his stiletto out at the bandit's throat, and the man's panicked kicking became a terrified quivering.

"See this?" Locke hissed. The bandit nodded. "This is a knife. They have these, wherever the fuck you came from?" The man nodded again. "So you know I could just stick you right now and let you fall, right?"

"Please, please, don't...."

"Shut up and listen. This single line that you and I are dangling from right now. Single, solitary, alone! This wouldn't be the line you were just chopping at up there, would it?"

The man nodded vigorously, his good eye wide.

"Isn't that splendid? Well, if the shock of your fall didn't break it, we're probably safe for a little while longer." White light flashed somewhere above them and thunder rolled, louder than before. "Though I have been *much more comfortable*. So don't kick. Don't flail. Don't struggle, and don't do anything fucking stupid. Savvy?"

"Oh, no, sir, oh please..."

"Shut up already."

"Lo...er, Leocanto," said Jean. "I'm thinking this fellow deserves some flying lessons."

"I'm thinking the same thing," said Locke, "but *thieves prosper,* right, Jerome? Help me haul this stupid bastard back up there somehow."

"Oh, thank you, thank—"

"Know why I'm doing this, you witless woodland clown?"

"No, but I—"

"Shut it. What's your name?"

"Trav!"

"Trav what?"

"Never had no after-name, sir. Trav of Vo Sarmara is all."

"And you're a thief? A highwayman?"

"Yes, yes I am."

"Nothing else? Do any honest work?"

"Er, no, not for some time now..."

"Good. Then we are brothers of a sort. Look, my smelly friend, the thing you have to understand is that there *is* a

Thirteenth. He *does* have a priesthood, and I'm one of his priests, savvy?"

"If you say so...."

"No, shut up. I don't want you to agree with me; I want you to use your misplaced acorn of a brain before the squirrel comes looking for it again. I have a blade at your throat, we're seventy feet above the ground, it's pissing a nice hard rain, and you just tried to murder me. By all rights, I ought to give you a red smile from ear to ear and let you drop. Would you agree to *that*?"

"Oh, probably, sir, gods, I'm sorry...."

"Hush now, sweet moron. So you'd admit that I must have a pretty powerful reason for not satisfying myself with your death?"

"I, uh, I guess!"

"I'm a divine of the Crooked Warden, like I said. Sworn to the service and the mandates of the god of our kind. Seems kind of a waste to spit in the face of the god that looks out for you and yours, doesn't it? Especially since I'm not so sure I've been doing right by Him recently."

"Uh..."

"I *should* kill you. Instead, I'm going to try and save your life. All I want you to do is think about this. Do I still seem like a heretic to you?"

"Uh...oh, gods, sir, I can't think straight...."

"Well, nothing unusual there, I'd wager. Remember what I said. Don't flail, don't kick, don't scream. And if you try to fight, even the tiniest bit, our arrangement's off. Wrap your arms around my chest and shut up. We're a good long way from sitting pretty."

2

AT LOCKE'S urging, Jean went up first, hand-over-hand on the slick cliff face at about half his usual speed. Up top, he rapidly unknotted his own belay line from his belt and passed it down to Locke and his shaken passenger. Next he took his harness off and slid his main line along the cliff edge until it too was beside the dangling men. They certainly didn't look comfortable, but with all three good lines in their reach they were at least a bit safer.

Jean found his frock coat on the ground and threw it on, grateful for the added coverage even if it was as sopping wet as the rest of him was. He thought quickly. Trav seemed a fairly meatless fellow, and Locke was lightly built—surely they were no more than three hundred pounds together. Jean was sure he could hoist nearly as much to his chest, perhaps even above his head. But in the rain, with so much at stake?

His thoughts turned to the carriage, about a quarter-mile distant through the woods. A horse would be a vast improvement on even a strong man, but the time it would require, and the trouble inherent in unhooking, calming, and leading a beast whose master had been clubbed unconscious...

"Fuck it," he said, and went back to the cliff's edge. "Leocanto!"

"Still here, as you might have guessed."

"Can the two of you make one of my ropes good and fast to your belt?"

There was a brief muttered conversation between Locke and Trav.

"We'll manage," Locke yelled. "What do you have in mind?"

"Have the idiot hold tight to you. Brace your arms and legs against the cliff once you've lashed yourselves to one of my lines. I'll start hauling on it with all I've got, but I'm sure your assistance won't hurt."

"Right. You heard the man, Trav. Let's tie a knot. Mind where you put your hands."

When Locke looked up and gave Jean their private hand signal for *proceed,* Jean nodded. The secured rope was Jean's former belay line; he seized the working end just before the coil that lay on the wet ground and frowned. The sludge underfoot would make things even more interesting than they already were, but there was nothing else for it. He formed a bight in the rope, stepped into it, and let it slide tight around his waist. He then leaned back, away from the cliff, with one hand on the rope before him and one hand behind, and cleared his throat.

"Tired of dangling, or shall I let you have a few more minutes down there?"

"Jerome, if I have to cradle Trav here for one second longer than I absolutely must, I'm going to—"

"Climb away, then!" Jean dug his heels in, allowed himself to lean even farther back, and began to strain at the rope. Gods damn it, he was a powerful man, unusually strong, but why did moments always come along to remind him that he could be even stronger? He'd been slacking; no other word for it. He should find some crates, fill them with rocks, and heave them up a few dozen times a day, as he had in his youth.... Damn, would the rope ever move?

There. At last, after a long, uncomfortable interval of motionless heaving in the rain, Jean took a slow step back. And then another...and another. Haltingly, with an itching fire steadily rising in the muscles of his thighs, he did his best impression of a plowhorse, pushing deep furrows into the gritty gray mud. Finally, a pair of hands appeared at the edge of the cliff, and in a torrent of shouts and curses, Trav hoisted himself up over the top and rolled onto his back, gasping. Immediately the strain on Jean slackened; he maintained his previous level of effort and just a moment later Locke popped over the edge. He crawled to his feet, stepped over beside Trav, and kicked the would-be bandit in the stomach.

"You fucking jackass! Of all the stupid damn...how difficult would it have been to say, 'I'll lower a rope, tie your purses onto it and send them up, or I won't let you back up'? You don't tell your bloody victims you're just going to kill them outright! You come on reasonable first, and when you have the money you run!"

"Oh...ow! Gods, please; ow! You said you...wouldn't kill me!"

"And I meant it. I'm not going to kill you, you cabbage-brained twit; I'm just going to kick you until it stops feeling good!"

"Ow! Agggh! Please! Aaaaow!"

"I have to say, it's still pretty fascinating."

"Aiiiah! Ow!"

"*Still* enjoying myself."

"Oooof! Agh!"

Locke finally ceased pummeling the unfortunate Verrari, unbuckled his harness belt, and dropped it in the mud. Jean, breathing heavily, came up beside him and handed him his soaked coat.

"Thank you, Jerome." Having his coat back, sopping or no, seemed to salve some of Locke's wounded dignity. "As for you. Trav. Trav of Vo Sarmara, you said?"

"Yes! Oh, please, don't kick me again."

"Look here, Trav. Here's what you're going to do. First, tell no one about this. Second, don't fucking go anywhere near Tal Verrar. Got it?"

"Wasn't plannin' to, sir."

"Good. Here." Locke reached down into his left boot and drew out a very slender purse. He tossed it down beside Trav, where it landed with a jingling plop. "Should be ten volani in there. A healthy bit of silver. And you can... wait a minute, are you absolutely sure our driver's still alive?"

"Oh, gods yes! Honest truth, Master Leocanto, sir, he

was breathin' and moanin' after I thumped him, he surely was."

"So much the better for you, then. You can have the silver in that purse. When Jerome and I have left, you can come back and take whatever we leave. My vest and some of this rope, for sure. And listen to me very carefully. I saved your life today when I could have killed you in a heartbeat. Sound about right to you?"

"Yes, yes you did, and I'm so very—"

"Yes, shut up. Someday, Trav of Vo Sarmara, I may find myself back in these parts, and I may need something. Information. A guide. A bodyguard. Thirteen help me if it's you I have to turn to, but if anyone ever comes to you and whispers the name of Leocanto Kosta, you *jump at their word*, you hear?"

"Yes!"

"Your oath before the gods?"

"Upon my lips and upon my heart, before the gods, or strike me dead and find me wantin' on the scales of the Lady of the Long Silence."

"Good enough. Remember. Now fuck off in the direction of your choice, so long as it isn't back toward our carriage."

Jean and Locke watched him scamper away for a minute or two, until his cloaked figure had faded from view behind the shifting gray curtains of the downpour.

"Well," said Jean, "I think that's enough practice for one day, don't you?"

"Absolutely. The actual Sinspire job'll be a bloody ballroom dance compared to this. What say we just grab the two spare coils of rope and make for the carriage? Let Trav spend the rest of the afternoon out here untying knots."

"A lovely plan." Jean inspected his Wicked Sisters, recovered from the edge of the cliff, and gave them a possessive pat on their blades before slipping them into his coat pocket. "There, darlings. That ass might have dulled you a bit, but I'll soon have you sharpened up again."

"I hardly credit it," said Locke. "Nearly murdered by some halfwit country mudsucker. You know, I do believe that's the first time since Vel Virazzo that anyone's actually tried to kill either of us."

"Seems about right. Eighteen months?" Jean slipped one wet coil of rope around his shoulder and passed the other to Locke. Together, they turned and began to trudge back through the forest. "Nice to know that some things never really change, isn't it?"

CHAPTER SIX

BALANCE OF TRADES

1

"WHOEVER PUT THOSE assassins there obviously knew we used that path to get back to the Savrola," said Locke.

"Which doesn't mean all that much; we've used the docks often. Anyone could have seen us, and set them there to wait." Jean sipped his coffee and ran one hand idly over the battered leather cover of the small book he'd brought to breakfast. "Maybe for several nights. It wouldn't require any special knowledge or resources."

The Gilded Cloister was even quieter than usual at the seventh hour of the morning this Throne's Day. Most of the revelers and businessfolk who provided its custom would have been up late on the Golden Steps, and would not rise for several hours. By unspoken consent, Locke and Jean's breakfast this morning was designed for nervous nibbling: cold fillets of pickled shark meat with lemon, black bread and butter, some sort of brownish fish broiled in orange juice, and coffee—the largest ceramic pot the waiter could find to bring to the table. Both thieves were still having trouble adjusting to the sudden turnaround in their nights and days.

"Unless the Bondsmagi tipped *another* party off to our

presence here in Tal Verrar," said Locke. "They might even be helping them."

"If the Bondsmagi had been helping those two on the docks, do you really think we'd have survived? Come on. Both of us knew they were probably going to come after us for what we did to the Falconer, and if they just wanted us dead, we'd be smoked meat. Stragos is right about one thing—they must mean to toy with us. So I still say it's more likely that some third party took offense at something we've done as Kosta and de Ferra. That makes Durenna, Corvaleur, and Lord Landreval the obvious suspects."

"Landreval's been gone for months."

"That doesn't rule him out completely. The lovely ladies, then."

"I just . . . I honestly believe they'd come after us themselves—Durenna has a reputation with a sword, and I hear that Corvaleur's been in a few duels. Maybe they'd hire some help, but they're hands-on sorts."

"Did we bilk anyone important at Blind Alliances? Or some *other* game when we were playing our way up through the floors? Step on someone's toe? Fart noisily?"

"I can't imagine that we'd have missed someone disgruntled enough to hire assassins. Nobody likes to lose at cards, to be sure, but do any really sore losers stick out in memory?"

Jean scowled and sipped his coffee. "Until we know more, this speculation is useless. Everyone in the city is a suspect. Hell, everyone in the world."

"So in truth," said Locke, "all we really know is that whoever it is wanted us dead. Not scared off, not brought in for a little chat. Plain old dead. Maybe if we can ponder that, we might come up with a few—"

Locke stopped speaking the instant he saw their waitress approaching their booth—then looked more closely and

saw that it wasn't their waitress at all. The woman wearing
the leather apron and red cap was Merrain.

"Ah," said Jean. "Time to settle the bill."

Merrain nodded, and handed Locke a wooden tablet
with two small pieces of paper pinned to it. One was indeed the bill; the other had a single line written on it in
flowing script:

*Remember the first place I took you the night we met?
Don't waste time.*

"Well," said Locke, passing the note to Jean, "we'd love
to stay, but the quality of the service has sharply declined.
Don't expect a gratuity." He counted copper coins onto the
wooden tablet, then stood up. "Same old place as usual,
Jerome."

Merrain collected the wooden tablet and the money,
bowed, and vanished in the direction of the kitchens.

"I hope she doesn't take offense about the tip," said Jean
when they were out on the street. Locke glanced around in
every direction, and noticed that Jean was doing likewise.
Locke's sleeve-stilettos were a comforting weight inside
each arm of his coat, and he had no doubt that Jean was
ready to produce the Wicked Sisters with a twitch of his
wrists.

"Gods," Locke muttered. "We should be back in our
beds, sleeping the day away. Have we ever been *less* in control of our lives than we are at this moment? We can't run
away from the archon and his poison, which means we
can't just disengage from the Sinspire game. Gods know we
can't even see the Bondsmagi lurking, and we've suddenly
got assassins coming out of our assholes. Know something?
I'd lay even odds that between the people following us and
the people hunting us, we've become this city's principal
means of employment. Tal Verrar's entire economy is now
based on *fucking with us.*"

It was a short walk, if a nervous one, to the crossroads

just north of the Gilded Cloister. Cargo wagons clattered across the cobbles and tradesfolk walked placidly to their jobs. As far as they knew, Locke thought, the Savrola was the quietest, best-guarded neighborhood in the city, a place where nothing worse than the occasional drunk foreigner ever disturbed the calm.

Locke and Jean turned left at the intersection, then approached the door of the first disused shop on their right. While Jean kept a watch on the street behind them, Locke stepped up to the door and rapped sharply, three times. It opened immediately, and a stout young man in a brown leather coat beckoned them in.

"Stay away from the window," he said once he'd closed and bolted the door behind them. The window was covered with tightly drawn sailcloth curtains, but Locke agreed that there was no need to tempt fate. The only light in the room came from the sunrise, filtered soft pink through the curtains, enabling Locke to see two pairs of men waiting at the rear of the shop. Each pair consisted of one heavy, broad-shouldered man and one smaller man, and all four of the strangers were wearing identical gray cloaks and broad-brimmed gray hats.

"Get dressed," said the man in the leather coat, pointing to a pile of clothing on a small table. Locke and Jean were soon outfitted in their own matching gray cloaks and hats.

"New summer fashion for Tal Verrar?" said Locke.

"A little game for anyone trying to follow you," said the man. He snapped his fingers, and one set of gray-clad strangers moved to stand right behind the door. "I'll go out first. You stand behind these two, follow them out, then enter the third carriage. Understood?"

"What carri—" Locke started to say, but he cut himself off as he heard the clatter of hooves and wheels in the street immediately outside. Shadows passed before the window, and after a few seconds the man in the brown coat unbolted

the door. "Third carriage. Move fast," he said without turning around, and then he threw the door open and was out
into the street.

At the curb just outside the disused shop three identical
carriages were lined up. Each was black lacquered wood
with no identifying crests or banners, each had heavy
drapes drawn over its windows, and each was pulled by two
black horses. Even their drivers all looked vaguely similar,
and wore the same reddish uniforms under leather over-
coats.

The first pair of gray strangers stepped out the door and
hurried to the first carriage in line. Locke and Jean left the
disused shop a second later, hurrying to the rear carriage.
Locke caught a glimpse of the last team of gray strangers all
but running to the door of the middle carriage behind
them. Jean worked the latch on the rear carriage's door,
held it open for Locke, and flung himself inside afterward.

"Welcome aboard, gentlemen." Merrain lounged in the
right forward corner of the compartment, her waitress'
clothing discarded. She was now dressed as though for a
ride in an open saddle, in field boots, black breeches, a red
silk shirt, and a leather vest. Locke and Jean settled beside
one another in the seat across from her. Jean's slamming of
the door threw them into semidarkness, and the carriage
lurched into motion.

"Where the hell are we going?" Locke began to shrug off
his gray cloak as he spoke.

"Leave that on, Master Kosta. You'll need it when we get
out again. First we'll all tour the Savrola for a bit. Then
we'll split—one carriage to the Golden Steps, one to the
northern edge of the Great Gallery, and us to the docks to
catch a boat."

"A boat to where?"

"Don't be impatient. Sit back and enjoy the ride."

That was difficult, to say the least, in the hot and stuffy

compartment. Locke felt sweat running down his brow, and he grumpily removed his hat and held it in his lap. He and Jean attempted to pelt Merrain with questions, but she answered with nothing but noncommittal "hmmms" until they gave up. Tedious minutes passed. Locke felt the carriage rattling around several corners, then down a series of inclines that had to be the ramp from the upper heights of the Savrola to the sea-level docks.

"We're almost there," said Merrain after another few minutes had passed in uncomfortable, jouncing silence. "Hats back on. When the carriage stops, go straight to the boat. Take your seat at the rear, and for the gods' sake, if you see anything dangerous, duck."

True to her word, the carriage rattled to a halt just a few heartbeats later. Locke planted his hat over his hair once again, fumbled for the door mechanism, and squinted as it opened into bright morning light.

"Out," said Merrain. "Don't waste time."

They were down on the interior docks at the very northeastern tip of the Savrola, with a sheer wall of black Elderglass behind them and several dozen anchored ships on the gleaming, choppy water before them. One boat was lashed to the nearest pier, a sleek gig about forty feet long, with a raised and enclosed gallery at the stern. Two lines of rowers, five to a side, filled most of the rest of its space.

Locke hopped down from the carriage and led the way toward the boat, past a pair of alert men wearing cloaks as heavy as his own, quite inappropriate for the weather. They were standing at near attention, not lounging, and Locke caught a glimpse of a sword hilt barely hidden beneath one cloak.

He all but scampered up the flimsy ramp to the boat, hopped down into it, and threw himself onto the bench at the rear of the passenger gallery. The gallery, fortunately, was only enclosed on three sides; a decent forward view of their next little voyage would be vastly preferable to another trip inside a dark box. Jean was close behind him, but Merrain turned right, climbed through the mass of rowers, and seated herself in the coxswain's position at the bow.

The soldiers on the dock rapidly pulled back the ramp, unlashed the boat, and gave it a good push away from the dock with their legs. "Pull," said Merrain, and the rowers exploded into action. Soon the boat was creaking to their steady rhythm and knifing across the little waves of Tal Verrar's harbor.

Locke took the opportunity to study the men and women at the oars—they were all leanly muscled, all with hair neatly trimmed short, most with fairly visible scars. Not one of them looked to be younger than their midthirties. Veteran soldiers, then. Possibly even Eyes without their masks and cloaks.

"I have to say, Stragos' people put on a good production," said Jean. He then raised his voice. "Hey! Merrain! Can we take these ridiculous clothes off?"

She turned only long enough to nod, and then returned her attention to the waters of the harbor. Locke and Jean eagerly removed their hats and cloaks, and piled the clothing on the deck at their feet.

The ride across the water took about a third of an hour, as near as Locke could tell. He would have preferred to be free to study the harbor in all directions, but what he could see out the open front of the gallery revealed enough. First they headed southwest, following the curve of the inner docks, past the Great Gallery and the Golden Steps. Then they turned south, putting the open sea on their right, and sped toward a huge crescent island of a like size with the one on which the Sinspire sat.

Tal Verrar's southwestern crescent wasn't tiered. It was more like a naturally irregular hillside, studded with a number of stone towers and battlements. The huge stone quays and long wooden docks at its northwestern tip comprised the Silver Marina, where commercial vessels could put in for repairs or refitting. But past that, past the bobbing shapes of old galleons waiting for new masts or sails, lay a series of tall gray walls that formed enclosed bays. The tops of these walls supported round towers where the dark shapes of catapults and patrolling soldiers could be seen. The bow of their boat was soon pointed at the nearest of these huge stone enclosures.

"I'll be damned," said Jean. "I think they're taking us into the Sword Marina."

2

THE VAST stone walls of the artificial bay were gated with wood. As the boat approached, shouts rang out from the battlements above, and the clanking of heavy chains echoed off stone and water. A crack appeared in the middle of the gate, and then the two doors slowly swung inward, sweeping a small wave before them. As the boat passed through the gate, Locke tried to estimate the size of everything he was seeing; the opening itself had to be seventy or eighty feet wide, and the timbers of the doors looked to be as thick as an average man's torso.

Merrain called instructions to the rowers and they brought the boat in carefully, coasting gently up to a small wooden dock where a single man waited to receive them. The rowers had placed the boat at an angle, so that the end of the dock barely scraped the hull of the boat between the rowers and the passenger gallery.

"Your stop, gentlemen," called Merrain. "No time to tie up, I'm afraid. Be nimble or get wet."

"You're the soul of kindness, madam," said Locke. "I've shed any lingering regret about failing to leave a tip for you." He moved out of the gallery and to the gunwale on his right hand. There the stranger waited with one arm held out to assist him. Locke sprang up to the dock easily enough with the man's help, and the two of them in turn yanked Jean to safety.

Merrain's rowers backed water immediately; Locke watched as the gig made sternway, aligned itself with the gate, and then sped back out of the little bay at high speed. Chains rattled once again, and water surged as the gates drew closed. Locke glanced up and saw that teams of men were turning huge capstans, one on either side of the bay doors.

"Welcome," said the man who'd helped them out of the boat. "Welcome to the most foolish damn venture I ever heard of, much less got pressed into. Can't imagine whose wife you must've fucked to get assigned to this here suicide mission, sirs."

The man could have been anywhere between fifty and sixty; he had a chest like a tree stump and a belly that hung over his belt as though he were trying to smuggle a sack of grain beneath his tunic. Yet his arms and neck were almost scrawny in their wiriness, seamed with jutting veins and the scars of hard living. He had a round face, a wooly white beard, and a greasy streak of white hair that fell straight off the back of his head like a waterfall. His dark eyes were nestled in pockets of wrinkles under permanent furrows.

"That might've been a pleasant diversion," said Jean, "if we'd known we were going to end up here anyway. Who might you be?"

"Name's Caldris," said the old man. "Ship's master without a ship. You two must be Masters de Ferra and Kosta."

"Must be," said Locke.

"Let me show you around," said Caldris. "Ain't much to see now, but you'll be seeing a lot of it."

He led the way up a set of rickety stairs at the rear of the dock, which opened onto a stone plaza that rose four or five feet above the water. The entire artificial bay, Locke saw, was a square roughly one hundred yards on a side. Walls enclosed it on three sides, and at the rear rose the steep glass hillside of the island. There were a number of structures built on platforms sticking out from that hillside; storage sheds, armories, and the like, he presumed.

The gleaming expanse of water beside the plaza, now sealed off from the harbor once again by the wooden gates, was large enough to float several ships of war, and Locke was surprised to see that there was only one craft tied up. A one-masted dinghy, barely fourteen feet long, rocked gently at the plaza's side.

"Quite a bay for such a small boat," he said.

"Eh? Well, the ignorant need room in which to risk their lives without bothering anybody else for a while," said Caldris. "This here's our own private pissing-pond. Never you mind the soldiers on the walls; they'll ignore us. Unless we drown. Then they'll probably laugh."

"Just what is it," said Locke, "that you think we're doing here, Caldris?"

"I've got a month or so in which to turn two ignorant straight-legged fumble-thumb landlubbers into something resembling phony sea-officers. All gods as my witness, sirs, I suspect this is all gonna end in screaming and drowning."

"I might have taken offense at that, if I didn't know that every word you just called us was true," said Locke. "We *told* Stragos we didn't know the first damn thing about sailing."

"The Protector seems mighty set on having you out to sea regardless."

"How long have you been in his navy?" asked Jean.

"Been at sea forty-five years, maybe. In the Verrari navy even before there was archons; been in the Thousand-Day War, the old wars against Jerem, the war against the Ghostwinds Armada.... Seen a lot of shit, gentlemen.

Thought I had it sewn up—been master on archons' vessels for twenty years. Good pay. Even got a house coming, or so I thought. Before this shit. No offense."

"None taken," said Locke. "This some sort of punishment detail?"

"Oh, it's punishment, Kosta. It's punishment all right. Just weren't no crime done to earn it. Archon sort of volunteered me. Fuck me, but that's what all my loyalty bought. That and a taste of the archon's wine, so I can't just quit or run away on you. Poisoned wine. The waiting sort of poison. I take you to sea, outlive all this nonsense, I get the antidote. Maybe my house, if I'm lucky."

"The archon gave you poisoned wine?" said Locke.

"Didn't know it was poisoned, obviously. What was I supposed to do," Caldris spat, "not fuckin' drink it?"

"Of course not," said Locke. "We're passengers in the same boat, friend. Except it was cider with us. We had a hell of a thirst."

"Oh, really?" Caldris gaped. "Ha! Fuck me raw! Here I thought I was the biggest damn fool on the Sea of Brass. Here I thought I was the damnedest halfwit of a blind, useless...old...ah..."

He seemed to notice the glare Locke and Jean were giving him in unison, and he coughed loudly.

"Which is to say, sirs, that misery does love company, and I can see that we're all going to be real enthusiastic about this here do-or-die mission."

"Right. So, ah, tell us," said Jean. "Exactly how are we going to get on with this?"

"Well, first I reckon we talk; second I reckon we sail. I got just a few things to say before we tempt the gods, so open your ears. First, it takes five years or so to make a landsman into a halfway decent sailor. Ten to fifteen to make a halfway decent sea-officer. So fuckin' attend this: I ain't making no halfway decent sea-officers of you. I'm making shams. I'm making it so you're not embarrassed to talk rope and canvas around real sailors, and that's about it. Maybe, just maybe, that's what I can do to you in a month. So you can pretend to give orders while taking 'em from me. Taking 'em *good.*"

"Fair enough," said Locke. "The more you handle, the more comfortable we are, honest."

"I just don't want you to decide you're heroes who've learned the full business, so's you start changing sails and trim and courses without my leave. Do that and we're all gonna die, fast as a one-copper fuck in a one-whore cathouse. I hope that's clear."

"Not to get ahead of ourselves," said Jean, "but where the hell is this ship on which we would never, ever dare do anything like that?"

"It's around," said Caldris. "Getting a bit of finishing in another bay, just to help it hold together. For the time being, that there's the only vessel you're fit to board." He pointed at the dinghy. "That's what I'll learn you on."

"What does that little thing have to do with a real ship?"

"That little thing is what *I* learned on, Kosta. That little thing is where any real sea-officer starts. That's how you cop to the basics: hull, wind, and water. Know 'em on a boat and you can think it out on a ship. So, off with your coats and vests and fancy shit. Leave anything you mind getting wet, as I'm making no promises. Boots as well. You'll do this barefoot."

Once Locke and Jean had stripped down to their tunics and breeches, Caldris led them over to a large covered basket that sat on the stones near the docked dinghy. He undid the cover, reached in, and removed a live kitten.

"Hello, you monstrous little necessity."

"Mrrrrwwwwww," said the monstrous little necessity.

"Kosta." Caldris shoved the squirming kitten into Locke's arms. "Look after her for a few minutes."

"Um...why do you keep a kitten in that basket?" The kitten, dissatisfied with Locke's arms, decided to wrap her paws around his neck and experiment on it with her claws.

"When you go to sea, there's two necessities, for luck. First, you're courting an awful fate if you take a ship to sea without at least one woman officer. It's the law of the Lord of the Grasping Waters. His mandate. He's got a fixation for the daughters of the land; he'll smash any ship that puts to sea without at least one aboard. Plus, it's plain common sense. They're good officers. Decent plain sailors, but finer officers than you or I. Just the way the gods made 'em.

"Second, it's powerful bad luck to put out without cats on board. Not only as they kill the rats, but as they're the proudest creatures anywhere, wet or dry. Iono admires the little fuckers. Got a ship with women and cats aboard, you'll have the finest luck you can hope for. Now, our little boat's so small I reckon we're fine without no woman. Fishers and harbor boats go out all the time, no worries. But with the pair of you aboard, I'll be damned if I'm not bringing a cat. A little one suits a little vessel."

"So...we have to tend this kitten while we're out there risking our lives?"

"I'll throw you overboard before I'll lose her, Kosta." Caldris chuckled. "You think I'm lying, you just test me. But keep your breeches on; she'll be in the covered basket."

Speaking of the basket seemed to recall it to his mind. He reached into it again and drew out a small loaf of bread and a silver knife. Locke saw that the loaf had many small marks upon it, about the size of the muzzle of the little creature trying to slip out of his arms. Caldris didn't seem to care.

"Master de Ferra, hold out your right hand and don't whine."

Jean extended his right hand toward Caldris. Without hesitation, the sailing master slashed the knife across Jean's palm. The big man said nothing, and Caldris grunted as though pleasantly surprised. He turned Jean's palm upside down and smeared the bread with the blood trickling from the cut.

"Now you, Master Kosta. Keep that kitten still. Vile luck to cut her by accident. Plus she's armed, fore and aft."

A moment later, Caldris had made a shallow, stinging cut across Locke's right palm and was pressing the loaf of bread up against it as though to stanch the wound. When he seemed to decide that Locke had bled sufficiently, he smiled and moved to the edge of the stone plaza, overlooking the water.

"I know you both been passengers on ships," he said, "but passengers don't signify. Passengers ain't *involved*. Now you're gonna be involved, proper, so I got to make things right for us first."

He cleared his throat, knelt at the edge of the water, and put up his arms. In one hand he held the loaf of bread; in the other, the silver knife. "Iono! Iono Stormbringer! Lord of the Grasping Waters! Your servant Caldris bal Comar calls. Long you been pleased to show your servant mercy, and your servant kneels to show his devotion. Surely you know a mighty fuckin' mess waits over the horizon for him."

He tossed the bloody knife into the bay and said, "This is the blood of landsmen. All blood is water. All blood is yours. This is a knife of silver, metal of the sky, sky that touches water. Your servant gives you blood and silver to show his devotion."

He took the loaf of bread in both hands, tore it in half, and threw both halves into the water. "This is the bread of landsmen, that landsmen need to live! At sea, all life is yours. At sea, yours is the only mercy. Give your servant strong winds and open waters, Lord. Show him mercy in his passage. Show him the might of your will within the waves, and send him safe home again. Hail, Iono! Lord of the Grasping Waters!"

Caldris rose from his knees, groaning, and wiped a few smears of blood on his tunic. "Right. If that can't help, we never had a fuckin' chance."

"Beg pardon," said Jean, "but it seems to me you could have possibly mentioned us along with yourself...."

"Don't think nothing of it, de Ferra. I prosper, you prosper. I cop it, you're screwed. Praying for my health works to your full advantage. Now, put the cat in the basket, Kosta, and let's do some business."

A few minutes later, Caldris had Locke and Jean seated beside one another at the rear of the dinghy, which was still lashed firmly to several iron rings set into the stone of the plaza. The covered basket was sitting on the tiny deck of the dinghy at Locke's feet, occasionally emitting bumping and scratching noises.

"Right," said Caldris. "Far as the basics go, a boat is just a little ship and a ship is just a bigger boat. Hull goes in the water, mast points toward the sky."

"Of course," said Locke, as Jean nodded vigorously.

"The nose of your boat is called the bow, the ass is called the stern. Ain't no right and left at sea. Right is *starboard*, left is *larboard*. Say right or left and you're liable to get whipped. And remember, when you're directing someone else, it's the ship's starboard and larboard you're talking about, not your own."

"Look, little as we know, Caldris, I daresay we know that much," said Locke.

"Well, far be it from me to correct the young master," said Caldris, "but as this venture is somewhat in the way of completely fuckin' mad, and since all our lives are looking mighty cheap, I'm gonna start by presuming that you don't know water from weasel piss. Is that suitable by you, gentlemen?"

Locke opened his mouth to say something ill-advised, but Caldris went on.

"Now, unrack the oars. Slide 'em in the oarlocks. Kosta, you're starboard oar. De Ferra, you're larboard." Caldris unlashed the dinghy from the iron rings, threw the ropes into the bottom of the boat, and hopped down into it, landing just before the mast. He settled down onto his backside and grinned as the boat swayed. "I've locked the rudder tight for now. You two will do all our steering, gods help us.

"De Ferra, push us off from the quay. That's right. Nice and easy. Can't fly sails straight from the dockside; got to get some sea-room first. Plus there's no breeze behind these walls for us to use anyway. Row gently. Pay attention as I move around...look how I'm making us wobble. Don't like that, do you? You're turning green, Kosta."

"Hardly," muttered Locke.

"This is important. What I'm trying to tell you about now is called *trim*. Weight needs to be distributed sensible in a boat or a ship. I move to starboard, we heel over on Kosta's side. I move to larboard, we heel over even worse on de Ferra's side. Can't have that. That's why stowing cargo proper is so important on a ship. Gotta have balance fore and aft, starboard and larboard. Can't have the bow in the air or the stern higher than the mast. Looks silly, then you sink and die. That's basically what I mean when I says 'trim.' Now, time to learn how to row."

"We already know how to—"

"I don't care what you think you know, Kosta. Until further notice, we're gonna presume that you're too dumb to count to one."

Locke would later swear that they must have spent two or three hours rowing around in circles on that artificial bay, with Caldris crying out, "Hard a-larboard! Back water! Hard a-starboard!" and a dozen other commands, seemingly at random. The sailing master constantly shifted his weight, left and right, forward and center, to force them to fight for stability. To make things even more interesting, there was an obvious difference between the power of Jean's strokes and the power of Locke's, and they had to concentrate to avoid constantly turning to starboard. They were at it so long that Locke started in surprise when Caldris finally called for a halt to their labor.

" 'Vast rowing, you fuckin' toddlers." Caldris stretched and yawned. The sun was approaching the center of the sky. Locke's arms felt wrung out, his tunic was soaked through with sweat, and he fervently wished that he'd had less coffee and more actual food for breakfast. "Better than you was two hours ago, I'll give you that. That and not much else. You gotta know your starboard and larboard, fore and aft, boats and oars, like you know the width of your own cocks. Ain't no such thing as a calm or conve- nient emergency out on the blue."

The sailing master produced lunch from a leather sack at the bow of the dinghy, and they floated relaxingly in the middle of the enclosed square bay while they ate. The men shared black bread and hard cheese, while the kitten was let out to make quick work of a pat of butter in a stone crock. The skin that Caldris passed around was full of "pinkwa- ter," warm rainwater mixed with just enough cheap red wine to partly conceal its stale, leathery taste. Caldris took only a few sips, but the two thieves rapidly finished it off.

"So, our ship is waiting for us somewhere around here," said Locke when his thirst was temporarily beaten down, "but where are we going to get a crew?"

"A fine question, Kosta. I wish I knew the answer. The archon said the matter is being attended to, that's all."

"I suspected you'd say something like that."

"No sense in dwelling on what's beyond our power at the moment," said Caldris. The sailing master lifted the kitten, who was still licking her greasy nose and paws, and stuck her back into the basket with surprising tenderness. "So, you've done some rowing. I'll get those men up top to open the gate, take the rudder, and we're gonna head out and see if we can catch enough breeze to hoist some canvas. You two have any money in the things you left ashore?"

"Some," said Locke. "Maybe twenty volani. Why?"

"Then I'll bet you twenty volani that you two are gonna capsize us at least once before the sun goes down."

"I thought you were here to teach us how to do things the right way?"

"I am. And I damn well will! It's just that I know first-time sailors too well. Make the bet and the money's as good as mine. Hell, I'll pay up a full solari against your twenty silvers if I'm wrong."

"I'm in," said Locke. "Jerome?"

"We've got the kitten and a blood blessing on our side," said Jean. "Underestimate us at your peril, sailing master."

3

IT HAD been refreshing, at first, to work for a while in completely soaked tunic and breeches. After they'd righted the dinghy and rescued the kitten, of course.

But now the sun was lowering in the west, casting a golden halo around the dark outlines of the battlements and towers above the Sword Marina, and the gentle harbor breeze had begun to chill Locke despite the lingering heat of the summer air.

He and Jean were rowing the dinghy toward the open gate to their private bay; Caldris had been happy to earn his twenty volani, but not happy enough that he was willing to trust them with the sails again.

"'Vast rowing," said Caldris as they finally drifted near the edge of the stone plaza. Caldris tended to the business of tying them up again while Locke stowed his oar and breathed a deep sigh of relief. Every muscle in his back seemed to slide painfully against those surrounding it, as though someone had thrown grit in between them. He had a headache from the glare of sun on water, and his old wound in his left shoulder was demanding attention above and beyond his other aches.

Locke and Jean clambered stiffly out of the boat and stretched while Caldris, clearly amused, uncovered the basket and plucked the bedraggled kitten out of it. "There, there," he said, allowing it to nestle within his crossed arms. "The young masters didn't mean anything by that soaking they gave you. They got it just as bad."

"Mrrrrrrrreeeeew," it said.

"I fancy that means 'fuck you,'" said Caldris, "But at least we've got our lives. So what do you think, sirs? An educational day?"

"I hope we've shown some aptitude, at least," groaned Locke, kneading a knot in the small of his back.

"Baby steps, Kosta. As far as sailors go, you haven't even learned to suck milk from a tit yet. But now you know starboard from larboard, and I'm twenty volani richer."

"Indeed," sighed Locke as he fetched his coat, vest, neckcloths, and shoes from the ground. He tossed a small leather purse to the sailing master, who dangled it at the kitten and cooed as though to a small child.

Locke happened to glance over at the gate while he was throwing his coat on over his damp tunic, and he saw Merrain's gig slip into the artificial bay. She was seated at the bow again, looking as though they had parted ten minutes rather than ten hours before.

"Your ride back to civilization, gents." Caldris raised Locke's coin purse in a salute. "See you bright and early tomorrow. Only gets worse from here, so mind yourselves. Enjoy those nice beds while they're still available."

Merrain was completely unwilling to answer questions as the team of ten soldiers rowed them back to the docks beneath the Savrola, which suited Locke's mood. He and Jean commiserated over their aches and pains while lounging, as best the space allowed, in the rear gallery.

"I could sleep for about three days, I think," said Locke.

"Let's order a big dinner when we get back, and some baths to take the knots out. After that, I'll race you to unconsciousness."

"Can't," Locke sighed. "Can't. I have to go see Requin tonight. By now, he probably knows Stragos pulled us in again a few nights ago. I need to talk to him before he gets annoyed. And I need to give him the chairs. *And* I need to somehow tell him about all of this, and convince him not to strangle us with our own intestines if we leave for a few months."

"Gods," said Jean. "I've been trying not to think about that. You just barely convinced him that we've been assigned to the Sinspire to go after his vault; what can you say that will make this whole out-to-sea thing plausible?"

"I have no idea." Locke massaged the aching vicinity of his old shoulder wound. "Hopefully the chairs will put him in a forgiving mood. If not, you'll get the bill for cleaning my brains off his plaza stones."

When the rowers finally pulled the boat up alongside the Savrola docks, where a carriage was waiting with several guards, Merrain left the bow and made her way back to where Locke and Jean were sitting.

"Seventh hour of the morning tomorrow," she said, "I'll have a carriage at the Villa Candessa. We'll vary your movement for a few mornings for safety's sake. Stay at your inn this evening."

"Out of the question," said Locke. "I have business on the Golden Steps tonight."

"Cancel it."

"Go to hell. How do you propose to stop me?"

"You might be surprised." Merrain rubbed her temples as though she felt a headache coming on, then sighed. "You're sure you can't cancel it?"

"If I cancel my business tonight, you-know-who at the Sinspire is likely to cancel *us*," said Locke.

"If you're worried about Requin," she said, "I could simply arrange for quarters to be found in the Sword Marina. He'd never be able to reach you there; you'd be safe until your training was finished."

"Jerome and I have sunk two years in this bloody city into our plans for Requin," said Locke. "We intend to finish them. Tonight is critical."

"On your head be it, then. I can send a carriage with some of my men. Can it wait two hours?"

"If that's what it takes, fine." Locke smiled. "In fact, send two. One for me, one for cargo."

"Don't push your—"

"Excuse me," said Locke, "but is the money coming out of *your* pocket? You want to protect me, surround me with your agents, fine—I accept. Just send two carriages. I'll be on my best behavior."

"So be it," she said. "Two hours. No sooner."

4

THE WESTERN horizon had swallowed the sun, and the two moons visible in the cloudless sky were soft red, like silver coins dipped in wine. The driver of the carriage rapped three times on the roof to announce their arrival at the Sinspire, and Locke moved the window curtain back over the corner he'd been peeking out of.

It had taken time for the pair of carriages to thread their way out of the Savrola, across the Great Gallery, and through the bustling traffic of the Golden Steps. Locke had found himself alternately stifling yawns and cursing the bumpy ride. His companion, a slender swordswoman with a well-used rapier resting across her legs, had steadfastly ignored him from her position on the opposite seat.

Now, as the carriage jostled to a halt, she preceded him out the door, tucking her weapon under a long blue coat that hung to her calves. After she'd scanned the warm night for trouble, she beckoned wordlessly for Locke to follow.

As per Locke's instructions, the carriage driver had turned onto the cobbled drive that led to a courtyard behind the Sinspire. Here, a pair of converted stone houses held the tower's primary kitchens and food storage areas. By the light of red and gold lanterns bobbing on unseen lines, Sinspire attendants were coming and going in squads—carrying forth elaborate meals and returning with empty platters. The smell of richly seasoned meat filled the air.

Locke's bodyguard continued to look around, as did the two soldiers atop the carriage, each dressed in nondescript coachman's uniforms. The second carriage, the one carrying Locke's suite of chairs, rattled to a halt behind the first. Its team of gray horses stamped their feet and snorted, as though the scent of the kitchens was not to their taste. A heavyset Sinspire attendant with thinning hair hurried over to Locke and bowed.

"Master Kosta," he said, "apologies, sir, but this is the service courtyard. We simply cannot receive you in the accustomed style here; the front doors are far more suited to—"

"I'm in the right place." Locke put one hand on the attendant's shoulder and slipped five silver volani into the man's vest pocket, letting the coins clink against one another as they slipped from his hand. "Find Selendri, as quickly as you can."

"Find…uh…well…"

"Selendri. She stands out in a crowd. Fetch her now."

"Uh . . . yes, sir. Of course!"

Locke spent the next five minutes pacing in front of his carriage while the swordswoman tried to look casual and keep him within a few steps at the same time. Surely nobody would be foolish enough to try anything, he thought—not with five people at his beck and call, not here in the very heart of Requin's domain. Nonetheless, he was relieved to finally see Selendri step out the service door, wearing a flame-colored evening gown that made the brass of her artificial hand look molten where it reflected orange.

"Kosta," she said. "To what do I owe the distraction?"

"I need to see Requin."

"Ah, but does Requin need to see *you*?"

"Very much," said Locke. "Please. I do need to see him in person. And I'm going to need some of your stronger attendants; I've brought gifts that need careful handling."

"Gifts?"

Locke showed her to the second carriage and opened the door. She spared a quick glance at Locke's bodyguard, then stroked her brass hand with her flesh hand while she pondered the contents of the compartment.

"Are you entirely sure that such obvious bribery is the solution to your problems, Master Kosta?"

"It's not like that, Selendri. It's rather a long story. In fact, he'd be doing me a favor if he'd accept them. He has a tower to decorate. All I have is a rented suite and a storage room."

"Interesting." She closed the door to the second carriage, turned away, and began walking back toward the tower. "I can't wait to hear this. You'll come up with me. Your attendants stay here, of course."

The swordswoman looked as though she might utter a protest, so Locke shook his head firmly and pointed sternly at the first carriage. The glare she returned made him glad that she was bound by orders to protect him.

Once inside the Sinspire, Selendri gave whispered orders to the heavyset attendant, then led Locke through the usual busy crowds, up to the service area on the third floor. Soon enough they were locked away inside the darkness of the climbing closet, slowly rising to the ninth floor. Locke was surprised to feel her actually turn toward him.

"Interesting bodyguard you've found for yourself, Master Kosta. I didn't know you rated an Eye of the Archon."

"Er, neither did I. I suspected, but I didn't know. What makes you so sure?"

"Tattoo on the back of her left hand. A lidless eye in the center of a rose. She's probably not used to going about in common clothes; she should have worn gloves."

"You must have sharp eyes. Eye. Sorry. You know what I mean. I saw it, but I didn't give it much thought."

"Most people aren't familiar with the sigil." She turned away from him once again. "I used to have one just like it on my own left hand."

"I . . . well. That's . . . I had no idea."

"The things you don't know, Master Kosta. The things you simply *do not* know . . ."

Gods damn it, Locke thought. She was trying to unnerve him, returning her own *strat péti* for his effort to engage her sympathy the last time they'd been this close. Did everyone in this damn city have a little game?

"Selendri," he said, trying to sound earnest and a bit hurt, "I have never desired anything more than to be a friend to you."

"As you're a friend to Jerome de Ferra?"

"If you knew what he'd done to me, you'd understand. But as you seem to want to flaunt your secrets, I think I'll just keep a few of my own."

"Please yourself. But you might remember that my opinion of you will ultimately be a great deal more *final* than your opinion of me."

Then the climbing closet creaked to a halt, and she squeezed past him into the light of Requin's office. The master of the Sinspire looked up from his desk as Selendri led Locke across the floor; Requin's optics were tucked into the collar of his black tunic, and he was poring over a large pile of parchment.

"Kosta," he said. "This is timely. I need some explanation from you."

"And you're certainly going to get it," said Locke. Shit, he thought, I hope he hasn't found out about the assassins on the docks. I have too damn much to explain as is. "May I sit?"

"Grab your own chair."

Locke selected one from against the wall and set it down before Requin's desk. He surreptitiously rubbed the sweat of his palms away on his breeches as he sat down. Selendri bent over beside Requin and whispered in his ear at length. He nodded, then stared at Locke.

"You've had some sun," he said.

"Today," said Locke. "Jerome and I were sailing in the harbor."

"Pleasant exercise?"

"Not particularly."

"A pity. But it seems you were on the harbor several nights ago. You were spotted returning from the Mon Magisteria. Why have you waited to bring the events of that visit to my attention?"

"Ah." Locke felt a rush of relief. Perhaps Requin simply didn't know there was any relevant link between Jean, himself, and the two dead assassins. A reminder that Requin wasn't all-knowing was exactly what Locke needed at that moment, and he smiled. "I presumed that if you wanted to know sooner, one of your gangs would have hauled us here for a conversation."

"You should make a little list, Kosta, titled *People It's Safe for Me to Antagonize*. My name will not appear on it."

"Sorry. It wasn't exactly by design; Jerome and I have had a need over the past few days to go from sleeping with the sunrise to rising with it. And the reason for that *does* have something to do with Stragos' plans."

At that moment, a Sinspire attendant appeared at the head of the stairs leading up from the eighth floor. She bowed deeply and cleared her throat.

"Begging your pardon, master and mistress. Mistress ordered Master Kosta's chairs brought up from the court-yard."

"Do so," said Requin. "Selendri mentioned these. What's this, then?"

"I know it's going to look more crass than it really is," said Locke, "but you'd be doing me a favor, quite honestly, by agreeing to take them off my hands."

"Take them off your ... oh my."

A burly Sinspire attendant came up the stairs, carrying one of Locke's chairs before him with obvious caution. Requin rose from his desk and stared.

"Talathri Baroque," he said. "Surely, it's Talathri Baroque ... you, there. Put those in the center of the floor. Yes, good. Dismissed."

Four attendants deposited four chairs in the middle of Requin's floor, and then retreated back down the stairwell, bowing before they left. Requin paid them no heed; he stepped around the desk and was soon examining a chair closely, running a gloved finger over its lacquered surface.

"Reproduction ...," he said slowly. "Beyond any doubt ... but absolutely beautiful." He returned his attention to Locke. "I wasn't aware that you were familiar with the styles I collect."

"I'm not," said Locke. "Never heard of the Talathri Whatever before now. A few months ago, I played cards with a drunk Lashani. His credit was...strained, so I agreed to accept my winnings in goods. I got four expensive chairs. They've been in storage ever since because, honestly, what the hell am I going to do with them? I saw the things you keep up here in your office, and I thought perhaps you might want them. I'm glad they suit. Like I said, you're the one doing me a favor if you take them."

"Astonishing," said Requin. "I've always thought about having a suite of furniture crafted in this style. I love the Last Flowering. This is quite a thing to part with."

"They're wasted on me, Requin. A fancy chair is a fancy chair, as far as I know. Just be careful with them. For some reason, they're shear-crescent wood. Safe enough to sit in, but don't abuse them."

"This is...most unexpected, Master Kosta. I accept. Thank you." Requin returned, with obvious reluctance, to his chair behind his desk. "This doesn't slip you out of your need to deliver on your end of our agreement. Or to continue your explanation." The smile on his face diminished, no longer reaching his eyes.

"Of course not. But, concerning that...look, Stragos has a jar of fire oil up his ass about something. He's sending Jerome and I away for a bit, on business."

"Away?" The guarded courtesy of a moment earlier was gone; the single word was delivered in a flat, dangerous whisper.

Here goes. Crooked Warden, throw your dog a scrap.

"To sea," said Locke. "To the Ghostwinds. Port Prodigal. On an errand."

"Strange. I don't recall moving my vault to Port Prodigal."

"It relates to that." But how? "We're...after something."

Shit. Not nearly good enough. "Someone, actually. Have you ever . . . ah, ever . . ."

"Ever *what?*"

"Ever heard of . . . a man named . . . Calo . . . Callas?"

"No. Why?"

"He's, ah . . . well, the thing is, I feel foolish about this. I thought maybe you'd have heard about him. I don't know if he even exists. He might be nothing more than a tall tale. You're *sure* you don't recall hearing the name before?"

"Certain. Selendri?"

"The name means nothing," she said.

"Who is he supposed to be, then?" Requin folded his gloved hands tightly together.

"He's . . ." What would do it? What would sensibly draw us away from this place if we're here to break the vault? Oh . . . Crooked Warden, of course! ". . . a lockbreaker. Stragos' spies have a file on him. Supposedly, he's the best, or he was, back in his day. An artist with a pick, some sort of mechanical prodigy. Jerome and I are expected to entice him out of retirement so he can apply himself to the problem of your vault."

"What's a man like that doing in Port Prodigal?"

"Hiding, I imagine." Locke felt the corners of his mouth drawing upward and suppressed an old familiar glee; once a Big Lie was let out in the world, it seemed to grow on its own and needed little tending or worry to bend to the situation. "Stragos says that the Artificers have tried to kill him several times. He's their antithesis. If he's real, he's the gods-damned anti-artificer."

"Strange that I've never heard of him," said Requin, "or been asked to find and remove him."

"If you were the Artificers," said Locke, "would you want to spread knowledge of his capabilities to someone in a position to make the best possible use of them?"

"Hmmm."

"Hell." Locke scratched his chin and feigned distracted consideration. "Maybe someone *did* ask you to find him and remove him. Just not by that name, and not with that description of his skills, you know?"

"But why, of all his agents, would you and Jerome—"

"Who else is guaranteed to come back or die trying?"

"The alleged poison. Ah."

"We have two months, maybe less." Locke sighed. "Stragos warned us not to dally. We're not back by then, we get to find out how skilled his personal alchemist is."

"The service of the archon seems a complicated life, Leocanto."

"Fucking tell me about it. I liked him much better when he was just our unknown paymaster." Locke rolled his shoulders and felt some of his sore back muscles protest. "We leave inside the month. That's what the day-sailing is about. We'll slip in with the crew of an independent trader once we've had some training, so we don't stand out as the land-huggers we are. No more late nights gaming for us, until we get back."

"You expect to succeed?"

"No, but one way or another, I'm damn well coming back. Maybe Jerome can even have an 'accident' on the voyage. Anyhow, we'll be storing our wardrobes at the Villa Candessa. And we'll be leaving every centira we currently have on your ledgers right where they are. My money and Jerome's. Hostage against my return, as it were."

"And if you do return," said Selendri, "you might bring back a man who can genuinely aid the archon's design."

"*If* he's there," said Locke, "I'll be bringing him straight back here first. I expect you'll want to have a frank discussion with him about the health benefits of accepting a counteroffer."

"Assuredly," said Requin.

"This Callas," said Locke, letting excitement rise in his

voice, "he could be our key to getting Stragos over the coals. He could be an even *better* turncoat than I am."

"Why, Master Kosta," said Selendri, "I doubt that anyone could be a more enthusiastic turncoat than you."

"You know damn well what I'm enthusiastic about," said Locke. "But that's that. Stragos hasn't told us anything else at the moment. I just wanted to get rid of those damn chairs and let you know we'd be leaving for a while. I assure you, I'll be back. If it's in my power at all, I'll be back."

"Such assurances," mused Requin. "Such earnest assurances."

"If I wanted to cut and run," said Locke, "I would have done it already. Why come tell you all this first?"

"Obvious," said Requin, smiling gently. "If this is a ploy, it could buy you a two-month head start during which I wouldn't think to go looking for you."

"Ah. An excellent point," said Locke. "Except that I'd expect to start dying horribly around then, head start or no."

"So you claim."

"Look. I'm deceiving the archon of Tal Verrar on your behalf. I'm deceiving Jerome gods-damned de Ferra. I need allies if I'm going to get out of this shit. I don't *care* if you two trust me; I *have* to trust you. I am showing you my hand. No bluff. Now, again, you tell me how we proceed."

Requin casually riffled the edges of the parchment pile on his desk, then matched gazes with Locke. "I expect to hear the archon's further plans for you immediately. No delays. Make me wonder where you are again, and I'll have you fetched. With finality."

"Understood." Locke made a show of swallowing and wringing his hands together. "I'm sure we'll be seeing him again before we leave. I'll be here the night after any meeting, no later."

"Good." Requin pointed in the direction of the climbing

closet. "Leave. Find this Calo Callas, if he exists, and bring him to me. But I *don't* want dear Jerome slipping over a rail while you're out at sea. Understand? Until Stragos is in hand, that privilege is mine to deny."

"I . . ."

"No 'accidents' for Master de Ferra. You satisfy that grudge on my sufferance. That's the bargain."

"If you put it that way, understood, of course."

"Stragos has his promised antidote." Requin took up a quill and returned his attention to his parchments. "I want my own assurance of your enthusiastic return to my fair city. You want to slaughter your calf, you tend him for a few months first. Tend him *very well.*"

"Of . . . of course."

"Selendri will show you out."

5

"HONESTLY, IT could have gone much worse," said Jean as he and Locke pulled at their oars the next morning. They were out in the main harbor, clipping over the gentle swells near the Merchants' Crescent. The sun had not yet reached its noon height, but the day was already hotter than its predecessor. The two thieves were sweat-drenched.

"Sudden miserable death is indeed much worse," said Locke. He stifled a groan; today, the exercise was troubling not only his back and shoulder but the old wounds that covered a substantial portion of his left arm. "But I think that's the last dregs of Requin's patience. Any more strangeness or complication . . . Well, hopefully, this is as odd as Stragos' plans are going to get."

"Can't move the boat by flapping your mouths," yelled Caldris.

"Unless you want to chain us to these oars and beat a drum," said Locke, "we converse as we please. And unless you wish us to drop dead, you should consider an early lunch."

"Oh dear! Does the splendid young gentleman not find the working life agreeable?" Caldris was sitting in the bow with his legs stretched out toward the mast. On his stomach, the kitten was curled into a dark ball of sleeping contentment. "The first mate here wants me to remind you that where we're going, the sea don't wait on your pleasure. You might be up twenty hours straight. You might be up *forty*. You might be on deck. You might be working a pump. Time comes to do what's necessary, you'll fucking well do it, and you'll do it until you drop. So we're gonna row, every day, until your expectations are right where they should be. And today we're gonna take a late lunch, not an early one. Hard a-larboard!"

6

"EXCELLENT WORK, Master Kosta. Fascinating and bloody unorthodox. By your reckoning, we're somewhere near the latitudes of the Kingdom of the Seven Marrows. A touch on the warm side for Vintila, don't you think?"

Locke slipped the backstaff, a four-foot pole with an awkward arrangement of vanes and calipers on the forward end, off his shoulder and sighed.

"Can you not see the sun-shadow on your horizon vane?"

"Yes, but—"

"I admit, the device ain't exactly as precise as an arrow-shot. But even a land-sucker should be able to do better than that. Do it again, just like I showed you. Horizon and sun-shadow. And be grateful you're using a Verrari Quadrant; the old cross-staffs made you look right at the sun instead of away from it."

"Beg pardon," said Jean, "but I'd always heard this device referred to as a Camorri Quadrant."

"Bullshit," said Caldris. "This here's a Verrari Quadrant. Verrari invented it, twenty years back."

"That claim," said Locke, "must take some of the sting out of getting the shit walloped out of you in the Thousand-Day War, eh?"

"You sweet on Camorri, Kosta?" Caldris put a hand on the backstaff. Locke realized with a start that his anger wasn't bantering. "I thought you was Talishani. You got a reason to fuckin' speak up for Camorr?"

"No, I was just—"

"Just what, now?"

"Forgive me." Locke realized his mistake. "I didn't think. It's not just history to you, is it?"

"All thousand days and then some," said Caldris. "I was there all the fuckin' way."

"My apologies. I suppose you lost friends."

"You damn well suppose right." Caldris snorted. "Lost a ship from under me. Lucky not to be devilfish food. Bad times." He removed his hand from Locke's backstaff and composed himself. "I know you didn't mean anything, Kosta. I'm ... sorry, too. Those of us who bled in that fight didn't exactly think we was losing it when the Priori gave in. Partly why we had such hopes for the first archon."

"Leocanto and I have no reason to love Camorr," said Jean.

"Good." Caldris clapped Locke on the back and seemed to relax. "Good. Keep it that way, eh? Now! We're lost at sea, Master Kosta! Find our latitude!"

It was the fourth day of their training with the Verrari sailing master; after their customary morning of torture at the oars, Caldris had led them out to the seaward side of the Silver Marina. Perhaps five hundred yards out from the glass island, still within the sweep of calmed sea provided by the city's encircling reefs, there was a flat-topped stone platform in forty or fifty feet of translucent blue-green water. Caldris had called it the Lubber's Castle; it was a training platform for would-be Verrari naval and merchant sailors.

Their dinghy was lashed to the side of the platform, which was perhaps thirty feet on a side. Spread across the stones at their feet were an array of navigational devices: backstaffs, cross-staffs, hourglasses, charts and compasses, a Determiner's Box, and a set of unfathomable peg-boards that Caldris claimed were used for tracking course changes. The kitten was sleeping on an astrolabe, covering up the symbols etched into its brass surface.

"Friend Jerome was tolerably good at this," said Caldris. "But he's not to be the captain; you are."

"And I thought *you* were to handle all the important tasks, on pain of gruesome death, as you've only mentioned ten score times."

"I am. You're mad if you think that's changed. But I need you to understand just enough not to gawk with your thumb up your ass when I say this or do that. Just know which end to hold, and be able to read a latitude that doesn't put us off by half the fucking world."

"Sun-shadow and horizon," muttered Locke.

"Indeed. Later on tonight, we'll use the old-style staff for the only thing it's still good for—taking your reading from the stars."

"But it's just past noon!"

"Right," said Caldris. "We're in for a good long haul today. There's books and charts and maths to do, and more sailing and rowing, then more books and charts. Late to bed, you'll be. Better get comfortable with this here Lubber's Castle." Caldris spat on the stones. "Now fetch that fucking latitude!"

7

"WHAT'S IT mean if we broach?" said Jean.

It was late in the evening of their ninth day with Caldris, and Jean was soaking in a huge brass tub. Despite the warmth of their enclosed chambers at the Villa Candessa, he'd demanded hot water, and it was still sending up wisps of curling steam after three-quarters of an hour. On a little table beside the tub was an open bottle of Austershalin brandy (the 554, the cheapest readily available) and both of the Wicked Sisters.

The shutters and curtains of the suite's windows were all drawn tight, the door was bolted, and Locke had wedged a chair up beneath its handle. That might provide a few seconds' additional warning if someone tried to enter by force. Locke lay on his bed, letting two glasses of brandy loosen the knots in his muscles. His knives were set out on the nightstand, not three feet from his hands.

"Ah, gods," he said. "I know this. It's . . . something . . . bad?"

"To meet strong winds and seas abeam," said Jean, "taking them on the side, rather than cutting through them with the bow."

"And that's bad."

"Powerful bad." Jean was paging through a tattered copy of Indrovo Lencallis' *Wise Mariner's Practical Lexicon, with Numerous Enlightening Examples from Honest History.* "Come on, you're the captain of the ship. I'm just your skull-cracker."

"I know. Give me another." Locke's own copy of the book was currently resting underneath his knives and his glass of brandy.

"Hmmm." Jean flipped pages. "Caldris says to put us on a beam reach. What the hell's he talking about?"

"Wind coming in perpendicular to the keel," muttered Locke. "Hitting us straight on the side."

"And now he wants a broad reach."

"Right." Locke paused to sip his brandy. "Wind neither blowing right up our ass nor straight on the side. Coming from one of the rear quarters, at forty-five degrees or so to the keel."

"Good enough." Jean flipped pages again. "Box the compass. What's the sixth point?"

"Hard east. Gods, this is just like dinner with Chains back home."

"Right on both counts. South a point."

"Um, east by south."

"Right. South another point."

"Southeast east?"

"And another point."

"Ah, gods." Locke grabbed his glass and downed the rest of his brandy in one gulp. "Southeast by go-fuck-yourself. That's enough for tonight."

"But—"

"I am the captain of the bloody ship," said Locke, rolling over onto his stomach. "My orders are to drink your brandy and go to bed." He reached out, pulled a pillow completely over his head, and was fast asleep in moments. Even in his dreams he was tying knots, bracing sails, and finding latitudes.

8

"I WAS not aware," said Locke the next morning, "that I had joined your navy. I thought the whole idea was to run away from it."

"A means to an end, Master Kosta."

The archon had been waiting for them in their private bay within the Sword Marina. One of his personal boats (Locke remembered it from the glass caverns beneath the Mon Magisteria) was tied up behind their dinghy. Merrain and half a dozen Eyes had been in attendance. Now Merrain was helping Locke try on the uniform of a Verrari naval officer.

The tunic and breeches were the same dark blue as the doublets of the Eyes. The coat, however, was brownish red, with stiff black leather sewn along the forearms in approximation of bracers. The single neck-cloth was dark blue, and gleaming brass devices in the shape of roses over crossed swords were pinned to his upper arms just below the shoulders.

"I don't have many fair-haired officers in my service," said Stragos, "but the uniform is a good fit. I'll have another made by the end of the week." Stragos reached out and adjusted some of Locke's details—tightening his neck-cloth, shifting the hang of the empty scabbard at his belt. "After that, you'll wear it for a few hours each day. Get used to it. One of my Eyes will instruct you in how to carry yourself, and the courtesies and salutes we use."

"I still don't understand why—"

"I know." Stragos turned to Caldris, who, in his master's presence, had lost his customary vulgar impishness. "How are they doing in their training, sailing master?"

"The Protector is already well aware," said Caldris slowly, "of my general opinion concerning this here mission."

"That's not what I asked."

"They are ... less hopeless than they were, Protector. Somewhat less hopeless."

"That will do, then. You still have nearly three weeks to mold them. I daresay they already look better acquainted with hard work under the sun."

"Where's our ship, Stragos?" asked Locke.

"Waiting."

"And where's our crew?"

"In hand."

"And why the hell am I wearing this uniform?"

"Because it pleases me to make you a captain in my navy. That's what's meant by the twin roses-over-swords. You'll be a captain for one night only. Learn to look comfortable in the uniform. Then learn to be patient waiting for your orders."

Locke scowled, then placed his right hand on his scabbard and crossed his left arm, with a clenched fist, across his chest. He bowed from the waist at the precise angle he'd seen Stragos' Eyes use on several occasions. "Gods defend the archon of Tal Verrar."

"Very good," said Stragos. "But you're an officer, not a common soldier or sailor. You bow at a shallower angle."

He turned and walked toward his boat. The Eyes formed ranks and marched after him, and Merrain began pulling the uniform hurriedly off Locke.

"I return you gentlemen to Caldris' care," said the archon as he stepped down into the boat. "Use your days well."

"And just when in the name of the gods do we get to learn how this all fits together?"

"All in good time, Kosta."

9

TWO MORNINGS later, when the gates swung wide to admit Merrain's boat to the private bay in the Sword Marina, Locke and Jean were surprised to discover that their dinghy had been joined during the night by an actual ship.

A soft warm rain was falling, not a proper squall from the Sea of Brass but an annoyance blowing in from the mainland. Caldris waited on the stone plaza in a light oilcloak, with rivulets of water streaming from his unprotected hair and beard. He grinned when the boat delivered Locke and Jean, lightly clad and bootless.

"Look you both," Caldris yelled. "Here she is in person. The ship we're damn likely to die on!" He clapped Locke on the back and laughed. "She's styled the *Red Messenger*."

"Is she now?" The vessel was quiet and still, sails furled, lamps unlit. There was something unfathomably melancholy about a ship in such a condition, Locke thought. "One of the archon's, I presume?"

"No. It seems the gods have favored the Protector with a chance to be bloody economical with this mission. You know what stiletto wasps are?"

"Only too well."

"Some idiot tried to put into port with a hive in his hold, not too long ago. Gods know what he was planning with it. That got him executed, and the ship was ruled droits of the archonate. That nest of little monsters got burned."

"Oh," said Locke, sniggering. "I'm very sure it was. Thorough and incorruptible, the fine customs officers of Tal Verrar."

"Archon had it careened," continued Caldris. "Needed new sails, some shoring up, fresh lines, bit of caulking. All the insides got smoked with brimstone, and she's been renamed and rechristened. Still plenty cheap, compared to offering up one of his own."

"How old is she?"

"Twenty years, near as I can tell. Hard years, likely, but she'll hold for a few more. Assuming we bring her back. Now show me what you've learned. What do you think she is?"

Locke studied the vessel, which had two masts, a very slightly raised stern deck, and a single boat stored upside down at its waist. "Is she a *caulotte*?"

"No," said Caldris, "she's more properly a *vestrel*, what you'd also call a brig, a very wee one. I can see why you'd say *caulotte*. But let me tell you why you're off on the particulars. . . ."

Caldris launched into a number of highly technical explanations, pointing out things about leeward main braces and cross-jacks that Locke only half understood in the manner of a visitor to a foreign city listening to eager directions from a fast native talker.

"... she's eighty-eight feet, stem to stern, not counting the bowsprit, of course," finished Caldris.

"I hadn't truly realized before now," said Locke. "Gods, I'm to actually command this ship."

"Ha! No. You are to *feign* command of this ship. Don't get blurry-eyed on me, now. All you do is tell the crew what *my* proper orders are. Hurry aboard."

Caldris led them up a ramp and onto the deck of the *Red Messenger,* and while Locke gazed around, absorbed in every visible detail, a gnawing unease was growing in his stomach. He'd taken all the minutiae of shipboard life for granted on his single previous (and bedridden) voyage, but now every knot and ring-bolt, every block and tackle, every shroud and line and pin and mechanism might hold the key to saving his life . . . or foiling his impersonation utterly.

"Damn," he muttered to Jean. "Maybe ten years ago, I might have been dumb enough to think this was going to be easy."

"It's not getting any easier," said Jean, squeezing Locke on his uninjured shoulder. "But we're not yet out of time to learn."

They paced the full length of the ship in the warm drizzle, with Caldris alternately pointing things out and demanding answers to difficult questions. They finished their tour at the *Red Messenger*'s waist, and Caldris leaned back against the ship's boat to rest.

"Well," he said, "you do learn fast, for lubbers. I can give you that much. Notwithstanding, I've taken shits with more sea wisdom than the pair of you combined."

"Come ashore and let us try to teach you *our* profession some time, goat-face."

"Ha! Master de Ferra, you'll fit in just fine in that wise. Maybe you'll never truly know shit from staysails, but you've got the manner of a grand first mate. Now, up the ropes. We're visiting the maintop this morning while this fine weather holds."

"The maintop?" Locke stared up the mainmast, dwindling into the grayness above, and squinted as rain fell directly into his face. "It's bloody raining!"

"It has been known to rain at sea. Ain't nobody passed you the word?" Caldris stepped over to the starboard main shrouds; they passed down just the opposite side of the deck railing, and were secured by deadeyes to the outer hull itself. Grunting, the sailing master hoisted himself up onto the rail and beckoned for Locke and Jean to follow. "The poor bastards on your crew will be up there in all weather. I'm not taking you out to sea as virgins to the ropes, so get your asses up after me!"

They followed Caldris up into the rain, carefully stepping into the ratlines that crossed the shrouds to provide footholds. Locke had to admit that nearly two weeks of steady hard exercise had given him more wind for a task like this, and begun to mitigate the pain of his old wounds. Still, the strange and faintly yielding sensation of the rope ladder was like nothing familiar to him, and he was only too happy when a dark yardarm loomed out of the drizzle just above them. A few moments later, he scampered up to join Jean and Caldris on a circular platform that was blessedly firm.

"We're two-thirds up, maybe," said Caldris. "This yard carries the main course." Locke knew by now that he was referring to the ship's primary square sail, not a navigational plan. "Farther up, you got your topsails and t'gallants. But this is fine enough for now. Gods, you think you got it bad today, can you imagine climbing up here with the ship bucking side to side like a bull making babies? Ha!"

"Can't be as bad," Jean whispered to Locke, "as some fucking idiot toppling off and landing on one of us."

"Will I be expected," said Locke, "to come up here frequently?"

"You got unusually sharp eyes?"

"I don't think so."

"Hell with it, then. Nobody'll expect it. Captain's place is on deck. You want to see things from a distance, use a glass. You'll have top-eyes hugging the mast farther up to do your spotting."

They took in the view for a few more minutes, and then thunder rumbled in the near distance, and the rain stiffened.

"Down we go, I think." Caldris rose to his knees and prepared to slide over the side. "There's tempting the gods, and then there's tempting the gods."

Locke and Jean reached the deck again with no trouble, but when Caldris jumped down from the shrouds he was breathing raggedly. He groaned and massaged his upper left arm. "Damn. I'm too old for the tops. Thank the gods the master's place is on the decks, too." Thunder punctuated his words. "Come on, then. We'll use the main cabin. No sailing today; just books and charts. I know how much you love those."

10

BY THE end of their third week with Caldris, Locke and Jean had begun to nurture guarded hopes that their brush with the two dockside assassins would not be repeated. Merrain continued to escort them each morning, but they were given some freedom at night provided they went armed and ventured no farther than the interior waterfront of the Arsenale District. The taverns there were thick with the archon's soldiers and sailors, and it would be a difficult place for someone to lurk unnoticed in ambush.

At the tenth hour of the evening on Duke's Day (which of course, Jean corrected himself, the Verrari called Council's Day), Jean found Locke staring down a bottle of fortified wine at a back table in the Sign of the Thousand Days. The place was spacious and cheerfully lit, noisy with the bustle of healthy business. It was a naval bar—all the best tables, under hanging reproductions of old Verrari battle pennants, were filled with officers whose social status was clear whether or not they were wearing their colors. Common sailors drank and gamed at the penumbra of tables surrounding them, and the few outsiders congregated at the little tables around Locke.

"I thought I might find you here," said Jean, taking the seat across from Locke. "What do you think you're doing?"

"I'm working. Isn't it obvious?" Locke seized the wine bottle by its neck and gestured toward Jean. "This is my hammer." He then rapped his knuckles against the wooden tabletop. "And this is my anvil. I am beating my brains into a more pleasant shape."

"What's the occasion?"

"I just wanted half a night to be something other than the captain of a phantom fucking sailing expedition." He spoke in a controlled whisper, and it was plain to Jean that he was not yet drunk, but more possessed of an earnest desire to be so. "My head is full of little ships, all going round and round gleefully making up new names for the things on their decks!" He paused to take a sip, then offered the bottle to Jean, who shook his head. "I suppose you've been diligently studying your *Lexicon*."

"Partly." Jean turned himself and his chair a bit toward the wall, to allow him to keep an unobtrusive eye on most of the tavern. "I've also penned some polite little lies to

Durenna and Corvaleur; they've been sending notes to the Villa Candessa, asking when we'll come back to the gaming tables so they can have another go at butchering us."

"I do so hate to disappoint the ladies," said Locke, "but tonight I'm on leave from everything. No 'Spire, no archon, no Durenna, no *Lexicon,* no navigational tables. Just simple arithmetic. Drink plus drinker equals drunk. Join me. Just for an hour or two. You know you could use it."

"I do. But Caldris grows more demanding with every passing day; I fear we'll need clear heads on the morrow more than we'll need clouded ones tonight."

"Caldris' lessons aren't clearing our heads. Quite the opposite. We're taking five years of teaching in a month. It's all jumbling up inside me. You know, before I stepped in here tonight I bought half a peppered melon. The stall woman asked which of her melons I wished cut, the one on the left or the right. I replied, 'The larboard!' My own throat has turned traitorously nautical on me."

"It is something like a madman's private language, isn't it?" Jean slipped his optics out of his coat pocket and onto the end of his nose so he could examine the faint etching on Locke's wine bottle. An indifferent Anscalani vintage, a blunt instrument among wines. "So intricate in its convolutions. Say you have a rope lying on the deck. On Penance Day it's just a rope lying on the deck; after the third hour of the afternoon on Idler's Day it's a half-stroke babble-gibbet, and then at midnight on Throne's Day it becomes a rope again, unless it's raining."

"Unless it's raining, yes, in which case you take your clothes off and dance naked round the mizzenmast. Gods, yes. I swear, Je…Jerome, the next person who tells me something like, 'Squiggle-fuck the rightwise cock-swatter with a starboard jib' is going to get a knife in the throat. Even if it's Caldris. No more nautical terms tonight."

"You seem to be three sheets to the wind."

"Oh, that's your death warrant signed, then, four-eyes." Locke peered down into the depths of his bottle, like a hawk eyeing a mouse in a field far below. "There's altogether too much of this stuff not yet in me. Get a glass and join in. I want to be a barking public embarrassment as soon as possible."

There was a commotion at the door, followed by a general stilling of conversation and a rise in murmuring that Jean recognized from long experience as very, very dangerous. He looked up warily and saw that a party of half a dozen men had just set foot inside the tavern. Two of them wore the partial uniforms of constables, under cloaks, without their usual armor or weapons. Their companions were dressed in plain clothing, but their bulk and manner told Jean that they were all prime examples of that creature commonly known as the city watchman.

One of them, either fearless or possessed of the sensibilities of a dull stone, stepped up to the bar and called for service. His companions, wiser and therefore more nervous, began to whisper back and forth. Every eye in the tavern was upon them.

There was a scraping sound as a tough-looking woman at one of the officers' tables pushed her chair back and slowly stood up. Within seconds, all of her companions, uniformed or otherwise, were standing beside her. The motion spread across the bar in a wave; first the other officers, and then the common sailors, once they saw that the weight of numbers would be eight-to-one in their favor. Soon enough, four dozen men and women were on their feet, saying nothing, simply staring at the six men by the door. The tiny knot of folk around Locke and Jean stayed planted in their seats; at the very least, if they remained where they were, they would be far out of the main line of trouble.

"Sirs," said the oldest barkeeper on duty as his two

younger associates reached surreptitiously beneath the counter for what had to be weapons. "You've come a long way now, haven't you?"

"What do you mean?" If the constable at the bar wasn't feigning puzzlement, thought Jean, he was dimmer than a snuffed candle. "Came from the Golden Steps, is all. Fresh off duty. Got a thirst and a fair bit of coin to fill it."

"Perhaps," said the barkeep, "another tavern would be more to your taste this evening."

"What?" The man seemed at last to become aware of the fact that he was the focal point of a waiting mob's attention. As always, thought Jean, there were two sorts in a city watch—the ones that had eyes for trouble in the backs of their heads, and the ones that used their skulls to store sawdust.

"I said...," the barkeep began, clearly losing patience.

"Hold," said the constable. He put both hands up toward the patrons of the tavern. "I see what's what. I already had a few tonight. You got to forgive me; I don't mean nothing. Aren't we all Verrari here? We just want a drink, is all."

"Lots of places have drinks," said the barkeep. "Lots of more suitable places."

"We don't want no trouble for anyone."

"Wouldn't be any trouble for *us*," said a burly man in naval tunic and breeches. His table-mates shared an evil chuckle. "Find the fucking door."

"Council dogs," muttered another officer. "Oathless gold-sniffers."

"Hold on," said the constable, shaking off the grasp of a friend who was trying to pull him to the door. "Hold on, I said we didn't mean nothing. Dammit, I meant it! Peace. We'll be on our way. Have a round on me, all of you. Everyone!" He shook out his purse with trembling hands. Copper and silver coins rattled onto the wooden bar.

"Barkeep, a round of good Verrari dark for anyone who wants it, and keep what's left."

The barkeeper flicked his gaze from the unfortunate constable to the burly naval officer who'd spoken earlier. Jean guessed the man was one of the senior officers present, and the barkeep was looking to him for a judgment.

"Groveling suits you," the officer said with a crooked grin. "We won't touch a drink with you, but we'll be happy to spend your money once you're out that door for good."

"Of course. Peace, friends, we didn't mean nothing." The man looked as though he might babble on, but two of his comrades grabbed him by the arms and dragged him out the door. There was a general outburst of laughter and applause when the last of the constables had vanished into the night.

"Now that's how the navy adds money to its budget," yelled the burly officer. His table-mates laughed, and he grabbed his glass and held it up toward the rest of the tavern. "The archon! Confusion to his enemies at home and abroad."

"The archon," chorused the other officers and sailors. Soon enough, they were all settling down into good humor once again, and the eldest barkeep was counting the constable's money while his assistants set out rows of wooden cups beside a tapped cask of dark ale. Jean frowned, calculating in his head. Drinks for roughly fifty people, even plain dark ale, would set the constable back at least a quarter of his monthly pay. He'd known many men who'd have chanced a chase and a beating before parting with that much hard-earned coin.

"Poor drunk idiot," he sighed, glancing at Locke. "Still want to make yourself a barking public embarrassment? Seems they've already got one in these parts."

"Maybe I'll just hold fast after this bottle," said Locke.

"Hold fast is a nautical—"

"I know," said Locke. "I'll kill myself later."

The two younger barkeeps circulated with large trays, passing out wooden cups of dark ale, first to the officers, who seemed mostly indifferent, and then to the ordinary sailors, who received them with enthusiasm. Seemingly as an afterthought, one of them eventually made his way to the corner where Locke and Jean and the other civilians sat.

"Sip of the dark stuff, sirs?" He set cups down before Locke and Jean and, with dexterity approaching that of a juggler, dashed salt into them from a little glass shaker. "Courtesy of the man with more gold than brains." Jean slid a copper onto his tray to be sociable, and the man nodded his appreciation before moving on to the next table. "Sip of the dark stuff, madam?"

"Clearly, we need to come here more often," said Locke, though neither he nor Jean touched their windfall ale. Locke, it seemed, was content to drink his wine, and Jean, consumed by thoughts of what Caldris might challenge them with the next day, felt no urge to drink at all. They passed a few minutes in quiet conversation, until Locke finally stared down at his cup of ale and sighed.

"Salted dark ale just isn't the thing to follow punched-up wine," he mused aloud. A moment later, Jean saw the woman seated behind him turn and tap him on the shoulder.

"Did I hear you right, sir?" She looked to be a few years younger than Locke and Jean, vaguely pretty, with bright scarlet forearm tattoos and a deep suntan that marked her as a dockworker of some sort. "Salted dark not to your taste? I don't mean to be bold, but I've just run dry over here...."

"Oh. Oh!" Locke turned, smiling, and passed his cup of ale to her over his shoulder. "By all means, help yourself. My compliments."

"Mine as well," said Jean, passing it over. "It deserves to be appreciated."

"It will be. Thank you kindly, sirs."

Locke and Jean settled back into their conference of whispers.

"A week," said Locke. "Maybe two, and then Stragos wants us gone. No more theoretical madness. We'll be living it, out there on the gods-damned ocean."

"All the more reason I'm glad you've decided not to get too bent around the bottle this evening."

"A little self-pity goes a long way these days," said Locke. "And brings back memories of a time I'd rather forget."

"There's no need for you to keep apologizing for . . . that. Not to yourself and certainly not to me."

"Really?" Locke ran one finger up and down the side of the half-empty bottle. "Seems I can see a different story in your eyes, whenever I make the acquaintance of more than a glass or two. Outside a Carousel Hazard table, of course."

"Now, hold on—"

"It wasn't meant as an unkindness," Locke said hurriedly. "It's just the truth, is all. And I can't say you're wrong to feel that way. You . . . What is it?"

Jean had looked up, distracted by a wheezing sound that was rising behind Locke. The dockworker had half risen out of her chair, and was clutching at her throat, fighting for breath. Jean immediately stood up, stepped around Locke, and took her by the shoulders.

"Easy, madam, easy. A little too much salt in the ale, eh?" He spun her around and gave her several firm slaps on the back with the heel of his right hand. To his alarm, she continued choking—in fact, she was sucking in absolutely nothing now with each futile attempt at a breath. She turned and clutched at him with desperate strength; her eyes were wide with terror, and the redness of her face had nothing to do with her suntan.

Jean glanced down at the three empty ale cups on the table before her, and a sudden realization settled in his gut like a cold weight. He grabbed Locke with his left hand and all but heaved him out of his chair.

"Back against the wall," he hissed. "Guard yourself!" Then he raised his voice and shouted across the tavern, "Help! This woman needs help!"

There was a general tumult; officers and sailors alike came to their feet, straining to see what was happening. Elbowing through the mass of patrons and suddenly empty chairs came an older woman in a black coat, with her stormcloud-colored hair drawn into a long tight tail with silver rings. "Move! I'm a ship's leech!"

She seized the dockworker from Jean's arms and gave her three sharp blows against her back, using the bottom edge of her clenched fist.

"Already tried," cried Jean. The choking woman was flailing against him and the leech alike, shoving at them as though they were the cause of her troubles. Her cheeks were wine-purple. The leech managed to snake a hand around the dockworker's neck and clutch at her windpipe.

"Dear gods," the woman said, "her throat's swelled up hard as a stone. Hold her to the table. Hold her down with all your strength!"

Jean shoved the dockworker down on her tabletop, scattering the empty ale cups. A crowd was forming around them; Locke was looking at it uneasily, with his back to the wall as Jean had insisted. Looking frantically around, Jean could see the older barkeeper, and one of his assistants . . . but one was missing. Where the hell was the one who'd served them those cups of ale?

"Knife," the leech shouted at the crowd. "Sharp knife! Now!"

Locke conjured a stiletto out of his left sleeve and passed it over. The leech glanced at it and nodded—one edge was visibly dull, but the other, as Jean knew, was like a scalpel. The leech held it in a fencer's grip and used her other hand to force the dockworker's head back sharply.

"Press her down with everything you've got," she said to Jean. Even with the full advantage of leverage and mass, Jean was hard-put to keep the thrashing young woman's upper arms still. The leech leaned sharply against one of her legs, and a quick-witted sailor stepped up behind her to grab the other. "A thrash will kill her."

As Jean watched in horrified fascination, the leech pressed the stiletto down on the woman's throat. The dockworker's corded neck muscles stood out like those of a stone statue, and her windpipe looked as prominent as a tree trunk. With gentleness that Jean found awe-inspiring, given the situation, the leech cut a delicate slice across the windpipe just above the point where it vanished beneath the woman's collarbones. Bright red blood bubbled from the cut, then ran in wide streams down the sides of the woman's neck. Her eyes were rolling back in her head, and her struggles had become alarmingly faint.

"Parchment," the leech shouted, "find me parchment!"

To the barkeeper's consternation, several sailors immediately began ransacking the bar, looking for anything resembling parchment. Another officer shoved her way through the crowd, plucking a letter from within her coat. The leech snatched it, rolled it into a tight, thin tube, and then shoved it down the slit in the dockworker's throat, past the bubbling blood. Jean was only partially aware that his jaw was hanging open.

The leech then began pounding on the dockworker's chest, muttering a series of ear-scalding oaths. But the dockworker was limp; her face was a ghastly shade of plum, and the only movement visible was that of the blood streaming out around the parchment tube. The leech ceased her struggles after a few moments and sat down against the edge of Locke and Jean's tables, gasping. She wiped her bloody hands against the front of her coat.

"Useless," she said to the utterly silent crowd. "Her warm humors are totally stifled. I can do nothing else."

"Why, you've killed her," shouted the eldest barkeeper. "You cut her fucking throat right where we could all see it!"

"Her jaw and throat are clenched tight as iron," said the leech, rising in anger. "I did the only thing I possibly could to help her!"

"But you cut her—"

The burly senior officer Jean had seen earlier now stepped up to the bar, with a cadre of fellow officers at his back. Even across the room, Jean could see a rose-over-swords somewhere on every coat or tunic.

"Jevaun," he said, "are you questioning Scholar Almaldi's competence?"

"No, but you saw—"

"Are you questioning her *intentions*?"

"Ah, sir, please—"

"Are you naming a physiker of the archon's warrant," the officer continued in a merciless voice, "our sister-officer, a murderer? Before witnesses?"

The color drained from the barkeeper's face so quickly Jean almost wanted to look behind the bar, to see if it had pooled there. "No, sir," he said with great haste. "I say nothing of the sort. I apologize."

"Not to me."

The barkeeper turned to Almaldi and cleared his throat. "I beg your absolute pardon, Scholar." He looked down at his feet. "I'm...I've not seen much blood. I spoke in wretched ignorance. Forgive me."

"Of course," said the leech coldly as she shrugged out of her coat, perhaps finally realizing how badly she'd bloodied it. "What the hell was this woman drinking?"

"Just the dark ale," said Jean. "The salted Verrari dark."

And it was meant for us, he thought. His stomach twisted.

His words caused a new eruption of anger throughout the crowd, most of whom had, of course, been recently drinking the very same ale. Jevaun put up his arms and waved for silence.

"It was good, clean ale from the cask! It was tasted before it was drawn and served! I would serve it to my grandchildren!" He took an empty wooden cup, held it up to the crowd, and drew a full draught of dark beer from the cask. "This I *will* declare to witnesses! This is a house of honest quality! If there is some mischief afoot, it was nothing of my doing!" He drained the cup in several deep gulps and held it up to the crowd. Their murmuring continued, but their angry advance on the bar was halted.

"It's possible she had a reaction," said Almaldi. "An allergy of some sort. If so, it would be the first I've ever seen of anything like it." She raised her voice. "Who else feels poorly? Sore necks? Trouble breathing?"

Sailors and officers looked at one another, shaking their heads. Jean offered a silent prayer of thanks that nobody seemed to have seen the dockworker taking the fatal cups of ale from himself and Locke.

"Where the hell is your other assistant?" Jean shouted to Jevaun. "I counted two before the ale was served. Now you have only one!"

The eldest barkeeper whipped his head from side to side, scanning the crowd. He turned to his remaining assistant with a horrified look on his face. "I'm sure Freyald is just scared shitless by the commotion, right? Find him. Find him!"

Jean's words had had precisely the effect he'd desired; sailors and officers alike scattered angrily, looking for the missing barkeeper. Jean could hear the muffled trilling of watch whistles somewhere outside. Soon enough constables would be here in force, sailors' bar or no. He nudged Locke and gestured at the back door of the tavern, through which several others, plainly expecting much complication, had already slipped out.

"Sirs," said Scholar Almaldi as Locke and Jean moved past her. She wiped Locke's stiletto clean on the sleeve of her already-ruined coat and passed it back to him. He nodded as he took it.

"Scholar," he said, "you were superb."

"And yet completely inadequate," she said, running her bloodstained fingers carelessly through her hair. "I'll see someone dead for this."

Us, if we linger here much longer, thought Jean. He had a nasty suspicion that the hands of the city watch would offer no safety if he and Locke vanished into them.

Further arguments were erupting throughout the room by the time Jean finally managed to use his bulk to knock a path for himself and Locke to the tavern's rear entrance. It led to an unlit alley, running away in either direction. The clouds had settled across the black sky, blotting out the moons, and Jean slipped a hatchet reflexively into his right hand before he'd taken three steps into the night. His trained ears told him the watch whistles were about a block to the west and moving fast.

"Freyald," said Locke as they moved through the darkness together. "That rat bastard barkeep. That ale was aimed at us, sure as a crossbow quarrel."

"That was my conclusion," said Jean. He led Locke across a narrow street, over a rough stone wall, and into a silent courtyard that appeared to border on warehouses. Jean crouched behind a partially shattered crate, and his adjusting eyes saw the black shape of Locke flatten against a nearby barrel.

"Things are worse," said Locke. "Worse than we thought. What are the odds that half a dozen city watch wouldn't know which bars were safe for off-duty hours? What are the odds that they would come to the wrong fucking *neighborhood*?"

"Or drop that much pay on drinks for a bar full of the archon's people? They were just cover. Probably they didn't even know what they were covering for."

"It still means," whispered Locke, "that whoever's after us can pull strings in the city watch."

"It means Priori," said Jean.

"Them or someone close to them. But why?"

There was the sudden scuff of leather on stone behind them; Locke and Jean went silent in unison. Jean turned in time to see a large dark shape hop the wall behind them, and the slap of heels on cobbles told him that a man of some weight had just landed.

In one smooth motion, Jean slipped out of his coat, swung it in a high arc, and brought it down over the man's upper body. While the shadowy shape struggled with the coat, Jean leapt up and cracked the top of his opponent's head with the blunt end of his hatchet. He followed this with a punch to the solar plexus, folding the man in half. It was child's play after that to guide the man facefirst to the ground with a shove on the back.

Locke shook a tiny alchemical lamp, little more than a thumb-sized vial, to life. He shielded the wan glow against his body and let the light fall in only one direction, on the man Jean had subdued. Jean obligingly took back his coat, revealing a tall, well-muscled fellow with a shaven head. He was dressed nondescriptly in the fashion of a coachman or servant, and he threw a gloved hand across his face as he moaned in pain. Jean set the blade of his hatchet just beneath the man's jaw.

"M-master de Ferra...de Ferra, no, please," the man whispered. "Sweet gods. I'm with Merrain. I'm to...look after you."

Locke seized the man's left hand and peeled his leather glove off. By the pale lamplight, Jean saw a tattoo on the back of the stranger's hand, an open eye in the center of a rose. Locke sighed and whispered, "He's an Eye."

"He's a bloody fool," said Jean, glancing around them before setting his hatchet down quietly. He rolled the man onto his back. "Easy, friend. I pulled the blow to your head, but not to your stomach. Just lie there and breathe for a few minutes."

"I've been hit before," huffed the stranger, and Jean could see that tears of pain gleamed on his cheeks. "Gods. I marvel at the thought that you need protecting at all."

"We clearly do," said Locke. "I saw you in the Thousand Days, didn't I?"

"Yes. And I saw you give up your glasses of ale to that poor woman. Oh, fuck, my stomach is like to burst."

"It will pass," said Jean. "Did you see where that missing barkeep went?"

"I saw him enter the kitchen, and I never looked for him to come back. Didn't have any reason to at the time."

"Shit." Locke scowled. "Knowing Merrain, does she have soldiers nearby against need?"

"Four in an old warehouse just a block south." The Eye gasped several times before continuing. "I was to take you there in case of trouble."

"This qualifies," said Locke. "When you can move, take us to them. We need to reach the Sword Marina in one piece. And then I'll need you to carry a message to her. Can you reach her tonight?"

"Within the hour," the man said, rubbing his stomach and staring up at the starless sky.

"Tell her we wish to take her up on her earlier offer of . . . room and board."

Jean rubbed his beard thoughtfully, then nodded.

"I'll send a note to Requin," said Locke. "I'll tell him

we're leaving in a day or two. We won't be around much longer than that, in truth. I'm no longer confident we can walk the streets. We can demand an escort to fetch our things from the Villa Candessa tomorrow, close our suite, put most of our clothes into storage. Then we'll hide in the Sword Marina."

"We have orders to guard your lives," said the Eye.

"I know," said Locke. "About the only thing we're sure of is that for the time being, your master means to use us, not kill us. So we'll rely on his hospitality." Locke passed the soldier's glove back to him. "For now."

11

TWO CARRIAGES of Eyes, dressed in plain fashion, accompanied Locke and Jean when they packed their personal effects at the Villa Candessa the next morning.

"We're heartily sorry to see you go," said the chief steward as Locke scratched Leocanto Kosta's signature onto a last few scraps of parchment. "You've been superb guests; we hope that you'll consider us again the next time you visit Tal Verrar."

Locke had no doubt the inn had been glad of their business; at five silvers a day for a year and a half, plus the price of additional services, he and Jean had left behind a pile of solari large enough to purchase a decent-sized house of their own and hire capable staff.

"Pressing matters compel our presence elsewhere," muttered Locke coldly. He rebuked himself in his thoughts a moment later—it wasn't the steward's fault they were being chased from comfort by Stragos, Bondsmagi, and bloody mysterious assassins. "Here," he said, fishing three solari out of his coat and setting them down on the desk. "See that this is split evenly and passed out to everyone on staff." He turned his palm up, and with a minor bit of legerdemain conjured another gold coin. "And this for your-self, to express our compliments for your hospitality."

"Return *anytime*," said the steward, bowing deeply.

"We shall," said Locke. "Before we go, I'd like to arrange to have some of our wardrobe stored indefinitely. You can be certain we'll be back to claim it."

While the steward happily scrawled the necessary orders on a parchment, Locke borrowed a square of the Villa Candessa's pale blue formal stationery. On this he wrote, *I depart immediately by the means previously discussed. Rely upon my return. I remain deeply grateful for the forbearance you have shown me.*

Locke watched the steward seal it in the house's black wax, and said, "See that this is delivered without fail to the master of the Sinspire. If not personally, then only to his majordomo, Selendri. They will want it immediately."

Locke suppressed a smile at the slight widening of the steward's eyes. The suggestion that Requin had a vested personal interest in the contents of the note would do much to speed it safely on its way. Nonetheless, Locke still planned to send another copy later through one of Stragos' agents. No sense in taking chances.

"So much for those fine beds," said Jean as he carried their two trunks of remaining possessions out to the waiting carriages. They had kept only their implements of thieving—lockpicks, weapons, alchemical dyes, disguise items—plus a few hundred solari in cold metal, and a few sets of tunics and breeches to take to sea. "So much for Jerome de Ferra's money."

"So much for Durenna and Corvaleur," said Locke with a tight smile. "So much for looking over our shoulders everywhere we go. Because, in truth, we're stepping into a cage. But just for a few days."

"No," said Jean thoughtfully as he stepped up into a

carriage door held open by a bodyguard. "No, the cage goes on, much farther than that. It goes wherever we go."

12

THEIR TRAINING with Caldris, which resumed that afternoon, only grew more arduous. The sailing master walked them from end to end of the ship, drilling them in the operation of everything from the capstan to the cooking box. With the help of a pair of Eyes, they unlashed the ship's boat, hoisted it over the side, and retrieved it. They pulled the gratings from the main-deck cargo hatches and practiced sending barrels up and down with various arrangements of block and tackle. Everywhere they went, Caldris had them tying knots and naming obscure devices.

Locke and Jean were given the stern cabin of the *Red Messenger* for their living quarters. At sea, Jean's compartment would be separated from Locke's by a thin wall of stiffened canvas—and Caldris' equally tiny "cabin" would be just across the passage—but for now they made the space into tolerably comfortable bachelor accommodations. The necessity of their enclosure seemed to impress upon them both the utter seriousness of their situation, and they redoubled their efforts, learning confusing new things with speed they had not required since they had last been under the tutelage of Father Chains. Locke found himself falling asleep with his copy of the *Lexicon* for a pillow nearly every night.

Mornings they sailed their dinghy west of the city, within the glass reefs but with increasing confidence that only somewhat eclipsed actual skill. Afternoons, Caldris would call out items and locations on the deck of the ship and expect them to run to each place he named.

"Binnacle," the sailing master cried, and Locke and Jean raced together for the small wooden box just beside the ship's wheel that held a compass and several other navigational aids. No sooner had they touched it than Caldris cried, "Taffrail," which was easy enough—the stern rail at the very end of the ship. Next, Caldris shouted, "Craplines!" Locke and Jean ran past the bemused kitten, who lounged on the sunlit quarterdeck licking her paws. They were grimacing as they ran, for the craplines were what they'd be bracing themselves against when they crawled out onto the bowsprit to relieve themselves into the sea. More commodious methods of shitting were for rich passengers on larger vessels.

"Mizzenmast," bellowed Caldris, and Locke and Jean both fetched up short, breathing heavily.

"Ship doesn't bloody have one," said Locke. "Just foremast and mainmast!"

"Oh, clever you! You've undone my subtle ruse, Master Kosta. Get your bloody uniform and we'll let you act the peacock for a few hours."

The three men worked together across the days to define a system of hand and verbal signals, with Locke and Jean making a few sensible adaptations from their existing private language.

"Privacy on a ship at sea is about as real as fucking fairy piss," Caldris grumbled one afternoon. "I might not be able to give you clear spoken instructions with gods-know-who watching and listening. We'll work with lots of nudges and whispers. If you know something complicated is coming up, best thing to say is just—"

"Let's see if you know your business, Caldris!" Locke found that the Verrari naval uniform was a great aid when it came to conjuring an authoritative voice.

"Right. That or something like it. And if one of the sailors cops technical and wants your opinion on something you don't know..."

"Come now, Imaginary Seaman, surely I don't have to spell it out for you like a child?"

"Right, good. Give me another one."

"Gods damn you, I know this ship's lines like the back of my hand!" Locke looked down his nose at Caldris, which was only possible because his leather boots added an inch and a half to his height. "And I know what she's capable of. Trust my judgment or feel free to start swimming."

"Yes. A fine job, Master Kosta!" The sailing master squinted at Locke and scratched his beard. "Where *does* Master Kosta go when you do that? What *exactly* is it you do for a living, Leocanto?"

"I do this, I suppose. I'm a professional pretender. I... act."

"On the stage?"

"Once upon a time. Jerome and I both. Now I suppose we make this ship our stage."

"Indeed you do." Caldris moved to the wheel (which was actually a pair of wheels, joined by a mechanism below the deck, to allow more than one sailor to exert their strength against it in hard weather), evading a brief attack on his bare feet from the kitten. "Places!"

Locke and Jean hurried to the quarterdeck to stand near him, ostensibly aloof and concentrating on their own tasks, while remaining close enough to pick up on a whisper or a prompting gesture.

"Imagine us beating to windward with the breeze coming in across the larboard bow," said Caldris. It was necessary to imagine, for in the enclosed little bay not the slightest breeze stirred. "The time has come for us to tack. Just sound off the steps. I need to know you've got them down."

Locke pictured the operation in his head. No square-rigged ship could sail straight into the wind. To move a desired direction against the breeze required sailing at something like a forty-five degree angle to it, and switching over at intervals to present different sides of the bow to the wind. It was in effect a series of zigzags, tack after tack, arduously clawing in a desired direction. Each changeover, from larboard tack to starboard tack or vice versa, was a delicate operation with many opportunities for disaster.

"Master Caldris," he bellowed, "we shall put the ship about. The wheel is yours."

"Very good, sir."

"Master de Ferra!"

Jean gave three short blasts on the whistle he wore, as Locke did, around his neck. "All hands! All hands ready to put the ship about!"

"Master Caldris," said Locke. "Neatness counts. Seize your wheel. Put your helm down."

Locke waited a few seconds for dramatic effect, then yelled, "Helm a-lee!"

Caldris mimed hauling the wheel in the direction of the ship's lee side, in this case the starboard, which would tilt the rudder in the opposite direction. Locke conjured a vivid mental picture of the sudden press of water against it, forcing the ship into a turn to larboard. They would be coming into the eye of the wind, feeling its full force; an error at this point could "lock them in irons," stalling all progress, stealing power from rudder and sails alike. They would be helpless for minutes, or worse—an error like that in heavy weather could flip them, and ships were not acrobats.

"Imaginary Sailors! Tacks and sheets!" Jean waved his arms and hollered his instructions to the invisible deckhands. "Smartly now, you slothful dogs!"

"Master de Ferra," called Locke, "that Imaginary Sailor is not minding his duty!"

"I'll fuckin' kill you later, you cabbage-brained pig-rapist! Seize your rope and wait for my word!"

"Master Caldris!" Locke whirled toward the sailing

master, who was nonchalantly sipping from a leather skin of pinkwater. "Hard over!"

"Aye, sir." He belched and set the skin down on the deck at his feet. "By your word, hard over."

"Up mainsail," cried Locke.

"Bowlines off! Braces off!" Jean blew another blast on his whistle. "Yards around for the starboard tack!"

In Locke's mind, the ship's bow was now tilting past the heart of the wind; the larboard bow would become their lee, and the wind would blow in across the starboard side of the ship. The yards would be rapidly rebraced for the sails to take advantage of the wind's new aspect, and Caldris would be frantically reversing his wheel's turn. The *Red Messenger* would need to stabilize her new course; if she was pushed too far to larboard, they might find themselves moving in the opposite of their intended direction, with the sails braced improperly to boot. They would be lucky to be merely embarrassed by such a fiasco.

"Hard over," he yelled again.

"Aye sir," cried Caldris. "Heard the captain fine the first time."

"Lines on! Braces on!" Jean blew his whistle yet again. "Haul off all, you fuckin' maggots!"

"We're now on the starboard tack, Captain," said Caldris. "Surprisingly, we didn't lose her in stays and we'll all live to see another hour."

"Aye, no bloody thanks to this useless cur of an Imaginary Sailor!" Locke mimed grabbing a man and forcing him to the deck. "What's your gods-damned problem, you work-shirking little orlop worm?"

"First mate de Ferra beats me cruelly," cried Jean in a squeaky voice. "He is a monstrous bad fellow, who makes me wish I'd taken priest's orders and never set foot aboard!"

"Of course he does! It's what I pay him for." Locke

mimed hefting a blade. "For your crimes, I swear you'll die on this very deck, unless you can answer two bloody questions! First—where the hell is my *nonimaginary* crew? And second, why in the name of all the gods am I supposed to practice wearing this damned uniform?"

He was startled out of his act by the sound of applause from behind him. He whirled to see Merrain standing just beside the entry port at the ship's rail; she'd come up the ramp in absolute silence.

"Oh, wonderful!" She smiled at the three men on deck, stooped down, and plucked up the kitten, who'd moved immediately to attack Merrain's fine leather boots. "Very convincing. But your poor invisible sailor doesn't have the answers you seek."

"Are you here to name someone who does?"

"On the morrow," she said, "the archon orders you to take the sails of one of his private boats. He wishes to see a demonstration of your skills before you receive your final orders for sea. He and I will be your passengers. If you can keep our heads above water, he'll show you where your crew is. And why we've had you practicing with that uniform."

CHAPTER SEVEN

CASTING LOOSE

1

THERE WAS ONE GUARD PACING the dock at the base of the lonely island. His soft yellow lamp cast rippling light across the black water as Locke threw him a rope from within the little launch. Rather than tying them up, the guard thrust his lantern down toward Locke, Jean, and Caldris, and said, "This dock is strictly off . . . oh, gods. My apologies, sir."

Locke grinned, feeling the authority of the full Verrari captain's uniform enfold him like nothing so much as a warm blanket. He grabbed a piling and heaved himself up onto the dock while the guard saluted him awkwardly with his lantern hand crossed over his chest.

"Gods defend the archon of Tal Verrar," said Locke. "Carry on. It's your job to challenge strange boats at night, soldier."

While the soldier tied the launch to a piling, Locke reached down and helped Jean up. Moving gracefully in the now-familiar costume, Locke then stepped around behind the dock guard, unfurled a leather crimper's hood from within his jacket, slammed it down over the soldier's head, and cinched the drawstring tight.

"Gods know there's none stranger than ours that you're ever likely to see."

Jean held the soldier by his arms while the drugs inside the hood did their job. He lacked the constitution of the last man Locke had tried to knock out with such a hood, and sagged after just a few seconds of muffled struggle. When Locke and Jean tied him firmly to the piling at the far corner of the dock and stuffed a rag in his mouth, he was sleeping peacefully.

Caldris clambered out of the boat, picked up the guard's lantern, and began pacing with it in his place.

Locke stared up at the stone tower that was their objective; seven stories tall, its battlements were orange-lit by alchemical navigation beacons warning ships away. Ordinarily there would be guards up there as well, watching the waters and the dock, but the hand of Stragos was already at work. Nothing moved atop the tower.

"Come on, then," Locke whispered to Jean. "Let's get inside and do some recruiting."

2

"IT'S CALLED Windward Rock," Stragos said. He pointed at the stone tower that jutted from the little island, perhaps a single arrow-flight from the line of hissing white surf that marked Tal Verrar's outer barrier of glass reefs. They floated at anchor in seventy feet of water, a good mile west of the Silver Marina. The warm morning sun was just rising over the city behind them, making tiers of soft light from its layers of foggy haze.

True to Merrain's word, Stragos had arrived at dawn in a thirty-foot launch of polished black wood, with comfortable leather seats at the stern and gold-gilded scrollwork on every surface. Locke and Jean were given the sails under Caldris' minimal supervision, while Merrain sat in the bow. Locke had wondered if she was ever comfortable any-where else.

They had sailed north, then rounded the Silver Marina and turned west, chasing the last blue shadow of the night sky on the far horizon.

They rode on for a few minutes, until Merrain whistled for everyone's attention and pointed to her left, across the starboard bow. A tall, dark structure could be seen rising above the waves in the distance. Orange lights glowed at its peak.

Soon enough they had dropped anchor to regard the lonely tower. If Stragos had no praise for Locke and Jean's handling of the vessel, neither did he offer any criticism.

"Windward Rock," said Jean. "I've heard of it. Some sort of fortress."

"A prison, Master de Ferra."

"Will we be visiting it this morning?"

"No," said Stragos. "You'll be returning and landing soon enough. For now, I just wanted you to see it ... and I wanted to tell you a little story. I have in my service a par-ticularly unreliable captain, who has until now done a splendid job of concealing his shortcomings."

"Words cannot express how truly sorry I am to hear that," said Locke.

"He will betray me," said Stragos. "His plans for months have been leading up to a grand and final betrayal. He will steal something of great value from me and turn it against me for all to see."

"You should have been watching him more closely," Locke muttered.

"I have been," said Stragos. "And I am right now. The captain I speak of is you."

3

WINDWARD ROCK had only one set of doors, iron-bound, eleven feet tall, locked and guarded from the inside. A small panel in the wall beside them slid open as Locke and Jean approached, and a head silhouetted by lamplight appeared behind it. The guardswoman's voice was devoid of banter: "Who passes?"

"An officer of archon and Council," said Locke with ritual formality. "This man is my boatswain. These are my orders and papers."

He passed a set of documents rolled into a tight tube to the woman behind the door. She slid the panel closed over her watch-hole, and Locke and Jean waited in silence for several minutes, listening to the rushing passage of surf over the nearby reefs. Two moons were just coming up, gilding the southern horizon with silver, and the stars dusted the cloudless sky like confectioners' sugar thrown against a black canvas.

Finally, there was a metallic clatter, and the heavy doors swung outward on creaking hinges. The guardswoman stepped out to meet them, saluting, but not returning Locke's papers.

"My apologies for the delay, Captain Ravelle. Welcome to Windward Rock."

Locke and Jean followed her into the tower's entrance hall, which was divided into two halves by a wall of black iron bars running from floor to ceiling across its breadth. On the far side of these bars, a man behind a wooden desk had control of whatever mechanism closed the gates—they clattered shut behind Locke and Jean after a few seconds.

The man, like the woman, wore the archon's blue under ribbed black leather armor: bracers, vest, and neck-guard. He was clean-shaven and handsome, and he waited behind the bars as the female guard approached to pass him Locke's papers.

"Captain Orrin Ravelle," she said. "And boatswain. Here with orders from the archon."

The man studied Locke's papers at length before nodding and passing them back through the bars. "Of course. Good evening, Captain Ravelle. This man is your boatswain, Jerome Valora?"

"Yes, Lieutenant."

"You're to view the prisoners in the second vault? Anyone in particular?"

"Just a general viewing, Lieutenant."

"As you will." The man slid a key from around his neck, opened the only gate set into the wall of iron bars, and stepped out toward them smiling. "We're pleased to render any aid the Protector requires, sir."

"I very much doubt that," said Locke, letting a stiletto slip into his left hand. He reached out and gave the female guard a slash behind her right ear, across the unprotected skin between her leather neck-guard and her tightly coifed hair. She cried out, whirled, and had her blackened-steel saber out of its scabbard in an instant.

Jean was tackling the male guard before her blade was even out; the man uttered a surprised choking noise as Jean slammed him against the bars and gave him a sharp chop to the neck with the edge of his right hand. The leather armor robbed the blow of its lethal possibilities without dulling the shock of impact. Gasping, the guard was easily pinned from behind by Jean, who immobilized his arms and held him in a grip like iron.

Locke darted backward out of the female guard's reach as she slashed with her blade. Her first attack was swift and nearly accurate. Her second was a bit slower, and Locke had no trouble avoiding it. She readied a third swing and misstepped, tripping over her own feet. Her mouth hung open in confusion.

"You...fucker...," she muttered. "Poi...poi...son."

Locke winced as she toppled facefirst to the stone floor; he'd meant to catch her, but the stuff on the blade was faster than he'd expected.

"You bastard," coughed the lieutenant, straining uselessly in Jean's hold, "you killed her!"

"Of course I didn't kill her, you twit. Honestly, you people...pull a blade anywhere around here and everyone assumes straightaway that you've killed someone." Locke stepped up before the guard and showed him the stiletto. "Stuff on the edge is called witfrost. You have a good hard sleep all night, wake up around noon. At which time you'll feel like hell. Apologies. So do you want it in the neck or in the palm of your hand?"

"You...you gods-damned traitor!"

"Neck it is." Locke gave the man his own shallow cut just behind his left ear and barely counted to eight before he was hanging in Jean's arms, limper than wet silk. Jean set the lieutenant down gently and plucked a small ring of iron keys from his belt.

"Right," said Locke. "Let's pay a visit to the second vault."

4

"RAVELLE DIDN'T exist until a month ago," said Stragos. "Not until I had you to build the lie around. A dozen of my most trusted men and women will swear after the fact that he was real; that they shared assignments and meals with him, that they spoke of duties and trifles in his company.

"My finnickers have prepared orders, duty rosters, pay vouchers, and other documents, and seeded them throughout my archives. Men using the name of Ravelle have rented rooms, purchased goods, ordered tailored uniforms delivered to the Sword Marina. By the time I'm dealing with the consequences of your betrayal, he'll seem real in fact and memory."

"Consequences?" asked Locke.

"Ravelle is going to betray me just as Captain Bonaire betrayed me when she took my *Basilisk* out of the harbor seven years ago and raised a red banner. It's going to happen again . . . twice to the same archon. I will be ridiculed in some quarters, for a time. Temporary loss for long-term gain." He winced. "Have you not considered the public reaction to what I'm arranging, Master Kosta? I certainly have."

"Gods, Maxilan," said Locke, toying absently with a knot on one of the lines bracing the vessel's relatively small mainsail. "Trapped out at sea, feigning mastery in a trade for which I'm barely competent, fighting for my life with your fucking poison in my veins, I shall endeavor to keep you in my prayers for the sake of your hardship."

"Ravelle is an ass, too," said the archon. "I've had that specifically written into his back history. Now, something you should know about Tal Verrar—the Priori's constables guard Highpoint Citadel Gaol in the Castellana. The majority of the city's prisoners go there. But while Windward Rock is a much smaller affair, it's mine. Manned and provisioned only by my people."

The archon smiled. "That's where Ravelle's treachery will reach the point of no return. That, Master Kosta, is where you'll get your crew."

5

TRUE TO Stragos' warning, there was an additional guard to be disarmed in the first cell level beneath the entrance hall, at the foot of a wide spiral staircase of black iron. The stone tower overhead was for guards and alchemical lights; Windward Rock's true purpose was served by three ancient stone vaults that went down far beneath the sea, into the roots of the island.

The man saw them coming and took immediate alarm; no doubt Locke and Jean descending alone was a breach of procedure. Jean relieved him of his sword as he charged up the steps, kicked him in the face, and pinned him, squirming, on his stomach. Jean's month of exercise at Caldris' whim seemed to have left his strength more bullish than ever, and Locke almost pitied the poor fellow struggling beneath his friend. Locke reached over, gave the guard a touch of witfrost, and whistled jauntily.

That was it for the night shift—a skeleton force with no cooks or other attendants. One guard at the docks, two in the entrance hall, one on the first cell level. The two on the roof, by Stragos' direct order, would have sipped drugged tea and fallen asleep with the pot between them. They'd be found by their morning relief with a plausible excuse for their incapacity—and another lovely layer of confusion would be thrown over the whole affair.

There were no boats kept at Windward Rock itself, so even if prisoners could conceivably escape from iron-barred cells set into the weeping walls of the old vaults, and win free through the barred entrance hall and lone reinforced door, they'd face a swim across a mile of open water (at least), watched with interest by many things in the depths eager for a meal.

Locke and Jean ignored the iron door leading to the cells of the first level, continuing down the spiraling staircase. The air was dank, smelling of salt and unwashed bodies. Past the iron door on the second level, they found themselves in a vault divided into four vast cells, long and low-ceilinged, two on each side with a fifteen-foot corridor down the middle.

Only one of these cells was actually occupied; several dozen men lay sleeping in the pale green light of barred alchemical globes set high on the walls. The air in here was positively rank, dense with the odors of unclean bedding, urine, and stale food. Faint tendrils of mist curled around the prisoners. A few wary pairs of eyes tracked Locke and Jean as they stepped up to the cell door.

Locke nodded to Jean, and the bigger man began to pound his fist against the bars of the door. The clamor was sharp, echoing intolerably from the dripping walls of the vault. Disturbed prisoners rose from their dirty pallets, swearing and hollering.

"Are you men comfortable in there?" Locke shouted to be heard above the din. Jean ceased his pounding.

"We'd be lots more comfortable with a nice sweet Verrari captain in here for us to fuck sideways," said a prisoner near the door.

"I have no patience to speak of," said Locke, pointing at the door he and Jean had come through. "If I walk back out that door, I won't be coming back."

"Piss off, then, and let us sleep," said a scarecrow of a man in a far corner of the cell.

"And if I won't be coming back," said Locke, "then none of you poor bastards will ever find out why vaults one and three have prisoners in every cell . . . while *this* one is completely empty save for yourselves."

That got their attention. Locke smiled.

"That's better. My name is Orrin Ravelle. Until a few minutes ago, I was a captain in the navy of Tal Verrar. And the reason you're here is because *I* selected you. Every last one of you. *I* selected you, and then I forged the orders that got you assigned to an empty cell vault."

6

"I CHOSE forty-four prisoners, originally," said Stragos. They stared at Windward Rock in the light of the morning sun. A boat of blue-coated soldiers was approaching it in the distance, presumably to relieve the current shift of guards. "I had the second cell vault cleared, except for them. All the orders signed 'Ravelle' are plausible, but upon scrutiny, the signs of forgery will become evident. I can use that later as a plausible excuse to arrest several clerks whose loyalties aren't...straightforward enough for my taste."

"Efficient," said Locke.

"Yes." Stragos continued, "These prisoners are all prime seamen, taken from ships that were impounded for various reasons. Some have been in custody for a few years. Many are actually former crewmen of your *Red Messenger,* lucky not to be executed along with their officers. Some of them might even have past experience at piracy."

"Why keep prisoners at the Rock?" asked Jean. "In general, I mean?"

"Oar fodder," answered Caldris. "Handy thing to keep on hand. War breaks out, they'll be offered full pardons if they agree to work as galley rowers for the duration. The Rock tends to have a couple galleys' worth, most of the time."

"Caldris is entirely correct," said Stragos. "Now, as I said, some of those men have been in there for several years, but none of them have ever had to endure conditions like those of the past month. I have had them deprived, of everything from clean bedding to regular meals. The guards have been cruel, disturbing their sleeping hours with loud noises and buckets of cold water. I daresay by now that there isn't a man among them that doesn't hate Windward Rock, hate Tal Verrar, and hate *me.* Personally."

Locke nodded slowly. "And that's why you expect them to greet Ravelle as their savior."

7

"YOU'RE THE one responsible for shoving us into this hell, you fuckin' Verrari ass-licker?"

One of the prisoners stepped up to the bars and clutched them; the depredations of the cell vault had yet to whittle away a build frighteningly close to that of the heroic statuary of old. Locke guessed he was a recent arrival; his muscles looked carved from witchwood. His skin and hair were black enough to shrug off the pale green light, as though in disdain.

"I'm the one responsible for moving you to this vault," said Locke. "I didn't lock you up in the first place. I didn't arrange for the treatment you've been receiving."

"*Treatment*'s a fancy fuckin' word for it."

"What's your name?"

"Jabril."

"Are you in charge?"

"Of what?" Some of the man's anger seemed to ebb, transmuting to tired resignation. "Nobody's in fuckin' charge behind iron bars, *Captain* Ravelle. We piss where we sleep. We don't keep bloody muster rolls or duty shifts."

"You men are all sailors," said Locke.

"Was sailors," said Jabril.

"I know what you are. You wouldn't be here otherwise. Think about this—thieves get let out. They go to West Citadel, they work at hard labor, they slave until they rupture or get pardoned. But even they get to see the sky. Even their cells have windows. Debtors are free to go when their debts are paid. Prisoners of war go home when the war's over. But you poor bastards...you're penned up here against need. You're cattle. If there's a war, you'll be chained to oars, and if there's no war ... well."

"There's always war," said Jabril.

"Seven years since the last one," said Locke. He stepped up to the bars just across from Jabril and looked him in the eyes. "Maybe seven years again. Maybe never. You really want to grow old in this vault, Jabril?"

"What's the bloody alternative ... Captain?"

"Some of you came from a ship," said Locke. "Impounded recently. Your captain tried to smuggle in a nest of stiletto wasps."

"The *Fortunate Venture,* aye," said Jabril. "We was promised high heaps of gold for that job."

"Fucking things killed eight men on the voyage," said another prisoner. "We thought we'd inherit their shares."

"Turns out they was lucky," said Jabril. "They didn't have to take no share of this gods-damned place."

"The *Fortunate Venture* is riding at anchor in the Sword Marina," said Locke. "She's been rechristened the *Red Messenger.* Refurbished, resupplied, careened, and smoked. She's been prettied up. The archon means to take her into his service."

"Good for the bloody archon."

"I'm to command her," said Locke. "She's at my disposal. I have the keys, as it were."

"What the fuck do you want, then?"

"It's half past midnight," said Locke, lowering his voice to a stage whisper that echoed dramatically to the back of the cell. "Morning relief won't arrive for more than six hours. And every guard on Windward Rock is ... currently ... unconscious."

The entire cell was full of wide eyes. Men heaved themselves up from their sleeping pallets and pressed closer to the bars, forming an unruly but attentive crowd.

"I am leaving Tal Verrar tonight," said Locke. "This is

the last time I will ever wear this uniform. I am quits with the archon and everything he stands for. I mean to take the *Red Messenger,* and for that I need a crew."

The mass of prisoners exploded into a riot of shoving and jabbering. Hands thrust out at Locke through the bars, and he stepped back.

"I'm a topman," one of the prisoners yelled, "fine topman! Take me!"

"Nine years at sea," hollered another. "Do anything!"

Jean stepped up and pounded on the cell door again, bellowing, *"Quiiiieeeett!"*

Locke held up the ring of keys Jean had taken from the lieutenant in the entrance hall.

"I sail south on the Sea of Brass," he said. "I make for Port Prodigal. This is not subject to vote or negotiation. You sail with me, you sail under the red flag. You want off when we reach the Ghostwinds, you can have it. Until then, we're on the watch for money and plunder. No room for shirkers. The word is equal shares."

That would give them something to ponder, Locke thought. A freebooter captain more commonly took two to four shares from ten of any plunder got at sea. Just the thought of equal shares for all would quell a great many mutinous urges.

"Equal shares," he repeated above another sudden outburst of babble. "But you make your decision here and now. Take oath to me as your captain and I will free you immediately. I have means to get you off this rock and over to the *Red Messenger.* We'll have hours of darkness to clear the harbor and be well away. If you don't want to come, fine. But no courtesies in that case. You'll stay here when we're gone. Maybe the morning relief will be impressed with your honesty...but I doubt it. Who among you will desist?

None of the prisoners said anything.

"Who among you will go free, and join my crew?"

Locke winced at the eruption of shouts and cheers, then allowed himself a wide, genuine grin.

"All gods as your witness!" he shouted. "Upon your lips and upon your hearts."

"Our oath is made," said Jabril, while those around him nodded.

"Then stand upon it, or pray to die, and be damned and found wanting on the scales of the Lady of the Long Silence."

"So we stand," came a chorus of shouts.

Locke passed the ring of keys over to Jean. The prisoners watched in an ecstasy of disbelief as he found the proper key, slid it into the lock, and gave it a hard turn to the right.

8

"THERE IS one problem," said Stragos.

"Just one?" Locke rolled his eyes.

"There are only forty left of the forty-four I selected."

"How will that suit the needs of the ship?"

"We've got food and water for a hundred days with sixty," said Caldris. "And she can be handled well with half that number. Once we've got them sorted out, we'll do fine for hands at the lines."

"So you will," said Stragos. "The missing four are women. I had them placed in a separate cell. One of them developed a gaol-fever, and soon they all had it. I had no choice but to move them to shore; they're too weak to lift their arms, let alone join this expedition."

"We're for sea with not a woman aboard," said Caldris. "Will not Merrain be coming with us, then?"

"I'm afraid," she said sweetly, "that my talents will be required elsewhere."

"This is mad," cried Caldris. "We taunt the Father of Storms!"

"You can find women for your crew in Port Prodigal, perhaps even good officers." Stragos spread his hands. "Surely you'll be fine for the duration of a single voyage down."

"Would that it were mine to so declare," said Caldris, a haunted look in his eyes. "Master Kosta, this is a poor way to start. We must have cats. A basket of cats, for the *Red Messenger*. We need what luck we can steal. All gods as your witness, you *must not fail* to have cats at that ship before we put to sea."

"Nor shall I," said Locke.

"Then it's settled," said Stragos. "Heed this now, Kosta. Concerning the . . . depth of your deception. In case you have any misgivings. None of the men you'll be taking from Windward Rock have ever served in my navy, so they've little notion of what to expect from one of my officers. And soon enough you'll be Ravelle the pirate rather than Ravelle the naval captain, so you may tailor the impersonation as you see fit, and worry little over small details."

"That's good," said Locke. "I've got enough of those crammed into my head just now."

"I have one last stipulation," Stragos continued. "The men and women who serve at Windward Rock, even those who are not party to this scheme, are among my finest and most loyal. I will provide means for you to disable them without rendering permanent harm. *In no way* are they to be otherwise injured, not by you nor your crew, and gods help you if you leave any dead."

"Curious sentiments for a man who claims to be no stranger to risks."

"I would send them into battle at any time, Kosta, and lose them willingly. But none who wear my colors honestly are to die as part of this; that much my honor compels me to grant them. You are supposed to be professionals. Consider this a test of your professionalism."

"We're not bloody murderers," said Locke. "We kill for good reason, when we kill at all."

"So much the better," said Stragos. "That is all I have to say, then. This day is yours to do with as you see fit. Tomorrow evening, just before midnight, you'll land on Windward Rock and start this business."

"We need our antidote," said Locke. Jean and Caldris nodded.

"Of course. You three will get your last vials just before you leave. After that...I shall expect your first return within two months. And a report of your progress."

9

LOCKE AND Jean managed a ragged muster of their new crew just inside the entrance hall. Jean had to demonstrate his physical strength to several men who attempted to vent their frustrations on the sleeping guards.

"I said you touch them at your peril," Locke snarled for the third time. "Let them be! If we leave them dead behind us, we'll lose all sympathy with anyone. Let them live, and Verrari will be laughing about this for months to come.

"Now," he said, "move out quietly to the dockside. Take your ease, stretch your legs, have a good long look at the sea and sky. I've a boat to fetch before we can be away. For the sake of us all, keep your mouths shut."

They mostly obeyed this admonition, breaking up into little whispering groups as they moved out of the tower. Locke noticed that some of the men hung back near the door, their hands on the stones, as though afraid to step out beneath the open sky. He couldn't say he blamed them after months or years in the vault.

"That's lovely," said Jabril, who fell into step beside

Locke as they approached the dock where Caldris paced with his lantern. "Fuckin' lovely. Almost as lovely as not having to smell us all at once."

"You'll be crammed together again soon enough," said Locke.

"Aye. Same but different."

"Jabril," said Locke, raising his voice, "in time, as we come to know one another's strengths, we can hold proper votes for some of the officers we'll need. For now, I'm naming you acting mate."

"Mate of what?"

"Mate of whatever." Locke grinned and slapped him on the back. "I'm not in the navy anymore, remember? You'll answer to Jerome. Keep the men in order. Take the weapons from that soldier tied to the dock, just in case we need to pull a little steel this evening. I don't expect a fight, but we should be ready."

"Good evening, Captain Ravelle," said Caldris. "I see you've fetched them out just as you planned."

"Aye," said Locke. "Jabril, this is Caldris, my sailing master. Caldris, Jabril is acting mate under Jerome. Listen up!" Locke raised his voice without shouting, lest it echo across the water to unseen ears. "I came with a boat for six. I have a boat for forty nearby. I need two men to help me row. Won't be half an hour, and then we'll be away."

Two younger prisoners stepped forward, looking eager for anything that would relieve the tedium of what they'd been through.

"Right," said Locke as he stepped down into their little boat, after Caldris and the two sailors. "Jerome, Jabril, keep order and quiet. Try to sort out those who can work right away from those who will need a few days to recover their strength."

Anchored half a mile out from Windward Rock was a long launch, invisible in the moonlight until Caldris' lantern found it from about fifty yards away. Locke and Caldris worked quickly to rig the boat's small sail; then, slowly but surely, they steered their way back toward the prison with the two ex-prisoners rowing the little boat beside them. Locke glanced around nervously, spotting a sail or two gleaming palely on the far horizons, but nothing closer.

"Listen well," he said when the launch was tied up below the dock and surrounded by his would-be crew. He was pleasantly surprised at how quickly they'd settled down to the business at hand. Of course, that made sense—they were the crews of impounded ships, not hard cases imprisoned for individual crimes. It didn't make saints of them, but it was nice to have something unforeseen working in his favor for once.

"Able hands take the oars. Don't be shy if you're less than able for the time being; I know some of you have been down there too damn long. Just sit down in the middle of the launch and take it easy. You can recover yourselves on the voyage out. We've plenty to eat."

That lent them some cheer. Once at sea, Locke knew, the state of their rations might easily approach that of the prison slop they were leaving behind, but for a fair few days they'd have a supply of fresh meat and vegetables to look forward to.

In good order the former prisoners clambered aboard the launch; soon the gunwales were lined with those claiming to be able-bodied, and oars were being slipped into their locks. Jabril took the bow, waving up at Locke and Caldris when all was in readiness.

"Right," said Locke. "The *Messenger* is anchored south of the Sword Marina on the seaward side, wanting nothing save her crew. One guard stands watch for the night, and I'll deal with him. Just follow us and go aboard once I've done that; the nets are lowered over the side and the defenses are stowed."

Locke took the bow of the small boat and struck what he hoped was an appropriately regal posture. Jean and Caldris took the oars, and the last two prisoners sat at the stern, one of them holding Caldris' lantern.

"Say farewell to Windward Rock, boys," said Locke. "And bid fuck-you to the archon of Tal Verrar. We're bound for sea."

10

A SHADOW within shadows watched the two boats depart.

Merrain moved out of her position beside the tower and gave a small wave as the low gray shapes diminished into the south. She loosed the black silk scarf that had covered her lower face and pushed back the hood of her black jacket; she had lain in the shadows beside the tower for nearly two hours, waiting patiently for Kosta and de Ferra to finish their business. Her own boat was stashed beneath a rocky overhang on the east side of the island, little more than a cockleshell of treated leather over a wood frame. Even in moonlight, it was all but invisible on the water.

She padded quietly into the entrance hall of the prison, finding the two guards much where she expected, carelessly strewn about in the grip of witfrost sleep. True to the archon's wishes, Kosta and de Ferra had prevented anyone from harming them.

"Alas for that," she whispered, kneeling over the lieutenant and running a gloved finger across his cheeks. "You're a handsome one."

She sighed, slipped a knife from its sheath within her jacket, and cut the man's throat with one quick slash. Moving back to avoid the growing pool of blood, she wiped the blade on the guard's breeches and contemplated the woman lying across the entrance hall.

The two atop the tower could live; it wouldn't be plausible for anyone to have climbed the stairs and gone for them. But she could do the one on the dock, the two here, and the one who was supposed to be downstairs.

That would be enough, she reckoned—it wasn't that she desired Kosta and de Ferra to fail. But if they *did* return successful in their mission, what was to stop Stragos from assigning them another task? His poison made tools of them indefinitely. And if they *could* return victorious, well ... men like that were better off dead if they couldn't be put to use on behalf of the interests she served.

Resolved, she set about finishing the job. The thought that for once it would be entirely painless was a comfort in her work.

11

"CAPTAIN RAVELLE!"

The soldier was one of those handpicked by the archon to be in on some part of the deception. He feigned surprise as Locke appeared on the *Red Messenger*'s deck, followed by Jean, Caldris, and the two ex-prisoners. The launch full of men was just butting up against the ship's starboard side.

"I didn't expect you back this evening, sir. . . . Sir, what's going on?"

"I have reached a decision," said Locke, approaching the soldier. "This ship is too fine a thing for the archon to have. So I am relieving him of its care and taking it to sea."

"Now hold on ... hold on, sir, that's not funny."

"Depends on where you're standing," said Locke. He stepped up and delivered a feigned punch to the soldier's stomach. "Depends on *if* you're standing." By arrangement, the man did a very credible impression of having received a devastating blow, and fell backward to the deck, writhing. Locke grinned. Let his new crew whisper of *that* amongst themselves.

The crew in question had just started to come up the boarding nets on the starboard side. Locke relieved the soldier of his sword, buckler, and knives, then joined Jean and Caldris at the rail to help the men up.

"What's to be done with the launch, Captain?" Jabril said as he came over the side.

"It's too damn big to carry with us on this little bitch," said Locke. He jerked a thumb over his shoulder at the "subdued" guard. "We'll set him adrift in it. Jerome!"

"Aye, sir," said Jean.

"Get everyone up and muster all hands at the waist. Master Caldris! You know the vessel best for now; give us light."

Caldris fetched alchemical lamps from a locker near the wheel, and with Locke's help he hung them about the deck until they had more than enough soft golden light to work by. Jean produced his little whistle and blew three short blasts. In moments, he had the crew herded into the middle of the ship's waist, before the mainmast. Before them all, Locke stood, stripped off his Verrari officer's coat, and pitched it over the side. They applauded.

"Now, we must have haste without carelessness," he said. "Those of you that do not believe yourselves fit for work, hands up! No shame, lads."

Locke counted nine hands. Most of the men who raised them were visibly aged or far too slender for good health, and Locke nodded. "We hold no grudge for your honesty. You'll take up your share of work once you're fit again. For now, find a spot on the main deck below, or beneath the forecastle. There's mats and canvas in the main hold. You may sleep or watch the fun as you see fit. Now, can anyone among you claim to be any sort of cook?"

One of the men standing behind Jabril raised a hand.

"Good. When the anchor's up, get below and have a look at the stores. We've a brick firebox at the forecastle, plus an alchemical stone and a cauldron. We'll want a hell of a meal once we're out past the glass reefs, so show some initiative. And tap a cask of ale."

The men began cheering at that, and Jean blew his whistle to quiet them down.

"Come, now!" Locke pointed to the darkness of the Elderglass island looming behind them. "The Sword Marina's just the other side of that island, and we're not away yet. Jerome! Capstan bars and stand by to haul up anchor. Jabril! Fetch rope from Caldris and help me with this fellow."

Together, Locke and Jabril hoisted the "incapacitated" soldier to his feet. Locke tied a loose but very convincing knot around his hands with a scrap of rope provided by Caldris; once they were gone, the man could work himself free in minutes.

"Don't kill me, Captain, please," the soldier muttered.

"I would never," said Locke. "I need you to carry a message to the archon on my behalf. Tell him that he may kiss Orrin Ravelle's ass, that my commission is herewith resigned, and that the only flag his pretty ship will fly from now on is red."

Locke and Jabril hoisted the man over the side of the entry port and dropped him the nine feet into the bottom of the launch. He yelped in (no doubt genuine) pain and rolled over, but seemed otherwise okay.

"Use those exact words," Locke cried, and Jabril laughed. "Now! Master Caldris, we shall make for sea!"

"Very good, Captain Ravelle." Caldris collared the four men nearest to him and began leading them below. Under his guidance, they would keep the anchor cable moving smoothly toward its tier on the orlop.

"Jerome," said Locke, "hands to the capstan to raise anchor!"

Locke and Jabril joined all the remaining able-bodied members of the crew at the capstan, where the last of the heavy wooden bars were being slid into their apertures. Jean blew on his whistle, and the men crammed together shoulder-to-shoulder on the bars. "Raise anchor! Step-and-on! Step-and-on! Push it hard; she'll be up ere long!" Jean chanted at the top of his lungs, giving them a cadence to stamp and shove by. The men strained at the capstan, many of them weaker than they would have liked or admitted, but the mechanism began to turn and the smell of wet cable filled the air.

"Heave-and-up! Heave-and-up! Drop the anchor and we'll all be fucked!"

Soon enough they managed to heave the anchor up out of the water, and Jean sent a party forward to the starboard bow to secure it. Most of the men stepped away from the capstan groaning and stretching, and Locke smiled. Even his old injuries still felt good after the exercise.

"Now," he shouted, "who among you sailed this ship when she was the *Fortunate Venture*? Step aside."

Fourteen men, including Jabril, separated themselves from the others.

"And who among you were fair topmen?"

That got him seven raised hands; good enough for the time being.

"Any of you not familiar with this ship nonetheless comfortable up above?"

Four more men stepped forward, and Locke nodded. "Good lads. You know where you'll be, then." He grabbed one of the non-topmen by the shoulder and steered him toward the bow. "For'ard watch. Let me know if anything untoward pops up in front of us." He grabbed another man and pointed to the mainmast. "Get a glass from Caldris;

you'll be masthead watch for now. Don't look at me like that; you won't be fucking with the rigging. Just sit still and stay awake.

"Master Caldris," he bellowed, noting that the sailing master was back on deck, "southeast by east through the reef passage called Underglass!"

"Aye, sir, Underglass. I know the very one." Caldris, of course, had plotted their course through the glass reefs in advance and carefully instructed Locke in the orders to give until they were out of sight of Tal Verrar. "Southeast by east."

Jean gestured at the eleven men who'd volunteered for duty up on the heights of the yardarms, where the furled sails waited, hanging in the moonlight like the thin cocoons of vast insects. "Hands aloft to loose topsails and t'gallants! On the word, mind you!"

"Master Caldris," shouted Locke, unable to disguise his mirth, "now we shall see if you know your business!"

The *Red Messenger* moved south under topsails and topgallants, making fair use of the stiff breeze blowing west off the mainland. Her bow sliced smoothly through the calm dark waters, and the deck beneath their feet heeled only the tiniest bit to starboard. It was a good start, thought Locke—a good start to a mad venture. When he had settled most of his crew in temporary positions, he stole a few minutes at the taffrail, watching the reflections of two moons in the gentle ripple of their wake.

"You're enjoying the hell out of yourself, Captain Ravelle." Jean stepped up to the taffrail beside him. The two thieves shook hands and grinned at one another.

"I suppose I am," Locke whispered. "I suppose this is the most lunatic thing we've ever done, and so we're *entitled* to bloody well enjoy ourselves."

"Crew seems to have bought the act for now."

"Well, they're still fresh from the vault. Tired, underfed,

excited. We'll see how sharp they are when they've had a few days of food and exercise. Gods, at least I didn't call anything by the wrong name."

"Hard to believe we're actually doing this."

"I know. Barely seems real yet. Captain Ravelle. First Mate Valora. Hell, you've got it easy. I've got to get used to people calling me 'Orrin.' You get to stay a 'Jerome.'"

"I saw little sense in making things harder for myself. I've got you to do that for me."

"Careful, now. I can order you whipped at the rail."

"Ha! A navy captain, maybe. A pirate first mate doesn't have to stand for that." Jean sighed. "You think we'll ever see land again?"

"I damn well mean to," said Locke. "We've got pirates to piss off, a happy return to arrange, Stragos to humble, antidotes to find, and Requin to rob blind. Two months at sea and I may even begin to have the faintest notion *how*."

They stared for a while at Tal Verrar sliding away behind them, at the aura of the Golden Steps and the torchglow of the Sinspire slowly vanishing behind the darker mass of the city's southwestern crescent. Then they were passing through the navigational channel in the glass reefs, away to the Sea of Brass, away to danger and piracy. Away to find war and bring it back for the archon's convenience.

12

"SAIL AHOY! Sail two points off the larboard bow!"

The cry filtered down from above on the third morning of their voyage south. Locke sat in his cabin, regarding his blurry reflection in the dented little mirror he'd packed in his chest. Before departure, he'd used a bit of alchemy from his disguise kit to restore his hair to its natural color, and now a fine shadow in much the same shade was appearing on his cheeks. He wasn't yet sure if he'd shave it, but with the shout from above, his concern for his beard vanished. In a moment he was out of the cabin, up the awkward steps of the dim companionway, and into the bright light of morning on the quarterdeck.

A haze of high white clouds veiled the blue sky, like wisps of tobacco smoke that had drifted far from the pipes of their progenitors. They'd had the wind on their larboard beam since reaching open sea, and the *Red Messenger* was heeled over slightly to starboard. The constant swaying and creaking and deck-slanting were utterly alien to Locke, who'd been confined to a cabin by infirmity on his last—and only previous—sea voyage. He flattered himself that the trained agility of a thief went some way toward feigning sea legs, but he avoided scampering around too much, just in case. At least he appeared to be immune to seasickness this time out, and for that he thanked the Crooked Warden fervently. Many aboard had not been so lucky.

"What passes, Master Caldris?"

"Compliments of a fine morning, Captain, and the masthead watch says we got white canvas two points off the larboard bow."

Caldris had the wheel to himself this morning, and he drew light puffs from a cheap sheaf of cut-rate tobacco that stank like sulfur. Locke wrinkled his nose.

Sighing inwardly and stepping with as much care as he could manage, Locke brought out his seeing glass and hurried forward, up the forecastle and to the rail on the larboard bow. Yes, there it was—hull down, a minute speck of white, barely visible above the dark blue of the distant horizon. When he returned to the quarterdeck, Jabril and several other sailors were lounging around, waiting for his verdict.

"Do we give her the eyeball, Captain?" Jabril seemed merely expectant, but the men behind him looked down-right eager.

"Looking for an early taste of those equal shares, eh?" Locke feigned deep consideration, turning toward Caldris long enough to catch the sailing master's private signal for an emphatic no. As Locke had expected—and he could give legitimate reasons without prompting.

"Can't do it, lads. You know better than that. We've not yet begun to set our own ship to rights; little sense in taking a fight to someone else's. A quarter of us are still unfit for work, let alone battle. We've got fresh food, a clean ship, and all the time in the world. Better chances will come. Hold course, Master Caldris."

"Hold course, aye."

Jabril accepted this; Locke was discovering that the man had a solid core of sense and a fair knowledge of nearly every aspect of shipboard life, which made him Locke's superior in that wise. He was a fine mate, another bit of good fortune to be grateful for. The men behind Jabril, now . . . Locke instinctively knew they needed some occupying task to help mitigate their disappointment.

"Streva," he said to the youngest, "heave the log aft. Mal, you mind the minute-glass. Report to Master Caldris. Jabril, you know how to use a recurved bow?"

"Aye, Captain. Shortbow, recurved, longbow. Decent aim with any."

"I've got ten of them in a locker down in the aft hold. Should be easy to find. Couple hundred arrows, too. Rig up some archery butts with canvas and straw. Mount them at the bow so nobody gets an unpleasant surprise in the ass. Start sharpening up the lads in groups, every day when the weather allows. Time comes to finally pay a visit to another ship, I'll want good archers in the tops."

"Fine idea, Captain."

That, at least, seemed to restore excitement to the sailors who were still milling near the quarterdeck. Most of them followed Jabril down a hatchway to the main deck. Their interest in the matter gave Locke a further thought.

"Master Valora!"

Jean was with Mirlon, their cook, scrutinizing something at the little brick firebox abutting the forecastle. He waved in acknowledgment of Locke's shout.

"By sunset I want to know that every man aboard knows where all the weapons lockers are. Make sure of it yourself."

Jean nodded and returned to whatever he was doing. By Locke's reckoning, the idea that Captain Ravelle wanted every man to be comfortable with the ship's weapons— aside from the bows, there were hatchets, sabers, clubs, and a few polearms—would be far better for morale than the thought that he would prefer keeping them locked up or hidden.

"Well done," said Caldris quietly.

Mal watched the last few grains in the minute-glass bolted to the mainmast run out, then turned aft and shouted, "Hold the line!"

"Seven and a half knots," Streva hollered a moment later.

"Seven and a half," said Caldris. "Very well. We've been making that more or less steady since we left Verrar. A good run."

Locke snuck a glance at the pegs sunk into the holes on Caldris' navigational board, and the compass in the binnacle, which showed them on a heading just a hairsbreadth west of due south.

"A fine pace if it holds," muttered Caldris around his cigar. "Puts us in the Ghostwinds maybe two weeks from today. Don't know about the captain, but getting a few days ahead of schedule makes me *very* bloody comfortable."

"And will it hold?" Locke spoke as softly as he could without whispering into the sailing master's ear.

"Good question. Summer's end's an odd time on the Sea of Brass; we got storms out there somewhere. I can feel it in my bones. They're a ways off, but they're waiting."

"Oh, splendid."

"We'll make do, Captain." Caldris briefly removed his cigar, spat something brown at the deck, and returned it to between his teeth. "Fact is, we're doing just fine, thank the Lord of the Grasping Waters."

13

"KILL 'IM, Jabril! Get 'im right in the fuckin' 'eart!"

Jabril stood amidships, facing a frock coat (donated from Locke's chest) nailed to a wide board and propped up against the mainmast, about thirty feet away. Both of his feet touched a crudely chalked line on the deck planks. In his right hand was a throwing knife, and in his left was a full wine bottle, by the rules of the game.

The sailor who'd been shouting encouragement burped loudly and started stomping the deck. The circle of men around Jabril picked up the rhythm and began clapping and chanting, slowly at first, then faster and faster. "Don't spill a drop! Don't spill a drop! Don't spill a *drop*! Don't spill a *drop*! *Don't spill a drop!*"

Jabril flexed for the crowd, wound up, and flung the knife. It struck dead center in the coat, and up went a cheer that quickly turned to howls. Jabril had sloshed some of the wine out of the bottle.

"Dammit!" he cried.

"*Wine-waster,*" shouted one of the men gathered around him, with the fervor of a priest decrying the worst sort of blasphemy. "Pay the penalty and put it where it belongs!"

"Hey, at least I hit the coat," said Jabril with a grin. "You nearly killed someone on the quarterdeck with your throw."

"Pay the price! Pay the price! Pay the price!" chanted the crowd.

Jabril put the bottle to his lips, tipped it all the way up, and began to guzzle it in one go. The chanting rose in volume and tempo as the amount of wine in the bottle sank. Jabril's neck and jaw muscles strained mightily, and he raised his free hand high into the air as he sucked the last of the dark red stuff down.

The crowd applauded. Jabril pulled the bottle from his lips, lowered his head, and sprayed a mouthful of wine all over the man closest to him. "Oh no," he cried, "I *spilled* a drop! Ah ha ha ha ha!"

"My turn," said the drenched sailor. "I'm gonna lose on purpose and spill a drop right back, mate!"

Locke and Caldris watched from the starboard rail of the quarterdeck. Caldris was taking a rare break from the wheel; Jean currently had it. They were sailing along in a calm, muggy dusk just pleasant enough for Caldris to separate himself from the ship's precious helm by half a dozen paces.

"This was a good idea," said Locke.

"Poor bastards have been under the boot for so long, they deserve a good debauch." Caldris was smoking a pale blue ceramic pipe, the finest and most delicate thing Locke had ever seen in his hands, and his face was lit by the soft glow of embers.

At Caldris' suggestion, Locke had had large quantities of wine and beer (the *Red Messenger* was amply provisioned with both, and for a crew twice this size) hauled up on deck, and he'd offered a choice of indulgences to every man on board. A double ration of fresh roasted pork—courtesy of the small but well-larded pig they'd brought with them—for those who would stay sober and on watch, and a drunken party for those who wouldn't. Caldris, Jean, and Locke were sober, of course, along with four hands who'd chosen the pork.

"It's things like this that makes a ship seem like home," said Caldris. "Help you forget what a load of tedious old shit life out here can be."

"It's not so bad," said Locke, a bit wistfully.

"Aye, says the captain of the fuckin' ship, on a night sent by the gods." He drew smoke and blew it out over the rail. "Well, if we can arrange a few more nights like this, it'll be bloody grand. Quiet moments are worth more than whips and manacles for discipline, mark my words."

Locke gazed out across the black waves and was startled to see a pale white-green shape, glowing like an alchemical lantern, leap up from the waves and splash back down a few seconds later. The arc of its passage left an iridescent afterimage when he blinked.

"Gods," he said, "what the hell is *that*?"

There was a fountain of the things, now, about a hundred yards from the ship. They flew silently after one another, appearing and disappearing above the surf, casting their ghostly light on black water that returned it like a mirror.

"You really are new to these waters," said Caldris. "Those are flit-wraiths, Kosta. South of Tal Verrar, you see 'em all about. Sometimes in great schools, or arches leapin' over the water. Over ships. They've been known to follow us about. But only after dark, mind you."

"Are they some kind of fish?"

"Nobody rightly knows," said Caldris. "Flit-wraiths can't be caught. They can't be *touched*, as I hear it. They fly right through nets, like they was ghosts. Maybe they are."

"Eerie," said Locke.

"You get used to 'em after a few years," said Caldris. He drew smoke from his pipe, and the orange glow strengthened momentarily. "The Sea of Brass is a damned strange place, Kosta. Some say it's haunted by the Eldren. Most say it's just plain haunted. I've seen things. Saint Corella's fire, burnin' blue and red up on the yardarms, scaring the piss outta the top-watch. I sailed over seas like glass and seen... a city, once. Down below, not kidding. Walls and towers, white stone. Plain as day, right beneath our hull. In waters that our charts put at a thousand fathoms. Real as my nose it was, then gone."

"Heh," said Locke, smiling. "You're pretty good at this. You don't have to toy with me, Caldris."

"I'm not toying with you one bit, Kosta." Caldris frowned, and his face took on a sinister cast in the pipe-light. "I'm telling you what to expect. Flit-wraiths is just the beginning. Hell, flit-wraiths is almost friendly. There's things out there even I have trouble believing. And there's places no sensible ship's master will ever go. Places that are... wrong, somehow. Places that *wait* for you."

"Ah," said Locke, recalling his desperate early years in the old and rotten places of Camorr, and a thousand looming, broken buildings that had seemed to wait in darkness to swallow small children. "Now there I grasp your meaning."

"The Ghostwind Isles," said Caldris, "well, they're the worst of all. In fact, there's only eight or nine islands human beings have actually set foot on, and come back to tell about it. But gods know how many more are hiding down there, under the fogs, or what the fuck's on 'em." He paused before continuing. "You ever hear of the three settlements of the Ghostwinds?"

"I don't think so," said Locke.

"Well." Caldris took another long puff on his pipe. "Originally there was three. Settlers out of Tal Verrar touched there about a hundred years ago. Founded Port Prodigal, Montierre, and Hope-of-Silver.

"Port Prodigal's still there, of course. Only one left. Montierre was doing well until the war against the Free Armada. Prodigal's tucked well back in a fine defensive position; Montierre wasn't. After we did for their fleet, we paid a visit. Burnt their fishing boats, poisoned their wells, sank their docks. Torched everything standing, then torched the ashes. Might as well have just rubbed the name 'Montierre' off the map. Place ain't worth resettling."

"And Hope-of-Silver?"

"Hope-of-Silver," said Caldris, lowering his voice to a whisper. "Fifty years ago, Hope-of-Silver was larger than Port Prodigal. On a different island, farther west. Thriving. That silver wasn't just a hope. Three hundred families, give or take.

"Whatever happened, happened in one night. Those three hundred families, just . . . gone."

"Gone?"

"Gone. Vanished. Not a body to be found. Not a bone for birds to pick at. Something came down from those hills, out of that fog above the jungle, and gods know what it was, but it took 'em all."

"Merciful hells."

"If only," said Caldris. "A ship or two poked around after it happened. They found one ship from Hope-of-Silver itself, drifting offshore, like it'd put out in a real hurry. On it, they found the only bodies left from the whole mess. A few sailors. All the way up the masts, up at the very tops." Caldris sighed. "They'd lashed themselves there to escape whatever they'd seen . . . and they were all found dead by their own weapons. Even where they were, they killed themselves rather than face whatever was comin' for 'em.

"So pay attention to this, Master Kosta." Caldris gestured at the circle of relaxed and rowdy sailors, drinking and throwing knives by the light of alchemical globes. "You sail a sea where shit like that happens, you can see the value of making your ship a happy home."

14

"NEED A word, Captain Ravelle."

A day had passed. The air was still warm and the sun still beat down with palpable force when not behind the clouds, but the seas were higher and the wind stiffer. The *Red Messenger* lacked the mass to knife deep into the turbulent waves without shuddering, and so the deck beneath Locke's feet became even less of a friend.

Jabril—recovered from his close engagement with a wine bottle—and a pair of older sailors approached Locke as he stood by the starboard rail late in the afternoon, holding tight and trying to look casual. Locke recognized the older sailors as men who'd declared themselves unfit at the start of the voyage; days of rest and large portions had done them good. Locke, in light of the ship's understrength complement, had recently authorized extra rations at every meal. The notion was popular.

"What do you need, Jabril?"

"Cats, Captain."

The bottom fell out of Locke's stomach. With heroic effort, he managed to look merely puzzled. "What about them?"

"We been down on the main deck," said one of the older sailors. "Sleeping, mostly. Ain't seen no cats yet. Usually the little buggers are crawlin' around, doin' tricks, lookin' to curl up an' sleep on us."

"I asked around," said Jabril. "Nobody's seen even one. Not on the main deck, not up here, not on the orlop. Not even in the bilges. You keepin' em in your cabin?"

"No," said Locke, picturing with perfect clarity the sight of eight cats (including Caldris' kitten) lounging contentedly in an empty armory shack above their private bay back at the Sword Marina. Eight cats sparring and yowling over bowls of cream and plates of cold chicken.

Eight cats who were undoubtedly *still* lounging in that shack, right where he'd forgotten them, the night of the fateful assault on Windward Rock. Five days and seven hundred miles behind them.

"Kittens," he said quickly. "I got a pack of kittens for this trip, Jabril. I reckoned a ship with a new name could do with new cats. And I can tell you they're a hell of a shy bunch—I myself haven't seen one since I dumped them on the orlop. I expect they're just getting used to us. We'll see them soon enough."

"Aye, sir." Locke was surprised at the relief visible on the faces of the three sailors. "That's good to hear. Bad enough we got no women aboard until we get to the Ghostwinds; no cats would be plain awful."

"Couldn't tolerate no such offense," whispered one of the older sailors.

"We'll put out some meat every night," said Jabril. "We'll keep poking around the decks. I'll let you know soon as we find one."

"By all means," said Locke.

Seasickness had nothing to do with his sudden urge to throw up over the side the moment they were gone.

15

ON THE evening of their fifth day out from Tal Verrar, Caldris sat down for a private conversation in Locke's cabin with the door locked.

"We're doing well," the sailing master said, though Locke could see dark circles like bruises under his eyes. The old man had slept barely four hours a day since they'd reached the sea, unable to trust the wheel to Locke or Jean's care without supervision. He'd finally cultivated a fairly responsible master's mate, a man called Bald Mazucca, but even he was lacking in lore and could only be trained a little each day, with Caldris' attention so divided.

They continued to be blessed by the behavior of the rest of the crew. The men were still fresh with vigor for any sort of work following their escape from prison. A half-assed carpenter and a decent sailmaker had been found, and one of Jabril's friends had been optimistically voted quartermaster, in charge of counting and dividing plunder when it came. The infirm were gaining health with speed, and several had already joined watches. Lastly, the men no longer gathered to stare nervously across the ship's wake, looking for any hint of pursuit on the sea behind them. They seemed to think that they had evaded Stragos' retribution... and of course they could never be told that none would be forthcoming.

"This is your doing," said Locke, patting Caldris on the shoulder. He berated himself for not thinking beforehand of what a strain the voyage would put on the older man. Mazucca would have to be shaped more quickly, and he and Jean would need to pick up whatever slack they could in their inept fashion. "Even with a glassy sea and a fine breeze, there's no way in hell we'd have pulled this off so far without you."

"Strong weather coming, though," said Caldris. "Weather that will test us. Summer's end, like I said, shit blows up that's like to knock you halfway round the world. Might spend days riding it out with bare poles, throwing up until there ain't a dry spot in the holds." The sailing master sighed, then gave Locke a curious look. "Speaking of holds, I heard the damnedest things the past day or two."

"Oh?" Locke tried to sound nonchalant.

"Ain't nobody seen a cat, not on any of the decks. Not a one has come up from wherever they are, not for anything, ale or milk or eggs or meat." Sudden suspicion clouded his brow. "There are cats down there . . . right?"

"Ah," said Locke. His sympathy for Caldris from a moment earlier remained like a weight on his heart. For once, he found himself completely unwilling to lie, and he massaged his eyes with his fingers as he spoke. "Ah. No, the cats are all safe and sound in their shack in the Sword Marina, right where I left them. Sorry."

"You fucking jest," said Caldris in a flat, dead voice. "Come now. Don't bloody lie to me about this."

"I'm not." Locke spread his palms before him and shrugged. "I know you told me it was important. I just . . . I had a hundred things to do that night. I meant to fetch them, honest."

"*Important?* I told you it was *important*? I told you it was fucking critical, is what I told you!" Caldris kept his voice at a whisper, but it was like the sound of water boiling against hot coals. Locke winced. "You have imperiled our *souls*, Master Kosta, our very gods-damned souls. We have no women and no cats and no proper *captain*, I remind you, and hard weather sits upon our course."

"Sorry, honestly."

"Honestly, indeed. I was a fool to send a land-sucker to fetch cats. I should have sent cats to fetch me a land-sucker! They wouldn't have disappointed me."

"Now, surely, when we reach Port Prodigal—"

"*When* is an audacious assumption, Leocanto. For long before then the crew will cop wise to the fact that our cats are not merely shy, but *imaginary*. If they decide the cats have died off, they will just assume that we are cursed and abandon the ship when we touch land. If, however, the absence of smelly little bodies leads them to deduce that their fuckin' captain in fact brought *none*, they will hang you from a yardarm."

"Ouch."

"You think I jest? They will *mutiny*. If we see another sail on that horizon, in any direction, we must give chase. We must bring a fight. You know why? *So we can take some of their bloody cats*. Before it's too late."

Caldris sighed before continuing, and suddenly looked ten years older. "If it's a summer's-end storm coming up on us," said Caldris, "it'll be moving north and west, faster than we can sail. We'll have to pass through it, for we cannot outrun it by beating up to the east. It'll catch us still, and it'll only catch us tired. I'll do my damnedest, but you'd better pray in your cabin tonight for one thing."

"What's that?"

"Cats falling from the bloody sky."

16

OF COURSE, no convenient rain of screeching felines was forthcoming that night, and when Locke made his first appearance on the quarterdeck the next morning, there was an ugly ghost-gray haze looming on the southern horizon like the shadow of an angry god. The bright medallion of the sun rising in the otherwise clear sky only made it seem more sinister. The starboard heel of the deck was yet more pronounced, and walking to anywhere on the larboard bow felt almost like going up a small hill. Waves slapped the hull and were pulverized to spray, filling the air with the smell and taste of salt.

Jean was drilling a small group of sailors with swords and polearms at the ship's waist, and Locke nodded knowingly, as though he caught every nuance of their practice and approved. He toured the deck of the *Red Messenger,* greeting sailors by name, and tried to ignore the feeling that Caldris' gaze was burning holes in the back of his tunic.

"A fine morning to you, Captain," muttered the sailing master when Locke approached the wheel. Caldris looked ghoulish in the bright sunlight: his hair and beard washed whiter, his eyes sunken in deeper shadow, every line on his face newly re-etched by the hand of whatever god claimed him.

"Did you sleep last night, Master Caldris?"

"I found myself strangely unable, Captain."

"You must rest sometime."

"Aye, and the ship must generally stay above the waves, or so I've heard it suggested."

Locke sighed, faced the bow, and studied the darkening southern sky. "A summer's-end storm, I daresay. Been through enough of them in my time." He spoke loudly and casually.

"Soon enough you'll be in one more, Captain."

Locke spent the afternoon counting stores in the main hold with Mal as his scribe, marking little lines on a wax tablet. They ducked and weaved through a forest of salted meat in treated cloth sacks, hung from the beams in the hold and swaying steadily with the increasing motion of the ship. The hold was danker already from constant occupation by the crew; those who had been inclined to sleep in the more open space beneath the forecastle had abandoned it as the promise of hard weather had loomed. Locke was certain he smelled piss; someone was either too lazy or too frightened to crawl out and use the craplines. That could get ugly.

The whole sky was a cataract of haze-gray by the fourth hour of the afternoon. Caldris, slumped against the mast for a brief respite while Bald Mazucca and another sailor held the wheel, ordered sails trimmed and lanterns passed around from the storm lockers. Jean and Jabril led parties belowdecks to ensure that their cargo and equipment was all properly stowed. A weapons locker flying open, or a barrel tumbling around in a rocking ship, would send hapless sailors to meet the gods.

After dinner, at Caldris' whispered insistence, Locke ordered those sailors who'd dipped into the ship's store of tobacco to smoke their last until further notice. Open flames would no longer be tolerated anywhere; alchemical lanterns would provide all of their light, and they would use the hearthstone or—more likely—take cold meals. Locke promised an extra half of a wine ration each night if that became necessary.

A premature darkness had infused the sky by the time Locke and Jean could sit down for a quiet drink in the stern cabin. Locke closed the shutters over his stern windows, and the compartment seemed smaller than ever. Locke regarded the dubious comforts of this symbol of Ravelle's authority: a padded hammock against the larboard bulkhead, a pair of stools, his sword and knives hung on the wall by storm clasps. Their "table" was a flat wooden board atop Locke's chest. Sad as it was, it was princely compared to the glorified closets claimed by Jean and Caldris, or the way the men seemed to burrow in cargo and canvas matting on the main deck.

"I'm so sorry about the cats," said Locke.

"I could have remembered as well," said Jean. Unspoken was the obvious statement that he'd trusted Locke enough not to feel that he needed to concern himself. Jean might be doing his best to stay polite, but guilt twisted in Locke's stomach more sharply for it.

"No sharing this blame," said Locke, sipping his warm ale. "I'm the captain of the bloody ship."

"Don't be grandiose." Jean scratched his belly, which had been reduced by his recent activity to a much less dramatic curve than it had once possessed. "We'll think of something. Hell, if we spend a few days plowing through a storm, the men won't have time to worry about anything except when and how hard to piss their breeches."

"Hmmm. Storm. Fine opportunity for one of us to

misstep and look a fool in front of the men. More likely to be me than you."

"Quit brooding." Jean grinned. "Caldris knows what he's doing. He'll haul us through somehow."

There was a sudden heavy impact on the cabin door. Locke and Jean jumped up from their stools in unison, and Locke darted for his weapons. Jean shouted, "What passes?"

"Kosta," came a faint voice, followed by a feeble rattling, as though someone was trying and failing to work the latch.

Jean pulled the door open just as Locke finished buckling on his sword-belt. Caldris stood at the bottom of the companionway, clutching the doorframe for support, swaying on his feet. The amber glow of Locke's cabin lamp revealed wretched details: Caldris' eyes were bloodshot and rolling upward, his mouth hung open, and his waxy skin was glazed with sweat.

"Help, Kosta," he whispered, wheezing with a sound that was painful just to hear.

Jean grabbed him and held him up. "Damn," he muttered. "He's not just tired, Leo...Captain. He needs a bloody physiker!"

"Help...Kosta," moaned the sailing master. He clawed at his left upper arm with his right hand, and then at his left breast. He squeezed his eyes shut and winced.

"Help me?" Locke put a hand beneath Caldris' chin; the man's pulse was wild and erratic. "What do you mean, help me?"

"No." Caldris grimaced with concentration, sucking in a harsh breath between each word. "Help. *Me*. Kosta!"

"Lay him on the table," said Jean, and together he and Locke pressed the old man down onto his back.

"Sweet gods," said Locke, "is it the poison? I don't feel any different."

"Nor I," said Jean. "I think . . . I think his heart is seizing up. I've seen it before. Shit. If we can calm him down, maybe get him to drink something—"

But Caldris moaned again, dug feebly at the left side of his chest with both hands, and shuddered. His hands fell limp. One long, strangled exhalation escaped from his throat, and Locke, in rising horror, felt frantically around the base of his neck with the fingers of both hands.

"His pulse is gone," Locke whispered.

A soft rattle on the cabin roof, gentle at first but quickly rising in tempo, told them that the first drops of rain were beginning to fall on the ship. Caldris' eyes, fixed on the ceiling, were lifeless as glass.

"Oh, *shit*," said Jean.

II

CARDS UP THE SLEEVE

"Gamblers play just as lovers make love and
drunkards drink—blindly and of necessity, under
domination of an irresistible force."

Jacques Anatole Thibault

CHAPTER EIGHT

SUMMER'S END

1

DARK WATER ACROSS THE BOW, water at the sides, water in the air, falling with the weight of lead pellets against Locke's oilcloak. The rain seemed to come first from one side and then another, never content to fall straight down, as the *Red Messenger* rocked back and forth in the gray hands of the gale.

"Master Valora!" Locke held fast to the safety lines knotted around the mainmast (as they were knotted all around the deck) and bellowed down the main-deck hatch. "How much water in the well?"

Jean's answer came up a few moments later. "Two feet!"

"Very good, Master Valora!"

Locke caught a glimpse of Bald Mazucca staring at him, and he suppressed a feeling of unease. He knew that Caldris' sudden death the day before had been taken by the crew as an omen of the worst sort; they were openly muttering about women and cats, and the focal point of all their unkind attention was one Orrin Ravelle, whose status as captain and savior was steadily fraying. Locke turned toward the helmsman and found him once again squinting ahead into the stinging rain, seemingly absorbed in his duty.

Two cloaked sailors stood at the second wheel behind Mazucca; in seas this strong control of the rudder could easily fly free from the grip of a single man. Their faces were dark shadows within their hoods; they had nothing friendly to say to Locke, either.

The wind screamed through the lines and yards overhead, where most of the sails were tightly furled. They continued to push vaguely southwest under the press of nothing but close-reefed topsails. They were heeled over so far to starboard that Mazucca and his assistants were not merely standing in wait at their wheels. The crashing sea demanded their constant, tedious concentration to keep the ship stable, and still the sea was rising.

A rush of gray-green water ran over Locke's bare toes and he sucked in breath; he'd abandoned his boots for the more certain footing of unprotected feet. Locke watched that water roll across the deck, unwelcome but constant guest, before it poured away down the scuppers and leaked past the edges of the storm-canvas laid beneath the hatch gratings. In truth the water was warm, but here in the sunless heart of the storm, with the wind like knives in the air, his imagination made it seem cold.

"Captain Ravelle!"

Jabril was approaching along the larboard rail, storm lantern in one night-black hand. "It might've been advisable to take down the fuckin' topgallant masts a few hours ago," he shouted.

Since Locke had risen that morning, Jabril had offered at least half a dozen rebukes and reminders without prompting. Locke stared upward at the very tips of the main and foremasts, nearly lost in the swirling haze overhead. "I gave it some thought, Jabril, but it didn't seem necessary." According to some of what Locke had read, even without sails flying from their yards, the topgallant masts might give unwanted leverage to deadly storm winds, or even be lost over the side as the vessel bucked and heaved. He'd been too busy to think of striking them down.

"It'll seem pretty gods-damned necessary if they come down and take more of the rigging with them!"

"I might have them struck down in a while, Jabril, if I think it proper."

"If you think it proper?" Jabril gaped at him. "Are you bereft of your bloody senses, Ravelle? The time to strike the bastards was hours ago; now the hands we have are in sore need elsewhere, and the fuckin' weather's up! We might try it only were the ship in peril...but damn me, she might soon be! Have you not been out this far on the Sea of Brass before, Captain?"

"Aye, of course I have." Locke sweated within his oilcloak. Had he known the real extent of Jabril's sea-wisdom, he might have tasked the man with minding such details, but now it was too late, and some of his incompetence was laid bare. "Forgive me, Jabril. Caldris was a good friend. His loss has left me a bit off-kilter!"

"Indeed! As the loss of the fuckin' ship might leave us all more than a touch *off-kilter,* sir." Jabril turned and began making his way forward along the larboard rail, then after a few seconds whirled back to Locke. "You and I both know for a damn truth there's not a single bloody cat on board, Ravelle!"

Locke hung his head and clung to the mizzen. It was too much to hope that Mazucca and the hands standing behind him hadn't heard that. But of course, at his glance, they said nothing and betrayed nothing, staring fixedly ahead into the storm, as though trying to imagine he were not there at all.

2

BELOWDECKS WAS a nightmare. At least on deck one had masts and crashing seas to offer some perspective on one's place. Down here, in the enveloping fug of sweat, urine, and vomit, the shuddering walls themselves seemed to tilt and lurch at malicious whim. Streams of water poured down from hatchways and gratings, despite the weather precautions the crew had taken. The main deck echoed with the muffled howling of the wind, and the clanking sound of the pumps rose from the orlop below.

Those pumps were fine Verrari gearwork, capable of heaving water up and dashing it over the side at some speed, but they demanded eight-man shifts in seas like this, and the labor was backbreaking. Even a crew in good health would have found the job onerous; it was just plain bad luck for this bunch that so few of them had come out of prison at anything near their full strength.

"The water gains, Captain," said a sailor Locke couldn't recognize in the near darkness. He'd popped his head up the hatchway from the orlop. "Three feet in the well. Aspel says we busted a seam somewhere; says he needs men for a repair party."

Aspel was their approximation of a ship's carpenter. "He'll have them," Locke said, though from where, he knew not. Ten doing important work on deck, eight at the pumps...damn near their time to be relieved, too. Six or seven still too bloody weak to be of any use save as ballast. A squad in the orlop hold with Jean, resecuring casks of food and water after three had come loose and broken open. Eight sleeping fitfully on the main deck just a few feet away, having been up all night. Two with broken bones, trying to dull the pain with an unauthorized ration of wine. Their rudimentary scheme of watches was unraveling in the face of the storm's demands, and Locke struggled to subsume a sharp pang of panic.

"Fetch Master Valora from the orlop," he said at last. "Tell him he and his men can look to the stores again once they've given Aspel a hand."

"Aye, sir."

"Captain Ravelle!"

Another shout rose from below as the first sailor disappeared, and Locke stood over the hatchway to answer. "What passes?"

"Our time at the bloody pumps, sir! We can't keep up this gods-damned pace forever. We need relief. And we need food!"

"You shall have them both," said Locke, "in but ten minutes." Though from where, again, he knew not; all his choices were sick, injured, exhausted, or otherwise engaged. He turned to make his way back up to the deck. He could swap the deck-watch and the men at the pumps; it would bring joy to neither group, but it might serve to nudge the ship ahead of total disaster for a few more precious hours.

3

"WHAT DO you mean, you haven't been turning the glasses?"

"Captain Ravelle, sir, beggin' your double-fuckin' pardon, but we ain't had no time to turn the glasses nor mind the log since... hell, I suppose I can't say. A while now."

Bald Mazucca and his mate looked more like they were clinging to his wheel for dear life than steering the ship with it. Two teams of two had the wheels; the air was a frenzy of howling wind and stinging rain. The sea, cresting twenty feet or more, slammed past the bow again and again, washing the deck white and sluicing past Locke's ankles. At long last they'd been forced to abandon a southerly course, and now they were dead west before the wind, pulled by one lonely storm forecourse. They scudded again and again through waves high as houses.

A bolt of yellow flitting past in the periphery of Locke's vision was a storm-lantern flying free and vanishing over the side, soon to be a curiosity for the fish far below.

Locke hauled himself over to the binnacle and flipped through the damp pages of the master's log; the last hasty entry read:

> *3rd hr afternoon 7 Festal 78 Morgante s/sw 8 kts*
> *please may Iono spare these souls*

Locke couldn't remember when it had last felt like the third hour of the afternoon. The storm turned high noon dark as the insides of a shark's gullet, and the crackle of lightning gave uncanny illumination to what might have been deep evening. They were as unfixed in time as they were in place.

"At least we know we're somewhere on the Sea of Brass," he shouted above the din. "We'll be through this mess soon enough, and then we'll take sightings to fix our latitude."

If only that was as easily done as said. Fear and exhaustion had set Locke's senses reeling; the world was gray and whirling in every direction, and he'd thrown up his last cold meal at the taffrail . . . gods knew when. Hours before, probably. If Bondsmage of Karthain had appeared on deck at that moment and offered to use magic to steer the ship to safety, Locke might have kissed their boots.

There was a sudden terrible sound overhead; an explosive crack followed by the warbling hiss of a broken line lashing the air. Seconds later came a louder crash, and then a *snap-snap-snap* like the noise of a whip biting flesh.

" 'Ware above," cried Jabril from somewhere forward;

Locke and the ship seemed to lurch at once from another hammering wave. It was this loss of footing that saved Locke's life. A shadow swooped past his left shoulder as he slipped to the wet deck, sputtering. There was a splintering crash, screams, and sudden blackness as something slick and yielding enshrouded him.

Sail canvas! Locke shoved at it, working his way out from beneath it. Strong hands grabbed his forearms and hauled him to his feet. They belonged to Jean, who was braced against the starboard quarterdeck rail. Locke had slid a few feet to his right with the fall. Muttering thanks, he turned to see exactly what he feared.

The main topgallant mast had torn away. Its stays must have been snapped by some trick of wind or the ship's tumult. It had plunged forward and down, unfurling and trailing sail from its yard as it went, before a mess of tangled rigging had snapped it backward like a pendulum just above the deck. It covered the wheels, and the four men previously manning them were nowhere to be seen. Locke and Jean moved in unison, fighting across wet canvas and torn rope while smaller pieces of debris continued to rain down around them. Already Locke could feel the ship moving in an unhealthy fashion beneath them. The wheels must be seized, the rudder put right instantly.

"All hands," Locke cried with every ounce of conviction he possessed. "All hands on deck! All hands to save the ship!"

Jean heaved against the fallen topgallant spar, bracing himself against the mainmast, letting loose a howl of sheer exertion. Wood and canvas shifted, then crashed to the deck. Some of the handles of the two wheels had been reduced to splinters, but the wheels themselves were substantially intact. Locke could now see Bald Mazucca crawling slowly to his feet behind them; another man lay on deck with the top of his head plainly smashed in.

"Seize the wheel," Locke cried, looking around for more help. "Seize the bloody wheel!" He found himself tangled with Jabril.

"Captain," Jabril hollered straight into his face, "we are like to broach!"

Oh good, thought Locke, at least I know what that means. He gave Jabril a shove toward the wheels, and grabbed onto one beside Jean. "Helm a-larboard," Locke coughed, confident of that much. Groaning with strain, he and Jean fought to heave the wheel in the proper direction. The *Red Messenger* was slipping to lee at an angle, down into the troughs of the waves; in moments she'd be broadside to them and all but lost. A dark wave, impossibly heavy, surged over the starboard rail and doused them all, the merest foretaste of what awaited failure.

But the resistance of the wheel lessened as Jabril found his place behind them and heaved; in seconds he was joined by Mazucca, and inch by straining inch Locke felt the ship's stern come round again to larboard, until her bow was knifing into the waves once more. They'd bought time to contemplate the disaster the toppling mast had made of the rigging.

Men boiled out of the deck hatches, inhuman shapes in the dancing light of storm-lanterns. Lightning scorched the darkness above them. Orders were issued, from Locke and Jean and Jabril, with no heed paid to whose was the higher authority. The minutes became hours, and the hours felt like days. They fought on together in an eternity of gray chaos, cold and exhausted and terrified, against the screaming winds above and the hammering waters below.

4

"THREE FEET of water in the well and holding, Captain."

Aspel delivered his report with a makeshift bandage wrapped around his head, the sleeve of someone's jacket roughly slashed from its parent garment.

"Very good," said Locke, holding himself up at the mainmast much as Caldris had days before. Every joint and muscle in Locke's body announced their discomfort; he felt like a rag doll full of broken glass, and he was soaked in the bargain. But in that he was no different from any of the survivors aboard the *Red Messenger*. As Chains had once said, feeling like you wanted desperately to die was fine evidence that you had yet to do so.

The summer's-end storm was a receding line of darkness on the northwestern horizon; it had spit them out a few hours earlier. Here, the seas were running at five or six feet and the skies were still ashen gray, but this was a paradise following the tempest. Enough funereal light filtered down from above for Locke to guess that it was day, after some fashion.

He surveyed the shambles of the deck; lifelines and debris from the rigging were tangled everywhere. Scraps of canvas fluttered in the wind, and sailors were tripping over fallen block and tackle, cursing as they went. They were a crew of ghosts, haggard and clumsy with fatigue. Jean labored at the forecastle to conjure their first warm meal in living memory.

"Damnation," Locke muttered. Their escape had not been without price: three swept clean overboard, four seriously injured, two dead including Caldris. Mirlon, the cook, had been the man at the wheel when the main topgallant mast had crashed down upon him like a divine spear and shattered his skull.

"No, Captain," said Jabril from behind him. "Not if we can do right by them."

"What?" Locke whirled, confused.... Suddenly he remembered. "Oh, yes, of course."

"The fallen, Captain," said Jabril, enunciating as though to a child. "The fallen haunt our decks and cannot rest until we send them off proper."

"Aye," said Locke. "Let's do that."

Caldris and Mirlon lay by the larboard entry port, wrapped in canvas. Pale packages bound with tarred rope, awaiting their final send-off. Locke and Jabril knelt beside them.

"Say the words, Ravelle," muttered Jabril. "You can do that much for them. Send their souls on down to Father Stormbringer and give them rest."

Locke stared at the two wrapped corpses and felt a new pain in his heart. Nearly overcome with fatigue and shame, he put his head in his hands and thought quickly.

By tradition, ships' captains could be proclaimed lay priests of Iono, with a minimum of study at any proper temple to the Father of Grasping Waters. At sea, they could then lead prayers, perform marriages, and even give death-blessings. While Locke knew some interior ritual of Iono's Temple, he wasn't consecrated in Iono's service. He was a priest of the Crooked Warden, and here at sea, a thousand miles out into Iono's domain, aboard a ship that was already damned for spurning His mandates . . . there was no way in heavens or hells Locke could presume to give these men Iono's rest. For the sake of their souls, he'd have to invoke the only power he had any pull with.

"Crooked Warden, Unnamed Thirteenth, your servant calls. Place your eyes upon the passing of this man, Caldris bal Comar, Iono's servant, sworn to steal goods beneath the red flag, therefore sharing a corner of your kingdom—"

"What are you *doing*?" Jabril hissed, seizing Locke by the arm. Locke shoved him backward.

"The only thing I can do," said Locke. "The only honest blessing I can give these men, understand? Don't fucking interfere again." He reached back down to touch Caldris' wrapped body. "We deliver this man, body and spirit, to the realm of your brother Iono, mighty lord of the sea." Locke figured a little flattery never went amiss in these matters. "Lend him aid. Carry his soul to She who weighs us all. This we pray with hopeful hearts."

Locke gestured for Jabril's help. The muscular man remained deadly silent as they lifted Caldris' body together and heaved it out the entry port. Even before he heard the splash, Locke reached back down to the other canvas bundle.

"Crooked Warden, Thiefwatcher, your servant calls. Place your eyes upon the passing of this man, Mirlon, Iono's servant, sworn to steal goods beneath a red flag, therefore sharing a corner of your kingdom..."

5

THE MUTINY came the next morning, while Locke slept senseless in his hammock, still wearing the wet clothes that had seen him through the storm.

He was awakened by the sound of someone slamming his door and shooting home the bolt. Bleary-eyed and gasping in confusion, he all but fell out of his hammock and had to use his sea chest to push himself unsteadily to his feet.

"Arm yourself," said Jean, backing away from the door with both of his hatchets in hand. "We've got a problem."

That brought Locke to full wakefulness sharply enough. He buckled on his sword-belt in haste, noting with satisfaction that the heavy shutters over his stern windows were still drawn. Light peeked in around the edges; was it day already? Gods, he'd slept the whole night away in one dreamless blink.

"There's, ah, some of them that aren't happy with me, aren't there?"

"None of them are happy with us."

"I think they're surely angrier with me than they are with you. I think you could still make it as one of them; it's my blood they'll be after, and you can claim to be as much my dupe as they were. Take me out to them. You might still pull this scheme off and get the antidote from Stragos."

"Are you *mad*?" Jean glared back at Locke, but didn't step away from the door.

"You're a strange fellow, brother." Locke contemplated his Verrari sea-officer's saber uneasily; in his hands it would be no less a showpiece than it was now, in its scabbard. "First you want to punish yourself for something that's not your fault, and now you won't let me slip you out of a mistake that's entirely mine."

"Who the hell are you to lecture me, Locke? *First* you insist that I stay despite the real danger I pose to you, now you beg me to betray you for gain? Fuck you. You're ten pints of crazy in a one-pint glass."

"That describes us both, Jean." Locke smiled despite himself; there was something refreshing in being returned to danger of his own making after the indifferent malice of the storm. "Though you're more of a carafe than a pint glass. I knew you wouldn't buy it."

"Too gods-damned right."

"I will say, I would've liked to see Stragos' face when we did whatever we were going to do to him," said Locke. "And I would've liked to know what it was when the clever moment came."

"Well," said Jean, "as long as we're wishing, I would have liked a million solari and a parrot that speaks Throne Therin. But they're not coming, take my meaning?"

"Maybe the fact that this scuppers Stragos' precious little plan is fuck-you enough."

"Now, Locke." Jean sighed, and his voice softened. "Maybe they'll want to talk first. And if they want to talk to *you*, with your wits about you, we might still have a chance."

"Doubtless you're the only man aboard this ship who'd still express confidence in anything I do," Locke sighed.

"*Ravelle!*" The shout came from the companionway.

"You didn't kill any of them yet, did you, Jean?"

"Not yet, no."

"*Ravelle! I know you're in there, and I know you can hear me!*"

Locke stepped up to the cabin door and shouted back through it. "Marvelously clever, Jabril! You've tracked me unerringly to the cabin in which I've been fast asleep and motionless all bloody night. Who tipped you off?"

"We have all the bows, Ravelle!"

"Well, damn," said Locke. "You must have gotten into the weapon lockers, then. I suppose I was hoping we could have one of those pleasant dancing mutinies, or maybe a singing-and-card-games mutiny, you know?"

"There's thirty-two of us as can still move, Ravelle! Two of you in there, no food, no water...the ship's ours. How long do you figure on staying in there?"

"It's a fine place," shouted Locke. "Got a hammock, a table, nice view out the stern...big door between us and the rest of you...."

"Which we can smash at any time, and you know it." Jabril lowered his voice; a creak of shifting weight in the companionway told Locke he'd stepped right up to the other side of the door. "You're glib, Ravelle, but glib's no good against ten bows and twenty blades."

"I'm not the only man in here, Jabril."

"Aye. And believe me, there's not one among us who'd like to face Master Valora; not with fuckin' four-to-one odds. But the odds is better than that. Like I said, we got all the bows. You want it to come down hard, we'll do what it takes."

Locke bit the inside of his cheek, thinking. "You swore an oath to me, Jabril. An oath to me as your captain! After I gave you your *lives* back."

"We all did, and we meant it, but you're not what you said you was. You're no sea-officer. Caldris was the real thing, gods rest him, but I don't know what the fuck you are. You deceived us, so the oath don't stand."

"I see." Locke pondered, snapped his fingers, and continued. "So you would have kept to the oath, had I...ah, been what I claimed to be?"

"Aye, Ravelle. Fuckin' right we would've."

"I believe you," said Locke. "I believe you're no oath-breaker, Jabril. So I have a proposal. Jerome and I are willing to come peaceably out of the cabin. We'll come up on the deck, and we'll talk. We'll be pleased to hear your grievances, every last one. And we'll keep our hands empty, so long as you swear an oath to give us that much. Safe conduct to the deck, and an open talk. For everyone."

"Won't be no 'hearing grievances,' Ravelle. It'll just be us telling you how it's to be."

"As you wish," said Locke. "Call it whatever you like. Give me your oath of safe passage, and it'll happen. We'll come out right now."

Locke strained for several seconds to hear anything from the companionway. At last, Jabril spoke.

"Come up with empty hands," he said, "and don't make no unkind moves, especially not Valora. Do that, and I swear before all the gods, you'll come up to the deck safe. Then we'll talk."

"Well," whispered Jean, "at least you got us that much."

"Yeah. Maybe just a chance to die in the sunlight rather than the shade, though." He considered changing out of his wet clothes before going up on deck, then shook his head. "Hell with it. Jabril!"

"Aye?"

"We're opening the door."

6

THE WORLD above the deck was one of rich blue skies and bright sunlight; a world Locke had almost forgotten over the previous days. He marveled at it, though Jabril led them to the waist under the eyes of thirty men with drawn swords and nocked arrows. Lines of white foamed on the sea at the horizons, but around the *Red Messenger* the waves rolled softly, and the breeze was a welcome kiss of warmth against Locke's skin.

"I'll be damned," he whispered. "We sailed right back into summer again."

"Stands to reason that we got blown a ways south even in the storm," said Jean. "We must have passed the Prime Divisor. Latitude naught."

The ship was still something of a shambles; Locke spotted makeshift and incomplete repairs everywhere. Mazucca stood calmly at the wheel, the only unarmed man on deck. The ship was making steerage way under nothing but its main topsail. The mainmast rigging would need one hell of a sorting out before it would carry any useful canvas; the fallen topgallant mast was nowhere to be seen.

Locke and Jean stood before the mainmast, waiting. Up on the forecastle, men were looking down on them from behind their bows. Thankfully, none of them had drawn their strings back—they looked nervous, and Locke trusted neither their judgment nor their muscle tone. Jabril leaned back against the ship's boat and pointed at Locke.

"You fuckin' lied to us, Ravelle!"

The crew shouted and jeered, shaking their weapons,

hurling insults. Locke held up his hand to speak, but Jabril cut him off. "You said it yourself, down below. I got you to bloody admit it, so say it again, for all to hear. *You ain't no sea-officer.*"

"It's true," said Locke. "I'm not a sea-officer. That should be obvious to everyone by now."

"What the hell are you, then?" Jabril and the men seemed genuinely confused. "You had a Verrari uniform. You got in and out of Windward Rock. The archon took this ship, and you got it back. What's the gods-damned game?"

Locke realized that an unsatisfactory answer to this question would have hard consequences; those things really did add up to a mystery too considerable to brush off. He scratched his chin, then put up his hands. "Okay, look. Only *some* of what I told you was a lie. I, ah, I really *was* an officer in the archon's service, just not a *naval* officer. I was one of his captains of intelligence."

"Intelligence?" cried Aspel, who held a bow atop the forecastle. "What, you mean spies and things like that?"

"Exactly," said Locke. "Spies. And things like that. I hate the archon. I was sick of his service. I figured . . . I figured with a crew and a ship I had a sure way to get the hell out and give him grief at the same time. Caldris came along to do all the real work, while I was learning."

"Aye," said Jabril. "But that's not what happened. You didn't just lie to us about what you was." He turned his back to Locke and Jean to address the crew. "He brought us out to sea without a woman aboard the ship!"

Scowls, catcalls, rude gestures, and no few hand-signs against evil. The crew were not well pleased to be reminded of that subject.

"Hold fast," shouted Locke, "I meant to bring women with us; I had four women on my list. Didn't you see them at Windward Rock? Other prisoners? They all went down with a fever. They had to be put back ashore, don't you see?"

"If that was you," shouted Jabril, "maybe you thought of it once, but what did you do to fix it when they fell sick?"

"The archon took the bloody prisoners, not me," said Locke. "I had to work with what that left me. It left me *you*!"

"So it did," said Jabril, "and then you fuckin' brought us out here without *one single cat* neither!"

"Caldris told me to get some," said Locke. "Forgive me, I just . . . I said I'm not a sailor, right? I got busy sneaking out of Tal Verrar and I left them behind. I didn't understand!"

"Indeed," said Jabril. "You had no business out here if you didn't know the bloody mandates! Because of you, this ship is cursed! We're lucky to be alive, those of us that *is*. Five men paid for what was rightly your sin! Your ignorance of what's due Iono Stormfather by those that sail his waters!"

"Lord of the Grasping Waters shield us!" said another sailor.

"Our misfortune's been made by you," Jabril continued. "You admit your lies and ignorance. I say this ship ain't clean till we get you off her! What's the word of all?"

There was a loud, immediate, and unanimous chorus of agreement; the sailors shook their weapons at Locke and Jean as they cheered.

"That's that," said Jabril. "Drop your weapons on the deck."

"Wait," said Locke. "You said we'd talk, and I'm not finished!"

"I brought you on deck safe, and we did talk. Talk's finished, oath's paid off." Jabril folded his arms. "Lose your weapons!"

"Now—"

"Archers!" yelled Jabril. The men atop the forecastle took aim.

"What's the choice?" Locke shouted angrily. "Disarm so we can *what*?"

"Keep your arms and die bleeding on this deck," said Jabril. "Or disarm, and swim as far as you can. Let Iono be your judge."

"Quick and painful or slow and painful. Right." Locke unbound his sword-belt and let it drop to the deck. "Master Valora had nothing to do with my cock-ups. I dragged him into this same as you!"

"Now, wait a fucking minute . . . ," said Jean, as he set the Wicked Sisters respectfully down at his feet.

"What say you, Valora?" Jabril looked around for objections from the crew and saw none. "Ravelle's the liar. Ravelle admits the crime is his; away with him and the curse is lifted fair. You'd be welcome to stay."

"He swims, I swim," Jean growled.

"He worth that much to you?"

"I don't have to bloody well explain myself."

"So be it. That I respect," said Jabril. "Time to go."

"No," shouted Locke as several sailors advanced, swords held at guard. "No! I have one thing to say first."

"You had your say. Stormfather'll judge what else there is."

"When I found you," said Locke, "you were in a vault. Under a fucking *rock*. You were locked away beneath iron and stone! You were fit to die or to push oars for the archon's pleasure. You were dead and rotting, every last miserable one of you!"

"Heard this already," said Jabril.

"Maybe I'm not a sea-officer," said Locke. "Maybe I deserve this; maybe you're doing right to punish the man that's brought you this misfortune. But I am also the man who freed you. *I am the man who gave you any life you have.* You spit on that gift before the gods to do this to me!"

"You saying you want the arrows, then?" said Aspel, and the men around him laughed.

"No," said Jabril, holding up his hands. "No. There's a point. This ain't a happy ship in the eyes of the gods, that's for bloody sure. Our luck is tight-drawn as it is, even once we're rid of him. He needs to die for the crimes he's done; for his lies and his ignorance and the men who won't see land again. But he did free us." Jabril looked around and bit his lip before continuing. "We *do* owe him for that. I say we give them the boat."

"We need that boat," hollered Mazucca.

"Lots of boats in Port Prodigal," said Streva. "Maybe we can take one as plunder on the way down there."

"Aye, that and cats," shouted another sailor.

"Open boat," said Jabril. "No food, no water, says I. They go in as they are now. Let Iono take them as and when he will. What's the word of all?"

The word of all was another outburst of enthusiastic approval. Even Mazucca gave in and nodded.

"Just a longer swim, in the end," said Locke.

"Well," whispered Jean, "at least you talked them into that much."

7

THE SHIP'S boat was unlashed, hoisted out, and plopped over the starboard side into the deep blue waters of the Sea of Brass.

"They get oars, Jabril?" One of the sailors had been assigned the task of removing the water cask and rations from the boat, and he'd pulled out the oars as well.

"Think not," said Jabril. "Iono moves them if he wants them moved. We leave them to float; that was the word."

Parties of armed sailors lined up fore and aft to prod Locke and Jean toward the starboard entry port. Jabril followed close behind. When they reached the edge, Locke saw that the boat was tied up with one knotted line that would allow them to climb down.

"Ravelle," said Jabril quietly. "You really hold with the Thirteenth? You really one of his divines?"

"Yeah," said Locke. "It was the only honest blessing I could give for their sakes."

"I suppose that makes sense. Spies, things like that." Jabril slipped something cold beneath Locke's tunic, against the small of his back, sliding it precariously into the top of his breeches. Locke recognized the weight of one of the stilettos from his belt.

"Stormfather maybe takes you fast," whispered Jabril, "or maybe he lets you float. Long fuckin' time. Until you decide you just plain had *enough*...you know?"

"Jabril," said Locke, "...thank you. I, ah, wish I could have been a better captain."

"I wish you'd been any kinda captain at all. Now get over the fuckin' side and be gone."

So it was that Locke and Jean watched from the gently bobbing boat as the *Red Messenger* limped on, southwest by west under tattered sail, leaving them in the middle of nowhere under a midafternoon sun that Locke would have given ten thousand solari for just a day or two earlier.

One hundred yards, two hundred, three...their former ship slowly made way across the rippling sea, at first with what must have been half the crew gazing astern, watching. But soon enough they lost interest in the dead men in their wake. Soon enough they returned to the task of keeping their precious little wooden world from succumbing to its wounds.

Locke wondered who would inherit the stern cabin, Jean's hatchets, their unusual tools, and the five hundred solari stashed at the bottom of his personal chest—a mixture of their last funds and Stragos' financing.

Thieves prosper, he thought.

"Well, splendid," he said, stretching his legs as best he could. He and Jean faced each other from opposite rowing benches of a boat built for six. "Once again we've engineered a brilliant escape from immediate peril, and stolen something of value to take with us. This boat must be worth two solari."

"I just hope that whoever ends up with the Wicked Sisters bloody well chokes," said Jean.

"What, on the hatchets?"

"No, on anything. Whatever's convenient. I should've thrown them out the cabin window rather than let someone else have them. Gods."

"You know, Jabril slipped me a stiletto as I went off."

Jean seemed to ponder the implications of this for a moment, then shrugged. "When a smaller boat comes along, at least we'll have a weapon to board and carry her."

"Are you, ah, comfortable back there in the stern cabin?"

"I am," said Jean. He got off the bench, slid sideways, and crammed himself into the stern with his back against the starboard gunwale. "Bit tight, but luxurious trimmings."

"That's good," said Locke, pointing to the middle of the boat. "Hope it doesn't get more cramped when I install the hanging garden and the library right about there."

"Already took that into account." Jean leaned his head back and closed his eyes. "Hanging garden can go in on top of my bathhouse."

"Which can double as a temple," said Locke.

"You think that necessary?"

"I do," said Locke. "I daresay the two of us are going to be doing a hell of a lot of praying."

They floated in silence for many minutes. Locke also closed his eyes, breathed deep of the tangy air, and listened to the faint whisper of the waves. The sun was a warm and welcome pressure on the top of his head, and this above all conspired to lull him into a half-dozing state as he sat. He looked within for some hint of anguish and found only a hollow numbness; he seemed to have relaxed into relief at this final collapse of all his plans. Nobody else to fool, no more secrets to keep, no duties required of him or Jean as they drifted, merely drifted, waiting for the gods to make their next whim known.

Jean's voice recalled him to the present after some unguessable interval had passed, and he blinked as he re-opened his eyes to the bright gleam of sun on water.

"Locke," said Jean, evidently repeating himself, "sail ho, three points off the starboard bow!"

"Ha-ha, Jean. That would be the *Red Messenger,* sailing away from us forever. Surely you remember her."

"No," said Jean, more insistent. "*Fresh* sail ho, three points off the starboard bow!"

Locke glanced over his right shoulder, squinting. The *Red Messenger* was still plainly visible, now about three-quarters of a mile distant. And there, off to the left of his former ship, hard to see at first against the bright fusion of sea and sky—yes, a dusty white square just cresting the horizon.

"I'll be damned," said Locke. "Looks like our lads are going to have their first chance at some plunder."

"If only it'd had the courtesy to show up yesterday!"

"I'll wager I would have screwed things up regardless. But . . . can you imagine those poor bastards grappling their prey, leaping over the rails, swords in hand, screaming, 'Your cats! Give us all your gods-damned cats!' "

Jean laughed. "What a bloody mess we've unleashed. At least we'll have some entertainment. This'll be damn awkward with the *Messenger* in such a state. Maybe they'll come back for us and beg us to lend a hand."

"They'd beg *you*, maybe," said Locke.

As Locke watched, the *Messenger*'s forecourse shuddered into existence, an unfolding square of white. Straining, he could just see tiny figures dashing to and fro on the deck and in the rigging. His former ship put her bow a touch to larboard, bringing the wind onto her larboard quarter.

"She's limping like a horse with a broken ankle," said Jean. "Look, they won't trust the mainmast with any canvas. Can't say I blame them." Jean scrutinized the scene for a few moments more. "Their new friend's coming up north-northwest, I think. If our lads sneak west and look harmless enough, maybe...otherwise, that new ship's got plenty of room to run west or south. If she's in any decent shape at all, *Messenger*'ll never catch her."

"Jean...," said Locke, very slowly, a bit hesitant to trust his own naval judgment. "I don't...I don't think escape is anywhere on their minds. Look, they're straight on for the *Messenger*."

The next few minutes confirmed this. Indeed, the newcomer's sails soon doubled in size, and Locke could see the faintest line of the hull beneath them. Whatever she was, she was angled well north of west, fit to cut straight across the path of the *Red Messenger*.

"And she's fast," said Jean, clearly fascinated. "Look at her come on! I'd bet my own liver the *Messenger*'s not even making four knots. She's doing twice that or more."

"Maybe they just don't give a whit for the *Messenger*," said Locke. "Maybe they can see she's wounded and they're just going to fly right past."

"A 'kiss my ass and fare-thee-well,'" said Jean. "Pity."

The newcomer grew steadily; blurry shapes became a sleek dark hull, billowing sails, the thin lines of masts.

"Two masts," said Jean. "Brig, flying *loads* of canvas."

Locke felt an unexpected urgency; he tried to restrain his excitement as the *Messenger* plodded feebly to the southwest while the newcomer steadily gained on her. Now the strange vessel showed her starboard side to them. As Jean had said, she had two masts, as well as a swift low profile and a hull so black she gleamed.

A dark speck appeared in midair above her stern. It moved upward, expanded, and burst apart into a huge fluttering flag—a banner of solid crimson, bright as fresh-spilled blood.

"Oh, gods," cried Locke. "You have to be fucking kidding!"

The newcomer raced on, foam-capped water surging at her bow, closing the gap with the *Red Messenger* with every passing second. Low white shapes appeared from behind her—boats crammed with the dark specks of sailors. The new ship swung round to the *Messenger*'s lee like a hungry beast cutting off her prey's escape; meanwhile, her boats knifed across the gleaming water to launch their attack from windward. Whatever Jabril and his crew did to try and foil their entrapment, it wasn't enough; chorus after chorus of belligerent cheers echoed faintly across the water, and little black specks were soon swarming up the *Messenger*'s sides.

"No!" Locke was unaware that he'd leapt to his feet until Jean pulled him back down hastily. "Oh, you bastards! You rotten, miserable, skulking bastards! You can't take my fucking ship—"

"Which was already taken," said Jean.

"I come a thousand miles to shake your bloody hands," Locke screamed, "and you show up two *hours* after they put us overboard!"

"Not even half that," said Jean.

"Bloody fucking limp-cocked witless laggard *pirates*!"

"Thieves prosper," said Jean, biting his knuckles as he snorted with laughter.

The battle, if it could be called that, didn't last five minutes. Someone on the quarterdeck brought the *Messenger* around, luffing straight into the wind, killing what little speed she'd had. All her sails were taken in, and she soon drifted gently with one of the marauder's boats tied up at her side. Another boat hurried back to the ship that had birthed it. That vessel, under a far lazier press of sail than it had set out to snatch up the *Messenger,* then came round on a starboard tack and began to bear down in the general direction of Locke and Jean—an ominous monster toying with its next tiny meal.

"I think this might be one of those 'good news, bad news,' situations," said Jean, cracking his knuckles. "We may need to ready ourselves to repel boarders."

"With what? One stiletto and hurtful insinuations about their mothers?" Locke clenched his fists; his anger had become excitement. "Jean, if we get aboard that ship and talk our way into her crew, we're back in the game, by the gods!"

"They might just mean to kill us and take the boat."

"We'll see," said Locke. "We'll see. First we'll exchange courtesies. Have ourselves some diplomatic interaction."

The pirate vessel came on slowly as the sun sank toward the west and the color of sky and water alike seemed to deepen by a shade. She was indeed black-hulled, witch-wood, and larger than the *Red Messenger* even at a glance. Sailors crowded her yardarms and deck railings; Locke felt a pang of envy to see such a large and active crew. She sliced majestically through the water, then luffed up as orders were shouted from the quarterdeck. Sails were reefed with precise and rapid movements; she slowed to a crawl, blocked their view of the *Red Messenger,* and presented her larboard side at a distance of about twenty yards.

"Ahoy the boat," cried a woman at the rail. She was rather short, Locke could see—dark-haired, partially armored, backed up by at least a dozen armed and keenly interested sailors. Locke felt his skin crawl under their scrutiny, and he donned a cheerful mask.

"Ahoy the brig," he shouted. "Fine weather, isn't it?"

"What do you two have to say for yourselves?"

Locke rapidly considered the potential advantages of the pleading, cautious, and cocky approaches, and decided that cocky was the best chance they had of making a memorable impression. "Avast," he cried, standing up and hoisting his stiletto over his head, "you must perceive we hold the weather gauge, and you are luffed up with no hope of escape! Your ship is ours, and you are all our prisoners! We are prepared to be gracious, but don't test us."

There was an outbreak of laughter on the deck of the ship, and Locke felt his hopes rise. Laughter was good; laughter like that rarely preceded bloody slaughter, at least in his experience.

"You're Captain Ravelle," shouted the woman, "aren't you?"

"I, ah, see my reputation precedes me!"

"Previous crew of your previous ship might have mentioned you."

"Shit," Locke muttered.

"Would you two care to be rescued?"

"Yes, actually," said Locke. "That would be a damn polite thing for you to do."

"Right, then. Have your friend stand up. Both of you get all your clothes off."

"*What?*"

An arrow hissed through the air, several feet above their heads, and Locke flinched.

"Clothes off! You want charity, you entertain us first! Get your big friend up and get naked, both of you!"

"I don't believe this," said Jean, rising to his feet.

"Look," shouted Locke as he began to slip out of his tunic, "can we just drop them in the bottom of the boat? You don't want us to throw them overboard, right?"

"No," said the woman. "We'll keep 'em plus the boat, even if we don't keep you. Breeches off, gentlemen! That's the way!"

Moments later Locke and Jean stood, precariously balanced in the wobbling boat, stark naked with the rising evening breeze plainly felt against their backsides.

"Gentlemen," yelled the woman. "What's this? I expect to see some sabers, and instead you bring out your stilettos!"

The crew behind her roared with laughter. Crooked Warden! Locke realized others had come up along the larboard rail. There were more sailors just standing there pointing and howling at him and Jean than there were in the entire crew of the *Red Messenger*.

"What's the matter, boys? Thoughts of rescue not enticing enough? What's it take to get a rise out of you down there?"

Locke responded with a two-handed gesture he'd learned as a boy, one guaranteed to start fights in any city-state in the Therin world. The crowd of pirates returned it, with many creative variations.

"Right, then," cried the woman. "Stand on one leg. Both of you! Up on one!"

"*What?*" Locke put his hands on his hips. "Which one?"

"Just pick one of two, like your friend's doing," she replied.

Locke lifted his left foot just above the rowing bench, putting his arms out for balance, which was becoming steadily harder to keep. Jean did the same thing beside him, and Locke was absolutely sure that from any distance they looked a perfect pair of idiots.

"Higher," said the woman, "that's sad. You can do better than that!"

Locke hitched his knee up half a foot more, staring defiantly up at her. He could feel the vibrations of fatigue and the unstable boat alike in his right leg; he and Jean were seconds away from capping embarrassment with embarrassment.

"Fine work," the woman shouted. "Make 'em dance!"

Locke saw the dark blurs of the arrows flash across his vision before he heard the flat snaps of their release. He dove to his right as they thudded into the middle of the boat, realizing half a second too late that they'd not been aimed at flesh and blood. The sea swallowed him in an instant; he hit unprepared and upside down, and when he kicked back to the surface he gasped and sputtered at the unpleasant sensation of salt water up his nose.

Locke heard rather than saw Jean spit a gout of water as he came up on the other side of the boat. The pirates were roaring now, falling over themselves, holding their sides. The short woman kicked something, and a knotted rope fell through an entry port in the ship's rail.

"Swim over," she yelled, "and pull the boat with you."

By clinging to the gunwales and paddling awkwardly, Locke and Jean managed to push the little boat over to the ship, where they fell into shadow beneath her side. The end of the knotted rope floated there, and Jean gave Locke a firm shove toward it, as though afraid they might yank it up at any second.

Locke hauled himself up against the fine-grained black wood of the hull, wet and naked and fuming. Rough hands grasped him at the rail and heaved him aboard. He found himself looking at a pair of weathered leather boots, and he sat up.

"I hope that was amusing," he said, "because I'm going to—"

One of those boots struck him in the chest and shoved him back down to the deck. Wincing, he thought better of standing and instead studied the boot's owner. The woman was not merely short—she was petite, even from the perspective of someone literally beneath her heel. She wore a frayed sky-blue tunic over a loose black leather vest decorated with slashes that had more to do with near misses than high fashion. Her dark hair, which piled curl upon curl, was tightly bound behind her neck, and the belt at her waist carried a minor arsenal of fighting knives and sabers. There was obvious muscle on her shoulders and arms, an impression of strength that made Locke quickly stifle his anger.

"Going to *what*?"

"Lie here on the deck," he said, "and enjoy the fine afternoon sun."

The woman laughed; a second later Jean was pulled up over the side and thrown down beside Locke. His black hair was plastered to his skull, and water streamed from the bristles of his beard.

"Oh my," said the woman. "Big one and a little one. Big one looks like he can handle himself a bit. You must be Master Valora."

"If you say so, madam, I suppose I must be."

"Madam? Madam's a shore word. Out here to the likes of you, it's *lieutenant*."

"You're not the captain of this ship, then?"

The woman eased her boot off Locke's chest and allowed him to sit. "Not even hardly," she said.

"Ezri's my first," said a voice behind Locke. He turned, slowly and carefully, to regard the speaker.

This woman was taller than the one called Ezri, and broader across her shoulders. She was dark, with skin just a few shades lighter than the hull of her ship, and she was striking, but not young. There were lines about her eyes and mouth that proclaimed her somewhere near forty. Those eyes were cold and that mouth was hard—clearly, she didn't share Ezri's sense of mischief about the two un-clothed prisoners dripping water on her deck.

Her night-colored braids, threaded with red and silver ribbons, hung in a mane beneath a wide four-cornered cap, and despite the heat she wore a weather-stained brown frock coat, lined along the insides with brilliant gold silk. Most astonishingly, an Elderglass mosaic vest hung un-buckled beneath her coat. That sort of armor was rarely seen outside of royal hands—each little slat of Elderglass had to be joined by a latticework of metal, since humans knew no arts to meld the glass to itself. The vest glittered with reflected sunlight, more intricate than a stained-glass window—a thousand fingernail-sized chips of gleaming glory outlined in silver.

"Orrin Ravelle," she said. "I've never heard of you."

"Nor should you have," said Locke. "May we have the pleasure of your acquaintance?"

"Del," she said, turning away from Locke and Jean to look at Ezri, "get that boat in. Give their clothes the eye, take anything interesting, and get them dressed again."

"Your will, Captain." Ezri turned and began giving in-structions to the sailors around her.

"As for you two," the captain said, returning her gaze to the two drenched thieves, "my name is Zamira Drakasha. My ship's the *Poison Orchid*. And once you're dressed, someone will be along to haul you below and throw you in the bilge hold."

CHAPTER NINE

THE POISON ORCHID

1

THEIR PRISON WAS AT THE very bottom of the *Poison Orchid,* on what was ironically the tallest deck on the ship, a good ten feet from lower deck to ceiling. However, the pile of barrels and oilcloth sacks crammed into the compartment left nothing but a coffin-dark crawlspace above their uneven surface. Locke and Jean sat atop this uncomfortable mass of goods with their heads against the ceiling. The lightless room stank of muck-soaked orlop ropes, of moldering canvas, of stale food and ineffective alchemical preservatives.

This was technically the forward cargo stowage; the bilge proper was sealed behind a bulkhead roughly ten feet to their left. Not twenty feet in the opposite direction the curved black bow of the ship met wind and water. The soft waves they could hear were lapping against the ship's sides three or four feet above their heads.

"Nothing but the friendliest people and the finest accommodations on the Sea of Brass," said Locke.

"At least I don't feel too disadvantaged by the darkness," said Jean. "Lost my bloody optics when I took that tumble into the water."

"Thusfar today, we've lost a ship, a small fortune, your hatchets, and now your optics."

"At least our setbacks are getting progressively smaller." Jean cracked his knuckles, and the sound echoed strangely in the darkness. "How long do you suppose we've been down here?"

"Hour, maybe." Locke sighed, pushed himself away from the starboard bulkhead, and began the laborious process of finding a vaguely comfortable niche to slide into, amidst barrel-tops and sacks of hard, lumpy objects. If he was going to be bored, he might as well be bored lying down. "But I'd be surprised if they mean to keep us here for good. I think they're just...marinating us. For whatever comes next."

"You making yourself comfortable?"

"I'm fighting the good fight." Locke shoved a sack out of the way, and at last had enough space to rest in. "That's better."

A few seconds later, there came the creaking tread of many pairs of feet just overhead, followed by a scraping noise. The grating to the deck above (which had been wrapped in oilcloth to seal them in darkness) was being pulled. A wan light intruded into the blackness, and Locke squinted.

"Doesn't that just figure," he muttered.

"Cargo inspection," came a familiar voice from above. "We're looking for anything out of place. You two qualify."

Jean crawled over to the pale square of light and looked up. "Lieutenant Ezri?"

"Delmastro," she said. "Ezri Delmastro, hence Lieutenant Delmastro."

"My apologies. Lieutenant *Delmastro*."

"That's the spirit. How do you like your cabin?"

"Could smell worse," said Locke, "but I think I'd have to spend a few days pissing on everything to get there."

"Stay alive until our supplies start to run low," said Delmastro, "and you'll drink some things that'll make this stench a happy memory. Now, usually I'd drop a ladder, but it's only three feet. I think you can manage. Come up slow; Captain Drakasha's got a sudden eagerness to have a word with you."

"Does that offer include dinner?"

"You're lucky it includes clothes, Ravelle. Get up here. Smallest first."

Locke crawled past Jean and heaved himself up through the hatch, into the moderately less stifling air of the orlop deck. Lieutenant Delmastro waited with eight of her crewfolk, all armed and armored. Locke was seized from behind by a burly woman as he stood up in the passageway. A moment later Jean was helped up and held by three sailors.

"Right." Delmastro seized Jean's wrists and snapped a pair of blackened-steel manacles around them. It was Locke's turn next; she fit the cold restraints and fastened them without gentleness. Locke gave the manacles a quick professional appraisal. They were oiled and rust-free, and too tight to wiggle out of even if he had time to make some painful adjustments to his thumbs.

"Captain's finally had a chance to talk to some of your old crew at length," said Delmastro. "Mighty curious, is what I'd call her."

"Ah, that's wonderful," said Locke. "Another fine chance to explain myself to someone. How I do so love *explaining* myself."

Their wary escort herded them along, and soon they were on deck in the very last light of dusk. The sun was just passing beneath the western horizon, a bloodred eye closing lazily under lids of faintly red cloud. Locke gulped the fresh air gratefully, and was again struck by the impression of population that hung about the *Poison Orchid*. She was crammed with crew, men and women alike, bustling about below or working on deck by the light of an increasing number of alchemical lanterns.

They had come up amidships. Something clucked and fluttered in a dark box—a chicken coop, Locke realized—just forward of the mainmast. At least one bird was pecking the mesh of its cage in agitation.

"I sympathize," whispered Locke.

The *Orchid* crewfolk led him to the stern a few steps ahead of Jean. On the quarterdeck, just above the companionway leading down to the stern cabins, a group of sailors once again restrained Jean at some signal from Delmastro.

"This invitation's for Ravelle only," she said. "Master Valora can wait up here until we see how this is to go."

"Ah," said Locke. "Will you be comfortable up here, Jerome?"

"'Cold walls do not a prison make,'" recited Jean with a smile, "'nor iron bands a bondsman.'"

Lieutenant Delmastro looked at him strangely, and after a few seconds replied, "'Bold words from the tongues of the newly chained will fly—like sparks from flint, with as much real heat, and as long a life.'"

"You know *The Ten Honest Turncoats*," said Jean.

"As do you. *Very* interesting. And . . . completely beside the point." She gave Locke a gentle push toward the companionway. "Stay here, Valora. Lift a finger in an unfriendly fashion and you'll die where you stand."

"My fingers will be on their best behavior."

Down the companionway Locke stumbled, into a dark space nearly the twin of that on the *Red Messenger,* though larger. If Locke's quick estimate was correct, the *Poison Orchid* was half again as long as his former ship. There were little canvas-door cabins, two to a side, and a sturdy witchwood door to the stern cabin, currently closed tight. Ezri pushed Locke firmly aside and knocked on this door three times.

"It's Ezri, with the question mark," she shouted.

A moment later the door was unbolted from within, and Delmastro motioned for Locke to precede her.

Captain Drakasha's cabin, in contrast to "Ravelle's," showed every evidence of long, comfortable habitation. Richly lit by faceted alchemical jewel-lamps in gold frames, the space was piled with layers of tapestries and silk pillows. Several sea chests supported a lacquered tabletop covered with empty dishes, folded maps, and navigational instruments of obvious quality. Locke felt a pang when he saw his own chest, wide open on the floor beside Drakasha's chair.

The shutters had been drawn away from the stern windows. Drakasha sat before them, her coat and armor discarded, holding a girl of three or four on her knees. Through the windows, Locke could see the *Red Messenger,* shadowed in the growing darkness, crawling with the bobbing lights of what must be repair parties.

Locke glanced to his left to see who'd opened the door, looked down, and found himself meeting the gaze of a curly-haired boy who looked barely older than the girl held by Zamira. Both children had her coal-black hair, and something of her features, but their skin was somewhat lighter, like desert sand in shadow. Ezri tousled the boy's hair affectionately as she nudged Locke farther into the cabin, and the boy stepped away shyly.

"There," said Zamira, ignoring the newcomers for the moment and pointing out the stern windows. "Can you see that, Cosetta? Do you know what that is?"

"Ship," said the little girl.

"That's right." Zamira smiled. . . . No, Locke corrected himself, she positively smirked. "Mommy's *new* ship. From which Mommy has taken a lovely little pile of *gold*."

"Gold," said the little girl, clapping.

"Indeed. But look at the ship, love. Look at the ship. Can

you tell mommy what those tall things are? Those tall things that reach for the sky?"

"They ... um ... ha! No."

"No, you don't know, or no, you are being mutinous?"

"Moot nust!"

"Not on Mommy's ship, Cosetta. Look again. Mommy's told you what they are before, hasn't she? They reach for the sky, and they carry the sails, and they are the ..."

"Mast," said the girl.

"Masts. But close enough. And how many are there? How many *masts* does Mommy's new little ship have? Count them for Mommy."

"Two."

"How clever you are! Mommy's new ship has two masts, yes." Zamira leaned close to her daughter's face, so that they were touching noses, and Cosetta giggled. "Now," said Zamira, "find me something else that comes in *two*."

"Um ..."

"Here in the cabin, Cosetta. Find Mommy *two* of something."

"Um ..."

The girl looked around, sticking most of her left hand into her mouth as she did so, before seizing upon the pair of sabers that rested, in their scabbards, against the wall just beneath the stern window.

"Sword," said Cosetta.

"That's right!" Zamira kissed her on the cheek. "Mommy has *two* swords. At least where you can see them, love. Now, will you be a good girl and go above with Ezri? Mommy needs to speak to this man alone for just a bit. Paolo will go, too."

Ezri moved across the cabin to take Cosetta into her arms, and the little girl clung to her with obvious pleasure. Paolo followed Ezri like a shadow, keeping the lieutenant between himself and Locke, peeking out from behind her legs when he dared to look at all.

"You sure you want to be alone back here, Captain?"

"I'll be fine, Del. Valora's the one I'd be worried about."

"He's manacled, with eight hands standing by."

"Good enough, I think. And the *Red Messenger*'s men?"

"All under the forecastle. Treganne's giving them the eyeball."

"Fine. I'll be along soon enough. Take Paolo and Cosetta off to Gwillem and let them sit on the quarterdeck. Nowhere near the rails, mind."

"Aye."

"And tell Gwillem that if he tries to give them unwatered beer again I'll cut his heart out and piss in the hole."

"I'll quote that in full, Captain."

"Off with the lot of you. If you give Ezri and Gwillem any trouble, loves, Mommy will *not* be pleased."

Lieutenant Delmastro withdrew from the cabin, taking the two children and closing the door behind her. Locke wondered how to approach this meeting. He knew next to nothing about Drakasha; no weak spots to exploit, no prejudices to twist. Coming clean about the various layers of deception he was working under was probably a mistake. Best to act fully as Ravelle, for the time being.

Captain Drakasha picked up her sheathed sabers and turned her full regard upon Locke for the first time. He decided to speak first, in a friendly fashion.

"Your children?"

"How *little* escapes the penetrating insight of the veteran intelligence officer." She slid one of her sabers out of its scabbard with a soft metallic hiss and gestured toward Locke with it. "Sit."

Locke complied. The only other chair in the cabin was next to the table, so he settled into it and folded his manacled hands in his lap. Zamira eased herself into her own chair, facing him, and set the drawn saber across her knees.

"Where I come from," she said, "we have a custom concerning questions asked over a naked blade." She had a distinct, harmonious accent, one that Locke couldn't place. "Are you familiar with it?"

"No," said Locke, "but I think the meaning is clear."

"Good. Something is wrong with your story."

"Nearly *everything* is wrong with my story, Captain Drakasha. I had a ship and a crew and a pile of money. Now I find myself hugging a sack of potatoes in a bilge hold that smells like the bottom of an unwashed ale cup."

"Don't hope for a lasting relationship with the potatoes. I just wanted you out of the way while I spoke to some of the *Messenger*'s crewmen."

"Ah. And how is my crew?"

"We both know they're not your crew, Ravelle."

"How is *the* crew?"

"Tolerably well, little thanks to you. They lost the nerve for a fight as soon as they saw our numbers. Most of them seemed downright eager to surrender, so we took the *Messenger* with nothing more than a few bruises and some hurt feelings."

"Thank you for that."

"We weren't kind for your sake, Ravelle. In fact, you're damned fortunate we were even nearby. I like to cruise the wake of the summer's-end storms. They tend to spit out juicy morsels in no condition to refuse our hospitality."

Drakasha reached down into Locke's sea chest, shuffled the contents, and withdrew a small packet of papers. "Now," she said, "I want to know who Leocanto Kosta and Jerome de Ferra are."

"Cover identities," said Locke. "False faces we used for our work back in Tal Verrar."

"In the archon's service?"

"Yes."

"Nearly everything in here is signed 'Kosta.' Small letters of credit and reference ... work order for some chairs ... receipt for clothing in storage. The only document with the name Ravelle on it is this commission as a Verrari sea-officer. Should I be calling you Orrin or Leocanto? Which one's the false face?"

"You might as well just call me Ravelle," said Locke. "I've been on the officer's list under that name for years. It's how I drew my pay."

"Are you Verrari-born?"

"Mainland. A village called Vo Sarmara."

"What did you do before you served the archon?"

"I was what you'd call a patient man."

"Is that a profession now?"

"I mean a master of scales and balances, for a merchant syndicate. I was the *patient man* because I did the *weighting,* you see?"

"Droll. A syndicate in Tal Verrar?"

"Yes."

"So you surely worked for the Priori."

"That was part of the, ah, original incentive for Stragos' people to bring me into their fold. After my usefulness as an agent in the syndicate hit a wall, I was given new duties."

"Hmm. I spoke at length with Jabril. Long enough to have no trouble believing that your naval commission really is a fake. Do you have *any* experience under arms?"

"No formal military training, if that's what you mean."

"Curious," said Drakasha, "that you had the authority to lay claim to a ship of war, even a small one."

"When we move slowly enough to avoid upsetting anyone, captains of intelligence have excessive powers of requisition. Or at least we *did.* I suspect my remaining peers will be shackled with a bit of unwanted oversight because of what I've done."

"Tragic. Still . . . it's curious again that when you were at my feet you had to ask my name. I'd have thought that my identity would be obvious to anyone in Stragos' service. How long were you with him?"

"Five years."

"So you came after the Free Armada was lost. Nonetheless, as a Verrari—"

"I had a vague description of you," said Locke. "Little more than your name and the name of your ship. I can assure you, had the archon ever thought to have your portrait painted for our benefit, no man in his service would stay ignorant of your looks."

"Excellent form. But you would do well to consider me dead to flattery."

"That's a pity. I'm *so* good at it."

"A third curious thing occurs to me. You seemed genuinely surprised to see my children aboard."

"It's, ah, merely that I found it strange you'd have them with you. Out here at sea. Company to the hazards of . . . all this."

"Where else might I be expected to keep an eye on them?" Zamira fingered the hilt of her drawn saber. "Paolo's four. Cosetta's three. Is your intelligence *really* so out of date that you didn't know about them?"

"Look, my job was in-city operations against the Priori and other dissenters. I didn't pay much attention to naval affairs beyond drawing my official salary."

"There's a bounty of five thousand solari on my head. Mine, and every other captain that survived the War for Recognition. I know that accurate descriptions of myself and my family were circulated in Tal Verrar last year; I got my hands on some of the leaflets. Do you expect me to believe that someone in your position could be this ignorant?"

"I hate to sting your feelings, Captain Drakasha, but I told you. I was a landsman—"

"Are."

"... am and was, and my eyes were on the city. I had little enough time to study the basics of survival when I started getting ready to steal the *Messenger.*"

"Why do that, though? Why steal a ship and go to sea? Something *completely* outside your confessed experience? If you had your eyes on the land and the city, why didn't you *do* something involving the land or the city?"

Locke licked his lips, which had become uncomfortably dry. He'd pounded a dossier of background information on Orrin Ravelle into his head, but the character had never been designed for an interrogation from this perspective. "It might sound odd," said Locke, "but it was the best I *could* do. As it turned out, my fake commission as a sea-officer gave me the most leverage to hurt the archon. Stealing a ship was a grander gesture than stealing, say, a carriage."

"And what did Stragos do to earn this *grand gesture?*"

"I've sworn an oath never to speak of the matter."

"Convenient."

"Just the opposite," said Locke. "As I wish I could put you at ease."

"At ease? How could anything you've told me put me at ease? You lie, and add flourishes to old lies, and refuse to discuss your motives for embarking on an insane venture. If you won't give me answers, I have to presume that you're a danger to this vessel, and that I risk offending Maxilan Stragos by taking you in. I can't afford the consequences. I think it's time to put you back where I found you."

"The hold?"

"The open sea."

"Ah." Locke frowned, then bit the inside of his right cheek to contain a laugh. "Ah, Captain Drakasha, that was *very* well done. Amateurish, but creative. Someone without my history might have fallen for it."

"Damn." Drakasha smiled tightly. "I should have drawn the curtains over the stern windows."

"Yes. I can see your people swarming over the *Messenger* as we speak. I presume your prize crew is unfucking the rigging so she can make more than a toddler's crawl, right? If you gave one speck of rat shit for offending the archon, you'd be sinking that ship, not refurbishing it for sale."

"True," said Drakasha.

"Which means—"

"Which *means* that I'm still asking questions, Ravelle. Tell me about your accomplice, Master Valora. A particular friend?"

"An old associate. He helped me in Tal Verrar with . . . objectionable work."

"Just an associate?"

"I pay him well and trust him with my business, yes."

"Curiously educated." Zamira pointed up at the cabin ceiling; a narrow skylight had vents slightly cracked to let in air from the quarterdeck. "I heard him and Ezri quoting Lucarno to one another a few minutes ago."

"*The Tragedy of the Ten Honest Turncoats*," said Locke. "Jerome is . . . fond of it."

"He can read. According to Jabril, he's not a seaman, but he can do complex sums. He speaks Vadran. He uses trader's terms and knows his way around cargo. So I'd guess that he comes from prosperous merchant stock."

Locke said nothing.

"He was with you before you worked for the archon, wasn't he?"

"He was a servant of the Priori, yes." It seemed that fitting Jean into Drakasha's presumptions wouldn't be as hard as Locke had feared. "I brought him with me when I joined the archon's cause."

"But not as a friend."

"Just a very good agent."

"My appropriately amoral spy," said Drakasha. She stood up, moved beneath the skylight, and raised her voice. "On deck, there!"

"Aye, Captain?" Ezri's voice.

"Del, bring Valora down here."

A few moments later, the door to the cabin swung open and Jean entered, followed by Lieutenant Delmastro. Captain Drakasha suddenly unsheathed her second saber. The empty scabbards clattered to the deck, and she pointed one blade at Locke.

"The instant you rise from that chair," she said, "you die."

"What's going—"

"Quiet. Ezri, I want Valora *dealt with*."

"Your will, Captain."

Before Jean could do anything, Ezri gave him a sharp kick to the back of his right knee, so fast and well placed that Locke winced. She followed this up with a hard shove, and Jean fell to his hands and knees.

"I might still have a use for you, Ravelle. But I can't let you keep your agent." Drakasha took a step toward Jean, raising her right-hand saber.

Locke was out of the chair before he could help himself, throwing himself at her, trying to tangle her arms in his manacle chain.

"*No!*" he screamed. The cabin spun wildly around him, and then he was on the floor with a dull ache coursing through his jaw. His mind, working a second or two behind the pace of events, gradually concluded that Drakasha had bashed his chin with the hilt of one of her sabers. He was now on his back, with that saber hovering just above his neck. Drakasha seemed ten feet tall.

"Please," Locke sputtered. "Not Jerome. It's not necessary."

"I know," said Drakasha. "Ezri?"

"Looks like I owe you ten solari, Captain."

"You should've known better," said Drakasha, grinning. "You heard what Jabril had to say about these two."

"I did, I did." Ezri knelt over Jean, a look of genuine concern on her face. "I just didn't think Ravelle had it in him."

"This sort of thing rarely goes just one way."

"Should've known that, too."

Locke raised his hands and pushed Drakasha's blade aside. She yielded. He rolled over, stumbled to his knees, and grabbed Jean by one arm, ignoring his throbbing jaw. He knew it wasn't broken, at least.

"Are you okay, Jerome?"

"Fine," said Jean. "Scraped my hands a bit."

"I'm sorry," Ezri said.

"No worries," said Jean. "That was a good hit. Not much else you could have done to knock down someone my size." He stumbled to his feet with Locke and Ezri's help. "A kidney punch, maybe."

Ezri showed off the set of iron knuckles around the fingers of her right hand. "That was the contingency plan."

"Damn, am I glad you didn't do that. But you could've....I might have fallen backwards if you hadn't shoved fast enough. Hooking one foot around my shin from behind—"

"Thought about it. Or a good stiff jab to the sensitive spot in your armpit—"

"And an arm twist, yeah. That would've—"

"But I *don't* trust that against someone so big; the leverage is wrong unless—"

Drakasha cleared her throat loudly, and Jean and Ezri fell silent, almost sheepishly.

"You lied to me about Jerome, Ravelle." She retrieved her sword-belt and slid her sabers into their scabbards with a pair of sharp clacks. "He's no hired agent. He's a friend. The sort who'd refuse to let you get thrown off a ship by yourself. The sort *you'd* try to protect, even though I told you it would mean your death."

"Clever," said Locke, feeling a faint warmth rising on his cheeks. "So that's what this was all about."

"More or less. I needed to know what sort of man you were before I decided what to do with you."

"And what have you decided?"

"You're reckless, vain, and too clever by half," she said. "You suffer from the delusion that your prevarications are charming. And you're just as willing as Jerome is to die stupidly on behalf of a friend."

"Yeah," he said. "Well . . . perhaps I've grown fond of the ugly lump over the years. Does that mean we're going back to the hold, or to the open sea?"

"Neither," said Drakasha. "You're going to the forecastle, where you'll eat and sleep with all the other crewmen from the *Red Messenger*. I'll peel your other lies apart at leisure. For the time being, I'm satisfied that if you've got Jerome to look after, you'll be sensible."

"And so we're what? Slaves?"

"No one aboard this ship takes slaves," said Drakasha with a dangerous edge in her voice. "We do execute our fair share of smart-asses, however."

"I thought I was a charming prevaricator."

"Grasp this," said Drakasha. "Your whole world consists of the few inches of empty deck I allow you, and you're gods-damned lucky to have them. Ezri and I will explain the situation to all of you at the forecastle."

"And our things? The papers, I mean? The personal documents? Keep the gold, but—"

"Keep it? You really *mean* that? What a sweetheart this

man is, Ezri." Drakasha used her right boot to tip the cover of Locke's sea chest closed. "Let's call your papers a hostage to your good behavior. I have a shortage of blank parchment, and two children who've recently discovered the joys of ink."

"Point thoroughly taken."

"Ezri, haul them up on deck and get their manacles off. Let's get back to acting as though we have somewhere important to be."

2

ON THE quarterdeck they were met by a harried-looking woman of middle years, short and broad, with a finger-length halo of white hair above the lines of a face that had obviously contributed many years of scowls to the world. Her wide, predatory eyes were in constant motion, like an owl unable to decide whether it was bored or hungry.

"You might have caught a less wretched bunch, had you looked nearly anywhere," she said without preamble.

"And you might have noticed it hasn't exactly been a buyer's market for prizes recently." Zamira bore the woman's manner with the ease of what must have been a very old familiarity.

"Well, if you want to use frayed hemp to weave a line, don't blame the rope maker when it snaps."

"I know better than to blame you for anything, Scholar. It leads to weeks of misery for everyone. How many?"

"Twenty-eight at the forecastle," she said. "Eight had to be left aboard the prize. Broken bones in every case. Not safe to move them."

"Will they last to Port Prodigal?"

"Assuming their ship does. Assuming they do as I told them, which is a bold—"

"That's the best we can do for them, I'm sure. Condition of the twenty-eight?"

"I'm sure you heard me say 'wretched,' which derives from a state of wretchedness, which is in turn caused by their being wretches. I could use a number of other highly technical terms, only some of them completely imaginary—"

"Treganne, my patience is as long-vanished as your good looks."

"Most of them are still suffering from long enclosure. Poor sustenance, little exercise, and nervous malaise. They've been eating better since leaving Tal Verrar, but they're exhausted and battered. A handful are in what I'd call decent health. An equal number are not fit for any work at all until I say otherwise. I won't bend on that . . . Captain."

"I won't ask you to. Disease?"

"Miraculously absent, if you mean fevers and contagions. Also little by way of sexual consequences. They've been locked away from women for months, and most of them are Eastern Therin. Very little inclination to lie with one another, you know."

"Their loss. If I have further need of you—"

"I'll be in my cabin, obviously. And mind your children. They appear to be steering the ship."

Locke stared at the woman as she stamped away. One of her feet had the hollow, heavy sound of wood, and she walked with the aid of a strange cane made of stacked white cylinders. Ivory? No—the spine of some unfortunate creature, fused together with shining seams of metal.

Drakasha and Delmastro turned toward the ship's wheel, a doubled affair like the one aboard the *Messenger*, currently tended by an unusually tall young man who was all sharp, gangling angles. At either side stood Paolo and

Cosetta, not actually touching the wheel but mimicking his movements and giggling.

"Mumchance," said Drakasha as she stepped over and pulled Cosetta away from the wheel, "where's Gwillem?"

"Craplines."

"I *told* him he was on sprat duty," said Ezri.

"I'll have his fucking eyes," said Drakasha.

Mumchance seemed unruffled. "Man's gotta piss, Captain."

"Gotta piss," mumbled Cosetta.

"Hush." Zamira reached around Mumchance and snatched Paolo back from the wheel as well. "Mum, you know full well they're not to touch the wheel or the rails."

"They wasn't touching the wheel, Captain."

"*Nor* are they to dance at your side, cling to your legs, or in any other way assist you in navigating the vessel. Clear?"

"Savvy."

"Paolo," said Drakasha, "take your sister back to the cabin and wait for me there."

"Yes," said the boy, his voice as faint as the sound of two pieces of paper sliding together. He took Cosetta's hand and began to lead her aft.

Drakasha hurried forward once again, past small parties of crewfolk working or eating, all of whom acknowledged her passing with respectful nods and waves. Ezri pushed Locke and Jean along in her wake.

Near the chicken coops, Drakasha crossed paths with a rotund but sprightly Vadran a few years older than herself. The man was wearing a dandified black jacket covered in tarnished brass buckles, and his blond-gray hair was pulled into a billowing ponytail that hung to the seat of his breeches. Drakasha grabbed him by the front of his tunic with her left hand.

"Gwillem, what part of 'watch the children for a few minutes' did Ezri fail to make clear?"

"I left them with Mum, Captain—"

"They were your problem, not his."

"Well, you trust him to steer the ship, why not trust him to—"

"I do trust him with my loves, Gwillem. I just have a peculiar attachment to having orders followed."

"Captain," said Gwillem in a low voice, "I had to drop some brown on the blue, eh? I could've brought them to the craplines, but I doubt you would have approved of the education they'd have received."

"Hold it in, for Iono's sake. I only took a few minutes. Now go pack your things."

"My things?"

"Take the last boat over to the *Messenger* and join the prize crew."

"Prize crew? Captain, you know I'm not much good—"

"I want that ship eyeballed and inventoried, bowsprit to taffrail. Account for everything. When I haggle with the Shipbreaker over it, I want to know exactly how far the bastard is trying to cheat me."

"But—"

"I'll expect your written tally when we rendezvous in Port Prodigal. We both know there was hardly any loot to sling over and count today. Get over there and earn your share."

"Your will, Captain."

"My quartermaster," Zamira said when Gwillem had trudged away, swearing. "Not bad, really. Just prefers to let work sort of *elude* him whenever possible."

At the bow of the ship was the forecastle deck, raised perhaps four and a half feet above the weather deck, with broad stairs on either side. In between those stairs a wide, uncovered opening led to a dark area that was half compartment and half crawlspace beneath the forecastle. It was seven or eight yards long by Locke's estimate.

The forecastle deck and stairs were crowded with most of the *Red Messenger*'s men, under the casual guard of half a dozen of Zamira's armed crewfolk. Jabril, sitting next to Aspel at the front of the crowd, seemed deeply amused to see Locke and Jean again. The men behind him began to mutter.

"Shut up," said Ezri, taking a position between Zamira and the newcomers. Locke, not quite knowing what to do, stood off to one side with Jean and waited for instructions. Drakasha cleared her throat.

"Some of us haven't met. I'm Zamira Drakasha, captain of the *Poison Orchid*. Lend an ear. Jabril told me that you took ship in Tal Verrar thinking you were to be pirates. Anyone having second thoughts?"

Most of the *Messenger*'s men shook their heads or quietly muttered denials.

"Good. I *am* what your friend Ravelle pretended to be," Drakasha said, reaching over and putting one of her arms around Locke's shoulders. She smiled theatrically, and several of the *Messenger*'s less-battered men chuckled. "I have no lords or masters. I fly the red flag when I'm hungry and a false flag when I'm not. I have one port of call: Port Prodigal in the Ghostwinds. Nowhere else will have me. Nowhere else is *safe*. You live on this deck, you share that peril. I know some of you don't understand. Think of the world. Think of *everywhere in the world* that isn't this ship, save one rotten little speck of misery in the blackest asshole of nowhere. That's what you're renouncing. Everything. Everyone. Everywhere."

She released Locke, and seemed to note the somber expressions of the *Messenger*'s crew with approval. She pointed at Ezri.

"My first mate, Ezri Delmastro. We call her 'lieutenant' and so do you. She says it, I back it. Never presume otherwise.

"You've met our ship's physiker. Scholar Treganne tells me you could be worse and you could be better. There'll be rest for those that need it. I can't use you if you're in no condition to work."

"Are we being invited to join your crew, Captain Draksaha?" asked Jabril.

"You're being offered a chance," said Ezri. "That's all. After this, you're not prisoners, but you're not free men. You're what we call the scrub watch. You sleep here, in what we call the undercastle. Worst place on the ship, more or less. If there's a filthy shit job to be had, you'll do it. If we're short blankets or clothes, you'll go without. You're last for meals and drinks."

"Every member of my crew can give you an order," said Drakasha, picking up as Ezri finished. Locke had a notion that they'd honed this routine together over time. "And every one of them will expect to be obeyed. We've no formal defaults; cop wise or slack off and someone will just beat the hell out of you. Raise enough fuss that I have to notice and I'll throw you over the side. Think I'm kidding? Ask someone who's been here a while."

"How long do we have to be on the scrub watch?" asked one of the younger men near the back of the crowd.

"Until you prove yourselves," said Drakasha. "We raise anchor in a few minutes and sail for Port Prodigal. Anyone who wants to leave when we get there, be gone. You won't be sold; this isn't a slaving ship. But you'll get no pay save drink and rations. You'll walk away with empty pockets, and in Prodigal, slavery might be kinder. At least someone would give a shit that you lived or died.

"If we cross paths with another sail on the way down," she continued, "I'll give thought to taking her. And if we fly a red flag, that's your chance. You'll go in first; you'll board the prize before any of us. If there's fire or bows or razor nets or gods-know-what, you'll taste it first and bleed first.

If you survive, grand. You're crew. If you refuse, we dump you in Port Prodigal. I only keep a scrub watch on hand as long as I have to."

She nodded to Ezri.

"As of now," said Delmastro, "you can have the forecastle and the weather deck far back as the mainmast. Don't go below or touch a tool without instructions. Touch a weapon, or try to take one from one of the crew, and I guarantee you'll die on the instant. We're touchy about that.

"You want to get cozy with a member of the crew, or they offer to get cozy with you, do what you will as long as you're off duty and you stay off the bloody weather deck. Out here, what's given is given. You try to take something by force, you'd better pray you die in the attempt, because we're touchy about that, too."

Zamira took over again and pointed at Locke and Jean. "Ravelle and Valora will be rejoining you." A few of the men grumbled, and Zamira rested her hands on her saber hilts. "Mind your fucking manners. You put them over the side and vowed to let Iono be their judge. I showed up about an hour later. That settles that; anyone who thinks they know better than the Lord of the Grasping Waters can jump over the rail and take it up with Him in person."

"They're scrub watch like the rest of you," said Ezri.

Still, the men didn't seem particularly enthusiastic, and Zamira cleared her throat. "This is an equal-shares ship."

That got their attention.

"Ship's quartermaster goes by the name of Gwillem. He counts the take. Thirty percent goes to the ship so we don't slink about with rotting canvas and cordage. Rest gets split evenly, one share per beating heart.

"You don't touch a centira from what we already took out of your old ship. No apologies there. But if you get your chance on the way to Port Prodigal, and you're crew when we sell the *Messenger* off to the Shipbreaker, you'll get a share of that, and that'll set you up nicely. *If* you're crew."

Locke had to admire her for that; it was a sensible policy, and she'd brought it into the lecture at a moment calculated to deflect dissension and worry. Now the *Red Messenger* wouldn't just be an unhappy memory vanishing over the horizon in the hands of a prize crew; it might be a waiting pile of silver.

Zamira turned and headed aft, leaving Delmastro to finish the show. As murmurs of conversation began to rise, the petite lieutenant yelled, "Shut up! That's the business, then. There'll be food in a while and a half-ration of beer to settle you down some. Tomorrow I'll start sorting those of you with particular skills and introducing you to some work.

"There's *one* last thing the captain didn't mention." Ezri paused for several seconds and made sure that everyone was listening attentively. "The younger Drakashas. Captain has a boy and a girl. Mostly they're in her cabin, but sometimes they've got the run of the ship. What they are to you is *sacred.* I mean this, more than I mean anything else I've said tonight. Say so much as an *unkind word* to them and I'll nail your cock to the foremast and leave you there to die of thirst. The crew thinks of them as family. If you have to break your neck to keep them safe, then it's in your best interest to break your bloody neck."

Delmastro seemed to take everyone's silence as a sign that they were duly impressed, and she nodded. A moment later, Drakasha's voice sounded from the quarterdeck, magnified by a speaking trumpet: "Up anchor!"

Delmastro lifted a whistle that hung around her neck on a leather cord and blew it three times. "At the waist," she hollered in an impossibly loud voice, "ship capstan bars! Stand by to raise anchor! Scrub watch to the waist, as able!"

At her urging, most of the *Messenger*'s former crew rose and began shuffling toward the *Orchid*'s waist. A large work party was already gathering there, between the foremast and the chicken coops, fitting long capstan bars in their places by lantern light. A woman was scattering sand on the deck from a bucket. Locke and Jean fell in with Jabril, who smiled wryly.

"Evening, Ravelle. You look a bit . . . demoted."

"I'm happy enough," said Locke. "But honestly, Jabril, I leave the *Messenger* in your hands for what, an hour? And look what happens."

"It's a bloody improvement," said someone behind Locke.

"Oh, I agree," said Locke, deciding that the next few days might be infinitely more pleasant for everyone if Ravelle were to swallow anything resembling pride over his brief career as a captain. "I agree with all my gods-damned heart."

Ezri shoved her way through the gathering crowd and vaulted atop the capstan barrel; it was wide enough that she could sit cross-legged upon it, which she did. She blew her whistle twice more and yelled, "Rigged below?"

"Rigged below," rose an answering cry from one of the hatches.

"Take your places," said Ezri. Locke squeezed in next to Jean and leaned against one of the long wooden bars; this capstan was wider than the one aboard the *Messenger*, and an extra twenty or so sailors could easily crowd in to work it. Every place was filled in seconds.

"Right," said Ezri, "heave! Slow to start! Heave! Slow to start! Feet and shoulders! Faster, now—make the little bitch spin round and round! You know you want to!"

Locke heaved at his bar, feeling the grit shift and crunch beneath him, poking uncomfortably at the sensitive spots between his toes and the balls of his bare feet. But nobody else seemed to be complaining, so he bit his lip and bore it. Ezri was indeed spinning round and round; clank by clank, the anchor cable was coming in. A party formed at the larboard bow to secure it. After several minutes of shoving, Ezri brought the capstan party to a halt with one short blast on her whistle.

" 'Vast heaving," she cried. "Secure larboard anchor!"

"Cast to the larboard tack," came Drakasha's amplified voice; "fore and main topsails!"

More running, more whistles, more commotion. Ezri hopped to her feet atop the capstan and bellowed a quick succession of orders: "Hands aloft to loose fore and aft topsails! Brace mainyards round for the larboard tack! Foreyards braced abox!" There was more, but Locke stopped listening as he tried to make sense of what was happening. The *Poison Orchid* had been drifting by a single anchor in a calm sea, with a light breeze out of the northeast, and she'd drifted down so that the wind was dead ahead. What little he understood of Ezri's orders told him that the ship would be slipping a bit aback, then turning east and bringing the wind over her larboard bow.

"Fore and aft watches, at the rails! Top-eyes, wide awake, now!" Ezri leapt down onto the deck. Dark shapes were surging up the ratlines hand-over-hand; blocks and tackles creaked in the growing darkness, and still more crew were coming up through the hatches to join the tumult. "Scrub watch! Scrub watch, get to the undercastle and stay out of the bloody way! *Not* you two." Ezri grabbed Locke and Jean as they moved with the *Messenger*'s men, and she pointed them aft. "Tool locker, under the starboard stairs abaft the mainmast. Get brooms and sweep all this sand back into its bucket. After you unship the capstan bars."

They did just that, tedious work by wavering alchemical

light, frequently interrupted by busy or discourteous crewfolk. Locke worked with a scowl until Ezri stepped up between him and Jean and whispered, "Don't mind this. It'll make things a hell of a lot easier with your old crew."

Damned if she wasn't right, Locke thought; a little extra humiliation heaped on Ravelle and Valora might be just the thing to stifle the old crew's resentment.

"My compliments," he whispered.

"I know my business," she said brusquely. "See everything back to where you found it, then go to the undercastle and stay there."

Then she was gone, into the work parties overseeing a dozen delicate operations. Locke returned the brooms to the tool locker, then threaded his way forward with Jean just behind. Overhead, canvas snapped and rolled, ropes creaked as strain was added or adjusted, and men and women called softly to one another as they worked with nothing but thin air for dozens of yards beneath them.

The *Poison Orchid* slid slowly onto the larboard tack. She put the last faint halo of the lost sun behind her, as though sailing out of some ghostly golden portal, and gathered way beneath the first stars of evening, which waxed steadily brighter in the inky eastern sky.

Locke was pleasantly surprised to discover that Jabril had held a spot for him and Jean; not one of the more desirable ones near the entrance to the undercastle, but enough spare deck to squeeze up against the larboard bulkhead, in relative darkness. Others with more favorable positions seemed not to begrudge them a moment of space as they crawled and stumbled past. One or two men muttered greetings; at worst, a few, like Mazucca and Aspel, maintained an unfriendly silence.

"Looks like you two really have joined the rest of us galley slaves," said Jabril.

"Galley slaves is what we'd be, if Ravelle hadn't gotten us outta Windward Rock," said someone Locke didn't recognize. "May be a dumb fuck, but we should show him fellowship for that."

Thanks for speaking up when we were being thrown off the ship, Locke thought.

"Aye, I agree about the dumb fuck part," said Mazucca.

"And we'll *all* mind the fellowship part," said Jean, using the slow, careful voice he reserved for people he was trying to avoid hitting. "Orrin's not alone, is he?"

"Dark in here," said Mazucca. "Lots of us, squeezed in together. You think you can move fast enough, Valora? You think you can stay awake long enough for it to matter? Twenty-eight on two—"

"If it was clear deck between you and me," said Jean, "you'd piss your breeches the moment I cracked my knuckles."

"Jerome," said Locke, "easy. We can all—"

There was the sound of a scuffle in the darkness, and a heavy thud. Mazucca gave a strangled squawk.

"Baldy, you stupid bastard," hissed an unknown voice, "you raise a hand against them and Drakasha will *kill* you, savvy?"

"You'll make it worse for all of us," said Jabril. "You never heard of Zamira Drakasha? Piss her off and we might lose our chance to be crew. You do that, Mazucca, you find out what twenty-eight on *one* feels like. Fuckin' promise."

There were murmurs of agreement in the darkness, and a sharp gasp as whoever had been holding Mazucca let go.

"Peace," he gasped. "I won't... I won't ruin things. Not me."

The night was warm, and the heat of thirty men in close confinement rapidly grew stifling despite the small ventilation grating in the middle of the forecastle deck. As Locke's eyes adjusted to the darkness, he became able to pick out the shadowed shapes of the men around him more clearly. They lay or sat flank to flank like livestock. The ship reverberated with activity around them. Feet pounded the forecastle deck; crewfolk moved about and laughed and shouted on the deck below. There was a slapping hiss of waves parting before the bow, and the constant sound of toil and shouted orders from aft.

In time, there was a cursory meal of lukewarm salted pork and half a leather jack of skunkish swill vaguely descended from ale. The food and drink were passed awkwardly through the crowd; knees and elbows met stomachs and foreheads on a continual basis until everyone was dealt with. Then came the equally punishing task of passing jacks and tin bowls back, and then of men crawling over one another to use the craplines. Locke finally settled for good into his sliver of deck space against Jean's back, and had a sudden thought.

"Jabril, did anyone find out what day it is?"

"Twelfth of Festal," said Jabril. "I asked Lieutenant Delmastro when I was brought aboard."

"Twelve days," muttered Jean.

"Yeah," Locke sighed. Twelve days gone. Not two weeks since they'd set out, with every man here deferring to him and Jean as heroes. Twelve days for the antidote to wane in strength. Gods, the archon . . . how the hell was he going to explain what had happened to the ship? Some nautical technicality?

"Squiggle-fucked the rightwise cock-swabber with a starboard jib," he whispered to himself, "when I should've used a larboard jib."

"What?" muttered Jean and Jabril simultaneously.

"Nothing."

Soon enough the old instincts of a Catchfire orphan asserted themselves. Locke made a pillow of the crook of his left arm and closed his eyes. In moments the noise and heat and bustle of the men around him, and the thousand noises of the unfamiliar ship, were nothing more than a vague background to his light but steady sleep.

CHAPTER TEN

ALL SOULS IN PERIL

1

BY THE SEVENTEENTH OF FESTAL, Jean had come to dread the sight and smell of the ship's vinegar as much as he'd come to appreciate his glimpses of her lieutenant.

His morning task, on most days, was to fill one bucket with the foul red stuff and another with seawater, and set to swabbing the deck and bulkheads along the full length of the main deck, at least where he could reach. Fore and aft were long compartments called crew berths, and one would be in use at any given time, crammed with four or five dozen people in and out of hammocks, their snores mingling like the growls of caged beasts. That berth Jean would carefully avoid, instead swabbing out ship's stores (what the crew called the "delicates room," for its rack of glass bottles under netting), the main-deck hold and armory, and the empty crew berth—though even when empty each berth contained a mess of barrels, crates, and nettings that had to be laboriously shifted.

Once the reek of watered vinegar was fully mingled with the usual belowdecks stench of old food, bad liquor, and all things unwashed, Jean would usually move throughout the lowest two decks, the orlop and the bilge, swinging a large yellow alchemical light before him to help dissipate the miasmas that caused disease. Drakasha was a great one for the health of her crew; most of the sailors pierced their ears with copper to ward off cataracts and drank pinches of white sand in their ale to strengthen their bellies against rupture. The lower decks were lighted at least twice a day, much to the amusement of the ship's cats. Unfortunately, this meant climbing, crawling, scrambling, and shoving past all manner of obstacles, including busy crewfolk. Jean was always careful to be polite and make his obeisance by nodding as he passed.

This crew was always in motion; this ship was always alive. The more Jean saw and learned on the *Poison Orchid*, the more convinced he became that the maintenance schedule he'd set as first mate of the *Red Messenger* had been hopelessly naïve. No doubt Caldris would have spoken up eventually, had he lived long enough to notice.

There seemed to be no such thing, in Captain Drakasha's opinion, as a state of adequate repair for a ship at sea. What was checked or inspected one watch was checked again the next, and the next, day after day. What was braced was then rebraced, what could be mended was remended. The pump and capstan mechanisms were greased daily with fat scraped from the cooking pots; the masts were "slushed" top to bottom with the same brown gunk, for protection against the weather. Sailors wandered in constant, attentive parties, inspecting plank seams or wrapping canvas around rigging where the ropes chafed against one another.

The Orchids were divided into two watches, Red and Blue. They would work in six-hour shifts, one watch minding the ship while the other rested. The Red watch, for example, had duty from noon till the sixth hour of the evening, and would come back on duty from midnight till the sixth hour of the morning. Crew on the off watch could do as they pleased, unless the call of "all hands" summoned them to the deck for some strenuous or dangerous undertaking.

The scrub watch didn't fit into this scheme; the former men of the *Red Messenger* were worked from dawn to dusk, and took their meals after they were dismissed, rather than around noon with the actual crew.

For all their grumbling, Jean didn't get the sense that the Orchids genuinely resented their new shipmates. In fact, he suspected that the ex-Messengers were taking up most of the less interesting chores, leaving the Orchids that much more time to sleep, or mend personal effects, or gamble, or fuck without a hint of shame in their hammocks or under their blankets. The lack of privacy aboard ship was still a major astonishment to Jean; he was neither a prude nor a virgin, but his idea of *the right place* had always involved stone walls and a firmly locked door.

A lock would mean little on a ship like this, where most any noise was a shared noise. There were a pair of men on the Blue watch who could be heard from the taffrail if they were doing it in the forward berth, and a woman on the Red watch who screamed the damnedest things in Vadran, usually just as Jean was drifting off to sleep on the deck above her. He and Locke had puzzled over her grammar and concluded that she didn't actually speak Vadran. Sometimes, her performances were followed by applause.

That aside, the crew seemed to take pride in their discipline. Jean witnessed no fights, few serious arguments, and no out-of-place drunkenness. Beer or wine was had in a respectable fashion at every meal, and by some complicated scheme that Jean had yet to work out, each member of the crew was allowed, about once a week, to go on what was called the Merry Watch, a sort of watch-within-a-watch. The Merry Watch would set up on the main deck, and be allowed a bit of freedom at the ship's waist (especially for throwing up). They could drink more or less as they saw fit, and were excused even from all-hands calls until they'd recovered.

"It's not...exactly what I expected," said Jean as Ezri stood at the larboard rail one morning, pretending not to watch him touch up the gray paint on the bottom of the ship's smallest boat. She did that, every now and again. Was he imagining things? Was it his quoting Lucarno? He'd avoided quoting anything else at her, even when the opportunity had presented itself. Better to be a mystery, in his book, than to make a cheap refrain of something that had caught her attention.

Thirteen gods, he thought with a start, am I angling myself for a pass at her? Is she—

"Pardon?" she said.

Jean smiled. Somehow he'd guessed she wouldn't mind his speaking without invitation. "Your ship. It's not exactly what I expected. From what I read."

"From what you *read*?" She laughed, crossed her arms, and regarded him almost slyly. "What'd you read?"

"Let me think." He dipped his brush in the gray alchemical slop and tried to look busy. "*Seven Years between the Gale and the Lash.*"

"Benedictus Montcalm," she said. "Read that one. Mostly bullshit. I think he traded drinks for stories off real sailors until he had his fill."

"How about *True and Accurate History of the Wanton Red Flag*?"

"Suzette vela Ducasi! I know her!"

"Know her?"

"Know *of* her. Crazy old bitch wound up in Port Prodigal. Scribes for coppers, drinks every coin she gets. Barely speaks decent Therin anymore. Just haunts the gutter and curses her old publishers."

"Those are all the books I can remember," said Jean. "Not much of a taste for histories, I'm afraid. So, how'd you manage to read everything you have?"

"Ahhh," she said, tossing her hair backward with a flick of her neck. She wasn't scrawny, thought Jean—no angles on Ezri, just healthy curves and muscle. Had to be healthy, to knock him down as she had, even by surprise. "Out here, the past is a currency, Jerome. Sometimes it's the only one we have."

"Mysterious."

"Sensible."

"You already know a bit about me."

"And fair's fair, is it? Thing is, I'm a ship's officer and you're a dangerous unknown."

"That sounds promising."

"I thought so too." She smiled. "More to the point, I'm a ship's officer and you're scrub watch. You're not even real yet." She framed him with her hands and squinted. "You're just a sort of hazy *something* on the horizon."

"Well," he said, and, aware that he sounded like a nitwit even as he repeated himself, "ah, well."

"But you were curious."

"I was?"

"About the ship."

"Oh. Yeah, I was. I just wondered . . . now that I've seen a fair bit of it—"

"Where's the singing, where's the dancing on the yardarms, where's the ale casks fore and aft, where's the drinking and puking sunrise to sunset?"

"More or less. Not exactly a navy, you know."

"Drakasha *is* former navy. Syrune. She doesn't talk about it much, but she doesn't try to hide her accent anymore. She did, once."

Syrune, thought Jean, an island empire even more easterly than Jerem and Jeresh; proud and insular dark-skinned folk who took their ships seriously. If Drakasha was one of them, she'd come from a tradition of sea-officers that some said was as old as the Therin Throne.

"Syrune," he said. "That explains some things. I thought the past was a currency?"

"She'd've let you have that bit for free," said Ezri. "Trust me, if history's a coin, she's sitting on a gods-damned fortune."

"So she, uh, bends the ship to her old habits?"

"More like we let ourselves be bent." Ezri gestured to him to keep painting, and he returned to work. "Brass Sea captains are special. They have status, on the water and off. There's a council of them in Prodigal. But each ship . . . the brethren sort of go their own way. Some captains get elected. Some only rule when it's time to take arms. With Drakasha . . . she rules because we know she's our best chance. At anything. They don't fuck around in Syrune."

"So you keep naval watches, and drink like nervous husbands, and mind your manners?"

"You don't approve?"

"Gods' blood, I damn well approve. It's just tidier than I imagined, is all."

"You wouldn't call anything we do *naval* if you'd ever served on a real ship of war. Most of our crew have, and this is a slacker's paradise by comparison. We keep our habits because most of us have been aboard other pirate ships, too. Seen the leaks that gain a little bit every day. Seen the mechanisms rusting. Seen the rigging fraying. What good's slacking all the time if the ship comes apart beneath you while you sleep?"

"So you're a prudent bunch."

"Yeah. Look, the sea either makes you prudent, or it kills you. Drakasha's officers take an oath. We're sworn that this ship goes down in battle, or by the will of the gods. Not for want of work, or canvas, or cord. That's a holy vow." She stretched. "And not for want of paint, either. Give the whole thing another coat, and look sharp about it."

Officers. Jean reviewed the *Orchid*'s officers as he worked, to keep his mind off Ezri. There was Drakasha, obviously. She kept no watch but appeared when and as she saw fit. She seemed to be on deck at least half the day, and materialized like magic when anything interesting happened. Beneath her, Ezri . . . dammit, no thoughts concerning Ezri. Not now.

Mumchance, the sailing master, and his little crew of trusted wheelhands. Drakasha might allow ordinary crewfolk to hold the helm in steady weather, but for any operation of skill, it was Mum and his bunch or nobody. Roughly equal with Mum were the quartermaster—currently assigned to the *Red Messenger*—and the physiker, Treganne, who would likely never admit to being equal with anyone who didn't have a temple with their name on it. Drakasha had the great cabin, naturally, and the four highest officers were allowed little closet rooms in the companionway, canvas-walled things like his old cabin.

Then there was a carpenter, a sailmaker, a cook, and a boatswain. The only privilege of being a petty officer seemed to be the right to boss a few other crewfolk about from time to time. There was also a pair of . . . underlieutenants, Jean supposed. Ezri called them her watch chiefs, and they were Ezri when Ezri wasn't around. Utgar had the Red watch and a woman called Nasreen led the Blue, but Jean had yet to meet her, since she'd been entrusted with the *Messenger*'s prize crew.

It seemed that all the menial, back-and-forth mucking about was giving Jean—and the rest of the scrub watch—the chance to learn the ship's hierarchy, along with its layout. He supposed that was by design.

The weather had been consistent since their capture. Steady light breezes from the northeast, clouds that came and went like a tavern dancer's favor, endless low waves that made the sea gleam like a million-faceted sapphire. The sun was a pounding heat by day, and enclosure stifled them at night, but Jean was conditioned to this work by now. He was as brown as Paolo and Cosetta. Locke, too, seemed to be making the best of it—tanned and bearded and genuinely wiry, for once, rather than merely slender. His size and an unwise boast about his agility had gotten him assigned to mast-slushing duty, foremast and main, each and every morning.

Their food still came late after each long day, and though charmless it was more than ample. They had a full liquor ration now, too. As much as Jean hated to admit it, even to himself, he didn't mind this turn of events so very much. He could work and sleep in confidence that the people ruling the ship knew their business; he and Locke no longer had to run everything on improvisation and prayer. If not for the damned log, with its relentless record of day after day passing them by, day after day of the antidote waning, it would have been a good time. A good and time-less interval, with Lieutenant Delmastro to puzzle over.

But neither he nor Locke could stop counting the days.

2

ON THE eighteenth of Festal, Bald Mazucca snapped.

He'd given no warning; though he'd been sullen in the undercastle each night, he was one among many tired and short-tempered men, and he'd made no further threats toward anyone, crew or scrub watch.

It was dusk, two or three hours into the Blue watch's duty, and lanterns were going up across the ship. Jean was sitting next to Locke by the chicken coops, unraveling old rope into its component yarns. Locke was shredding these into a pile of rough brown fibers. Tarred, this stuff would become oakum, and be used for everything from caulking seams to stuffing pillows. It was a miserably tedious job, but the sun was almost gone and the end of duty for the day was nearly at hand.

There was a clatter from somewhere near the undercastle, followed by swearing and laughter. Bald Mazucca stomped into sight, carrying a mop and a bucket, with a crewman Jean didn't recognize at his heels. The crewman said something else that Jean didn't catch, and then it happened—Mazucca whirled and flung the heavy bucket at him, catching him right in the face. The crewman fell on his backside, stunned.

"Gods *damn* you," Mazucca cried, "d'you think I'm a fuckin' child?"

The crewman fumbled at his belt for a weapon—a short club, Jean saw. But Mazucca's blood was up, and the crewman was still recovering from the blow. In a moment, Mazucca had kicked him in the chest and snatched the club for himself. He raised it above his head, but that was as far as he got. Three or four crewfolk hit him simultaneously, knocking him to the deck and wrestling the club from his hand.

Heavy footsteps beat rapidly from the quarterdeck to the waist. Captain Drakasha had come without being summoned.

As she flew past, Jean—his rope work quite forgotten—felt his stomach flutter. She had *it*. She wore it like a cloak. The same aura that he'd once seen in Capa Barsavi, something that slept inside until it was drawn out by anger or need, so sudden and so terrible. Death itself was beating a tread upon the ship's planks.

Drakasha's crewfolk had Mazucca up and pinned by the arms. The man who'd been hit by the bucket had retrieved his club and was rubbing his head nearby. Zamira came to a halt and pointed at him.

"Explain yourself, Tomas."

"I was...I was...sorry, Cap'n. Just having some fun."

"He's been hounding me all fuckin' afternoon," said Mazucca, subdued but nowhere near calm. "Hasn't done a lick of work. Just follows me around, kicks my bucket, takes my tools, messes up my shit and sets me to fixing it again."

"True, Tomas?"

"I just...it was just fun, Cap'n. Teasing the scrub watch. Didn't mean nothing. I'll stop."

Drakasha moved so fast Tomas didn't even have time to flinch until he was already on his way back to the deck, his nose broken. Jean had noted the elegant upward sweep of her arm and the precise use of the palm—he'd been on the receiving end of that sort of blow at least twice in his life. Tomas, stupid ass that he was, had his sympathy.

"Agggh," said Tomas, spraying blood.

"The scrub watch are like tools," said Drakasha. "I expect them to be kept in a useful trim. Maintained. You want to have fun, you make sure it's responsible fun. I'm halving your share of the *Red Messenger* loot, and your share of the sale." She gestured to the women standing behind him. "You two. Haul him aft and find Scholar Treganne."

As Tomas was being dragged toward the quarterdeck for a surprise visit to the ship's physiker, Drakasha turned to Mazucca.

"You heard my rules, first night you were on my ship."

"I know. I'm sorry, Captain Drakasha, he just—"

"You did hear. You *did* hear what I said, and you understood."

"I did, I was angry, I—"

"Death to touch a weapon. I made that clear as a cloudless sky, and you did it anyway."

"Look—"

"I've got no use for you," she said, and her right arm darted out to close around Mazucca's throat. The crewfolk released him, and he locked his hands around Drakasha's forearm, to no avail. She began dragging him toward the starboard rail. "Out here, you lose your head, you make one dumb gods-damned mistake, you can take the whole ship down. If you can't keep your wits when you've been told what's at stake, clear and simple, you're just ballast."

Kicking and gagging, Mazucca tried to fight back, but Drakasha hauled him inexorably toward the side of the weather deck. About two yards from the rail, she gritted her teeth, drew her right arm back, and flung Mazucca forward, putting the full power of hip and shoulder into the push. He hit hard, flailing for balance, and toppled backward. A second later there was the sound of a splash.

"This ship has ballast enough."

Crewfolk and scrub watch alike ran to the starboard rail. After a quick glance at Locke, Jean got up to join them. Drakasha remained where she was, arms at her side, her sudden rage evaporated. In that, too, she seemed like Barsavi. Jean wondered if she would spend the rest of the night sullen and brooding, or even drinking.

The ship had been making a steady four or five knots, and Mazucca didn't appear to be a strong swimmer. He was already five or six yards to the side of the ship, and fifteen or twenty yards back, off the quarterdeck. His arms and head bobbed against the rippling darkness of the waves, and he hollered for help.

Dusk. Jean shuddered. A hungry time on the open sea. The hard light of day drove many things deep beneath the waves, made the water nearly safe for hours on end. All that changed at twilight.

"Shall we fish him out, Captain?" A crewman had stepped up beside her, and he spoke in a voice so low that only those nearby could hear.

"No," said Drakasha. She turned and began to walk

slowly aft. "Sail on. Something will be along for him soon enough."

3

ON THE nineteenth, at half past noon, Drakasha shouted for Locke to come to her cabin. Locke ran aft as fast as he could, visions of Tomas and Mazucca vivid in his mind.

"Ravelle, what the unhallowed hells *is* this?"

Locke paused to take in the scene. She'd rigged her table in the center of the cabin. Paolo and Cosetta were seated across from one another, staring at Locke, and a deck of playing cards was spread in an unfathomable pattern between them. A silver goblet was tipped over in the middle of the table... a goblet too large for little hands. Locke felt a flutter of anxiety in the pit of his stomach, but looked closer nonetheless.

As he'd suspected... a mouthful or so of pale brown liquor had spilled onto the tabletop from the goblet, and fallen across a card. That card had dissolved into a puddle of soft, completely unmarked gray material.

"You took the cards out of my chest," he said. "The ones in the double-layered oilcloth parcel."

"Yes."

"And you were drinking a fairly strong liquor with your meal. One of your children spilled it."

"Caramel brandy, and I spilled it myself." She produced a dagger and poked at the gray material. Although it had a liquid sheen, it was hard and solid, and the tip of the dagger slid off it as though it were granite. "What the hell *is* this? It's like... alchemical cement."

"It *is* alchemical cement. You didn't notice that the cards smelled funny?"

"Why the hell would I smell playing cards?" She

frowned. "Children, don't touch these anymore. In fact, go sit on your bed until Mommy can wash your hands."

"It's not dangerous," said Locke.

"I don't care," she said. "Paolo, Cosetta, put your hands in your laps and wait for Mommy."

"They're not really cards," said Locke. "They're alchemical resin wafers. Paper-thin and flexible. The card designs are actually painted on. You wouldn't believe how expensive they were."

"Nor would I care. What the hell are they *for*?"

"Isn't it obvious? Dip one in strong liquor and it dissolves in a few seconds. Suddenly you've got a little pat of alchemical cement. Mash up as many cards as you need. The stuff dries in about a minute, hard as steel."

"Hard as steel?" She eyed the gray splotch on her fine lacquered tabletop. "How does it come off?"

"Um . . . it doesn't. There's no solvent. At least not outside of an alchemist's lab."

"What? Gods damn it, Ravelle—"

"Captain, you're being unfair. I didn't ask you to take those cards out and play with them. Nor did I spill liquor on them."

"You're right," said Drakasha with a sigh. She looked tired, Locke thought. The faint frown lines around her mouth looked as though they'd had a long recent workout. "Gather these up and throw them overboard."

"Captain, please. *Please.*" Locke held his hands out toward her. "Not only are they expensive, they'd be . . . damned impossible to duplicate. It'd take months. Let me just roll them back up in oilcloth and put them in the chest. Please think of them as part of my papers."

"What do you use them for?"

"They're just part of my little bag of tricks," he said. "All I have left of it, really. One last, important little trick. I swear to you, they're absolutely no threat to you and your ship.... You have to spill booze on them, and even then they're just an annoyance. Look, if you save them for me, and find me some knives with scalpel edges, I'll devote all my time to getting that shit off your table. Prying from the sides. Even if it takes all week. Please."

As it turned out, it took him ten hours, scraping away with infinite care atop the forecastle, as though he were performing surgery. He worked without rest, first by sunlight and then by the glow of multiple lanterns, until the devilishly hard stuff had been scraped off with nothing but a ghost upon the lacquer to show for it.

When he finally claimed his minuscule sleeping space, he knew his hands and forearms would ache well into the next day.

It was worth it, and had been worth every minute of work, to preserve the existence of that deck of cards.

4

ON THE twentieth, Drakasha gave up on the easterly course and put them west by north with the wind on the starboard beam. The weather held; they cooked by day and sweated by night, and the ship sailed beneath streams of flit-wraiths that hung over the water like arches of ghostly green light.

On the twenty-first, as the promise of dawn was just graying the eastern sky, they had their chance to prove themselves.

Locke was knocked out of a too-short sleep by an elbow to the ribs. He awoke to confusion; the men of the scrub watch were shifting, stumbling, and muttering all around him.

"Sail ho," said Jean.

"Heard it from the masthead just a minute ago," said

someone near the door. "Two points off the starboard quarter. That's well east and a little north of us, hull down."

"That's good," said Jabril, yawning. "The dawn glimpse."

"Dawn?" It still seemed dark, and Locke rubbed his sleep-blurred eyes. "Dawn already? Since I no longer have to pretend to know what the hell I'm doing, what's a dawn glimpse?"

"Sun's coming up over the horizon, see?" Jabril seemed to relish the chance to lecture Locke. "Over in the east. We're still in shadow over here, to the west a' them. Hard to see us, but we got a good eye on them with that faint light behind their masts, savvy?"

"Right," said Locke. "Seems like a good thing."

"We're for her," said Aspel. "We'll move in and take her. This ship is loaded with crew, and Drakasha's a bloody-handed bitch."

"It's a fight for us," said Streva. "We'll go first."

"Aye, and prove ourselves," said Aspel. "Prove ourselves and be quits with this scrub watch shit."

"Don't be tying silver ribbons on your cock just yet," said Jabril. "We don't know her heading, or what speed she makes, or what her best point of sailing is. She might be a ship of war. Might even be part of a squadron."

"Be fucked, Jabbi," said someone without real malice. "Don't you want to be gone from scrub watch?"

"Hey, time comes to board her, I'll row the boat naked and attack the bastards with my good fuckin' looks. Just wait and see if she's prey, is all I'm sayin'."

There was noise and commotion on deck; orders were shouted. The men at the entrance strained to hear and see everything.

"Delmastro's sending people up the lines," said one of them. "Looks like we're going to come north a few points. They're doing it quick-like."

"Nothing's more suspicious than a sudden change of sail, if they see us," said Jabril. "She wants us to be nearer their course before we're spotted, so it looks natural."

Minutes passed; Locke blinked and settled back down against his familiar bulkhead. If action wasn't imminent, there was always time for a few more minutes of sleep. From the groaning and shuffling around him, he wasn't alone in that opinion.

He awoke a few minutes later—the sky seen through the ventilation hatch was lighter gray—to Lieutenant Delmastro's voice coming from the undercastle entrance.

"...where you are for now. Keep quiet and out of sight. It's about five minutes to the switchover from Red to Blue, but we're suspending regular watches for action. We'll be sending Red down in bits and pieces, and half of Blue will come up to replace them. We want to look like a merchant brig, not a prowler with a heavy crew."

Locke craned his neck to look out over the shadowy shapes around him. Just past Delmastro, in the predawn murk, he could see crewfolk at the waist wrestling several large barrels toward the ship's larboard rail.

"Smoke barrels on deck," called a woman.

"No open flames on deck," shouted Ezri. "No smoking. Alchemical lights only. Pass the word."

Minutes passed, and the light of dawn grew steadily. Locke nonetheless found his eyelids creeping back downward. He sighed relaxed, and—

"On deck there," came a shout from the foremast head. "Send to the captain she's got three masts, and she's northwest by west. Topsails."

"Aye, three masts, northwest by west, topsails," shouted Ezri. "How does she bear?"

"Broad on the starboard beam, aft a point maybe."

"Keep sharp. Is she still hull down?"

"Aye."

"The moment she lifts her skirts over that horizon, you peek and tell us what's under them." Ezri returned to the undercastle and pounded loudly on the bulkhead beside the entrance. "Scrub watch, rouse up. Stretch your legs and use the craplines, then get back under here. Be quick. We'll be fighting or running soon enough. Best to have your innards in good order."

It was less like moving with a crowd than being squeezed from a tube. Locke found himself pushed onto deck, and he curled his back and stretched. Jean did likewise, then stepped up beside Delmastro. Locke raised an eyebrow; the little lieutenant seemed to tolerate Jean's conversation to the same extent that she disdained his. So long as one of them was getting information from her, he supposed.

"Do you really think we'll be running?" asked Jean.

"I'd prefer not." Delmastro squinted over the rail, but even from Locke's perspective the new ship couldn't be seen on deck just yet.

"You know," said Jean, "it's to be expected that you won't see anything from down there. You should let me put you on my shoulders."

"A *short joke*," said Delmastro. "How remarkably original. I've never heard the like in all my days. I'll have you know I'm the tallest of all my sisters."

"Sisters," said Jean. "Interesting. A bit of your past for free?"

"Shit," she said, scowling. "Leave me alone, Valora. It's going to be a busy morning."

Men were returning from the craplines. Now that the press had lessened, Locke climbed the stairs and made his way forward to do his own business. He had sufficient unpleasant experience by now to elbow his way to the weather side—damned unfortunate things could happen to those on the lee craplines in any kind of wind—of the little wooden brace, which crossed the bowsprit just a yard or two out from the forepeak. It had ratlines hanging beneath it like a miniature yardarm, and against these Locke braced his feet while he undid his breeches. Waves pounded white against the bow, and spray rose to splash the backs of his legs.

"Gods," he said, "to think that pissing could be such an adventure."

"On deck, there," came the cry from the foremast a moment later. "She's a flute, she is. Round and fat. Holding course and sail as before."

"What colors?"

"None to be seen, Lieutenant."

A flute. Locke recognized the term—a round-sterned merchantman with a homely curved bow. Handy for cargo, but a brig like the *Orchid* could dance around it at will. No pirate or military expedition would make use of such a vessel. As soon as they could draw her in, it seemed they'd have their fight.

"Ha," he muttered, "and here I am, caught with my breeches down."

5

THE SUN rose molten behind their target, framing the low black shape in a half-circle of crimson. Locke was on his knees at the starboard rail of the forecastle, trying to stay unobtrusive. He squinted and put a hand over his eyes to cut the glare. The eastern sky was a bonfire aura of pink and red; the sea was like liquid ruby spreading in a stain from the climbing sun.

A dirty black smear of smoke rose from the lee side of the *Poison Orchid*'s waist, a few yards wide, an ominous intrusion into the clean dawn air. Lieutenant Delmastro was tending the smoke barrels herself. The *Orchid* was making way under topsails with her main and forecourses furled; conveniently, it was both a logical plan of sail for this breeze and the first precaution they would have taken if the ship were really on fire.

"Come on, you miserable twits," said Jean, who was seated beside him. "Glance left, for Perelandro's sake."

"Maybe they do see us," said Locke. "Maybe they just don't give a damn."

"They haven't changed a sail," said Jean, "or we would've heard about it from the lookouts. They must be the most incurious, myopic, dim-witted buggers that ever set canvas to mast."

"On deck there!" The foremast lookout sounded excited. "Send to the captain she's turning to larboard!"

"How far?" Delmastro stepped away from her smoke barrels. "Is she coming about to head right for us?"

"No, she's come about three points around."

"They want to have a closer look," said Jean, "but they're not hopping into the hammock with us just yet."

There was a shout from the quarterdeck, and a moment later Delmastro blew her whistle three times.

"Scrub watch! Scrub watch to the quarterdeck!"

They hurried aft, past crewfolk removing well-oiled bows from canvas covers and stringing them. As Delmastro had promised, about half the usual watch was on deck; those involved in preparing weapons were crouched down or hiding behind the masts and the chicken coops. Drakasha was waiting for them at the quarterdeck rail, and she started speaking the moment they arrived.

"They still have time and room enough to put about. It's a flute, and I doubt they could run from us forever in any weather, but they could make us work for the catch. My guess is six or seven hours, but who wants to be bored for that long? We'll pose as a charter brig on fire and see if we can't entice them to do the sociable thing.

"I offered a chance to prove yourselves, so you're the teeth of the trap. You'll fight first. Good on you if you come back. If you don't want to fight, get under the forecastle and stay scrub watch until we're quits with you.

"As for me, I woke up hungry this morning. I mean to have that fat little prize. Who among you would fight for a place on my ship?"

Locke and Jean thrust their arms into the air, along with everyone nearby. Locke glanced quickly around and saw that nobody seemed to be declining their chance.

"Good," said Drakasha. "We've three boats, seating about thirty. You'll have them. Your task will be to look innocent at first; stay near the *Orchid*. At the signal, you'll dash out and attack from the south."

"Captain," said Jabril, "what if we can't take her ourselves?"

"If numbers or circumstances are against you, hold fast to whatever scrap of deck you can. I'll bring the *Orchid* alongside and grapple to her. Nothing that ship carries can stand against a hundred fresh boarders."

A fine comfort that'll be, to those of us already dead or dying, Locke thought. The reality of what they were about to do had only just come home to him, and he felt an anxious fluttering in his stomach.

"Captain!" One of the lookouts was hailing from the maintop. "She's sent up Talishani colors!"

"She might be lying," muttered Jabril. "Decent bluff. If you're going to fly a false flag, Talisham's got a bit of a navy. And nobody's at war with 'em right now."

"Not *too* clever, though," said Jean. "If she had escorts in sight, why not fly it at all times? Only someone with cause to be worried hides their colors."

"Aye. Them and pirates." Jabril grinned.

Captain Drakasha shouted across the crowd. "Del! Have

one of your smoke barrels sent over to the starboard rail. Just forward of the quarterdeck stairs."

"You want smoke from the weather rail, Captain?"

"A good smudge right across the quarterdeck," said Drakasha. "If they want to chat with signal flags, we need an excuse to keep mum."

The lanky sailing master, holding the wheel a few feet behind Drakasha, cleared his throat loudly. She smiled, then seemed to have an idea. Turning to a sailor on her left, she said, "Get three signal pennants from the flag chest and let them fly from the stern. Yellow over yellow over yellow."

"All souls in peril," said Jean. "That's a come-hither look, and no fooling."

"I thought it was just a distress signal," said Locke.

"Should've read the book more closely. Three yellow pennants says we're so hard up that we'll legally grant them salvage rights to anything we don't carry on our persons. They save it, they own it."

Delmastro and her crew had moved a smoke barrel into position at the starboard rail, and lit it with a bit of twist-match. Gray tendrils of smoke began to snake up and over the quarterdeck, chasing the darker black cloud rising from the lee side. At the taffrail, a pair of sailors was sending up three fluttering yellow pennants.

"Extra lookouts aloft and at the rails to give Mumchance a hand," called Drakasha. "Archers up one at a time. Keep your weapons down in the tops; stay out of sight if you can, and play meek until I give the signal."

"Captain!" The mainmast lookouts were shouting down once more. "She's turned to cut our path, and she's adding sail!"

"Funny how tender-hearted they get as soon as they see that signal," said Drakasha. "Utgar!"

A fairly young Vadran, the skin of his shaved head red-baked over a braided black beard, appeared just beside Lieutenant Delmastro.

"Hide Paolo and Cosetta on the orlop deck," said Zamira. "We're about to cause an argument."

"Aye," he said, and hurried up the quarterdeck stairs.

"As for you," said Drakasha, returning her attention to the scrub watch, "hatchets and sabers are set out at the foremast. Take your choice and wait to help send the boats down."

"Captain Drakasha!"

"What is it, Ravelle?"

Locke cleared his throat and offered a silent prayer to the Nameless Thirteenth that he knew what he was doing. The time for a gesture was now; if he didn't do something to restore a bit of prestige to Ravelle, he'd end up as just another member of the crew, shunned for his past failure. He needed to be respected if he expected to achieve any part of his mission. That meant a grand act of foolishness.

"It's my fault that these men nearly died aboard the *Messenger*. They were my crew, and I should have looked after them better. I'd like the chance to do that now. I want . . . the first seat on the lead boat."

"You expect me to let you command the attack?"

"Not command," said Locke. "Just go up the side first. Whatever's there to bleed us, let it bleed me first. Maybe I can spare whoever comes up next."

"That means me as well," said Jean, placing a hand on Locke's shoulder, somewhat protectively. "I go where he goes."

Gods bless you, Jean, thought Locke.

"If it's your ambition to stop a crossbow bolt," said Drakasha, "I won't say no." She seemed a bit taken aback, however, and she gave the tiniest fraction of an approving nod to Locke as the crowd began to break up and head forward for their weapons.

"Captain!" Lieutenant Delmastro stepped forward, her hands and forearms covered in soot from the smoke barrels. She glanced at Locke and Jean as she spoke. "Just who *is* leading the cutting-out boats anyway?"

"Free-for-all, Del. I'm sending one Orchid per boat to hold them; what the scrub watch does after they climb the sides is their business."

"I want the boats."

Drakasha stared at her for several seconds, and said nothing. She was wreathed in gray smoke from the waist down.

"I had nothing to do when we took the *Messenger,* Captain," Delmastro said hastily. "In fact, I haven't had any real fun with a prize for weeks."

Drakasha flicked her gaze over Jean and frowned. "You crave an indulgence."

"Aye. But a useful one."

Drakasha sighed. "You have the boats, Del. Mind you, Ravelle gets his wish."

Translation: If he takes an arrow for anyone, make sure it's you, thought Locke.

"You won't regret it, Captain. Scrub watch! Arm yourselves and meet me at the waist!" Delmastro dashed up the quarterdeck stairs, past Utgar, who was leading the Drakasha children along with one clinging tightly to either hand.

"You're a bold and stupid fellow, Ravelle," said Jabril. "I think I almost like you again."

"...at least he can fight, we know that much," Locke heard one of the other men saying. "You should've seen him take care of the guard the night we got the *Messenger.* Pow! One little punch folded him right up. He'll show us a thing or two this morning. You wait."

Locke was suddenly very glad he'd already pissed everything he had to piss.

At the waist, an older crew-woman stood watch on small barrels packed full of the promised hatchets and sabers. Jean drew out a pair of hatchets, hefted them, and frowned as Locke hesitated before the barrels.

"You have any idea what you're doing?" he whispered.

"None whatsoever," said Locke.

"Take a saber and try to look comfortable."

Locke drew a saber and gazed at it as though immensely satisfied.

"Anyone with a belt," shouted Jean, "grab a second weapon and tuck it in. You never know when you or someone else might need it."

As half a dozen men took his advice, he sidled up to Locke and whispered again. "Stay right beside me. Just... keep up with me and stand tall. Maybe they won't have bows."

Lieutenant Delmastro returned to their midst, wearing her black leather vest and bracers, as well as her knife-packed weapon belt. Locke noticed that the curved hand-guards of her sabers were studded with what looked like jagged chips of Elderglass.

"Here, Valora." She tossed a leather fighting collar to Jean and held her tightly tailed hair up to leave her neck fully exposed. "Help a girl out."

Jean placed the collar around her neck and clasped it behind her head. She tugged it once, nodded, and put up her arms. "Listen up! Until we make an unfriendly move, you're wealthy passengers and land-sucking snobs, sent out in the boats to save your precious skins."

A pair of crewmen were making the rounds of the scrub watch, handing out fine hats, brocaded jackets, and other fripperies. Delmastro seized a silk parasol and shoved it into Locke's hands. "There you go, Ravelle. That might de-flect some harm."

Locke shook the folded parasol over his head with exaggerated belligerence, and got some nervous laughter in exchange.

"Like the captain said, it'll be one Orchid per boat, to make sure they come back even if you don't," said Delmastro. "I'll take Ravelle and Valora with me, in the little boat you donated from the *Messenger*. Plus you and you." She pointed to Streva and Jabril. "Whatever else happens, we're first to the side and first up."

Oscarl, the boatswain, appeared with a small party of assistants carrying lines and blocks to begin rigging hoisting gear.

"One thing more," said Delmastro. "If they ask for quarter, give it. If they drop their weapons, respect it. If they carry on fighting, slaughter them where they fucking stand. And if you start to feel sorry for them, just remember what signal we had to fly to get them to lend aid to a ship on fire."

6

FROM THE water, the illusion of that fire seemed complete to Locke's eyes. All the smoke barrels were going now; the ship trailed a black-and-gray cloud that all but enveloped its quarterdeck. The figure of Zamira appeared now and again, her spyglass briefly catching the sun before she vanished back into the darkness. A team of crewmen had rigged small pumps and canvas hoses amidships (at the rail, where they could best be seen), and they were directing streams of water at the cloud of smoke, though actually doing nothing but washing the deck.

Locke sat at the bow of the little boat, feeling vaguely ridiculous with his parasol in hand and a cloth-of-silver jacket draped over his shoulders like a cape. Jean and Jabril shared the forward rowing bench, Streva and Lieutenant Delmastro were behind them, and a very small crewman named Vitorre—little more than a boy—crouched in the stern to take over from them when they boarded the flute.

That ship, her curiously round and wallowing hull-curves now plainly visible, was angled somewhat away from them to the north. Locke estimated that it would cross paths with the *Poison Orchid,* or very nearly so, in about ten minutes.

"Let's start rowing for her," said Delmastro. "They'll expect it by now."

Their boat and the two larger ones had been keeping station about a hundred yards southeast of the *Orchid.* As the four rowers in the lead boat began to pull north, Locke saw the others catch their cue and follow.

They bobbed and slipped across the foot-high waves. The sun was up and its heat was building; it had been half past the seventh hour of the morning when they'd left the ship. The oars creaked rhythmically in their locks; now they were abreast with the *Orchid,* and the newcomer was about half a mile to their northeast. If the flute caught wind of the trap and tried to flee to the north, the ship would loose canvas to fly after it. If it tried to flee south, however, it would be up to the boats to slip into its path.

"Ravelle," said Delmastro, "at your feet, the breaching shears. You see them?"

Locke looked down. Tucked away beneath his seat was an ugly-looking hinged device with a pair of wooden handles. These handles worked a metal jaw.

"I think so."

"Bows aren't our biggest problem. The most trouble they can give us is if they rig razor nets against boarding; we'll slash ourselves to pieces trying to climb on deck. If those nets are rigged, you *must* use those shears to cut a slit for us to get in."

"Or die trying," he said. "I think I get it."

"But the good news is, rigging razor nets is a pain in the

ass. And they won't be up at all if they're expecting to send out boats and receive passengers. If we can just get close enough before we tip our hand, they won't have time to use them."

"What's the signal to tip our hand?"

"You won't miss it. Trust me."

7

ZAMIRA DRAKASHA stood at the starboard quarter-deck rail, taking a break from the smoke. She studied the approaching flute through her glass; there was elaborate ornamentation on the stubby forepeak, and a somewhat whimsical gold-and-black paint scheme along her tall sides. That was agreeable; if she was well maintained she was likely to be carrying a respectable cargo and a bit of coin.

A pair of officers stood at the bow, studying her ship through their own glasses. She waved in what she hoped was an encouraging fashion, but received no response.

"Well, fine," she muttered. "You'll be rendering your courtesies soon enough."

The small dark shapes of crew rushed about on the flute, now just a quarter mile distant. Her sails were shuddering, her hull elongating in Zamira's view—were they running? No, just killing momentum, turning a point or two to starboard, aiming to get close but not *too* close. She could see a pump-and-hose team at work amidships, shooting a stream of water upward to wet the flute's lower sails. Very sensible, when coming anywhere near a fire at sea.

"Signal party," she said, "stand ready."

"Aye, Captain," came a chorus of voices from within the smoke-shrouded portion of the quarterdeck.

Her own boats were cutting the waves between the two

ships. There was Ravelle in the lead with his parasol, looking a bit like a thin silver mushroom with a soft white cap. And there was Valora, and there was Ezri...damn it. Ezri's request had given her little choice but to acquiesce or look foolish in front of the scrub watch. There'd be words for that little woman...if the gods blessed Zamira enough to send her lieutenant back alive.

She studied the flute's officers, who'd moved from the bow to the larboard rail. Wide fellows, it seemed, a bit overdressed for the heat. Her eyes were not what they'd been twenty-five years ago.... Were they prodding one another, looking more intently through their glasses?

"Captain?" asked a member of the signal party.

"Hold," she said. "Hold..." Every second closed the gap between the *Orchid* and her victim. They'd slowed and turned, but leeway would bring them closer still...closer still. One of them pointed, then grabbed the other by the shoulder and pointed again. Their glasses flew up in unison.

"Ha!" Zamira cried. Not a chance they could slip away now. She felt new zeal lending strength to her every step and motion; she felt half her years seem to fall from her shoulders. *Gods,* the moment they realized just how fucked they were was always sweet. She slammed her spyglass shut, snatched her speaking trumpet from the deck, and hollered across the length of the ship.

"Archers ready at the tops! All hands on deck! All hands on deck and man the starboard rail! Stifle smoke barrels!"

The *Poison Orchid* shuddered; seven dozen hands were pounding up the ladders, surging out of the hatchways, armed and armored, screaming as they came. Archers stepped out from behind the masts, knelt on their fighting platforms, and nocked arrows to their gleaming bows.

Zamira didn't need her glass to see the shapes of officers and crew running about frantically on the flute's deck.

"Let's give 'em something that'll really make 'em piss their breeches," she shouted, not bothering with the speaking trumpet. *"Hoist our crimson!"*

The three yellow pennants streaming above the quarterdeck shuddered, then plummeted straight down into the gray haze. From out of the last of the black and boiling smoke rose a broad red banner, bright as the morning sun looming above a storm.

8

"WITH A will," shouted Lieutenant Delmastro, "with a will!" As the bloodred flag rose to its full prominence above the stern of the *Orchid* and the first of the horde of maniacally cheering crewfolk began to crowd her starboard rail, the three boats surged across the waves.

Locke shed his parasol and jacket, tossing them overboard before remembering that they were worth quite a bit of money. He breathed in excited gasps, glancing over his shoulder at the fast-approaching side of the flute, a sheer wooden surface that loomed like a floating castle. Dear gods, he was going into battle. What the fuck was the *matter* with him?

He bit the insides of his cheeks for concentration and held on to the gunwales with white knuckles. *Damn* it, this was no grand gesture. He couldn't afford this. He breathed deep to steady himself.

Locke Lamora was small, but the Thorn of Camorr was larger than any of this. The Thorn couldn't be touched by blade or spell or scorn. Locke thought of the Falconer, bleeding at his feet. He thought of the Gray King, dead beneath his knife. He thought of the fortunes that had run through his fingers, and he smiled.

Steadily, carefully, he drew his saber and began to wave it in the air. The three boats were nearly abreast now, slashing white triangles of wake on the sea, a minute from their target. Locke meant to hit it wearing the biggest lie of his life like a costume. He might be dead in a few moments, but until then, by the gods, he was the Thorn of Camorr. He was Captain Orrin *fucking* Ravelle.

"Orchids! Orchids!" He made a statue of himself at the bow of the boat, thrusting with his saber as though he meant to ram the flute and punch a hole in her side all by himself. "Pull for the prize! Pull for yourselves! Follow me, Orchids! *Richer and cleverer than everyone else!*"

The *Poison Orchid* slipped ahead of the last of her smoke, streaming gray lines from her quarterdeck, as though evading the grasp of some godlike ghostly hand. The teeming crewfolk at her rail cheered again, and then fell silent together. The ship's sails began to flutter. Drakasha was tacking, with haste, to bring the ship sharply around to starboard. If she pulled it off she would snug up, on the larboard tack, right alongside the flute at knife-fighting distance.

The sudden silence of the Orchids allowed Locke to hear noises from the flute for the first time—orders, panic, arguments, consternation. And then, over everything else, a tinny and desperate voice shouting through a speaking trumpet:

"Save us! For the love of the gods, please ... please get over here and save us!"

"Shit. That's a little different than what we usually get," said Delmastro.

Locke had no time to think; they were up to the flute's hull, bumping hard against the wall of wet planks on her lee side. The ship was slightly heeled over, creating the illusion that she was about to topple and crush them. Miraculously, there were shrouds and a boarding net within easy reach. Locke leapt for the net, sword arm raised.

"Orchids," he cried as he climbed the rough, wet hemp in an exaltation of fear. "Orchids! Follow me!"

The moment of truth; his left hand found the deck at the top of the boarding net. Gritting his teeth, he swept upward with his saber, clumsily and viciously, in case anyone was waiting at the edge of the deck. Then he heaved himself up, rolled under the rail—he'd missed the entry port by a few yards—and stumbled to his feet, screaming like a madman.

The deck was all chaos, and none of it meant for him. There were no razor nets, no archers, no walls of polearms or swords waiting to receive the boarders. Crewmen and -women ran about in a panic. An abandoned fire hose lay on the deck at Locke's feet like a dead brown snake, gurgling seawater into a spreading puddle.

A crewman skidded through that puddle and slammed into him, flailing. Locke raised his saber, and the crewman cringed, throwing up his hands to show that they were empty.

"We tried to surrender," the crewman gasped. "We tried! They wouldn't let us! Gods, help us!"

"Who? *Who* wouldn't let you surrender?"

The crewman pointed to the ship's raised quarterdeck, and Locke whirled to see what was there.

"Aw, *hell*," he whispered.

There had to be at least twenty of them, all men, cast from the same mold. Tanned, stocky, muscular. Their beards were neatly trimmed, their shoulder-length hair bound in rattling strings of beads. Their heads were wrapped with bright green cloths, and Locke knew from past experience that what looked like thin, dark sleeves covering their arms was actually holy verse, tattooed so thickly in black and green ink that every trace of the skin beneath was lost.

Jeremite Redeemers. Religious maniacs who believed

that they were the only possible salvation for the sins of their wicked island. They made themselves living sacrifices to the Jeremite gods, wandering the world in exile groups, living polite as monks until someone, anyone, threatened them.

Their sacred vow was to kill or be killed when offered violence; to die honorably for Jerem, or to ruthlessly exterminate anyone who raised a hand against them. All of them were looking very, very intently at Locke.

"The heathen offers a red cleansing!" A Redeemer at the head of the group pointed at Locke and hoisted his brass-studded witchwood club. "Wash our souls in heathen blood! *Slay for holy Jerem!*"

Weapons high, they rushed the quarterdeck stairs and surged down them, fixed on Locke, all the while demonstrating just how madmen *really* screamed. A crewman tried to stumble out of their way and was swatted down, his skull cracking like a melon beneath the club of the leader. The others trampled his body as they charged.

Locke couldn't help himself. The spectacle of that onrushing, battle-hardened, completely insane death was so far beyond anything in his experience, he coughed out a burst of startled laughter. He was scared to the marrow, and in that there was sudden, absolute freedom. He raised his one useless saber and flung himself into a countercharge, feeling light as dust on a breeze, hollering as he ran. "Come, then! Face Ravelle! The gods have sent your doom, *motherfuckers!*"

He should have died a few seconds later. It was Jean, as usual, who had other plans.

The Jeremite leader bore down on Locke, twice his weight worth of murderous fanatic, blood and sunlight gleaming on the studs of his raised club. Then there was a hatchet where his face had been, the handle protruding from the shattered hollow of an eye. Impact, not with the

club but with the suddenly senseless corpse, slammed
Locke to the deck and knocked the air from his lungs. Hot
blood sprayed across his face and neck, and he struggled
furiously to free himself from beneath the twitching body.
The deck around him was suddenly full of shapes kicking,
stomping, screaming, and falling.

The world dissolved into disconnected images and sensations. Locke barely had time to catalog them as they
flashed by.

Axes and spears meant for him sinking into the body of
the Jeremite leader. A desperate lunge with his saber, and
the shock of impact as it sank into the unprotected hollow
of a Redeemer's thigh. Jean hauling him to his feet. Jabril
and Streva pulling other Orchids onto the deck. Lieutenant
Delmastro, fighting beside Jean, turning a Redeemer's face
to raw red paste with the glass-studded guard of one of her
sabers. Shadows, movements, discordant shouts.

It was impossible to stay next to Jean; the press of
Redeemers was too thick, the number of incoming blows
too great. Locke was knocked down again by a falling body,
and he rolled to his left, slashing blindly, frantically as he
went. The deck and the sky spun around him until suddenly he was rolling into thin air.

The grating was off the main cargo hatch.

Desperately he checked himself, scrambling back to his
right before he toppled in. A glimpse into the main-deck
hold had revealed a trio of Redeemers there, too. He stumbled to his feet and was immediately attacked by another
Jeremite; parrying slash after slash, he sidestepped left and
tried to slip away from the edge of the cargo hatch. No
good; a second antagonist appeared, blood-drenched spear
at the ready.

Locke knew he'd never be able to fight or dodge the pair
of them with an open grate behind his feet. He thought
quickly. The flute's crew had been in the process of shifting

a heavy barrel from the main-deck hold when the attack had come. That cask, four or five feet in diameter, hung in a netting above the mouth of the cargo hatch.

Locke lashed out wildly at his two opponents, aiming only to force them back. Then he spun on his heels and leapt for all he was worth. He struck the hanging cask with a head-jarring thud and clung to the netting, his legs kicking like those of a man treading water. The cask swung like a pendulum as he scrambled atop it.

From here, he briefly enjoyed a decent view of the action. More Orchids were pouring into the fray from the ship's larboard side, and Delmastro and Jean were pushing the main body of Redeemers back up the quarterdeck stairs. Locke's side of the deck was a tangled swirl of opponents; green cloths and bare heads above weapons of every sort.

Suddenly, the Jeremite with the spear was jabbing at him, and the blackened-steel head of the weapon bit wood inches from his leg. Locke flailed back with his saber, realizing that his suspended haven wasn't as safe as he'd hoped. There were shouts from below; the Redeemers in the hold had noticed him, and meant to do something about him.

It was up to him to do something crazy first.

He leapt up, holding fast to one of the lines by which the cask was suspended from a winding-tackle, and dodged another spear thrust. No good trying to cut all the lines leading down from the tackle. That could take minutes. He tried to remember the patterns of ropes and blocks Caldris had drilled into him. His eyes darted along the single taut line that fell from the winding-tackle to a snatch-block at one corner of the cargo hatch. Yes—that line led across the deck, disappearing beneath the throng of combatants. It would run to the capstan, and if it was cut . . .

Gritting his teeth, he gave the taut line a good slash with the forte of his blade, feeling the saber bite hemp. A thrown hatchet whizzed past his shoulder, missing by the width of his little finger. He slashed the line again, and again, driving the blade with all the force he could muster. At the fourth stroke, it unraveled with a snap, and the weight of the cask broke it clean in two. Locke rode the barrel down into the hold, his eyes squeezed firmly shut. Someone screamed, saving him the trouble of doing so himself.

The cask struck with a resounding crash. Locke's momentum smacked him down hard against its upper surface. His chin struck wood and he was tossed sideways, landing in an undignified heap on the deck. Warm, smelly liquid washed over him—beer. The cask was gushing it.

Locke climbed back to his feet, groaning. One Redeemer hadn't moved fast enough, and was splayed out beneath the cask, clearly dead. The other two had been knocked sideways by the impact, and were feeling around groggily for their weapons.

He stumbled over and slit their throats before they knew he was even back on his feet. It wasn't fighting, just thief's work, and he did it mechanically. Then he blinked and looked around for something to clean the blade on; an old and natural thief's habit that nearly got him killed.

A heavy dark shape splashed into the beer beside him. One of the Jeremites who'd been troubling him above, the one with the spear, had leapt the six or seven feet down into the hold. But the gushing beer was treacherous; the Redeemer's feet went out from under him as he landed, and he toppled onto his back. Coldly resigned, Locke drove his saber into the man's chest, then pried the spear from his dying hands.

"Undone by drink," he whispered.

The fight continued above. For the moment, he was alone in the hold with his shoddy little victory.

Four dead, and he'd cheated every one, using luck and surprise and plain skullduggery to do what would have been impossible in a stand-up fight. Knowing that they would never have given or accepted quarter *should* have made it easier, but the wild abandon of a few minutes before had drained clean away. Orrin Ravelle was a fraud after all; he was plain Locke Lamora once again.

He threw up behind a pile of canvas and netting, using the spear to hold himself up until the heaving stopped.

"Gods *above!*"

Locke wiped his mouth as Jabril and a pair of Orchids slipped down through the cargo hatch, holding to the rim of the deck rather than leaping. They didn't seem to have caught him puking.

"Four of 'em," continued Jabril. His tunic had been partly torn away above a shallow cut on his chest. "Fuck me, Ravelle. I thought *Valora* scared the piss out of me."

Locke took a deep breath to steady himself. "Jerome. Is he all right?"

"Was a minute ago. Saw him and Lieutenant Delmastro fighting on the quarterdeck."

Locke nodded, then gestured aft with his spear. "Stern cabin," he said. "Follow me. Let's finish this."

He led them down the length of the flute's main deck at a run, shoving unarmed, cowering crewfolk out of the way as he passed. The armored door to the stern cabin was shut, and behind it Locke could hear the sound of frantic activity. He pounded on the door.

"We know you're in there," he yelled, and then turned to Jabril with a tired grin. "This seems awfully familiar, doesn't it?"

"You won't get through that door," came a muffled shout from within.

"Give it some shoulder," said Jabril.

"Let me try being terribly clever first," said Locke. Then,

raising his voice: "First point, this door may be armored, but your stern windows are glass. Second point, open this fucking door by the count of ten or I'll have every surviving crewman and woman put to death on the quarterdeck. You can listen while you're doing whatever it is you're doing in there."

A pause; Locke opened his mouth to begin counting. Suddenly, with the ratcheting clack of heavy clockwork, the door creaked open and a short, middle-aged man in a long black jacket appeared.

"Please don't," he said. "I surrender. I would have done it sooner, but the Redeemers wouldn't have it. I locked myself in after they chased me down here. Kill me if you like, but spare my crew."

"Don't be stupid," said Locke. "We don't kill anyone who doesn't fight back. Though I suppose it's nice to know you're not a complete asshole. Ship's master, I presume?"

"Antoro Nera, at your service."

Locke grabbed him by his lapels and began dragging him toward the companionway. "Let's go on deck, Master Nera. I think we've dealt with your Redeemers. What the hell were they doing aboard, anyway? Passengers?"

"Security," muttered Nera. Locke stopped in his tracks.

"Are you that fucking dim-witted, that you didn't know they'd go berserk the first time someone dangled a fight in front of their noses?"

"I didn't want them! The owners insisted. Redeemers work for nothing but food and passage. Owners thought...perhaps they'd scare off anyone looking for trouble."

"A fine theory. Only works if you advertise their presence, though. We didn't know they were aboard until they were charging us in a fucking phalanx."

Locke went up the companionway, dragging Nera behind him, followed by Jabril and the others. They emerged into the bright light of morning on the quarterdeck. One of the men was hauling down the flute's colors, and he was knee-deep in bodies.

There were at least a dozen of them. Redeemers, mostly, with their green head-cloths fluttering and their expressions strangely satisfied. But here and there were unfortunate crewfolk, and at the head of the stairs a familiar face—Aspel, the front of his chest a bloody ruin.

Locke glanced around frantically and sighed when he saw Jean, apparently untouched, crouched near the starboard rail. Lieutenant Delmastro was at his feet, her hair unbound, blood running down her right arm. As Locke watched, Jean tore a strip of cloth from the bottom of his own tunic and began binding one of her wounds.

Locke felt a pang that was half relief and half melancholy; usually it was *him* that Jean was picking up in bloody pieces at the end of a fight. Ducking away from Jean had been a matter of split-second necessity in the heat of the struggle. He realized that he was strangely disquieted that Jean hadn't followed him, relentlessly at his heels, looking after him as always.

Don't be an ass, he thought. Jean had his own bloody problems.

"Jerome," he said.

Jean's head darted around, and his lips nearly formed an "L" sound before he got himself under control. "Orrin! You're a mess! Gods, are you all right?"

A mess? Locke looked down and discovered that nearly every inch of his clothing was soaked in blood. He ran a hand over his face. What he'd taken for sweat or beer came away red on his palm.

"None of it's mine," he said. "I think."

"I was about to come looking for you," said Jean. "Ezri...Lieutenant Delmastro..."

"I'll be fine," she groaned. "Bastard tried to hit me with a mizzenmast. Just knocked the wind out of me."

Locke spotted one of the huge brass-studded clubs lying on the deck near her, and just beyond it, a dead Redeemer with one of Delmastro's characteristic sabers planted in his throat.

"Lieutenant Delmastro," said Locke, "I've brought the ship's master. Allow me to introduce Antoro Nera."

Delmastro pushed Jean's hands away and crawled past him for a better view. Lines of blood ran from cuts on her lip and forehead.

"Master Nera. Well met. I represent the side that's still standing. Appearances to the contrary." She grinned and wiped at the blood above her eyes. "I'll be responsible for arranging larceny once we've secured your ship, so don't piss me off. Speaking of which, what ship is this?"

"*Kingfisher*," said Nera.

"Cargo and destination?"

"Tal Verrar, with spices, wine, turpentine, and fine woods."

"That and a fat load of Jeremite Redeemers. No, shut up. You can explain later. Gods, Ravelle, you *have* been busy."

"Too fucking right," said Jabril, slapping him on the back. "He killed four of them himself in the hold. Rode a beer cask down on one, and must've fought the other three straight up." Jabril snapped his fingers. "Like *that*."

Locke sighed, and felt his cheeks warming. He reached up and put a bit of the blood back where he'd found it.

"Well," said Delmastro, "I won't say that I'm not surprised, but I am pleased. You're not fit to tend so much as a fishing boat, Ravelle, but you can lead boarding parties whenever you like. I think we just redeemed about half of Jerem."

"You're too kind," said Locke.

"Can you get this ship into order for me? Clear the decks of crewfolk and put them all under guard at the forecastle?"

"I can. Will she be all right, Jerome?"

"She's been smacked around and cut up a bit, but—"

"I've had worse," she said. "I've had worse, and I've certainly given it back. You can go with Ravelle if you like."

"I—"

"Don't make me hit you. I'll be fine."

Jean stood up and came over to Locke, who shoved Nera gently toward Jabril.

"Jabril, would you escort our new friend to the forecastle while Jerome and I scrape up the rest of his crew?"

"Aye, be pleased to."

Locke led Jean down the quarterdeck stairs, into the tangle of bodies amidships. More Redeemers, more crewfolk...and five or six of the men he'd pulled out of Windward Rock three weeks before. He was uncomfortably aware that the survivors all seemed to be staring at him. He caught snatches of their conversation:

"...laughing, he was..."

"Saw it as I came up the side. Charged them all by himself..."

"Never seen the like." That was Streva, whose left arm looked broken. "Laughed and laughed. Fucking fearless."

"...'the gods send your doom, motherfuckers.' That's what he told them. I heard it...."

"They're right, you know," whispered Jean. "I've seen you do some brave and crazy shit, but that was...that was—"

"It was all crazy and none brave. I was out of my fucking head, get it? I was so scared shitless I didn't know what I was doing."

"But in the hold below—"

"I dropped a cask on one," said Locke. "Two more got their throats slit while they were still dumb. The last was kind enough to slip in beer and make it easy. Same as always, Jean. I'm no bloody warrior."

"But now they think you are. You pulled it off."

They found Mal, slumped against the mainmast, unmoving. His hands were curled around the sword buried in his stomach, as though he were trying to keep it safe. Locke sighed.

"I have what you might call mixed feelings about that right now," he said.

Jean knelt down and pushed Mal's eyelids closed. "I know what you mean." He paused, seeming to weigh his words before continuing. "We have a serious problem."

"Really? Us, problems? What *ever* could you mean?"

"These people are our people. These people are *thieves*. Surely you see it too. We can't sell them out to Stragos."

"Then we'll die."

"We both know Stragos means to kill us anyway—"

"The longer we string him along," said Locke, "the closer we get to pulling off some part of our mission, the closer we are to a real antidote. The more time we get, the greater the chance he'll slip . . . and we can do something."

"We can do something by siding with our own kind. Look around you, for the gods' sake. *All* these people do to live is steal. They're us. The mandates we live by—"

"Don't fucking lecture *me* about propriety!"

"Why not? You seem to need it—"

"I've done my duty by the men we brought from Tal Verrar, Jean. But they and *all* of these people are strangers. I aim to have Stragos weeping for what he's done, and if I have to spare them to achieve that, by the gods, I'll spare them. But if I have to sink this ship and a dozen like it to bring him down, I'll damn well do that, too."

"Gods," Jean whispered. "Listen to yourself. I thought *I*

was Camorri. You're the pure essence. A moment ago you were morose for the sake of these people. Now you'd fucking drown them all for the sake of your revenge!"

"*Our* revenge," said Locke. "*Our* lives."

"There has to be another way."

"What do you propose, then? Stay out here? Spend a merry few weeks in the Ghostwinds, and then politely *die*?"

"If necessary," said Jean.

The *Poison Orchid*, under reduced sail, drew near the stern of the *Kingfisher*, putting herself between the flute and the wind. The men and women lining the *Orchid*'s rail let loose with three raucous cheers, each one louder than the last.

"Hear that? They're not cheering the scrub watch," said Jean. "They're cheering their own. That's what we are, now. Part of all this."

"They're str—"

"They're not *strangers*," said Jean.

"Well." Locke glanced aft, at Lieutenant Delmastro, who'd risen to her feet and taken the *Kingfisher*'s wheel. "Maybe some of them are less strange to you than they are to me."

"Now, wait just a—"

"Do what you have to do to pass the time out here," said Locke, scowling. "But don't forget where you come from. Stragos is our business. *Beating him* is our business."

" 'Pass the time'? Pass the gods-damned *time*?" Jean sucked in an angry breath. He clenched his fists, and for a second looked as though he might grab Locke and shake him. "Gods, I see what's twisting under your skin. Look, *you* may be resigned to the fact that the *only* woman you'll ever consider is years gone. But you've been screwed down so tight about that, for so long, that you seem to think the rest of the world keeps your habits."

Locke felt as though he'd been stabbed. "Jean, don't you even—"

"Why not? Why *not*? We carry your precious misery with us like a holy fucking relic. *Don't* talk about Sabetha Belacoros. *Don't* talk about the plays. *Don't* talk about Jasmer, or Espara, or any of the schemes we ran. I lived with her for nine years, same as you, and I've pretended she doesn't fucking exist to *avoid upsetting you*. Well, I'm not you. I'm not content to live like an oath-bound monk. *I have a life outside your gods-damned shadow.*"

Locke stepped back. "Jean, I don't . . . I didn't—"

"And quit calling me *Jean,* for fuck's sake."

"Of course," said Locke coldly. "Of course. If we keep this up we'll be breaking character for good. I can prowl below myself. You get back to Delmastro. She's holding on to that wheel to stay on her bloody feet."

"But—"

"*Go,*" said Locke.

"Fine." Jean turned to leave, then paused one last time. "But understand—*I can't do it.* I'll follow you to any fate, and you know it, but I can't fuck these people over, even for our own sake. And even if you think it's for our sake . . . I can't let *you* do it, either."

"What the hell does that mean?"

"It means you have a lot to think about," said Jean, and he stomped away.

Small parties of sailors had begun slipping over from the *Orchid.* Utgar rushed up to Locke, red-faced with excitement, leading a group of crewfolk carrying lines and fend-offs to help hold the ships alongside one another.

"Sweet Marrows, Ravelle, we just found out about the Redeemers," Utgar said. "Lieutenant told us what you did. Fuckin' amazing! A job well done!"

Locke glanced at the body of Mal resting against the mainmast, and at Jean's back as he approached Delmastro with his hands out to hold her up. Not caring who saw, he flung his saber down at the deck planks, where it stuck tip-first, quivering from side to side.

"Oh, indeed," he said. "It seems I win again. *Hooray* for winning."

CHAPTER ELEVEN

ALL ELSE, TRUTH

1

"BRING THE PRISONERS FORWARD," said Captain Drakasha.

It was full night on the deck of the *Poison Orchid,* and the ship rode at anchor beneath a star-pierced sky. The moons had not yet begun to rise. Drakasha stood at the quarterdeck rail, backlit by alchemical lamps, wearing a tarpaulin for a cloak. Her hair was covered by a ludicrous woolen wig, vaguely resembling the ceremonial hairpiece of a Verrari magistrate. The deck fore and aft was crowded with shadowed crewfolk, and in a small clear space amidships stood the prisoners.

Nineteen men from the *Red Messenger* had survived the morning's fight. Now all nineteen stood, bound hands and feet, in an awkward bunch at the ship's waist. Locke shuffled forward behind Jean and Jabril.

"Clerk of the court," said Drakasha, "you have brought us a *sad* lot."

"A sad lot indeed, Your Honor." Lieutenant Delmastro appeared beside the captain, clutching a rolled scroll and wearing a ridiculous wig of her own.

"As wretched a pack of dissolute, cockless mongrels as I've ever seen. Still, I suppose we must try them."

"Indeed we must, ma'am."

"With what are they charged?"

"Such a litany of crimes as turns the blood to jam." Delmastro opened the scroll and raised her voice as she read. "Willful refusal of the kind hospitality of the archon of Tal Verrar. Deliberate flight from the excellent accommodations provided by said archon at Windward Rock. Theft of a naval vessel with the stated intention of applying it to a life of piracy."

"Disgraceful."

"Just so, Your Honor. Now the next bit is rather confusing; some are charged with mutiny, while others are charged with incompetence."

"Some this, some that? Clerk of the court, we cannot *abide* untidiness. Simply charge everyone with everything."

"Understood. The mutineers are now incompetent and the incompetent are also mutineers."

"Excellent. Very excellent, and so *very* magisterial. No doubt I shall be quoted in books."

"Important books too, ma'am."

"What else do these wretches have to answer for?"

"Assault and larceny beneath the red flag, Your Honor. Armed piracy on the Sea of Brass on the twenty-first instant of the month of Festal, this very year."

"Vile, grotesque, and contemptible," shouted Drakasha. "Let the record show that I feel as though I may swoon. Tell me, are there any who would speak in defense of the prisoners?"

"None, ma'am, as the prisoners are penniless."

"Ah. Then under whose laws do they claim any rights or protections?"

"None, ma'am. No power on land will claim or aid them."

"Pathetic, and not unexpected. Yet without firm guidance from their betters, perhaps it's only *natural* that these rodents have shunned virtue like a contagious disease. Perhaps some small chance of clemency may be forthcoming."

"Unlikely, ma'am."

"One small matter remains, which may attest to their true character. Clerk of the court, can you describe the nature of their associates and consorts?"

"Only too vividly, Your Honor. They willfully consort with the officers and crew of the *Poison Orchid*."

"Gods above," cried Drakasha, "did you say *Poison Orchid*?"

"I did indeed, ma'am."

"They are guilty! Guilty on every count! Guilty in every particular, guilty to the utmost and final extremity of all possible human culpability!" Drakasha tore at her wig, then flung it to the deck and jumped up and down upon it.

"An excellent verdict, ma'am."

"It is the judgment of this court," said Drakasha, "solemn in its authority and unwavering in its resolution, that for crimes upon the sea the sea shall have them. Put them over the side! And may the gods not be too hasty in conferring mercy upon their souls."

Cheering, the crew surged forth from every direction and surrounded the prisoners. Locke was alternately pushed and pulled along with the crowd to the larboard entry port, where a cargo net lay upon the deck with a sail beneath it. The two were lashed together at the edges. The ex-Messengers were shoved onto the netting and held there while several dozen sailors under Delmastro's direction moved to the capstan.

"Make ready to execute sentence," said Drakasha.

"Heave up," cried Delmastro.

A complex network of pulleys and tackles had been

rigged between the lower yards of the foremast and main-mast; as the sailors worked the capstan, the edges of the net drew upward and the Orchids holding the prisoners stepped back. In a few seconds the ex-Messengers were off the deck, squeezed together like animals in a trap. Locke clung to the rough netting to avoid slipping into the center of the tangled mass of limbs and bodies. There was a gener-ally useless bout of shoving and swearing as the net swung out over the rail and swayed gently in the darkness fifteen feet above the water.

"Clerk of the court, execute the prisoners," said Drakasha.

"Give 'em a drop, aye!"

They wouldn't, thought Locke, at the very same mo-ment they did.

The net full of prisoners plunged, drawing unwilling yelps and screams from the throats of men who'd done murderous battle on the *Kingfisher* in relative silence. The pull on the edges of the net slackened as it fell, so at least they had more room to tumble and bounce when they hit the surface of the water—or, more accurately, the strangely yielding barrier of net and sail canvas with the water be-neath it like a cushion.

They rolled around in a jumbled, shouting mass for a second or two while the edges of their trap settled down into the waves, and then the warm dark water was pouring in around them. Locke felt a brief moment of genuine panic—hard not to when the knots binding hands and feet were very real—but after a few moments the edges of the net-backed sail began to draw upward again, until they were just above the surface of the ocean. The water still trapped with the prisoners was about waist-deep to Locke, and now the sail canvas formed a sort of shielded pool for them to stand and flounder about in.

"Everyone all right?" That was Jean; Locke saw that he'd

claimed the edge of the net directly across from him. There were half a dozen shoving, splashing men between them. Locke scowled at the realization that Jean was quite content to stay where he was.

"Fuckin' jolly," muttered Streva, holding himself upright by one arm. The other had been lashed to the front of his chest in a crude sling. Several of the ex-Messengers were nursing broken bones, and nearly all of them had cuts and bruises, but not one had been excused from this ritual by his injuries.

"Your Honor!" Locke glanced up at the sound of Delmastro's voice. The lieutenant was peering down at them from the larboard entry port with a lantern in one hand; their net was resting in the water three or four feet from the *Orchid*'s dark hull. "Your Honor, they're not drowning!"

"What?" Drakasha appeared next to Delmastro with her false wig back on her head, now more wildly askew than ever. "You rude little *bastards*! How dare you waste this court's time with this ridiculous refusal to be executed! Clerk, help them drown!"

"Aye, ma'am, immediate drowning assistance. Deck pumps at the ready! Deck pumps away!"

A pair of sailors appeared at the rail with the aperture of a canvas hose held between them. Locke turned away just as the gush of warm salt water started pounding down on them all. Not so bad, he thought, just seconds before something more substantial than water struck the back of his head with a wet, stinging smack.

Bombardment with this new indignity—greased oakum, Locke quickly realized—was general and vigorous. Crewfolk had lined the rail and were flinging it down into the netted prisoners, a veritable rain of rags and rope fragments that had the familiar rancid stink of the stuff he'd spent several mornings painting the masts with. This assault continued for several minutes, until Locke had no idea where the grease ended and his clothes began, and the water in their little enclosure was topped with a sliding layer of foulness.

"Unbelievable," shouted Delmastro. "Your Honor, they're still there!"

"Not drowned?"

Zamira appeared at the rail once again and solemnly removed her wig. "Damnation. The sea refuses to claim them. We shall have to bring them back aboard."

After a few moments, the lines above them drew taut and the little prison of net and canvas began to rise from the water. Not a moment too soon, it seemed—Locke shuddered as he felt something large and powerful brush against the barrier beneath his feet. In seconds they were mercifully above the tips of the waves and creaking steadily upward.

But their punishment was not yet over; they hung once more in the darkness when the net was hoisted above the rail, and were not brought back in above the deck.

"Free the spinning-tackle," shouted Delmastro.

Locke caught sight of a small woman shimmying out onto the tangle of ropes overhead. She pulled a restraining pin from the large wooden tackle by which the net was suspended. Locke recognized the circular metal bearing within the tackle; heavily greased, it would allow even awkward and weighty cargoes to be spun with ease. Cargoes like *them*.

Crewfolk lined the rail and began to grab at the net and heave it along; in moments the prisoners were spinning at a nauseating rate, and the world around them flew by in glimpses—dark water . . . lamps on the deck . . . dark water . . . lamps on the deck . . .

"Oh, gods," said someone, a moment before he noisily threw up. There was a sudden scramble away from the poor fellow, and Locke clung grimly to his place at the edge of the net, trying to ignore the kicking, shuddering, spinning mass of men.

"Clean 'em up," shouted Delmastro. "Deck pumps away!"

The hard stream of salt water gushed into their midst once more, and they spun furiously. Locke intersected the spray every few seconds as each rotation of the net brought him around. His dizziness grew and grew as the minutes passed, and though it was becoming extremely fashionable, he focused every speck of dignity on simply not throwing up.

So intense was his dizziness and so swift was their deliverance that he didn't even realize they'd been swung back onto the deck until the net he was clinging to collapsed into slackness. He toppled forward, onto netting and canvas above good, hard planks once again. The net had ceased spinning, but the world took its place, rotating in six or seven directions at once, all of them profoundly unpleasant. Locke closed his eyes, but that didn't help. It merely made him blind as well as nauseous.

Men were crawling over him, moaning and swearing. A pair of crewfolk reached down and heaved Locke to his feet; his stomach nearly surrendered at that point and he coughed sharply to fight back his nausea. Captain Drakasha was approaching, her false wig and cloak discarded, and she was tilted at a funny angle.

"The sea won't have you," she said. "The water refuses to swallow you. It's not yet your time to drown, praise Iono. Praise Ulcris!"

Ulcris was the Jereshti name for the god of the sea, not often heard in Therin lands or waters. There must be more eastern islanders aboard than I realized, thought Locke.

"Lord of the Grasping Waters shield us," chanted the crew.

"So you're here with us between all things," said Drakasha. "The land won't have you and the sea won't claim you. You've fled, like us, to wood and canvas. This deck's your firmament; these sails are your heavens. This is all the world you get. This is all the world you *need*."

She stepped forward with a drawn dagger. "Will you lick my boots to claim a place on it?"

"*No!*" the ex-Messengers roared in unison. They'd been coached on this part of the ritual.

"Will you kneel and kiss my jeweled ring for mercy?"

"*No!*"

"Will you bend your knees to pretty titles on pieces of paper?"

"*No!*"

"Will you pine for land and laws and kings, and cling to them like a mother's tit?"

"*No!*"

She stepped up to Locke and handed him the dagger.

"Then free yourself, brother."

Still unsteady, and grateful for the aid of the crewfolk beside him, Locke used the blade to saw through the rope that bound his hands, and then bent over to cut the rope between his ankles. That accomplished, he turned and saw that all of the ex-Messengers were more or less upright, most of them held by one or two Orchids. Close at hand he could see several familiar faces—Streva, Jabril, a fellow called Alvaro . . . and just behind them, Jean, watching him uneasily.

Locke hesitated, then pointed to Jabril and held out the blade.

"Free yourself, brother."

Jabril smiled, took the blade, and was finished with his bonds in a moment. Jean glared at him. Locke closed his eyes, not wanting to make further eye contact, and listened as the dagger made its passage through the group, from hand to hand. "Free yourself, brother," they murmured, one after another. And then it was done.

"Unbound by your own hands, you are outlaw brethren of the Sea of Brass," said Captain Drakasha, "and crewmen of the *Poison Orchid.*"

2

EVEN AN experienced thief will find occasion to learn new tricks if he lives long enough. That morning and afternoon, Locke had learned how to properly loot a captured ship.

Locke finished his last circuit belowdecks, reasonably certain there were no more *Kingfisher* crewfolk to round up, and stomped up the companionway to the quarterdeck. The bodies of the Redeemers there had been moved aside and stacked at the taffrail; the bodies of those from the *Poison Orchid* had been carried down to the waist. Locke could see several of Zamira's crewfolk respectfully covering them with sail canvas.

He quickly surveyed the ship. Thirty or forty Orchids had come aboard, and were taking control of the vessel everywhere. They were up the ratlines, with Jean and Delmastro at the wheel, tending the anchors, and guarding the thirty or so surviving *Kingfisher* crewfolk atop the forecastle deck. Under Utgar's supervision, the wounded Kingfishers and Orchids had been carried down to the waist near the starboard entry port, where Captain Drakasha and Scholar Treganne were just coming aboard. Locke hurried toward them.

"It's my arm, Scholar. Hurts something awful." Streva used his good arm to support his injured limb as he winced and held it out for Treganne's inspection. "I think it's broken."

"Of course it's broken, you cretinous turd," she said,

brushing past him to kneel beside a Kingfisher whose tunic was completely soaked in blood. "Keep waving it like that and it'll snap right off. Sit down."

"But—"

"I work from worst chance to best," Treganne muttered. She knelt on the deck beside the injured Kingfisher, using her cane to brace herself until she was on both knees. Then she gave the cane a twist. The handle separated from the cane's full length, revealing a dagger-sized blade that Treganne used to slice the sailor's tunic open. "I can move you up on my list by kicking your head a couple times. Still want prompt attention?"

"Um...no."

"You'll keep. Piss off."

"There you are, Ravelle." Captain Drakasha stepped past Treganne and the injured and grabbed Locke by the shoulder. "You've done well for yourself."

"Have I?"

"You're as useless as an ass without a hole when it comes to running a ship, but I've heard the damnedest things about how you fought just now."

"Your sources exaggerate."

"Well, the ship's ours and you gave us her master. Now that we've plucked our flower, we need to sip the nectar before bad weather or another ship comes along."

"Will you be taking the *Kingfisher* as a prize?"

"No. I don't like having more than one prize crew out at a time. We'll shake her down for valuables and useful cargo."

"Then burn her or something?"

"Of course not. We'll leave the crew stores enough to make port and watch them scamper for the horizon. You look confused."

"No objections, Captain, it's just...not as downright bastardly as I was expecting."

"You don't think we respect surrenders because we're kindly people, do you, Ravelle?" Drakasha grinned. "I don't have much time to explain, but it's like this. If not for those gods-damned Redeemers, these people"—she waved a hand at the injured Kingfishers waiting for Treganne's attention—"wouldn't have given or taken a scratch. Four out of five ships we take, I'd say, if they can't rig razornets and get bows ready, they just roll right over for it. They know we'll let 'em slip off with their lives once we're done. And the common sailors don't own one centira of the cargo, so why should they swallow a blade or a crossbow bolt for it?"

"I guess it does make sense."

"To more people than us. Look at this shambles. Redeemers for security? If those maniacs hadn't been available for free, this ship wouldn't have any real guards. I guarantee it. No sense in it for the owners. These long voyages, four or five months from the far east back to Tal Verrar with spices, rare metals, wood—an owner can lose two ships out of three, and the one that arrives will pay for the two that don't. With profit to spare. And if they get the actual ship back, even sans cargo, so much the better. That's why we don't sink and burn like mad. As long as we show some restraint, and don't get too close to civilization, the folks holding the purse strings think of us as a natural hazard, like the weather."

"So with the, ah, plucking and sipping the nectar bit, where do we start?"

"Most worthwhile thing at hand is the ship's purse," said Drakasha. "Master keeps it for expenses. Bribes and so forth. Finding it's always a pain in the ass. Some throw it overboard; others hide it somewhere dank and unlikely. We'll probably have to slap this Nera around for a few hours before he spits truth."

"Damnation." Behind them, Treganne let her patient slump to the deck and began wiping her bloody hands on his breeches. "No good on this one, Captain. I can see straight through to his lungs behind the wound."

"He's dead for sure?" said Locke.

"Well, heavens, I wouldn't know, I'm just the fucking physiker. But I heard in a bar once that dead is the *accepted* thing to be when your lungs are open to daylight," said Treganne.

"Uh...yes. I heard the same thing. Look, will anyone else here die without your immediate full attention?"

"Not likely."

"Captain Drakasha," said Locke, "Master Nera has something of a soft heart. Might I take the liberty of suggesting a plan...?"

A few moments later, Locke returned to the waist, holding Antoro Nera by one arm. The man's hands had been bound behind his back. Locke gave him a good shove toward Zamira, who stood with one saber unsheathed. Behind her, Treganne worked feverishly over the corpse of the newly deceased sailor. The slashed and bloody tunic had been disposed of, and a clean one drawn over the corpse's chest. Only a small red spot now marked the lethal wound, and Treganne gave every impression that the unmoving form was still within her power to save.

Drakasha caught Nera and set her blade against his upper chest.

"Pleased to make your acquaintance," she said, sliding the curved edge of her weapon toward Nera's unprotected neck. He whimpered. "Your ship's badly out of trim. Too much weight of gold. We need to find and remove the master's purse as quick as we can."

"I, uh, don't know exactly where it is," said Nera.

"Right. And I can teach fish to fart fire," said Drakasha. "You get one more chance, and then I start throwing your injured overboard."

"But...please, I was told—"

"Whoever told you anything wasn't *me*."

"I . . . I don't—"

"Scholar," said Drakasha, "can you do anything for the man you're working on?"

"He won't be dancing anytime soon," said Treganne, "but yes, he'll pull through."

Drakasha shifted her grip on Nera and held him by his tunic collar with her free hand. She took two steps to her right and, barely looking, drove her saber down into the dead sailor's neck. Treganne flinched backward and gave the corpse's legs a little push to make it look as though they'd kicked. Nera gasped.

"Medicine is such an uncertain business," said Drakasha.

"In my cabin," said Nera. "A hidden compartment by the compass above my bed. Please . . . please don't kill any more of—"

"I didn't, actually," said Drakasha. She withdrew her saber from the corpse's throat, wiped it on Nera's breeches, and gave him a quick kiss on the cheek. "Your man died a few minutes ago. My leech says she can save the rest of your injured without trouble."

She spun Nera around, slashed the rope that bound his hands, and shoved him toward Locke with a grin. "Return him to his people, Ravelle, and then kindly relieve his secret compartment of its burden."

"Your will, Captain."

After that, they began taking the *Kingfisher* apart more eagerly than newlyweds tearing off layers of formal clothing in their first moment of privacy. Locke felt his fatigue vanishing as he became absorbed in what was essentially one vast robbery, for more physical material than he'd ever stolen before in his life. He was passed from duty to duty among Orchids who laughed and clowned with real spirit, but worked with haste and precision for all that.

First they snatched up anything portable and reasonably valuable—bottles of wine, Master Nera's formal wardrobe, bags of coffee and tea from the galley, and several crossbows from the *Kingfisher*'s tiny armory. Drakasha herself appraised the ship's collection of navigational instruments and hourglasses, leaving Nera the bare minimum required to safely work his vessel back to port.

Next, Utgar and the boatswain scoured the flute from stem to stern, using the surviving scrub watch as mules to haul off stores and equipment of nautical use: alchemical caulk, good sail canvas, carpenter's tools, barrels of pitch, and loop after loop of new rope.

"Good shit, hey," said Utgar, as he weighed Locke down with about fifty pounds of rope and a box of metal files. "Much too expensive in Port Prodigal. Always best to get it at what we call the broadside discount."

Last but not least came the *Kingfisher*'s cargo. All the main-deck hatch gratings were pulled, and a nearly incomprehensible network of ropes and pulleys was rigged on and between the two ships. By noon, crates and casks and oilcoth-wrapped bundles were being lighted along to the *Poison Orchid*. It was everything Nera had promised and more—turpentine, oiled witchwood, silks, crates of fine yellow wine padded with sheepskins, and barrel after barrel of bulk spices. The smell of cloves, nutmeg, and ginger filled the air; after an hour or two of work at the hoists Locke was brown with a sludge that was half sweat and half powdered cinnamon.

At the fifth hour of the afternoon Drakasha called a halt to the forcible transfusion of wealth. The *Poison Orchid* rode lower in the gleaming water and the lightened flute rolled freely, hollowed out like an insect husk about to fall from a spider's jaws. Drakasha's crew hadn't stripped her clean, of course. They left the Kingfishers their casks of water, salted meat, cheap ale, and pink-piss ration wine. They even left a few crates and parcels of valuables that were too deeply or inconveniently stowed for Drakasha's taste— nonetheless, the sack was thorough. Any land-bound merchant would have been well pleased to have a ship unloaded at the dock with such haste.

A brief ceremony was held at the taffrail of the *Kingfisher*; Zamira blessed the dead of the two vessels in her capacity as a lay priestess of Iono. Then the corpses went over the side, sewn into old canvas with Redeemer weapons weighing them down. The Redeemers themselves were then thrown overboard without a word.

"Ain't disrespectful," said Utgar when Locke whispered to him about this. "Far as they believe, they get consecrated and blessed and all that fine stuff by their own gods the moment they die. No hard feelings if you just tip the heathens over the side afterward. Helpful thing to know if you ever have to kill a bunch of 'em again, hey?"

At last, the day's long business was truly concluded; Master Nera and his crew were released to tend to their own fortunes once again. While Drakasha's archers kept watch from their perches on the yardarms, the network of lines and fend-offs between the two ships was pulled apart. The *Poison Orchid* hauled up her boats and loosed her sails. In minutes, she was making seven or eight knots to the southwest, leaving the *Kingfisher* adrift in disarray behind her.

Locke had seen little of Jean all day, and both of them had seemed to work to studiously preserve their separation. Just as Locke had thrown himself into manual labor, Jean had remained with Delmastro on the quarterdeck. They didn't come close enough to speak again until the sun fell beneath the horizon, and the scrub watch was herded together and bound for their initiation.

3

ALL THE new initiates and half the ship's old company were on the Merry Watch, fueled by rack after rack of the fine eastern wines they'd plucked from the *Kingfisher*. Locke recognized some of the labels and vintages. Stuff that wouldn't sell in Camorr for less than twenty crowns a bottle was being sucked down like beer, or poured into the hair of celebrating men and women, or simply spilled on deck. The Orchids, men and women alike, were mixing eagerly with the ex-Messengers now. Dice games and wrestling matches and song-circles had erupted spontaneously. Propositions spoken and unspoken were everywhere. Jabril had vanished belowdecks with a crew-woman at least an hour before.

Locke took it all in from the shadows of the starboard side, just below the raised quarterdeck. The starboard stairs weren't flush with the rail; there was space enough for a lean person to wedge comfortably between the two. "Ravelle" had been greeted warmly and eagerly enough when he'd circulated on deck, but now that he'd found a cozy exile nobody seemed to be missing him. In his hands was a large leather jack full of blue wine that was worth its weight in silver, untouched.

Across the great mass of laughing, drinking sailors, Locke could make out Jean at the ship's opposite rail. While Locke watched, the shape of a woman, much shorter, approached him from behind and reached out toward him. Locke turned away.

The water slipped past, a black gel topped with curls of faintly phosphorescent foam. The *Orchid* was setting a good pace through the night. Laden, she yielded less than before to the chop of the sea, and was parting these little waves like they were air.

"When I was a lieutenant apprentice," said Captain

Drakasha, "on my first voyage with an officer's sword, I lied to my captain about stealing a bottle of wine."

She spoke softly. Startled, Locke looked around and saw that she was standing directly over him, at the forward quarterdeck rail.

"Not just me," she continued. "All eight of us in the apprentices' berth. We 'borrowed' it from the captain's private stores and should have been smart enough to pitch it over the side when we'd finished."

"In the . . . navy of Syrune, this was?"

"Her Resplendent Majesty's Sea Forces of Syrune Eternal." Drakasha's smile was a crescent of white against darkness, faint as the foam topping the waves. "The captain could have had us whipped, or reduced in rank, or even chained up for formal trial on land. Instead she had us strike down the royal yard from the mainmast. We had a spare, of course. But she made us scrape the varnish off the one we'd taken down. . . . This is a spar of oak, you know, ten feet long and thick as a leg. The captain took our swords and said they'd be restored if and only if we ate the royal yard. Tip to tip, every last splinter."

"*Ate* it?"

"A foot and a quarter of sturdy oak for each of us," said Drakasha. "How we did it was our business. It took a month. We tried everything. Shaving it, scraping it, boiling it, pulping it. We had a hundred tricks to make it palatable, and we forced it down, a few spoonfuls or chips a day. Most of us got sick, but we ate the yard."

"Gods."

"When it was over, the captain said she'd wanted us to understand that lies between shipmates tear the ship apart, bit by bit, gnawing at it just as we'd gnawed the royal yard down to nothing."

"Ah." Locke sighed and at last took a sip of his warm, excellent wine. "I take it this means I'm due for a bit more dissection, then?"

"Come join me at the taffrail."

Locke rose, knowing it wasn't a request.

4

"I NEVER knew that dispensing justice could be so tiring," said Ezri, appearing at Jean's right elbow as he stood staring out over the *Orchid*'s larboard rail. One of the moons was just starting to rise in the south, half a silver-white coin peeking above the night horizon, as though lazily considering whether it was worth rising at all.

"You've had a long day, Lieutenant." Jean smiled.

"Jerome," she said, reaching out to set a hand upon his right forearm, "if you call me 'lieutenant' again tonight, I'll kill you."

"As you wish, Lieu...La...something-other-than-'Lieutenant'-that-starts-with-'Lieu,' honest.... Besides, you already tried to execute me once this evening. Look how that turned out."

"Best way possible," she said, now leaning against the rail beside him. She wasn't wearing her armor, just a thin tunic and a pair of calf-length breeches without hose or shoes. Her hair was free, waves of dark curls rustling in the breeze. Jean realized that she was putting most of her weight against the rail and trying hard not to show it.

"Uh, you got a little too close to a few blades today," he said.

"I've been closer. But you, now...you're...you're a very good fighter, do you know that?"

"It's been s—"

"Gods, how wretched was that? Of *course* you're a good fighter. I meant to say something much wittier, honest."

"Then consider it said." Jean scratched his beard and felt

a warm, welcome sort of nervousness fluttering in his stomach. "We can both pretend. All of the, um, effortlessly witty nonsense I've been practicing on the barrels in the hold for days has taken flight, too."

"Practicing, hmmm?"

"Yeah, well. . . . That Jabril, he's a sophisticated fellow, isn't he? Need a bit of conversation to catch his attention, won't I?"

"What?"

"Didn't you know I only fancied men? *Tall* men?"

"Oooh, I kicked you to the deck once, Valora, and I'm about to—"

"Ha! In your condition?"

"My *condition* is the only thing saving your life at the moment."

"You wouldn't dare heap abuse on me in front of half the crew—"

"Of course I would."

"Well, yes. True."

"Look at this lovely, noisy mess. I don't think anyone would even notice if I set you on fire. Hell, down in the main-deck hold there's couples going at it packed tighter than spears in the arms lockers. You want real peace and quiet any time tonight, closest place you might find it is two or three hundred yards off one of the bows."

"No, thanks. I don't know how to say 'stop eating me' in shark."

"Well then, you're stuck here with us. And we've been waiting for you lot to get off the scrub watch for long enough." She grinned up at him. "Tonight everyone gets to know everyone else."

Jean stared at her, eyes wide, not knowing what to say or do next. Her grin became a frown.

"Jerome, am I . . . doing something wrong?"

"Wrong?"

"You keep sort of moving away. Not just with your body, but with your neck. You keep..."

"Oh, hell." Jean laughed, reached out to put a hand on her shoulder, and felt himself burst into an uncontrollable twit-grin when she reached up to hold it there. "Ezri, I lost my optics when you...made us swim, the day we came aboard. I'm what they call near-blind. I guess I didn't realize it, but I've been fidgeting to keep you in focus."

"Oh, gods," she whispered. "I'm sorry."

"Don't be. Keeping you in focus is worth the trouble."

"I didn't mean—"

"I know." Jean felt the anxious pressure in his stomach migrating upward to fill his chest, and he took a deep breath. "Look, we almost got killed today. Fuck these games. Do you want to have a drink with me?"

5

"WATCH," SAID Drakasha.

Locke stood at the taffrail, looking down into the ship's phosphorescent wake between the glow of two stern lanterns. Those lanterns were glowing glass orchids the size of his head, transparent petals drooping delicately toward the water.

"Gods," said Locke, shuddering.

Between the wake and the lanterns, there was just enough light for him to spot it—a long black shadow sliding beneath the *Poison Orchid*'s trail of disturbed water. Forty or fifty feet of something sinuous and sinister, using the ship's wake to conceal itself. Captain Drakasha had one boot up on the taffrail and an expression of casual pleasure on her face.

"What the hell is it?"

"Five or six possibilities," said Drakasha. "Might be a whaleworm or a giant devilfish."

"Is it *following* us?"

"Yes."

"Is it ... um, dangerous?"

"Well, if you drop your drink over the rail, don't jump in after it."

"Don't you think you should maybe let it have a few arrows?"

"I might, if only I were sure that this was the fastest it could swim."

"Good point."

"Fling arrows at all the strange things you see out here, Ravelle, and all you do is run out of arrows." She sighed and glanced around to ensure that they were more or less alone. The closest crewman was at the wheel, eight or nine yards forward. "You made yourself very useful today."

"Well, the alternative just didn't suit."

"I thought I was abetting a suicide when I agreed to let you lead the boats."

"You nearly were, Captain. It was ... Look, it was inches from disaster the whole way, that fight. I don't even remember half of it. The gods blessed me by allowing me to avoid soiling my breeches. Surely you know what it's like."

"I do. I also know that sometimes these things aren't accidents. You and Master Valora have ... excited a great deal of comment for what you did in that battle. Your skills are unusual for a former master of weights and measures."

"Weighing and measuring is a *boring* occupation," said Locke. "A man needs a hobby."

"The archon's people didn't hire you by accident, did they?"

"What?"

"I said I'd peel this strange fruit you call a story, Ravelle, and I have been. My initial impression of you wasn't favorable. But you've ... done better. And I think I can understand how you kept your old crew in thrall despite your ignorance. You seem to have a real talent for improvised dishonesty."

"Weighing and measuring is a very, *very* boring—"

"So you're a master of a sedentary occupation who just *happened* to have a talent for espionage? And disguise? And command? Not to mention your skill at arms, or that of your close and unusually educated friend Jerome?"

"Our mothers were so very proud of us."

"You weren't hired away from the Priori by the archon," said Drakasha. "You were double agents. Planted provocateurs, *intended* to enter the archon's service. You didn't steal that ship because of some insult you won't speak of; you stole it because your orders were to damage the archon's credibility. To do something big."

"Uh..."

"Please, Ravelle. As if there could be any other reasonable explanation."

Gods, what a temptation, Locke thought. A mark actually inviting me to step into her own misconception, free and clear. He stared at the phosphorescent wake, at the mysterious something swimming beneath it. What to do? Take the opening, cement the Ravelle and Valora identities in Drakasha's mind, work from there? Or...his cheeks burned as the sting of Jean's rebuke rose again in his memory. Jean hadn't just criticized him on theological grounds, or because of Delmastro. It was a matter of approaches. Which would be more effective?

Treat this woman as a mark, or treat her as an ally?

Time was running out. This conversation was the point of decision; follow his instincts and play her, or follow Jean's advice and...attempt to trust her. He thought furiously. His own instincts—were they always impeccable? Jean's instincts—arguments aside, had Jean ever done anything but try to protect him?

"Tell me something," he said very slowly, "while I weigh a response."

"Perhaps."

"Something half the size of this ship is probably staring at us as we speak."

"Yes."

"How do you *stand* it?"

"You see things like this often enough, you get used—"

"Not just that. Everything. I've been at sea a grand total of six or seven weeks in my life. How long have *you* been out here?"

She stared at him, saying nothing.

"Some things about myself," said Locke, "I won't tell you just because you're the captain of this ship, even if you throw me back in the hold or pitch me over the side. Some things . . . I want to know who I'm *talking to* first. I want to talk to Zamira, not to Captain Drakasha."

Still she remained silent.

"Is that asking so very much?"

"I'm nine and thirty," she said at last, very quietly. "I first sailed when I was eleven."

"Nearly thirty years, then. Well, like I said, I've been out here a few *weeks*. And in that time—storms, mutiny, sea-sickness, battles, flit-wraiths . . . hungry damn *things* lurking all over the place, waiting for someone to dip a toe in the water. It's not that I haven't enjoyed myself at times; I have. I've learned things. But . . . thirty years? And children as well? Don't you find it all . . . chancy?"

"Do you have children, Orrin?"

"No."

"The instant I decide that you are presuming to lecture me on their behalf, this conversation *will* end with you going over this rail to make the acquaintance of whatever's down there."

"That's not at *all* what I meant. It's just—"

"Have people on land acquired the secret of living forever? Have they abolished accidents? Have they ceased to have *weather* in my absence?"

"Of course not."

"How much more danger are my children *truly* in than some poor bastard conscripted to fight in his duke's wars? Or some penniless family dying of a plague with their neighborhood quarantined, or burnt to the ground? Wars, disease, taxes. Bowing heads and kissing boots. There's plenty of hungry damn *things* prowling on land, Orrin. It's just that the ones at sea tend not to wear crowns."

"Ah—"

"Was *your* life a paradise before you sailed the Sea of Brass?"

"No."

"Of course not. Listen well. I thought that I'd grown up in a hierarchy where *mere* competence and loyalty were enough to maintain one's station in life," she whispered. "I gave an oath of service and imagined that oath was binding in both directions. I was a *fool*. And I had to kill an awful lot of men and women to escape the consequences of that foolishness. Would you really ask me to place my trust, and my hopes for Paolo and Cosetta, in the same bullshit that nearly killed me before? Which system of laws should I bend to, Orrin? Which king or duke or empress should I trust like a mother? Which of them is a better judge of my life's worth than I am? Can you point them out to me, write a letter of introduction?"

"Zamira," said Locke, "*please* don't make me out to be some sort of advocate for things that I'm not; it seems to me that my whole life has been spent in the willful disdain of what you're talking about. Do I strike you as a law-and-order sort of fellow?"

"Admittedly not."

"I'm just curious, is all. I do appreciate this. Tell me

now—what about the Free Armada? Your so-called War for Recognition? Why profess such hatred for . . . laws and taxes and all those strictures, if that was essentially what you were fighting to emplace down here?"

"Ah." Zamira sighed, removed her four-cornered hat, and ran her fingers through her breeze-tossed hair. "Our infamous Lost Cause. Our personal contribution to the glorious history of Tal Verrar."

"Why did you start it?"

"Bad judgment. We all hoped . . . Well, Captain Bonaire was persuasive. We had a leader, a plan. Open mines on new islands, tap some of the safe forests for wood and resin. Pillage as we liked until the other powers on the Sea of Brass came wringing their hands to the bargaining table, and then beat the shit out of them with authorized trade. We imagined a realm without tariffs. Montierre and Port Prodigal swelling up with merchants and their imported fortunes."

"Ambitious."

"Idiotic. I was newly escaped from one sour allegiance and I leapt right into another. We believed Bonaire when she said that Stragos didn't have the clout to come down and mount a serious fight."

"Oh. Hell."

"They met us at sea. Biggest action I ever saw, and the soonest lost. Stragos put hundreds of Verrari soldiers on his ships to back the sailors; we never stood a chance in close action. Once they had the *Basilisk* they stopped taking prisoners. They'd board a ship, scuttle it, and move on to the next. Their archers put shafts into anyone in the water, at least until the devilfish came.

"I needed every trick I had just to get the *Orchid* out. A few of us straggled back to Prodigal, beat to hell, and even before we got there the Verrari pounded Montierre into the sand. Five hundred dead in one morning. After that, they sailed back home and I imagine there was a lot of dancing, fucking, and speeches."

"I think," said Locke, "you can take a city like Tal Verrar...and you can threaten its purse strings *or* its pride, and get away with it. But not if you threaten both at once."

"You're right. Maybe Stragos *was* impotent when Bonaire left the city; whatever he was, we united Tal Verrar's interests behind him. We summoned him up like some demon out of a story." She folded her arms over her hat and leaned forward, resting her elbows against the taffrail. "So, we stayed outlaws. No flowering for the Ghostwinds. No glorious destiny for Port Prodigal. This ship is our world now, and I only take her in when her belly's too full to prowl.

"Am I making myself clear, Orrin? I don't regret how I've lived these past few years. I move where I will. I set no appointments. I guard no borders. What land-bound king has the freedom of a ship's captain? The Sea of Brass provides. When I need haste, it gives me winds. When I need gold, it gives me galleons."

Thieves prosper, thought Locke. The rich remember.

He made his decision, and gripped the rail to avoid shaking.

"Only gods-damned fools die for lines drawn on maps," said Zamira. "But nobody can draw lines around my ship. If they try, all I need to do to slip away is set more sail."

"Yeah," said Locke. "But...Zamira, what if I were forced to tell you that that may no longer be the case?"

6

"HAVE YOU really been practicing on barrels, Jerome?"

They'd laid claim to a bottle of Black Pomegranate brandy from one of the crates broken open amidst the revelers, and taken it back to their spot by the rail.

"Barrels. Yes." Jean took a sip of the stuff, dark as distilled night, with a sting like nettles beneath the sweetness. He passed the bottle back to her. "They never laugh, they never ridicule you, and they offer no distractions."

"Distractions?"

"Barrels don't have breasts."

"Ah. So what have you been *telling* these barrels?"

"This bottle of brandy," said Jean, "is still too full for me to begin embarrassing myself like that."

"Pretend I'm a barrel, then."

"Barrels don't have br—"

"So I've heard. Find the nerve, Valora."

"You want me to pretend that you're a barrel so I can tell you what I was telling barrels back when I was pretending they were you."

"Precisely."

"Well." He took another long sip from the brandy bottle. "You have . . . you have such hoops as I have never seen in any cask on any ship, such shiny and well-fit hoops—"

"Je*rome*—"

"And your staves!" He decided it was a good time to take another drink. "Your staves . . . *so* well planed, so tightly fit. You are as fine a cask as I have ever seen, you marvelous little barrel. To say nothing of your bung—"

"Ahem. So you won't share your sweet nothings?"

"No. I am utterly emboldened in my cowardice."

" 'Man! What a mouse he is made by conversation,' " Ezri recited. " 'Scorns gods, dares battle, and flinches from a maid's rebuke! Merest laugh from merest girl is like a dagger felt, and like a dagger, makes a lodging of his breast. Turns blood to milkwater and courage to faint memory.' "

"Ohhhhh, Lucarno, is it?" Jean tugged at his beard thoughtfully. " 'Woman, your heart is a mapless maze. Could I bottle confusion and drink it a thousand years, I could not confound myself so much as you do between waking and breakfast. You are grown so devious that serpents would applaud your passage, would the gods but give them hands.'"

"I like that one," she said. "*The Empire of Seven Days*, right?"

"Right. Ezri, forgive my asking, but how the hell do you—"

"It's no more odd than the fact that you know any of this." She took the bottle from him, tipped it back for a long draught, and then raised her free hand. "I know. I'll give you a hint. 'I have held the world from meridian to meridian in my hands and at my whim. I have received the confessions of emperors, the wisdom of magi, the lamentations of generals.'"

"You had a library? You *have* a library?"

"Had," she said. "I was the sixth of six daughters. I imagine the novelty wore off. Mother and father could afford live companions for the older five. I made do with all the dead playmates in mother's books." With her next drink she drained the last of the bottle, and with a grin she tossed it overboard. "So what's your excuse?"

"My education was, ah, eclectic. Did you ever... When you were little, do you remember a toy of wooden pegs, in various shapes, that would fit into matching holes on a wooden frame?

"Yes," she said. "I got my sisters' when they tired of it."

"You might say that I was trained to be a professional square peg in a round hole."

"Really? Is there a guild for that?"

"We've been working on getting a charter for years."

"Did you have a library as well?"

"After a fashion. Sometimes we'd... borrow someone else's without their knowledge or cooperation. Long story. But there's one other reason. I'll give you a verse of your own to guess. 'After dark,'" he recited with a flourish, "'an ass with an audience of one is called a husband; an ass with an audience of two hundred is called a success.'"

"You were...on stage," she said. "You were a player! Professionally?"

"Temporarily," said Jean. "Very temporarily. I was... well...we..." He glanced aft and instantly regretted it.

"Ravelle," Ezri said, then looked at Jean curiously. "You and he were...you two are having some sort of disagreement, aren't you?"

"Can we not talk about him?" Jean, feeling bold and nervous at once, put a hand on her arm. "Just for tonight. Can he not exist?"

"We can indeed not talk about him," she said, shifting herself so that her weight rested against his chest rather than the rail. "Tonight," she said, "*nobody* else exists."

Jean stared down at her, suddenly acutely aware of the beat of his own heart. The rising moonlight in her eyes, the feel of her warmth against him, the smell of brandy and sweat and salt water that was uniquely hers—suddenly the only thing he was capable of saying was, "Uhhhhhh..."

"Jerome Valora," she said, "you magnificent idiot, must I draw you a diagram?"

"Of—"

"Take me to my cabin." She curled the fabric of his tunic in one fist. "I have the privilege of walls and I intend to use it. At length."

"Ezri," Jean whispered, "never in a hundred, never in a thousand years would I say no, but you were cut half to ribbons today, and you can barely stand—"

"I know," she said. "That's the only reason I'm confident I'm not going to *break* you."

"Oh, for that I'm going to—"

"I certainly hope you will." She threw her arms wide. "First get me there."

He picked her up with ease; she settled into his arms

and wrapped hers around his neck. As Jean swung away from the rail and headed for the quarterdeck stairs, he found himself facing an arc of thirty or forty Merry Watch revelers. They raised their arms and began cheering wildly.

"Put your names on a list," hollered Ezri, "so I can kill you all in the morning!" She smiled and turned her eyes back to Jean. "Or maybe it'll have to wait for the afternoon."

7

"JUST LISTEN," said Locke. "Listen, please, with as open a mind as you can manage."

"I'll do my best."

"Your, ah, deduction about Jerome and myself is commendable. It does make sense, but for the parts that I've concealed until now. Starting with myself. I'm not a trained fighter. I'm a bloody *miserable* fighter. I have tried to be otherwise, but the gods know, it's always comedy or tragedy before I can blink."

"That—"

"Zamira. Heed this. I didn't kill four men with anything resembling skill. I dropped a beer cask on a man too dumb to look up. I slit the throats of two more who got knocked aside by the cask. I did the fourth when he slipped in beer. When everyone else found the bodies, I let them make their own assumptions."

"But I know for a fact that you charged those Redeemers all by yourself—"

"Yes. People who are about to die frequently go out of their minds. I should have died ten seconds into that fight, Zamira. It was Jerome who made it otherwise. Jerome and *only* Jerome."

At that moment, a loud cheer abruptly rose above the noise of the near carnival at the ship's waist. Locke and

Zamira both turned in time to see Jean appear at the top of the quarterdeck stairs with Lieutenant Delmastro in his arms. Neither of them so much as glanced aft at Locke and the captain; a few seconds later they were vanishing down the companionway.

"Well," said Zamira, "to win that heart, even for a night, your friend Jerome must be even more extraordinary than I thought."

"He is extraordinary," Locke whispered. "He continues to save my life, time and time again, even when I don't deserve it." He returned his gaze to the *Orchid*'s roiling, glowing, monster-haunted wake. "Which is always, more or less."

Zamira said nothing, and after a few moments Locke continued.

"Well, after he did it again this morning, I slipped and fumbled and ran like hell until the fight was over. That's all. Panic and dumb luck."

"You still led the boats. You still went up first, not knowing what was waiting for you."

"All bullshit. I'm a bullshit artist, Zamira. A false-facer. An actor, an impersonator. I didn't have any noble motives when I made that request. My life just wasn't worth much if I didn't do something utterly crazy to win back some respect. I faked every second of composure anyone glimpsed this morning."

"The fact that you consider that extraordinary only tells me that it really *was* your first actual battle."

"But—"

"Ravelle, anyone in command feigns ease when death is near. We do it for those around us, and we do it for ourselves. We do it because the sole alternative is to die cringing. The difference between an experienced leader and an untested one is that *only* the untested one is shocked at how well they can pretend when their hand is forced."

"I don't believe this," said Locke. "When I first came aboard, I couldn't impress you enough to make you spit in my face. Now you're making my excuses for me. Zamira, Jerome and I never worked for the Priori. I've never even met a Priori except in passing. The fact is that we're still working for Maxilan Stragos as we speak."

"*What?*"

"Jerome and I are thieves. Professional, independent thieves. We came to Tal Verrar on a very delicate job of our own design. The archon's . . . intelligence services figured out who and what we were. Stragos poisoned us, a latent poison for which only he can supply the antidote. Until we get it or secure some other remedy, we're his puppets."

"To what possible end?"

"Stragos handed us the *Red Messenger,* allowed us to take a crew from Windward Rock, and built up a parchment trail concerning an imaginary disgruntled officer named Orrin Ravelle. He gave us our sailing master—the one whose heart seized on us before we hit the storm—and sent us out here on his business. That's how we got the ship. That's how we tweaked Stragos' nose in such an unlikely fashion. All was to his design."

"What's he after? Someone in Port Prodigal?"

"He wants the same thing you gave him last time you crossed paths. He's all but at war with the Priori, and he's feeling his years. If he's going to seize anything resembling popularity ever again, the time is now. He needs an enemy outside the city to bring his army and navy back into favor. That's *you,* Zamira. Nothing would be more convenient for Stragos than a wider outbreak of piracy near his city in the next few months."

"Which is *exactly* why the Brass Sea captains have avoided going anywhere near Tal Verrar for the last seven years! We learned our lesson the bitter way. If he comes looking for a brawl, we'll duck and run before we'll grant him one."

"I know. And so does he. Our job—our *mandate*—is to find some way to stir up trouble down here regardless. To get you to fly the red flag close enough for common Verrari to see it from the public outhouses."

"How the hell did you ever plan on accomplishing this?"

"I had some half-assed idea to spread rumors, offer bribes. If you hadn't hit the *Messenger,* I would have tried to kindle a mess myself. But that was before we had any hint to the real state of things out here. Now Jerome and I obviously need your help."

"To do what?"

"To buy time. To convince Stragos that we're succeeding on his behalf."

"If you think for one second that I'll do anything to aid the archon—"

"I don't," said Locke, "and if you think for one second that I truly mean to aid him, you haven't been listening. Stragos' antidote is supposedly good for two months. That means Jerome and I *must* be in Tal Verrar in five weeks to get another sip. And if we have no progress to claim, he may simply decide to fold his investment in us."

"If you have to leave us to return to Tal Verrar," she said, "that's unfortunate. But you can find an independent trader in Port Prodigal; they're never more than a few days apart. We have arrangements with a number of them that call in Tal Verrar and Vel Virazzo. You'll have enough money from your shares to buy passage."

"Zamira, you have more wit than this. Listen. I have spoken personally to Stragos several times. Been lectured, is more the word. And I *believe* him. I believe that this is his last chance to put his foot down on the Priori and truly rule Tal Verrar. He needs an enemy, Zamira. He needs an enemy that he knows he can crush."

"Then it would be madness to acquiesce to his plan by provoking him."

"Zamira, this fight is coming to you regardless of your intentions. You are *all he has*. You are the only foe that suits. He's already sacrificed a ship, a veteran sailing master, a galley crew's worth of prisoners, and a considerable amount of his own prestige just to put Jerome and me in play. As long as we're out here, as long as you're helping us, then you'll know exactly where his plans rest, because we'll be running them from your ship. If you ignore us, I have no idea what he'll try next. All I know is that he *will* have other designs, and you won't be privy to them."

"What good will it do me," said Zamira, "to play along with you, and rouse Tal Verrar to the point that Stragos achieves his desire? We couldn't best his fleet seven years ago, with twice our present numbers."

"You're not the weapon," said Locke. "Jerome and I are the weapons. We have access to Stragos. All we need is an answer to the poison and we'll turn on the son of a bitch like a scorpion in his breechclout."

"For this I dangle my ship, my crew, and my children in easy reach of an enemy far beyond my strength?"

"Zamira, you spoke of the Sea of Brass as though it were a fairy kingdom, infinitely mutable, but you are lashed tight to Port Prodigal and you must know it. I don't doubt that you could sail for any port in the world and fetch it safely, but could you live anywhere else as you do here? Sell your goods and captured ships as easily? Pay your crew so regularly? Know the waters and your fellow outlaws so well? Lurk in trade lanes half as far from the navy of any great power?"

"This is the strangest conversation I have had in years," said Zamira, returning her hat to her head. "And probably the strangest request anyone has ever made of me. I have no way of knowing if anything you say is true. But I know this ship, and how fast she can run, if all else fails. Even Port Prodigal."

"That is, of course, one option. Ignore me. Wait until Stragos finds some other way to have his war, or a likeness of a war. And then fly. To some other sea, some harder life. You said yourself you can't beat the archon's navy; you can't strike at Stragos by force of arms. So consider this— every other choice you have will sooner or later turn into withdrawal and retreat. Jerome and I represent the sole means of attack that you will ever possess. With your help, we could destroy the archonate forever."

"How?"

"That's . . . sort of a work in progress."

"Possibly the least reassuring thing you've—"

"If nothing else," interrupted Locke, "we *know* that there are powerful forces in Tal Verrar balanced against the archon. Jerome and I could contact them, involve them somehow. If the archonate were abolished, the Priori would hold Tal Verrar by the purse strings. The last thing they'd want is embroilment in a useless war that might create another popular military hero."

"Standing here at the stern of my ship, weeks away from Tal Verrar, how can you speak with any certainty of what can be done with that city's merchants and politicians?"

"You said yourself that I had a talent for dishonesty. I often think it the only skill I have worthy of recommendation."

"But—"

"Drakasha, this is intolerable!"

Locke and Zamira whirled, once again in unison, to find Scholar Treganne standing at the head of the companionway. She stepped toward them, limping without the support of her cane, and in her outthrust arms wriggled a chitinous black nightmare, multilegged and gleaming in the lantern light. A spider the size of a cat. She held it belly outward, and its gleaming fangs twitched indignantly.

"Dear gods, it certainly is," said Locke.

"Treganne, what the hell is Zekassis doing out of her cage?"

"Your lieutenant has commenced an assault on the partition between our quarters," hissed Treganne. "Intolerable noise and commotion! She was lucky to shatter only one cage with all of her knocking about, and luckier still that I was there to restrain this blameless lady—"

"So... wait, you keep that thing in your quarters?" Locke was relieved to discover that it hadn't been prowling the ship, but only marginally so.

"Where do you think woundsilk comes from, Ravelle? Quit flinching; Zekassis is a delicate and timid creature."

"Treganne," said Drakasha, "as a physiker, you must be familiar with the courtship habits of the adult human female."

"Yes, but six feet from my head is an insufferable intrusion—"

"Treganne, in my opinion, interrupting Ezri at the moment would be an insufferable intrusion. The quartermaster's compartment across the passage is open. Fetch the carpenter to give Zek temporary accommodations, and pitch your hammock in Gwillem's space."

"I shall remember this indignity, Drakasha—"

"Yes, for approximately ten minutes, until some new vexation arises to claim your full attention."

"Should Delmastro do herself some injury through her exertions," said Treganne primly, "she may find another physiker to serve her needs. And I daresay that she may use her own abdomen to spin silk for her bandages—"

"I'm sure Ezri's abdomen is otherwise occupied, Scholar. Please find someone to build that thing a home for the night. You won't need to say much to convince them of your urgency."

As Treganne stomped off in a huff with her delicate and timid creature waving its legs in protest, Locke turned back to Zamira with one eyebrow raised.

"Where did you ever—"

"The punishment for insolence to the Nicoran royal family is to be hung out to starve in an iron cage. We were in Nicora doing a bit of smuggling; Treganne was hanging there doing a bit of dying. Most of the time I don't regret cutting her down."

"Well. What do you say to my—"

"Mad proposal?"

"Zamira, I don't need you to sail into Tal Verrar harbor. Just give me something to buy another few months of Stragos' indulgence. Sack a ship or two near Tal Verrar. Quick and easy work. You know Jerome and I will be the first over the side for you. Just ... let them run for the city and spread a bit of panic. Then send us in one night by boat, let us do our business, and we'll be back with a better idea of how to turn the situation—"

"Attack ships flying the Verrari flag, then get close enough to the city to let you slip in by boat? Wait at anchor with a five thousand solari bounty on my head—"

"Now *that* is an injustice, Zamira, whatever else I've done to merit suspicion. If Jerome and I merely wanted to slip back to Tal Verrar, why would we have risked our necks in your attack this morning? And if I wanted to continue deceiving you or spying on you, why didn't I just play along with your conclusion that we were agents of the Priori?

"Jerome and I quarreled this morning. If you spoke to Jabril before you pulled me out of your hold, you must know that I'm a divine of the Thirteenth, the Crooked Warden. You're ... our people, more or less. Our kind. It's a matter of propriety. Jerome insisted that we tell you the truth, that we needed you as willing allies and not as dupes. I'm ashamed to say that I was too angry to agree. But he was right, and it's not just fucking sentiment, it's hard truth. I don't think Jerome and I can pull this off unless you aid us with full knowledge of what we're up to. And if you can't or won't do that, I think you've got a hell of a mess coming your way. Soon."

Drakasha settled her right hand on the pommel of one of her sabers and closed her eyes, looking tired and vexed.

"Before anything else," she said at last, "apart from all other considerations, we need to put in at Port Prodigal. I have cargo to sell, stores to buy, a prize to dispose of, and crew to meet up with. We're several days out, and will be several days there. I will think on what you've said. One way or another, I'll give you an answer after we've done our business there."

"Thank you."

"So it's Leocanto, then?"

"Just keep calling me Ravelle," said Locke. "Easier for everyone."

"So be it. You're on the Merry Watch and you won't be shifted back to duty watches until tomorrow afternoon. I suggest you make good use of the night."

"Well." Locke glanced down at his leather cup of blue wine, suddenly thinking that maybe he could do with a few more, and perhaps a dice game to lose himself in for a few hours. "If the gods are kind I already have. Good night, Captain Drakasha."

He left her alone at the taffrail, silently studying the monster that lurked in the *Orchid*'s wake.

8

"DID THAT hurt?" whispered Ezri, tracing a finger across the sweat-slick skin above Jean's ribs.

"Did it hurt? Gods above, woman, no, that was—"

"I don't mean that." She gave him a firm poke in the scar that arced across his abdomen beneath his right breast. *"That."*

"Oh, that. No, it was wonderful. Someone came after me with a pair of Thieves' Teeth. Felt like a warm breeze on a fine spring day. I loved every second of—oof!"

"Ass!"

"Where did you get such sharp elbows? You grind those things against a whetstone, or—oof!"

Ezri lay on top of Jean on the demi-silk hammock that took up most of the space in her compartment. It was just barely long enough for him to lie with one arm above his head (brushing the interior bulkhead of the ship's starboard side), and he could have spanned its width between his outstretched arms. An alchemical trinket the size of a coin provided a faint silver light. Ezri's witchwood-dark curls were touched with fey highlights; scattered strands gleamed like threads of spider silk in moonlight. He ran his hands through that damp forest of hair, massaged her warm scalp with his fingernails, and she let her muscles go slack with a gratifying moan of relaxation.

The motionless air in the compartment was thick with sweat and the trapped heat of their first endless, frantic hour together. The place was also, Jean noticed for the first time, utterly wrecked. Their clothes were scattered in purest chaos. Ezri's weapons and few possessions littered the deck like navigational hazards. A small net containing a few books and scrolls hung from a ceiling beam and tilted toward the compartment door, indicating that the whole ship was heeled over to larboard.

"Ezri," he muttered, staring at the stiffened canvas partition that formed their left-hand "wall." A pair of large feet and a pair of small feet had given it a serious denting. "Ezri, whose cabin did we nearly kick our way into a little while ago?"

"Oh . . . Scholar Treganne's. Who told you to stop doing that to my hair? Oh, much better."

"Will she be pissed off?"

"More so than usual?" Ezri yawned and shrugged. "She's free to find a lover of her own and kick it back whenever she pleases. I'm too preoccupied to be diplomatic." She kissed Jean's neck, and he shivered. "Besides. Night hasn't nearly run its course yet. We may yet kick the whole damn thing down if I have my way, Jerome."

"Then it's your way we'll have," said Jean, gently shifting the weight of her body until they were lying on their sides, face-to-face. He ran his hands as carefully as he could over the stiff bandages on her upper arms, the only thing she couldn't in good sense take off. His hands moved to her cheeks, and then to her hair. They kissed for the sort of endless moment that only exists between lovers whose lips are still new territory to each other.

"Jerome," she whispered.

"No. Do something for me, Ezri. In private. Never call me that."

"Why not?"

"Call me my real name." He kissed her neck, put his lips to one of her ears, and whispered into it.

"Jean . . . ," she repeated.

"Gods, yes. Say that again."

"Jean Estevan Tannen. I like that."

"Yours and yours alone," Jean whispered.

"Something in return," she said. "Ezriane Dastiri de la Mastron. Dame Ezriane of the House of Mastron. Nicora."

"Really? You have an estate or something?"

"Doubt it. Spare daughters who run away from home don't tend to receive holdings." She kissed him again, then ruffled his beard with her fingertips. "In fact, with the letter

I left Mother and Father, I'm sure I was disinherited at the best possible speed."

"Gods. I'm sorry."

"Don't be." She moved her fingers down to his chest. "These things happen. You keep moving. You find things here and there that help you forget."

"You do indeed," he whispered, and then they were too busy to talk for a good long while.

9

LOCKE WAS pulled out of his vivid thicket of dreams by a number of things: the rising heat of day, the pressure of three cups of wine in his bowels, the moans of the hungover men around him, and the sharp prick of claws from the heavy little creature sleeping on the back of his neck.

Struck by a sudden foggy memory of Scholar Treganne's spider, he gasped in horror and rolled over, clutching at whatever was clinging to him. He blinked several times to clear the veil of slumber from his eyes, and found himself struggling not with a spider but with a kitten, narrow-faced and black-furred.

"The hell?" Locke muttered.

"Mew," the kitten retorted, locking gazes with him. It had the expression common to all kittens, that of a tyrant in the becoming. *I was comfortable, and you dared to move,* those jade eyes said. *For that you must die.* When it became apparent to the cat that its two or three pounds of mass were insufficient to break Locke's neck with one mighty snap, it put its paws on his shoulders and began sharing its drool-covered nose with his lips. He recoiled.

"That's Regal," said someone to Locke's left.

"Regal? No, it's ridiculous." Locke tucked the kitten under his arm like a dangerous alchemical device. Its fur was thin and silky, and it began to purr noisily. The man who'd spoken was Jabril; Locke raised his eyebrows when he saw that Jabril was lying on his back, stark naked.

"His name," said Jabril. "Regal. He's got that white spot on his throat. And a wet nose, right?"

"The very one."

"Regal. You been adopted, Ravelle. Ain't that ironic?"

"My life's ambition realized at last." Locke glanced around the half-empty undercastle. Several of the new Orchids were snoring loudly; one or two were crawling to their feet, and at least one was sleeping contentedly in a pool of his own vomit. Or so Locke assumed. Jean was nowhere to be seen.

"And how was your evening, Ravelle?" Jabril pushed himself up on both elbows.

"Virtuous, I think."

"My condolences." Jabril smiled. "You ever met Malakasti from the Blue watch? Got the sorta red hair and the daggers tattooed on her knuckles? Gods, I don't think she's human."

"You vanished early from the party, I'll say that."

"Yeah. She had some demands. And some friends." Jabril massaged his temples with his right hand. "That boatswain from Red watch, fellow with no fingers on his left hand. Had no idea they taught gods-fearing Ashmiri lads them sorts of tricks. Whew."

"Lads? I didn't know you, ah, stalked that particular quarry."

"Yeah, well, seems I'll try anything once." Jabril grinned. "Or five or six times, as it turns out." He scratched his belly and seemed to become aware of his lack of clothes for the first time. "Hell. I remember owning breeches as recently as yesterday. . . ."

Locke emerged into sunlight a few minutes later with Regal still tucked under his arm. As Locke stretched and yawned, the cat did the same, attempting to wriggle out of

Locke's grasp and presumably climb back atop his head. Locke held the tiny fellow up and stared at him.

"I'm not getting attached to you," he said. "Find someone else to share your drool with." Well aware that any mistreatment of the little fellow might get him thrown over the side, he set the kitten down and nudged him with a bare foot.

"You sure you're authorized to give orders to that cat?" Locke turned to find Jean standing on the forecastle steps, just finishing pulling a tunic on. "Gotta be careful. He might be a watchmate."

"If he acknowledges any rank, I think he puts himself somewhere between Drakasha and the Twelve." Locke stared up at Jean for several seconds. "Hi."

"Hello..."

"Look, there's a lot of tedious 'I was an ass' sort of conversation to stumble through, and I'm still feeling a bit victimized by that blue wine, so let's just assume—"

"I'm sorry," said Jean.

"No, that's my job."

"I meant...we really found our jagged edges again, didn't we?"

"If there's one thing a battle isn't, it's calming on the nerves. I don't blame you for...what you said."

"We can think of something," said Jean, quietly and urgently. "Something together. I know you're not...I didn't mean to insult your..."

"I deserved it. And you were right. I spoke to Drakasha last night."

"You did?"

"I told her." Locke grimaced, stretched again, used the motion to cover a series of hand signals. Jean followed, his eyebrows rising.

Didn't mention Bondsmagi, Sinspire, Camorr, real names. All else, truth.

"Really?" said Jean.

"Yes." Locke stared down at the deck. "I said you were right."

"And how did she—"

Locke mimed a roll of the dice, and shrugged. "We're for Port Prodigal before anything else happens," he said. "Chores to do. Then she said . . . she'll let us know."

"I see. And so . . ."

"Did you have a good night?"

"Gods, yes."

"Good. About, ah, what I said yesterday—"

"You don't need—"

"I do. It was the *dumbest* of all the things I said yesterday. Dumbest and least fair. I know I've been . . . hopeless for so long I wear it like armor. I don't begrudge you anything you have. Savor it."

"I do," said Jean. "Believe me, I do."

"Good. I'm no one you want to learn from."

"Uh, so—"

"All's well, Master Valora." Locke smiled, pleased to feel the corners of his mouth creeping up of their own volition. "But that wine I was talking about . . ."

"Wine? Did you—"

"Craplines, Jerome. I need to piss before my innards explode. You're blocking the stairs."

"Ah." Jean stepped down and slapped Locke on the back. "My apologies. Free yourself, brother."

CHAPTER TWELVE

PORT PRODIGAL

1

THE *POISON ORCHID* BORE WEST by south through muggy air and moderate seas, and the days rolled by for Locke in a rhythm of chores.

He and Jean were placed on the Red watch, which had been put under Lieutenant Delmastro's direct oversight in Nasreen's absence. Grand initiation ceremonies did nothing to sate the ship's appetite for maintenance; the masts still needed to be slushed, the seams checked and rechecked, the decks swept, the rigging adjusted. Locke oiled sabers from the weapons lockers, heaved at the capstan to shift cargo for better trim, served ale at the midevening meals, and pulled rope fragments to oakum until his fingers were red.

Drakasha acknowledged Locke with terse nods, but said nothing, and summoned him to no more private conversations.

As full crew, the ex-Messengers had the right to sleep more or less where they would. Some opted for the main hold, especially those who claimed willing hammock-partners among the old Orchids, but Locke found himself comfortable enough with the now-roomier undercastle. He won a spare tunic in a game of dice and used it as a pillow, a luxury after days of bare deck alone. He slept like a stone statue after finishing each night's watch just before the red light of dawn.

Jean, of course, slept elsewhere after the night watches.

They had no sightings through the twenty-fifth of the month, when the winds shifted and began to blow strongly from the south. Locke had collapsed into his usual spot against the undercastle's larboard wall at sunrise, and then snored for several hours in the fashion of the eminently self-satisfied until some sort of commotion awoke him and he found Regal draped across his neck.

"Gah," he said, and the kitten took this as a signal to perch his forepaws on Locke's cheeks and begin poking his wet nose directly between Locke's eyes. Locke seized the kitten, sat up, and blinked. His skull felt full of cobwebs; something had definitely woken him prematurely.

"Was it you?" he muttered, frowning and rubbing the top of Regal's skull with two fingers. "We have to stop meeting like this, kid. I'm not getting attached to you."

"Land ho," came a faint cry from outside the undercastle. "Three points off the larboard bow!" Locke set Regal down, gave him an unambiguous nudge toward some other snoring sleeper, and crawled out into the morning light.

Activity on deck seemed normal; nobody was rushing about, or delivering urgent messages to Drakasha, or even crowding the rail to try to spot the approaching land. Someone slapped Locke on the back and he turned to find himself facing Utgar, who had a coil of rope slung over his shoulder. The Vadran nodded in a friendly fashion.

"You look confused, Red watch."

"It's just—I heard the cry. I thought there'd be more excitement. Will that be Port Prodigal?"

"Nah. It's the Ghostwinds, right, but we're just fetching

the edges. Miserable places. Asp Island, Bastard Rock, the Opal Sands. Nowhere we'd want to touch. Two days yet to Prodigal, and with the winds like this, we're not getting in the way we'd like, hey?"

"What do you mean?"

"You'll see." Utgar grinned, enjoying some private knowledge. "You'll see for damn sure. Get your beauty sleep, right? You're back on the masts in two hours."

2

THE GHOSTWIND Isles gradually crowded in around the *Orchid* like a gang of muggers savoring their slow approach to a target. The horizon, once clear, sprouted islands thick with mist-capped jungle. Tall black peaks rumbled intermittently, belching lines of steam or smoke into the heavy gray skies. Rain washed down in sheets, not the merciless storms of the high seas but rather the indifferent sweat of the tropics, blood-warm and barely pushed by the jungle breeze.

The waters lightened with their passage west, from the cobalt of the deeps to sky blue to translucent aquamarine. The place was teeming with life; birds wheeled overhead, fish darted through the shallows in silver clouds, and sinuous shapes larger than men shadowed them. They stalked languidly in the *Orchid*'s wake as well: scythe sharks, blue widowers, bad-luck reefmen, daggerfins. Eeriest of all were the local wolf sharks, whose sand-colored backs made them vanish into the pale haze below the ship. It took a keen eye to spot the ghostly incongruities that betrayed their lurking, and they had the disconcerting habit of circling beneath the craplines.

Locke thanked the gods that they weren't jumpers.

For a day and a half they sailed on, heeling over to dodge the occasional reef or smaller island. Drakasha and

Delmastro seemed to know the area by heart and muttered over Drakasha's charts only at rare intervals. Locke began to glimpse human detritus on the shoals and rocks—here a weathered mast, there the skeletal ribs of an ancient keel on the sandy bottom. On one afternoon watch, he spotted hundreds of crablike things the size of dogs congregating on the overturned bottom of a ship's hull. As the *Orchid* passed, the creatures fled from their artificial reef en masse, making the water around it froth white. In moments they had vanished completely.

Locke went off that watch a few hours later, aware of a steadily growing tension in the crew around him. Something had changed. Drakasha paced the quarterdeck ceaselessly, ordered extra lookouts to the mastheads, and held whispered conferences with Delmastro and Mumchance.

"She won't tell me what's going on," said Jean after Locke dropped what he thought was a subtle hint. "She's all lieutenant and no Ezri at the moment."

"That in itself tells us something," said Locke. "Tells us to curb our good cheer."

Drakasha mustered all hands at the evening watch change. All the Orchids—one vast, sweaty, anxious mass of men and women—fixed their eyes on the quarterdeck rail and waited for the captain's words. The sun was a disk of burning copper crowning jungle heights dead ahead; the colors of fire were creeping up layer by layer through the clouds, and all around them the islands were falling into shadow.

"Well," said Drakasha, "here it is, plain. The winds have been steady as hell these past few days, out of the south. We can drop anchor in Prodigal tonight, but we can't make it through the Trader's Gate."

There was a general murmur from the crowd. Lieutenant Delmastro, stepping up beside the captain, placed a hand on her weapons belt and hollered, "Quiet! Perelandro's piss, most of us have been here before."

"So we have," said Drakasha. "Stout hearts, Orchids. We'll do the usual. Red watch, take some ease. Expect an all-hands call in a few hours. After that, nobody sleeps, nobody drinks, nobody fucks until we're safe home again. Blue watch, you have the duty. Del, see to the newcomers. Run it all down for them."

"Run *what* down?" Locke looked around, asking the question to the air as the crew dispersed.

"Two passages to get to Port Prodigal," said Jabril. "First, Trader's Gate, that's north of the city. Twelve miles long, say. Twists and turns, shoals all over the place. Slow going at the best of times, but with a hard south wind, piss on it. It'll take us days."

"So what the hell are we doing?"

"Second way, from the west. Half as long. Still twisty, but ain't near so bad. Especially with this wind. But it don't get used if anyone can help it. They call it the Parlor Passage."

"Why?"

"Because there's something there," said Lieutenant Delmastro, pushing her way through the little crowd, ex-Messengers all, that had gathered around Jabril. Locke saw her give Jean's arm the briefest squeeze, and then she continued. "Something...lives there."

"Something?" Locke couldn't keep a hint of irritation out of his voice. "Is the ship in danger?"

"No," said Delmastro.

"Let me be more specific, then. Are those of us *aboard* her in danger?"

"I don't know," said Delmastro, sharing a glance with Jabril. "Will something come aboard the ship? No. Absolutely not. Might you...feel like *leaving* the ship? I can't say. Depends on your temperament."

"I'm not sure I'd enjoy the close attention of anything swimming in these waters," said Locke.

"Good. Then you probably don't have anything to worry about." Delmastro sighed. "All of you, think on what the captain said. A bit of rest is the thing; you'll be called up halfway through your usual off-watch, so snatch what you can." She stepped up beside Jean, and Locke overheard her whisper, "I certainly intend to."

"I'll, ah, find you later then, Jerome." Locke smiled despite himself.

"You going to catch a nap?" asked Jean.

"Bloody hell, no. I expect to twiddle my thumbs and go steadily out of my skull until called for duty. Maybe I can find someone to share a hand of cards—"

"Doubt it," said Delmastro. "Your reputation . . ."

"Unjust persecution for my good fortune," said Locke.

"Yeah, well, maybe you should consider a public streak of bad luck. Word to the wise." She blew Locke a mocking little kiss. "Or whatever you are, Ravelle."

"Oh, steal Jerome and go do your worst to him." Locke folded his arms and grinned; Delmastro's loosening up toward him had been a welcome change over the previous few days. "I'll be judging your performance by how pissed Treganne is when we see her next. Hell, that's how I can amuse myself. I'll solicit wagers on how riled up you two can get the Scholar—"

"You do *anything* of the sort," said Delmastro, "and I'll chain you to an anchor by your precious bits and have you dragged over a reef."

"No, this is a good scheme," said Jean. "We could place our own bets with him, then rig the contest—"

"This ship has *two* anchors, Valora!"

3

DUSK WAS approaching by the time Jean and Ezri crept back up to the quarterdeck. Drakasha stood near the taffrail, cradling Cosetta in her left arm and holding a small silver cup in her right.

"You must drink it, love," whispered Drakasha. "It's a special nighttime drink for pirate princesses."

"No," muttered Cosetta.

"Are you not a pirate princess?"

"No!"

"I think you are. Be good—"

"Don't want!"

Jean thought back to his time in Camorr, and to how Chains had sometimes behaved when one of the young Gentlemen Bastards had decided to throw a fit. They'd been much older than Cos, true, but children were children and Drakasha looked hollow-eyed with worry.

"My, my," he said loudly, approaching the Drakashas so that Cosetta could see him. "That looks *very* good, Captain Drakasha."

"It does look very good," she said, "and it tastes better than it looks—"

"Feh," said Cosetta. "Ahhhhh! No!"

"You *must*," said her mother.

"Captain," said Jean, pretending to be entranced by the silver cup, "that looks *so* wonderful. If Cosetta doesn't want it, I'll have it."

Drakasha stared at him, and then smiled. "Well...," she said, sounding grudging, "if Cosetta doesn't want it, I suppose I have no choice." She slowly moved the cup away from Cosetta and toward Jean, and the little girl's eyes grew wide.

"No," she said. "No!"

"But you don't want it," said Drakasha with an air of finality. "Jerome does. So it's going away, Cosetta."

"Mmmm," said Jean. "I'll drink it straightaway."

"No!" Cosetta stretched for the cup. "No, no, no!"

"Cosetta," said Drakasha sternly, "if you want it, you must drink it. Do you understand?"

The little girl nodded, her mouth an "O" of concern, her fingers straining to reach the suddenly invaluable prize. Zamira held the silver cup to Cosetta's lips and the little girl drained it with urgent greed.

"Very good," said Drakasha, kissing her daughter on the forehead. "Very, very good. Now I'm going to take you down so you and Paolo can go to sleep." She slipped the empty silver cup into a coat pocket, slung Cosetta round to the front of her chest, and nodded at Jean. "Thank you for that, Valora. Deck is yours, Del. Just a few minutes."

"She hates doing that," said Ezri quietly when Drakasha had vanished down the companionway.

"Feeding Cos for the night?"

"It's milk of poppy. She puts them both to sleep . . . for the Parlor Passage. No way in hell she wants them awake when we go through it."

"What the hell is going to—"

"It's hard to explain," said Ezri. "It's easier just to get it over with. But you'll be fine; I know you will." She ran one hand up and down his back. "You manage to survive *me* in my poorer moods."

"Ah," said Jean, "but when a woman has your heart, she doesn't have poor moods. Only interesting moods . . . and *more* interesting moods."

"Where I was born, obnoxious flatterers were hung out to dry in iron cages."

"I can see why you ran away. You inspire such flattery that any man who talked to you at length would have been caged up after—"

"You are *beyond* obnoxious!"

"I need to do something to keep my mind off whatever's coming—"

"What we just did below wasn't enough?"

"Well, I suppose we could always go back down and—"

"Alas that the biggest bitch on this ship isn't even Drakasha or myself, but duty." She kissed Jean on the cheek. "You want something to keep yourself busy, you can get started with preparations for the passage. Get to the for'ard lantern locker and bring me the alchemical lights."

"How many?"

"All of them," she said. "Every last one you can find."

4

THE TENTH hour of the evening. Night fell like a cloak over the Ghostwinds; and the *Poison Orchid,* under topsails, stood in to the Parlor Passage gilded in white and amber light. A hundred alchemical lanterns had been shaken to life and placed around the ship's entire hull, a few in the rigging but most beneath the rail, casting rippling facets of false fire on the dark water just below.

"By the deep six," called one of the two sailors Drakasha had placed at the sides, where they cast their lead lines to gauge the amount of water between the ship's hull and the sea bottom. Six fathoms; thirty-six feet. The *Orchid* could slip through far shallower straits than that.

Ordinarily, soundings were occasional and one leadsman would suffice to take them. Now the men, two of her oldest and most experienced, cast their lines and called the results continually. What's more, each of them was watched by a small party of . . . minders, was the best word Jean could come up with. Sailors who were armed and armored.

Strange precautions had been ordered all over the ship. The small, elite crew who waited above to work the sails had safety lines lashed around their waists; they would dangle like pendulums if they fell, but at least they'd probably live. Real fires were extinguished, smoking strictly forbidden. Drakasha's children slept in her cabin with the stern shutters locked and the companionway door guarded. Drakasha herself had her Elderglass mosaic vest buckled on, and her sabers hung ready in their scabbards.

"A quarter less six," called a leadsman.

"Fog coming up," said Jean. He and Locke stood at the starboard rail of the quarterdeck. Drakasha paced nearby, Mumchance had the wheel, and Delmastro stood by the binnacle with a small rack of precision timing glasses.

"That's how it starts," said Mumchance.

The *Orchid* was entering a mile-wide channel between cliffs that rose to about half the height of the masts and were surmounted by dark jungle that rose and faded into the blackness. There were faint sounds of things unseen in that jungle; screeches, snapping, rustling. The ship's arcs of lanterns made the waters around them clear for fifty or sixty feet, and at the edges of that gleaming circle Jean saw threads of gray mist beginning to curl out of the water.

"And a half five," came the cry from the starboard leadsman.

"Captain Drakasha." Utgar stood at the taffrail, log-line pinched between his fingers. "Four knots, hey."

"Aye," said Drakasha. "Four knots, and our stern's even with the mouth of the passage. Give me ten minutes, Del."

Delmastro nodded, flipped one of her glasses over, and kept watch as sand began to trickle from the upper chamber to the lower. Drakasha moved to the forward quarterdeck rail.

"Heed this," she said to the crewfolk working or waiting on deck. "If you start to feel peculiar, stay away from the rails. If you cannot abide the deck, go below. This is a chore we must endure, and we've come through it before. You *cannot* be harmed if you stay on the ship. Hold fast to that thought. *Do not leave the ship.*"

The mist was rising now, layering upon itself. The shadowy outlines of cliffs and jungles beyond were swiftly vanishing. Before them was nothing but blackness.

"Ten, Captain," said Delmastro at last.

"By the mark five," cried one of the leadsmen.

"Mum, put your helm down." Drakasha used a stick of charcoal to scrawl a quick note on a folded parchment. "Two spokes a-lee."

"Aye, Captain, helm a-lee by two."

At the sailing master's slight adjustment to the wheel, the ship leaned to larboard. Sailors overhead made faint adjustments to sails and rigging acting on instructions Drakasha had drilled into them before they'd entered the passage.

"Give me twelve minutes, Del."

"Aye, Captain, twelve it is."

As those twelve minutes passed, the fog grew thicker, like smoke from a well-fed fire. It closed on either side, a swirling gray wall that seemed to lock their own light and sound in a bubble, closing off all hint of the outside world. The creak of the blocks and rigging, the slap of the water on the hull, the babble of voices—all these familiar things echoed flatly, and the jungle noises vanished. Still the fog encroached, until it crossed the ephemeral line of well-lit water created by the lanterns. Visibility in any direction now died at forty feet.

"Twelve, Captain," said Delmastro.

"Mum, put up your helm," said Drakasha, staring at the compass in the binnacle. "Helm a-weather. Bring us northwest by west." She shouted to the crewfolk at the waist, "Make ready to shift yards! Northwest by west, wind to the larboard quarter!"

There were several minutes of activity as the ship came

slowly around to its new course and the crew rebraced the yards. All the while, Jean became more convinced that he wasn't imagining the sound-dampening nature of the fog. The noise of their activity simply died when it hit that shroud. In fact, the only evidence of a world beyond the mist was the wet, earthy smell of jungle blowing in with the warm breeze across the quarterdeck.

"By the mark seven," called a leadsman.

"Twenty-two minutes, Del."

"Aye," said Delmastro, turning her glasses like an automaton.

The next twenty-two minutes passed in claustrophobic silence, punctuated only by the occasional flutter of sail canvas and the shouts of the leadsmen. Tension built as the minutes crawled by, until—

"Time, Captain."

"Thanks, Del. Mum, put your helm down. Bring us southwest by west." She raised her voice. "Lively, now! Tacks and sheets! To the larboard tack, southwest by west!"

Sails shuddered, and crewfolk ran about swearing and working ropes as the ship heeled back onto the larboard tack. They spun at the heart of the fog; the jungle-scented breeze seemed to rotate around them like a boxer dancing around an opponent, until Jean could feel it against his left cheek.

"Hold steady, Mum," said Drakasha. "Ezri, fifteen minutes."

"Fifteen, aye."

"Here it fucking comes," muttered Mumchance.

"Belay that crap," said Drakasha. "Only thing truly dangerous out here is us, got it?"

Jean felt a prickling sensation on the skin of his forehead. He reached up and wiped away the sweat that was beading there.

"A quarter less five," called a leadsman.

Jean, whispered a faint voice.

"What, Orrin?"

"Huh?" Locke was gripping the rail with both hands and barely spared a glance for Jean.

"What did you want?"

"I didn't say anything."

"Are you—"

Jean Tannen.

"Oh gods," said Locke.

"You too?" Jean stared at him. "A voice—"

"Not from the air," whispered Locke. "More like . . . you know who. Back in Camorr."

"Why is it saying my—"

"It's not," said Drakasha in a low, urgent voice. "We all hear it talking to us. We all hear our own names. Hold fast."

"Crooked Warden, I will fear no darkness for the night is yours," muttered Locke, pointing the first two fingers of his left hand into the darkness. The Dagger of the Thirteenth, a thief's gesture against evil. "Your night is my cloak, my shield, my escape from those who hunt to feed the noose. I will fear no evil, for you have made the night my friend."

"Bless the Benefactor," said Jean, squeezing Locke's left forearm. "Peace and profit to his children."

Jean . . . Estevan . . . Tannen.

He *felt* the voice, realizing somehow that the impression of sound was just a trick he played upon himself, an echo in his ears. He felt its intrusion into his awareness like the brush of insect legs against his skin. He wiped his forehead again, and realized that he was sweating profusely, even for the warm night.

Forward, someone started sobbing loudly.

"Twelve," Jean heard Ezri whispering. "Twelve more minutes."

The water is cool, Jean Tannen. You...sweat. Your clothes itch. Skin...itch. But the water is cool.

Drakasha squared her shoulders and strolled down the quarterdeck steps to the waist. She found the sobbing crewman, hauled him gently to his feet, and gave him a pat on the back. "Chins up, Orchids. This isn't flesh and blood. This isn't a fight. Stand fast."

She sounded bold enough. Jean wondered how many of her crew knew or guessed that she drugged her children rather than put them through this.

Was it merely Jean's imagination, or was the fog lightening to starboard? The haze was no thinner, but the darkness behind it seemed to abate...to acquire a sickly luminescence. A whispering hiss of water grew into a steady, rhythmic pulse. Waves breaking over shoals. The black water rippled at the edge of their little circle of light.

"The reef," muttered Mumchance.

"By the deep four," called a leadsman.

Something stirred in the fog, the faintest impression of movement. Jean peered at the swirling gloom, straining to catch it again. He rubbed at his chest, where his sweat-soaked tunic seemed to irritate the skin beneath.

Come to the water, Jean Tannen. Water so cool. Come. Lose tunic, lose sweat, lose itch. Bring...the woman. Bring her with you to the water. Come.

"Gods," whispered Locke, "whatever's out there knows my real name."

"Mine as well," said Jean.

"I mean, it's not calling me 'Locke.' It knows my *real* name."

"Oh. Shit."

Jean stared down at the black water and heard the sound of it breaking over the unseen reef. It couldn't be cool...it had to be as warm as everything else in this damn place. But the sound...the sound of those waves was not so unpleasant. He listened, entranced for several seconds, then raised his head lethargically and stared into the fog.

Something was there, for the briefest instant—a dark shape visible through the curtains of mist. Man-sized. Tall, thin, and motionless. Waiting there, atop the reef.

Jean shuddered violently, and the shape disappeared. He blinked as though waking from a daydream. The fog was now as dark and solid as ever, the imagined light gone, the hissing rush of water over shoals no longer so pleasing to his ears. Sweat ran in itching streams down his neck and arms, and he welcomed the distraction, scratching himself furiously.

"By the…by the, ah, deep four…and a quarter four…," murmured a leadsman.

"Time," said Ezri, seeming to come out of a daze of her own. "Time, time!"

"Surely not," muttered Locke. "That wasn't…but a few minutes."

"I looked down and the sands were run out. I don't know when it happened." She raised her voice urgently. "Captain! Time!"

"Rouse up, rouse up!" Drakasha bellowed as though the ship were under attack. "Tacks and sheets! Come west by north! Wind to the larboard quarter, brace the yards!"

"West by north, aye," said Mumchance.

"I don't understand," said Ezri, staring at her timing glasses. Jean saw that her blue tunic was soaked with sweat, her hair was matted, and her face was slick. "I was watching the glasses. It was like…I just blinked, and… all the time was gone."

The deck was alive with vigorous commotion. Once more the breeze shifted, the fog swirled around them, and Mumchance settled them onto their new course with precise, almost delicate shifts of his wheel.

"Gods," said Ezri. "That one was as bad as I can remember."

"Never been like that before," added Mumchance.

"How much longer?" asked Jean, not ashamed to sound anxious.

"That's our last turn," said Ezri. "Assuming we didn't slip south far enough that we run aground on something in these next few minutes, it's straight on west by north all the way to Port Prodigal."

They slipped on through the dark waters, and gradually the strange sensations on Jean's skin ebbed. The fog withdrew, first opening into cleaner darkness before the ship, and then unraveling behind them. The light from the lanterns seemed to pour back out into the night, unrestrained, and the reassuring noise of the jungle on either side of the channel returned.

"By the deep eight," came a leadsman's shout.

"That's the main channel," said Drakasha, ascending the steps to the quarterdeck once again. "Well done, everyone." She turned to look out over the waist. "Take in most of the lanterns. Leave a few out for navigation, so we don't surprise anyone coming into the harbor. Keep the leads going." She reached out and put her arms on Mumchance and Ezri, squeezing their shoulders. "I know I said no drinking, but I think we could all do with a brace."

Her gaze fell on Locke and Jean. "You two look as though you could use a job. Fetch up an ale cask and serve it out at the mainmast." She raised her voice to a shout. "Half a cup for anyone who wants it."

As Jean hurried forward with Locke close behind, he was pleased to feel the tension of a few moments earlier evaporating. Crewfolk were smiling again, chattering away at one another, even laughing here and there. A few kept to themselves, arms folded and eyes downcast, but even they seemed relieved. The only odd thing about the scene, Jean realized, was how assiduously most of them seemed to be trying to keep their attention focused on the ship and the people around them.

More than an hour would pass before many of them would allow themselves to glance out at the water again.

5

IF YOU could stand on air a thousand feet above Port Prodigal, this midnight, you would see a tenuous ribbon of light set like a jewel in the midst of boundless tropical darkness. Clouds veil the moons and the stars. Even the thin red lines of volcanic flow that sometimes ignite the far horizons are missing; those dark mountains smolder tonight without visible fire.

Prodigal claims a long beach on the north side of a vast, hilly island. Miles of ancient rain forest recede into the night behind it; not a speck of light burns anywhere within that grim expanse.

The broad harbor, enclosed on all sides, is uncommonly friendly to ships once they slip through either of the arduous passages that bring them from the sea. There are no reefs, no smaller islands, no navigational hazards marring the sandy white bottom of the bay. At the eastern end of town the water shallows to waist depth, while in the west even heavy ships may all but kiss the shore and keep eight or nine fathoms beneath their keels.

A forest of masts rocks gently above these depths, a floating hodgepodge of docks, boats, working ships, and hulls in every state of disrepair. There are two loosely defined anchorages serving Port Prodigal—first, the Graveyard, where float the hundreds of hulls and wrecks that will never move on the open sea again. East of that, claiming all the larger, newer docks, lies the Hospital, so-called because its patients may yet live.

6

A BELL began tolling, its slow clang echoing off the water, as soon as the *Poison Orchid* emerged from the Parlor Passage.

Locke stared over the ship's larboard rail, toward the lights of the city and their rippling reflections on the bay.

"Harbor watch'll ring that damn thing until we drop anchor." Jabril had taken note of his curiosity and taken the rail beside him. "Gotta let everyone know they're on the job so they keep getting paid their liquor ration."

"You spend much time here, Jabril?"

"Born here. Prison in Tal Verrar is what I got the one time I tried to see some other oceans."

Dropping anchor in Prodigal Bay had none of the ceremony Locke had seen elsewhere; no shore pilots, no customs officers, not even a single curious fisherman. And, to his surprise, Drakasha didn't take the *Orchid* all the way in. They settled about half a mile offshore, furled sails, and kept their lanterns burning.

"Drop a boat to larboard," ordered Drakasha, peering at the city and its anchorages through her glass. "Then rig razor nets at the starboard. Keep lanterns burning. Dismiss Blue watch below but have sabers ready at the masts. Del, get Malakasti, Dantierre, Big Konar, and Rask."

"Your will, Captain."

After helping a work party heave one of the ship's larger boats over the side, Locke approached Drakasha on the quarterdeck and found her still studying the town through her glass.

"I take it you have reason for caution, Captain?"

"We've been out for a few weeks," said Drakasha, "and things change. I've got a big crew and a big ship, but neither of them is the biggest there is."

"Do you see something that makes you nervous?"

"Not nervous. Curious. Looks like most of us are home for once. See that line of ships, at the eastern docks, closest to us? Four of the council captains are in town. Five, now that I'm back." She lowered her glass and looked sidelong at him. "Plus two or three independent traders, near as I can tell."

"I really hope it doesn't come to that," he said quietly.

At that moment Lieutenant Delmastro returned to the quarterdeck, armed and armored, with four sailors in tow.

Malakasti, a thin woman with more tattoos than words in her vocabulary, had a shipwide reputation as a knife fighter. Dantierre was a bearded, balding Verrari who favored tattered nobleman's silks; he'd gone outlaw after a long career as a professional duelist. Big Konar, true to his name, was the largest slab of human flesh aboard the *Orchid*. And Rask—well, Rask was a type that Locke recognized almost immediately, a murderer's murderer. Drakasha, like many *garristas* back in Camorr, would keep him on a short leash, and give him his head only when she needed blood on the wall. *Lots* of blood on the wall.

A brutal crew, none of them young and none of them new to Drakasha's command. Locke pondered this while all hands were briefly mustered at the waist.

"Utgar has the ship," Drakasha announced. "We're not putting in tonight. I'm taking Del and a shore party to sound out the town. If all's well, we'll have a busy few days...and we'll start divvying up the shares tomorrow evening. Try not to gamble it all away to your watchmates before it's even in your hands, eh?

"In the meantime, Red watch, mind the ship. Razor nets on starboard stay up until we come back. Post lookouts up every mast and keep an eye on the waterline. Blue watch, some of you sleep near the arms lockers if you're so inclined. Keep daggers and clubs at hand." To Utgar, she said more quietly, "Double guard on my cabin door all night."

"Aye, Captain."

Drakasha vanished into her cabin for a few moments. She reemerged in her Elderglass mosaic vest, with her sabers in fine jeweled scabbards, gleaming emeralds in her ears, and gold rings over the black leather gloves on her hands. Locke and Jean confronted her together, as unobtrusively as they could.

"Ravelle, I do not have time—"

"Captain," said Locke, "you've put together a bruising crew because you're out to scare someone who might give you trouble, haven't you? And if they're too stupid to take a hint, you want people who can end things quick. I strongly, *strongly* suggest that Jerome would serve you well on both counts."

"I...hmmm." She stared at Jean, as though only just noticing the width of his shoulders and upper arms. "That might just add the finishing touch. All right, Valora, you fancy a short night out?"

"I do," said Jean. "But I work best as part of a team. Orrin is just the man to—"

"You two think you're *so* clever," said Drakasha. "But—"

"I mean it," said Jean hurriedly. "Humble apologies. But you've seen what he does. You'll have a pile of strongarms at your back; bring him for...situations unforeseen."

"Tonight is delicate business," said Drakasha. "Misstepping in Port Prodigal after midnight is like pissing on an angry snake. I need—"

"Ahem," said Locke. "Originally, we're from Camorr."

"Be on the boat in five minutes," said Drakasha.

7

DRAKASHA TOOK the bow, Delmastro the stern, and everyone else an oar. At a stately pace they scudded across the calm surface of the bay.

"At least that jackass finally stopped ringing the bell," muttered Jean. He had taken a spot on the last rowing bench, next to Big Konar, so he could chat with Ezri. She was trailing one of her hands in the water.

"Is that wise?" Jean asked.

"What, fiddling with the water?" Ezri hooked a thumb over her shoulder in the direction of the Parlor Passage outlet. "You can't see them by night, but at the entrances to the bay there are rows of huge white stones set across the bottom. Regular lines of them."

"Eldren stones," muttered Konar.

"They don't bother us," said Ezri, "but nothing else will pass them. Not one single thing lives in this bay; you can swim at dusk with bloody cuts on your feet and nothing will come along for a taste."

"But not too close to the docks. Piss," said Konar, almost apologetically.

"Well, damn," said Jean. "That sounds nice."

"Sure, I guess," said Ezri. "Makes fishing a pain in the ass. Little boats crowd the Trader's Gate passage and muck up the works there more than usual. Speaking of mucking up the works..."

"Mmm?"

"I don't see the *Red Messenger* anywhere."

"Ah."

"But she was crawling like a snail," she said. "And we do have some interesting company in her place."

"Such as?"

"See that first row of ships? Starboard to larboard, that's *Osprey*, Pierro Strozzi's lugger. His crew's tiny and so's his ambition, but he could sail a barrel through a hurricane. Next to that, *Regal Bitch*, captain Chavon Rance. Rance is a pain in the ass. Has a real temper. Next is *Draconic*, Jacquelaine Colvard's brig. She's reasonable, and she's been out here longer than anyone.

"That big three-master on the far end is the *Dread Sovereign*, Jaffrim Rodanov's lady. Nasty piece of work. Last I saw she was on the beach getting careened, but now she looks ready for sea."

With six people pulling at the oars, they made short work of the trip. In just a few moments they were alongside a crumbling stone jetty. As Jean secured his oar, he spied a man's corpse bobbing gently in the water.

"Ah," said Ezri. "Poor bastard. That's the mark of a lively night in these parts."

Drakasha's shore party tied the boat to the very end of the jetty and went up as though boarding an enemy vessel, with wary hearts and hands near their weapons.

"Holy gods," exclaimed a mostly toothless drunk cradling a wineskin in the middle of the jetty. "It's Drakasha, isn't it?"

"It is. Who are you?"

"Banjital Vo."

"Well," said Drakasha, "Banjital Vo, I'm making you responsible for the safety of the boat we just tied up."

"But...I—"

"If it's here when we come back, I'll give you a Verrari silver. If anything's happened to it, I'll ask around for you, and when I find you I'll pull your gods-damned eyes out."

"I'll...I'll keep it like it were my own."

"No," said Drakasha, "keep it like it's *mine*."

She led them off the jetty and up a gently sloping sand path bordered by canvas tents, roofless log cabins, and partially collapsed stone buildings. Jean could hear the snores of sleeping people within those decrepit structures, plus the soft bleat of goats, the growls of mongrel dogs, and the flutter of agitated chickens. A few cookfires had burned down to coals, but there were no lanterns or alchemical lights hung out anywhere on this side of town.

A pungent stream of piss and night soil was trickling

down the right-hand side of the path, and Jean stepped carefully to avoid it, as well as a sprawled corpse damming the flow about fifty yards up from the jetty. The occasional semilucid drunk or pipe smoker stared at them from various nooks and shadows, but they weren't spoken to until they crested a rise and found stones beneath their feet once again.

"Drakasha," shouted a corpulent man in leathers with blackened-iron studs, "welcome back to civilization!" The man carried a dim lantern in one hand and a bronze-ringed club in the other. Behind him was a taller fellow, scruffy and potbellied, armed with a long oak staff.

"Handsome Marcus," said Drakasha. "Gods, you get uglier every time I come back. Like someone's slowly sculpting an ass out of a human face. Who's the new charmer?"

"Guthrin. Wise lad decided to give up sailing and join the rest of us big swinging cocks in the glamorous life."

"Yeah? Well," Drakasha said, holding out a closed fist and shaking it so that the coins inside clinked against one another, "I found these in the road. They belong to you?"

"I got a happy home for 'em right here. See now, Guthrin, that's the style. Show this lady some favor and she returns the compliment. Fruitful voyage, Captain?"

"Belly so full we can't swim anymore, Marcus."

"Good on you, Captain. You'll want to hear from the Shipbreaker, then?"

"Nobody *wants* to hear from that waste of a working asshole, but if he wants to open his purse and bend over, I've got a little something in wood and canvas for his collection."

"I'll pass the word. You in for the night?"

"Toehold, Marcus. Just here to fly the flag."

"Fine idea." He glanced around briefly, and then his voice grew more serious. "Chavon Rance has the high table at the Crimson. Just so you can look all-knowing when you walk in the door."

"Obliged to you."

When the two men had strolled on their way down the path toward the jetty, Jean turned to Ezri. "Guards of some sort?"

"Maintainers," she said. "More like a gang. Sixty or seventy of them, and they're what we have for order around here. Captains pay them a little out of every load they bring in, and they beat the rest of their living out of public nuisances. You can pretty much do as you like, long as you hide the bodies and don't burn anything down or wake up half the city. Do that and the Maintainers come out to do a bit of maintaining."

"So what's 'flying the flag,' exactly?"

"Gotta play these games sometimes," said Ezri. "Let everyone in Prodigal know that Zamira's back, that she's got a hold full of swag, that she'll kick their heads in for looking at her cross-eyed. You know? Especially her brother and sister captains."

"Ah. I'm with you."

They entered the city proper; here, at least, were the lights they'd seen from out in the bay, pouring from open windows and doors on both sides of the street. The buildings here had started as respectable stone homes and shops, but time and mischief had marked their faces. Broken windows were covered over with planking from ships or scraps of tattered sailcloth. Many of the houses sprouted leaning wooden additions that looked unsafe to approach, let alone live in; others grew wattle-and-daub third or fourth stories like mushrooms from their old roofs.

Jean felt a sudden pang of grudging nostalgia. Drunkards lying senseless in the alleys. Larcenous children eyeing their party from the shadows. Maintainers in long leather coats thumping some poor bastard senseless behind a cart with no wheels. The sounds of swearing, argument, laughter, and ale sickness pouring from every open window and door . . . This place was, if not quite a fraternal relation to Camorr, at least a first cousin.

"Orchids," hollered someone from a second-story window. "Orchids!"

Zamira acknowledged the drunken shout with a casual wave, and turned right at a muddy crossroads. From the dark mouth of an alley a heavyset man stumbled, wearing nothing but soiled breeches. He had the glassy, unfocused eyes of a Jeremite powder-smoker, and in his right hand was a serrated knife the length and width of Jean's forearm.

"Coin or suck," said the man, threads of saliva dangling down his chin. "Don't care which. Got needs. Give us a—"

If he was oblivious to the fact that he was facing eight opponents, he wasn't oblivious to Rask knocking his blade hand aside and shoving him back into the alley by his neck. What happened next took only a few seconds; Jean heard a wet gurgle, and then Rask was stepping back out into the street, wiping one of his own knives on a rag. He threw this rag into the alley behind him and hooked his thumbs into his belt. Ezri and Drakasha seemed to think the incident not even worthy of comment, and they strolled on, casual as temple-goers on Penance Day morning.

"Here we are," said Ezri as they reached the top of another small hill. A wide, half-paved square, its muddy sections crisscrossed by overlapping wagon tracks, was dominated by a fat two-story building with a portico constructed around the chopped-off stern facing of an old ship. Time, weather, and no doubt countless brawls had scuffed and chipped its elaborate scrollwork, but people could be seen drinking and reveling behind the second-story windows, in what would have been the great cabin. Where the rudder had once been mounted was now a heavy double door, flanked by alchemical globes (the round thick kind that were nearly impossible to break) in an approximation of stern lanterns.

"The Tattered Crimson," Ezri continued. "It's either the heart of Port Prodigal or the asshole, depending on your perspective."

To the left of the entryway was a ship's longboat, mounted to the building by heavy wooden struts and iron chains. A few human arms and legs seemed to be sticking out of it. As Jean watched, the doors to the Tattered Crimson slammed outward and a pair of brutes emerged, carrying a limp old man between them. Without ceremony or pity, they heaved him into the boat, where his arrival caused some incoherent shouting and flailing of limbs.

"Now watch your step," said Ezri, grinning. "Get too drunk to stand and they throw you overboard. Some nights there's ten or twenty people piled up in that boat."

A moment later Jean was squeezing past those brutes, into the familiar smells of a busy tavern at an hour closer to dawn than dinner. Sweat, scalded meat, puke, blood, smoke, and a dozen kinds of bad ale and wine: the bouquet of the civilized nightlife.

The place looked to be constructed for a clientele that would be waging war not just on one another but on the bar and pantry. The bar itself, at the far side of the room, was enclosed from countertop to ceiling by iron panels, leaving only three narrow windows through which the staff could serve drinks and food like archers firing from murder-holes.

There were only floor tables down here, in the Jereshti fashion; low surfaces around which men and women sat, knelt, or lay on scuffed cushions. In the cavelike fug of the dimly lit room, they played cards and dice, smoked, drank, arm wrestled, argued, and tried to laugh off the attention of the prowling heavies who were obviously looking for candidates to toss into the boat outside.

Conversation wavered as Drakasha's party appeared; cries of "Orchids!" and "Zamira's back!" could be heard. Drakasha nodded to the room at large and slowly turned her gaze up to the second floor.

Stairs went up either side of the common room; at the sides, the second floor was little more than a railed walkway. Above the bar and the entry, it expanded into wider balconies with Therin-style tables and chairs. Jean presumed that the "high table" was the one he'd glimpsed from the outside. A moment later Drakasha began to move toward the stairs that led in that very direction.

A sudden current of excitement rose in the air: too many conversations halted absolutely; too many eyes followed their passage. Jean cracked his knuckles and prepared himself for things to get interesting.

Atop those stairs was a railed alcove backed by the windows overlooking the darkened square from which they'd just come. Red silk banners hung in niches with alchemical globes behind them, giving off a low, vaguely ominous rose-tinted light. Two wide tables had been pushed together to accommodate a party of twelve, all clearly sailors and toughs much, Jean realized to his own amusement, like themselves.

"Zamira Drakasha," said the woman at the head of the table, rising from her chair. She was young, roughly Jean's own age, with the sun-browned skin and faint lines edging her eyes that told of years spent on the water. Her sand-colored hair was drawn back into three tails, and though shorter than Zamira she looked to outweigh her by about two stone. Tough and round, this one, with a well-worn saber hilt visible at her belt.

"Rance," said Drakasha, "*Chay.* It's been a long night, love, and you know full well you're sitting at my table."

"That's damn peculiar. It's got our drinks on top of it,

and our asses in its chairs. You think it's yours, maybe you should take it with you when you're out of town."

"When I'm away on my business, you mean. Fighting my ship, flying the red flag. You know where the sea is, right? You've seen other captains coming and going—"

"I don't have to break myself month in and month out, Drakasha. I just pick richer targets in the first place."

"You're not hearing me, Chay. I really don't care what sort of dog gnaws bones at my place when I'm gone," said Drakasha, "but when I come back I expect her to crawl under the table where she belongs."

Rance's people exploded out of their chairs, and she raised a hand, grinning fiercely. "Pull steel, you dusty cunt, and I'll kill you fair in front of witnesses. Then the Maintainers can haul your crew back to the docks for brawling and Ezri here can see how your brats like the taste of *her* tits—"

"Show your hand, Rance. You think you're fit to keep this spot?"

"Name the test and I'll leave you weeping."

"We're going to have the house brutes on us—," Jean whispered to Ezri.

"No," she said, waving him to silence. "Calling out isn't like plain brawling. Especially not between captains."

"For the table," shouted Drakasha, reaching for a half-empty bottle, "all the Crimson as our witness, the contest is drinks. First on her ass takes her sorry crew and moves down to the floor."

"I was hoping for something that'd take longer than ten minutes," said Rance. "But I accept. You be my guest with that bottle."

Zamira looked around, then snatched two small clay cups of equal size from places previously occupied by Rance's crewfolk. She tossed their contents onto the tabletop, then refilled them from the bottle. It was white Kodari brandy, Jean saw, rough as turpentine, packing quite a sting. Rance's crew backed up against the windows, and Rance herself came around the table to stand beside Zamira. She lifted one of the cups.

"One thing," said Zamira. "You're gonna take your first drink Syrune-fashion."

"What the hell's that?"

"Means you drink it through your fucking eyes." Drakasha's left arm was a blur as she whipped her own cup from the tabletop and dashed its contents into Rance's face. Before Rance could even scream, Drakasha's right arm came up just as fast. Her gloved fist, rings and all, met Rance's jaw with the sound of a cracking whip, and the younger woman hit the floor so hard the cups atop the table rattled.

"Are you on your ass down there, love, or is that your head? Anybody think there's a difference?" Drakasha stood over Rance and slowly tipped the contents of the second clay cup into her own mouth. She swallowed it all without flinching and tossed the cup over her shoulder.

"You said it was gonna be—"

Before Rance's angry crewman, probably her first mate, could finish his protest Locke stepped forward with his hand upraised.

"Zamira kept her oath. The test *was* a drink, and your captain's on her ass."

"But—"

"Your captain should've had the wit to be more specific," said Locke, "and she lost. You going to take her oath back *for* her?"

The man grabbed Locke by the front of his tunic. The two of them scuffled briefly and Jean darted forward, but before the situation went to hell Rance's sailor was hauled back, grudgingly but firmly, by his friends.

"Who the hell are you, anyway?" he shouted.

"Orrin Ravelle," said Locke.

"Never fucking heard of you."

"I think you'll remember me, though." Locke dangled a small leather pouch in front of the man. "Got your purse, prickless."

"You *motherfu*—"

Locke gave the purse a hard toss backward, and it landed somewhere down among the hundred or so patrons watching the action on the balcony with eyes wide and mouths open.

"*Oops,*" said Locke, "but I'm sure you can rely on all the upstanding folks down there to keep it safe for you."

"Enough!" Zamira reached down, grabbed Rance by the collar, and hoisted her to a sitting position. "Your captain called it and your captain lost. *Is she your captain?*"

"Yes," said the man, scowling.

"Then keep her oath." Zamira dragged Rance to the head of the stairs and knelt in front of her. "Not such a very regal bitch after all, eh, Chay?"

Rance reared back to spit blood in Drakasha's face, but the older captain's slap was faster, and the blood spewed out across the stairs.

"Two things," said Zamira. "First, I'm calling the council for tomorrow. I'll expect to see you there at the usual place and time. Nod your silly head."

Rance nodded, slowly.

"Second, I don't have brats. I have a daughter and a son. And if you *ever* forget that again, I'll carve your fucking bones into toys for them."

With that, she heaved Rance down the stairs. By the time she landed in a heap at the bottom, her chagrined crew was hurrying after her, under the triumphant stares of Drakasha's party.

"See you around . . . Orrin Ravelle," said the purseless sailor.

"Valterro," said Zamira sternly, "this was all business. Don't make it personal."

The man looked no happier, but he moved off with the rest of Rance's crew.

"That bit about your children sounded very personal," whispered Jean.

"So I'm a hypocrite," muttered Drakasha. "You want to protest, you can take a drink Syrune-fashion." Zamira moved to the rail overlooking the main floor and raised her voice to a shout. "Zacorin! You hiding down there somewhere?"

"Hiding's the word, Drakasha," came a voice from behind the windows of the armored bar. "War over yet?"

"If you've got a cask of anything that doesn't taste like pig sweat, send it up. And some meat. And Rance's bill. Poor dear needs all the help she can get."

There was an outbreak of laughter across the floor. Rance's crew, carrying her out by her arms and legs, didn't look even vaguely amused.

"So that's that," said Zamira, settling into the chair Rance had just vacated. "Make yourselves comfortable. Welcome to the high table at the Tattered Crimson."

"Well," said Jean as he took a seat between Locke and Ezri, "did that go as you hoped?"

"Oh yeah." Ezri smirked at Drakasha. "Yeah, I'd say our flag is *flown*."

8

THEY DID their best to look relaxed and amused for the better part of an hour, helping themselves to the Crimson's mediocre dark ale and all the better liquors Rance's crew had left behind. Grease-blanketed duck was the dish of the evening; most of them treated it as decoration, but Rask and Konar gradually brutalized it down to a pile of bones.

"So what do we do now?" asked Locke.

"Word'll go out to all the usual vultures that we're back in," said Drakasha. "Less than a day or two and they'll be courting us. Liquor and rations will go first; always easiest to sell. Nautical spares and stores we keep for ourselves. As for the silks and finer things, those independent traders moored at the Hospital docks are our friends in that regard. They'll try to clean us out for fifteen to twenty percent of market value. Good enough for us—then they haul it back across the sea and sell it at full price with innocent smiles on their faces."

"What about the *Messenger*?"

"When she shows up, the Shipbreaker will pay us a visit. He'll offer us piss in a clay bowl and we'll talk him up to piss in a wooden jug. Then she's his problem. She's worth maybe six thousand solari with her rigging intact; I'll be lucky to take him for anything near two. His crew will take her east and sell her to some eager merchant for about four; undercutting his competition and carving a fat profit at the same time."

"Hell," said Lieutenant Delmastro, "some of the ships on the Sea of Brass routes have been taken and resold three or four times."

"This Shipbreaker," said Locke, feeling a scheme in the birthing, "I take it the fact that his trade is also his name means he doesn't have any competitors?"

"All dead," said Delmastro. "The ugly and publicly instructive way."

"Captain," said Locke, "how long will all of this take? It's nearly the end of the month, and—"

"I'm well aware of what day it is, Ravelle. It takes as long as it takes. Maybe three days, maybe seven or eight. While we're here everyone on the crew gets at least one chance at a day and night ashore, too."

"I—"

"I haven't forgotten the matter you're concerned about," Drakasha said. "I'll bring it to the council tomorrow. After that, we'll see."

"Matter?" Delmastro looked genuinely confused. Locke had been half expecting Jean to have told her by now, but apparently they'd been spending their private time in a wiser and more diverting fashion.

"You'll find out tomorrow, Del. After all, you'll be at the council with me. No more on the subject, Ravelle."

"Right." Locke sipped beer and held up a finger. "Something else, then. Let me request a few things of you in private before this Shipbreaker comes calling. Maybe I can help you squeeze a higher price out of the fellow."

"He's not a fellow," said Drakasha. "He's as slippery as a pus-dipped turd and about as pleasant."

"So much the better. Think on Master Nera; at least let me make the attempt."

"No promises," said Zamira. "I'll hear you, at least."

"Orchids," boomed a deep-voiced man as he appeared at the top of the stairs. "Captain Drakasha! You know they're still pulling Rance's teeth out of the walls downstairs?"

"Rance fell ill with a sudden bout of discourtesy," said Zamira. "Then she just fell. Hello, Captain Rodanov."

Rodanov was one of the largest men Locke had ever seen; he must have been just shy of seven feet. He was about Zamira's age, and somewhat round in the belly. But his long, muscle-corded arms looked as though they'd be about right for strangling bears, and the fact that he didn't deign to carry a weapon said much. His face was long and heavy-jawed, his pale hair receding, and his eyes were bright with the satisfied humor of a man who feels himself equal to the world. Locke had seen his type before, among the better *garristas* of Camorr, but none so towering; even Big Konar could only outdo him in girth.

Incongruously, his huge hands were wrapped around a pair of delicate wine bottles, made of sapphire-colored glass with silver ribbons below their corks. "I took a hundred bottles of last year's Lashani Blue out of a galleon a few months ago. I saved a few because I knew you had a taste for it. Welcome back."

"Welcome to the table, Captain." At Drakasha's gesture, Ezri, Jean, Locke, and Konar shuffled one chair to the left, leaving the chair next to Zamira open. Jaffrim settled into it and passed her the wine bottles. When she offered her right hand he kissed it, then stuck out his tongue.

"Mmm," he said. "I always wondered what Chavon would taste like."

He helped himself to a disused cup as Zamira laughed. "Who's closest to the ale cask?"

"Allow me," said Locke.

"Most of you I've met," said Rodanov. "Rask, of course, I'm shocked as hell you're still alive. Dantierre, Konar, good to see you. Malakasti, love, what's Zamira got that I haven't? Wait, I'm not sure I want to know. And *you*." He slipped an arm around Lieutenant Delmastro and gave her a squeeze. "I didn't know Zamira still let children run free on deck. When are you going to reach your growth?"

"I grew in all the right directions." She grinned and feigned a punch to his stomach. "You know, the only reason people think your ship's a three-master is because you're always standing on the quarterdeck."

"If I take my breeches off," said Rodanov, "it suddenly looks as though she's got *four*."

"We might believe that if we hadn't seen enough naked Vadrans to know better," said Drakasha.

"Well, *I'm* no shame to the old country," said Rodanov as Locke passed him a cup full of beer. "And I see you've been picking up new faces."

"Here and there. Orrin Ravelle, Jerome Valora. This is Jaffrim Rodanov, captain of the *Dread Sovereign*."

"Your health and good fortune," said Rodanov, raising his cup. "May your foes be unarmed and your ale unspoiled."

"Foolish merchants and fine winds to chase them on," said Zamira, raising one of the wine bottles he'd given her.

"Did you have a good sweep this time out?"

"Holds are fit to bust," said Drakasha. "And we pulled in a little brig, about a ninety-footer. Ought to be here by now, actually."

"That the *Red Messenger*?"

"How'd you—"

"Strozzi came in just yesterday. Said he swooped down on a brig with bad legs and was about to pluck her when he found one of your prize crews waving at him. This was about sixty miles north of Trader's Gate, just off the Burning Reach. Hell, they might be crawling through Trader's Gate as we speak."

"More power to them, then. We came in through the Parlor."

"Not good," said Rodanov, looking less than pleased for the first time since he'd come up. "Heard some strange things about the Parlor lately. His Eminence the Fat Bastard—"

"Shipbreaker," Konar whispered to Locke.

"—sent a lugger east last month and says it got lost in a storm. But I hear from reliable lips that it never made it out of the Parlor."

"I thought speed would be the greater virtue coming in," said Drakasha, "but next time back, I'll use the Gate if it takes a week. You can pass that around."

"It'll be my advice, too. Speaking of which, I hear you want to call the council tomorrow."

"There's five of us in town. I've got . . . curious business from Tal Verrar. And I want a closed meeting."

"One captain, one first," said Rodanov. "Right. I'll pass the word to Strozzi and Colvard tomorrow. I take it Rance already knows?"

"Yes."

"She might not be able to speak."

"She won't need to," said Drakasha. "I'm the one with the story to tell."

"So be it," said Rodanov. " 'Let us speak behind our hands, lest our lips be read as the book of our designs, and let us find some place where only gods and rats may hear our words aloud.' "

Locke stared at Rodanov; that was Lucarno, from—

"*The Assassin's Wedding*," said Delmastro.

"Yeah, easy," said Rodanov with a grin. "Nothing more difficult sprang to mind."

"What a curiously theatrical bent you Brass Sea reavers seem to have," said Jean. "I knew Ezri had a taste—"

"I only quote Lucarno for her," said Rodanov. "I myself hate the bastard. Mawkish sentiment, obvious self-satisfaction, and so many little puns about fucking so all the Therin Throne's best-dressed twits could feel naughty in public. Meanwhile the Bondsmagi and my ancestors rolled dice to see who got to burn the empire down first."

"Jerome and I are both very fond of Lucarno," said Delmastro.

"And that is because you don't know any better," said Rodanov. "Because the plays of the early Throne poets are kept in vaults by pinheads while Lucarno's merest specks of vomit are exalted by anyone with coins to waste on scribes and bindery. His plays aren't preserved, they're *perpetrated*. Mercallor Mentezzo—"

"Mentezzo's all right," said Jean. "His verse is fair, but he uses the chorus like a crutch and always throws the gods in at the end to solve everyone's problems—"

"Mentezzo and his contemporaries *built* Therin Throne drama from the Espardri model," said Rodanov, "invigorating dull temple rituals with relevant political themes. The limitations of their structure should be forgiven; by comparison, Lucarno had their entire body of work to build upon, and all he added to the mix was tawdry melodrama—"

"Whatever he added, it's enough that four hundred years after the scourging of Therim Pel, Lucarno is the *only* playwright with Talathri's formal patronage whose work is still preserved in its entirety and regularly prepared in new editions—"

"An appeal to the tastes of the groundlings is *not* equivalent to a valid philosophical analysis of the works in question! Lucestra of Nicora wrote in her letters to—"

"Begging everyone's pardon," said Big Konar, "but it ain't polite to have an argument if nobody else knows what the *fuck* you're arguing about."

"I have to admit that Konar is right," said Drakasha. "I can't tell if you two are about to pull steel or found a mystery cult."

"Who the hell are you?" asked Rodanov, his eyes fixed on Jean. "I haven't had anyone to discuss this with for years."

"I had an unusual childhood," said Jean. "Yourself?"

"The, ah, prevailing vanity of my youth was that the Therin Collegium needed a master of letters and rhetoric named Rodanov."

"What happened?"

"Well, there was a certain professor of rhetoric, see, who'd come up with a foolproof way to run a betting shop out of the Hall of Studious Reflection. Gladiator pits, collegium boat races, that sort of thing. He used his students as message runners, and since money can be used to buy beer, that made him our personal hero. Of course, when he had to flee the city it was whips and chains for the rest of us, so I signed on for shit-work aboard a merchant galleon—"

"When was this?" interrupted Locke.

"Hell, this was back when the gods were young. Must be twenty-five years."

"This professor of rhetoric...was his name Barsavi? Vencarlo Barsavi?"

"How the *hell* could you possibly know that?"

"Might have...crossed paths with him a few times." Locke grinned. "Traveling in the east. Vicinity of Camorr."

"I heard rumors," said Rodanov. "Heard the name once or twice, but never made it to Camorr myself. Barsavi, really? Is he still there?"

"No," said Jean. "No, he died a couple of years ago, is what I heard."

"Too bad." Rodanov sighed. "Too damn bad. Well...I can tell I've detained you all for too long nattering about people who've been dead for centuries. Don't take me too seriously, Valora. A pleasure to meet you. You as well, Ravelle."

"Good to see you, Jaffrim," said Zamira, rising from her chair along with him. "Until tomorrow, then?"

"I'll expect a good show," he said. "Evening, all."

"One of your fellow captains," said Jean as Rodanov descended the stairs. "Very interesting. So why didn't he want our table, then?"

"*Dread Sovereign*'s the biggest ship any Port Prodigal captain has ever had," said Zamira, slowly. "And she's got the biggest crew by far. Jaffrim doesn't need to play the games the rest of us do. And he knows it."

There was no conversation at the table for several minutes, until Rask suddenly cleared his throat and spoke in a low, gravelly voice.

"I saw a play once," he said. "It had this dog that bit a guy in the balls—"

"Yeah," said Malakasti. "I saw that, too. 'Cause the dog loves sausage, and the man is always feeding him sausage, and then he takes his breeches off—"

"Right," said Drakasha. "The very next person who mentions a play of any sort is going to swim back to the *Orchid*. Let's go see how badly our friend Banjital Vo wanted his silver."

9

REGAL WOKE Locke the next day just in time for the noon watch change. Locke plucked the kitten off the top of his head, stared into his little green eyes, and said, "This may come as quite a shock to you, but there is just no way in all the hells that I'm getting attached to you, you sleep-puncturing menace."

Locke yawned, stretched, and walked out into a soft warm rain falling from a sky webbed by cataracts of cloud. "Ahhh," he said, stripping to his breeches and letting the rain wash some of the smell of the Tattered Crimson from his skin. It was strange, he reflected, how the myriad stinks of the *Poison Orchid* had become familiar, and the smell of the sort of places he'd spent years in had become intrusive.

Drakasha had shifted the *Orchid* to a position just off one of the long stone piers in the Hospital anchorage, and Locke saw that a dozen small boats had come up along the larboard side. While five or six armed Blue watch held the entry port, Utgar and Zamira were negotiating vigorously with a man standing atop a launch filled with pineapples.

The early afternoon was consumed by the coming and going of boats; assorted Prodigals appeared offering to sell everything from fresh food to alchemical drugs, while representatives from the independent traders came to inquire about the goods in the hold and view samples under Drakasha's watchful eye. The *Orchid* temporarily became a floating market square.

Around the second hour of the afternoon, just as the rain was abating and the sun burning through the clouds above, the *Red Messenger* appeared out of the Trader's Gate passage and dropped anchor beside the *Orchid*. Nasreen, Gwillem, and the prize crew came back aboard, along with several of the ex-Messengers who'd recovered enough to move around.

"What the hell is *he* doing here?" one of them hollered when he saw Locke.

"Come with me," said Jabril, putting an arm around the man's shoulder. "Nothin' I can't explain. And while I'm at it, I'll tell you about a thing called the scrub watch...."

Scholar Treganne ordered a boat lowered so she could visit the *Messenger* and examine the injured still aboard her. Locke helped hoist the smallest boat down, and while he was doing so Treganne crossed paths with Gwillem at the entry port.

"We've traded cabins," she said gruffly. "I've got your old compartment, and you can have mine."

"What? *What?* Why?"

"You'll find out soon enough."

Before the Vadran could ask any more questions, Treganne had clambered over the side and Zamira had taken him by the arm.

"What sort of bid will the Shipbreaker open with for her?"

"Two silvers and a cup of cowpox scabs," said Gwillem.

"Yes, but what can I reasonably talk him up to?"

"Eleven or twelve hundred solari. He's going to need two new topgallant masts, as the fore was sprung as well. It just didn't come down. New yards, some new sails. She's had work done recently, and that's a help, but a look at her timbers will show her age. She's got maybe ten years of use left in her."

"Captain Drakasha," said Locke, stepping up beside Gwillem. "If I may be so bold—"

"This scheme you were talking about, Ravelle?"

"I'm sure I can squeeze at least a few hundred more solari out of him."

"Ravelle?" Gwillem frowned at him. "Ravelle, the former captain of the *Red Messenger*?"

"Delighted to meet you," said Locke, "and all I need to borrow, Captain, are some better clothes, a few leather satchels, and a pile of coins."

"What?"

"Relax. I'm not going to spend them. I just need them for show. And you'd better let me have Jerome as well."

"Captain," said Gwillem, "why is Orrin Ravelle alive and a member of the crew and asking you for money?"

"Del!" hollered Drakasha.

"Right here," she said, appearing a moment later.

"Del, take Gwillem aside and explain to him why Orrin Ravelle is alive and a member of the crew."

"But why is he asking you for money?" said Gwillem. Ezri grabbed him by the arm and pulled him away.

"My people expect to be paid for the *Messenger*," said Drakasha. "I need to be sure whatever you're scheming won't actually make things worse."

"Captain, in this matter I'd be acting *as* a member of your crew—lest you forget, I have a share of what we get for the *Messenger*, too."

"Hmmm." She looked around and tapped her fingers on the hilt of one of her sabers. "Better clothes, you say?"

10

THE SHIPBREAKER'S agents, primed by rumors from the night before, were swift to spot the new sail in Prodigal Bay. At the fifth hour of the afternoon, an ornate barge rowed by banks of slaves pulled alongside the *Red Messenger*.

Drakasha waited to receive the occupants of the barge with Delmastro, Gwillem, and two dozen armed crewfolk. First up the side was a squad of guards, men and women sweating beneath armor of boiled leather and chain. Once they'd swept the deck with their eyes, a team of slaves leapt aboard and rigged lines to haul a hanging chair from barge to ship. Sweating furiously, they strained to heave this chair and its occupant up to the entry port.

The Shipbreaker was exactly as Drakasha remembered. An old, paper-skinned Therin so distended with fat that it looked as though he'd popped his seams and his viscous flesh was pouring out into the world around him. His jowls ended somewhere below the middle of his neck, his fingers were like burst sausages, and his wattles had so little firmament behind them they quivered when he blinked. He managed to rise from his chair, with the help of a slave at either hand, but he didn't look remotely comfortable until another slave produced a wide lacquered shelf, a sort of portable table. This was set before him, and he heaved his massive belly atop it with a groan of relief.

"A limping brig," he said to no one in particular. "One t'gallant mast gone and the other one fit for firewood. Somewhat aged. A lady whose fading charms are ill concealed by recent layers of paint and gilt. *Oh*. Forgive me, Zamira. I did not see you standing there."

"Whereas I felt the ship heel over the instant you came aboard," said Drakasha. "She was tough enough to pull through a summer's-end storm even in the hands of an incompetent. Her lines are clean, topgallant masts are cheap, and she's sweeter by far than most of the heaps you haul to the east."

"Heaps procured for me by captains like yourself. Now,

I'll want to peek under her breeches and see if she has any quim left to speak of. Then we can discuss the size of the favor I'll be doing you."

"Pose all you like, old man. I'll have a fair price for a fair ship."

"Fair she is," said Leocanto Kosta, choosing that moment to emerge from his lurking place within the companionway. The *Orchid*'s little store of fine clothing had furnished him with a veneer of wealth. His mustard-brown coat had cloth-of-silver cuffs, his tunic was unstained silk, his breeches were passable, and his shoes were polished. They were also large enough for a man of Jerome's build, but Kosta had stuffed them with rags to help them fit. One couldn't have everything.

A borrowed rapier hung from his belt, and several of Zamira's rings gleamed on his fingers. Behind him came Jerome, dressed as the Dutiful Manservant of Common Demeanor, carrying three heavy leather satchels over his shoulder. The speed with which they'd assumed these roles led Zamira to infer they'd used them elsewhere.

"M'lord," said Drakasha. "Have you finished your inspection?"

"I have. And, as I said, fair. Not excellent, but hardly a deathtrap. I can see fifteen years in her, with a bit of luck."

"Who the fuck might you be?" The Shipbreaker regarded Kosta with eyes like a bird suddenly confronted by a rival's beak just as it's about to seize a worm.

"Tavrin Callas," said Kosta. "Lashain."

"A peer?" asked the Shipbreaker.

"Of the Third. You don't need to use my title."

"Nor will I. Why are you sniffing around this ship?"

"Your skull must be softer than your belly. I'm angling to buy her from Captain Drakasha."

"*I* am the one who buys ships in Prodigal Bay."

"By what, the writ of the gods? I'm in funds and that's all that signifies."

"Your funds won't help you swim, boy—"

"*Enough*," said Drakasha. "Until one of you pays for it, this is my ship you're standing on."

"You're very far from home, pup, and you cross me at your—"

"You want this ship, you pay full weight of metal for it," Drakasha seethed, her irritation genuine. The Shipbreaker was powerful and useful, but in a contest of sheer force any Brass Sea captain could crush him beneath their heel. Lack of competition led him to presume too much upon the patience of others. "If Lord Callas tenders the best offer, I'll take it from him. Are we through being foolish?"

"I'm prepared to buy my ship," said Kosta.

"Now hold it, Captain," said Delmastro on cue. "We know the Shipbreaker can pay. But we've yet to see the lordship's coin."

"Del's right," said Drakasha. "We use letters of credit to wipe our asses down here, Lord Callas. You'd best have something heavy in those bags."

"Of course," said Kosta, snapping his fingers. Jerome stepped forward and dropped one satchel on the deck at Drakasha's feet. It landed with a jangling clink.

"Gwillem," she said, motioning him forward. He crouched over the satchel, unbound its clasps, and revealed a pile of gold coins—in actuality, a combination of Zamira's ship's purse and the funds Leocanto and Jerome had brought to sea. Gwillem lifted one, held it up to the sunlight, scratched it, and bit it. He nodded.

"The real thing, Captain. Tal Verrar solari."

"Seven hundred in that bag," said Kosta, which was the cue for Jerome to throw the second one down on the deck beside it. "Seven hundred more."

Gwillem unclasped the second satchel, allowing the Shipbreaker to see that it, too, was apparently brimming with gold. At least it was for five or six layers of solari above a silk pocket filled with silvers and coppers. The third satchel was as much a sham, but Zamira hoped that Kosta wouldn't have to make his point again.

"And from that," said Leocanto, "I'll give you one thousand to commence."

"The edges of his coins could be shaved," said the Shipbreaker. "This is intolerable, Drakasha. Bring scales from your ship, and I'll have mine fetched up."

"These coins are pristine," said Kosta, gritting his teeth. "Every last one. I know you'll check them, Captain, and I know what my life would be worth if you found any of them debased."

"But—"

"Your deep concern for my welfare is noted, Shipbreaker," said Drakasha. "But Lord Callas is entirely correct and I judge him sincere. He offers a thousand. Do you wish to better that?"

"Legs are open, old man," said Leocanto. "Can you really get it up?"

"One thousand and ten," said the Shipbreaker.

"Eleven *hundred*," said Kosta. "Gods, I feel like I'm playing cards with my stablehands."

"Eleven hundred," wheezed the Shipbreaker, "and fifty."

"Twelve hundred."

"I have yet to even examine her timbers—"

"Then you should have hauled yourself across the bay faster. Twelve hundred."

"Thirteen!"

"That's the spirit," said Kosta. "Pretend you can keep up with me. Fourteen hundred."

"Fifteen," said the Shipbreaker. "I warn you, Callas, if you push this price higher there will be consequences."

"Poor old lardbucket, forced to make do with a merely ridiculous profit rather than an obscene one. Sixteen hundred."

"Where did you *come* from, Callas?"

"Booked passage on an independent trader."

"Which one?"

"None of your gods-damned business. I'm good for sixteen. What are—"

"*Eighteen*," hissed the Shipbreaker. "Are you running out of purses, you Lashani pretender?"

"Nineteen," said Kosta, injecting a note of concern into his voice for the first time.

"Two thousand solari."

Leocanto made a show of conferring briefly with Jerome. He looked down at his feet, muttered, "Fuck you, old man," and gestured for Jerome to collect the satchels from the deck.

"To the Shipbreaker," said Zamira, suppressing a huge smile. "For two thousand."

"Ha!" The Shipbreaker's face became contorted with triumph that looked nearly painful. "I could buy ten of you on a whim, whelp. If I ever felt the need to scabbard my cock in something foreign and useless."

"Well, you won," said Leocanto. "Congratulations. I'm ever so chagrined."

"You should be," said the Shipbreaker. "Since you're suddenly standing on my ship. Now I'd like to hear what you'll bid to keep me from having you spitted over a fire—"

"Shipbreaker," said Drakasha, "until I see two thousand solari in my hands, like all *hells* is this your ship."

"Ah," said the old man. "A technicality." He clapped his hands and his slaves sent the hoist-chair back to the barge, presumably to be loaded with gold.

"Captain Drakasha," said Kosta, "thank you for your indulgence, but I know when it's time to withdraw—"

"Del," said Drakasha, "show Lord Callas and his man to one of our boats. Lord Callas, you're welcome to stay for dinner in my cabin. After that we can...send you back where you belong."

"Indebted to you, Captain." Kosta bowed more deeply than strictly necessary, and then vanished through the entry port with Delmastro and Jerome.

"Gut the wet-eared little prick," said the Shipbreaker, loudly. "Keep his money."

"I'm content with yours," said Zamira. "Besides—I'm rather taken with the idea of having a *genuine* Lashani baron convinced that he owes me his life."

The Shipbreaker's slaves transferred bag after bag of coins to the deck of the *Messenger*, silver and gold, until the agreed-upon price was heaped at Zamira's feet. Gwillem would count it all at leisure, of course, but Zamira felt no anxiety about fraud or debasing. The sacks would contain exactly what they were supposed to, by the logic "Tavrin Callis" had espoused a few minutes earlier. The Shipbreaker kept a dozen well-equipped mercenaries at his fortified estate on the edge of town, but if he cheated a captain he'd have pirates after him in platoons, and his running days were a distant memory.

Drakasha left the Messenger in the hands of the Shipbreaker's guards and slaves, and was back aboard the *Orchid* within half an hour, feeling the contentment that always came with seeing a prize sold off. One less complication to plan around—now her entire crew would be back on one hull, shares would be made, the ship's purse substantially enriched. The injured ex-Messengers who hadn't been with them for the *Kingfisher* sacking presented a slight problem, but to a man they'd opted for the temporary indignity of the scrub watch, if the alternative was to be left in Prodigal in ill health.

"Ravelle, Valora," she said, finding the pair of them sitting in the undercastle shade, talking and grinning along with Del and a dozen crewfolk. "That went better than I expected."

"Seven or eight hundred more than what we might have had otherwise," said Gwillem with surprise.

"That much more fat to marble everyone's cut," said Valora.

"Until the bastard spends some money to check up on the independent traders," said Del, one eyebrow raised in mingled admiration and disbelief. "When he discovers that nobody's brought any Lashani noble anywhere near Prodigal recently—"

"Of course he'll figure out what happened, sooner or later." Kosta waved a hand dismissively. "That's the beauty of it. That sort of uptight, self-loving, threat-making little tyrant...well, you can play 'em like a piece of music. Never in a thousand years would he run around letting anyone else know that you suckered him in broad daylight with such a simple trick. And with the profit margin he scrapes out of every ship he takes from you, there's just no way in hell he'll hit back with anything but fussy words."

"He's got no power to push, if pushing's what comes to his mind," said Zamira. "I call the deed well done. Doesn't mean you can lounge around in those fancy clothes all evening, though. Get them stowed again."

"Of course...Captain."

"And whether or not the Shipbreaker bites his tongue, I think it best to keep you two out of sight for the rest of our time here. You're both confined to the ship."

"What? But—"

"I believe," said Drakasha in an amused but firm tone of voice, "that it might not be wise to let a pair such as you off the leash too frequently. I'll give you a little something extra from the ship's purse for your trouble."

"Oh, fair enough." Kosta began removing the more delicate components of his fine costume. "I suppose I've got no particular urge to get my throat slit in an alley, anyway."

"Wise lad." Zamira turned to Delmastro. "Del, let's get a list together for tonight's Merry Watch. They can go ashore with us when we head in for the council. Let's say ... half the ship's company. Make it fair."

"Right," said Del. "And until we come back from that meeting, they can wait in the boats, conveniently watching for trouble, can't they?"

"Exactly," said Zamira. "Same as all the other crews, I expect."

"Captain," Del whispered almost into Zamira's ear, "what the hell is this meeting about?"

"Bad business, Ezri." She glanced at Leocanto and Jerome, smiling and joking with one another, oblivious of her scrutiny. "Bad if it's true. Bad if it's not."

She put an arm on Ezri's shoulder; this young woman who'd turned her back on life as a pampered Nicoran aristocrat, who'd risen from scrub watch to first mate, who'd nearly been killed a dozen times in half that many years to keep Zamira's precious *Orchid* afloat. "Some of the things you'll hear tonight concern Valora. I can't guess what you two have spoken of in private ... in those rare interludes where you two spend your private moments *speaking*—"

Ezri thrust out her chin, smiled, and didn't deign to blush.

"—but what I have to say may not please you."

"If there's anything to be settled between us," said Ezri softly, "I trust him to settle it. And I'm not afraid to hear anything."

"My Ezri," said Zamira. "Well then, let's get dressed to go meet the relations. Armor and sabers. Oil your scabbards and whet your knives. We might need the tools to make some parting arguments if the conversation goes poorly."

CHAPTER THIRTEEN

POINTS OF DECISION

1

A MILE OF LONELY BEACH separates Port Prodigal from the ruins of its fallen stone sentinel: Castana Voressa, Fort Glorious.

Built to dominate the northern side of the bay serving Fort Glorious before a shift in the fortunes of the Ghostwinds brought an equivalent change to the city's name, the fort would not now suffice to ward off an attack with vulgar language, let alone the blades and arrows of a hostile force.

To say that it was constructed cheaply would be an injustice to skinflint stonemasons; several whole shiploads of Verrari granite blocks were diverted into the home-building trade for wine money by bored officials far from home. Grand plans for walls and towers became grand plans for a wall, and finally modest plans for a smaller wall with barracks, and as a capstone to the entire affair the garrison of soldiers intended for those barracks was lost in transit to a summer's-end storm.

The only useful remnant of the fort is a circular stone pavilion about fifty yards offshore, linked to the main ruins by a wide stone causeway. This was intended to be a platform for catapults, but none ever came. Nowadays, when the pirate captains of Port Prodigal call a council to discuss their affairs, this pavilion is always the place and dusk is always the time. Here the captains do business in private, standing on the stones of a Verrari empire that never was, atop the frustrated ambitions of a city-state that had nonetheless frustrated their own ambitions seven years before.

2

IT BEGAN as every such meeting Zamira could remember; under the purple-red sky of sunset, with lanterns set out atop the old stones, with the humid air thick as an animal's breath and the biting insects out in force.

There was no wine, no food, and no sitting when the council of captains was called. Sitting only made people more inclined to waste time. Discomfort stripped sentiment from everyone's words and brought them to the heart of their problems with haste.

To Zamira's surprise, she and Ezri were the last to arrive. Zamira glanced around at her fellow captains, nodding cordially as she eyed them all in turn.

First there was Rodanov, armed now, with his first mate Ydrena Koros, a trim blond woman only slightly taller than Ezri. She had the poise of a professional duelist and a reputation with the wide-bladed Jereshti scimitar.

Beside them stood Pierro Strozzi, an amiable bald fellow pushing fifty, waited on by his lieutenant, called Eartaker Jack for what he liked to slice from the heads of his fallen foes. It was said that he tanned them and sewed them into elaborate necklaces, which he kept locked in his cabin.

Rance was there, with Valterro at her shoulder as usual. The right side of Rance's jaw was several wince-inducing shades of black and green, but she was standing on her own two feet, and at least had the courtesy not to glare at Zamira when she thought Zamira was watching.

Last but not least was Jacquelaine Colvard, the so-called "Old Woman of the Ghostwinds," still elegant in her mid-sixties, if gray-haired and sun-scorched like old leather. Her current protégé, and therefore lover, was Maressa Vicente, whose fighting and sailing qualities were not yet generally known. The young woman certainly looked capable enough.

Until one of them walked away, then, they were effectively sealed off here from the rest of the world. Parties from their crews, about half a dozen from each ship, mingled uneasily at the end of the causeway. No one else would be permitted to walk upon it until they finished.

So, Zamira thought, how will we do this?

"Zamira," said Rodanov, "you're the one who called the council. Let's hear what's on your mind."

Straight to the action, then.

"Not so much on my mind, Jaffrim, as on all of our heads. I have evidence that the archon of Tal Verrar may have inconvenient plans for us once again."

"Once again?" Rodanov made fists of his huge hands. "It was *Bonaire* who had the inconvenient plans, Zamira; we should have expected Stragos to do what any one of us would have done in his place—"

"I haven't forgotten so much as a day of that war, Jaffrim." Zamira felt her hackles rise despite her determination to be patient. "You know very well that I've come to call it a mistake."

"The Lost Cause," snorted Rodanov. "More like the Dumb Fucking Idea. Would that you'd seen it for folly at the time!"

"Would that you'd done more than *talk* at the time,"

said Strozzi mildly. "Talked and sailed away when the archon's fleet darkened the horizon."

"I never joined your damned Armada, Pierro. I offered to try and draw some of his ships off, and that much I did. Without my help you'd have lost the weather gauge sooner and been flanked from the north. Chavon and I would be the only captains standing here—"

"*Stand off,*" shouted Zamira. "I called the council, and I have more to tell. I didn't bring us here to salt old wounds."

"Speak on," said Strozzi.

"A month ago a brig left Tal Verrar. Her captain stole her from the Sword Marina."

There was a general outburst of muttering and head-shaking at that. Zamira smiled before continuing. "For crew, he stole into Windward Rock and emptied a vault full of prisoners. His intention, and theirs, was to sail south and join us in Port Prodigal. To fly the red flag."

"Who could steal one of the archon's ships from a guarded harbor?" Rodanov spoke as if he only half believed the possibility. "I'd like to meet him."

"You have," said Zamira. "His name is Orrin Ravelle."

Valterro, previously silent behind Captain Rance, sputtered. "*That* fucking little—"

"Quiet," said Zamira. "Lost your purse last night, didn't you? Ravelle has fast hands. Fast hands, a quick mind, a talent for command, and a way with a blade. He earned his way onto my crew by killing four Jeremite Redeemers by himself." Zamira felt vaguely amused to be talking Kosta up with the same half-truths he'd worked so hard to disabuse her of.

"Yet you said he had his own ship," said Rodanov.

"Yes. The *Red Messenger,* sold off to the Shipbreaker just this afternoon. Pierro, you saw it off the Burning Reach a few days ago, didn't you?"

"Indeed."

"There I was, going about my business, innocently scooping up prizes here and there on the Sea of Brass," said Zamira, "when I happened upon Ravelle's *Messenger*. Interrupted his plans, to say the least. I poked holes in his story until I squeezed it all out of him, more or less."

"What story is that?" Rance sounded as though she had a collection of small rocks in her mouth, but she made herself understood.

"Think about it, Rance. Who is Ravelle? One man—a thief, clearly. Trained to do many unusual things. But could one man sail a brig out of the gated harbors in the Sword Marina? Could one man break into Windward Rock, overcome every guard there, free an entire vault full of prisoners, and pack them off in his brig, conveniently stolen the very same night?"

"Uh," said Rance. "Well, possibly—"

"He didn't do it alone." Colvard spoke for the first time, quietly, but her voice drew the eyes of everyone on the pavilion. "Stragos must have let him escape."

"Precisely," said Zamira. "Stragos let him escape. Stragos gave him a crew of prisoners eager for any sort of freedom. Stragos gave him a ship. And he did all this knowing full well that Ravelle would sail south. Come down to join us in our trade."

"He wanted an agent among us," said Strozzi, uncharacteristically excited.

"Yes. More than that." Zamira gazed around the circle of pirates, ensuring that she had their undivided attention before she continued. "He *has* an agent among us. Aboard my ship. Orrin Ravelle and his companion Jerome Valora are currently in the archon's service."

Ezri whipped her head around to stare at Zamira, mouth open. Zamira squeezed her arm unobtrusively.

"Kill them," said Colvard.

"The situation is more complicated and more grave than that," said Zamira.

"Grave indeed, for these two men you speak of. I find it best to make corpses of complications."

"Had I discovered their deceit on my own, it would already be done. But Ravelle is the one who confessed these things to me. He and Valora are, by his claim, entirely unwilling agents. Stragos gave them a latent poison, to which he alone supposedly holds the antidote. Another month will bring them due for their next dose."

"Death would be a favor, then," mumbled Rance. "That bastard will never let them be anything but puppets."

Rodanov waved for her to pipe down. "What, to hear it from Ravelle's lips, was their mission? To spy on us, I presume?"

"No, Jaffrim." Zamira put her hands behind her back and began to slowly pace the center of the pavilion. "Stragos wants us to do him the favor of flying the red flag in sight of Tal Verrar again."

"That makes *no* sense," said Strozzi.

"It does when you consider the archon's needs," said Colvard.

"How?" Rance and Strozzi spoke in unison.

"I hear that things are brittle between the archon and the Priori," said Colvard. "If something were to come along and put a fright into the fine citizens of Tal Verrar, their regard for the army and navy would rise."

"Stragos needs a foe from outside Tal Verrar," said Zamira. "He needs it with all haste, and he needs to be assured that his forces can kick it around with a will." She spread her arms wide, toward her fellow captains and their mates. "We might as well be painted like archery butts."

"There's no profit," said Strozzi, "in bringing a fight to us—"

"For those that take their profit in coin, you're right. But for Stragos, it means everything. He gambled a ship, a crew of prisoners, and his very reputation on Ravelle's mission. You don't think he's serious? He made a laughingstock of himself by allowing a 'pirate' to escape from his secure harbors, all so he could wait to redeem himself by crushing us later." Zamira brought her fists together. "That was Ravelle's task—convince us, trick us, lie to us, bribe us. And if we couldn't be made to serve, his plan was to do it himself, in the *Messenger*."

"Then our course is obvious," said Rodanov. "We don't give Stragos a damn thing. We don't dance around his noose. We keep five hundred miles between ourselves and Tal Verrar, as we have since the war. If need be, we play meek for a few months." He reached over and gave Strozzi's paunch a hearty slap. "We live off our fat."

"If we do that much," said Ydrena Koros, "begging your pardon, Captain. This evidence of yours, Captain Drakasha—the word of these two men seems thinner than—"

"Not just their word," said Zamira. "Think, Koros. They had the *Red Messenger*. Its crew, the survivors of which are now *my* crew, did indeed come from Windward Rock. The archon sent them, all right."

"I concur," said Colvard, "though I also agree with Jaffrim that standing down from provocation is the wisest—"

"*Would* be wisest," interrupted Zamira, "if Stragos was doing this on a whim. But he's not, is he? He's in the fight of his life. His very position is at stake. He needs us."

She paced the center of the pavilion again, reminded of the "arguments" she'd put forth over the years in her pretend turns as a magistrate for initiation rituals. Were these theatrics any more convincing? She hoped to the gods they were.

"If we tip Ravelle and Valora over the side and ignore

them," she said, "or shy away from Tal Verrar, Stragos will try something else. Some other scheme to trick us into a fight, or to convince his people that we're bringing one. Only next time, the gods may not see fit to allow the instruments of his design to fall into our hands. We'll be blind."

"There's more hypothesis here," said Rodanov, "than just about anything I ever heard at the collegium."

"The *Red Messenger* and the prisoners do indicate that Stragos took a gamble," said Colvard. "That he took a gamble indicates that he can't move openly or with confidence. Knowing what we do of the situation in Tal Verrar...I'd say this threat is real. If Stragos requires an enemy, we are the only suitor at this dance that fits his need. What else can he do? Pick a fight with Balinel? Camorr? Lashain? *Karthain?* I hardly think so."

"What would you have us do, Zamira?" Rodanov folded his arms and scowled.

"We possess the means to strike back at the archon."

"We *can't* fight the Verrari navy," said Rodanov. "Nor can we storm the damn city, summon lightning from the sky, or ask the gods to politely dispose of Stragos for us. So by what means may we 'strike back'? Wound his feelings with vicious letters?"

"Ravelle and Valora are expected to report directly to him when they receive their antidote."

"They have access to him," said Colvard. "An assassination!"

"For which they suffer the blame, assuming they live," mused Strozzi.

"Good for them," said Rodanov. "And what, you wished our consent to take them back to Tal Verrar and let them loose? By all means let fly. I'd be happy to lend them a pair of knives."

"There is, from the perspective of Ravelle and Valora, only one minor complication. That they would prefer to acquire a permanent antidote, and *then* do away with Stragos."

"Alas," said Rance, "we so rarely realize our desires in life—"

"Tell them that we have an antidote," said Colvard. "Convince them that we have the means to free them from their condition. Then set them loose upon the archon.... Whether they survive the assassination or not will be of no consequence."

Ezri opened her mouth to disagree, and Zamira fixed her with the most withering glare in her long-practiced arsenal.

"Marvelously devious," said Zamira, when she was certain that Ezri would mind herself. "But too convenient. In their position, would you ever believe such a claim?"

"My skull is beginning to spin," said Strozzi. "What the hell do you wish to do, Zamira?"

"I wish," she said, enunciating each word very carefully, "for none of you to be alarmed if I should find it necessary to raise a bit of ruckus in the immediate vicinity of Tal Verrar."

"And thereby call down our destruction," shouted Rodanov. "Do you want to see Port Prodigal sacked like Montierre? Do you want to see us scattered halfway across the world, and our unguarded trade routes filled with angry Verrari warships?"

"If I do anything," said Zamira, "discretion would be—"

"Impossible," growled Rodanov. "This will finish the job Stragos began when he crushed the Free Armada. This will destroy our way of life!"

"Or *preserve* it." Zamira put her hands on her hips. "If Stragos is determined to push us, he will push us, whether we would dance his tune or no. I have aboard my ship our means, our *only* means, of taking the fight to him. If Stragos is knocked aside, the archonate falls with him. And if the Priori rule Tal Verrar, we can loot this sea at our own merry pace until the day we die."

"Why," said Strozzi, "would you want to play along with the archon's design, even with . . . discretion?"

"Ravelle and Valora aren't saints," said Zamira. "They're not looking to throw their lives away for our benefit. They want to live, and to do that they need time. If Stragos believes they're hard at work on his behalf, he'll grant them the weeks or months necessary to find a solution. And in the meantime, he's likely to stay his other plans."

"Those weeks and months may instead be time enough for him to rouse his city," said Rodanov.

"You must trust me to be delicate," said Zamira. "As brother and sister captains, that's what I'm asking in the end. No matter what you hear from Tal Verrar—trust my judgment."

"A significant request," said Colvard. "You ask no aid from any of us?"

"I can't think of anything that would be *more* counterproductive than for all of us to show up one morning off Tal Verrar, can you? The archon would have his war in about ten minutes. So leave this task to me. A risk to my ship alone."

"A risk to us all," said Rodanov. "You're asking us to put our fates, and that of Port Prodigal, in your hands. Without any oversight."

"How has it been otherwise, these past seven years?" She stared around the circle at each captain in turn. "Each of us has *always* been at the mercy of the others. Any one of us could have raided too far north, attacked a ship carrying someone's royal cousin, murdered too many sailors, or simply grown too greedy to ignore. We've been in peril all the way. I'm merely doing you the courtesy of pointing it out in advance for once."

"And if you fail?" asked Rance.

"If I fail," said Zamira. "There'll be no penalty for you to levy. I'll already be dead."

"Our oaths of noninterference," said Colvard. "That's what you want, isn't it? A promise to keep our swords in their scabbards while you throw the most important rule of our . . . association out your stern window."

"In lieu of any better alternatives," said Zamira, "yes. That's exactly what I'm asking for."

"And if we say no?" Rodanov spoke quietly. "If we, four against one, forbid this?"

"Then we come to a line that we all fear to cross," said Zamira, matching his stare.

"*I* won't forbid it," said Rance. "I'll vow to keep my hands off you, Zamira. If you sweat for my gain, so much the better. And if you die in the process, I'll mourn you not."

"I'll give my oath as well," said Colvard. "Zamira's right. Our collective safety at any given time depends on whichever one of us is the bloody craziest. If there's a chance to kick Maxilan off his pedestal, I pray for your success."

"Obviously Zamira Drakasha votes with Zamira Drakasha," Zamira said, turning her gaze to Rodanov and Strozzi.

"I don't like any of this," said Strozzi. "But if things go to shit, no ship afloat on this sea can run like my *Osprey*." He smiled and cracked his knuckles. "What the hell. You wave your skirt at the archon and see if he's up for a fondle. I won't be anywhere near it."

"It seems," said Rodanov once all eyes had turned to him, "that I have the opportunity to be . . . unsociable." He sighed and rubbed his forehead. "I don't think any of this is wise—but if I may take your promise of discretion to be as binding as my oath of noninterference . . . very well. Go spring this insane scheme."

"Thank you," said Zamira, feeling a warm flush of relief from head to toe. "Wasn't that easier than cutting one another to pieces?"

"This needs to stay between us," said Colvard. "I don't ask for an oath; I *expect* it. Stragos may have other eyes and ears in Prodigal. If this gets out to anyone not standing here, the time we've spent at this meeting—not to mention Zamira's mission—will be an utter waste."

"Right," said Strozzi. "Silence. All gods as our witness."

"All gods as our witness," the others echoed.

"Will you leave immediately?" asked Colvard.

"My crew needs a night ashore. I can't ask them back out without that much. I'll send them in halves, sell off the rest of my swag as fast as I can. Clear the harbor in two or three days."

"Three weeks to Tal Verrar," said Rodanov.

"Right," said Zamira. "No point in any of this if our lads drop dead en route. I intend to be hasty." She stepped up to Rodanov, put one hand on his right cheek, and stood on her toes to kiss his other. "Jaffrim, have I ever let you down?"

"Never since the war," said Rodanov. "Ah, shit. Even that was a poor thing to say. Don't put me on the spot like this, Zamira. Just . . . don't fuck this up."

"Hey," said Colvard, "how can I get some of that attention?"

"I'm feeling generous, but keep your hands to yourself if you prefer to keep them attached." She smiled, kissed Colvard in the middle of her wrinkled forehead, and gave the old woman a hug. Gingerly, because it took pains to accommodate all the swords and daggers the two of them were wearing.

Always thus, thought Zamira. Always thus in this life.

3

UTGAR WAS the one waiting at the entry port to offer a hand when Zamira and Ezri went back up the side of the *Poison Orchid*. It was half past the tenth hour of the evening.

"Welcome back, Captain. How you be?"

"I've spent the day arguing with the Shipbreaker and the council of captains," Zamira muttered. "I require my children and I require a drink. Ezri—"

"Yes?"

"You, Ravelle, Valora. My cabin, immediately."

Once in her cabin, Zamira threw her coat, sabers, Elderglass vest, and hat haphazardly onto her hammock. She settled onto her favorite chair with a groan and welcomed Paolo and Cosetta onto her lap. She lost herself in the familiar smell of their curly dark hair, and gazed with absolute satisfaction at their little fingers as she caught them in her own rough hands. Cosetta's, still so tiny and uncertain...Paolo's, growing longer and more dexterous by the week. Gods, they were growing too fast, too fast.

Their familiar chatter calmed her to the marrow; apparently Paolo had spent the afternoon fighting monsters that lived in her sea chest, while Cosetta now had plans to grow up to be king of the Seven Marrows. Zamira briefly considered explaining the difference between a king and a queen, and deemed it not worth the effort; contradicting Cos would only lead to days of circular argument.

"Be king! Seven marers!" the little girl said, and Zamira nodded solemnly.

"Remember your poor family when you come into your kingdom, darling."

The door opened, and Ezri appeared with Kosta and Valora...or should that be de Ferra? Damn these layered aliases.

"Lock the door," said Zamira. "Paolo, fetch Mommy four glasses. Ezri, can you do the business on one of those bottles of Lashani Blue? They're right behind you."

Paolo, overawed at his responsibility, set four small tumblers out on the lacquered table atop the sea chests. Kosta and de Ferra found seats on floor cushions, and Ezri made quick work of the waxed cork sealing the bottle. The smell of fresh lemons filled the cabin, and Ezri filled each tumbler to the brim with wine the color of the ocean depths.

"Alas, I'm bereft of toasts," said Zamira. "Sometimes one merely needs a drink. Have at it." Holding Cos with her left arm, Zamira downed her wine in one go, relishing the mingled tastes of spice and citrus, feeling the prickles of icy heat slide down her throat.

"Want," said Cosetta.

"This is a Mommy drink, Cos, and you wouldn't like its taste."

"Want!"

"I said—oh, very well. Can't fear the fire if you don't scald your fingertips." She poured the merest dash of the blue wine into her tumbler and handed it carefully to Cos. The girl took it up with an expression of the utmost solemnity, tipped it back into her mouth, and then dropped it on the tabletop with a clatter.

"Like *piss*," she hollered, shaking her head.

"There are some drawbacks," said Zamira as she caught the tumbler before it went over the edge, "to raising children among sailors. But then I myself am no doubt making the largest contribution to her vocabulary."

"*Piiiisssss*," yelled Cosetta, giggling and immensely pleased with herself. Zamira shushed her.

"I have a toast," said Kosta, smirking and raising his glass. "To clear perception. I have just now, after all these weeks, realized who the *real* captain of this vessel is."

De Ferra chuckled and clinked tumblers with him. Ezri, however, left her wine untouched on the table before her and stared down at her hands. Zamira resolved to make this quick; Ezri clearly needed to be alone with Jerome.

"It's like this, Ravelle," said Zamira. "I didn't know I'd be arguing for your plan until I found myself doing so."

"So you're taking us—"

"Back to Tal Verrar. Yes." She poured herself another tumbler of wine and took a more conservative sip. "I've convinced the council not to panic if stories come down from the north concerning the mischief we're about to work."

"Thank you, Captain. I—"

"Don't thank me with words, Ravelle." Zamira sipped her wine again and set the tumbler down. "Thank me by keeping your side of the bargain. Find a way to kill Maxilan Stragos."

"Yes."

"Let me make something else clear." Zamira carefully turned Cosetta in her arms so that the little girl was looking out across the table, straight at Kosta. "Everyone aboard this ship will be risking their life to give you your chance at this scheme. *Every single person.*"

"I . . . I understand."

"If time passes, and we can't find a solution for what Stragos has done to you . . . well, your access to him can't last forever. I'll do everything in my power to help you before it comes to that. But if there's no other alternative, if time runs out and the only way you can take him down is to sacrifice yourself—I won't expect to see you again, do you understand?"

"If it comes to that," said Kosta, "I'll drag him to the judgment of the gods with my bare hands. We'll go together."

"Gods," said Cosetta. "Bare hands!"

"Piss!" shouted Kosta, hoisting his tumbler toward Cosetta, who nearly came apart at the joints with the resulting fit of giggles.

"*Thank you*, Ravelle, for this gift of a daughter who will now be up all night repeating that word..."

"Sorry, Captain. So, when do we leave?"

"Half the crew goes ashore tonight, and the other half tomorrow. We'll be scraping them up in heaps the day after, those that want to stay with us. Hopefully we can be rid of our swag tomorrow. So...two days. Two and a half, maybe. Then we'll see how the *Orchid* flies."

"Thanks, Captain."

"And that's all," Zamira said. "My children are up too late, and I intend to claim the privilege of snoring as loudly as I wish once you're all out of my cabin."

Kosta was the first to take the hint, draining his glass and leaping to his feet. De Ferra followed, and was about to leave when Ezri spoke in a quiet voice. "Jerome. May I see you in my cabin? Just for a few minutes?"

"A few minutes?" Jerome grinned. "Tsk, Ezri, when did you become such a pessimist?"

"Now," she said, wiping the smile from his face. Chagrined, he helped her to her feet.

A moment later, the door to her cabin clicked shut, leaving Zamira alone with her family in one of the quiet interludes that were so damnably rare. For a few brief moments every night, she could imagine that her ship was traveling neither to nor from danger, and she could imagine herself more mother than captain, alone with the ordinary concerns of her children—

"Mommy," said Paolo without any warning, "I want to learn how to fight with a sword."

Zamira couldn't help herself; she stared at him for several seconds, and then cracked up laughing. Ordinary?

Gods, how could any child born to this life be anything re-sembling ordinary?

"Sword," hollered Cosetta, possible future king of the Seven Marrows. "Sword! Sword!"

4

"EZRI, I—"

He saw the slap coming, but it never occurred to him for an instant to try to prevent the blow from landing. She put all of her muscle into it, which was saying something, and tears blurred Jean's vision.

"Why didn't you *tell* me?"

"Tell you—"

She was sobbing now, but her next punch landed on his right arm with undiminished force.

"Ow," he said. "What? What?"

"Why didn't you tell me?"

It was almost a shout; he spread his hands to catch her fists. A punch from her to the ribs or solar plexus and he'd feel it for hours.

"Ezri, please. Tell you what?" He knelt on the narrow floor of her compartment, kissing her fingertips while she tried to yank her hands back. At last he let her, and knelt before her, arms lowered.

"Ezri, if you need to hit me, then by the gods hit me. If that's what you need, I won't fight you for a second. Not ever. Just . . . tell me what you want."

She balled her fists, and Jean braced himself for another swing, but she sank to her knees and wrapped her arms around his neck. Her tears were hot on his cheeks.

"How could you not tell me?" she whispered.

"Anything you want to know, I'll tell you now, just—"

"The poison, Jean."

"Oh," he moaned, slumping sideways against the rear wall of the cabin. She slid with him. "Oh, *shit*."

"You selfish *bastard*, how could you not—"

"Drakasha told the council of captains our story," Jean said numbly. "You were there to hear it."

"From her, not you! How could you do that to me?"

"Ezri, please, it's—"

"You are the only thing," she whispered through the iron grip of her embrace, "the only thing on this whole fucking *ocean* that's mine, Jean Tannen. I don't own this ship. Hell, I don't own this cabin. I don't have a buried fucking treasure. I have no family and no title, not anymore. And then I finally got to take something in return—"

"And it turns out I have . . . one significant flaw."

"We can do something," she said. "We can find someone. Physikers, alchemists—"

"Tried, Ezri. Alchemists and poisoners. We need the antidote from Stragos, or an actual sample of his poison from which to create one."

"And didn't I deserve to know? What if you'd—"

"Dropped dead in here one night? Ezri, what if a Redeemer had put his sword through my skull, or the crew had just murdered me on the day we met?"

"That's not you," she said. "That's not how someone like you dies. I know, I just know—"

"Ezri, you've seen every one of my scars. You know I'm not—"

"This is *different*," she said. "This is something you can't just fight."

"Ezri, I *am* fighting it. I have been fighting it, every single day since the archon put the fucking thing in me. Leocanto and I count the days, do you understand? I would lie awake at night the first few weeks, and I was sure I could feel it, doing something in me." He gulped, and felt his own tears pouring down his face. "Look, when I'm in here it doesn't exist, understand? When I'm with you I can't feel it. I don't *care* about it. This is...it's like a different world. How could I tell you? How could I ruin that?"

"I would kill him," she whispered. "Stragos. Gods, if he was here right now I'd cut his fucking throat—"

"I'd help. Believe me—"

She released her arms from around his neck and they knelt there in the semidarkness, staring at each other.

"I love you, Jean," she whispered at last.

"I love you, Ezri." Saying it was like allowing some sudden release of pressure behind his heart; it felt like breathing in at last after ages spent underwater. "You're like no one else I've ever met."

"I can't let you die," she said.

"It's not you.... You can't—"

"I can do what I damn well please," she said. "I can get you to Tal Verrar. I can buy you time to get what you need from Stragos. I can help you kick his ass."

"Ezri," said Jean, "Drakasha's right. If I can't get what I need from him...taking Stragos down is more important—"

"*Don't* say it."

"I'll do it," he said. "It only makes sense. Gods, I don't want to, but if I have no choice I'll trade myself for him."

"Damn you," she whispered, and faster than he could react she leapt to her feet, seized him by the front of his tunic, and slammed him against the starboard bulkhead. "You will not! Not if we beat him, Jean Tannen. Not if we *win*."

"But if I have no choice—"

"Make a new choice, you son of a bitch." She pinned him to the bulkhead with a kiss that was pure alchemy, and his hands found their way down her tunic, down to her breeches, where he unhitched her weapons belt with as much gratuitous fondling of the areas not covered by it as he could manage.

She took the belt from his hands and flung it against one of the stiffened canvas walls, where it struck with a clattering racket and slid to the floor. "If there is no way, make a way, Jean Tannen. Losers don't fuck in this particular cabin."

He picked her up, making a seat for her from his crossed arms, and whirled her around so that her back was against the bulkhead and her feet were dangling. He kissed her breasts through her tunic, grinning at her reaction. He stopped to put his head against her chest; felt the rapid flutter of her heart beneath his left cheek.

"I would have told you," he whispered. "Somehow."

"Somehow, indeed. 'Man,'" she said, "'What a mouse he is made by conversation—'"

"Oh, it's not enough that I have to take this from you, now I have *Lucarno* chastising me—"

"Jean," she interrupted, pressing his head more firmly against her with a hug. "Stay with me."

"What?"

"This is a good life," she whispered. "You suit it. *We* suit it. After we deal with Stragos . . . stay with me."

"I like it here," said Jean. "Sometimes I think I could stay forever. But there are . . . other places I could show you. Other things we could do."

"I'm not sure I'd adjust well to life on land—"

"Land has its pirates, same as the sea," he murmured between kisses. "I'm one of them. You could—"

"Belay this. We don't have to decide anything now. Just . . . think on what I said. I didn't bring you in here for negotiations."

"What did you bring me here for?"

"Noise," she whispered, starting to pull his tunic off. "Lots and lots of noise."

5

JUST BEFORE the midnight change of watches, Gwillem emerged from his new quarters into the narrow corridor between the ship's four smaller cabins. Scowling, clad only in his breechclout and a hastily thrown-on vest, he stepped across to the door of his old compartment. Bits of flannel rag were stuffed into his ears.

He pounded on the door several times. When no answer was forthcoming, he knocked again and hollered, "Treganne, you bitch, I'll get you for this!"

6

"ARE HER preparations almost complete, then?"

The two men met in the roofless ruins of a stone cottage, south of the city proper, so close to the edge of the eerie jungle that not even drunks and gazers would crawl out to it for shelter. It was near midnight, and a hard rain was falling, warm as spit.

"Got all our junk sold just this afternoon. Been taking on water and ale like crazy. More than enough food already. Once we scrape up everyone that wants to get scraped up tomorrow, I'm sure we're gone."

Jaffrim Rodanov nodded, and for the hundredth time cast his gaze around the broken house and its shadows. Anyone close enough to listen through the noise of the rain would have to be close enough to spot, he reckoned.

"Drakasha said...disturbing things when she called the council. What's she told you about her plans once she's back at sea?"

"Nothing," said the other man. "Peculiar. Usually she gives us a good week to get our skulls busted and our purses sucked dry. She's got a fire under her ass, and it's a mystery to the rest of us."

"Of course," said Rodanov. "She wouldn't tell you any-thing until you were on your way. But she's said nothing about the archon? About Tal Verrar?"

"No. So what do you think she's—"

"I know exactly what she's doing. I'm just not entirely convinced it's wise." Rodanov sighed. "She might call down a heap of shit on everyone in the Ghostwinds."

"So now you—"

"Yeah." Rodanov passed a purse over, giving it a shake so the coins within could be heard. "Just like we discussed. Keep your eyes open. Note what you see. I'll want to hear about it after."

"And the other thing?"

"Got it here," said Rodanov, hefting an oilcloth satchel with a heavy weight inside. "You're *sure* you have a place where this cannot be found—"

"My sea chest. Privilege of rank, right? Got a false bot-tom."

"Good enough." Rodanov passed the satchel over.

"And if I have to . . . use this thing . . ."

"Again, like we discussed. Three times what I just paid you, waiting for you once it's done."

"I want more than that," said the man. "I want a place aboard the *Sovereign*."

"Of course." Rodanov extended his hand, and the other man met his grip. They shook in the traditional Vadran fashion, clasping each other's forearms. "You know I can al-ways use a good man."

"You're using him right now, hey? Just want to be sure I got a place to call home when all this is over. One way or another."

Utgar's grin was the faintest crescent of white against the shadows.

7

NORTH BY east on the Sea of Brass, with the wet southern wind on the starboard quarter, the *Poison Orchid* dashed across the waves like a racing mare at last given her head. It was the third day of Aurim.

After a day lost laboriously navigating the twisting, rock-choked passage called the Trader's Gate, they had spent two more dodging reefs and islands, until the last jungle-crowned dome and the last volcanic smoke of the Ghostwinds had been sunk beneath the horizon.

"This is the game," said Drakasha, addressing the group she'd assembled on the quarterdeck. Delmastro, Treganne, Gwillem, Utgar, Nasreen, Oscarl, and all the skilled mates—carpenters, sailmakers, and so forth. Mumchance listened from his place at the wheel, and Locke listened from the quarterdeck stairs, along with Jean and a half dozen off-watch sailors. If they hadn't exactly been invited to hear the captain's little speech, neither had they been dissuaded. There was no point, when news would travel across a ship faster than fire.

"We're bound for Tal Verrar," said Drakasha. "We're going to allow our new friends Ravelle and Valora to conduct a bit of sneaky business ashore."

"Bounty," said Mumchance.

"He's right," said Gwillem. "Begging your pardon, Captain, but if we haul up in sight of Tal Verrar—"

"If the *Poison Orchid* drops anchor, aye, I'm worth a lot of money. But if we make some adjustments to my pretty ship here and there, alter the sail plan a bit, swap my stern lanterns for something plainer, and paint a false name in huge damn letters at the stern..."

"What shall we call her, Captain?" asked the carpenter.

"I'm partial to *Chimera*."

"That's cheeky," said Treganne. "But what's the gain for the rest of us in this 'sneaky business,' Drakasha?"

"Nothing I care to discuss before the deed is done," said Drakasha. "But the gain for all of us will be substantial. You might say we're going out with the blessing of the whole council of captains."

"Then why aren't they out here lending a hand?" asked Nasreen.

"Because there's only one captain who's best at what she does." Drakasha gave an exaggerated curtsy. "Now, back to duties or to slacking, as you were. Spread the word to everyone."

Locke was slacking a few minutes later, alone with his thoughts at the larboard rail, when Jean took the spot beside him. The sea and sky alike were bronzing around the setting sun, and the warm ocean air was nonetheless refreshing after the sweaty atmosphere of the Ghostwinds.

"You feel anything strange?" asked Jean.

"What, about the—oh, you mean the poison. No. Can't say that I feel any better or worse than I have for a while. But, ah, I'm sure I'll try to get a message to you if I start vomiting up newts or something. Assuming you could hear anyone knocking at that cabin door—"

"Oh, gods. Not you, too. Ezri nearly tipped Gwillem over the taffrail—"

"Well, let's be honest, people will notice the sort of racket that generally accompanies an attack upon the ship—"

"And now *you* are about to have a sudden accident—"

"...by Jeremite Redeemers mounted on cavalry steeds. Where do you find the energy?"

"She makes it easy," said Jean.

"Ah."

"She's asked me to stay," said Jean, looking down at his hands.

"Aboard the ship? Once all of this is over? Assuming there's anything left of us?"

Jean nodded. "And by me, I'm sure she meant you as well—"

"Oh, of course she did," said Locke, not entirely curbing his reflexive tone of sarcasm. "What did you say?"

"I asked her ... I thought maybe she could come with us."

"You love her." Locke nodded to himself before Jean could answer. "You're not just marking time while we're out here. You've really fallen off the cliff, haven't you?"

"Yeah," Jean whispered.

"She's good," said Locke. "She's got wits and fire. She has a real taste for taking things away from people at sword-point, which is an asset in my book. And at least her you can trust at your back in a fight—"

"I've *always* trusted you—"

"To *be* at your back in a fight, sure. But her you can trust not to embarrass everyone before it's over. You two won the day on the *Kingfisher,* not me. And I saw how she got kicked around—most people would have hugged their hammocks for a few days after that. She's too damn stubborn to stop moving. You two really are a good match."

"You make it sound like it's her or you—"

"Of course it doesn't have to be. But things will change—"

"Change, yes. And *improve.* This doesn't have to mean the end of anything."

"Take her with us? Three against the world? Start up the whole thing again, rebuild a gang? Haven't we had this conversation before?"

"Yes, and—"

"I was doing my best impression of a drunken asshole at the time. I know." Locke put his left hand atop Jean's right. "You're right. Things can change, and improve. We've seen it happen to other people; maybe it can happen to us for once. Soon as we finish the Sinspire game, we'll be richer than hell, and no longer welcome in Tal Verrar's polite society. She could come with us...or you could stay with her...."

"I don't know yet," said Jean. "Neither of us knows. We've decided to deal with the question by ignoring it for the duration of the voyage."

"Excellent idea."

"But I want—"

"Listen. When the time comes, you make whatever choice you need to, and you don't think about me, understand? It *is* a fine match. Maybe you could do better—"

Locke grinned to let Jean know that there was no actual need to knock his brains out of his skull.

"—but I know for a solid fact that she couldn't. *Ever.*" So saying, he squeezed Jean's hand. "I'm happy for you. You've gone and stolen something back from this whole dead-end distraction Stragos has shoved us into. Hold it tight."

There seemed nothing else to say, so they stood listening to the cries of the circling gulls and watched the sun sink into the far horizon, bleeding its fire into the sea. Eventually, heavy footsteps sounded on the quarterdeck stairs behind them.

"My boys," said Drakasha, appearing behind them and draping her arms across their shoulders, "just the pair I wanted to speak with. I'm removing you from afternoon watch duty with all the other Reds."

"Um...that's generous," said Locke.

"No it isn't. From now on, you're detached to the carpenter's mercy for afternoons. Since we're slipping into Tal Verrar for your benefit, most of the alterations to the *Orchid* are going to be your responsibility. Painting, carving, rigging—you two will be rather busy."

"Wow," said Locke, "that sounds like an absolutely *grand* way to spend the voyage."

It wasn't.

8

"LAND HO," cried the early evening foremast watch. "Land and fire one point on the starboard bow!"

"Fire?" Locke looked up from his hand in the card game that had broken out in the undercastle. "Shit!" He dropped his cards to the deck, forfeiting his seven-solari bet for the round. Nearly a year's pay for an honest Verrari laborer; common stakes for the games that took place after shares were paid out. There was a lot of spare coinage floating around the ship, since they'd left Port Prodigal in such a hurry.

Emerging from the undercastle, he nearly slammed into Delmastro.

"Lieutenant, is that Tal Verrar?"

"Has to be."

"And the fire? Is that certain?" Fire in the city could mean some sort of disaster, or it could mean civil war. Chaos. Stragos might already be dead, or besieged, or even victorious—and therefore in no further need of Locke or Jean.

"It's the twenty-first, Ravelle."

"I know what bloody day it is; I just—oh. Oh!"

The twenty-first of Aurim; the *Festa Iono,* the grand pageant of the Lord of the Grasping Waters. Locke sighed with relief. Away from the usual rhythms of the city, he'd all but forgotten about the holiday. At the *Festa Iono,* the Verrari gave thanks for Iono's influence on the city's fortunes by ceremonially burning old ships while thousands of drunkards made a mess of the streets and canals. Locke had only ever seen it from the balconies of the Sinspire, but it was a lively time. Hell, that would make slipping into the city easier; there'd be a thousand things going on to keep the watch busy.

"All hands," came the cry from astern. "All hands at the waist! Captain wants a word!"

Locke grinned. In the event of an all-hands call during a card game, the game had to stop, and everyone with a stake in the pot got it back. His seven solari would be returning home soon enough.

The Orchids mustered noisily at the waist, and after a few minutes were waved to silence by Drakasha. The captain set an empty cask beside the mainmast, and Lieutenant Delmastro leapt atop it, wearing a respectable overcoat from the ship's store of fine clothing.

"For the rest of the night," she shouted, "we're the *Chimera,* and we've never even heard of the *Poison Orchid.* I'm the captain! I'll be pacing the quarterdeck if anyone needs anything, and Drakasha will be in her cabin unless things go to hell.

"If another ship hails us, I'll be the one that answers. The rest of you pretend that you don't speak Therin. Our task is to deliver two of our new friends to shore, for a job that'll be important to us all. Ravelle, Valora—we'll send you out in the same boat you donated to our cause all those weeks ago." She paused to allow a sudden outburst of chatter to die off. "We should drop anchor in the next two hours. If you're not back by sunrise, this ship will be gone—and we'll never come within five hundred miles of this city again."

"We understand," said Locke.

"Once the anchor's down," continued Delmastro, "I'll want double watches aloft. Rig razor nets on both sides for a quick raise, but leave them down. Lay polearms at the sides, up against the rails, and ready sabers at both the masts. If a customs boat or anything else carrying a uniform tries to pay us a visit, we'll invite them aboard and detain them for the night. If anything more than that troubles us, we repel boarders, lay on the canvas, and run like hell."

There was a general murmur of approval to that idea.

"That's it. Stand in to Tal Verrar. Mumchance, put us about a mile off the Emerald Galleries. And raise an Ashmiri gray ensign at the taffrail."

Ashmere, though lacking a merchant or military fleet of its own, did a brisk business in registrations of convenience for smugglers, bounty-privateers, and tariff-dodging merchants. Nobody would look twice at them for the sake of that ensign. More importantly, nobody would approach merely for the sake of making small talk with fellow countrymen far from home. Locke approved. And anchoring in the waters southeast of the city would give them a good approach to the Castellana, so they could drop in on Stragos without lurking too close to the crowded marinas or the main anchorage.

"Hey," said Utgar, slapping Locke and Jean on the backs, "you two, what the hell are you getting yourselves into? You want a bodyguard?"

"Ravelle's the only bodyguard I need," said Jean with a smirk.

"Fair enough. I'll give you that. But what are you sticking your noses into, hmm? Something dangerous?"

"Probably not," said Locke. "Look, Drakasha will spin the full tale, probably sooner than you think. For tonight, let's just say we're on ordinary errands."

"Saying hello to Grandmother," said Jean. "Paying off Uncle's gambling debts. Picking up three loaves of bread and a bushel of onions at the Night Market."

"Fine, fine. Keep your secrets. Rest of us'll stay behind and be bored, right?"

"Not likely," said Locke. "This ship's full of little surprises, isn't it?"

"True enough," said Utgar, chuckling. "True enough, hey. Well, be careful. Eyes of the gods upon you and all that."

"Thanks." Locke scratched his beard, and then snapped his fingers. "Hell. I nearly forgot something. Jerome, Utgar, see you in a bit."

He jogged aft, dodging Blue watch work parties and bored Reds helping haul forth weapons from the arms lockers. He took the quarterdeck stairs in two quick leaps, slid down the companionway rails, and knocked loudly on Drakasha's cabin door.

"It's open," she shouted.

"Captain," said Locke, closing the door behind him, "I need to borrow the money that was in my sea chest again."

Drakasha was lounging on her hammock with Paolo and Cosetta, reading to them from a heavy book that looked an awful lot like a *Wise Mariner's Practical Lexicon.* "Technically, that money got cut up into shares," she said, "but I can give you the equivalent out of the ship's purse. All of it?"

"Two hundred and fifty solari should do. Oh. It, um, won't be coming back with me."

"Fascinating," she said. "That's a definition of 'borrow' that doesn't exactly compel me to get up from this hammock. On your way out—"

"Captain, Stragos is just one half of tonight's business. I need to keep Requin purring, too. He has the power to crush this scheme like an insect if I don't. Besides—if I tickle his fancy, there's one more useful item I might be able to squeeze out of him, now that I think of it."

"So you need a bribe."

"Between friends we call them considerations. Come on, Drakasha. Consider it an investment in our desired outcome."

"For the sake of my peace and quiet, fine. I'll have it waiting for you when you leave the ship."

"You're too—

"I am not even remotely too kind. Begone."

9

THEY'D BEEN away for seven weeks that felt like a lifetime.

Standing at the larboard rail, staring once again at the islands and towers of Tal Verrar, Locke felt anxiety and melancholy mingling like liquors. The clouds were low and dark above the city, reflecting the orange light of the festival fire burning in the main anchorage.

"Ready for this?" asked Jean.

"Ready and sweating heavily," said Locke.

They were dressed in borrowed finery, linen caps, and cloaks. The cloaks were too warm, but not so rare on the streets of many neighborhoods; they meant that the wearer was probably carrying weapons, and not to be trifled with. Hopefully, the added clothing would help protect them from a casual glimpse by anyone inconvenient who might recognize them.

"Heave out," cried Oscarl, in charge of the party putting their boat over the side. With the creak of rope and tackle, the little craft swung out into darkness and splashed down into the water. Utgar shimmied down the boarding net to unfasten everything and prepare the oars. As Locke stepped to the entry port and prepared to go down, Delmastro caught his arm.

"Whatever else happens," she whispered, "just bring him back."

"I won't fail," said Locke. "And neither will he."

"Zamira said to give you this." Delmastro passed over a

heavy leather purse, packed tight with coins. Locke nodded his gratitude and slipped it into an inner cloak pocket.

As Locke crawled down to the boat, he passed Utgar, who gave a cheery salute and kept climbing. Locke hopped down into the boat, but continued clinging to the boarding net so he could stand upright. He glanced up, and by the light of the ship's lanterns he saw Jean and Ezri saying farewell with a kiss. She whispered something to him, and then they parted.

"This is infinitely preferable to the last time we shared this boat alone," said Jean as they settled onto the rowing bench and fit the oars to their locks.

"You told her your real name, didn't you?"

"What?" Jean's eyes grew wide, and then he scowled. "Is that a guess?"

"I'm not much of a lip-reader, but the last thing she said to you had one syllable, not two."

"Oh," sighed Jean. "Well, aren't *you* the clever little bastard."

"Yes on all three counts, actually."

"I did, and I'm not sorry—"

"Gods, I'm not angry, Jean. I'm just showing off." They began to row together, pulling hard, driving the boat across the dark, choppy water toward the channel between the Galezzo District and the Emerald Galleries.

Minutes of rowing passed without conversation; the oars creaked, the water splashed, and the *Poison Orchid* fell away to stern, the whiteness of her furled sails vanishing into the darkness, until all that remained of her was a faint constellation of lantern lights.

"The alchemist," said Locke, without any warning.

"Huh?"

"Stragos' *alchemist*. He's the key to this mess."

"If by 'key' you mean 'cause'—"

"No, listen. How likely is it that Stragos is ever going to

just accidentally leave us the glasses he uses to give us our antidote? Or let a dose slip out of his pocket?"

"Easy question," said Jean. "It's bloody impossible."

"Right. So it's no use waiting for him to make a mistake—we've got to make contact with that alchemist."

"He's one of the archon's personal retinue," said Jean. "Maybe the most important person in Stragos' service, if Stragos makes a habit of doing this frequently. I doubt he has a nice, convenient, out-of-the way house where we can pay him a visit. He probably lives at the Mon Magisteria."

"But there's got to be something we can do," said Locke. "The man has to have a price. Think of what we've got at the Sinspire, or what we could get with Drakasha's help."

"I'll admit it's the best idea yet," said Jean. "Which isn't saying much."

"Eyes wide, ears open, and hope in the Crooked Warden," Locke muttered.

On this side of the city, Tal Verrar's inner harbor was thick with pleasure boats, barges, and hired gondolas. The wealthy (and the not-so-wealthy who didn't care whether or not they woke up without a centira the next day) were in full migration from the professional crescents to the bars and coffeehouses of the Emerald Galleries. Locke and Jean slipped into the stream and rowed against the prevailing current, dodging larger vessels and exchanging choice vulgarities with the shouting, leering, bottle-throwing customers on some of the rowdier barges.

Having dished out more abuse than they'd received, they slipped at last between the Artificers' Crescent and the Alchemists' Crescent, admiring the vivid blue and green fireballs that the alchemists were hurling, presumably in support of the festa (though one never knew) forty or fifty feet into the air over their private docks. The prevailing wind was toward Locke and Jean, and as they rowed they found themselves pursued by a brimstone-scented rain of sparks and burnt paper scraps.

Their destination was easy enough to find; at the northwestern end of the Castellana lay the entrance grotto to the Elderglass caverns from which they'd emerged with Merrain, the first night she'd kidnapped them on the archon's behalf.

Security at the archon's private landing had been enhanced. As Locke and Jean rowed around the final bend into the prismatic glass hollow, a dozen Eyes hefted crossbows and knelt behind curved iron shields, five feet high, set into the floor to provide cover. Behind them a squad of regular Verrari soldiers manned a ballista, a minor siege engine capable of shattering their boat with a ten-pound quarrel. An Eye officer pulled a chain leading into a wall aperture, presumably ringing an alarm above.

"Use of this landing is forbidden," shouted the officer.

"Please listen carefully," shouted Locke. The dull roar of the waterfall high above echoed throughout the cavern, and there was no room for error. "We have a message for the waiting lady."

Their boat bumped up against the edge of the landing. It was disconcerting, thought Locke, having so many crossbows large and small dedicated to their intimidation. However, the Eye officer stepped over and knelt beside them. His voice echoed metallically through the speaking holes of his featureless mask.

"You're here on the waiting lady's business?"

"We are," said Locke. "Tell her precisely this: 'Two sparks were kindled, and two bright fires returned.'"

"I shall," said the officer. "In the meantime..."

After carefully setting their crossbows down, half a dozen Eyes stepped out from behind their shields to haul Locke and Jean out of their boat. They were restrained and patted down; their boot daggers were confiscated, along with Locke's bag of gold. An Eye examined it, and then passed it to the officer.

"Solari, sir. Confiscate it?"

"No," said the officer. "Take them to the waiting lady's chamber, and give it back. If money alone could kill the Protector, the Priori would have already done it, eh?"

10

"YOU DID *what* to the *Red Messenger*?"

Maxilan Stragos was red-faced with wine, exertion, and surprise. The archon was dressed more sumptuously than Locke had ever seen him, in a vertically striped cape of sea-green silk that alternated with cloth-of-gold strips, over a coat and breeches that also gleamed gold. He wore rings on all ten of his fingers, set alternately with rubies and sapphires, very close approximations of the Tal Verrar colors. He stood before Locke and Jean in a tapestry-walled chamber on the first floor of the Mon Magisteria, attended by a pair of Eyes. If Locke and Jean had not been granted chairs, neither had they been trussed up. Or placed in the swelter-ing chamber.

"We, ah, used it to initiate successful contact with pi-rates."

"By *losing* it to them."

"In a word, yes."

"And Caldris is dead?"

"For some time."

"Now tell me, Lamora, just what sort of reaction were you hoping for when you brought me this news?"

"Well, a fucking heart attack would have been nice, but I'd settle for a bit of patience while I explain further."

"Yes," said the archon. "Do."

"When the *Messenger* was taken by pirates, all of us aboard were made prisoners." Locke had decided that the specific details of injuries and scrub watches and so forth could be safely left out of the story.

"By whom?"

"Drakasha."

"Zamira lives, does she? With her old *Poison Orchid*?"

"Yes," said Locke. "It's in fine condition, and in fact it's currently riding at anchor about two miles, um..." He pointed with a finger at what he believed to be south. "...that way."

"She dares?"

"She's practicing an obscure technique called 'disguise,' Stragos."

"So you're... part of her crew now?"

"Yes. Those of us taken from the *Messenger* were given a chance to prove our intentions by storming the next prize Drakasha took. You won't see the *Messenger* again, as it's been sold to a sort of, um, wrecker baron. But at least now we're in a position to give you what you want."

"Are you?" The expression on Stragos' face went from annoyance to plain avarice in an eyeblink. "How... refreshing to hear you deliver such a report, in lieu of vulgarity and complaint."

"Vulgarity and complaint are my special talents. But listen—Drakasha has agreed to drum up the scare you want. If we get our antidote tonight, by the end of the week you'll have reports of raids at every point of the compass. It'll be like dropping a shark in a public bath."

"What do you mean, precisely, by 'Drakasha has agreed'?"

Improvising a fictional motive for Zamira was elementary; Locke could have done it in his sleep. "I told her the truth," he said. "The rest was easy. Obviously, once our job is done, you'll send your navy south to kick sixteen shades of shit out of every Ghostwind pirate you find. *Except* the one that actually started the mess, who will conveniently hunt elsewhere for a few months. And once you've got your grand little war sewn up, she goes back home to find that her former rivals are on the bottom of the ocean. Alas."

"I see," said Stragos. "I would have preferred not to have her aware of my actual intentions—"

"If there are any survivors in the Ghostwinds," said Locke, "she can hardly speak of her role in the matter to them, can she? And if there are *no* survivors . . . who can she talk to at all?"

"Indeed," muttered Stragos.

"However," said Jean, "if the two of us don't return quite soon, the *Orchid* will head for the open sea, and you'll lose your one chance to make use of her."

"And I will have wasted the *Messenger,* and poisoned my reputation, and endured the abuse of your company, all for nothing. Yes, Tannen, I'm well aware of the angles of what you no doubt believe to be a terribly clever argument."

"Our antidote, then?"

"You've not earned a final cure yet. But you'll have the consequences further postponed."

Stragos pointed to one of the Eyes, who bowed and left the room. He returned a few moments later and held the door open for two people. The first was Stragos' personal alchemist, carrying a domed silver serving tray. The second was Merrain.

"Our two bright fires *have* returned," she said. She was dressed in a long-sleeved gown that matched the sea-green portions of Stragos' cape, and her slender waist was accented by a tight cloth-of-gold sash. Threaded into her hair was a circlet of red and blue rose blossoms.

"Kosta and de Ferra have earned another temporary sip of life, my dear." He held out his arm and she crossed over to him, taking his elbow in the light and friendly fashion of a chaperone rather than a lover.

"Have they, now?"

"I'll tell you about it when we return to the gardens."

"Some sort of Festa Iono affair, Stragos? You've never struck me as the celebratory type," said Locke.

"For the sake of my officers," said Stragos. "If I throw galas for them, the Priori spread rumors that I am profligate. If I do nothing, they whisper that I am austere and heartless. Regardless, my officers suffer far more in society when they have no private functions from which to exclude their jealous rivals. Thus I put my gardens to use, if nothing else."

"I weep again for your hardship," said Locke. "Forced by cruel circumstance to throw garden parties."

Stragos smiled thinly and gestured at his alchemist. The man swept the dome from the silver tray, revealing two white-frosted crystal goblets full of familiar pale amber liquid.

"You may have your antidote in pear cider tonight," said the archon. "For old times' sake."

"Oh, you funny old bastard." Locke passed a goblet to Jean, emptied his in several gulps, and then tossed it into the air.

"Heavens! I slipped."

The crystal goblet struck the stone floor with a loud clang rather than a shattering explosion into fragments. It bounced once and rolled into a corner, completely unharmed.

"A little gift from the master alchemists." Stragos looked extraordinarily amused. "Hardly Elderglass, but just the thing to deny rude guests their petty satisfactions."

Jean finished his own cider and set his glass back down on the bald man's serving tray. One of the Eyes fetched the other goblet, and when they were both covered by the silver dome once again, Stragos dismissed his alchemist with a wave.

"I...um...," said Locke, but the man was already out the door.

"This evening's business is concluded," said Stragos. "Merrain and I have a gala to return to. Kosta and de Ferra, you have the most important part of your task ahead of you. Please me...and I may just yet make it worth your while."

Stragos led Merrain to the door, turning only to speak to one of his Eyes. "Lock them in here for ten minutes. After that, escort them back to their boat. Return their weapons and see that they're on their way. With haste."

"I...but...*damn*," Locke sputtered as the door slammed closed behind the two Eyes.

"Antidote," said Jean. "That's all that matters for now. Antidote."

"I suppose." Locke put his head against one of the room's stone walls. "Gods. I hope our visit to Requin goes more smoothly than this."

11

"SERVICE ENTRANCE, you ignorant bastard!"

The Sinspire bouncer came out of nowhere. He doubled Locke over his knee, knocking the wind out of him in one cruel slam, and hurled him back onto the gravel of the lantern-lit courtyard behind the tower. Locke hadn't even stepped inside, merely approached the door after failing to spot anyone he could easily bribe for an audience with Selendri.

"Oof," he said as the ground made his acquaintance.

Jean, guided more by loyal reflex than clear thinking, got involved as the bouncer came forth to offer Locke further punishment. The bouncer growled and swung a too-casual fist at Jean, who caught it in his right hand and then broke several of the bouncer's ribs with the heel of his left.

Before Locke could say anything, Jean kicked the bouncer in the groin and swept his legs out from beneath him.

"Urrrrgh-*ack*," the man said as the ground made his acquaintance.

The next attendant out the door had a knife; Jean broke the fist that held it and bounced the attendant off the Sinspire wall like a handball from a stone court surface. The next six or seven attendants who surrounded them, unfortunately, had short swords and crossbows.

"You have no idea who you're fucking with," said one of them.

"Actually," came a harsh feminine whisper from the service entrance, "I suspect they do."

Selendri wore a blue-and-red silk evening gown that must have cost as much as a gilded carriage. Her ruined arm was covered by a sleeve that led down to her brass hand, while the fine muscles and smooth skin of her other arm were bare, accentuated by gold and Elderglass bangles.

"We caught them trying to steal into the service entrance, mistress," said one of the attendants.

"You caught us getting *near* the service entrance, you dumb bastard." Locke rose to his knees. "Selendri, we need to—"

"I'm sure you do," she said. "Let them go. I'll deal with them myself. Act as though nothing happened."

"But he . . . gods, I think he broke my ribs," wheezed the first man Jean had dealt with. The other was unconscious.

"If you agree that nothing happened," said Selendri, "I'll have you taken to a physiker. Did anything happen?"

"Unnnh . . . no. No, mistress, nothing happened."

"Good."

As she turned to reenter the service area, Locke stumbled to his feet, clutching his stomach, and reached out to grab her gently by the shoulder. She whirled on him.

"Selendri," he whispered, "we cannot be seen on the gaming floors. We have—"

"Powerful individuals rather upset about your failure to give them a return engagement?" She knocked his hand away.

"Forgive me. And yes, that's exactly it."

"Durenna and Corvaleur are on the fifth floor. You and I can take the climbing closet from the third."

"And Jerome?"

"Stay here in the service area, Valora." She pulled them both in through the service entrance so tray-bearing attendants, studiously ignoring the injured men on the ground, could get on with earning festival-night tips from the city's least inhibited.

"Thank you," said Jean, taking a half-hidden spot behind tall wooden racks full of unwashed dishes.

"I'll give instructions to ignore you," said Selendri. "As long as you ignore *my* people."

"I'll be a saint," said Jean.

Selendri grabbed a passing attendant with no serving tray and whispered a few terse instructions into his ear. Locke caught the words "dog-leech" and "dock their pay." Then he was following Selendri into the crowd on the ground floor, hunched over as though trying to shrink down beneath his cloak and cap, praying that the next and only person who'd recognize him would be Requin.

12

"SEVEN WEEKS," said the master of the Sinspire. "Selendri was so sure we'd never see you again."

"Three weeks down and three weeks back," said Locke. "Barely spent a week in Port Prodigal itself."

"You certainly look as though you passed some time on deck. Working for your berth?"

"Ordinary sailors attract much less notice than paying passengers."

"I suppose they do. Is that your natural hair color?"

"I think so. Swap it as often as I have and you start to lose track."

The wide balcony doors on the eastern side of Requin's office were open, but for a fine mesh screen to keep out insects. Through it, Locke could see the torchlike pyres of two ships in the harbor, surrounded by hundreds of specks of lantern-light that had to be spectators in smaller craft.

"They're burning four this year," said Requin, noticing that the view had caught Locke's attention. "One for each season. I think they're just finishing the third. The fourth should go up soon, and then all will be well. Fewer people in the streets, and more crowding into the chance houses."

Locke nodded, and turned to admire what Requin had done with the suite of chairs he'd had crafted for him. He tried to keep a smirk of glee off his face, and managed to look only vaguely appreciative. The four replica chairs were placed around a thin-legged table in a matching style, holding bottles of wine and an artful flower arrangement.

"Is that—"

"A replica as well? I'm afraid so. Your gift spurred me to have it made."

"My gift. Speaking of which..."

Locke reached beneath his cloak, removed the purse, and set it down atop Requin's desk.

"What's this?"

"A consideration," said Locke. "There are an awful lot of sailors in Port Prodigal with more coins than card sense."

Requin opened the satchel and raised an eyebrow. "Handsome," he said. "You really *are* trying very hard not to piss me off, aren't you?"

"I want my job," said Locke. "Now more than ever."

"Let's discuss your task, then. Does this Calo Callas still exist?"

"Yes," said Locke. "He's down there."

"Then why the hell didn't you bring him back with you?"

"He's out of his fucking mind," said Locke.

"Then he's useless—"

"No. *Not* useless. He feels persecuted, Requin. He's delusional. He imagines that the Priori and the Artificers have agents on every corner in Port Prodigal, every ship, every tavern. He barely leaves his house." Locke took pleasure at the speed with which he was conjuring an imaginary life for an imaginary man. "But what he *does* inside that house. What he has! Locks, hundreds of them. Clockwork devices. A private forge and bellows. He's as insatiable about his trade as he ever was. It's all he has left in the world."

"How is a madman's detritus significant?" asked Selendri. She stood between two of Requin's exquisite oil paintings, leaning against the wall with her arms folded.

"I experimented with all kinds of things back when I thought I might have a chance to crack this tower's vault. Acids, oils, abrasives, different types of picks and tools. I'd call myself a fair judge of mechanisms as well as lockbreaking. And the things this bastard can do, the things he builds and invents, even with a magpie mind—" Locke spread his hands and shrugged theatrically. "Gods!"

"What will it take to bring him here?"

"He wants protection," said Locke. "He's not averse to leaving Port Prodigal. Hell, he's eager to. But he imagines death at every step. He needs to feel that someone with power is reaching out to put him under their cloak."

"Or you could just hit him over the head and haul him back in chains," said Selendri.

"And risk losing his actual cooperation forever? Worse—*deal* with him on a three-week voyage after he wakes up? His mind is delicate as glass, Selendri. I wouldn't recommend knocking it around."

Locke cracked his knuckles. Time to sweeten the pitch.

"Look, you *want* this man back in Tal Verrar. He'll drive you mad. You may even have to appoint some sort of nurse or minder for him, and you'll definitely have to hide him from the Artificers. But the things he can do could make it worthwhile a hundred times over. He's the best lockbreaker I've ever seen. He just needs to believe that I truly represent you."

"What do you suggest?"

"You have a wax sigil, on your ledgers and letters of credit. I've seen it, making my deposits. Put your seal on a sheet of parchment—"

"And incriminate myself," said Requin. "No."

"Already thought about that," said Locke. "Don't write a name on it. Don't date it, don't sign it to anyone, don't even add your usual 'R.' Just write something pleasant and totally nonspecific. 'Look forward to comfort and hospitality.' Or, 'Expect every due consideration.'"

"Trite bullshit. I see," said Requin. He removed a sheet of parchment from a desk drawer, touched a quill to ink, and scrawled a few sentences. After sprinkling the letter with alchemical desiccant, he looked back at Locke. "And this childish device will be sufficient?"

"As far as his fears are concerned," said Locke, "Callas *is* a child. He'll grab at this like a baby grabbing for a tit."

"Or a grown man," muttered Selendri.

Requin smiled. Gloved as always, he removed the glass cylinder from a small lamp atop his desk, revealing a candle at its heart. With this, he heated a stick of black wax, which he allowed to drip into a pool on the sheet of parchment. At last, he withdrew a heavy signet ring from a jacket pocket and pressed it into the wax.

"Your bait, Master Kosta." He passed the sheet over. "The

fact that you're skulking at the service entrance and trying to hide beneath that cloak both suggest you're not planning on staying in the city for long."

"Back south in a day or two, as soon as my shipmates finish offloading the, ah, completely legitimate and responsibly acquired cargo we picked up in Port Prodigal." That was a safe lie; with dozens of ships offloading in the city every day, at least a few of them had to be carrying goods from criminal sources.

"And you'll bring Callas back with you."

"Yes."

"If the sigil isn't sufficient, promise him anything else reasonable. Coin, drugs, drink, women. Men. Both. And if that's not enough, take Selendri's suggestion and let me worry about his state of mind. Don't come back empty-handed."

"As you wish."

"What then, for you and the archon? With Callas in hand, you'll likely be back to this scheme for my vault. . . ."

"I don't know," said Locke. "I'll be at least six or seven weeks away before I can come back with him; why don't you ponder how I can best serve you in that time? Whatever plan you deem suitable. If you want me to turn him over to the archon as a double agent, fine. If you want me to tell the archon that he died or something . . . I just don't know. My skull aches. You're the man with the big picture. I'll look forward to new orders."

"If you can stay this polite," said Requin, hefting the purse, "bring me Callas, and continue to be so satisfied with your place in the scheme of things . . . you may well have a future in my service."

"I appreciate that."

"Go. Selendri will show you out. I still have a busy night lying in wait for me."

Locke let a bit of his actual relief show in his expression.

This web of lies was growing so convoluted, so branching, and so delicate that a moth's fart might knock it to pieces—but the two meetings of the night had bought what he and Jean needed.

Another two months of life from Stragos, and another two months of tolerance from Requin. All they needed to do now was steal back to their boat without complication, and row themselves to safety.

13

"WE'RE BEING followed," said Jean as they crossed the Sinspire service courtyard. They were headed back toward the maze of alleys and hedgerows from which they'd come, the little-used block of gardens and service paths behind the lesser chance houses. Their boat was tied up at a pier along the inner docks of the Great Gallery; they'd snuck up to the top of the Golden Steps on rickety stairs, ignoring the lift-boxes and streets on which a thousand complications might lurk.

"Where are they?"

"Across the street. Watching this courtyard. They moved when we moved, just now."

"Shit," muttered Locke. "If only this city's entire population of lurking assholes shared one set of balls, so I could kick it repeatedly."

"At the edge of the courtyard, let's make a really obvious, sudden dash for it," said Jean. "Hide yourself. Whoever comes running after us—"

"Gets to explain some things the hard way."

At the rear of the courtyard was a hedge twice Locke's height. An archway surrounded by empty crates and casks led to the dark and little-used backside of the Golden Steps. About ten yards from this archway, acting in unison by some unspoken signal, Locke and Jean broke into a sprint.

Through the arch, into the shadowed alley beyond; Locke knew they had just moments to hide themselves. They needed to be far enough from the courtyard to prevent any of the Sinspire attendants from glimpsing a scuffle. Past the backs of gardens and walled lawns they ran, scant yards from buildings where hundreds of the richest people in the Therin world were losing money for fun. At last they found two stacks of empty casks on either side of the alley—the most obvious ambush spot possible, but if their opponents thought they were hell-bent on escape, they might just ignore the possibility.

Jean had already vanished into his place. Locke pulled his boot dagger, feeling the hammer of his own heartbeat, and crouched behind the casks on his side of the alley. He threw his cloaked arm across his face, leaving only his eyes and forehead exposed.

The rapid slap of leather on stones, and then—two dark shapes flew past the piles of casks. Locke deliberately delayed his own movement half a heartbeat, allowing Jean to strike first. When the pursuer closest to Locke turned, startled by the sound of Jean's attack on his companion, Locke slipped forward, dagger out, filled with grim elation at the thought of finally getting some answers to this business.

His grab for the attacker was good; he slipped his left arm around the man's neck at the exact instant he shoved his blade up against the soft junction of neck and chin on the other side. "Drop your weapon or I'll—" was all he had time to say, however, before the man did the absolute worst thing possible. He jerked forward in an attempt to break Locke's hold, perhaps reflexively, not realizing the angle at which Locke's blade was poised. Whether it was supreme optimism or miserable foolishness, Locke would never know, as the man sliced half the contents of his neck open and died that instant, spewing blood. A weapon clattered to the stones from his limp fingers.

Locke put his hands up in disbelief and let the corpse drop, only to find himself facing Jean, who was breathing heavily over the unmoving form of his own opponent.

"Wait a minute," said Locke, "you mean—"

"Accident," said Jean. "I caught his knife, we fought a bit, and he got it beneath his own rib cage."

"Gods damn it," Locke muttered, flicking blood from his right hand. "You try to keep a bastard alive, and look what happens—"

"Crossbows," said Jean. He pointed to the ground, where Locke's adjusting eyes could see the dim shapes of two small hand crossbows. Alley-pieces, the sort of thing you used within ten yards or not at all. "Grab them. There may be more of them after us."

"Hell." Locke grabbed one of the bows and gingerly handed the other to Jean. The little quarrels might be poisoned; the thought of handling someone else's envenomed weapon in the dark made his skin crawl. But Jean was right; they'd need the advantage if they had other pursuers.

"I say discretion is a pastime for other people," said Locke. "Let's run our asses off."

They sprinted at a wild tear through the forgotten places of the Golden Steps, north to the edge of the vast Elderglass plateau, where they scrambled down flight after flight of nauseatingly wobbly wooden steps, glancing frantically above and below for pursuit or ambush. The world was a dizzy whirl around Locke by the middle of the staircase, painted in the surreal colors of fire and alien glass. Out on the harbor the fourth and final ship of the festival was bursting into incandescence, a sacrifice of wood and pitch and canvas before hundreds of small boats packed with priests and revelers.

Down to the feet of the stairs and across the wooden

platforms of the inner docks they stumbled, past the occasional drunkard or beggar, waving their daggers and crossbows wildly. Before them was their pier, long and empty,
home only to a long stack of crates. No beggars, no drunks.
Their boat bobbed welcomingly on the waves, just a hundred feet away now, brightly lit by the glare of the inferno.

Stack of crates, Locke thought, and by then it was too
late.

Two men stepped from the shadows as Locke and Jean
passed, from the most obvious ambush spot possible.

Locke and Jean whirled together; only the fact that they
were carrying their stolen crossbows in their hands gave
them any chance to bring them up in time. Four arms flew
out; four men standing close enough to hold hands drew
on their targets. Four fingers quivered, each separated from
their triggers by no more than the width of a single droplet
of sweat.

Locke Lamora stood on the pier in Tal Verrar with the
hot wind of a burning ship at his back and the cold bite of
a loaded crossbow's bolt at his neck.

14

HE GRINNED, gasping for breath, and concentrated on
holding his own crossbow level with the left eye of his opponent; they were close enough that they would catch most
of one another's blood, should they both twitch their fingers
at the same time.

"Be reasonable," said the man facing him. Beads of
sweat left visible trails as they slid down his grime-covered
cheeks and forehead. "Consider the disadvantages of your
situation."

Locke snorted. "Unless your eyeballs are made of iron,
the disadvantage is mutual. Wouldn't you say so, Jean?"

Jean and his foe were toe-to-toe with their crossbows

similarly poised. Not one of them could miss at this range, not if all the gods above or below the heavens willed it otherwise.

"All four of us would seem ... to be up to our balls in quicksand," said Jean between breaths.

On the water behind them, the old galleon groaned and creaked as the roaring flames consumed it from the inside out. Night was made day for hundreds of yards around; the hull was crisscrossed with the white-orange lines of seams coming apart. Smoke boiled out of those hellish cracks in little black eruptions, the last shuddering breaths of a vast wooden beast dying in agony. The four men stood on their pier, strangely alone in the midst of light and noise that was drawing the attention of the entire city. Nobody in the boats was paying any attention to them.

"Lower your piece, for the love of the gods," said Locke's opponent. "We've been instructed not to kill you, if we don't have to."

"And I'm sure you'd be honest if it were otherwise, of course," said Locke. His smile grew. "I make it a point never to trust men with weapons at my windpipe. Sorry."

"Your hand will start to shake long before mine does."

"I'll rest the tip of my quarrel against your nose when I get tired. Who sent you after us? What are they paying you? We're not without funds; a happy arrangement could be reached."

"Actually," said Jean, "I know who sent them."

"What? Really?" Locke flicked a glance at Jean before locking eyes with his adversary once again.

"And an arrangement has been reached, but I wouldn't call it happy."

"Ah ... Jean, I'm afraid you've lost me."

"No." Jean raised one hand, palm out, to the man opposite him. He then slowly, carefully shifted his aim to his left—until his crossbow was pointing at Locke's head. The man he'd previously been threatening blinked in surprise. "You've lost *me,* Locke."

"Jean," said Locke, the grin vanishing from his face, "this isn't funny."

"I agree. Hand your piece over to me."

"Jean—"

"Hand it over now. Smartly. You there, are you some kind of moron? Get that thing out of my face and point it at him."

Jean's former opponent licked his lips nervously, but didn't move. Jean ground his teeth together. "Look, you sponge-witted dock ape, I'm doing your job for you. Point your crossbow at my gods-damned partner so we can get off this pier!"

"Jean, I would describe this turn of events as *less than helpful,*" said Locke, and he looked as though he might say more, except that Jean's opponent chose that moment to take Jean's advice.

It seemed to Locke that sweat was now cascading down his face, as though his own treacherous moisture were abandoning the premises before anything worse happened.

"There. Three on one." Jean spat on the pier. "You gave me no choice but to cut a deal with the employer of these gentlemen before we set out—gods damn it, *you* forced *me.* I'm sorry. I thought they'd make contact before they drew down on us. Now give your weapon over."

"Jean, what the *hell* do you think you're—"

"Don't. *Don't* say another fucking thing. Don't try to finesse me; I know you too well to let you have your say. Silence, Locke. Finger off the trigger and *hand it over.*"

Locke stared at the steel-tipped point of Jean's quarrel, his mouth open in disbelief. The world around him seemed to fade to that tiny, gleaming point, alive with the orange reflection of the inferno blazing in the anchorage behind him. Jean would have given him a hand signal if he were lying.... Where the hell was the hand signal?

"I don't believe this," he whispered. "This is impossible."

"This is the last time I'm going to say this, Locke." Jean ground his teeth together and held his aim steady, directly between Locke's eyes. "Take your finger off the trigger and hand over your gods-damned weapon. *Right now.*"

III

CARDS ON THE TABLE

"I am hard pressed on my right; my center is giving way;
situation excellent. I am attacking."

General Ferdinand Foch

CHAPTER FOURTEEN

SCOURGING THE SEA OF BRASS

1

JAFFRIM RODANOV WADED in the shallows by the hull of an overturned fishing boat, listening to the waves break against its shattered planks as they washed over his ankles. The sand and water of Prodigal Bay were pristine this far from the city. No layers of night soil slimed the water, no rusting metal scraps or pottery shards littered the bottom. No corpses floated as grim rafts for squawking birds.

Twilight, on the seventh day of Aurim. Drakasha gone for a week now. A thousand miles away, Jaffrim thought, a mistake was being made.

Ydrena whistled. She was leaning against the hull of the abandoned fishing boat, neither too close nor too far from him, merely emphasizing by her presence that Rodanov was not alone, and that his attendance at this meeting was known to his crew.

Jacquelaine Colvard had arrived.

She left her first mate beside Ydrena, shrugged out of her own boots, and waded into the water without hiking up her breeches. Old and unbent Colvard, who'd been sacking ships in these waters when he'd been a boy with his nose buried in musty scrolls. Before he'd even seen a ship that wasn't inked onto a sheet of parchment.

"Jaffrim," she said. "Thank you for humoring me."

"There's only one thing you could want to talk about at the moment," said Rodanov.

"Yes. And it's on your mind too, isn't it?"

"It was a mistake to give Drakasha our oaths."

"Was it?"

Rodanov hooked his thumbs into his sword-belt and looked down at the darkening water, the ripples where his pale ankles vanished into it. "I was generous when I should have been cynical."

"So you fancy yourself the only one who had the power to forbid this?"

"I could have withheld my oath."

"But then it would have been four against one, with you as the one," said Colvard, "and Drakasha would have gone north looking over her shoulder all the way."

Rodanov felt a cold excitement in his gut.

"I've noticed curious things, these past few days," she continued. "Your crew has been spending less time in the city. You've been taking on water. And I've seen you on your quarterdeck, testing your instruments. Checking your backstaffs."

His excitement rose. Out here alone, had she come to confront him or abet him? Could she be mad enough to put herself in his reach, if it was the former?

"You know, then," he said at last.

"Yes."

"Do you intend to talk me out of it?"

"I intend to see that it's done right."

"Ah."

"You have someone aboard the *Poison Orchid*, don't you?"

Though taken aback, Rodanov found himself in no mood to dissemble.

"If you'll tell me how you know," he said, "I won't insult you by denying it."

"It was an educated guess. After all, you tried to place someone aboard my ship once."

"Ah," he said, sucking air through his teeth. "So Riela didn't die in a boat accident after all."

"Yes and no," said Colvard. "It happened in a boat, at least."

"Do you—"

"Blame you? No. You're a cautious man, Jaffrim, as I am a fundamentally cautious woman. It's our shared caution that brings us here this evening."

"Do you want to come with?"

"No," said Colvard. "And my reasons are practical. First, that the *Sovereign* is ready for sea while the *Draconic* is not. Second, that two of us putting out together would cause... an inconvenient degree of speculation when Drakasha fails to return."

"There'll be speculation regardless. And there'll be confirmation. My crew won't bite their tongues forever."

"But anything could have happened, to bring one and one together on the high seas," said Colvard. "If we put out in a squadron, collusion will be the only reasonable possibility."

"And I suppose it's just coincidence," said Jaffrim, "that even several days since you first spotted my preparations, the *Draconic* still isn't ready for sea?"

"Well—"

"Spare me, Jacquelaine. I was ready to do this before we came here tonight. Just don't imagine that you've somehow *finessed* me into going in your place."

"Jaffrim. Peace. So long as this arrow hits the target, it doesn't matter who pulls back the string." She unbound her gray hair and let it fly free about her shoulders in the muggy breeze. "What are your intentions?"

"Obvious, I should think. Find her. Before she does enough damage to give Stragos what he wants."

"And should you run her down, what then? Polite messages, broadside to broadside?"

"A warning. A last chance."

"An ultimatum for *Drakasha*?" Her frown turned every line on her face near-vertical. "Jaffrim, you know too well how she'll react to any threat. Like a netted shark. If you try to get close to a creature in that state, you'll lose a hand."

"A fight, then. I suppose we both know it'll come to that."

"And the outcome of that fight?"

"My ship is the stronger and I have eighty more souls to spare. It won't be pretty, but I intend to make it mathematical."

"Zamira slain, then."

"That's what tends to happen—"

"Assuming you allow her the courtesy of death in battle."

"Allow?"

"Consider," said Colvard, "that while Zamira's course of action is too dangerous to tolerate, her logic was impeccable in one respect."

"And that is?"

"Merely killing her, plus this Ravelle and Valora, would only serve to bandage a wound that already festers. The rot will deepen. We need to sate Maxilan Stragos' ambition, not just foil it temporarily."

"Agreed. But I'm losing my taste for subtlety as fast as I'm depleting my supply, Colvard. I'm going to be blunt with Drakasha. Grant me the same courtesy."

"Stragos needs a victory not for the sake of his own vanity, but to rouse the people of his city. If that victory is lurk-

ing in the waters *near* Tal Verrar, and if that victory is colorful enough, what need would he have to trouble us down
here?"

"We put a sacrifice on the altar," Rodanov whispered.
"We put *Zamira* on the altar."

"After Zamira does some damage. After she raises just
enough hell to panic the city. If the notorious pirate, the *infamous* rogue Zamira Drakasha, with a five-thousand solari
bounty on her head, were to be paraded through Tal Verrar
in chains...brought to justice so quickly after foolishly
challenging the city once again..."

"Stragos victorious. Tal Verrar united in admiration."
Rodanov sighed. "Zamira hung over the Midden Deep in a
cage."

"Satisfaction in every quarter," said Colvard.

"I may not be able to take her alive, though."

"Whatever you hand over to the archon would be of
equal value. Corpse or quick, alive or dead, he'll have his
trophy, and the Verrari would swarm the streets to see it. It
would be best, I suspect, to let him have what's left of the
Poison Orchid as well."

"I do the dirty work. Then hand him the victor's lau-
rels."

"And the Ghostwinds will be spared."

Rodanov stared out across the waters of the bay for
some time before speaking again. "So we presume. But we
have no better notions."

"When will you leave?"

"The morning tide."

"I don't envy you the task of navigating the *Sovereign*
through the Trader's Gate—"

"I don't envy myself. I'll take the Parlor Passage."

"Even by day, Jaffrim?"

"Hours count. I refuse to see any more wasted." He
turned for shore, to retrieve his boots and be on his way.

"Can't buy in for the last hand if you don't get there in time to take a chair."

2

FEELING THE hot sting of sudden tears in his eyes, Locke slipped his finger away from the trigger of the alley-piece and slowly put it up in the air.

"Will you at least tell me why?" he said.

"Later." Jean didn't lower his own weapon. "Give me the crossbow. Slowly. *Slowly!*"

Locke's arm was shaking; the nervous reaction had lent an unwanted jerkiness to his movements. Concentrating, trying to keep his emotions under control, Locke passed the bow over to Jean.

"Good," said Jean. "Keep your hands up. You two brought rope, right?"

"Yeah."

"I've got him under my bolt. Tie him up. Get his hands and his feet, and make the knots tight."

One of their ambushers pointed his own crossbow into the air and fumbled for rope in a jacket pocket. The other lowered his bow and produced a knife. His eyes had just moved from Locke to his associate when Jean made his next move.

With his own bow in one hand and Locke's in the other, he calmly pivoted and put a bolt into the head of each of their attackers.

Locke heard the sharp *twak-twak* of the double release, but it took several seconds for full comprehension of its meaning to travel from his eyes to the back of his skull. He stood there shaking, jaw hanging open, while the two strangers spurted blood, twitched, and died. One of them reflexively curled a finger around the trigger of his weapon.

With a final *twak* that made Locke jump, a bolt whizzed into the darkness.

"Jean, you—"

"How difficult was it to *give me the damn weapon?*"

"But you ... you said—"

"I said..." Jean grabbed him by his lapels and shook him. "What do you mean 'I said,' Locke? Why were you paying attention to what I was saying?"

"You didn't—"

"Gods, you're shaking. You believed me? How could you *believe* me?" Jean released him and stared at him, aghast. "I thought you were just playing along too intently!"

"You didn't give me a hand signal, Jean! What the hell was I supposed to think?"

"Didn't give you a hand signal? I flashed you the 'lying' sign, plain as that bloody burning ship!"

"You did not—"

"I did! As if I could forget! I can't believe this! How could you ever think... Where did you think I'd found the *time* to broker a deal with anyone else? We've been on the same damn ship for two months!"

"Jean, without the signal—"

"I did give it to you, you twit! I gave it when I did the whole cold, reluctant betrayer bit! 'Actually, I know who sent them.' Remember?"

"Yeah—"

"And then the hand signal! The 'Oh, look, Jean Tannen is lying about betraying his best friend in the whole fucking world to a couple of Verrari cutthroats' signal! Shall we practice that one more often? Do we really need to?"

"I *didn't see* a signal, Jean. Honest to all the gods."

"You missed it."

"Missed it? I—yeah, look, fine. I missed it. It was dark, crossbows everywhere, I should've known. I should've known we didn't even need it. I'm sorry."

He sighed, and looked over at the two bodies, feathered shafts sticking grotesquely out of their motionless heads.

"We really, really needed to interrogate one of those bastards, didn't we?"

"Yes," said Jean.

"It was . . . bloody good shooting, regardless."

"Yes."

"Jean?"

"Mm?"

"We should *really* be running like hell right now."

"Oh. Yes. Let's."

3

"AHOY THE ship," cried Locke as the boat nudged up against the *Poison Orchid*'s side. He released his grip on the oars with relief; Caldris would have been proud of the pace they'd set in scudding out of Tal Verrar, through a flotilla of priestly delegations and drunkards, past the flaming galleon and the blackened hulks of the previous sacrifices, through air still choked with gray haze.

"Gods," said Delmastro as she helped them up the entry port, "what happened? Are you hurt?"

"Got my feelings dented," said Jean, "but all this blood has been borrowed for the occasion."

Locke glanced down at his own finery, smeared with the life of at least two of their attackers. He and Jean looked like drunken amateur butchers.

"Did you get what you needed?" asked Delmastro.

"What we needed? Yes. What we might have wanted? No. And from the goddamn mystery attackers that won't give us a moment's peace in the city? Far too much."

"Who's this, then?"

"We have no idea," said Locke. "How do the bastards

know where we are, or who we are? It's been nearly two months! Where were we indiscreet?"

"The Sinspire," said Jean, a bit sheepishly.

"How were they waiting for us at the docks, then? Pretty bloody efficient!"

"Were you followed back to the ship?" asked Delmastro.

"Not that we could tell," said Jean, "but I think we'd be fools to linger."

Delmastro nodded, produced her whistle, and blew the familiar three sharp notes. "At the waist! Ship capstan bars! Stand by to weigh anchor! Boatswain's party, ready to hoist the boat!"

"You two look upset," she said to Locke and Jean as the ship became a whirlwind of activity around them.

"Why shouldn't we be?" Locke rubbed his stomach, still feeling a dull ache where the Sinspire bouncer had struck him. "We got away, sure, but someone pinned a hell of a lot of trouble on us in return."

"You know what I like to do when I'm in a foul mood?" said Ezri sweetly. "I like to sack ships." She raised her finger and pointed slowly across the deck, past the hustling crewfolk, out to sea, where another vessel could just be seen, lit by its stern lanterns against the southern darkness. "Oh, look—there's one right now!"

They were knocking on Drakasha's cabin door just moments later.

"You wouldn't be standing on two legs if that blood was yours," she said as she invited them in. "Is it too much to hope that it belongs to Stragos?"

"It is."

"Pity. Well, at least you came back. That's reassuring."

Paolo and Cosetta were tangled together on their little bed, snoring peacefully. Drakasha seemed to see no need to whisper in their presence. Locke grinned, remembering that he'd learned to sleep through some pretty awful distractions at their age, too.

"Did you make any real progress?" asked Drakasha.

"We bought time," said Locke. "And we got out of the city. The issue was in doubt."

"Captain," said Delmastro, "we were sort of wondering if we could get started on the next part of this whole scheme a bit early. Like right now."

"You want to do some boarding and socializing?"

"There's a likely suitor waiting to dance about two miles south by west. Away from the city, outside the reefs—"

"And the city's a bit absorbed in the festa at the moment," added Locke.

"It'd just be a quick visit, like we've been discussing," said Ezri. "Rouse them up, make 'em piss their breeches, loot the purse and the portable goods, throw things overboard, cut some chains and cripple the rigging—"

"I suppose we have to start somewhere," said Drakasha. "Del, send Utgar down to borrow some of my silks and cushions. I want a makeshift bed rigged for the children in the rope locker. If I'm going to wake them up to hide them, it's only fair."

"Right," said Delmastro.

"What's the wind?"

"Out of the northeast."

"Put us around due south, bring it onto the larboard quarter. Reefed topsails, slow and steady. Tell Oscarl to hoist out the boats, behind our hull so our friend can't see them in the water."

"Aye, Captain." Delmastro shrugged out of her overcoat, left it on Drakasha's table, and ran from the cabin. A few seconds later Locke could hear commotion on deck, Oscarl shouting about how they'd only just been told to raise the boat, and Delmastro yelling something about soft-handed, slack-witted idlers.

"You two look ghastly," said Zamira. "I'll have to get a new sea chest to separate the blood-drenched finery from the clean. Confine yourselves to wearing reds and browns next time."

"You know, Captain," said Locke, staring down at the blood-soaked sleeves of his jacket, "that sort of gives me an idea. A really, really *amusing* idea . . ."

4

JUST PAST the second hour of the morning, with Tal Verrar finally shuddering into a drunken slumber and the festa fires extinguished, the *Poison Orchid* in her costume as the *Chimera* crept past the *Happy Pilchard*. She passed the battered, sleepy little ketch at a distance of about two hundred yards, flying a minimal number of navigational lanterns and offering no hail. That wasn't entirely unusual, in waters where not one act of piracy had been reported for more than seven years.

In darkness, it was impossible to see that the *Orchid*'s deck carried no boats.

Those boats slowly emerged from the ship's larboard shadow, and at a silent signal their rowers exploded into action. With the haste of their passage they turned the dark sea white. Three faint, frothy lines reached out from *Orchid* to *Pilchard*, and by the time the lone watchman on at the ketch's stern noticed anything, it was far too late.

"Ravelle," cried Jean, who was the first up the ketch's side. "Ravelle!" Still dressed in his blood-spattered finery, he'd wrapped a scrap of red linen around his head and borrowed an iron-shod quarterstaff from one of the *Orchid*'s arms lockers. Orchids scrambled up behind him—Jabril and Malakasti, Streva and Rask. They carried clubs and saps, leaving their blades sheathed at their belts.

Three boats' worth of pirates boarded from three

separate directions; the ketch's meager crew was swept into the waist by shouting, club-waving lunatics, all hollering a name that was meaningless to them, until at last they were subdued and the chief of their tormentors came aboard to exalt in his victory.

"The name's Ravelle!"

Locke paced the deck before the thirteen cringing crewfolk and their strange blue-robed passenger. Locke, like Jean, had kept his bloody clothing and topped it off with a red sash at his waist, a red bandanna over his hair, and a scattering of Zamira's jewelry for effect. "Orrin Ravelle! And I've come back to pay my respects to Tal Verrar!"

"Don't kill us, sir," pleaded the captain of the little vessel, a skinny man of about thirty with the tan of a lifelong mariner. "We ain't even from Tal Verrar, just calling so our charter can—"

"You are interrupting critical hydrographic experiments," shouted the blue-robed man, attempting to rise to his feet. He was shoved back down by a squad of leering Orchids. "This information is vital to the interest of all mariners! You cut your own throat if you—"

"What the hell's a critical hydrographic experiment, old man?"

"By examining seafloor composition—"

"Seafloor composition? Can I *eat* that? Can I *spend* it? Can I take it back to my cabin and fuck it sideways?"

"No and no and most *certainly* no!"

"Right," said Locke. "Toss this fucker over the side."

"You ignorant bastards! You hypocritical apes. Let go— *let go of me*!" Locke was pleased to see Jean stepping in to perform the duty of heaving the robed scholar off the deck; not only would the man be scared witless, but Jean would control the situation precisely to keep him from actually getting hurt.

"Oh, please, sir, don't do that," said the *Pilchard*'s captain. "Master Donatti's harmless sir, please—"

"Look," said Locke, "is everyone on this tub an idiot besides me? Why would I sully the soles of my boots with a visit to this embarrassment unless you had something I wanted?"

"The, um, hydrographic experiments?" asked the captain.

"*Money!*" Locke seized him by the front of his tunic and heaved him to his feet. "I want every valuable, every drinkable, every consumable this overgrown *dinghy* has to offer, or you can watch the old bastard drown! How's that for a *hydrographic experiment*?"

5

THEY DIDN'T clear such a bad haul for such a little ship; obviously, Donatti had paid well to be carried around for his experiments, and been unwilling to sail without many of the comforts of home. A boat laden with liquors, fine tobacco, silk pillows, books, artificers' instruments, alchemical drugs, and bags of silver coins was soon sent back to the *Orchid*, while "Ravelle's" pirates finished sabotaging the little ship.

"Rudder lines disabled, sir," said Jean about half an hour after they'd boarded.

"Halyards cut, braces cut," shouted Delmastro, plainly enjoying her role as an ordinary buccaneer for this attack. She strolled along the larboard rail with a hatchet, chopping things seemingly at whim. "Whatever the hell that was, cut!"

"Sir, please," pleaded the captain, "that'll take ages to fix. You got all the valuables already...."

"I don't want you to die out here," said Locke, yawning in feigned boredom at the captain's pleas. "I just want to have a few quiet hours before this news gets back to Tal Verrar."

"Oh, sir, we'll do what you ask. Whatever you want; we won't tell no one—"

"*Please*," said Locke. "Cling to some dignity, Master Pilchard. I *want* you to talk about this. All over the place. Use it to leverage sympathy from whores. Maybe get a few free drinks in taverns. Most importantly, repeat my name. Orrin Ravelle."

"O-orrin Ravelle, sir."

"Captain Orrin Ravelle," said Locke, drawing a dagger and placing it against the captain's throat. "Of the good ship *Tal Verrar Is Fucked*! You stop in and let them know I'm in the neighborhood!"

"I, uh, I will, sir."

"Good." Locke dropped the man back to the deck and stowed his dagger. "Then let's call it quits. I'll let you have your amusing little toy ship back now."

Locke and Jean met briefly at the stern before boarding the last boat back to the *Orchid*.

"Gods," said Jean, "the archon is going to *love* this."

"Well, we didn't lie to him, did we? We promised pirate attacks at every compass point. We just didn't say they'd all feature Zamira as the major attraction." Locke blew a kiss to the city, spread across the northern horizon. "Happy festa, Protector."

6

"IF THERE'S one thing I never particularly need to do again in my life," said Locke, "it's dangle here all day painting this bloody ship's ass."

At the third hour of the afternoon the next day, Locke and Jean were hanging from crude rope swings secured to the *Poison Orchid*'s taffrail. Now that last night's hasty coat of dark paint had forever blotted out the *Chimera*, they were laboriously christening the ship with a new moniker, *Delight*. Their hands and tunics were spattered with thick silver gobs.

They had gotten as far as *Delig*, and Paolo and Cosetta were making faces at them through the stern windows of Zamira's cabin.

"I think piracy's a bit like drinking," said Jean. "You want to stay out all night doing it, you pay the price the next day."

The *Orchid* had turned north that morning a comfortable forty or fifty miles west of the city; Drakasha had cleared the area of their *Pilchard* raid with haste, and decided to spend the day at a remove, brushing up her old wooden girl's new disguise. Or, more accurately, turning that duty over to Locke and Jean.

They finally managed to put the "light" into *Delight* around the fourth hour of the afternoon. Thirsty and sunbaked, they were hauled up to the quarterdeck by Delmastro, Drakasha, and Nasreen. After they'd gulped down proffered mugs of lukewarm cask water, Drakasha beckoned for them to follow her down to her cabin.

"Last night was well done," she said. "Well done and nicely confusing. I don't doubt the archon will be rather vexed."

"I'd pay something to be a fly on a tavern wall in Tal Verrar these next few days," said Locke.

"But it's also given me a thought, on our general strategy."

"Which is?"

"You told me that captain and crew of the ketch weren't Verrari—that will curb some of the impact of their story. There'll be questions about their reliability. Ignorant rumors and mutterings."

"Right..."

"So what we've just done will fester," said Zamira. "It will cause comment, speculation, and a great deal of aggravation to Stragos, but it won't cause a panic, or have the Verrari rioting in the streets for his intercession. In a way, as our first bit of piracy on his behalf, it's a bit of a botch job."

"You wound our professional pride," said Jean.

"And my own! But consider this...perhaps what we need is a string of similarly botched jobs."

"This sounds like it's going to have a very entertaining explanation," said Locke.

"Del told me this afternoon that you two are pinning your hopes for a solution on Stragos' personal alchemist; that you can somehow secure his assistance by making him a private offer."

"That's true enough," said Locke. "It's one of the aspects of last night's visit to the Mon Magisteria that didn't go very well."

"So obviously what we need to do," said Drakasha, "is give you another chance to make this alchemist's acquaintance. Another plausible reason to visit the Mon Magisteria, soon. Good little servants, eager to hear their master's opinion on how their work is progressing."

"Ahhh," said Locke. "And if he's looking to shout at us, we can be sure he'll at least let us in for a chat."

"Exactly. So. What we need to do ... is something colorful. Something striking, something that is *undeniably* a sincere example of our best efforts on Stragos' behalf. But ... it can't threaten Tal Verrar directly. Not to the point that Stragos would feel it a useful step in his intended direction."

"Hmmm," said Jean. "Striking. Colorful. Nonthreatening. I'm not entirely sure these concepts blend well with the piratical life."

"Kosta," said Drakasha, "you're staring at me very

strangely. Do you have an idea, or did I leave you out in the sun for too long today?"

"Striking, colorful, and not threatening Tal Verrar *directly*," Locke whispered. "Gods! Captain Drakasha, you would so honor me if you would consent to one humble suggestion...."

7

MOUNT AZAR was quiet this morning, the twenty-fifth of Aurim, and the sky above Salon Corbeau was blue as a river's depths, unmarked by the old volcano's gray smoke. It was another mild winter on the northern Brass Coast, in a climate more reliable than Verrari clockwork.

"New swells coming in," said Zoran, chief dock attendant of the morning watch.

"I don't see any more waves than what we already got." Giatti, his more junior counterpart, stared earnestly across the harbor.

"Not swells, you idiot, *swells*. Gentlefolk. The landed and larded class." Zoran adjusted his olive-green tabard and brushed it clean, wishing that he didn't have to wear Lady Saljesca's damned felt hat. It made him look taller, but it generated sweat without keeping it out of his eyes.

Beyond the natural rock walls of Salon Corbeau's harbor, a stately new brig, a two-master with a dark witchwood hull, had joined the two Lashani feluccas at anchor in the gentle sea. A longboat was coming in from the newcomer; four or five of the quality rowed by a dozen oarsmen.

As the longboat pulled up alongside the dock, Giatti bent down and began uncoiling a rope from one of the dock pilings. When the bow of the boat was secure, Zoran stepped to its side, bowed, and extended his hand to the first young woman to rise from her seat.

"Welcome to Salon Corbeau," he said. "How are you styled, and how must you be announced?"

The short young woman, unusually tanned for someone of her station, smiled prettily as she took Zoran's hand. She wore a forest-green jacket over a matching set of frilled skirts; the color set her curly, chestnut-colored hair off rather well. She seemed to be wearing rather less makeup and jewelry than might be expected, however. A poorer relative of whoever owned the ship?

"Forgive me, madam, but I must know whom I'm announcing." She stepped safely onto the dock, and he released his grip on her hand. To his surprise, she didn't release hers, and in one smooth motion she was up against him with the menacing weight of a blackened-steel dagger touching the crook of his thigh. He gasped.

"Heavily armed pirates, party of ninety-eight," the woman said. "Scream or fight back and you're going to be one surprised eunuch."

8

"STAY CALM," said Delmastro as Locke led Jean, Streva, Jabril, and Big Konar up onto the dock. "We're all friends here. Just a wealthy family coming up for a visit to your lovely little village. City. Thing." She kept her knife between herself and the older dock attendant, so there was no chance of anyone seeing it from more than a few feet away. Konar took the younger dock attendant, placing one arm around his shoulder as though they knew each other, and muttered something into his ear that made the color drain from the poor fellow's face.

Slowly, carefully, the Orchids all made their way onto the dock. At the heart of the group, those wearing layers of fine clothing tried not to make too much noise, laden down as they were with an arsenal of clattering weapons beneath their cloaks and skirts. It had been too much to suppose that the dock attendants wouldn't notice sabers and hatchets in the belts of the rowers.

"Here we are, then," said Locke.

"Looks like a nice place," said Jean.

"Looks are most assuredly deceiving. Now we just wait for the captain to get things started."

9

"EXCUSE ME? Excuse me, sir?"

Zamira Drakasha, alone in the *Orchid*'s smallest boat, stared up at the bored-looking guard behind the ornamented gunwale of the yacht closest to her ship. That yacht, about fifteen yards long, had a single mast and banks of four oars per side. Those oars were locked upward now, poised like the wings of a stuffed and mounted bird. Just abaft the mast was a tentlike pavilion with faintly fluttering silk walls. This tent was between the guard and the mainland.

The guard peered down at her, squinting. Zamira was wearing a thick, shapeless yellow dress that was almost a robe. She'd left her hat in her cabin, and pulled the bangles and ribbons out of her hair.

"What do you want?"

"My mistress has left me to tend to chores on her ship, while she takes her pleasure ashore," said Zamira. "I have several heavy things to move, and I was wondering if I could beg for your help."

"You want me to come over there and be a mule for you?"

"It would be so kind of you."

"And, ah, what are you prepared to do in exchange?"

"Why, offer my heartfelt thanks to the gods for your

goodness," said Zamira, "or perhaps I could brew you some tea?"

"You have a cabin over there?"

"Yes, by the kindness of my mistress—"

"A few minutes alone with you and that mouth of yours, and I'd be happy to move your shit for you."

"How . . . how *inappropriate*! My mistress will—"

"Who's your mistress, then?"

"The Lady-in-Becoming Ezriane de la Mastron, of Nicora—"

"Nicora? Ha! As if anyone would give a shit. Get lost."

The guard turned away, chuckling to himself.

"Ah," said Zamira. "So be it. I know when I'm not wanted."

She reached forward and moved the dun-colored tarpaulin on the bottom of the boat, just ahead of her feet. Beneath it was the heaviest crossbow in the *Poison Orchid*'s arsenal, carrying a barbed steel bolt the length of her upper arm.

"And I simply *do not care*."

The guard was no doubt flustered by the sudden emergence, two seconds later, of a crossbow quarrel's point from his sternum. Zamira wondered if he had time to speculate on the location of the rest of the bolt before he collapsed, the upper and lower halves of his spine no longer on speaking terms.

Zamira pulled the yellow dress up and over her head, then tossed it into the back of the boat. Beneath it she wore her Elderglass vest, light tunic and breeches, boots, and a pair of slender leather bracers. Her sword-belt was at her waist, empty; she reached beneath her rowing bench, pulled out her sabers, and slid them into their scabbards. She rowed her little boat up against the yacht's side and waved to Nasreen, who stood at the *Orchid*'s bow. Two crewfolk climbed over the brig's side and dove into the water.

The swimmers were alongside a minute later. Zamira helped them out of the water and sent them forward to man one of the sets of oars. She then pulled the pins to release the yacht's anchor chains; no sense in wasting time hoisting it up. With her two sailors rowing and Zamira manning the rudder, it took just a few minutes to shift the yacht behind the *Poison Orchid*.

Her crew began to come quietly down onto the yacht, armed and armored, looking completely incongruous as they squeezed themselves onto the fragile, scrollwork-covered vessel. Zamira counted forty-two before she felt the boat could take no more; crewfolk were crouched on deck, stuffed into the cabin, and manning all the oars. This would do; nearly two-thirds of her crew on shore to handle the main attack, and the other third on the *Orchid* to hit the vessels in the harbor.

She waved at Utgar, who would be in charge of that last duty. He grinned and left the entry port to begin his final preparations.

Zamira's rowers brought the yacht out and around the *Orchid*; they turned to larboard just past her stern and pointed themselves straight toward the beach. Beyond that the buildings and tiered gardens of the rich little valley could be seen, laid out neat as food before a banquet.

"Who brought the finishing touch?" Zamira asked.

One of her crewmen unfolded a red silk banner and began securing it to the ensign halyard dangling from the yacht's mast.

"Right, then." Zamira knelt at the bow of the yacht and gave her sword-belt a habitual adjustment. "Oars, with a will! Put us on that beach!"

As the yacht surged forward across the temporarily calm waters of the bay, Zamira noticed a few small figures atop the nearby cliffs finally taking alarm. One or two of them ran toward the city; it looked as though they'd arrive about the same time Zamira expected to feel the sand of the beach beneath her boots.

"That's it," she shouted. "Send up the red and let's have some music!"

As the scarlet banner shot up the halyard and caught the wind, every Orchid on the yacht let loose with a wild, wordless howl. Their yells echoed throughout the harbor, the disguised Orchids at the dock began seizing weapons, every visible person on the cliffs was now fleeing for the city, and Zamira's sabers flashed in the sunlight as she drew them for action.

It was the very definition of a beautiful morning.

10

"WAS IT *absolutely necessary* to sack Salon Corbeau so thoroughly?" said Stragos.

Locke and Jean were seated in the archon's office, surrounded by the faint shadowy flutterings of his thousand mechanical insects. It might just have been the shadows of the low-lit room, but it seemed to Locke that the lines on Stragos' face had deepened in the days since he'd last seen him.

"It was loads of fun. You have some particular attachment to the place?"

"Not for my own sake, Lamora—it's just that I had the clear impression that you were going to focus your activities on shipping in the vicinity of Tal Verrar."

"Salon Corbeau is generally considered to be in the vicinity of—"

"Is it a *ship*, Lamora?"

"There were ships in the harbor—"

"I have the gods-damned numbers here, from my

agents," said Stragos. He stabbed at a piece of parchment with two fingers. "Two feluccas sunk. Forty-six yachts, pleasure barges, and smaller craft, burned or sunk. One hundred and eighteen slaves stolen. Nineteen of Countess Saljesca's private guard slain, sixteen wounded. The vast majority of Salon Corbeau's residences and guest villas burnt, the gardens all but destroyed. Her replica stadium gutted. Miscellaneous damages and losses exceeding ninety-five thousand solari at a first estimate. About the only things you missed were a few shops and Lady Saljesca's residence itself!"

Locke smirked. That had been by design; after Saljesca's most important guests had fled to her fortresslike manor and barricaded themselves there with her remaining soldiers, attacking the manor would have been fruitless; the Orchids would have been slaughtered beneath the walls. But with their only opposition bottled up atop the valley, Drakasha's crew had been free to run amok for more than an hour, looting and burning the valley at leisure. They'd lost only four crewfolk in the attack.

As for the shops, well—Locke had specifically requested that the area surrounding the Baumondain family business be left alone.

"We didn't have time to hit everything," he said. "And now that Salon Corbeau's more or less ruined, some of those artisans might see fit to settle in Tal Verrar. Safer down here, with you and your military around, right?"

"How can you spend your time executing a raid like that so efficiently," said Stragos, "when your efforts toward my primary design are so perfunctory?"

"I object—"

"One attack by Orrin Ravelle—*thank you* for that, by the way—the night of the festa, against an Iridani ketch hired by a mad eccentric. Two more reported attacks, both in the vicinity of Salon Corbeau, one by Ravelle and one by the unknown "Captain de la Mastron." Does Drakasha fear to take credit for her own work?"

"We're trying to create the impression of multiple pirates at work—"

"What you are trying is my patience. You have stolen no major cargos, burned no ships at sea, nor even murdered any crewfolk. You content yourselves with money and portable valuables, you humiliate and frighten your prisoners, you do little more than vandalize their vessels, and then you vanish."

"We can't weigh ourselves down with heavier cargo; we've got a lot of roaming to do."

"It seems to me that you have a fair bit of *killing* to do," said Stragos. "The city is more bemused now than concerned; I continue to suffer in the public eye for the Ravelle affair, but few fear that this spree of...hooliganism truly bodes ill for Verrari trade.

"Even the sack of Salon Corbeau has failed to arouse anxiety. Your recent attacks give the impression that you now fear to approach the city again; that these waters remain safe." Stragos glared before continuing. "Were I purchasing goods from a tradesman, at the moment, I would not be well pleased with their quality."

"The difference, of course," said Locke, "is that when I get fitted for, say, new jackets, I don't *poison* my tailor until he has the length of the sleeves right—"

"My life and fortunes are at stake," said Stragos, rising from his chair. "And so are yours, dependent upon your success. I require butchers, not jesters. Take ships within sight of my city's walls. Put their crews to the sword. Take their cargo or burn it—the time has come to be *serious*. That and that alone will stir this city to its foundations.

"Do not return," he said, emphasizing every word, "until you have spilled blood in these waters. Until you have become a scourge."

"So be it," said Locke. "Another sip of our antidote—"

"No."

"If you wish us to work with absolute confidence—"

"You will *keep*," said Stragos. "Like pickled eggs in a jar. It has been less than two weeks since your last dose. You are in no danger for six more."

"But—wait, Archon." Jean interrupted him as he was turning to leave. "One thing more. When we came to this city on the night of the festa, we were attacked again."

Stragos' eyes narrowed. "The same assassins as before?"

"If you mean the same mystery, yes, we think so," said Jean. "Some lurked in wait for us at the docks after we visited Requin. If they received a tip-off concerning our presence in the city, they moved damned fast."

"And the only place we went," added Locke, "before visiting the Golden Steps was *here*."

"My people had nothing to do with it," said Stragos. "Indeed, this is the first I have heard of the matter."

"We left four dead behind us," said Jean.

"Unremarkable. The constables found nearly thirty bodies throughout the city after the festa; there are always arguments and robberies to supply them." Stragos sighed. "Obviously, this is nothing of my doing, and I have nothing more to tell you on the matter. I presume you'll be returning straight to your ship when you leave."

"At speed," said Locke. "Staying as far from the islands as we can."

"The complications of some previous malfeasance have obviously come back to ensnare you," said Stragos. "Now leave. No more antidote and no more consultation. You extend your lease on fair health again only once you send panicked merchants to my gates, begging for help because death lurks beyond these harbors. Go now and *do your job*."

He whirled and left without a further word. A moment

later a squad of Eyes marched in through the main door and waited expectantly.

"Well, damn," muttered Jean.

11

"WE'LL GET the bastard," said Ezri as they lay together in her cabin that night. The *Poison Orchid,* now calling itself the *Mercurial,* was treading heavy seas about twenty miles southwest of Tal Verrar, and the two of them clung to one another as they rocked back and forth in the hammock.

"With difficulty," said Jean. "He won't see us now until we do some serious work on his behalf . . . and if we do that, we might push things to the point that he no longer needs us. We'll get a knife, rather than an antidote. Or . . . if it comes to that, he'll get the knife—"

"Jean, I don't want to hear that," she said. "Don't talk about it."

"It's got to be faced, love—"

"I don't believe it," she said. "I don't. There's *always* a way to attack or a way to escape. That's the way it is out here." She rolled over on top of him and kissed him. "I told you not to give up, Jean Tannen, and the thing about me is I *get* my way."

"Gods," whispered Jean, "how did I ever live before I met you?"

"Sadly, poorly, miserably," she said. "I make everything so much better. It's why the gods put me here. Now quit moping and tell me something pleasant!"

"Something pleasant?"

"Yeah, slackwit, I've heard that other lovers sometimes tell one another pleasant things when they're alone—"

"Yes, but with you it's sort of on pain of death, isn't it?"

"It could be. Let me find a saber—"

"Ezri," he said with sudden seriousness. "Look—when this is over, Stragos and all, Leocanto and I might be... very rich men. If our other business in Tal Verrar goes well."

"Not if," she said. "When."

"All right," he said. "*When* it does... you really could come with us. Leo and I spoke about it a bit. You don't have to choose one life or another, Ezri. You can just sort of... go on leave for a bit. We all could."

"What do you mean?"

"We could get a yacht," said Jean, "in Vel Virazzo, there's this place—the private marina, where all the swells keep their boats and barges. They usually have a few for sale, if you've got a few hundred solari on hand, which we intend to. We have to go to Vel Virazzo anyway, to sort of... finish our business. We could have a boat fitted out in a couple of days, and then just... poke around a bit! Drift. Enjoy ourselves. Pretend to be useless gentlefolk for a while."

"And come back to all this later, you mean?"

"Whenever you wanted," said Jean. "Have it as you like. You always get your way, don't you?"

"Live on a yacht for a while with you and Leocanto," she said. "No offense, Jean, you're passable for a landsman, but by his own admission Leocanto couldn't con a shoe across a puddle of piss—"

"What do you think we'd be bringing you along for, hmmm?"

"Well, I would have imagined that *this* had something to do with it," she said, moving her hands strategically to a more interesting location.

"Ah," he said, "and so it does, but you could sort of be honorary captain, too—"

"Can I name the boat?"

"As if you'd let anyone else do it!"

"All right," she whispered. "If that's the plan, that's the plan. We'll do it."

"You really mean—"

"Hell," she said, "with just the swag we pulled from Salon Corbeau, everyone on this crew can stay drunk for months when we get back to the Ghostwinds. Zamira won't miss me for a while." They kissed. "Half a year." They kissed again. "Year or two, maybe."

"Always a way to attack," Jean mused between kisses, "always a way to escape."

"Of course," she whispered. "Hold fast, and sooner or later you'll always find what you're after."

12

JAFFRIM RODANOV paced the quarterdeck of the *Dread Sovereign* in the silvery-orange light of earliest morning. They were bound north by west with the wind on the starboard quarter, about forty miles southwest of Tal Verrar. The seas were running at five or six feet.

Tal Verrar. Half a day's sailing to the city they'd avoided like a colony of slipskinners these past seven years; to the home of a navy that could crush even his powerful *Sovereign* if roused to anger. There was no genuine freedom in these waters, only a vague illusion. Fat merchant ships he could never touch; a rich city he could never sack. Yet he could live with that. It was *grand,* provided only that the freedom and the plunder of the southern seas could remain.

"Captain," said Ydrena, appearing on deck with a chipped clay mug of her usual brandy-laced morning tea in one hand, "I don't mean to ruin a fine new morning—"

"You wouldn't be my first if I needed my ass kissed more than I needed my ship sailed."

"A week out here without a lead, Captain."

"We've seen two dozen sails of merchants, luggers, and pleasure galleys just these past two days," said Rodanov. "And we have yet to see a naval ensign. There's still time to find her."

"No quarrel with that logic, Captain. It's the finding her that's—"

"A royal pain in the ass. I know."

"It's not as though she'll be roaming around announcing herself as Zamira Drakasha of the *Poison Orchid*," said Ydrena, taking a sip of her tea. " 'Well met, we're infamous shipwreckers from the Ghostwinds; mind if we pull alongside for a visit?' "

"She can claim whatever name she likes," said Rodanov, "paint whatever she wants on her stern, mess with her sail plan until she looks like a constipated xebec, but she's only got one hull. Dark witchwood hull. And we've been seeing it for years."

"All hulls are dark until you get awful close, Captain."

"Ydrena, if I had a better notion, believe me, we'd be pursuing it." He yawned and stretched, feeling the heavy muscles in his arms flex pleasantly. "Only word we've got is a few ships getting hit, and now Salon Corbeau. She's circling out here somewhere, keeping west. It's what I'd do—more sea room."

"Aye," said Ydrena. "Such a very great *deal* of sea room."

"Ydrena," he said softly, "I've come a long way to break an oath and kill a friend. I'll go as far as it takes, and I'll haunt her wake as long as it takes. We'll quarter this sea until one of us finds the other."

"Or the crew decides they've had—"

"It's a good long haul till we cross that line. In the meantime, double all our top-eyes by night. Triple them by day. We'll put half the fucking crew up the masts if we have to."

"New sail ahoy," called a voice from atop the foremast. The cry was passed back down the deck, and Rodanov ran forward, unable to restrain himself. They'd heard the cry fifty times that week if they'd heard it once, but each time might be *the* time.

"Where away?"

"Three points off the starboard bow!"

"Ydrena," Rodanov shouted, "set more canvas! Straight for the sighting! Helm, bring us about north-northeast on the starboard tack!"

Whatever the sighting was, the *Dread Sovereign* was at home in wind and waters like this; her size and weight allowed her to crash through waves that would steal speed from lighter vessels. They would close with the sighting very soon.

Still, the minutes passed interminably. They came about to their new course, seizing the power of the wind now blowing from just abaft their starboard beam. Rodanov prowled the forecastle, waiting—

"Captain Rodanov! She's a two-master, sir! Say again, two masts!"

"Very good," he shouted. "Ydrena! First mate to the forecastle!"

She was there in a minute, pale blond hair fluttering in the breeze. She tossed back the last of her morning tea as she arrived.

"Take my best glass to the foretop," he said. "Tell me . . . as soon as you know anything."

"Aye," she said. "At least it's something to do."

The morning progressed with torturous slowness, but at least the sky was cloudless. Good conditions for spotting. The sun grew higher and brighter, until—

"Captain," hollered Ydrena. "Witchwood hull! That's a two-masted brig with a witchwood hull!"

He couldn't stand waiting passively anymore. "I'm coming up myself," he shouted.

Laboriously, he crawled up the foremast shrouds, to the

observation platform at the maintop, a place he'd left to smaller, younger sailors for many years. Ydrena was perched there, along with a crewman who shuffled aside to make room for him on the platform. Rodanov took the glass and peered at the ship on the horizon, stared at it until not even the most cautious part of himself would let him deny it.

"It's her," he said. "She's done something fancy to her sails, but that's the *Orchid*."

"What now?"

"Set every scrap of canvas we can bear," he said. "Steal as much of this ocean from her as we can before she recognizes us."

"Do you want to try and bring her up with signals? Offer parley, then jump her?"

" 'Let us speak behind our hands, lest our lips be read as the book of our designs,' " he said.

"More of your poetry?"

"Verse, not poetry. And no. She'll recognize us, sooner or later, and when she does she'll know *exactly* what our business is."

He passed the glass back to Ydrena, and prepared to go back down the shrouds.

"Straight on for her, cloaks off and weapons free. We can give her that much, for the last fight she'll ever have."

CHAPTER FIFTEEN

BETWEEN BRETHREN

1

"DOES JEROME KNOW that you're asking me to do this?"

"No."

Locke stood beside Drakasha at the taffrail, huddled close to her so they could converse privately. It was the seventh hour of the morning, more or less, and the sun was ascending into a cloudless bowl of blue sky. The wind was from the east, a touch abaft their starboard beam, and the waves were getting rowdy.

"And you feel that—"

"Yes, I do feel that I can speak for both of us," said Locke. "There's no other choice. We won't see Stragos again unless you do as he asks. And to be frank, if you do as he asks, I think our usefulness ends. We'll have one more chance at physical access to him. It's time to show this fucker how we used to do things in Camorr."

"I thought you specialized in dishonest finesse."

"I also do a brisk trade in putting knives to peoples' throats and shouting at them," said Locke.

"But if you request another meeting after we sink a few

ships for him, don't you think he'll be prepared for treachery? Especially in a palace crowded with soldiers?"

"All I have to do is get close to him," said Locke. "I'm not going to pretend I could fight my way through a wall of guards, but from six inches with a good stiletto, I'm the hand of Aza Guilla Herself."

"Hold him hostage, then?"

"Simple. Direct. Hopefully effective. If I can't trick an antidote out of him, or cut a deal with his apothecary, maybe I can frighten him half to death."

"And you honestly believe you've thought this through?"

"Captain Drakasha, I could barely sleep for pondering it. Why do you think I wandered back here to find you?"

"Well—"

"Captain!" The mainmast watch was hailing the deck. "Got action behind us!"

"What do you mean?"

"Sail maybe three points off the larboard quarter, at the horizon. Just came around real sudden. Went from sort of westerly to pointed right at us."

"Good eyes," said Drakasha. "Keep me informed. Utgar!"

"Aye, Captain?"

"Double the watch on each mast. On deck there! Make ready for a course change! Stand by tacks and braces! Wait for my word!"

"Real trouble, Captain?"

"Probably not," said Drakasha. "Even if Stragos had changed his mind since yesterday and decided to hunt us down now, a Verrari warship wouldn't be coming from that direction."

"Hopefully."

"Aye. So what we do is we change our own heading, nice and slow. If their course change was innocent, they'll sail merrily past." She cleared her throat. "Helm, come round northwest by north, smartly! Utgar! Get the yards braced for a wind on the starboard quarter!"

"Aye, Captain!"

The *Poison Orchid* slowly heeled even farther to larboard, until she was headed almost due northwest. The stiff breeze now blew across the quarterdeck, nearly into Locke's face. To the south he fancied that he could see tiny sails; from the deck the vessel was still hull-down.

A few minutes later came the shout. "Captain! She's come five or six points to her larboard! She's for us again!"

"We're off her starboard bow," said Drakasha. "She's trying to close with us. But that doesn't make sense." She snapped her fingers. "Wait. Might be a bounty-privateer."

"How could they know it's us?"

"Probably got a description of the *Orchid* from the crew of that ketch you visited. Look, we could only hope to disguise my girl for so long. These lovely witchwood planks of hers are too distinctive."

"So . . . how much of a problem is this?"

"Depends on who's got the speed. If she's a bounty-privateer, that's a profitless fight. She'll be carrying dangerous folk and no swag. So if we're the faster, I mean to show her our ass and wave farewell."

"And if not?"

"A profitless fight."

"Captain," hollered one of the top-eyes, "she's a three-master!"

"This just gets better and better," said Drakasha. "Go wake up Ezri and Jerome for me."

2

"BAD LUCK," said Delmastro. "Bad damned luck."

"Only for them, if I have my way," said Zamira.

The captain and her lieutenant stood at the taffrail, staring at the faint square of white that marked their pursuer's position on the horizon. Locke waited with Jean a few steps away, at the starboard rail. Drakasha had nudged the ship a few points south, so that they were traveling west-north-west with the wind fine on the starboard quarter, what she claimed was the *Orchid*'s best point of sail. Locke knew this was something of a risk; if their opponent was the faster, they could lay an intercepting course that would bring them up much sooner than a stern chase. The trouble was that such a chase to the north could not last; unlimited sea room existed only to their west.

"I'm not sure we're gaining any ground, Captain," said Delmastro after a few minutes of silence.

"Nor I. Damn this jumpy sea. If she's a three-master she may have the weight to carve a better speed out of it."

"Captain!" The cry from up the mainmast was even more urgent than usual. "Captain, she's not falling away, and ... Captain, beggin' pardon, but you might want to come and see this for yourself."

"See what?"

"If I ain't mad I've seen that ship before," shouted the watch-woman. "I'd swear it. I'd appreciate another set of eyes."

"I'll take a look," said Delmastro. "Mind if I fetch up your favorite glass?"

"Drop it, and I'll give your cabin over to Paolo and Cosetta."

Locke watched as Delmastro went up the mainmast a few minutes later armed with Zamira's pride and joy, a masterpiece of Verrari optics bound in alchemically treated leather. It was a few minutes more before her shout fell to the deck.

"Captain, that's the *Dread Sovereign*!"

"What? Del, are you absolutely sure?"

"Seen her often enough, haven't I?"

"I'm coming up myself!"

Locke exchanged a stare with Jean as Zamira leapt into the mainmast shrouds. A buzz of muttering and swearing had arisen among the crewfolk on deck. About a dozen abandoned their chores and headed aft, craning their necks for a glimpse of the sail in the south. They cleared away in alarm when Drakasha and Delmastro returned to the quarterdeck, looking grim.

"So it's him?" said Locke.

"It is," said Drakasha. "And if he's been looking for us for any length of time, it means he sailed not all that long after we did."

"So...he could be carrying a message or something, right?"

"No." Drakasha removed her hat and ran her other hand through her braids, almost nervously. "He opposed this plan more than anyone else on the council of captains. He didn't sail as long and as far as we did, to risk his ship within spitting distance of Tal Verrar, to deliver any message.

"I'm afraid we'll need to postpone our previous conversation, Ravelle. The point is moot until we're sure this ship will still be floating at the end of the day."

3

LOCKE STARED out across the whitecaps at the *Dread Sovereign,* now well over the horizon, fixed on them like a needle drawn toward a lodestone. It was the tenth hour of the morning, and Rodanov's progress at their expense was obvious.

Zamira slammed her glass shut and whirled away from the taffrail, where she'd been studying the same phenomenon.

"Captain," said Delmastro, "there must be something . . . if we can just keep him off until nightfall—"

"Then we'd have options, aye. But only a straight stern chase could buy us that much time, and if we fly north we'll find the coast long before dusk. Not to mention the fact that she's fresh-careened and we're past due. The plain truth is, we've already lost this race."

Drakasha and Delmastro said nothing to each other for several moments, until Delmastro cleared her throat.

"I'll, um, start getting things ready, shall I?"

"You'd better. Let the Red watch keep sleeping as long as you can, if any of them are still asleep."

Delmastro nodded, grabbed Jean by the tunic sleeve, and pulled him with her toward the main-deck cargo hatch.

"You mean to fight," said Locke.

"I have no *choice* but to fight. And neither do you, if you want to live to see dinner. Rodanov has nearly twice our numbers. You understand what a mess we're looking at."

"And it's all for my sake, more or less. I'm sorry, Captain—"

"Avast bullshit, Ravelle. I won't second-guess my decision to help you, so no one else gets to, either. This is Stragos' doing, not yours. One way or another his plans would have put us in a tight spot."

"Thank you for that, Captain Drakasha. Now . . . I know we've had our talk concerning the real extent of my skills in battle, but most of the crew probably still thinks I'm some sort of man-killer. I . . . I guess I'm saying—"

"You want a spot in the thick of it?"

"Yes."

"Thought you might ask. I already have a place for you," she said. "Don't think you'll have it easy."

She stepped away for a moment and shouted forward. "Utgar!"

"Aye, Captain?"

"Fetch the deep-sea lead and give me a cast!"

Locke raised his eyebrows by way of a question, and she said, "Need to know how much water we have beneath our feet. Then I'll know about how long it'll take the anchor to drop."

"Why would you want to drop an anchor?"

"On that matter, you'll just have to wait to be amazed. Along with Rodanov, hopefully...but that would be asking a great deal."

"Captain," Utgar yelled several minutes later, "got about ninety fathoms under us!"

"Right," she said. "Ravelle, I know you're off watch right now, but you were witless enough to wander back here and call attention to yourself. Grab a couple of Blues and bring up some ale casks from down below. Try to stay quiet for the sake of the Reds still sleeping. I'll call all hands in about an hour, and it's never wise to send people into a tussle like this with their throats too dry."

"I'll be happy to do that, Captain. About an hour, then? When do you think we'll be—"

"I mean to bring the fight before noon. Only one way to win when you're being chased by someone bigger and tougher than you are. Turn straight around, punch their teeth out, and hope the gods are fond of you."

4

"ALL HANDS," shouted Ezri one last time, "all hands at the waist! Idlers and lazy motherfuckers on deck! If you have watchmates still below, haul 'em up yourselves!"

Jean stood at the front of the crowd amidships, waiting for Drakasha to say her piece. She stood at the rail with Ezri, Nasreen, Utgar, Mumchance, Gwillem, and Treganne behind her. The scholar looked deeply annoyed that something as trivial as a murderous ship-to-ship fight could justify disrupting her usual habits.

"Listen well," shouted Drakasha. "The ship bearing down on us is the *Dread Sovereign*. Captain Rodanov has taken exception to our business in these waters, and he's come a long way to give us a fight."

"We can't fight that many people," shouted someone in the crowd.

"It's not as though we have a choice. They're closing to board now whether we like it or not," said Drakasha.

"But what if it's just you he's after?" A crewman Jean didn't recognize spoke up; to give him credit, he too was standing at the front of the crowd, right where Drakasha and all of her officers could see him. "We give you to him, we save ourselves a hell of a fight. This ain't a navy, and I got the right to be as fond of my life as—"

Jabril pushed through the crowd behind the man and punched him in the small of the back. The man fell writhing to the deck.

"We *don't* know that it's just Drakasha he wants," Jabril shouted. "Me, I ain't waitin' at the rail with my breeches down for someone to kiss my cock! Most of you know as well as I—if captain fights captain it ain't convenient to let two sides'a the story get back to Port Prodigal!"

"Hold, Jabril," said Zamira. She hurried down the quarterdeck stairs, stepped over to the would-be pragmatist, and helped him sit up. She then stood before her assembled crew, within reach of the first row. "Basryn here is right about one thing. This isn't a navy, so you do have the right to be fond of your own lives. I'm not your gods-damned empress. Anyone wants to try handing me over to Rodanov, I'm right here. Now's your chance."

When nobody stepped forward from the crowd, Drakasha heaved Basryn to his feet and looked him straight in the eyes. "Now, you can have the smallest boat," she said, "you and anyone else who wants to help you take it. Or you can stay."

"Ah, hell," he said, groaning. "I'm sorry, Captain. I guess . . . I guess I'd rather live as a coward than die a fool."

"Oscarl," said Drakasha, "when we're done here, get a party together and hoist out the small boat, on the quick. Anyone else wants off with Basryn, that's what I'm giving you. If Rodanov wins, take your chances. If I win . . . understand that we're at least fifty miles from land and you're not coming back aboard."

The man nodded, and that was that. Drakasha released him and he stumbled into the crowd, holding his back and ignoring the glares of those around him.

"Heed this, now," shouted Drakasha. "The sea isn't our friend today; that son of a bitch has more bite in the water than we do. A chase in any direction can't buy us more than a few hours. If we're going to settle this at kissing distance, I intend to set the terms of the courtship.

"We need to kill two for one just to have any of us left standing, so obviously we need to do better even than that. If we lock up with him so that one of our sides is against his bow, we can crowd in all around his boarding point and outnumber him at the only place it matters. That big fat crew of his won't mean a damn thing if he has to feed it piece by piece right through our teeth.

"So, at the waist, I'll put you in ranks, like the old Therin Throne legions. Swords and shields up front, spears and halberds behind. Don't take your sweet time. If you can't kill someone, knock them into the water. Just get them out of the damn fight!

"Del will choose our ten best archers and send you aloft to do the obvious. Five per mast. I wish I could send more, but we're going to need every blade on deck we can get.

"Ravelle, Valora, I'm going to give you a few crewfolk to form our flying company. Your job is the *Sovereign*'s boats.

They'll try and board us from all points of the compass once we're engaged at the waist, so you go wherever they go. One person on deck can keep five in a boat, provided you act with haste.

"Nasreen, you'll choose a party of three and stand by at the starboard anchor for my command. Once it's given, you'll guard the bow against boats and free Ravelle's party to fight elsewhere.

"Utgar, you're with me to load crossbows. Now, there's ale at the forecastle and I want to see the cask dry before we do this. Drink up, find your armor. If you've got mail or leathers you've been saving, pile it on. I don't care how much you sweat; you'll never need it again like you'll need it today."

Drakasha dismissed the crew by turning away from them and striding back up the quarterdeck stairs. Pandemonium erupted amidships; suddenly crewfolk were shoving past one another in all directions, some going for their armor and weapons, others headed for what might be their last drink in life.

Ezri vaulted the quarterdeck railing and shouted as she strode forward into the chaos, "Fire watches set double sand buckets! Rig the larboard razor net and hoist it high! Jerome, get your lazy ass up on the quarterdeck! Form up the flying company there!"

Jean waved and followed Drakasha up to the stern of the ship, where Utgar waited, looking nervous. Treganne was just descending the companionway stairs, muttering something about "bulk rates."

Suddenly, a low dark shape shot up the companionway and ran for Drakasha. She looked down in response to a sudden tug on her breeches and found Paolo clutching at her, unselfconsciously.

"Mommy, the noise!"

Zamira smiled and swept him up off the deck, cradling

him against the lapels of her jacket. She turned into the wind and let it push her hair out of her face. Jean could see that Paolo's eyes were on the *Dread Sovereign* as it heaved and swayed beneath the cloudless sky, implacably clawing across the distance between them.

"Paolo, love, Mommy needs you to help her hide you and your sister in the rope locker on the orlop deck, all right?"

The little boy nodded, and Zamira kissed him on the forehead, burying her nose in his tangle of short dark curls with her eyes closed.

"Oh, good," she said a moment later. "Because after that, Mommy needs to fetch her armor and her sabers. And then she needs to go board that lying motherfucker's ship and sink it like a stone."

5

JAFFRIM RODANOV was at the bow of his ship, the *Poison Orchid* steady in the center of his glass, when she suddenly whirled to larboard and pointed herself at him like an arrow. Her mainsails shivered and began to vanish as Drakasha's crew hauled them up for battle.

"Ah," he said. "There we go, Zamira. Doing the only sensible thing at last."

Rodanov had dressed for a fight, as usual, in a leather coat reinforced with mail inset at the back and the lapels. The nicks and creases in the battered old thing were always a comfort to him, a reminder that people had been trying and failing to kill him for years.

On his hands he wore his favored segmented blackened-steel gauntlets. In the confusion of a close melee, they could catch blades and break skulls. For the less personal work of actually forcing his way aboard the *Orchid,* he leaned on a waist-high iron-studded club. He folded his glass carefully and slipped it into a pocket, resolving to return it to the binnacle before the fight began. Not like the last time.

"Orders, Captain?"

Ydrena waited on the forecastle stairs, her own curved sword sheathed on her back, with the majority of his crew ready behind her.

"She's for us," boomed Rodanov. "I know this doesn't come easy, but Drakasha's raiding in Verrari waters. She'll call down hell on the life we all enjoy—unless we stop her now.

"Form up to starboard, as we planned. Shields up front. Crossbows behind. Remember, one volley, then throw 'em down and pull steel. Boat crews, over the starboard side once we're locked with the *Orchid*. Grapples ready at the waist and bow. Helm! You have your orders—make it perfect or pray you die in the fight.

"This day will be red! Drakasha is a foe to be reckoned with. But what are we, over all the winds and waters of the Sea of Brass?"

"*Sovereign!*" the crew shouted as one.

"Who are we, never boarded and never beaten?"

"*Sovereign!*"

"What do our enemies scream, when they speak the name of their doom at the judgment of the gods?"

"*Sovereign!*"

"We are!" He waved his club above his head. "And we have some surprises for Zamira Drakasha! Bring the cages forward!"

Three teams of six sailors apiece brought canvas-covered cages to the forecastle deck. These cages had wooden carrying handles set well beyond their steel-mesh sides. They were about six feet long, and half as wide and high.

"Nothing to eat since yesterday, right?"

"No," said Ydrena.

"Good." Rodanov double-checked the sections of the starboard rail his carpenter had weakened, so one good shove would knock them over for about a ten-foot length. A blemish on his beloved *Sovereign*, but one that could be fixed easily enough later. "Set them down over here. And kick the cages. Let's get them riled up."

6

THE TWO ships crashed through the waves toward each other, and for a second time Locke Lamora found himself about to get involved rather intimately in a battle at sea.

"Steady, Mum," called Drakasha, who stood peering out over the larboard quarterdeck rail. Locke and Jean waited nearby, armed with hatchets and sabers. Jean also had a pair of leather bracers liberated from the property of Basryn, who was nowhere to be seen since he alone had gone over the side with the small boat. *My boat,* Locke thought, somewhat bitterly.

For their "flying company," Locke and Jean had Malakasti, Jabril, and Streva, as well as Gwillem. All save the latter had shields and spears; the timid-looking quartermaster wore a leather apron stuffed with heavy lead bullets for the sling he carried in his left hand.

Most of the crew waited amidships, ranked as Drakasha had ordered; those with large shields and stabbing swords up front, those with polearms in back. The mainsails were drawn up, fire buckets were set out, the larboard entry port was protected by what Delmastro had called a "skinner net," and the *Poison Orchid* was rushing to the *Dread Sovereign*'s embrace like a long-separated lover.

Delmastro appeared out of the mess at the waist. She looked much as she had the first time Locke had ever seen her, with her leather armor on and her hair pulled back for action. Paying no heed to the weapons they were carrying at their belts, she leapt onto Jean, wrapping her arms and legs around him. He put his arms behind her back and they kissed until Locke chuckled out loud. Not the sort of thing one saw just before most battles, he imagined.

"This day is ours," she said when they parted at last.

"Try not to kill everyone over there before I even get involved, right?" Jean grinned down at her, and she handed him something in a small silk bag.

"What's this?"

"Lock of my hair," she said. "Meant to give it to you days ago, but we got busy with all the raiding. You know. Piracy. Hectic life."

"Thank you, love," he said.

"Now, if you find yourself in trouble wherever you go, you can hold up that little bag to whoever's bothering you, and you can say, 'You have no idea who you're fucking with. I'm under the protection of the lady who gave me this object of her favor.'"

"And that's supposed to make them stop?"

"Shit no, that's just to confuse them. Then you kill them while they're standing there looking at you funny."

They hugged again, and Drakasha cleared her throat.

"Del, if it's not too much trouble, we're planning to attack that ship just ahead of us, so could you—"

"Oh, yeah, the fight for our lives. I guess I could help you out for a few minutes, Captain."

"Luck, Del."

"Luck, Zamira."

"Captain," said Mumchance, "now—"

"*Nasreen!*" Drakasha bellowed at the top of her considerable voice. "*Starboard anchor away!*"

"Sound collision," called Delmastro a moment later. "All hands brace yourselves! Up aloft! Grab a mast, grab a line!"

Someone began to ring the foremast bell frantically. The

two ships were closing with astonishing speed. Locke and
Jean crouched on the larboard quarterdeck stairs, clinging
tight to the inner rail. Locke glanced over at Drakasha and
saw that she was counting something, mouthing each
number intently to herself. Curious, he tried to puzzle
them out and concluded she wasn't counting in Therin.

"Captain," said Mumchance, calm as someone ordering
coffee, "other ship—"

"Helm harda-larboard," Drakasha shouted. Mumchance
and his mate began manhandling the ship's wheel to the left.
Suddenly there was a creak and a snapping noise from the
bow; the ship shuddered end to end and was jerked to starboard as though caught in the teeth of a gale. Locke felt his
stomach protesting and clung to the rail with all of his
strength.

"Anchor party," yelled Drakasha, "cut the cable!"

Locke had an excellent view of the *Dread Sovereign*,
rushing down on them, scarcely a hundred yards away. He
gasped to think of that heavy ship's bowsprit plunging like
a spear into the *Orchid* or her massed crewfolk, but even as
he watched, the three-master heeled over to larboard, making a turn of her own.

Rodanov avoided a head-on collision, and Locke had to
guess that was intentional; while it might have done serious damage to the *Orchid*, it would have locked his ship
precisely where Zamira could best resist his boarders, and
possibly sunk both ships sooner or later.

What happened was spectacular enough; the sea
creamed white between the two vessels, and Locke heard
the protesting waves hissing like steam baking furiously
from hot coals. There was no way for the *Sovereign* or the
Orchid to shed all their forward momentum, but they slid
into each other along their sides with a rolling cushion of
water between them. The whole world seemed to shake as
they met; timbers creaked, masts shuddered, and high

overhead an Orchid was pitched from her position. She struck the *Sovereign*'s deck, becoming the first casualty of the battle.

"Spanker! Spanker!" Zamira cried, and everyone on the quarterdeck looked up in unison as the *Orchid*'s spanker sail was unfurled in the most unseamanlike fashion possible by the small crew detailed to it. Fluttering down to full extension, it was braced in place with desperate speed. Ordinarily, the fore-and-aft sail would never have been placed side-on to a wind, but in this case the stiff breeze from the east pushed against it by intention, heaving the *Orchid*'s stern away from contact with the *Dread Sovereign*. Mumchance hauled his wheel to starboard now, trying to help the process along.

There was a series of screams and snapping noises from forward; the *Dread Sovereign*'s bowsprit was destroying or fouling much of the forward rigging, but Drakasha's plan seemed to be working. That bowsprit hadn't punched a hole in the hull, and now Rodanov's starboard bow was the only part of his ship in contact with Drakasha's larboard side. From high above, Locke thought, the gods might have seen the two ships as drunken fencers, their bowsprits crossed but doing relatively little harm as they waved about.

Unseen things clawed the air with a snakelike hiss, and Locke realized that arrows were raining around him. The fight had well and truly begun.

7

"CLEVER SYRESTI bitch," muttered Rodanov, and he crawled back to his feet after the collision. Drakasha was using her spanker for leverage to prevent full broadside-to-broadside contact. So be it; he had his own advantages ready to play.

"Let 'em loose!" he shouted.

A crewman standing well back from the rear of the three cages (with shield bearers flanking him) pulled the rope that released their doors. These were set just inches back from the collapsible section of the rail, which had been conveniently knocked clean away when the ships met.

A trio of adult *valcona*—starving, shaken up, and pissed off beyond all measure—exploded from their confinement shrieking like the vengeful undead. The first thing they laid eyes on was the group of Orchids lining up across the way. Though heavily armed and armored, Zamira's people had no doubt expected to repel human boarders first.

The three attack birds launched themselves through the air and landed amidst shields and polearms, laying about with their beaks and their dagger-sized claws. Orchids screamed, shoved against one another, and caused utter chaos in their desperate struggle to either swing at or flee from the ferocious beasts.

Rodanov grinned fiercely. They'd been worth it—even though they'd cost too much in Prodigal, even though they'd stunk up the hold, even though they'd be dead soon enough. Every Orchid they mutilated was one less for his people to face, and it was always impossible to put a price on making your enemy shit their breeches.

"Away boats," he yelled. "Sovereigns! On me!"

8

THE SCREAMS from forward were more than human; Locke scrambled up the quarterdeck stairs on his hands and knees, straining to see what was going on. Brown shapes were flailing about within the packed masses of Zamira's "legions" along the larboard side. What the hell was that? Drakasha herself dashed past, twin sabers out, running for the point of greatest chaos.

Several sailors aboard Rodanov's ship hurled grappling

hooks across the gap between the vessels. A team of Drakasha's crewfolk, waiting for this, hurried to the larboard rail to sever the grappling lines with hatchets. One of them toppled with an arrow in his throat; the rest made short work of every line Locke could see.

A sharp, flat thwack told of an arrow landing nearby; Jean grabbed him by his tunic collar and hauled him all the way onto the quarterdeck. His "flying company" was crouched behind their small shields; Malakasti was using hers to cover Mumchance as well, who manned the wheel from a crouch. Someone screamed and fell from the rigging aboard the *Sovereign*; a second later Jabril cried, "Gah!" as an arrow struck splinters from the taffrail beside his head.

To Locke's surprise, Gwillem suddenly stood up in the midst of all this and, with a placid look on his face, began to whirl a bullet overhand in the cradle of his sling. As his arm went up he released one of the sling's cords, and a second later a bowman on the *Sovereign*'s quarterdeck fell backward. Jean pulled Gwillem back to the deck when the Vadran began to reach for another projectile.

"Boats," hollered Streva. "Boats coming around her!"

Two boats, each carrying about twenty sailors, were pulling fast from behind the *Dread Sovereign*, curving around to approach the *Orchid*'s stern. Locke wished mightily for a few arrows to season their passage, but the archers above had orders to ignore the boats. They were strictly the business of that legendary hero of the plunging beer cask, Orrin Ravelle.

He did, however, have one major advantage, and as usual its name was Jean Tannen. Sitting incongruously on the polished witchwood planks of the deck were several large round stones, plucked laboriously from the ship's ballast.

"Do the brute thing, Jerome," Locke shouted.

As the first boat of Sovereigns approached the taffrail, a pair of sailors armed with crossbows stood up to clear the way for a woman readying a grappling hook. Gwillem wound up and flung one of his stones downward, opening a bowman's head and toppling the body backward into the mess of would-be boarders. A moment later Jean stepped to the taffrail, hoisting a hundred-pound rock the size of an ordinary man's chest over his head. He hollered wordlessly and flung it down into the boat, where it shattered not just the legs of two rowers but the deck of the little craft itself. As water began to gush up through the hole, panic ensued.

Then crossbow bolts came from the second boat. Streva, caught up watching the travails of the first, took one in the ribs and fell backward onto Locke, who pushed the unfortunate young man away, knowing it was beyond his power to help. The deck was already bright red with blood. A moment later Malakasti gasped as an arrow from the *Sovereign*'s upper yards punched through her back; she fell against the taffrail and her shield went over the side.

Jabril pushed her spear away and yanked her down to the deck. Locke could see that the arrow had punctured one of her lungs, and the wet-sounding breaths she was fighting for now would be her last. Jabril, anguish on his face, tried to cover her with his body until Locke shouted at him, "More coming! Don't lose your fucking head!"

Gods-damned hypocrite, he thought to himself, heart hammering.

On the sinking boat below, another sailor wound up to toss a grappling hook. Gwillem struck again, shattering the man's arm. Yet another rock followed from Jean. That was it for the remaining Sovereigns; with the boat going down and corpses crowding the seats, the survivors were spilling over the side. They might be trouble again in a few minutes, but for now they were out of the fight.

So was a third of Locke's "company." The second enemy boat came on, wary enough of the stones to keep well back. It circled around the stern and darted for the starboard side, a shark with wounded prey.

9

ZAMIRA PULLED her saber from the body of the last *valcona* and hollered at her people along the larboard side, "Re-form! Re-form! Plug the fucking gap, there!"

Valcona! Damn Rodanov for a clever bastard; at least five of her people lay dead because of the bloody things, and gods knew how many more had been injured or shaken. He'd been *expecting* her to try and go broadside-to-bow; the beasts had been waiting like a spring-loaded trap.

And there he was—impossible to miss, nearly the size of two men, wearing a dark coat and those damned gauntlets of his. In his hands, a club that must have weighed twenty pounds. His people flooded around him, cheering, and they poured against her first rank through the gap Rodanov had somehow contrived in his starboard rail. The point of decision was exactly the mess she'd expected: stabbing spears, flailing shields, corpses and living fighters alike too pressed by the crowd on either side to move, except downward. Some slipped through the ever-changing gap between ships, to be drowned or ground to a pulp as the two vessels scraped together again.

"Crossbows," she yelled, "crossbows!"

Behind her spear-carriers, nearly every crossbow on the ship had been set out and loaded. The rear rank of waiting Orchids seized these and fired a ragged volley past the forward ranks; eight or nine of Rodanov's people toppled, but he himself seemed untouched. A moment later there was a return volley from the deck of the *Sovereign*; Rodanov had had the same idea. Screaming men and women fell out of

Zamira's lines with feathered shafts in their heads and chests, not one of them a person she could spare.

Sovereigns were attempting to hurtle the wider gap to the right of the main fight; some of them made it, and clung tenaciously to her rail, struggling to pull themselves up. She solved that problem herself, slashing faces and cracking skulls with the butts of her sabers. Three, four— more of them were coming. She was already gasping for breath. Not quite the tireless fighter she'd once been, she reflected ruefully. Arrows bit the air around her, more of Rodanov's people leapt, and it looked as though every single gods-damned pirate on the Sea of Brass was on the deck of the *Dread Sovereign*, lined up and waiting to storm her ship.

10

LOCKE'S "FLYING company" was now engaged at the starboard rail of the quarterdeck; while Mumchance and one of his mates wielded spears to fend off swimmers from any other angle, Locke, Jean, Jabril, and Gwillem tried to fight off the second boat.

This one was far sturdier than its predecessor; Jean's two hurled rocks had killed or injured at least five people, but failed to knock holes in the wood. Rodanov's crewfolk stabbed at them with boat hooks; it was an awkward duel between these and the spears of the Orchids. Jabril cried out as a hook gouged one of his legs, and he retaliated by stabbing a Sovereign in the neck.

Gwillem stood up and hurled a bullet down into the boat; he was rewarded for his effort by a loud scream. As he reached into his pouch for another, an arrow seemed to appear in his back as though by magic. He sagged forward against the starboard rail, and sling bullets rolled onto the deck, clattering.

"Shit," Locke yelled. "Are we out of big rocks?"

"Used them all," said Jean. A woman with a dagger in her teeth vaulted acrobatically up to the rail and would have made it over had Jean not bashed her in the face with a shield. She toppled into the water.

Jabril frantically swept with his spear as four or five Sovereigns at once got their hands up above the rail; two let go, but in a moment two more were rolling onto the deck, sabers in hand. Jabril fell onto his back and speared one in the stomach; Jean got his hands on Gwillem's sling and threw it around the throat of the other, garroting the man, just like old times in Camorr. Another sailor poked his head up and shoved a crossbow through the rails, aiming for Jean. Locke felt every inch the legendary hero of the plunging beer cask as he kicked the man in the face.

Rising screams from the water told of some new development; warily, Locke glanced over the edge. A roiling, gelatinous mass floated beside the boat like a translucent blanket, pulsing with a faint internal luminescence that was visible even by day. As Locke watched, a swimming man was drawn, screaming, into this mass. In seconds, the gelatinous substance around his legs clouded red and he began to spasm. The thing was drawing the blood out of his pores as a man might suck the juice from a pulpy fruit.

A death-lantern, drawn as ever to the scent of blood in the water. A gods-awful way to go, even for people Locke was actively trying to kill—but it and the others sure to come would take care of the swimmers. No more Sovereigns were climbing up the sides; the few left in the boat below were frantically trying to escape the thing in the water beside them. Locke dropped his spear and took a few much-needed deep breaths. A second later an arrow hit the rail two feet above his head; another hissed past it completely; a third struck the wheel. "Cover," he hollered, looking around frantically for a shield. A moment later Jean grabbed him and dragged him to the right, where he was holding Gwillem's body up before him. Jabril crawled behind the binnacle, while Mumchance and his mate mimicked Jean's ploy with Streva's body. Locke felt the impact as at least one arrow sank into the quartermaster's corpse.

"Might feel bad later about using the dead like this," hollered Jean, "but hell, there's certainly enough of them around."

11

YDRENA KOROS came over the rail and nearly killed Zamira with the first slash of her scimitar. The blade rebounded off Elderglass—still, Zamira burned at the thought that her guard had slipped. She struck back with both sabers; but Ydrena, small and lithe, had all the room she needed to parry one and avoid the other. So fast, so effortlessly fast—Zamira gritted her teeth. Two blades on one, and Koros still filled the air between them with a deadly silver blur; Zamira lost her hat and very nearly her neck, parrying only at the last second. Another slash hissed against her vest, a second sliced one of her bracers. *Shit*— she backed into one of her own sailors. There was nowhere else to go on the deck.

Koros conjured a curving, broad-bladed dagger in her left hand, feinted with it, and swept her scimitar at Zamira's knees. Zamira released her sabers and stepped into Koros' guard, putting them chest to chest. She grabbed Ydrena's arms with her own, forcing them out and down with all her strength. In that, at last, she had the advantage—that and one thing more. Fighting dirty usually prevailed over fighting prettily.

Zamira brought her left knee up into Ydrena's stomach. Ydrena sank; Zamira grabbed her hair and slammed her in the chin. The smaller woman's teeth made a sound like clattering billiard balls. Zamira heaved her to her feet and threw her backward, onto the sword of the Sovereign directly behind her. A brief look of surprise flared on the woman's blood-smeared face, then died with her. Zamira felt more relief than triumph.

She fetched her sabers from the deck where they'd fallen; as the sailor now in front of her pulled his sword from Ydrena and let her body drop, he suddenly found one of Zamira's blades in his chest. The battle ground on, and her actions became mechanical—her sabers rose and fell against the screaming tide of Rodanov's people, and the deaths ran together into one red cacophony. Arrows flew, blood slicked the deck beneath her feet, and the ships rolled and yawed atop the sea, lending a nightmarish shifting quality to everything.

It might have been minutes or ages before she found Ezri at her arm, pulling her back from the rail. Rodanov's people were falling back to regroup; the deck was thick with dead and wounded, her own survivors were all but standing on them as they stumbled into one another and fell back themselves.

"Del," gasped Zamira, "you hurt?"

"No." Ezri was covered in blood; her leathers had been slashed and her hair was partially askew, but otherwise she seemed to be correct.

"The flying company?"

"No idea, Captain."

"Nasreen? Utgar?"

"Nasreen's dead. Haven't seen Utgar since the fight started."

"Drakasha," came a voice above the moans and mutterings of the confusion on both sides. Rodanov's voice. "Drakasha! Cease fighting! Everyone, cease fighting! Drakasha, listen to me!"

12

RODANOV GLANCED at the arrow sunk into his right upper arm. Painful, but not the deep, grinding agony that told of a touch to the bone. He grimaced, used his left hand to steady the arrowhead, and then reached up with his right to snap the shaft just above it. He gasped, but that would do until he could deal with it properly. He hefted his club again, shaking blood onto the deck of the *Sovereign*.

Ydrena dead; gods-damn it, his first mate for five years, on the bloody deck. He'd laid about with his club to get to her side, splintering shields and beating aside spears. At least half a dozen Orchids to him, and he'd been their match—Dantierre he'd knocked clean over the side. But the fighting space was too narrow, the rolling of the ships unpredictable, his crewfolk too thin around him. Zamira'd suffered miserably, but at this confined point of contact he was stymied. A lack of brawling at the *Orchid*'s stern meant that the boats had probably fared the same. Shit. Half his crew was gone, at least. It was time to spring his second surprise. His calling a halt to the battle was the signal to bring it on. All in, now—last game, last hand, last turn of the cards.

"Zamira, don't make me destroy your ship!"

13

"GO TO hell, you oath-breaking son of a bitch! You come try again, if you think you still have any crewfolk willing to die in a hurry!"

Locke had left Jabril, Mumchance, and Mumchance's mate—along with the death-lanterns, he supposed—to guard the stern. He and Jean hurried forward, through the strangeness of air suddenly free from arrows, past the mounds of dead and wounded. Scholar Treganne stumped past, her false leg loud against the desk, single-handedly dragging Rask behind her. At the waist, Utgar stood, using a hook to pull up the main-deck cargo hatch grating. A leather satchel was at his feet; Locke presumed he was on some business for the captain and ignored him.

They found Drakasha and Delmastro at the bow, with about twenty surviving Orchids staring at twice their number of Sovereigns across the way. Ezri hugged Jean fiercely; she looked as though she'd been through a great deal of blood but not yet lost any of her own. Up here the *Orchid* seemed to have no deck; only a surface layer of dead and nearly dead. Blood drained off the sides in streams.

"Not me," shouted Rodanov.

"Here," yelled Utgar at the *Orchid*'s waist. "Here, Drakasha!"

Locke turned to see Utgar holding a gray sphere, perhaps eight inches in diameter, with a curiously greasy surface. He cradled it in his left hand, holding it over the open cargo hatch, and his right hand clutched something sticking out of the top of the sphere.

"Utgar," said Drakasha, "what the hell do you think you're—"

"Don't make a fucking move, right? Or you know what I'll do with this thing."

"Gods above," whispered Ezri, "I don't believe this."

"What the hell is that?" Locke asked.

"Bad news," she said. "Fucking awful news. That's a shipbane sphere."

14

JEAN LISTENED as she explained quickly.

"Alchemy, black alchemy, expensive as hell. You have to be fucking crazy to bring one to sea, same reason most captains shy away from fire-oil. But worse. Whole thing goes white-hot. You can't touch it; can't get close. Leave it on deck and it burns right through; down into the innards, and it sets *anything* on fire. Hell, it can probably set water on fire. Sure doesn't go out when you douse it."

"Utgar," said Drakasha, "you *motherfucker*, you traitor, how could—"

"Traitor? No. I'm Rodanov's man; am and have been since before I joined. His idea, hey? If I've done you good service, Drakasha, I've just been doing my job."

"Have him shot," said Jean.

"That thing he's holding is the twist-match fuse," said Ezri. "He moves his right hand, or we kill him and make that thing drop, it comes right out and ignites. *This* is what those damned things are for, get it? One man can hold a hundred prisoner if he just stands in the right spot."

"Utgar," she said. "Utgar, we're winning this fight."

"You might've been. Why do you think I stepped in?"

"Utgar, please. This ship is heaped with wounded. My children are down there!"

"Yeah. I know. So you'd best lay down your arms, hey? Back up against the starboard rail. Archers down from the masts. Everybody calm—and I'm sure for everyone but you, Drakasha, there's a happy arrangement waiting."

"Throats cut and over the side," shouted Treganne, who appeared at the top of the companionway with a crossbow in her hands. "That's the happy arrangement, isn't it, Utgar?" She stumped to the quarterdeck rail and put the crossbow to her shoulder. "This ship *is* heaped with wounded, and they're my responsibility, you bastard!"

"Treganne, *no*," Drakasha screamed.

But the scholar's deed was already done; Utgar seemed to jump and shudder as the bolt sank into the small of his back. The gray sphere tipped forward and fell from his left hand; his right hand pulled away, trailing a thin white cord.

He toppled to the deck, and his device vanished from sight into the hold below.

"Oh, *hell*," said Jean.

"No, no, no," Ezri whispered.

"Children," Jean found himself saying. "I can get them—"

Ezri stared at the cargo hatch, aghast. She looked at him, then back to the hatch.

"Not just them," she said. "Whole ship."

"I'll go," said Jean.

She grabbed him, wrapped her arms around his neck so tightly he could barely breathe, and whispered in his ear, "Gods damn you, Jean Tannen. You make this . . . you make it so hard."

And then she hit him in the stomach, harder than even he had thought possible. He fell backward, doubled in agony, realizing her intentions as she released him. He screamed in wordless rage and denial, reaching for her. But she was already running across the deck toward the hatch.

15

LOCKE KNOWS what Ezri means to do the instant he sees her make a fist, but Jean, his reflexes dulled by love or fatigue or both, plainly doesn't. And before Locke can do anything, she's hit Jean, and given him a shove backward so that Locke tumbles over him. Locke looks up just in time to see Ezri jump into the cargo hold, where an unnatural orange glare rises from the darkness a second later.

"Oh, Crooked Warden, damn it all to hell," he whispers, and he sees everything as time slows like cooling syrup—

Treganne at the quarterdeck rail, dumbfounded; clearly ignorant of what her erstwhile good deed has done.

Drakasha stumbling forward, sabers still in her hands, moving too slowly to stop Ezri or join her.

Jean crawling, barely able to move but willing himself after her with any muscle that will lend him force, one hand reaching uselessly after a woman already gone.

The crew of both ships staring, leaning on their weapons and on one another, the fight for a moment forgotten.

Utgar reaching for the bolt in his back, flailing feebly. It has been five seconds since Ezri leapt down into the cargo hold. Five seconds is when the screaming, the new screaming, starts.

16

SHE EMERGED from the main-deck stairs, holding it in her hands. No, more than that, Locke realized with horror—she must have known her hands wouldn't last. She must have cradled it close for that very reason.

The sphere was incandescent, a miniature sun, burning with the vivid colors of molten silver and gold. Locke felt the heat against his skin from thirty feet away, recoiled from the light, smelled the strange tang of scorched metal instantly. She ran, as best she could run; as she made her way toward the rail it became a jog, and then a desperate hop. She was on fire all the way, screaming all the way, unstoppable all the way.

She made it to the larboard rail and with one last convulsive effort, as much back and legs as what was left of her arms, she heaved the shipbane sphere across the gap to the *Dread Sovereign*. It grew in brightness even as it flew, a molten-metal comet, and Rodanov's crewfolk recoiled from it as it landed on their deck.

You couldn't touch such a thing, she'd said—well, clearly you could. But Locke knew you couldn't touch it and live. The arrow that took her in the stomach an eye-blink later was too late to beat her throw, and too late to do any real work. She fell to the deck, trailing smoke, and then all hell broke loose for the last time that morning.

"Rodanov," yelled Drakasha. "Rodanov!"

There was an eruption of light and fire at the waist of the *Dread Sovereign*; the incandescent globe, rolling to and fro, had at last burst. White-hot alchemy rained down hatches, caught sails, engulfed crewfolk, and nearly bisected the ship in seconds.

"If they would burn the *Sovereign*," shouted Rodanov, "all hands take the *Orchid*!"

"Fend off," cried Drakasha, "fend off and repel boarders! Helm hard a-larboard, Mum! Hard a-larboard!"

Locke could feel a growing new heat against his right cheek; the *Sovereign* was already doomed, and if the *Orchid* didn't disentangle from her shrouds and bowsprit and assorted debris, the fire would take both ships for a meal. Jean crawled slowly toward Ezri's body. Locke heard the sounds of new fighting breaking out behind them, and thought briefly of paying attention to it, but then realized that if he left Jean now he would never forgive himself. Or deserve forgiveness.

"Dear gods," he whispered when he saw her, "please, no. Oh, gods."

Jean moaned, sobbing, his hands held out above her. Locke didn't know where he would have touched her, either. There was so little *her* left—skin and clothing and hair burnt into one awful texture. And still she moved, trying feebly to rise. Still she fought for something resembling breath.

"Valora," said Scholar Treganne, hobbling toward them. "Valora don't, don't touch—"

Jean pounded the deck and screamed. Treganne knelt beside what was left of Ezri, pulling a dagger from her belt sheath. Locke was startled to see tears trailing down her cheeks.

"Valora," she said. "Take this. She's dead already. She needs you, for the gods' sake."

"No," sobbed Jean. "No, no, no—"

"Valora, *look at her,* gods damn it. She is beyond all help. Every second is an hour to her and she is *praying* for this knife."

Jean snatched the knife from Treganne's hand, wiped a tunic sleeve across his eyes, and shuddered. Gasping deep breaths despite the terrible smell of burning that lingered in the air, he moved the knife toward her, jerking in time with his sobs like a man with palsy. Treganne placed her hands over his to steady them, and Locke closed his eyes.

Then it was over.

"I'm sorry," said Treganne. "Forgive me, Valora. I didn't know—I didn't know what that thing was, what Utgar had. Forgive me."

Jean said nothing. Locke opened his eyes again, and saw Jean rising as though in a trance, his sobs all but stifled, the dagger still held loosely in his hand. He moved, as though he saw nothing of the battle still raging behind him, across the deck toward Utgar.

17

TEN MORE Orchids fell at the bow saving them, following Zamira's orders, shoving with all their might against the *Sovereign* with spears and boat hooks and halberds. Shoving to get her bowsprit and rigging clear of the *Orchid,* while Rodanov's survivors at the bow fought like demons to escape. But they did it, with Mumchance's help, and the two battered ships tore apart at last.

"All hands," shouted Zamira, dazed by the effort it suddenly required. "All hands! Tacks and braces! Put us west before the wind! Fire party to main hold! Get the wounded aft to Treganne!" Assuming Treganne was alive, assuming . . . much. Sorrow later. More hardship now.

Rodanov hadn't joined the final fight to board the *Orchid*; Zamira had last seen him running aft, fighting his way through the blaze and headed for the wheel. Whether in a last hopeless effort to save his ship or destroy hers, he'd failed.

18

"HELP," UTGAR whispered. "Help. Get it out. I can't reach it."

His movements were faint, and his eyes were going glassy. Jean knelt beside him, stared at him, and then brought the dagger down overhand into his back. Utgar took a shocked breath; Jean brought the knife down again and again while Locke watched; until Utgar was most certainly dead, until his back was covered in wounds, until Locke finally reached over and grabbed him by the wrist.

"Jean—"

"It doesn't help," said Jean, in a disbelieving voice. "Gods, it doesn't help."

"I know," said Locke. "I know."

"Why didn't you stop her?" Jean launched himself at Locke, pinning him to the deck, one hand around his throat. Locke gagged and fought back, and it did him about as much good as he expected. *"Why didn't you stop her?"*

"I tried," said Locke. "She pushed you into me. She knew what we'd do, Jean. She knew. Please—"

Jean released him and sat back as quickly as he had attacked. He looked down at his hands and shook his head. "Oh, gods, forgive me. Forgive me, Locke."

"Always," said Locke. "Jean, I am so, so sorry—I

wouldn't, I wouldn't have had it happen for the world. For the *world*, do you hear me?"

"I do," he said quietly. He buried his face in his hands and said nothing more.

To the southeast, the fire aboard the *Dread Sovereign* turned the sea red; it roared up the masts and sails, rained charred canvas like volcanic ash upon the waves, devoured the hull, and at last subsided into a billowing mountain of smoke and steam as the ship's charred hulk slipped beneath the waters.

"Ravelle," said Drakasha, placing a hand on Locke's shoulder and interrupting his reverie, "if you can help, I—"

"I'm fine," said Locke, stumbling to his feet. "I can help. Just maybe . . . leave Jerome—"

"Yes," she said. "Ravelle, we need—"

"Zamira, enough. Enough Ravelle this, Kosta that. Around the crew, sure. But my friends call me Locke."

"Locke," she said.

"Locke Lamora. Don't, ah—ahhh, who the hell would you tell anyway?" He reached up to set a hand on hers, and in a moment they had drawn one another into a hug. "I'm sorry," he whispered. "Ezri, Nasreen, Malakasti, Gwillem—"

"Gwillem?"

"Yeah, he—one of Rodanov's archers, I'm sorry."

"Gods," she said. "Gwillem was with the *Orchid* when I stole her. Last of the original crew. Ra—Locke. Mum has the wheel and we're safe for the moment. I need . . . I need to go down and see my children. And I need . . . I need you to look after Ezri. They can't see her like that."

"I'll take care of it," he said. "Look, go down. I'll take care of things on deck. We'll get the rest of the wounded back to Treganne. We'll get all the bodies covered up."

"Very good," said Zamira quietly. "You have the deck, Master Lamora. I'll return shortly."

I have the deck, thought Locke, staring around at the

shambles left by the battle: swaying rigging, damaged shrouds, splintered railings, arrows embedded damn near everywhere. Bodies crowded every corner of the waist and forecastle; survivors moved through them like ghosts, many of them hobbling on spears and bows for makeshift canes.

Gods. So this is what a command is. Staring consequences in the eye and pretending not to flinch.

"Jean," he whispered, crouching over the bigger man where he sat on the deck. "Jean, stay here. Stay as long as you like. I'll be close. I just need to take care of things, all right?"

Jean nodded, faintly.

"Right," said Locke, glancing around again, this time looking for the least injured. "Konar," he yelled. "Big Konar! Get a pump rigged, the first one you can find that works. Run a hose to this cargo hatch and give the main deck hold a good soak. We can't have anything smoldering down there. Oscarl! Come here! Get me sail canvas and knives. We've got to do something about all these... all these people."

All the crewfolk dead upon the deck. We've got to do something about them here, Locke thought. And then I'm going to do something about them in Tal Verrar. Once and for all.

CHAPTER SIXTEEN

SETTLING ACCOUNTS

1

"CROOKED WARDEN, Silent Thirteenth, your servant calls. Place your eyes upon the passing of this woman, Ezri Delmastro, Iono's servant and yours. Beloved of a man who is beloved by you." Locke's voice broke, and he struggled for self-control. "Beloved of a man who is my brother. We . . . we grudge you this one, Lord, and I don't mind saying so."

Thirty-eight left standing; fifty they'd put over the side, and the rest had been lost during the battle. Locke and Zamira shared the funeral duties. Locke's recitations had grown more numb with each one, but now, at this last ritual of the night, he found himself cursing the day he'd been chosen as a priest of the Crooked Warden. His presumed thirteenth birthday, under the Orphan's Moon. What power and what magic it had seemed back then. The power and the magic to give funeral orations. He scowled, buried his cynical thoughts for Ezri's sake, and continued.

"This is the woman who saved us all. This is the woman who beat Jaffrim Rodanov. We deliver her, body and spirit, to the realm of your brother Iono, mighty lord of the sea.

Lend her aid. Carry her soul to She who weighs us all. This we pray with hopeful hearts."

Jean knelt over the canvas shroud, and on it he placed a lock of dark brown hair. "My flesh," he whispered. He pricked his finger with a dagger, and let a red drop fall. "My blood." He leaned down to the unmoving head beneath the canvas, and left a lingering kiss. "My breath, and my love."

"These things bind your promise," said Locke.

"My promise," said Jean, rising to his feet. "A death-offering, Ezri. Gods help me to make it worthy. I don't know if I can, but gods help me."

Zamira, standing nearby, stepped up to take one side of the wooden plank holding Ezri's canvas-wrapped body. Locke took the other; Jean, as he'd warned Locke before the ceremony, was unable to help. He wrung his hands and looked away. In a moment it was over—Locke and Zamira tipped the plank, and the sailcloth shroud slid out the entry port, into the dark waves below. It was an hour past sunset, and at long last they were truly done.

The wordless circle of tired, mostly wounded crewfolk began to disperse, back to Treganne's fussing or their bare-bones watches. Rask had replaced Ezri, Nasreen, and Utgar alike for the time being; with his head swaddled in a thick linen bandage, he began grabbing the more able-bodied survivors and pointing out chores for their attention.

"And now?" asked Locke

"Now we limp, with the wind mostly against us, back to Tal Verrar." Zamira's voice was tired, but her gaze was level. "We had an understanding, before this. I've lost more than I bargained for, friends and crew both. We lack the strength to take so much as a fishing vessel now, so I'm afraid what remains is up to you."

"As we promised," said Locke. "Stragos. Yeah. Get us there, and I'll ... think of something."

"You won't have to," said Jean. "Just put in and send me off." He looked down at his feet. "Then leave."

"No," said Locke. "I won't just stay here while—"

"Only takes one for what I've got in mind."

"You just promised a death-offering—"

"She gets it. Even if it's *me,* she gets it."

"You think Stragos won't be suspicious to see just one of us?"

"I'll tell him you're dead. Tell him we had a fight at sea; that part's honest enough. He'll see me then."

"I won't let you go alone."

"And I won't let you come with. What do you think you can do, fight me?"

"Shut up, the pair of you," said Zamira. "Gods. Just this morning, Jerome, your friend here tried to convince me to let him do exactly what you're planning right now."

"What?" Jean glared at Locke and ground his teeth together. "You miserable little sneak, how could you—"

"What? How dare I contemplate what *you* were going to do to me? You self-righteous strutting cock, I'll—"

"What?" shouted Jean.

"—I'll throw myself at you, and you'll beat the shit out of me," said Locke. "And then you'll feel awful! How about that, huh?"

"I already feel awful," said Jean. "Gods, why can't you just let me do this? Why can't you give me this much? At least you'll be alive; you can try to find another alchemist, another poisoner. It's a better chance than I'll have."

"Like hell," said Locke. "That's not how we work, and if you wanted it otherwise, you should have left me bleeding to death in Camorr. I seem to recall being pretty set on it at the time."

"Yeah, but—"

"It's different when it's *you,* isn't it?"

"I—"

"Gentlemen," said Zamira, "or whatever you are. All other considerations aside, I gave my little boat to Basryn this afternoon so the bastard could die on the waves instead of on my ship. You'll have a hell of a time getting one of the other boats in to Tal Verrar by yourself, Jerome. Unless you propose to fly, for I'm not taking the *Orchid* more than a bowshot past the breakwater reefs."

"I'll swim if I bloody well have to—"

"Don't be stupid in your anger, Jerome." Drakasha grabbed him by the shoulders. "Be *cold*. Cold's the only thing that's going to work, if you're going to give me anything back for what's been done to my crew. For my *first mate*."

"Shit," Jean muttered.

"Together," said Locke. "You didn't leave me in Camorr, or Vel Virazzo. The hell if I'll leave you here."

Jean scowled, grabbed the rail, and stared down at the water. "It's a damn shame," he said at last. "All that money at the Sinspire. Pity we'll never get it out. Or the other things."

Locke grinned, recognizing the abrupt change of subject as Jean's way of salving his pride as he gave in.

"Sinspire?" said Zamira.

"We've left a few parts of our story untold, Zamira. Forgive us. Sometimes these schemes get a bit heavy to haul around. We, ah, have a few thousand solari on the books at the Sinspire. Hell, I'd let you have my share if there were any way to get it, but the point is moot."

"If only we'd found someone in the city to hold some of it for us," said Jean.

"No use wailing over spilled beer," said Locke. "I doubt we cultivated a single friend in Tal Verrar that we weren't hiring or tipping. Sure could use a fucking friend now." He joined Jean at the rail and pretended to be as absorbed in the sea as the bigger man did, but all he could think of were shrouded bodies splashing into the water.

Bodies falling, just as he and Jean had planned to use ropes, to fall safely out of—

"Wait a gods-damned minute," said Locke. "A friend. A friend. That's what we fucking need. We've spun Stragos and Requin like plates. Who haven't we even bothered to deal with in the past two years? Who have we been ignoring?"

"The temples?"

"Good guess, but no—who's got a direct stake in this bloody mess?"

"The Priori?"

"The Priori," said Locke. "Those fat, secretive, conniving bastards." Locke drummed his fingers against the rail, trying to push his sorrow out of his thoughts and will a dozen loose, improbable plans into one coherent scheme. "Think. Who'd we game with? Who'd we see at the Sinspire?"

"Ulena Pascalis."

"No. She just barely got her seat at the table."

"De Morella—"

"No. Gods, nobody takes him seriously. Who could move the Priori to do something absolutely rash? Who's been around long enough to either command respect or pull strings to enforce it? Inner Seven is what we need. The hell with everyone else."

Conjuring on the political realities of the Priori was akin to divination by chicken entrails, thought Locke. There were three tiers of seven in the merchant councils; the purpose of every seat on the lower two was public knowledge. Only the names of the Inner Seven were known—what hierarchy they held, what duties they performed was a mystery to outsiders.

"Cordo," said Jean.

"Old Cordo, or Lyonin?"

"Both. Either. Marius is Inner Seven; Lyonin's on his way up. And Marius is older than Perelandro's balls. If anyone could move the Priori, presumably as part of some insane thing you're dreaming up—"

"It's only half-insane."

"I know that fucking look on your face! I'm sure either Cordo's the one you want; pity we've never met the bastards." Jean stared at Locke with a wary expression. "You *do* have that look on your face. What do you mean to do?"

"I mean...what if I mean to have it all? Why are we plotting suicide as a first option? Why don't we at least *try* first? Get to Requin. Pull the job. Get to Stragos. Squeeze an answer or an antidote out of him. Then give it to him, one way or another." Locke mimed shoving a dagger into an invisible archon of Tal Verrar. It was so satisfying he mimed it again.

"How the hell do we do this?"

"That's a grand question," said Locke. "The best question you've ever asked. I know we need some things. First, the way it's been lately, every person in Tal Verrar is likely to be waiting for us at the docks with crossbows and torches. We need better disguises. Shoddiest priesthood of the twelve?"

"Callo Androno," said Jean.

"Begging His forgiveness, you got it," said Locke.

Callo Androno; Eyes on the Crossroads; god of travel, languages, and lore. His itinerant priests as well as his settled scholars disdained finery, taking pride in the roughness of their garments.

"Zamira," said Locke, "if there's anyone on board who can still push a needle and thread, we need two robes. Make them from sailcloth, spare clothes, anything. I hate to say it, but there's got to be a lot of spare clothing lying around now."

"The survivors will dice for the goods, and I'll share out

the coin among them," she said. "But I can claim a few things first."

"And we need something blue," said Locke. "The blue Androni headbands. As long as we wear those, we're holy men, not just ill-dressed vagrants."

"Ezri's blue tunic," said Jean. "It's . . . it'd be in her cabin, where she left it. It's a bit faded, but—"

"*Perfect,*" said Locke. "Now, Zamira, when we came back from our first visit to Tal Verrar with this ship, I gave you a letter for safekeeping. It has Requin's seal on it. Jerome, I need you to finesse that thing off like Chains showed us. You're better at it than me and it has to be good."

"I suppose I can try. I'm not sure . . . how good I can be at anything right now."

"I need your best. I need you to do it. For me. And for her."

"Where do you want the seal moved?"

"Clean parchment. Paper. Anything. Do you have one sheet, Zamira?"

"A full sheet? I don't think Paolo and Cosetta have left us any. But several of them are only partially scribbled on; I may be able to cut one in half."

"Do it. Jerome, you'll find some of the tools you need in my old sea chest, in Zamira's cabin. Can he use it, and some lanterns, Captain?"

"Paolo and Cosetta refuse to come out of the rope locker," said Zamira. "They're too upset. I've brought bed things and alchemical lights down for them. The cabin is at your disposal."

"You'll need your cards, too," said Jean. "Or so I presume."

"Hell yes, I mean to use the cards. I'll need them, plus the best set of gear we can scrape together. Daggers. Short lengths of cord, preferably demi-silk. Coin, Zamira—tight little purses of fifty or sixty solari in case we have to buy our way past a problem. And some coshes. If you don't have any, there's sand and sail canvas—"

"And a pair of hatchets," said Jean.

"There's two in my cabin. I took them out of your chest, actually."

"What?" A flicker of excitement actually crossed Jean's face. "You have them?"

"I needed a pair. I didn't know they were special; otherwise I'd have given them back when you came off the scrub watch—"

"Special? They're more like family than weapons," said Locke.

"So how does this all fall together, then?" said Jean.

"As I said, excellent question, one I intend to ponder at length—"

"We won't see Tal Verrar again until tomorrow night if this weather holds," said Zamira. "I guarantee you'll have a good long time to ponder. And you'll be doing most of it up the foremast as top-eyes. I still need you to make yourself useful."

"Of course," said Locke. "Of course. Captain, when we come in to Tal Verrar, bring us from the north, if you would. Whatever else we do, our first stop needs to be the Merchants' Quarter."

"Cordo?" asked Jean.

"Cordo," said Locke. "Older or Younger, I don't care. They'll see us if we have to crawl in through their gods-damned windows."

2

"WHAT THE—," said a portly, well-dressed servant who had the misfortune to walk around the corner, past the alcove containing the fourth-floor window Locke and Jean had just crawled in through.

"Hey," said Locke. "Congratulations! We're reverse burglars, here to give you fifty gold solari!" He tossed his coin purse at the servant, who caught it in one hand and gaped at its weight. In the next second and a half the man spent not raising an alarm, Jean coshed him.

They'd come in through the northwest corner of the top story of the Cordo family manor; battlements and iron spikes had made a climb to the roof unattractive. It was just shy of the tenth hour of the evening, a perfect mid-Aurim night on the Sea of Brass, and Locke and Jean had already squirmed through a thorny hedgerow, dodged three parties of guards and gardeners, and spent twenty minutes scaling the damp, smooth stone of Cordo Manor just to get this far.

Their makeshift priestly robes of Callo Androno, along with most of their other needs, were tucked into backpacks sewn with haste by Jabril. Possibly thanks to those robes, no one had loosed a crossbow bolt at them since they'd set foot on solid Verrari ground, but the night was young, thought Locke—so very, very young.

Jean dragged the unconscious servant into the window alcove and glanced around for other complications while Locke quietly slipped the double frosted-glass windows shut and rehitched their latch. Only a slender, carefully bent piece of metal had allowed him to open that latch; the Right People of Camorr called the tool a "breadwinner," because if you could get in and out of a household rich enough to own latching glass windows, your dinner was assured.

As it happened, Locke and Jean had stolen into just enough great houses much like this one—if none quite so vast—to know vaguely where to look for their quarry. Master bedchambers were often located adjacent to comforts like smoking rooms, studies, sitting parlors, and—

"Library," muttered Jean as he and Locke padded quietly down the right-hand corridor. Alchemical lights in tastefully curtained alcoves gave the place a pleasantly dim orange-gold glow. Through a pair of open doors in the middle of the hall, on their left, Locke could just glimpse shelves of books and scrolls. No other servants were in sight.

The library was a thing of minor wonder; there must have been a thousand volumes, as well as hundreds of scrolls in orderly racks and cases. Charts of the constellations, painted on alchemically bleached leather, decorated the few empty spots on the walls. Two closed doors led to other inner rooms, one to their left and one in front of them.

Locke flattened himself against the left-hand door, listening. He heard a faint murmur and turned to Jean, only to find that Jean had halted in his tracks next to one of the bookshelves. He reached out, plucked a slim octavo volume—perhaps six inches in height—from the stacks, and hurriedly stuffed it into his backpack. Locke grinned.

At that moment, the left-hand door opened directly into him, giving him a harmless but painful knock on the back of the head. He whirled to find himself face-to-face with a young woman carrying an empty silver tray. She opened her mouth to scream and there was nothing else for it; Locke's left hand shot out to cover her mouth while his right went for a dagger. He pushed her back into the room from which she'd come, and past the door Locke felt his feet sinking into plush carpet an inch deep.

Jean came through right behind him and slammed the door. The servant's tray fell to the carpet, and Locke pushed her aside. She fell into Jean's arms with an "Oooomph!" of surprise, and Locke found himself at the foot of a bed that was roughly ten feet on a side, draped in enough silk to sail a rather substantial yacht.

Seated on pillows at the far end of that bed, looking

vaguely comical with his thin body surrounded by so much empty, opulent space, was a wizened old man. His long hair, the color of sea foam, fell free to his shoulders above a green silk gown. He was sorting through a pile of papers by alchemical light as Locke, Jean, and the unwilling servant woman all barged into his quarters.

"Marius Cordo, I presume," said Locke. "For the future, might I suggest an investment in some artificer gearwork for your window latches?"

The old man's eyes went wide, and the papers scattered from his hands. "Oh, gods," he cried. "Oh, gods protect me! It's you!"

3

"OF COURSE it's me," said Locke. "You just don't know who the hell I am yet."

"Master Kosta, we can discuss this. You must know that I am a reasonable and extremely wealthy man—"

"All right, you *do* know who the hell I am," said Locke, disquieted. "And I don't give a shit about your money. I'm here to—"

"In my place, you would have done the same," said Cordo. "It was business is all, just business. Spare me, and let that too be a business decision, based on gain of gold, jewels, fine alchemicals—"

"Master Cordo," said Locke, "look, I—" He scowled, turned to the servant. "Is this man, ah, senile?"

"He's absolutely competent," she answered coldly.

"I assure you I am," roared Cordo. Anger changed his countenance utterly. "And I will not be put off from business by assassins in my own bedroom! Now, you will either kill me immediately or negotiate the price of my release!"

"Master Cordo," said Locke, "tell me two things, and be perfectly bloody clear about them both. First, how do you know who I am? Second, why do you think I'm here to kill you?"

"I was shown your faces," said Cordo, "in a pool of water."

"In a pool of—" Locke felt his stomach lurch. "Oh, *damn*, by a—"

"By a Karthani Bondsmage, representing his guild on a personal matter. Surely you now realize—"

"*You*," said Locke. "I'd have done the same in your place, is what you said. *You've* been sending those gods-damned assassins after us! Those fuckers at the docks, that barkeeper with the poison, those teams of men on festa night—"

"Obviously," said Cordo. "And you've been elusive, unfortunately. With a bit of help from Maxilan Stragos, I believe."

"Unfortunately? Unfortunately? Cordo, you have no idea what a lucky son of a bitch you are that they didn't succeed! What did the Bondsmagi tell you?"

"Come now. Surely your own plans—"

"Tell me in their words or I *will* kill you!"

"That you were a threat to the Priori, and that in light of sums paid for their services previously, they thought it in their best interests to tender a warning of your presence."

"To the Inner Seven, you mean."

"Yes."

"You *stupid* bastards," said Locke. "The Bondsmagi used you, Cordo. Think on that next time you consider giving them money. We—Master de Ferra and myself—are on their fuck-with list, and they tossed us between you and Stragos for a laugh. That's all! We didn't come here to do anything to the Priori."

"So you say—"

"Why aren't I murdering you right now, then?"

"A simultaneously pleasing and vexing point," said Cordo, biting his lip.

"The fact is," said Locke, "that for reasons which are forever going to remain way the hell beyond your understanding, I've broken into your manor to do one thing—give you the head of Maxilan Stragos on a platter."

"*What?*"

"Not literally. I have plans for that head, actually. But I know how gods-damned happy you'd be to have the archonate kicked over like an anthill, so I'm only going to say this once: I mean to remove Maxilan Stragos from power permanently, and I mean to do it tonight. I *must* have your help."

"But...you are some sort of agent of the archon—"

"Jerome and I are unwilling agents," said Locke. "Stragos' personal alchemist gave us a latent poison. So long as Stragos controls the antidote, we can serve him or die pretty awfully. But the fucker just had to keep pushing us, and now he's pushed too far."

"You could be...you could be provocateurs, sent by Stragos to—"

"What, test your loyalty? In what court, under what oath, before what law? Same question as before, this time in relation to the idiotic conjecture that I actually do Stragos' bidding—why aren't I murdering you, then?"

"As to that...a fair point."

"Here," said Locke, moving around the bed to sit beside Cordo. "Have a dagger." He tossed his blade into the old man's lap. At that moment, there was a pounding on the door.

"Father! Father, one of the servants is injured! Are you well? Father, I'm coming in!"

"My son has a key," said the elder Cordo as the click of it sounded in the door mechanism.

"Ah," said Locke, "I'll be needing this back, then." He

snatched his dagger again, stood beside Cordo, and pointed it at the old man in a vaguely threatening fashion. "Hold still. This won't take but a minute."

A well-built man in his midthirties burst into the room, an ornate rapier in his hands. Lyonis Cordo, second-tier Priori, his father's only heir, and a widower for several years. Perhaps the most eligible bachelor in all of Tal Verrar, all the more notable in that he rarely visited the Sinspire.

"Father! Alacyn!" Lyonis took a step into the room, brandishing his weapon with a flourish and spreading his arms to block the door. "Release them, you bastards! The household guards are roused, and you'll never make it down to the—"

"Oh, for Perelandro's sake, I'm not even going to pretend," said Locke. He passed the dagger back to the elder Cordo, who held it between two fingers like some sort of captured insect. "Look. There. What sort of whimsical assassin am I, then? Sheathe your sword, shut the door, and open your ears. We have a lot of business to discuss."

"I . . . but—"

"Lyonis," said the elder Cordo, "this man may be out of his mind, but as he says, neither he nor his partner are assassins. Put up your weapon and tell the guards to . . ." He turned to Locke suspiciously. "Did you *badly* injure any of my people breaking in, Kosta?"

"One slight bump on the head," said Locke. "Do it all the time. He'll be fine, whoever he was."

"Very well." Marius sighed and passed the dagger fussily back to Locke, who tucked it back into his belt. "Lyonis, tell the guards to stand down. Then be seated and lock the door again."

"May I go, if nobody's going to be doing any assassinating in these chambers?" asked Alacyn.

"No. Sorry. You've already heard too much. Take a seat

and get comfortable while you listen to the rest." Locke turned to the elder Cordo. "Look, for obvious reasons, she cannot leave this house until our business is done tonight, right?"

"Of all the—"

"No, Alacyn, he's right." The elder Cordo waved his hands placatingly. "Too much rides on this, and if you're loyal to me, you know it. If, forgive me, you're not, you know it all the more. I'll have you confined to the study, where you'll be comfortable. And I'll compensate you very, very handsomely for this, I promise."

Released by Jean, she sat down in a corner and folded her arms grumpily. Lyonis, looking as though he doubted his own sanity, briskly dismissed the squad of tough-looking brutes that pounded into the library a moment later, sheathed his rapier, and pulled the bedchamber door closed. He leaned back against it, his scowl matching Alacyn's.

"Now," said Locke, "as I was saying, by the end of this night, come hell or Eldren-fire, my partner and I will be in close physical proximity to Maxilan Stragos. One way or another, we are removing him from power. Possibly from life itself, if we have no choice. But in order to get there our way, we're going to need to demand some things of you. And you must understand, going in, that this is it. This is for real. Whatever your plans are to take the city from Stragos, have them ready to spring. Whatever your measures are to keep his army and navy tied down until you can remind them who pays their salaries, activate them."

"Remove Stragos?" Lyonis looked simultaneously awed and alarmed. "Father, these men are mad—"

"Quiet, Lyo." The elder Cordo raised his hand. "These men claim to be in a unique position to effect our desired change. And they have . . . declined to harm me for certain actions already taken against them. We will hear them out."

"Good," said Locke. "Here's what you need to under-stand. In a couple of hours, Master de Ferra and I are going to be arrested by the Eyes of the Archon as we leave the Sinspire—"

"Arrested?" said Lyonis. "How can you know—"

"Because I'm going to set an appointment," said Locke. "And I'm going to *ask* Stragos to have us arrested."

4

"THE PROTECTOR will not see you, nor will the wait-ing lady. Those are our orders."

Locke was sure he could feel the Eye officer's disdainful glare even through his mask.

"He will now," said Locke, as he and Jean pulled along-side the archon's landing in the smaller, more nimble boat they had talked out of the elder Cordo. "Tell him that we've done as he requested when we last met, and we *really* need to speak about it."

The officer took a few seconds to consider, then went for the signal chain. While they waited for a decision, Locke and Jean removed all of their weapons and gear, stashed it in their bags, and left those in the bottom of the boat. Eventually, Merrain appeared at the top of the landing stairs and beckoned; they were patted down with the usual thoroughness and escorted up to the archon's study.

Jean trembled at the sight of Stragos, who was standing behind his desk. Locke noticed Jean clenching and un-clenching his fists, so he squeezed his arm hard.

"Is this happy news?" asked the archon.

"Has anyone come in to report a fire at sea yesterday, around noon, anywhere west of the city?" asked Locke.

"Two merchant ships reported a large pillar of smoke on the western horizon," said Stragos. "No further news that I'm aware of, and no syndicate claiming any loss."

"They will soon enough," said Locke. "One ship, burnt and sunk. Not a survivor aboard. It was headed for the city and it was wallowing with cargo, so I'm sure it will be missed eventually."

"Eventually," said Stragos. "So what do you want now, a kiss on the cheek and a plate of sweetmeats? I told you not to trifle with me again until—"

"Think of our first sinking as earnest money," said Locke. "We've decided that we want to show our wine and drink it too."

"Meaning what, exactly?"

"We want the fruit of our efforts at the Sinspire," said Locke. "We want what we spent two years working for. And we want it tonight, before we do anything else."

"Well, you can't necessarily have it *tonight*. What, did you imagine I could give you some sort of writ, a polite request to Requin to allow you to carry out whatever your game is?"

"No," said Locke, "but we're going over there right now to pull it on him, and until we're safely away with our swag, not another ship gets sunk in your waters at the hands of the *Poison Orchid*."

"You *do not* dictate the terms of your employment to me—"

"I *do*, actually. Even if we are trusting you to give us our lives back when our enslavement to you is complete, we're no longer confident that the conditions in this city will allow us to pull our Sinspire scheme after you get your way. Think, Stragos. We certainly have been. If you mean to put the Priori squarely under your thumb, there could be chaos. Bloodshed and arrests. Requin's in bed with the Priori; his fortune needs to be intact if we're going to relieve him of any of it. So we want what's ours safely in our hands first, before we finish this affair for you."

"You arrogant—"

"Yes," Locke shouted. "Me. Arrogant. We still need our fucking antidote, Stragos. We still need it from your hands. And we *demand* another extension, if nothing else. Tonight. I want to see your alchemist standing beside you when we return here in a couple of hours."

"Of all the bloody—what do you mean, when you return here?"

"There's only one way for us to walk away safely from the Sinspire, once Requin knows we've taken him for a ride," said Locke. "We need to leave the Sinspire directly into the hands of your Eyes, who'll be waiting to arrest us."

"Why, before all the gods, would I have them do that?"

"Because once we're safely back here," said Locke, "we will slip out quietly, back to the *Poison Orchid*, and later this very night, we'll hit the Silver Marina itself. Drakasha has one hundred and fifty crewfolk, and we spent the afternoon taking two fishing boats to use as fire-craft. You wanted the crimson flag in sight of your city? By the gods, we'll put it in the *harbor*. Smash and burn as much as we can, and hit whatever's in reach on our way out. The Priori will be at your gates with bags of money, pleading for a savior. The people will riot if they don't get one. Is that immediate enough for you? We could do what you wanted. We could do it *tonight*. And a punitive raid for the Ghostwind Isles—well, how quickly can you pack your sea chest, Protector?"

"What are you taking from Requin?" asked Stragos, after a long, silent rumination.

"Nothing that can't be transported by one man in a serious hurry."

"Requin's vault is impenetrable."

"We know," said Locke. "What we're after isn't in it."

"How can I be sure you won't get yourselves uselessly killed while doing this?"

"I can assure you we will," said Locke, "unless we find immediate safety in the public, legal custody of your Eyes. And then we vanish, whisked away for crimes against the Verrari state, on a matter of the archonate's privilege. A privilege which you will soon be at leisure to flaunt. Come on, admit that it's bloody beautiful."

"You will leave the object of your desire with me," said the archon. "Steal it. Fine. Transport it here. But since you'll need your poison neutralized anyway, I will keep it for you until we part."

"That's—"

"A necessary comfort to myself," said Stragos, his voice laden with threat. "Two men who knew themselves to be facing certain death could easily flee, and then drink, binge, and whore themselves in comfort for several weeks before the end, if they suddenly found a large sum of money in their hands, couldn't they?"

"I suppose you're right," said Locke, feigning irritation. "Every single thing we leave with you—"

"Will be given scrupulous good care. Your investment of two years will be waiting for you at our parting of the ways."

"I guess we have no choice, then. Agreed."

"Then I will have a writ made out immediately for the arrest of Leocanto Kosta and Jerome de Ferra," said Stragos. "And I will grant this request—and then, by the gods, you and that Syresti bitch had better deliver."

"We will," said Locke. "To the utmost of our ability. An oath has been sworn."

"My soldiers—"

"Eyes," said Locke. "Send Eyes. There have to be agents of the Priori among your regulars; I'm staking my life on the fact that you keep more of an eye on your Eyes, as it were. Plus they scare the shit out of people. This is a shock operation."

"Hmmm," said Stragos. "The suggestion is reasonable."
"Then please listen carefully," said Locke.

5

IT FELT good to be stripping down to nothing.

Emerging from a long spell of false-facing could be like coming up for air after nearly drowning, Locke thought. Now all the baggage of their multitiered lies and identities was peeling away, sloughing off behind them as they pounded up the stairs to the Golden Steps one last time. Now that they knew the source of their mystery assassins, they had no need to sham as priests and skulk about; they could run like simple thieves with the powers of the city close on their heels.

Which was exactly what they were.

He and Jean should have been loving it, laughing about it together, reveling in their usual breathless joy at crime well executed. Richer and cleverer than everyone else. But tonight Locke was doing all the talking; tonight Jean struggled to keep his composure until the moment he could lash out, and gods help whoever got in his way when he did.

Calo, Galdo, and Bug, Locke thought. *Ezri.* All he and Jean had ever wanted to do was steal as much as they could carry and laugh all the way to a safe distance. Why had it cost them so many loved ones? Why did some stupid motherfucker *always* have to imagine that you could cross a Camorri with impunity?

Because you can't, Locke thought, sucking air through gritted teeth as the Sinspire loomed overhead, throwing blue-and-red light into the dark sky. You can't. We proved it once and we'll prove it again tonight, before all the gods.

6

"STAY CLEAR of the service entrance, you—oh, gods, it's you! Help!"

The bouncer who'd received Jean's painful ministrations to his ribs at their previous meeting recoiled as Locke and Jean ran across the service courtyard toward him. Locke saw that he was wearing some sort of stiff brace beneath the thin fabric of his tunic.

"Not here to hurt you," panted Locke. "Fetch . . . Selendri. Fetch her now."

"You're not dressed to speak with—"

"Fetch her now and earn a coin," said Locke, wiping sweat from his brow, "or stand there for two more seconds and get your fucking ribs rebroken."

Half a dozen Sinspire attendants gathered around in case of trouble, but they made no hostile moves. A few minutes after the injured bouncer had disappeared within the tower, Selendri came back out in his place.

"You two are supposed to be at sea—"

"No time to explain, Selendri. The archon has ordered us to be arrested. There's a squad of Eyes coming up to get us as we speak. They'll be here in minutes."

"*What?*"

"He figured it out somehow," said Locke. "He knows we've been plotting with you against him, and—"

"Don't speak of this here," Selendri hissed.

"Hide us. Hide us, please!"

Locke could see panic, frustration, and calculation warring on the unscarred side of her face. Leave them here to their fate, and let them spill everything they knew to the archon's torturers? Kill them in the courtyard, before witnesses, without the plausible explanation of an "accidental" fall? No. She had to take them in. For the moment.

"Come," she said. "Hurry. You and you, search them."

Sinspire attendants patted Locke and Jean down, coming up with their daggers and coin purses. Selendri took them.

"This one has a deck of cards," said an attendant after fishing in Locke's tunic pockets.

"He would," said Selendri. "I don't give a damn. We're going to the ninth floor."

Into the grandeur of Requin's shrine to avarice for one last time; through the crowds and the layers of smoke hanging like unquiet spirits in the air, up the wide spiraling stairs through the floors of increasing quality and risk.

Locke glanced about as they went up; was it his imagination, or were there no Priori preening in here tonight? Up to the fourth floor, up to the fifth—and there, naturally, he nearly walked into Maracosa Durenna, who gaped with a drink in her hand as Selendri and her guards dragged Locke and Jean past her. On Durenna's face, Locke could see more than bafflement or irritation—oh, gods. She was *pissed*.

Locke could only imagine how he and Jean looked to her—hairier, leaner, and burnt brown by the sun. Not to mention underdressed, sweaty, and clearly in a great deal of trouble with the house. He grinned and waved at Durenna as they ascended the stairs, and she passed out of view.

Up through the last floors, through the most rarefied layers of the house. Still no Priori—coincidence, or encouraging sign?

Up into Requin's office, where the master of the 'Spire was standing before a mirror, pulling on a long-tailed black evening coat trimmed in cloth-of-silver. He bared his teeth at the sight of Locke and Jean, the malice in his eyes easily a match for the fiery alchemical glare of his optics.

"Eyes of the Archon," said Selendri. "On their way to arrest Kosta and de Ferra."

Requin growled, lunged forward like a fencer, and back-handed Locke with astonishing force. Locke slid across the floor on his ass and slammed into Requin's desk. Knickknacks rattled alarmingly above him, and a metal plate clattered to the tiles.

Jean moved forward, but the two burly Sinspire attendants grabbed him by the arms, and with a well-oiled click Selendri had her concealed blades out to dissuade him.

"What did you do, Kosta?" roared Requin. He kicked Locke in the stomach, knocking him back against the desk once again. A wineglass fell from the desktop and shattered against the floor.

"Nothing," gasped Locke. "Nothing. He just *knew*, Requin; he knew we were conspiring against him. We had to run. Eyes on our heels."

"Eyes coming to my 'Spire," Requin growled. "Eyes that may be about to violate a rather important tradition of the Golden Steps. You've put me in a very tenuous situation, Kosta. You've fucked everything up, haven't you?"

"I'm sorry," said Locke, crawling to his hands and knees. "I'm sorry, there was nowhere else to run. If he...if he got his hands on us—"

"Quite," said Requin. "I'm going down to deal with your pursuers. You two will remain here. We'll discuss this the moment I get back."

When you come back, thought Locke, you'll have more of your attendants with you. And Jean and I will "slip" out the window.

It was time to do it.

Requin's boot heels echoed first against tile, then against the iron of his little staircase as he descended to the level below. The two attendants holding Jean released him, but kept their eyes on him, while Selendri leaned back atop

Requin's desk with her blades out. She stared coldly at Locke as he got back to his feet, wincing.

"No more sweet nothings to mutter in my ear, Kosta?"

"Selendri, I—"

"Did you know he was planning to kill you, Master de Ferra? That his dealings with us these past few months hinged on our *allowing* that to happen?"

"Selendri, listen, please—"

"I knew you were a poor investment," she said. "I just never realized the situation would turn so quickly."

"Yes, you were right. I was a bad investment, and I don't doubt that Requin will listen more closely to you in the future. Because I never wanted to kill Jerome de Ferra. Jerome de Ferra isn't a real person. Neither is Calo Callas.

"In fact," he said, grinning broadly, "you have just delivered us to *exactly* where we need to be, for the payoff to two long years of hard work, so we can *rob the fucking hell* out of you and your boss."

The next sound in the room was that of a Sinspire attendant hitting the wall, with the impression of one of Jean's fists reddening an entire side of his face.

Selendri acted with remarkable speed, but Locke was ready for her; not to fight, but simply to duck and weave, and to stay away from that bladed hand of hers. He vaulted over the desk, scattering papers, and laughed as the two of them feinted from side to side, dancing to see who would stumble past its protective bulk first.

"You die, then, Kosta," she said.

"Oh, and you were planning to spare us. Please. By the way—Leocanto Kosta's not real, either. So many little things you just *do not know,* eh?"

Behind them, Jean grappled with the second attendant. Jean slammed his forehead into the man's face, breaking his nose, and the man fell to his knees, burbling. Jean stepped behind him and drove his elbow down on the back of the man's neck with all of his upper body behind it. Involved as he was in avoiding Selendri, Locke winced at the noise the attendant's skull made as it struck the floor.

A moment later, Jean loomed behind Selendri, blood from the attendant's broken nose streaming down his face. She slashed with her blades, but Jean's anger had him in a rare, vicious form. He caught her brass forearm, folded her in half with a punch to the stomach, whirled her around, and held her by the arms. She writhed and fought for breath.

"This is a nice office," said Jean quietly, as though he'd just shaken hands with Selendri and her attendants rather than beaten the hell out of them. Locke frowned, but went on with the scheme—time was of the essence.

"Watch closely, Selendri, because I can only do this trick once," he said, producing his deck of fraudulent playing cards and shuffling them theatrically. "Is there a liquor in the house? A very strong liquor, the sort that brings tears to a man's eyes and fire to his throat?" He feigned surprise at the presence of a brandy bottle on the shelf behind Requin's desk, next to a silver bowl filled with flowers.

Locke seized the bowl, tossed the flowers on the floor, and set the empty container atop the desk. He then opened the brandy bottle and poured the brown liquor into the bowl, to a depth of about three fingers.

"Now, as you can see, I hold nothing in my hands save this perfectly normal, perfectly ordinary deck of perfectly unremarkable playing cards. Or *do* I?" He gave the deck one last shuffle and then dropped it into the bowl. The alchemical cards softened, distended, and began to bubble and foam. Their pictures and symbols dissolved, first into a color-streaked white mess, then into an oily gray goo. Locke found a rounded buttering knife on a small plate at a corner of the desk, and he used it to vigorously stir the gray goo until all traces of the playing cards had vanished.

"What the hell are you doing?" Selendri asked.

"Making alchemical cement," said Locke. "Little wafers of resin, painted to look like cards, formulated to react with strong liquor. Sweet gods above, you do *not* want to know what this cost me. Hell, I had no choice but to come rob you after I had it made."

"What do you intend—"

"As I know from vivid personal experience," said Locke, "this shit dries harder than steel." He ran over to the spot on the wall where the climbing closet would emerge, and he began to slather the gray goo all over the faint cracks that marked its door. "So once I paint it all over this lovely concealed entrance, and then pour it into the lock of the main door, why—in about a minute, Requin's going to need a battering ram if he wants to see his office again this evening."

Selendri tried to scream for help, but the damage to her throat was too much; it was a loud and eerie sound, but it didn't carry downstairs with the force she needed. Locke scampered down the iron stairs, closed the main doors to Requin's office, and hurriedly sealed the locking mechanism within a glob of already-firming cement.

"And now," he said when he returned to the center of the office, "the next curiosity of the evening, concerning this *lovely* suite of chairs with which I furnished our esteemed host. It turns out that I do know what the Talathri Baroque is after all, and that there *is* a reason why someone in his right mind would build such a nice thing out of a wood as fundamentally weak as shear-crescent."

Locke seized one of the chairs. He tore the seat cushion and its underlying panel off with his bare hands, exposing a shallow chamber within the seat packed tight with tools and equipment—knives, a leather climbing belt, clips and descenders, and assorted other implements. He shook these out onto the ground with a clatter, and then hoisted the chair above his head, grinning.

"It makes 'em so much easier to smash."

And that he did, bringing the chair down hard on Requin's floor. It shattered at all the joints, but didn't fly apart, because its splintered chunks were held together by something threaded through the hollow cavities within its legs and back. Locke fumbled with the wreckage for a few moments before successfully extracting several long lengths of demi-silk line.

Locke took one of these, and with Jean's help soon had Selendri tied into the chair behind Requin's desk. She kicked and spat and even tried to bite them, but it was no use.

Once she was secured, Locke picked a knife out of the pile of tools on the ground while Jean got to work smashing the other three chairs and extracting their hidden contents. As Locke approached Selendri with the blade in his hand, she gave him a contemptuous stare.

"I can't tell you anything meaningful," she said. "The vault is at the base of the tower, and you've just sealed yourselves up here. So frighten me all you like, Kosta, but I have no idea what you think you're doing."

"Oh, you think this is for you?" Locke smiled. "Selendri. I thought we knew each other better than that. As for the vault, who the hell said anything about it?"

"Your work to find a way in—"

"I lied, Selendri. I've been known to do that. You think I was really experimenting on clockwork locks and keeping notes for Maxilan Stragos? Like hell. I was sipping brandies on your first and second floors, trying to pull myself back together after I nearly got cut to pieces. Your vault's fucking impenetrable, sweetheart. I never wanted to go anywhere near it."

Locke glanced around, pretending to notice the room for the very first time.

"Requin sure does keep a lot of really expensive paintings on his walls, though, doesn't he?"

With a grin that felt even larger than it was, Locke stepped up to the closest one and began, ever so carefully, to cut it out of its surrounding frame.

7

LOCKE AND Jean threw themselves backward from Requin's balcony ten minutes later, demi-silk lines leading from their leather belts to the perfect anchor-noose knots they'd tied on the railing. There hadn't been enough room in the chairs for belay lines, but sometimes you couldn't get anywhere in life without taking little risks.

Locke hollered as they slid rapidly down through the night air, past balcony after balcony, window after window of bored, satisfied, incurious, or jaded gamers. His glee had temporarily wrestled his sorrow down. He and Jean fell for twenty seconds, using their iron descenders to avoid a headlong plummet, and for those twenty seconds all was right with the world, Crooked Warden be praised. Ten of Requin's prized paintings—lovingly trimmed from their frames, rolled up, and stuffed into oilcloth carrying tubes—were slung over his shoulder. He'd had to leave two on the wall, for lack of carrying cases, but once again space in the chairs had been limited.

After Locke had conceived the idea of going after Requin's fairly well-known art collection, he'd nosed around for a potential buyer among the antiquities and diversions merchants of several cities. The price he'd eventually been offered for his hypothetical acquisition of "the art objects" had been gratifying, to say the least.

Their slide ended on the stones of Requin's courtyard,

where the ends of their lines hung three inches above the ground. Their landing disturbed several drunk couples strolling the perimeter of the yard. No sooner were they shrugging out of their lines and harnesses than they heard the rush of heavily booted feet and the clatter of arms and armor. A squad of eight Eyes ran toward them from the street side of the Sinspire.

"Stand where you are," the Eye in the lead bellowed. "As an officer of archon and Council, I place you under arrest for crimes against Tal Verrar. Raise your hands and offer no struggle, or no quarter will be given."

8

THE LONG, shallow-draft boat drew up against the archon's private landing, and Locke found his heart hammering. Now came the delicate part, the ever-so-delicate part.

He and Jean were thrust from the boat by the Eyes surrounding them. Their hands were tied behind their backs, and they'd been relieved of their paintings. Those were carried, very carefully, by the last of the arresting Eyes to step off the boat.

The arresting officer stepped up to the Eye in command of the landing and saluted. "We're to take the prisoners to see the Protector immediately, Sword-prefect."

"I know," said the landing officer, an unmistakable note of satisfaction in his voice. "Well done, Sergeant."

"Thank you, sir. The gardens?"

"Yes."

Locke and Jean were marched through the Mon Magisteria, through empty hallways and past silent ballrooms, through the smells of weapon oil and dusty corners. At last they emerged into the archon's gardens.

Their feet crunched on the gravel of the path as they made their way through the deeply scented night, past the faint glow of silver creeper and the stuttering luminescence of lantern beetles.

Maxilan Stragos sat waiting for them near his boat-house, on a chair brought out for the occasion. With him were Merrain and—oh, how Locke's heart quickened—the bald alchemist, as well as two more Eyes. The arresting Eyes, led by their sergeant, saluted the archon.

"On their knees," said Stragos casually, and Locke and Jean were forced down to the gravel before him. Locke winced, and tried to take in the details of the scene. Merrain wore a long-sleeved tunic and a dark skirt; from his angle Locke could see that her boots weren't courtly fripperies, but black, flat-soled field boots, good for running and fight-ing. Interesting. Stragos' alchemist stood with a large gray satchel, looking nervous. Locke's pulse quickened once again at the thought of what might be in that bag.

"Stragos," said Locke, pretending that he didn't know exactly what was on the archon's mind, "another garden party? Your armored jackasses can untie us now; I doubt there are agents of the Priori lurking in the trees."

"I have sometimes wondered to myself," said Stragos, "precisely what it would take to humble you." He beckoned the Eye at his right side forward. "I have regretfully con-cluded that it's probably impossible."

The Eye kicked Locke in the chest, knocking him back-ward. Gravel slid beneath him as he tried to squirm away; the Eye reached down and yanked him back up by his tunic collar.

"Do you see my alchemist? Here, as you requested?" said Stragos.

"Yes," said Locke.

"That's what you get. All you will *ever* get. I have kept my word. Enjoy your useless glimpse."

"Stragos, you bastard, we still have work to do for—"

"I think not," said the archon. "I think your work is

already done. And at long last, I think I can see precisely why you so aggravated the Bondsmagi that they passed you into my care."

"Stragos, if we don't get back to the *Poison Orchid*—"

"My spotters have reported a ship answering that description anchored to the north of the city. I'll be out to fetch her soon enough, with half the galleys in my fleet. And then I'll have another pirate to parade through the streets, and a crew to drop into the Midden Deep one by one while all of Tal Verrar cheers me on."

"But we—"

"You have given me what I need," said Stragos, "if not in the manner in which you intended. Sergeant, did you encounter any difficulty in securing these prisoners from the Sinspire?"

"Requin refused to allow us entry to the structure, Protector."

"Requin refused to allow you entry to the structure," said Stragos, clearly savoring each word. "Thereby treating an informal tradition as though it had any precedence over my legal authority. Thereby giving me cause to send my troops in platoons, and do what the bought-and-paid-for constables won't—throw that bastard in a box, until we find out just how long he's willing to stay quiet about the activities of his good friends the Priori. Now I have my fighting chance. There's no need for you two to cause further violence in my waters."

"Stragos, you motherfucker—"

"In fact," said the archon, "there's no need for you two, at all."

"We had a deal!"

"And I would have kept to it, had you not scorned me in the one matter which could brook no disobedience!" Stragos rose from his chair, shaking with anger. "My instructions were to leave the men and women at Windward Rock alive! *Alive!*"

"But we—," began Locke, absolutely mystified. "We used the witfrost, and we did leave them—"

"With their throats cut," said Stragos. "Only the two on the roof lived; I presume you were too lazy to climb up and finish them off."

"We didn't—"

"Who else was raiding my island that night, Kosta? It's not exactly a shrine for pilgrims, is it? If you didn't do it, you allowed the prisoners to do it. Either way, the fault is yours."

"Stragos, I honestly don't know what you're talking about."

"That won't bring my four good men and women back, will it?" Stragos put his hands behind his back. "And with that, we're done. The sound of your voice, the tone of your arrogance, the sheer *effrontery* contained within that tongue of yours...you are sharkskin on my eardrums, Master Kosta, and you murdered honest soldiers of Tal Verrar. You will have no priest, no ceremony, and no grave. Sergeant, give me your sword."

The sergeant of the arresting Eyes stepped forward and drew his blade. He turned it hilt-first toward the archon.

"Stragos," said Jean. "One last thing."

Locke turned toward him, and saw that he was smiling thinly. "I'm going to remember this moment for the rest of my gods-damned life."

"I—"

Stragos never finished his sentence, since the Eye sergeant suddenly drew back his sword arm and slammed the hilt of the weapon into the archon's face.

9

THEY DID it like this.

The Eyes removed Locke and Jean from Requin's courtyard and shoved them into a heavy carriage with iron-
barred windows. Three entered the compartment with
them, two rode up top to tend the horses, and three stood
at the sides and rear, as outriders.

At the end of the street atop the highest tier of the
Golden Steps, where the carriage had to turn left to take the
switchback ramp down to the next level, another carriage
suddenly blocked its way. The Eyes yelled threats; the driver
of the other carriage apologized profusely and shouted that
his horses were uncommonly stubborn.

Then the crossbow strings began to snap, and the drivers and outriders toppled from their places, caught de-
fenseless in a storm of quarrels. Squads of constables in full
uniform appeared on the street to either side of the carriage, waving their staves and shields.

"Move along," they shouted at the wide-eyed by-
standers, the wisest of whom had already ducked for cover.
"Nothing to see here. Business of archon and Council."

As the bodies hit the cobblestones outside the carriage,
the door flew open and the three inside made a futile attempt
to aid their fallen comrades. Two more squads of constables,
with help from a number of private individuals in plain
dress who just *happened* to get involved at the same signal,
charged and overpowered them. One fought back so hard
that he was slain by accident; the other two were soon forced
down beside the carriage, and their bronze masks removed.

Lyonis Cordo appeared, wearing the uniform of an Eye,
complete in every detail save for the mask. He was followed
by seven more men and women in nearly complete costumes. With them was a young woman Locke didn't recognize. She knelt in front of the two captured Eyes.

"You I don't know," she said to the one on the right. Before the man had time to realize what was happening, a constable had passed a dagger across his throat and shoved him to the ground. Other constables were quickly dragging the rest of the bodies out of sight.

"You," said the woman, regarding the sole surviving Eye. "Lucius Caulus. You I know."

"Kill me now," said the man. "I'll give you nothing."

"Of course," said the woman. "But you have a mother. And a sister, who works in the Blackhands Crescent. And you have a brother-by-bonding on the fishing boats, and two nephews—"

"Fuck you," Caulus said. "You wouldn't—"

"While you watched. I would. I *will*. Every single one of them, and you'll be in the room the whole time, and they'll know that you could save them with a few words."

Caulus looked at the ground and began to sob. "Please," he said. "Let this stay between us—"

"Tal Verrar remains, Caulus. The archon isn't Tal Verrar. But I don't have time to play games with you. Answer my questions or we will find your family."

"Gods forgive me," said Caulus, nodding.

"Were you given any special code phrases or procedures to use when reentering the Mon Magisteria?"

"N-no..."

"What, exactly, were the orders that you heard given to your sergeant?"

When the brief interrogation was over, and Caulus carted off—alive, to keep him in fear of consequences should he be leaving anything out—along with the bodies, the false Eyes armed themselves with the weapons and harnesses of the real thing, and drew on the brass masks. Then the carriage was off again, speeding on its way to the boat waiting at the inner docks, lest any of Stragos' agents should get across the bay in time to warn of what they'd seen.

"That was about as good as we could hope for," said Lyonis, sitting inside the carriage with them.

"How good are those fake uniforms?" asked Locke.

"Fake? You misunderstand. The uniforms weren't the hard part; our sympathizers in Stragos' forces supplied us with these some time ago. It's the masks that are damned difficult. One per Eye, no spares; they keep them like family heirlooms. And they spend so much time looking at them even a close copy would be noticed." Cordo held up his mask and grinned. "After tonight, hopefully, we'll never see the damned things again. Now what the hell is in those oil-cloth tubes?"

"A gift from Requin," said Locke. "Unrelated personal business."

"You know Requin well?"

"We share a taste for the art of the late Therin Throne period," said Locke, smiling. "In fact, we've even exchanged some pieces of work recently."

10

AS LYONIS knocked the archon to the ground, the other false Eyes tore their masks off and took action. Locke and Jean slid out of the purely decorative knots at their wrists in less than a second.

One of Lyonis' men underestimated the skills of the real Eye he faced; he fell to his knees with most of his left side sliced open. Two more Priori pretenders closed in and harried the Eye until his guard slipped; they knocked him down and stabbed him several times. The other tried to run and fetch aid, but was slain before he could take five steps.

Merrain and the alchemist looked around, the alchemist far more nervously than Merrain, but two of Lyonis' people put them at swordpoint.

"Well, Stragos," said Lyonis, hauling the archon back to his knees, "warmest regards from the House of Cordo." He raised his arm, sword reversed to strike, and grinned.

Jean grabbed him from behind, threw him to the ground, and stood over him, seething. "The *deal*, Cordo!"

"Yeah," said Lyonis, still smiling where he lay on the ground. "Well, it's like this. You've done us quite a service, but we don't feel comfortable having loose ends running around. And there are now seven of us, and two of—"

"You *amateur* double-crossers," said Locke. "You make us professionals cringe. You think you're so fucking clever. I saw this coming about a hundred miles away, so I had a mutual friend offer an opinion on the subject."

Locke reached into his boot and pulled out a slightly crumpled, moderately sweaty half-sheet of parchment, folded into quarters. Locke passed this to Lyonis and smiled, knowing as the Priori unfolded it that he would read:

I WOULD TAKE IT AS A PERSONAL AFFRONT IF THE BEARERS OF THIS NOTE WERE TO BE HARMED OR HINDERED IN ANY WAY, ENGAGED AS THEY ARE UPON AN ERRAND OF MUTUAL BENEFIT. THE EXTENSION OF EVERY COURTESY TO THEM WILL BE NOTED AND RETURNED AS THOUGH A COURTESY TO MYSELF. THEY BEAR MY FULL AND ABSOLUTE TRUST.

R

All, of course, above Requin's personal seal.

"I know that you yourself are not fond of his chance house," said Locke. "But you must admit that the same is not generally true among the Priori, and many of your peers keep a great deal of money in his vault—"

"Enough. I take your point." Cordo rose to his feet and all but threw the letter back at Locke. "What do you ask?"

"I only want two things," said Locke. "The archon and his alchemist. What you do with this gods-damned city is entirely your business."

"The archon must—"

"You were about to gut him like a fish. He's my business now. Just know that whatever happens to him won't be an inconvenience for you."

The sound of shouting arose from the other side of the gardens. No, Locke corrected himself—the other side of the fortress.

"What the hell is that?" he asked.

"We have sympathizers at the Mon Magisteria's gate," said Cordo. "We're bringing people in to prevent anyone from leaving. They must be making their presence known."

"If you try to storm—"

"We're not storming the Mon Magisteria. Just sealing it off. Once the troops inside comprehend the new situation, we're confident they'll accept the authority of the councils."

"You'd better hope that's the case across Tal Verrar," said Locke. "But enough of this shit. Hey, Stragos, let's go have a chat with your pet alchemist."

Jean hoisted the archon—still clearly in shock—to his feet, and began to haul him over to where Merrain and the alchemist were standing under guard.

"You," said Locke, pointing at the bald man, "are about to start explaining a hell of a lot of things, if you know what's good for you."

The alchemist shook his head. "Oh, but I . . . I . . ."

"Pay close attention," said Locke. "This is the end of the archonate, understand? The whole institution is getting sunk in the harbor once and for all tonight. After this, Maxilan Stragos won't have the power to buy a cup of warm piss for all the gold in Tal Verrar. That will leave you with *nobody* to go crawling to as you spend the rest of your short, miserable life answering to the two men you fucking poisoned. Do you have a *permanent* antidote?"

"I . . . I carry an antidote for every poison I use in the archon's service, yes. Just in case."

"Xandrin, don't—," said Stragos. Jean punched him in the stomach.

"Oh, no. *Do,* Xandrin, do," said Locke.

The bald man reached into his satchel and held up a glass vial, full of transparent liquid. "One dose is what I carry. This is enough for one man—*do not* split it. This will cleanse the substance from the humors and channels of the body."

Locke took the vial from him, his hand trembling. "And this . . . how much will it cost to have another alchemist make more?"

"It's impossible," said Xandrin. "I designed the antidote to defy reactive analysis. Any sample subjected to alchemical scrutiny will be ruined. The poison and its antidote are my proprietary formulation—"

"Notes," said Locke. "Recipes, whatever you call the damn things."

"In my head," said Xandrin. "Paper is a poor keeper of secrets."

"Well then," said Locke, "until you cook us up another dose, it looks like you're fucking well coming with us. Do you like the sea?"

11

MERRAIN MADE her decision then. If the antidote couldn't be duplicated, and she could knock the vial to the ground . . . the troublesome anomalies Kosta and de Ferra were as good as dead. That would leave only Stragos and Xandrin.

If they were dealt with, all those with any direct knowledge of the fact that she served a master beyond Tal Verrar would be silenced.

She moved her right arm slightly, dropping the hilt of her poisoned dagger into her hand, and took a deep breath.

Merrain moved so fast that the false Eye standing to her side never even had the chance to raise his sword. Her sideways stab, not preceded by any telltale glance or lunge, took him in the side of the neck. She slid the blade sideways as she withdrew, tearing whatever she could in case the poison took a few extra seconds to do its work.

. 12

MERRAIN'S FIRST victim had just uttered a gasp of surprise when she moved again, slashing across the back of Xandrin's neck with a knife she'd produced from nowhere. Locke stared for a split second, startled; he counted himself fast, but if she'd been aiming for him he realized that he never would have seen the blow coming in time.

As Xandrin cried out and stumbled forward, Merrain kicked at Locke, a fast attack rather than a solid one. She caught his arm and the vial flew from his fingers; Locke barely had time to yell, "Shit!" before he was diving after it, heedless of the gravel he was about to skin himself against or anything else Merrain might care to do to him. He plucked the still-intact vial off the ground, uttered a whisper of thanks, and was then knocked aside as Jean rushed past, arms extended.

As he hit the ground with the vial clutched to his chest, Locke saw Merrain wind up and hurl her knife; Jean struck her at the moment of release, so that rather than impaling Stragos through the neck or chest as she'd clearly intended, she bounced her blade off the gravel at his feet. The archon flinched away from the weapon nonetheless.

Merrain, improbably, put up an effective struggle against Jean; she freed one arm from his grasp somehow and elbowed him in the ribs. Lithe and no doubt desperate as all hell, she kicked his left foot, broke his grip, and tried to stumble away. Jean retained enough of a hold on her tunic to tear off her left sleeve all the way to the shoulder; thrown off balance as it gave way, he fell to the ground.

Locke caught a flash of an elaborate, dark tattoo against the pale skin of Merrain's upper arm—something like a grapevine entwined around a sword. Then she was off like a crossbow bolt, darting into the night, away from Jean and the false Eyes who chased her in vain for a few dozen steps before giving up and swearing loudly.

"Well what the—oh, hell," said Locke, noticing for the first time that the false Eye Merrain had stabbed, along with Xandrin, was writhing on the ground with rivulets of foaming saliva trickling from the corners of his mouth. "Oh, shit, shit, *hell*," Locke shouted, bending helplessly over the dying alchemist. The convulsions ceased in just a few seconds, and Locke stared down at the single vial of antidote in his hands, a sick feeling in the pit of his stomach.

"No," said Jean from behind him. "Oh, gods, why did she do that?"

"I don't know," said Locke.

"What the hell do we do?"

"We . . . shit. Damned if I know that, either."

"You should—"

"Nobody's doing anything," said Locke. "I'll keep this safe. Once this is over, we'll sit down with it, have dinner, talk it over. We'll come up with something."

"You can—"

"Time to go," said Locke, lowering his voice to an urgent whisper. "Get what we came here for and go, before things get more complicated." Before troops loyal to the archon notice that he's having a bad night. Before Lyonis finds out that Requin is actually hunting for us as we speak. Before some other gods-damned surprise crawls out of the ground to bite us on the ass.

"Cordo," he shouted, "where's that bag you promised?"

Lyonis gestured to one of his surviving false Eyes, and the woman passed a heavy burlap sack to Locke. Locke shook it out—it was wider than he was, and nearly six feet long.

"Well, Maxilan," he said, "I offered you the chance to forget all of this, and let us go, and keep what you had, but you had to be a fucking asshole, didn't you?"

"Kosta," said Stragos, at least seeming to rediscover his voice, "I . . . I can give you . . ."

"You can't give me a gods-damned thing." Stragos seemed to be thinking of making an attempt for Merrain's dagger, so Locke gave it a hard kick. It skittered across the gravel and into the darkness of the gardens. "Those of us in our profession, those who hold with the Crooked Warden, have a little tradition we follow when someone close to us dies. In this case, someone who got killed as a result of this mad fucking scheme of yours."

"Kosta, don't throw away what I can offer—"

"We call it a death-offering," said Locke. "Means we steal something of value, proportional to the life we lost. Except in this case I don't think there's anything in the world that qualifies. But we're doing our best."

Jean stepped up beside him and cracked his knuckles.

"Ezri Delmastro," he said, very quietly, "I give you the archon of Tal Verrar."

He punched Stragos so hard that the archon's feet left the gravel. In a moment, he was stuffing the unconscious old man into the burlap sack. Another moment, and the sack was tied off, and slung over his shoulder like a bag of potatoes.

"Well, Lyonis," said Locke, "best of luck with your revolution, or whatever the hell it is. We're sneaking out of here before things have a chance to get any more interesting on us."

"And Stragos—"

"You'll never see him again," said Locke.

"Good enough, then. Are you leaving the city?"

"Not half fast enough for our gods-damned taste."

13

JEAN DUMPED him on the quarterdeck, under the eyes of Zamira and all the surviving crew. It had been a long and arduous trip back—first to retrieve their backpacks from Cordo's little boat, and then to dutifully retrieve Drakasha's ship's boat, and then to row nearly out to sea—but it had all been worth it. The entire *night* had been worth it, Locke decided, just to see the expression on Stragos' face when he found Zamira standing over him.

"Dr...r...akasha," he mumbled, then spit one of his teeth onto the deck. Blood ran in several streams down his chin.

"Maxilan Stragos, former archon of Tal Verrar," she said. "*Final* archon of Tal Verrar. Last time I saw you my perspective was somewhat different."

"As was...mine." He sighed. "What now?"

"There are too many debts riding on your carcass to buy them off with death," said Zamira. "We thought long and hard about this. We've decided that we're going to try to keep you around as long as we possibly can."

She snapped her fingers, and Jabril stepped forward, carrying a mass of sturdy, if slightly rusted, iron chains and cuffs in his arms. He dropped them on the deck next to Stragos and laughed as the old man jumped. The hands of other crewfolk seized him, and he began to sob in disbelief as his legs and arms were clamped, and as the chains were draped around him.

"You're going in the orlop, Stragos. You're going into the dark. And we're going to treat it as a special privilege, to carry you around with us wherever we go. In any weather, in any sea, in any heat. We're going to haul you a mighty long way. You and your irons. Long after your clothes fall off, I guarantee, you'll still have those to wear."

"Drakasha, please..."

"Throw him as far down as we got," she said, and half a dozen crewfolk began carrying him toward a main-deck hatch. "Chain him to the bulkhead. Then let him get cozy."

"Drakasha," he screamed, "you can't! You can't! I'll go mad!"

"*I know*," she said. "And you'll scream. Gods, how you'll wail down there. But that's okay. We can always do with a bit of music at sea."

Then he was carried below the *Poison Orchid*'s deck, to the rest of his life.

"Well," said Drakasha, turning to Locke and Jean. "You two delivered. I'll be damned, but you got what you wanted."

"No, Captain," said Jean. "We got what we went after, mostly. But we didn't get what we wanted. Not by a long gods-damned shot."

"I'm sorry, Jerome," she said.

"I hope nobody ever calls me that again," said Jean. "The name is Jean."

"Locke and Jean," she said. "All right, then. Can I take you two somewhere?"

"Vel Virazzo, if you don't mind," said Locke. "We've got some business to transact."

"And then you'll be rich men?"

"We'll be in funds, yes. Do you want some, for your—"

"No," she said. "You went into Tal Verrar and did the

stealing. Keep it. We've got swag enough from Salon Corbeau, and so few ways to split it now. We'll be fine. So what will you do after that?"

"We had a plan," said Locke. "Remember what you told me at the rail that night? If someone tries to draw lines around your ship, just . . . set more sail?"

Drakasha nodded.

"I guess you could say we're going to give it a try," said Locke.

"Will you need anything else, then?"

"Well," said Locke, "for safety's sake, given our past history . . . perhaps you'd let us consider borrowing one of your ship's cats?"

14

THEY MET the next day, at Requin's invitation, in what could only be described as the wreckage of his office. The main door was smashed off its hinges, the suite of chairs still lay broken across the floor, and of course almost all of the paintings on the walls had been sliced out of their frames. Requin seemed to derive a perverse pleasure in seating the seven Priori on fine chairs in the midst of the chaos and pretending that all was perfectly normal. Selendri paced the room behind the guests.

"Has everything gone more smoothly for you ladies and gentlemen since last night?" asked Requin.

"Fighting's ended in the Sword Marina," said Jacantha Tiga, youngest of the Inner Seven. "The navy is on the leash."

"The Mon Magisteria is ours," said Lyonis Cordo, standing in for his father. "All of Stragos' captains are in custody, except for two captains of intelligence—"

"We can't have another fucking Ravelle incident," said a middle-aged Priori.

"I've got people working on that issue myself," said Requin. "They won't go to ground within the city, I can promise that much."

"The ambassadors from Talisham, Espara, and the Kingdom of the Seven Marrows have publicly expressed confidence in the leadership of the council," said Tiga.

"I know," said Requin, smiling. "I forgave them some rather substantial debts last night, and suggested that they might make themselves useful to the new regime. Now, what about the Eyes?"

"About half of them are alive and in custody," said Cordo. "The rest are dead, with just a few thought to be trying to stir up resistance."

"They won't get far," said Tiga. "Loyalty to the old archonate won't buy food or beer. I expect they'll turn up dead here and there once they annoy the regulars too much."

"We'll have the rest quietly gotten rid of over the next few days," said Cordo.

"Now, I wonder," said Requin, "if that's really so very wise. The Eyes of the Archon represent a significant pool of highly trained and committed people. Surely there's got to be a better use for them than filling graves."

"They were loyal to Stragos alone—"

"Or perhaps to Tal Verrar, were you to ask them." Requin placed a hand over his heart. "My patriotic duty compels me to point this out."

Cordo snorted. "They were his shock troops, his body-guards, his torturers. They're useless to us, if not actively seditious."

"Perhaps, for all of his vaunted military understanding, our dear departed archon employed the Eyes inefficiently," said Requin. "Perhaps the business with the faceless masks was too much. They might have been better off in plain-clothes, as an enhancement to his intelligence apparatus, rather than terrorizing people as his enforcers."

"Maybe for *his* sake," said Tiga. "Had he done so, that intelligence apparatus might have foiled our move against him yesterday. It was a close thing."

"Still," said Cordo, "hard to keep a kingdom when you no longer have a king."

"Yes," said Tiga, "we're all so very impressed, Cordo. Subtly mention your involvement in passing as often as you like, please."

"At least I—"

"And more difficult *still* to keep a kingdom," interrupted Requin, "when you discard perfectly good tools left behind by the king."

"Forgive us our density," said Saravelle Fioran, a woman nearly as old as Marius Cordo, "but what precisely are you driving at, Requin?"

"Merely that the Eyes, properly vetted and retrained, could be a significant asset to Tal Verrar, if used not as shock troops but as . . . a secret constabulary?"

"Says the man in charge of the very people such a force would be charged with hunting down," scoffed Cordo.

"Younger Cordo," said Requin, "those are also the 'very people' whose interference with your family business is kept to an acceptable minimum through my involvement. They are the very people who were instrumental in delivering our victory yesterday—carrying your messages, filling the streets to detain army reinforcements, distracting Stragos' most loyal officers while some of you were allowed to approach this affair with the air of amateurs dabbling at lawn bowling."

"Not I—," said Cordo.

"No, not you. You did fight. But I flaunt my hypocrisy with a smile on my face, Lyonis. Don't you dare pretend, here in our highest privacy, that your disdain somehow absolves you for your involvement with the likes of me. You don't want to imagine a city with crime *unregulated* by the likes of me! As for the Eyes, I am not asking, I am telling. Those few who were true fanatics for Stragos can conveniently trip and land on swords, yes. The rest are too useful to throw away."

"On what grounds," said Tiga, "do you presume to lecture—"

"On the grounds that six of the seven people sitting here have seen fit to store goods and funds at the Sinspire vault. Items that, let us be frank, need not ever reappear in the event that I begin to feel anxious about our relationship.

"I have an investment in this city, the same as you. I would not take kindly to having a foreign power interrupt my affairs. To give Stragos his due, I cannot imagine that the army and navy in your hands will inspire a great deal of awe in our enemies, given what happened last time the Priori governed during a war. Therefore I see fit to hedge all of our bets."

"Surely we could discuss this in just a few days," said Lyonis.

"I think not. Inconveniences like our surviving Eyes have a habit of disappearing before arguments can broaden, don't they? It's a busy time. Messages might be lost, or misconstrued, and I'm sure there'd be a perfectly plausible reason for whatever happened."

"So what do you want?" asked Fioran.

"If you're going to take the Mon Magisteria as an administrative center for our shiny new government, I would imagine that a suite of offices would be a good start. Something nice and prestigious, before all the nice ones are gone. Plus I'll expect a rudimentary operating budget by the end of the week; I'll set down the rough finnicking myself. Salaries for the next year. Speaking of which, I will expect at least three or four positions within the hierarchy of this new organization to be placed entirely at my discretion. Salaries in the range of ten to fifteen solari per annum."

"So you can pass out sinecures to some of your jumped-up thieves," said Lyonis.

"So I can aid them in their transition to life as respectable citizens and defenders of Tal Verrar, yes," said Requin.

"Will this be your *own* transition to life as a respectable citizen?" asked Tiga.

"Here I thought I already was," said Requin. "Gods, no. I have no desire to turn away from the responsibilities I currently enjoy. But it just so happens that I have an ideal candidate in mind to head our new organization. Someone who shares my qualms about the manner in which Stragos employed his Eyes, and should be taken all the more seriously for the fact that she used to *be* one."

Selendri couldn't help smiling as the Priori turned in their seats to stare at her.

"Now, Requin, hold on," said Cordo.

"I see no need," said Requin. "I don't believe your six fellows are actually going to deny me this very minor and very patriotic request, are they?"

Cordo looked around, and Selendri knew what he was seeing on the faces of the other Priori; if he formally tried to stop this, he would be alone, and he would weaken not only his father's borrowed position but his own future prospects.

"I think her starting compensation should be something handsome, rather handsome," said Requin cheerfully. "And of course she'll require use of official carriages and barges. An official residence; Stragos had dozens of houses and manors at his disposal. Oh, and I think her office at the Mon Magisteria should be the nicest and most prestigious of all. Don't you?"

They kissed one another for a very long time, alone in the office once the Priori had left in various states of bemusement, worry, and aggravation. As he usually did, Requin removed his gloves to run the brown, pocked skin of his hands over her, over the matching scar tissue on her left-hand side as well as the healthy flesh on her right.

"There you are, my dear," he said. "I know you've been chafing here for some time, running up and down these tower steps, fetching and bowing for drunkards of quality."

"I'm still sorry for my failure to—"

"Our failure was entirely shared," said Requin. "In fact, I fell for Kosta and de Ferra's line of bullshit harder than you did—you retained your suspicion the whole way. Left to your own devices, you would have thrown them out the window early on and avoided the entire mess at the end, I'm sure."

She smiled.

"And those smirking Priori assume I'm inflicting one last grand sinecure on them where you're concerned." Requin ran his fingers through her hair. "Gods, are they in for a surprise. I can't wait to see you in action. You'll build something that will make my little coteries of *felantozzi* look tawdry."

Selendri stared around at the wreckage of the office. Requin laughed. "I suppose," he said, "that I have to admire the audacious little shits. To spend two years planning such a thing, and then the business with the chairs . . . and with my seal! My, Lyonis was throwing a fit. . . ."

"I'd have thought you'd be furious," said Selendri.

"Furious? I suppose I am. I was rather fond of that suite of chairs."

"I know how long you worked to acquire those paintings—"

"Ah, the paintings, yes." Requin grinned mischievously. "Well, as for that . . . the walls have been left somewhat underdecorated. How would you like to go down to the vault with me to start fetching out the real ones?"

"What do you mean, the real ones?"

EPILOGUE

RED SEAS UNDER RED SKIES

1

"What the hell do you mean, 'reproductions'?"

Locke sat in a comfortable, high-backed wooden chair in the study of Acastus Krell, Fine Diversions dealer of Vel Virazzo. He wrapped both hands around his slender glass of lukewarm tea to avoid spilling it.

"Surely you can't be unfamiliar with the term, Master Fehrwright," said Krell. The old man would have been stick-like if not for the grace of his movements; he paced his study like a dancer in a stage production, manipulated his magnifying lenses like a duelist striking a pose. He wore a loose brocaded gown of twilight-blue silk, and as he looked up now the hairless gleam of his head emphasized the eerily penetrating nature of his stare. This study was Krell's lair, the center of his existence. It lent him an air of authority.

"I am," said Locke, "in the matter of furniture, but as for paintings—"

"It's a rarer thing, to be sure, but there can be no doubt. I have never actually seen the original versions of these ten paintings, gentlemen, but there are *critical* incongruities in the pigments, brushstrokes, and general weathering of their surfaces. They are not genuine art objects of the Talathri Baroque."

Jean absorbed this morosely, hands folded before him, saying nothing and ignoring his tea. Locke tasted bile in the back of his throat.

"Explain," he said, struggling to keep his temper in check.

Krell sighed, his own aggravation clearly tempered by sympathy for their situation. "Look," he said, carefully holding up one of the paintings they'd stolen, an image of Therin Throne nobles seated at a gladiatorial game, receiving the tribute of a mortally wounded fighter. "Whoever painted this is a master artisan, a fantastically patient and skillful individual. It would have required hundreds of hours per painting, and the work must have been done with full access to the originals. Obviously, the ... gentleman from which you procured these objects had qualms about exposing the originals to danger. I'd wager my house and all of its gardens that they're in his vault."

"But the ... incongruities. How can you know?"

"The master artists patronized by the last court of the Therin Throne had a secret means to distinguish their works from those produced by artists serving lesser patrons. A fact not known outside the emperor's court until years after it fell. In their paintings, Talathri's chosen masters and their associates would deliberately create a very slight visual flaw in one corner of the work, by using brushstrokes whose size and direction jarred with those immediately surrounding them. The imperfection that proclaims perfection, as it were. Like the beauty mark some Vadrans favor for their ladies."

"And you can tell this at a glance?"

"I can tell well enough when I find no hint of it anywhere, on any of these ten works."

"Damnation," said Locke.

"It suggests to me," said Krell, "that the artist who created these—or their employer—so genuinely admired the original works that they refused to counterfeit their hidden marks of distinction."

"Well, that's very heartwarming."

"I can tell you require further proof, Master Fehrwright, and fortunately what remains is even clearer. First, the brightness of these pigments is impossible, given the state of alchemy four hundred years ago. The vibrancy of these hues bespeaks a contemporary origin. Lastly, and most damningly, there is no veneer of age upon these works. No fine cracks in the pigment, no discoloration from mold or sunlight, no intrusion of smoke into the overlying lacquers. The flesh of these works, as it were, is as distinct from the genuine article as my face would be from that of a ten-year-old boy." Krell smiled sadly. "I have aged to a fine old state. These have not."

"So what does this mean, for our arrangement?"

"I am aware," said Krell, settling into the chair behind his desk and setting the painting down, "that you must have undergone extraordinary hardship in securing even these facsimiles from the…gentleman in Tal Verrar. You have my thanks, and my admiration."

Jean snorted and stared at the wall.

"Your thanks," said Locke, "and your admiration, however well meant—"

"Are not legal tender," said Krell. "I'm not a simpleton, Master Fehrwright. For these ten paintings, I can still offer you two thousand solari."

"Two?" Locke clutched the armrests of his chair and leaned forward. "The sum we originally discussed was *thirty thousand*, Master Krell!"

"And for originals," said Krell, "I would have gladly paid that original sum; for genuine artifacts of the Last Flowering, I would have had buyers in distant locations completely unconcerned with the...potential displeasure of the gentleman in Tal Verrar."

"Two," muttered Locke. "Gods, we left more than that sitting at the Sinspire. Two thousand solari for two years is what you're offering us."

"No." Krell steepled his spindly fingers. "Two thousand solari for ten paintings. However much I regret what you might have endured to recover these objects, there were no hardship clauses in our agreement. I am paying for goods, not the process required to retrieve them."

"Three thousand," said Locke.

"Twenty-five hundred," said Krell, "and not a centira more. I *can* find buyers for these; each of them is still a unique object worth hundreds of solari, and well worth possessing or displaying. If pressed, after time passes, I can even attempt to sell them back to the gentleman in Tal Verrar, claiming that I procured them in some distant city. I don't doubt that he would be generous. But if you don't wish to accept my price...you are free to take them to a market square, or a tavern, perhaps."

"Twenty-five hundred," said Locke. "Damn it all to hell."

"So I suspect we shall be, Master Fehrwight, in our own good time. But now I'd like a decision. Do you accept the offer?"

2

"TWENTY-FIVE HUNDRED," said Locke for the fifteenth time as their carriage rattled toward Vel Virazzo's marina. "I don't fucking believe it."

"It's more than a lot of people have, I suppose," muttered Jean.

"But it's not what I promised," said Locke. "I'm sorry, Jean. I fucked up again. Tens of thousands, I said. Huge score. Put us back at the top of our games. Lashani noblemen. Gods above." He put his head in his hands. "Crooked Warden, why the hell do you ever listen to me?"

"It wasn't your fault," said Jean. "We did pull it off. We did get out with everything we planned. It's just...it was the wrong everything. There was no way we could know."

"Shit," said Locke.

Their carriage slowed, then creaked to a halt. There was a clatter and a scrape as their footman placed a wooden step, and then the door opened into daylight. The smell of the sea flooded into the compartment, along with the sound of crying gulls.

"Do you still...want to do this?" Locke bit his lip at Jean's lack of reaction. "I know...that she was meant to be here with us. We can just forget about it, leave it where it is, take carriages—"

"It's fine," said Jean. He pointed at the burlap bag on the seat beside Locke. The bag seemed to be undulating, possessed by a motive force within itself. "Besides, we went to the trouble of bringing a cat this time."

"I suppose we did." Locke poked the bag and smiled thinly at the resulting attack from inside. "But still, you—"

Jean was already rising to leave the carriage.

3

"MASTER FEHRWRIGHT! So pleased to finally make your acquaintance. And yours as well, Master—"

"Callas," said Locke. "Tavrin Callas. Forgive my friend; he's had a trying day. I'll conduct our business."

"Of course," said the master of Vel Virazzo's private yacht harbor. Here the pleasure barges and day-sailing vessels of Vel Virazzo's notable families—who could be counted on two hands without using all the available fingers—were kept under constant guard.

The harbormaster led them to the end of one of his

docks, where a sleek one-masted sailing vessel rocked gently on the swells. Forty feet long, lacquered teak and witchwood, trimmed with brass and silver. Her rigging was the finest new demi-silk, and her furled sails were the white of clean beach sand.

"Everything prepared according to your letters, Master Fehrwright," said the harbormaster. "I apologize for the fact that it required four days rather than three—"

"No matter," said Locke. He passed over a leather satchel containing solari he'd counted out in the carriage. "Balance of payment, in full, and the promised three-day bonus, for your work party. I've no reason to be stingy."

"You are entirely too kind," said the harbormaster, bowing as he accepted the heavy purse. Nearly eight hundred solari gone already.

"And the provisions?" asked Locke.

"Complete as specified," said the harbormaster. "Rations and water for a week. The wines, the oilcloaks and other emergency gear—all there, and checked by myself."

"Our dinner?"

"Coming," said the harbormaster. "Coming. I expected a runner several minutes ago. Wait—here's the boy now."

Locke glanced back toward their carriage. A small boy had just appeared from behind it, jogging with a covered basket larger than his chest cradled in his arms. Locke smiled.

"Our dinner concludes our business," he said as the boy approached and handed the basket up to Jean.

"Very good, Mater Fehrwright. Tell me, will you be putting out—"

"Immediately," said Locke. "We have...a great many things to leave behind."

"Will you require assistance?"

"We had expected a third," said Locke quietly. "But the two of us will suffice." He stared at their new boat, at the once-alien arrangement of sails, rigging, mast, tiller. "We're always sufficient."

It took them less than five minutes to load the boat with their baggage from the carriage; they had little to speak of. A few spare clothes, work tunics and breeches, weapons, and their little kit of thieves' conveniences.

The sun was settling into the west as Jean began to untie them from the dock. Locke hopped down onto the stern deck, a room-sized space surrounded by raised gunwales, and as his last act before their departure he opened the burlap sack and released the contents onto the boat.

The black kitten looked up at him, stretched, and began to rub himself against Locke's right boot, purring loudly.

"Welcome to your new home, kid. All that you survey is yours," said Locke. "But this doesn't mean I'm getting attached to you."

4

THEY ANCHORED a hundred yards out from the last of Vel Virazzo's lantern towers, and beneath their ruby light they had the dinner that Locke had promised.

They sat on the stern deck, legs folded, with a small table between them. They each pretended to be absorbed in their bread and chicken, in their shark fins and vinegar, in their grapes and black olives. Regal attempted to make war on their meal several times, and only accepted an honorable peace after Locke bribed him with a chicken wing nearly the size of his body.

They went through a bottle of wine, a nondescript Camorri white, the sort of thing that smooths a meal along without becoming its centerpiece. Locke tossed the empty bottle overboard and they started another, more slowly.

"It's time," Jean said at last, when the sun had moved so low in the west that it seemed to be sinking into the

starboard gunwale. It was a red moment, all the world from
sea to sky the color of a darkening rose petal, of a drop of
blood not yet dry. The sea was calm and the air was still;
they were without interruptions, without responsibilities,
without a plan or an appointment anywhere in the world.

Locke sighed, removed a glass vial of clear liquid from
his inner coat pocket, and set it on the table.

"We discussed splitting it," he said.

"We did," said Jean. "But that's not what we're doing."

"Oh?"

"You're going to drink it." Jean set both of his hands on
the table, palm down. "All of it."

"No," said Locke.

"You don't have a choice," said Jean.

"Who the hell do you think you are?"

"We can't take the chance of splitting it," said Jean, his
voice reasonable and controlled in just the fashion that told
Locke he was ready for instant action. "Better that one of us
be cured for certain, than for both of us to linger on and . . .
die like that."

"I'll take my chances with lingering on," said Locke.

"I won't," said Jean. "Please drink it, Locke."

"Or what?"

"Or you know what," said Jean. "You can't overpower
me. The reverse is definitely not true."

"So you'll—"

"Awake or unconscious," said Jean, "it's yours. I don't
care. Drink the fucking antidote, for the Crooked Warden's
sake."

"I can't," said Locke.

"Then you force me to—"

"You don't understand," said Locke. "I didn't say 'won't.'
I *'can't'*."

"What—"

"That's just water in a vial I picked up in town." Locke

reached once more into his pocket, withdrew an empty glass vial, and slowly set it down beside the fake. "I have to say, knowing me the way you do, I'm surprised you agreed to let me pour your wine."

5

"YOU *BASTARD*," Jean roared, leaping to his feet.

"Gentleman Bastard."

"You miserable fucking son of a *bitch*!" Jean was a blur as he moved, and Locke flinched backward in alarm. Jean snatched up the table and flung it into the sea, scattering the remnants of their dinner across the boat's deck. "How could you? How could you do that to me?"

"I can't watch you die," said Locke flatly. "I can't. You couldn't ask me to—"

"So you didn't even give me a choice!"

"You were going to fucking force-feed it to me!" Locke stood up, brushing crumbs and chicken-bone fragments from his tunic. "I *knew* you'd try something like that. Do you blame me for doing it first?"

"Now I get to watch you die, is that it? Her, and now you? And this is a *favor*?"

Jean collapsed onto the deck, buried his face in his hands, and began to sob. Locke knelt beside him and wrapped his arms around his shoulders.

"It is a favor," said Locke. "A favor to me. You save my life all the time because you're an idiot and you don't know any better. Let me . . . let me do it for you, just once. Because you actually deserve it."

"I don't understand any of this," Jean whispered. "You son of a fucking bitch, how can you do this? I want to hug you. And I want to tear your gods-damned head off. Both at once."

"Ah," said Locke. "Near as I can tell, that's the definition of 'family' right there."

"But you'll die," whispered Jean.

"It was always going to happen," said Locke. "It was always going to happen, and the only reason it didn't happen before now ... is ... you, actually."

"I hate this," said Jean.

"I do too. But it's done. I suppose I have to feel okay about it."

I feel calm, he thought. I guess I can say that. I feel calm.

"What do we do now?"

"Same as we planned," said Locke. "Somewhere, anywhere, laziest possible speed. Up the coast, just roaming. No one after us. No one in the way, no one to rob. We've never really done this sort of thing before." Locke grinned. "Hell, I honestly don't know if we'll be any *good* at it."

"And what if you—"

"When I do I do," said Locke. "Forgive me."

"Yes," said Jean. "And no. Never."

"I understand, I think," said Locke. "Get up and give me a hand with the anchor, would you?"

"What do you have in mind?"

"This coast is so gods-damned old," said Locke. "Falling apart. Seen it, seen everywhere like it. Let's see if we can't get this thing pointed somewhere else."

He stood up, keeping one of his hands on Jean's shoulder.

"Somewhere new."

AFTERWORD

Nautical enthusiasts, of both the armchair and the hands-on persuasion, are bound to have noticed that a great deal of folding, spindling, and mutilating has taken place within *Red Seas Under Red Skies* where the jargon of the sea is concerned.

In some instances I can claim the honorable excuses: that I have abstracted for the sake of reader comprehension or adjusted for the cultural and technological peculiarities of Locke's world. Others can only be explained by that most traditional affliction of authors—that I have screwed up somewhere and have no idea what I'm talking about. Things always work out best for the both of us, dear reader, when you can't tell the difference. Toward that end, my fingers are crossed.

This, then, concludes the second volume of the Gentleman Bastard sequence.

Scott Lynch
New Richmond, Wisconsin
January 26, 2007

ACKNOWLEDGMENTS

Once more to the amazing Jenny, for being so many things over the years—girlfriend, best friend, first reader, constructive critic, and, at long last, wife.

To Anne Groell, Gillian Redfearn, and Simon Spanton, not only for being generally and specifically brilliant, but for not murdering me.

To Jo Fletcher, again with the not murdering me. Cheers!

To everyone at Orion Books who made my first (one can only hope) trip to England a joy, and tolerated me despite my wretched state of illness; especially to Jon Weir, faithful whip-cracker and guide.

To all the UK booksellers who bent over backward promoting and talking up *The Lies of Locke Lamora* when it was just a newborn baby book, not yet walking on its own two feet, so many thanks.

To Desiree, Jeff, and Cleo.

To Deanna Hoak, Lisa Rogers, Josh Pasternak, John Joseph Adams, Elizabeth Bear, Sarah Monette, Jason McCray, Joe Abercrombie, Tom Lloyd, Jay Lake, GRRM, and so many others.

To Loki, Valkyrie, Peepit, Artemis, and Thor, the best contingent of small household mammals ever assembled.

ABOUT THE AUTHOR

SCOTT LYNCH was born in St. Paul, Minnesota, in 1978 and currently lives in Wisconsin with his wife and a small menagerie of household critters. He moonlights as a game designer and volunteer firefighter. This is his second novel.

Don't worry, fans; the saga is not over yet!
Don't miss out on the further exploits of
Locke and Jean in

THE REPUBLIC OF THIEVES
by Scott Lynch

Having pulled off the greatest heist of their career, Locke and his trusted partner in thievery, Jean, have escaped with a tidy fortune. But Locke's body is paying the price. Poisoned by an enemy from his past, he is slowly dying. And no physiker or alchemist can help him. Yet just as the end is near, a mysterious Bondsmagi offers Locke an opportunity that will either save him—or finish him off once and for all.

Magi political elections are imminent, and the factions are in need of a pawn. If Locke agrees to play the role, sorcery will be used to purge the venom from his body—though the process will be so excruciating he may well wish for death. Locke is opposed, but two factors cause his will to crumble: Jean's imploring—and the Bondsmagi's mention of a woman from Locke's past... *Sabetha*. The love of his life. His equal in skill and wit. And now his greatest rival.

Locke was smitten with Sabetha from his first glimpse of her as a young fellow-orphan and thief-in-training. But after a tumultuous courtship, Sabetha broke away. Now they will reunite in yet another clash of wills. For faced with his one and only match in both love and trickery, Locke must choose whether to fight Sabetha—or to woo her. It is a decision on which both their lives may depend.

Don't miss the next thrilling installment,
coming soon from Bantam Spectra!